Johnny Ludlow by Mrs Henry Wood

The Second Series

Ellen Price was born on 17th January 1814 in Worcester.

In 1836 she married Henry Wood, whose career in banking and shipping meant living in Dauphiné, in the South of France, for two decades. During their time there they had four children.

Henry's business collapsed and he and Ellen together with their four children returned to England and settled in Upper Norwood near London.

Ellen now turned to writing and with her second book 'East Lynne' enjoyed remarkable popularity. This enabled her to support her family and to maintain a literary career.

It was a career in which she would write over 30 novels including 'Danesbury House', 'Oswald Cray', 'Mrs. Halliburton's Troubles', 'The Channings' and 'The Shadow of Ashlydyat'.

Sadly, her husband, Henry died in 1866.

Ellen though continued to strive on. In 1867, she purchased the magazine 'Argosy', founded two years previously by Alexander Strahan. She was a prolific writer and wrote much of the magazine herself although she had some very respected contributors, amongst them Hesba Stretton and Christina Rossetti. Although she would gradually pare down writing for the magazine she continued to write novel after novel. Such was her talent that for a time she was, in Australia, more popular than Charles Dickens.

Apart from novels she was an excellent translator and a writer of short stories. 'Reality or Delusion?' is a staple of supernatural anthologies to this day.

Ellen Wood died of bronchitis on 10th February 1887. He estate was valued at a very considerable £36,000.

She is buried in Highgate Cemetery, London.

A monument to her in Worcester Cathedral was unveiled in 1916.

Index of Contents

CHAPTER I - LOST IN THE POST
CHAPTER II - A LIFE OF TROUBLE
CHAPTER III - HESTER REED'S PILLS
CHAPTER IV - ABEL CREW
CHAPTER V - ROBERT ASHTON'S WEDDING-DAY
CHAPTER VI - HARDLY WORTH TELLING
CHAPTER VII - CHARLES VAN RHEYN

CHAPTER VIII - MRS TODHETLEY'S EARRINGS
CHAPTER IX - A TALE OF SIN
CHAPTER X - A DAY OF PLEASURE
CHAPTER XI - THE FINAL ENDING TO IT
CHAPTER XII - MARGARET RYMER
CHAPTER XIII - THE OTHER EARRING
CHAPTER XIV - ANNE
CHAPTER XV - THE KEY OF THE CHURCH
CHAPTER XVI - THE SYLLABUB FEAST
CHAPTER XVII - SEEN IN THE MOONLIGHT
CHAPTER XVIII - ROSE LODGE
CHAPTER XIX - LEE, THE LETTER MAN

CHAPTER I

LOST IN THE POST

Many a true tale has been told of the disappearance of money in passing through the post. Sometimes the loss is never cleared up, but remains a mystery to the end. One of these losses happened to us, and the circumstances were so curious that they would have puzzled a bench of judges. It was a regular mystery, and could not be accounted for in any way.

If you chanced to read the first series of these papers, it may scarcely be necessary to recall certain points to your recollection—that Mr. Todhetley, commonly called the Squire, had two estates. The chief one, Dyke Manor, lay on the borders of Worcestershire and Warwickshire, partly in both counties; the other, Crabb Cot, was a smaller place altogether, and much nearer Worcester. Sometimes we stayed at one place, sometimes at the other. By an arrangement with Mr. Brandon, my guardian and the trustee to my property, I, Johnny Ludlow, lived with the Todhetleys. Mrs. Todhetley, the Squire's present wife, was my stepmother, my father having married her after my own mother's death. After my father's death—which took place speedily—she became the second wife of Squire Todhetley, and the stepmother of his only son and heir, Joseph. Two children were subsequently born to them, Hugh and Lena, to whom Joseph was of course half-brother. Joseph, unlike myself, had been old enough to resent the advent of a stepmother when she came. Indulged and haughty, he did not like the gentle control she brought; though she was good as gold, as loving to him as he would let her be, and kind to everybody. I don't say but that she was tall and thin as a lamp-post, with a mild face, given to having aches in it, scanty light hair, and kindly blue eyes; so she had not much to boast of in the way of appearance. Joe and I grew up together like brothers. He was several years the elder, and domineered over me absolutely. At school he was always called "Tod;" and I fell into the same habit. Perhaps that is sufficient explanation.

"And if you don't come back to-night, you had better send me a five-pound note in a letter," said Mrs. Todhetley.

"All right," replied the Squire.

This was said on the platform of Timberdale Station. We were staying at Crabb Cot, and were taking the train at Timberdale instead of that at South Crabb. The Squire was going to Worcester, and was taking Tod and myself with him. It was a fine morning in April, and Mrs. Todhetley and little Hugh had come with us through the Ravine for the sake of the walk. Our returning at night, or not, was left an open question, contingent upon the Squire's business at Worcester being over.

"Bring me a whip, and a new bird-cage for my thrush, and a pot of marmalade, papa," called out Hugh.

"What else would you like, sir?" retorted the Squire.

"You bring 'em, Joe."

"I dare say!" said Tod.

The train puffed off, drowning Hugh's further commands. We saw him throw his cap at the train, and Mrs. Todhetley holding him back from running after it.

"That young gentleman wants to be sent to school," remarked the Squire. "I'm afraid you two boys make him worse than he would be."

We reached Worcester about twelve, and went to the Star and Garter. The Squire had no end of matters on hand that day: but the two chief things that had brought him to Worcester were—to draw some money from the bank, and to negotiate with Mr. Prothero, a corn-dealer, for the sale of a load of wheat. Mr. Prothero was a close man to deal with: he wanted the wheat at one price, the Squire said it should only go at another: if he held out, the Squire meant to hold out, even though it involved staying the night in Worcester.

It was Wednesday; market-day. Not so large a market as the Saturday's, but the town looked pretty full. The first thing the Squire did was to go to the Old Bank. At the door he turned round and said there was no need for three of us to crowd into the place. However, we were then inside, and so went on with him.

He had something particular to say to Mr. Isaac, and asked for him. They were talking together in private for a minute or two, and then the Squire took out his cheque for fifty pounds, and laid it on the counter.

"How will you take it?" asked Mr. Isaac.

"In five-pound notes."

Mr. Isaac brought the money himself. The Squire put it in his pocket-book, and we said good-morning, and departed. There were shops to call at and people to see: and of course the market to walk through. You wouldn't get the Squire to keep himself out of the market-house, when in Worcester on market-day: he'd go about asking the price of butter and fowls like any old woman. A little after four o'clock we got back to the Star; and found Mr. Prothero had not made his appearance.

"Just like him!" cried the Squire. "His appointment was for four o'clock sharp. He means to hold out against my price; that's what he thinks to do. Let him! he won't get the wheat at less."

"I'd see him a jolly long way before he should have it at all," said haughty Tod. "Do you hear, sir?"

"Hold your tongue, Joe," was the Squire's answer.

"Anyway, sir, Prothero gives you more trouble than all the rest of the buyers put together. He's a stingy, close-fisted fellow."

"But his money's safe and sure. Prothero is a respectable man, Joe; his word's as good as his bond."

Half-past four, and no Prothero. The Squire began to fume a little: if he hated one thing more than another it was to be kept waiting.

"Look here, boys, I'll send that note to your mother," he said, taking out his pocket-book. "There's not much chance of our going home to-night at this rate. Ring, one of you, for some paper and envelopes."

Separating one of the notes from the roll Mr. Isaac had handed to him, he gave it to me to put up. I asked him if I should take down the number.

"I don't think it matters, Johnny."

But I took it down, perhaps through some unconscious instinct—for I don't suppose I am more cautious than other people. In my pocket was a letter from Anna Whitney: and I pencilled on it the number of the note.

"Write inside the envelope 'Not home till to-morrow,'" growled the Squire, forgetting that it could not be there till the morning. But he was in an ill-humour.

I wrote it at his bidding, enclosed the bank-note, and addressed the letter to Mrs. Todhetley at Crabb Cot. Tod and I went out to post it, and began laying plans as to how we should spend the evening at Worcester.

The post-office is not far from the Star, as everybody knows: and though we met a fellow who used to go to school with us, a doctor's son, and stayed talking with him, not ten minutes elapsed before we were back again. And behold in that short time there was a change in the programme. Old Prothero had been in, the bargain about the wheat was concluded, and the Squire intended to start for home as soon as dinner was over. Tod resented the change.

"Johnny and I were going to that advertised séance—or whatever they call the thing—on electro-biology, sir. It will be first-rate fun, they say."

"Very sorry for you and Johnny. You'll have to go home instead. Prothero has bought the wheat: and that's all I should have had to stay here for."

"At his own price!" cried Tod, rather mockingly.

"No, Mr. Joe; at mine."

"Well, it's an awful sell for us," grumbled Tod. "It's not so often we get a night at Worcester, that we should be done out of this chance."

"The fact is, I don't feel well," said the Squire, "and should most likely have gone home, whether Prothero had come in or not. I'm afraid I have caught cold, Joe."

There was not any more to be said. The Squire's colds were no joke: once he caught one, he would be downright ill; laid up for days. We went back by rail to Timberdale, and took a fly home.

The next morning the Squire did not get up. Sure enough he had a cold, and was feverish. At breakfast Mrs. Todhetley said one of us should go over to South Crabb and ask Mr. Cole to call and see him.

"Why, the pater hates doctors!" exclaimed Tod.

"I know he does," she answered. "But I feel sure that if he would only take remedies for his colds in time, they would not be so bad as they usually are, Joseph. Who's that?" she added—for she was seated where she could not see out, and had heard the gate click.

It was the postman: so I opened the glass doors.

"Only one, sir," said he, handing me the letter we had posted at Worcester the previous afternoon.

Mrs. Todhetley laughed as she opened it, saying it would have come sooner had we brought it with us. Looking to see that the bank-note was safe, she left it in the envelope on the breakfast-table.

"You may as well get it changed for me at Salmon's," she said, handing it to Tod as we were going out, "and then I need not disturb your father. But you must make haste back, for you know I want the money."

She had no money in the house except a few shillings: and this was why the note was to be posted to her if we stayed at Worcester. You are often run short of money in rural country places: it's quite different from town, where the banks are at hand.

We went through North Crabb, and met the doctor coming out at his door. Tod told him the Squire wanted some physicking.

"Caught a cold, has he?" cried Cole. "If he will only be reasonable and keep himself warm in bed, we'll soon have that out of him."

Cole lived close upon South Crabb—I think I've said so before. A few yards beyond his house the shops began. Salmon's was the fifth from the corner: a double shop, grocer's and draper's. The savings' bank was at Salmon's, and the post-office: he was the busiest tradesman in South Crabb, rather conceited over it, but very intelligent. His brother was in business at Timberdale. This is what occurred.

"Will you be good enough to change this five-pound note for me, Mr. Salmon?" said Tod, laying the note down on the grocer's counter, on the left of the door, behind which Salmon stood, his grey hair carefully brushed and a white apron on.

Salmon took the note up for a moment, and then unlocked the inner drawer of his till, where he kept his gold. He was counting out the five sovereigns when he paused; put them down, and picked up the note again quickly. I had seen his eyes fall on it.

"Where did you get this note from, sir?" asked he of Tod.

"From the Old Bank at Worcester."

"Well, it's one of them notes that was lost in the robbery at Tewkesbury, unless I'm much mistaken," cried Salmon, beginning to turn over the leaves of a small account-book that he fetched from the post-office desk. "Ay, I thought I was right," he adds, running his finger across some figures on one of the pages. "I had the numbers correct enough in my head."

"You must be out of your mind, Salmon," retorted Tod, in his defiant way. "That note was paid to my father yesterday at Worcester Old Bank."

"I don't think it was, sir."

"You don't think it was! Why, I was present. I saw Mr. Isaac count the notes out himself. Ten; and that was one of them."

"Mr. Isaac never counted out this note," persisted Salmon.

He smoothed it out on the counter as he spoke. I had not noticed it before: but it struck me now as I looked at it that it was not the note I had put into the envelope at Worcester. That was a new, crisp note; this was not crisp, and it looked a little soiled. Tod turned passionate over it: he was just like the Squire in some things.

"I don't understand your behaviour, Salmon. I can swear that this note was one given with the other nine at the bank yesterday, and given by Mr. Isaac."

Salmon shook his head. As much as to say he knew to the contrary.

"You'd better accuse Mr. Isaac of dealing in stolen notes—or me," cried hot Tod.

"You'd neither of you be likely to deal in them, Mr. Todhetley. There's a mistake somewhere. That's what it is. Mr. Isaac would be too glad to get this note into his possession to pay it away again. No people are more severe against money-robberies than bankers."

Salmon talked, and Tod talked; but they could not agree. The apprentice behind the counter on the drapery side listened with admiration, evidently not knowing which side to take. I spoke then, saying that the note did not appear to be the same as the one I had enclosed in the letter; and Tod looked as though he could have knocked me down for saying it. I had changed my clothes and had not Anna Whitney's letter with me.

"Tod, it is of no use your taking it up in this way. If the thing is so, it is. And it can soon be proved. I say I don't think it is the same note, or the same numbers."

"If I had taken down the numbers of a bank-note, I could remember what they were; so would any one but a muff, Johnny," said he, sarcastically.

"I don't remember what they were. But I do seem to remember that they were not these."

Tod flung out of the shop in a passion: to him it seemed impossible that anything could be wrong with a note had direct from the bank. As to its not being the same note, he scouted it utterly. Had it dropped through the envelope and changed itself en route from Worcester? he sarcastically demanded—coming in again to ask it.

Salmon was quietly going over the circumstances of the Tewkesbury robbery to me. About three weeks before, a butcher's shop was robbed in Tewkesbury—the till carried off in open day. It had gold and silver in it and two five-pound notes. The numbers of the notes happened to be known, and notice of them was circulated, to put people on their guard against taking them.

"Look here, Mr. Ludlow," said Salmon, showing me the numbers of the stolen notes written down in his book, and comparing the one with the bank-note we had taken to him. "It's the same, you see. Reason's reason, sir."

"But I don't see how it's practicable," cried Tod, coming round the least bit in the world, as he condescended to look himself at the numbers.

"Well, sir, neither do I—the facts being as you state them," acknowledged Salmon. "But here's the proof to stagger us, you observe. It's in black and white."

"There must be two notes with the same numbers," said Tod.

Salmon smiled: great in his assumption of superior knowledge.

"There never was yet, Mr. Todhetley."

"Who numbers the notes, I wonder? I suppose mistakes are not impossible to those who do it, any more than to other people."

"No fear of that, sir, with their system. The note has been changed in the post."

"Nonsense!" retorted Tod.

They'd have cavilled until night, with no result, one holding out against the other. Tod brought away the note and the five sovereigns—which Salmon offered. We could send over another note at leisure, he said. I examined the envelope after we had hastened home: it was the same we had posted at Worcester, and did not appear to have been tampered with.

Getting Anna Whitney's letter out of my best clothes' pocket, I brought it to Tod. The numbers were quite different from the note's. He stared like one bewildered: his eyes passing from those on the letter to those on the note.

"Johnny, this beats bull-baiting."

So it did—for mystification.

"Are you sure you copied the figures correctly, old fellow?"

"Now, Tod! Of course I did."

"Let us go up to the pater."

The pater was getting up, in defiance of old Cole and Mrs. Todhetley, and was dressed, up to his coat. He had a fire in his room and his white night-cap on. I told him about the note. Tod was outside, telling Mrs. Todhetley. He did not receive the news kindly.

"The note I gave you to put into the envelope was one of those stolen from the butcher at Tewkesbury! How dare you bring your rubbishing stories to me, Mr. Johnny!"

I tried to explain how it was—that it was not the same note; as the numbers proved. He would hear nothing at first, only went on at me, stamping his slippers and nodding his head, the big white tassel of the night-cap bobbing up and down. If Salmon dared to say he had sent him a stolen note to change, he'd teach Salmon what slander meant the next time the magistrates sat.

Tod came in then with Mrs. Todhetley. The Squire had talked himself quiet, and I got a hearing: showing him the numbers I had taken down outside Anna's letter and the numbers on the stolen bank-note. It brought him to reason.

"Why, bless my heart! How can they have been changed, Johnny?"

Taking the packet of notes out of his pocket-book, he went over their numbers. They were all consecutive, the nine of them; and so was the tenth, the one I had taken down. He pushed his night-cap back and stared at us.

"Did you two get larking yesterday and drop the letter on your way to the post?"

"We took it straight to the post, sir, and put it safely in."

"I don't know that I'd answer for that," stormed the Squire. "Once dropped in the street, there's no knowing who might pick it up, or what tricks might be played with it. Hold your tongues, you two. How else do you suppose it could have been done? We don't live in the days of miracles."

Off went his night-cap, on went his coat. Ringing the bell, he ordered the phaeton to be got ready on the instant, to take him to the station: he was going to Worcester. Mrs. Todhetley quite implored him not to go; as good as went down on her knees: he would increase his cold, and perhaps be laid up. But he wouldn't listen. "Hang the cold!" he said: "he had no cold; it was gone. People shouldn't have it to say that tricks could be played on him with impunity, and stolen notes substituted for honest ones."

"What a way he puts himself into!" laughed Tod, when he had ordered us off to make ready.

"I know somebody else who does just the same."

"You'll get it presently, Johnny."

Away we went to the station, Bob and Blister spanking along and Tod driving; the Squire, wrapped in about a dozen rugs and comforters, sitting beside him. The groom, Dwarf Giles, was behind with me: he would have to take the carriage back again. A train came up pretty soon, and we reached Worcester.

Of all commotions, the Squire made the worst. When he got to the bank, Mr. Isaac was out: would not be in till three o'clock: and that put the finishing stroke to the pater's impatience. Next he went to the Star, and told of the matter there, gathering half the house about him. The post-office was taken next. They seemed to know nothing whatever about the letter—and I don't think they did—had not particularly noticed it in sorting: could not have seemed to see less had they been in a fog at sea: except one thing, and that they'd swear to—that every letter posted at the office the previous day, and all other days, had been duly forwarded, untampered with, to its destination.

The first dawn of reason that fell over us was in the interview with Mr. Isaac. It was pleasant to be with any one so cheerfully calm. Taking the roll of five-pound notes in his hand, he pronounced them to be the same he had given us on the previous day; and the number I had dotted down to have been the one belonging to the tenth note.

"And is this one of those two stolen ones that were advertised?" demanded the Squire, putting it into Mr. Isaac's hands.

Mr. Isaac spoke with a clerk for a minute—perhaps referring to the numbers as Salmon had done—and came back saying that it was the note. So there we were: the matter laid, so far, to rest. Nothing could be more unsatisfactory. The Squire sat quite still, as if he had been struck dumb.

"I'm sure I shall never see daylight out of this," cried the Squire, in a sort of hopeless, mazy tone. "It's worse than conjuring."

Mr. Isaac was called away. The Squire fastened upon one of the old clerks, and went over the matter with him. He could not readily understand it.

"The note must have been changed, Mr. Todhetley," said he.

"Changed in the post?"

"Changed somewhere."

"But who did it?"

"That's the question."

The Squire could not tear himself away. Once out of the bank he would be nonplussed. He began casting a doubt on the Worcester post-office; the clerk retorted that there was a post-office at our end, Timberdale: and at that the Squire fired up. Each would have held out for the good faith of his respective post-office to the death. It put Tod and me in mind of the fable of the crows, each old mother saying that her own crow was the whitest. After glaring at one another for a bit through their spectacles, they shook hands and parted.

We arrived home to a late dinner at Crabb Cot, just as wise as we had left it in the morning. The Squire had an awful cold, though he wouldn't admit it. At nine o'clock he virtually gave in, went up to bed, and said Molly was to make him a basin of hot gruel, and we might put a drop of brandy in it.

The mode of conveying the letters from Worcester was this. The Timberdale bag, made up at the Worcester office, was brought out at night by the late train, and dropped at the Timberdale Station. The postmaster of Timberdale would be at the station to receive it, and carry it home.

His name was Rymer. A man of acknowledged respectability in the place, and of good connections, the son of a clergyman. He had been brought up for a surgeon, but somehow never had the chance to pass; and, years and years ago, opened a chemist and druggist's shop at Timberdale. Then he added other things: stationery, Christmas cards, valentines, boys' marbles, purses, and such like, which his wife attended to. In time he had the post-office. As to suspecting Rymer of doing anything wrong with the note, it was not to be thought of. He had two children: a son, who never seemed to do any good for himself, and if placed away from home would return to it again: and a daughter, a nice little girl of sixteen, who was as useful amidst the drugs and the post-office work as her father.

Timberdale had two letter-carriers. One for the place itself, the other for the country round. This last had a regular journey of it, for the farm-houses were scattered. There had always been talk that our two houses—the Squire's and old Coney's—ought not to be put in the Timberdale district of delivery, and why it was originally done nobody could make out; seeing that we were ever so far off Timberdale, and in Crabb parish. But people did not bestir themselves to alter it, and so the old custom went on. The country postman was Lee: a trustworthy old soul with shaky legs.

The next morning, Cole the surgeon came in, vexed. The Squire ought not to have got up at all the day before, he said, much less have gone to Worcester; and where was the use of his prescribing remedies if they were not attended to? Upon that, the Squire (after retorting that he should do as he pleased in spite of Cole and his remedies, and speaking in a sort of hoarse and foggy voice) told about posting the bank-note to Mrs. Todhetley, and what had come of it.

"Well, it's a strange thing," said Cole, when he had turned the news over in his mind. "What do you think, Johnny?"

He would often say to me when talking of things and people, "What do you think?" He had a theory that I saw more clearly than others, just as Duffham at Church Dykely had. I had nothing particular to think about this: it seemed a hopeless mystery.

"Lee's sure," said Cole, speaking of the postman; "so is Rymer. It could have been in no other hands on this side the journey."

"The Worcester people say it was not tampered with on their side."

"Have you questioned Rymer about it?"

"Not yet," croaked the Squire. "I meant to have gone to him to-day."

"Which you will not do!" cried Mr. Cole. "But now, look here: I wouldn't tell people at first that the exchanged note was one of those stolen ones, if I were you: not even Rymer. No one likes to be mixed up in robberies. You'd put folks on their guard at once; and any chance word of enlightenment, that might otherwise be dropped, would be kept in."

We did not quite take him. "I would not," repeated Cole.

"But we must inquire about it," said Tod. "What's to be said of the note?"

"Say that the bank-note you put in was changed en route for another one: that the numbers did not tally. That's all you need say at first."

Tod could not see any reason in the argument; but the Squire took up the idea eagerly, and ordered Tod to do as was suggested. He was unable to go to Timberdale himself, but was far too impatient to let it rest until another day, and so Tod was to be his deputy.

With at least a hundred suggestions and injunctions from the Squire—who only ceased when his voice disappeared completely—we set off, taking the way of the Ravine. It was a fine spring day: the trees were coming into leaf, the thorns and other bushes were budding: violets and primroses nestled at their feet. I picked some early cowslips for a ball for Lena, and some double white violets for Mrs. Todhetley.

Past Timberdale Court went we; past the church; past Jael Batty's and the other straggling cottages, and came to the village street. It was paved: and you can't say that of all villages.

Mr. Rymer was behind his counter: a thin, delicate-faced man, with a rather sad expression and mild brown eyes. In spite of his poor clothes and his white apron and the obscure shop he had served in for twenty years, his face had "gentleman" plainly stamped on it: but he gave you the idea of being too meek-spirited; as if in any struggle with the world he could never take his own part.

The shop was a double shop, resembling Salmon's at South Crabb in shape and arrangements. The drugs and chemicals were on the left-hand side as you entered; the miscellaneous wares on the other. Horse and cattle medicines were kept with the drugs: and other things too numerous to mention, such as pearl barley, pickles, and fish-sauce. The girl, Margaret Rymer, was serving a woman with a pennyworth of writing-paper when we went in, and a postage-stamp. Tod asked for Mr. Rymer.

He came forward from the little parlour, at one end of which was the desk where he did his postal work.

Upon Tod's saying that we wished to speak with him privately, he took us into the parlour. As we sat down opposite to him, I could not help thinking what a nice face he had. It was getting very careworn. A stranger would have given him more than his forty-five years: though the bright brown hair was abundant still. Tod told his story. The chemist looked thoroughly surprised, but open and upright as the day. I saw at once that no fault attached to him.

"A bank-note exchanged as it passed through the post!" he exclaimed. "But, Mr. Joseph Todhetley, the thing appears impossible."

"It appears so," said Tod. "I was just as unwilling to believe it at first: but facts are facts."

"I cannot see the motive," said Rymer. "Why should one bank-note be taken out of a letter, if another were substituted?"

Tod looked at me. Wanting to say that the other was a stolen note, and was no doubt put in to be got rid of. But the Squire had bound us down.

"Had the note been simply abstracted from the letter, we should be at no loss to understand that a thief had helped himself to it; but a thief would not put another note of the same value in its place," went on Rymer.

"Well, the facts are as I tell you, Mr. Rymer," returned Tod, impatient at being trammelled and having to tell so lame a tale. "One bank-note was taken out of the letter and another put in its place. We want you to help us unravel the mystery."

"I will help you to the utmost of my power," was Rymer's answer. "But—are you sure you have told me the circumstances correctly?"

"Quite sure," answered Tod. "The thing was done between Worcester post-office and our house. How it was done, and by whom, is the question."

"You enclosed the note in the letter yourself at Worcester on Wednesday afternoon, and put it into the post-office: when we delivered the letter at Crabb Cot yesterday morning, you found the note inside had been taken out and another put in? These are the circumstances?"

"Precisely so. Except that it was not I who enclosed the note and took down its number, but Johnny Ludlow. The Worcester office disclaims all knowledge of the matter, and so we are thrown on this side of the journey. Did you go to the station yourself for the letter-bag, Rymer?"

"I did, sir. I brought it home and sorted the letters at that desk, ready for the two men to take out in the morning. I used to sort all the letters in the morning, London and others: but lately I've done what we call the local bags—which come in before bed-time—at night. It saves time in the morning."

"Do you recollect noticing the letter for Crabb Cot?"

"I think I noticed it. Yes, I feel sure I did. You see, there's often something or other for you, so that it's not remarkable. But I am sure I did notice the letter."

"No one could have got to it in the night?"

"What—here?" exclaimed Rymer, opening his eyes in surprise that such a question should be put. "No, certainly not. The letter-bags are locked up in this desk, and I keep the key about me."

"And you gave them as usual to Lee in the morning?"

Mr. Rymer knitted his patient brow the least in the world, as if he thought that Tod's pursuing these questions reflected some suspicion on himself. He answered very meekly—going over the whole from the first.

"When I brought the Worcester bag in on Wednesday night, I was at home alone: my wife and daughter happened to be spending the evening with some friends, and the servant had asked leave to go out. I sorted the letters, and locked them up as usual in one of the deep drawers of the desk. I never unlocked it again until the last thing in the morning, when the other letters that had come in were ready to go out, and the two men were waiting for them. The letter would be in Lee's packet, of course—which I delivered to him. But Lee is to be depended on: he would not tamper with it. That is the whole history so far as I am connected with it, Mr. Joseph Todhetley. I could not tell you more if I talked till mid-day."

"What's that, Thomas? Anything amiss with the letters?" called out a voice at this juncture, as the inner door opened, that shut out the kitchen.

I knew it. Knew it for Mrs. Rymer's. I didn't like her a bit: and how a refined man like Rymer (and he was so in all respects) could have made her his wife seemed to me to be a seven days' wonder. She had a nose as long as from Timberdale to Crabb Ravine; and her hair and face were red, and her flounces gaudy. As common a woman as you'd see in a summer's day, with a broad Brummagem accent. But she was very capable, and not unkindly natured. The worst Timberdale said of her was, that she had done her best to spoil that ugly son of hers.

Putting her head, ornamented with yellow curl-papers, round the door-post, she saw us seated there, and drew it away again. Her sleeves were rolled up, and she had on a coarse apron; altogether was not dressed for company. Letting the door stand ajar, she asked again if anything was amiss, and went on with her work at the same time: which sounded like chopping suet. Mr. Rymer replied in a curt word or two, as if he felt annoyed she should interfere. She would not be put off: strong-minded women never are: and he had to give her the explanation. A five-pound bank-note had been mysteriously lost out of a letter addressed to Mrs. Todhetley. The chopping stopped.

"Stolen out of it?"

"Well—yes; It may be said so."

"But why do you call it mysterious?"

Mr. Rymer said why. That the bank-note had not, in one sense, been stolen; since another of the same value had been substituted for it.

Chop, chop, chop: Mrs. Rymer had begun again vigorously.

"I'd like to know who's to make top or tail of such a story as that," she called out presently. "Has anything been lost, or not?"

"Yes, I tell you, Susannah: a five-pound note."

Forgetting her curl-papers and the apron, Mrs. Rymer came boldly inside the room, chopping-knife in hand, and requested further enlightenment. We told her between us: she stood with her back against the door-post while she listened.

"When do you say this took place, young gents?"

"On Wednesday night, or Thursday morning. When the letter reached us at breakfast-time, the job was done."

She said no more then, but went back and chopped faster than ever. Tod and I had got up to go when she came in again.

"The odd part about it is their putting in a note for the same value," cried she. "I never heard of such a thing as that. Why not spend the other note, and make no bother over it?"

"You would be quite justified in doing so under the circumstances, Mr. Todhetley," said the quieter husband.

"But we can't," returned Tod, hotly—and all but said more than he was to say.

"Why not?" asked she.

"Because it's not ours; there, Mrs. Rymer."

"Well, I know what I'd say—if the chance was given me," returned she, resenting Tod's manner. "That the note found in the letter was the one put into it at Worcester. Changed in the post! It does not stand to reason."

"But, my dear—" her husband was beginning.

"Now, Thomas Rymer, that's what I think: and so would you, if you had a grain of sense beyond a gander's. And now good-morning, young gents: my pudding won't get done for dinner at this rate."

Mr. Rymer came with us through the shop to the door. I shook hands with him: and Tod's nose went up in the air. But I think it lies in what you see a man is, by mind and nature, whether he is your equal, and you feel proud to think he is so—not in the fact of his wearing an apron. There are some lords in the land I wouldn't half care to shake hands with as I would with Thomas Rymer.

"I hope you will pardon me for reverting to my first opinion, Mr. Todhetley," he said, turning to Tod— "but indeed I think there must be some mistake. Mrs. Rymer may be right—that the note found in the letter was the one put into it."

Tod flung away. The facts he had obstinately refused to believe at first, he had so fully adopted now, that any other opinion offended him. He was in a passion when I caught him up.

"To think that the pater should have sent us there like two fools, Johnny! Closing our mouths so that we could not speak the truth."

"Rymer only three parts believes it. His wife not at all."

"His wife be sugared! It's nothing to her. And all through the suggestion of that precious calf, Cole. Johnny, I think I shall act on my own judgment, and go back and tell Rymer the note was a stolen one."

"The pater told us not to."

"Stuff! Circumstances alter cases. He would have told it himself before he had been with Rymer two minutes. The man's hands are partly tied, you see; knowing only half the tale."

"Well, I won't tell him."

"Nobody asked you. Here goes. And the Squire will say I've done right."

Rymer was standing at his door still. The shop was empty, and there were no ears near. Tod lowered his voice, though.

"The truth is, Mr. Rymer, that the note, substituted in the letter for ours, was one of those two lost by the butcher at Tewkesbury. I conclude you heard of the robbery."

"One of those two!" exclaimed Rymer.

"Yes: Salmon at South Crabb recognized it yesterday when we were asking him to give change for it."

"But why not have told me this at once, Mr. Joseph?"

"Because the Squire and Cole, laying their wise heads together this morning, thought it might be better not to let that get abroad: it would put people on their guard, they said. You see now where the motive lay for exchanging the notes."

"Of course I do," said Mr. Rymer in his quiet way. "But it is very unaccountable. I cannot imagine where the treason lies."

"Not on this side, seemingly," remarked Tod: "The letter appears to have passed through no one's hands but Lee's: and he is safe."

"Safe and sure. It must have been accomplished at Worcester. Or—in the railway train," he slowly added. "I have heard of such things."

"You had better keep counsel at present as to the stolen note, Mr. Rymer."

"I will until you give me leave to speak. All I can do to assist in the discovery is heartily at Squire Todhetley's service. I'd transport these rogues, for my part."

We carried our report home—that the thing had not been, and could not have been, effected on the Timberdale side, unless old Lee was to be suspected: which was out of the question.

Time went on, and it grew into more of a mystery than ever. Not as to the fact itself or the stolen note, for all that was soon known high and low. The Worcester office exonerated itself from suspicion, as did the railway letter-van. The van let off its resentment in a little private sneering: but the office waxed hot, and declared the fraud must lie at the door of Timberdale. And so the matter was given up for a bad job, the Squire submitting to the loss of his note.

But a curious circumstance occurred, connected with Thomas Rymer. And, to me, his behaviour had seemed almost curious throughout. Not at that first interview—as I said, he was open, and, so to say, indifferent then; but soon afterwards his manner changed.

On the day following that interview, the Squire, who was very restless over it, wanting the thing to come to light in no time, sent me again to Rymer's, to know if he had learned any news. Rymer said he had not; and his manner was just what it had been the past day. I could have staked my life, if necessary, that the man believed what he said—that news must be looked for elsewhere, not at Timberdale. I am sure that he thought it impossible that the theft could have been effected after the letters came into his hands. But some days later on, when the whole matter had been disclosed, and the public knew as much about it as we did, the Squire, well of his cold, thought he would have a talk with Rymer himself, went over, and took me with him.

I shall not forget it. In Rymer's window, the chemical side, there was a picture of a bullock eating up some newly-invented cattle-food and growing fat upon it. It caught the Squire's eye. Whilst he stopped to read the advertisement, I went in. The moment Rymer saw me—his daughter called to him to come out of the parlour where he was at dinner—his face turned first red, and then as pale as death.

"Mr. Todhetley thought he would like to come and see you, Mr. Rymer."

"Yes, yes," he said, in an agitated sort of tone, and then he stooped to put some jars closer together under the counter; but I thought he knew how white he was, and wanted to hide it.

When the Squire came in, asking first of all about the new cattle-food, he noticed nothing. Rymer was very nearly himself then, and said he had taken the agency, and old Massock had ordered some of it.

Then they talked about the note. Rymer's tone was quite different from what it had been before; though whether I should have noticed it but for his white face I can hardly tell. That had made me notice him. He spoke in a low, timid voice, saying no more than he was obliged to say, as if the subject frightened him. One thing I saw—that his hands trembled. Some camomile blows lay on a white paper on the counter, and he began doing them up with shaky fingers.

Was his wife given to eavesdropping? I should have thought not—she was too independent for it. But there she was, standing just within the little parlour, and certainly listening. The Squire caught sight of her gown, and called out, "How d'ye do, Mrs. Rymer?" upon which she came forward. There was a scared look on her face also, as if its impudence had shrunk out of it. She did not stay an instant—just answered the Squire, and went away again.

"We must come to the bottom of the business somehow, you know, Rymer," concluded the Squire, as he was leaving. "It would never do to let the thief get off. What I should think is, that it must be the same fellow who robbed the butcher—"

"No, no," hastily interrupted Rymer.

"No! One of the gang, then. Any way, you'll help us all you can. I should like to bring the lot to trial. If you get to learn anything, send me word at once."

Rymer answered "Yes," and attended us to the door. Then the Squire went back to the cattle-food; but we got away at last.

"Thomas Rymer breaks, Johnny, I think. He doesn't seem in spirits somehow. It's hard for a man to be in a shop all day long, from year's end to year's end, and never have an hour's holiday."

Ever after this, when the affair was spoken of with Rymer, he showed more or less the same sort of shrinking—as if the subject gave him some terrible pain. Nobody but myself noticed it; and I only because I looked out for it. I believe he saw I thought something; for when he caught my eye, as he did more than once, his own fell.

But some curious circumstances connected with him have to be told yet. One summer evening, when it was getting towards dusk, he came over to Crabb Cot to see the Squire. Very much to the pater's surprise, Rymer put a five-pound note into his hand.

"Is the money found?" cried he, eagerly.

"No, sir, it is not found," said Rymer, in a subdued tone. "It seems likely to remain a mystery to the last. But I wish to restore it myself. It lies upon my conscience—being postmaster here—that such a loss should have taken place. With three parts of the public, and more, it is the Timberdale side that gets the credit of being to blame. And so—it weighs heavily upon me. Though I don't see how I could have prevented it: and I lie awake night after night, thinking it over."

The Squire stared for awhile, and then pushed back the note.

"Why, goodness, man!" cried he, when his amazement let him speak, "you don't suppose I'd take the money from you! What in the world!—what right have you to bear the loss? You must be dreaming."

"I should feel better satisfied," said poor Rymer, in his subdued voice of pain. "Better satisfied."

"And how do you think I should feel?" stamped the Squire, nearly flinging the note into the fire. "Here, put it up; put it up. Why, my good fellow, don't, for mercy's sake, let this bother take your senses away. It's no more your fault that the letter was rifled than it was mine. Well, this is a start—your coming to say this."

They went on, battling it out. Rymer praying him to take the note as if he'd pray his life away; the Squire accusing the other of having gone clean mad, to think of such a thing. I happened to go into the room in the middle of it, but they had not leisure to look at me. It ended in Rymer's taking back the note: it could not have ended in any other manner: the Squire vowing, if he did not, that he should go before the magistrates for lunacy.

"Get the port wine, Johnny."

Rymer declined to take any: his head was not accustomed to wine, he said. The Squire poured out a bumper and made him drink it: telling him he believed it was something of the kind his head wanted, or it would never have got such a wild notion into it as the errand he had come upon that evening.

A few minutes after Rymer had left, I heard the Squire shouting to me, and went back to the room. He had in his hand a little thin note-case of green leather, something like two leaves folded together.

"Rymer must have dropped this, Johnny, in putting it into his pocket. The note is in it. You had better run after him."

I took it, and went out. But which way had Rymer gone? I could see far along the solitary road, and it was light enough yet, but no one was in view, so I guessed he was taking the short-cut through the Ravine, braving the ghost, and I went across the field and ran down the zigzag path. Wasn't it gloomy there!

Well, it was a surprise! Thinking himself alone, he had sat down on the stump of a tree, and was sobbing with all his might: sobs that had prevented his hearing me. There was no time for me to draw back, or for him to hide his trouble. I could only hold out the green case and make the best of it.

"I am afraid you are in some great trouble, Mr. Rymer?"

He got up and was quiet at once. "The best of us have trouble at times, Master Johnny."

"What can I do for you?"

"Nothing. Nothing. Except forget that you have seen me giving way. It was very foolish of me: but there are moments when—when one loses self-control."

Either through his awkwardness or mine, the leaves of the case opened, and the bank-note fluttered out. I picked it up and gave it to him. Our eyes met in the gloom.

"I think you know," he whispered.

"I think I suspect. Don't be afraid: no one else does: and I'll never drop a hint to mortal man."

Putting my hand into his that he might feel its clasp, he took it as it was meant, and wrung it in answer. Had we been of the same age, I could have felt henceforth like his brother.

"It will be my death-blow," he whispered. "Heaven knows I was not prepared for it. I was unsuspicious as a child."

He went his way with his grief and his load of care, and I went mine, my heart aching for him. I am older now than I was then: and I have learnt to think that God sends these dreadful troubles to try us, that we may fly from them to Him. Why else should they come?

And I dare say you have guessed how it was. The time came when it was all disclosed; so I don't break faith in telling it. That ill-doing son of Rymer's had been the thief. He was staying at home at the time with one of the notes stolen from Tewkesbury in his possession: some of his bad companions had promised him a bonus if he could succeed in passing it. It was his mother who surreptitiously got the keys of the desk for him, that he might open it in the night: he made the excuse to her that there was a letter in the Worcester bag for himself under a false direction, which he must secure, unsuspected. To do Madam Rymer justice, she thought no worse: and it was she who in her fright, when the commotion arose about the Tewkesbury note, confessed to her husband that she had let Ben have the keys that night. There could be no doubt in either of their minds after that. The son, too, had decamped. It was to look for our letter he had wanted the keys. For he knew it might be coming, with the note in it: he was on the platform at Timberdale railway-station in the morning—I saw him standing there—and must have heard what Mrs. Todhetley said. And that was the whole of the mystery.

But I would have given the money from my own pocket twice over, to have prevented it happening, for Thomas Rymer's sake.

CHAPTER II

A LIFE OF TROUBLE

Mrs. Todhetley says that you may sometimes read a person's fate in their eyes. I don't know whether it's true. She holds to it that when the eyes have a sad, mournful expression naturally, their owner is sure to have a life of sorrow. Of course such instances may be found: and Thomas Rymer's was one of them.

You can look back and read what was said of him: "A thin, delicate-faced man, with a rather sad expression and mild brown eyes." The sad expression was in the eyes: that was certain: thoughtful, dreamy, and would have been painfully sad but for its sweetness. But it is not given to every one to discern this inward sadness in the look of another.

It was of no avail to say that Thomas Rymer had brought trouble upon himself, and marred his own fortune. His father was a curate in Warwickshire, poor in pence, rich in children. Thomas was apprenticed to a doctor in Birmingham, who was also a chemist and druggist. Tom had to serve in the shop, take out teeth, make up the physic, and go round with his master to fevers and rheumatisms. Whilst he was doing this, the curate died: and thenceforth Thomas would have to make his own way in the world, with not a soul to counsel him.

Of course he might have made it. But Fate, or Folly, was against him. Some would have called it fate, Mrs. Todhetley for one; others might have said it was folly.

Next door to the doctor's was a respectable pork and sausage shop, carried on by a widow, one Mrs. Bates. Rymer took to going in there of an evening when he had the time, and sitting in the parlour behind with Mrs. Bates and her two daughters. Failing money for theatres and concerts, knowing no friends to drop in to, young fellows drift anywhere for relaxation when work is done. Mrs. Bates, a good old motherly soul, as fat as her best pig, bade him run in whenever he felt inclined. Rymer liked her for her hearty kindness, and liked uncommonly the dish of hot sausages, or chops, that would come on the table for supper. The worst was, he grew to like something else—and that was Miss Susannah.

If it's true that people are attracted by their contrasts, there might have been some excuse for Rymer. He was quiet and sensitive, with a refined mind and person, and retiring manners. Susannah Bates was free, loud, good-humoured, and vulgar. Some people, it was said, called her handsome then; but, judging by what she was later, we thought it must have been a very broad style of beauty. The Miss Bateses were intended by their mother to be useful; but they preferred being stylish. They played "Buy a broom" and other fashionable tunes on the piano, spent time over their abundant hair, wore silks for best, carried a fan to chapel on Sundays, and could not be persuaded to serve in the shop on the busiest day. Good Mrs. Bates managed the shop herself with the help of her foreman: a steady young man, whose lodgings were up a court hard by.

Well, Tom Rymer, the poor clergyman's son, grew to be as intimate there as if it were his home, and he and Susannah struck up a friendship that continued all the years he was at the next door. Just before he was out of his time, Mrs. Bates died.

The young foreman somehow contrived to secure the business for himself, and married the elder Miss Bates off-hand. There ensued some frightful squabbling between the sisters. The portion of money said to be due to Miss Susannah was handed over to her with a request that she should find herself another home. Rymer came of age just then, and the first thing he did was to give her a home himself by making her his wife.

There was the blight. His prospects were over from that day. The little money she had was soon spent: he must provide a living how he could. Instead of qualifying himself for a surgeon, he took a situation as a chemist and druggist's assistant: and, later, set up for himself in the shop at Timberdale. For the first ten years of his married life, he was always intending to pass the necessary examinations: each year saying it should be done the next. But expenses came on thick and fast; and that great need with every one, present wants, had to be supplied first. He gave up the hope then: went on in the old jog-trot line, and subsided into an obscure rural chemist and druggist.

The son, Benjamin, was intended for a surgeon. As a preliminary, he was bound apprentice to his father in order to learn the mysteries of drugs and chemicals. When out of his time, he was transferred to a chemist and druggist's at Tewkesbury, who was also in practice as a medical man. There, Mr. Benjamin fell in with bad companions; a lapse that, in course of time, resulted in his coming home, changing the note in our letter for the stolen one, and then decamping from Timberdale. What with the blow the discovery itself was to Rymer, and what with the concealing of the weighty secret—for he had to conceal it: he could not go and inform against his own son—it pretty nearly did for him. Rymer tried to make reparation in one sense of the word—by the bringing of that five-pound bank-note to the Squire. For which the Squire, ignorant of the truth, thought him a downright lunatic.

For some months, after that evening, Thomas Rymer was to be seen in his shop as usual, growing to look more and more like a ghost. Which Darbyshire, the Timberdale doctor, said was owing to liver, and physicked him well.

But the physic did not answer. Of all obstinate livers, as Darbyshire said, Rymer's was about the worst he had ever had to do with. Some days he could not go into the shop at all, and Margaret, his daughter, had to serve the customers. She could make up prescriptions just as well as he, and people grew to trust her. They had a good business. It was known that Rymer's drugs were genuine; had direct from the fountain-head. He had given up the post-office, and the grocer opposite had taken to it—Salmon, who was brother to Salmon of South Crabb. In this uncertain way, a week ill, and a week tolerably well, Rymer continued to go on for about two years.

Margaret Rymer stood behind the counter: a neat little girl in grey merino. Her face was just like her father's; the same delicate features, the sweet brown eyes, and the look of innate refinement. Margaret belonged to his side of the house; there was not an atom of the Brummagem Bateses in her. The Squire, who remembered her grandfather the clergyman, said Margaret took after him. She was in her nineteenth year now, and for steadiness you might have trusted her alone right across the world and back again.

She stood behind the counter, making up some medicine. A woman in a coarse brown cloak with a showy cotton handkerchief tied on her head was waiting for it. It had been a dull autumn day: evening was coming on, and the air felt chilly.

"How much be it, please, miss?" asked the woman, as Margaret handed her the bottle of mixture, done up in white paper.

"Eighteenpence. Thank you."

"Be the master better?" the woman turned round from the door to inquire, as if the state of Mr. Rymer's health had been an afterthought.

"I think he is a little. He has a very bad cold, and is lying in bed to-day. Thank you for asking. Good-night."

When dusk came on, Margaret shut the street-door and went into the parlour. Mrs. Rymer sat there writing a letter. Margaret just glanced in.

"Mother, can you listen to the shop, please?"

"I can if I choose—what should hinder me?" responded Mrs. Rymer. "Where are you off to, Margaret?"

"To sit with my father for a few minutes."

"You needn't bother to leave the shop for that. I dare say he's asleep."

"I won't stay long," said Margaret. "Call me, please, if any one comes in."

She escaped up the staircase, which stood in the nook between the shop and the parlour. Thomas Rymer lay back in the easy-chair by his bit of bedroom fire. He looked as ill as a man could look, his face thin and sallow, the fine nose pinched, the mild brown eyes mournful.

"Papa, I did not know you were getting up," said Margaret, in a soft low tone.

"Didn't you hear me, child?" was his reply, for the room was over the shop. "I have been long enough about it."

"I thought it was my mother moving about."

"She has not been here all the afternoon. What is she doing?"

"I think she is writing a letter."

Mr. Rymer groaned—which might have been caused by the pain that he was always feeling. Mrs. Rymer's letters were few and far between, and written to one correspondent only—her son Benjamin.

That Benjamin was random and must be getting a living in any chance way, or not getting one at all, and that he had never been at home for between two and three years, Margaret knew quite well. But she knew no worse. The secret hidden between Mr. and Mrs. Rymer, that they never spoke of to each other, had been kept from her.

"I wish you had not got up," said Margaret. "You are not well enough to come down to-night."

He looked at her, rather quickly; and spoke after a pause.

"If I don't make an effort—as Darbyshire tells me—it may end in my becoming a confirmed invalid, child. I must get down while I can."

"You will get better soon, papa; Mr. Darbyshire says so," she answered, quietly swallowing down a sigh.

"Ay, I know he does. I hope it will be so, please God. My life has been only a trouble throughout, Margaret; but I should like to struggle with it yet for all your sakes."

Looking at him as he sat there, the firelight playing upon his worn face with its subdued spirit, you might have seen it was true—that his life had been a continuous trouble. Was he born to it? or did it only come upon him through marrying Susannah Bates? On the surface of things, lots seemed very unequally dealt out in this world. What had been the lot of Thomas Rymer? The poor son of a poor curate, he had known little but privation in his earlier years; then came the long drudgery of his apprenticeship, then his marriage, and the longer drudgery of his after-life. An uncongenial and unsuitable marriage—and he had felt it to the backbone. From twenty to thirty years had Rymer toiled in a shop late and early; never taking a day's rest or a day's holiday, for some one must always be on duty, and he had no help or substitute. Even on Sundays he must be at hand, lest his neighbours should be taken ill and want drugs. If he went to church, there was no certainty that his servant-maid—generally a stout young woman in her teens, with a black face and rough hair—would not astonish the congregation by flying up to his pew-door to call him out. Indeed the vision was not so very uncommon. Where, then, could have been Rymer's pleasure in life? He had none; it was all work. And upon the work came the trouble.

Just as the daughter, Margaret, was like her father, so the son, Benjamin, resembled his mother. But for the difference of years, and that his red hair was short and hers long, he might have put on a lace cap, and sat for her portrait. He was the eldest of the children; Margaret the youngest, those between had died. Seven years between children makes a difference, and Margaret with her gentleness had always been afraid of rough Benjamin.

But whether a child is ugly or handsome, it's all the same to the parents, and for some years the only white spot in Thomas Rymer's life had been the love of his little Benjamin. For the matter of that, as a child, Ben was rather pretty. He grew up and turned out wild; and it was just as great a blow as could have fallen upon Rymer. But when that horrible thing was brought home to him—taking the bank-note out of the letter, and substituting the stolen one for it—then Rymer's heart gave in. Ever since that time it had been as good as breaking.

Well, that was Thomas Rymer's lot in life. Some people seem, on the contrary, to have nothing but sunshine. Do you know what Mrs. Todhetley says?—that the greater the cloud here, the brighter will be the recompense hereafter. Looking at Thomas Rymer's face as the fire played on it—its goodness of expression, almost that of a martyr; remembering his prolonged battle with the world's cares, and his aching heart; knowing how inoffensive he had been towards his fellow-creatures, ever doing them a good turn when it lay in his power, and never an ill one—one could only hope that his recompense would be of the largest.

"Had many people in this afternoon, Margaret?"

"Pretty well, papa."

Mr. Rymer sighed. "When I get stronger—"

"Margaret! Shop."

The loud coarse summons was Mrs. Rymer's. Margaret's spirit recoiled from it the least in the world. In spite of her having been brought up to the "shop," there had always been something in her innate refinement that rebelled against it and against having to serve in it.

"A haperth o' liquorish" was the extensive order from a small child, whose head did not come much above the counter. Margaret served it at once: the liquorice, being often in demand, was kept done up in readiness. The child laid down the halfpenny and went out with a bang.

"I may as well run over with the letter," thought Margaret—alluding to an order she had written to London for some drug they were out of. "And there's my mother's. Mother," she added, going to the parlour-door, "do you want your letter posted?"

"I'll post it myself when I do," replied Mrs. Rymer. "Ain't it almost time you had the gas lighted? That shop must be in darkness."

It was so, nearly. But the gas was never lighted until really needed, in the interests of economy. Margaret ran across the road, put her letter into the post in Salmon's window, and ran back again. She stood for a moment at the door, looking at a huge lumbering caravan that was passing—a ménage on wheels, as seen by the light within its small windows. "It must be on its way to Worcester fair," she thought.

"Is it you, Margaret? How d'ye do?"

Some great rough man had come up, and was attempting to kiss her. Margaret started back with a cry. She would have closed the door against him; but he was the stronger and got in.

"Why, what possesses the child! Don't you know me?"

Every pulse in Margaret Rymer's body tingled to pain as she recognized him. It was her brother Benjamin. Better, than this, that it had been what she fancied—some rude stranger, who in another moment would have passed on and been gone for ever. Benjamin's coming was always the signal for discomfort at home, and Margaret felt half-paralyzed with dismay.

"How are the old folk, Maggie?"

"Papa is very ill," she answered, her voice slightly trembling. "My mother is well as usual. I think she was writing to you this afternoon."

"Governor ill! So I've heard. Upstairs a good deal, is he not?"

"Quite half his time, I think."

"Who attends here?"

"I do."

"You!—you little mite! Brought your knowledge of rhubarb to good use, eh? What's the matter with papa?"

"He has not been well for a long while. I don't know what it is. Mr. Darbyshire says"—she dropped her voice a little—"that he is sure there's something on his mind."

"Poor old dad!—just like him! If a woman came in with a broken arm, he'd take it to heart."

"Benjamin, I think it is you that he has most at heart," the girl took courage to say.

Mr. Benjamin laughed. "Me! He needn't trouble about me. I am as steady as old Time, Maggie. I've come home to stay; and I'll prove to him that I am."

"Come home to stay!" faltered Margaret.

"I can take care of things here. I am better able to do it than you."

"My father will not put me out of my place here," said Margaret, steadily. "He has confidence in me; he knows I do things just as he does."

"And for that reason he makes you his substitute! Don't assume, Miss Maggie; you'd be more in your place stitching wristbands in the parlour than as the presiding genius in a drug-shop. How d'ye do, mother?"

The sound of his voice had reached Mrs. Rymer. She did not believe her own ears, and came stealing forth to look, afraid of what she might see. To give Madam Rymer her due, she was quite as honest-natured as her husband; and the matter of the bank-note, the wrong use made of the keys she was foolish enough to lend surreptitiously to Mr. Benjamin, had brought her no light shock at the time. Ill-conduct in the shape of billiards, and beer, and idleness, she had found plenty of excuse for in her son; but when it came to felony, it was another thing altogether.

"It is him!" she muttered, as he saw her, and turned. "Where on earth have you sprung from?" demanded Mrs. Rymer.

"Not from the skies, mother. Hearing the governor was on the sick list, I thought I ought to come over and see him."

"None of your lies, Ben," said Mrs. Rymer. "That has not brought you here. You are in some disgraceful mess again."

"It has brought me here—and nothing else," said Ben: and he spoke truth. "Ashton of Timberdale—"

A faint groan—a crash as of breaking glass. When they turned to look, there was Rymer, fallen against the counter in his shock of surprise and weakness. His arm had thrown down an empty syrup-bottle.

And that's how Benjamin Rymer came home. His father and mother had never seen him since before the discovery of the trouble; for as soon as he had changed the bank-note in the letter, he was off. The affair had frightened him a little—that is, the stir made over it, of which he had contrived to get notice; since then he had been passably steady, making a living for himself in Birmingham as assistant to a surgeon and druggist. He had met Robert Ashton a short time ago (this was the account he now gave), heard from that gentleman rather a bad account of his father, and so thought it his duty to give up what he was about, and come home. His duty! Ben Rymer's duty!!

Ben was a tall, bony fellow, with a passably liberal education. He might not have been unsteady but for bad companions. Ben did not aid in robbing the butcher's till—he had not quite come to that—neither was he privy to it; but he did get persuaded into trying to dispose of one of the stolen notes. It had been the one desperate act of his life, and it had sobered him. Time, however, effaces impressions; from two to three years had gone on since then; nothing had transpired, never so much as a suspicion had fallen on Mr. Benjamin, and he grew bold and came home.

Timberdale rubbed its eyes with astonishment that next autumn day, when it woke up to see Benjamin Rymer in his father's shop, a white apron on, and serving the customers who went in, as naturally as though he had never left it. Where had he been all that while? they asked. Improving himself in his profession, coolly avowed Ben with unruffled face.

And so the one chance—rest of mind—for the father's return to health and life, went out. The prolonged time, passing without discovery, giving a greater chance day by day that it might never happen, could but have a beneficial effect on Mr. Rymer. But when Ben made his appearance, put his head, so to say, into the very stronghold of danger, all his sickness and his fear came back again.

Ben did not know why his father kept so poorly and looked so ill. Never a word, in his sensitiveness, had Mr. Rymer spoken to his son of that past night's work. Ben might suspect, but he did not know. Mr. Rymer would come down when he was not fit to do so, and take up his place in the shop on a stool. Ben made fun of it: in sport more than ill-feeling: telling the customers to look at the old ghost there. Ben made himself perfectly at home; would sometimes hold a levée in the shop if his father was out of it, when he and his friends, young men of Timberdale, would talk and laugh the roof off.

People talk of the troubles of the world, and say their name is legion: poverty, sickness, disappointment, disgrace, debt, difficulty; but there is no trouble the human heart can know like that brought by rebellious children. To old Rymer, with his capacity for taking things to heart, it had been as a long crucifixion. And yet—the instinctive love of a parent cannot die out: recollect David's grief for wicked Absalom: "Would God I had died for thee, O Absalom, my son, my son!"

Still, compared with what he used to be, Ben Rymer was steady. As the winter approached, there set in another phase of the reformation; for he pulled up even from the talking and laughing, and became as good as gold. You might have thought he had taken his dead grandfather, the clergyman, for a model, and was striving to walk in his steps. He went to church, read his medical works, was pleasant at home, gentle with Margaret, and altogether the best son in the world.

"Will it last, Benjamin?" his father asked him sorrowfully.

"It shall last, father; I promise it," was the earnestly-spoken answer. "Forget the past, and I will never, I hope, try you again."

Ben kept his promise throughout the winter, and seemed likely to keep it always. Mr. Rymer grew stronger, and was in business regularly, which gave Ben more leisure for his books. It was thought that a good time had set in for the Rymers; but, as Mrs. Todhetley says, you cannot control Fate.

One day, when we were again staying at Crabb Cot, I had to call at the shop for a box of "Household Pills," Rymer's own making. When any one was ailing at home, Mrs. Todhetley would administer a dose of these pills. But that Rymer was so conscientious a man, I should have thought they were composed of bread and pepper. Mrs. Todhetley pinned her faith to them, and said they did wonders.

Well, I had to go to Timberdale on other matters, and was told to call, when there, for a box of these delectable Household Pills. Mr. Rymer and his son stood behind the counter, the one making up his books, Ben pounding something in a mortar. Winter was just on the turn, and the trees and hedges were beginning to shoot into bud. Ben left his pounding to get the pills.

"Is this Mr. Rymer's? Halloa, Ben! All right. How goes it, old boy?"

The door had been opened with a burst, and the above words met our ears, in a tone not over-steady. They came from a man who wore sporting clothes, and his hat very much on one side. Ben Rymer stared in surprise; his mouth dropped.

But that it was early in the day, and one does not like to libel people, it might have been thought the gentleman had taken a little too much of something strong. He swaggered up to the counter, and held out his hand to Ben. Ben, just then wrapping up the box of pills, did not appear to see it.

"Had a hunt after you, old fellow," said the loud-voiced stranger. "Been to Birmingham and all kinds of places. Couldn't think where you'd hid yourself."

"You are back pretty soon," growled Ben, who certainly did not seem to relish the visit.

"Been back a month. Couldn't get on in the New World; its folks are too down for me. I say, I want a word with you. Can't say it here, I suppose?"

"No," returned Ben, rather savagely.

"Just come out a bit, Ben," resumed the stranger, after a short pause.

"I can't," replied Ben—and his tone sounded more like I won't. "I have my business to attend to."

"Bother business! Here goes, then: it's your fault if you make me speak before people. Gibbs has come out of hiding, and is getting troublesome—"

"If you will go outside and wait, I'll come to you," interrupted Ben at this, very quickly.

The man turned and swaggered out. Ben gave me the pills with one hand, and took off his apron with the other. Getting his hat, he was hastening out, when Mr. Rymer touched his arm.

"Who is that man, Benjamin?"

"A fellow I used to know in Tewkesbury, father."

"What's his name?"

"Cotton. I'll soon despatch him and be back again," concluded Ben, as he disappeared.

I put down half-a-crown for the pills, and Mr. Rymer left his place to give me the change. There had been a sort of consciousness between us, understood though not expressed, since the night when I had seen him giving way to his emotion in Crabb Ravine. This man's visit brought the scene back again. Rymer's eyes looked into mine, and then fell.

"Ben is all right now, Mr. Rymer."

"I could not wish him better than he is. It's just as though he were striving to atone for the past. I thought it would have killed me at the time."

"I should forget it."

"Forget it I never can. You don't know what it was, Mr. Johnny," he continued in a sort of frightened tone, a red spot coming into his pale thin cheeks, "and I trust you never will know. I never went to bed at night but to lie listening for a summons at my door—the officers searching for my son, or to tell me he was taken. I never rose in the morning but my spirit fainted within me, as to what news the day might bring forth."

Mr. Benjamin and his friend were pacing side by side in the middle of the street when I went out, probably to be out of the reach of eavesdroppers. They did not look best pleased with each other; seemed to be talking sharply.

"I tell you I can't and I won't," Ben was saying, as I passed them in crossing over. "What do you come after me for? When a fellow wants to be on the square, you won't let him. As to Gibbs—"

The voices died out of hearing. I went home with the pills, and thought no more about the matter.

Spring weather is changeable, as we English know only too well. In less than a week, a storm of sleet and snow was drifting down. In the midst of it, who should present himself at Crabb Cot at midday but Lee, the letter-carrier. His shaky old legs seemed hardly able to bear him up against the storm, as he came into the garden. I opened the door, wondering what he wanted.

"Please can I see the Squire in private, sir?" asked Lee, who was looking half angry, half rueful. Lee had never been in boisterous spirits since the affair of the bank-note took place. Like a great many more people, he grew fanciful with years, and could not be convinced but that the suspicion in regard to it lay on him.

"Come in out of the storm, Lee. What's up?"

"Please, Mr. Ludlow, sir, let me get to see the Squire," was all his answer.

The Squire was in his little room, hunting for a mislaid letter in the piece of furniture he called his bureau. As I shut old Lee in, I heard him, Lee, begin to say something about the bank-note and Benjamin Rymer. An instinct of the truth flashed over me—as sure as fate something connecting Ben with it had come out. In I shot again, to make one at the conference. The Squire was looking too surprised to notice me.

"It was Mr. Rymer's son who took out the good note and put in the bad one?" he exclaimed. "Take care what you say, Lee."

Lee stood near the worn hearthrug; his old hat, covered with snow-flakes, held between his hands. The Squire had put his back against the bureau and was staring at him through his spectacles, his nose and face a finer red than ordinary.

The thing had been tracked home to Benjamin Rymer by the man Cotton, Lee explained in a rambling sort of tale. Cotton, incensed at Rymer's not helping him to some money—which was what he had come to Timberdale to ask for—had told in revenge of the past transaction. Cotton had not been connected with it, but knew of the part taken in it by Rymer.

"I don't believe a syllable of it," said the Squire, stoutly, flinging himself into his bureau chair, which he twisted round to face the fire. "You can sit down, Lee. Where did you say you heard this?"

Lee had heard it at the Plough and Harrow, where the man Cotton had been staying. Jelf, the landlord, had been told it by Cotton himself, and Jelf in his turn had whispered it to Lee. That was last night: and Lee had come up with it now to Mr. Todhetley.

"I tell you, Lee, I don't believe a syllable of it," repeated the Squire.

"It be true as gospel, sir," asserted Lee. "Last night, when I went in to Jelf's for a drop of beer, being stiff all over with the cold, I found Jelf in a passion because a guest had gone off without paying part of his score, leaving nothing but a letter to say he'd send it. Cotton by name, Jelf explained, and a sporting gent to look at. A good week, Jelf vowed he'd been there, living on the best. And then Jelf said I had no cause to be looked down upon any longer, for it was not me that had done that trick with the bank-notes, but Benjamin Rymer."

"Now just stop, Lee," interrupted the Squire. "Nobody looked down upon you for it, or suspected you: neither Jelf nor other people. I have told you so times enough."

"But Jelf knows I thought they did, sir. And he told me this news to put me a bit at my ease. He—"

"Jelf talks at random when his temper's up," cried the Squire. "If you believe this story, Lee, you'll believe anything."

"Ben Rymer was staying at home at the time, sir," urged Lee, determined to have his say. "If he is steady now, it's known what he was then. He must have got access to the letters somehow, while they lay at his father's that night, and opened yours and changed the note. Cotton says Mr. Ben had had the stolen note hid about him for ever so long, waiting an opportunity to get rid of it."

"Do you mean to accuse Mr. Ben of being one of the thieves who robbed the butcher's till?" demanded the Squire, growing wrathful.

"Well, sir, I don't go as far as that. The man told Jelf that one of the stolen notes was given to young Rymer to pass, and he was to have a pound for himself if he succeeded in doing it."

The Squire would hardly let him finish.

"Cotton said this to Jelf, did he?—and Jelf rehearsed it to you?"

"Yes, sir. Just that much."

"Now look you here, Lee. First of all, to whom have you repeated this tale?"

"Not to anybody," answered Lee. "I thought I'd better bring it up here, sir, to begin with."

"And you'd better let it stop here to end with," retorted the Squire. "That's my best advice to you, Lee. My goodness! Accuse a respectable man's son of what might transport him, on the authority of a drunken fellow who runs away from an inn without paying his bill! The likeliest thing is that this Cotton did it himself. How else should he know about it? Don't you let your tongue carry this further, Lee, or you may find yourself in the wrong box."

Lee looked just a little staggered. A faint flush appeared in his withered face. The Squire's colour was at its fiercest. He was hard at the best of times to take in extraordinary tales, and utterly scouted this one. There was no man he had a greater respect for than Thomas Rymer.

"I hoped you might be for prosecuting, sir. It would set me right with the world."

"You are a fool, Lee. The world has not thought you wrong yet. Prosecute! I! Upon this cock-and-bull story! Mr. Rymer would prosecute me in turn, I expect, if I did. You'd better not let this get to his ears: you might lose your post."

"Mr. Rymer, sir, must know how wild his son has been."

"Wild! Most of the young men of the present day are that, as it seems to me," cried the Squire, in his heat. "Mine had better not let me catch them at it, though. I'd warm their ears well beforehand if I thought they ever would— Do you hear, Mr. Johnny?"

I had been leaning on the back of a chair in the quietest corner for fear of being sent away. When the Squire put himself up like this, he would say anything.

"To be a bit wild is one thing, Lee; to commit felony quite another: Rymer's son would be no more guilty of it than you would. It's out of all reason. And do you take care of your tongue. Look here, man: suppose I took this up, as you want me, and it was found to have been Cotton or some other gaol-bird who did it, instead of young Rymer: where would you be? In prison for defamation of character, if the Rymers chose to put you there. Be wise in time, Lee, and say no more."

"It might have been as you say, sir—Cotton himself; though I'm sure that never struck me," returned Lee, veering round to the argument. "One thing that made me believe it, was knowing that Ben Rymer might easily get access to the letters."

"And that's just the reason why you should have doubted it," contradicted the Squire. "He would be afraid to touch them because of the ease with which he could do it. Forgive you for coming up, you say?" added the Squire, as Lee rose with some humble words of excuse. "Of course I will. But don't forget that a word of this, dropped abroad, might put your place, as postman, in jeopardy."

"And that would never do," said Lee, shaking his head.

"I should think not. It's cold to-day, isn't it?"

"Frightful cold, sir."

"And you could come through it with this improbable story! Use your sense another time, Lee. Here, Johnny, take Lee into the kitchen, and tell them to give him some cold beef and beer."

I handed him over, with the order, to Molly; who went into one of her tantrums at it, for she was in the midst of pastry-making. The Squire was sitting with his head bent, looking as perplexed as an owl, when I got back to the room.

"Johnny—shut the door. Something has come into my mind. Do you recollect Thomas Rymer's coming up one evening, and wanting to give me a five-pound note?"

"Quite well, sir."

"Well; I—I am not so sure now that there's nothing in this fresh tale."

I sat down; and in a low voice told him all. Of the fit of sobbing in which I had found Rymer that same night in the Ravine; and that I had known all along it was the son who had done it.

"Bless my heart!" cried the Squire, softly, very much taken aback. "It's that, perhaps, that has been making Rymer so ill."

"He said it was slowly killing him, sir."

"Mercy on him!—poor fellow! An ill-doing scapegrace of a rascal! Johnny, how thankful we ought to be when our sons turn out well, and not ill! But I think a good many turn out ill nowadays. If you should live to have sons, sir, take care how you bring them up."

"I think Mr. Rymer must have tried to bring Ben up well," was my answer.

"Yes; but did the mother?" retorted the Squire. "More responsibility lies with them than with the father, Johnny; and she spoilt him. Take care, sir, how you choose a wife when the time comes. And there was that miserable lot the lad fell in with at Tewkesbury! Johnny, that Cotton must be an awful blackguard."

"I hope he'll live to feel it."

"Look here, we must hush this up," cried the Squire, sinking his voice and glancing round the room. "I wouldn't bring fresh pain on poor Rymer for the world. You must forget that you've told me, Johnny."

"Yes, that I will."

"It's only a five-pound note, after all. And if it were fifty pounds, I wouldn't stir in it. No, nor for five hundred; be hanged if I would! It's not I that would bring the world about Thomas Rymer's ears. I knew his father and respected him, Johnny; though his sermons were three-quarters of an hour long, sometimes; and I respect Thomas Rymer. You and I must keep this close. And I'll make a journey to Timberdale when this snow-storm's gone, Johnny, and frighten Jelf out of his life for propagating libellous tales."

That's where it ought to have ended. The worst is, "oughts" don't go for much in the world; as perhaps every reader of this paper has learned to know.

When Lee appeared the next morning with the letters as usual, I went out to him. He dropped his voice to speak, as he put them in my hand.

"They say Benjamin Rymer is off, sir."

"Off where?"

"Somewhere out of Timberdale."

"Off for what?"

"I don't know, sir. Jelf accused me of having carried tales there, and called me a jackass for my pains. He said that what he had told me wasn't meant to be repeated again, and I ought not to have gone telling it about, especially to the Rymers themselves; that it might not be true—"

"As the Squire said yesterday, you know, Lee."

"Yes, sir. I answered Jelf that it couldn't have been me that had gone talking to the Rymers, for I had not as much as seen them. Any way, he said, somebody had, for they knew of it, and Benjamin had gone off in consequence. Jelf's as cross over it as two sticks. It's his own fault; why did he tell me what wasn't true?"

Lee went off—looking cross also. After breakfast I related this to the Squire. He didn't seem to like it, and walked about thinking.

"Johnny, I can't stir in it, you see," he said presently. "If it got abroad, people might talk about compromising a felony, and all that sort of rubbish: and I am a magistrate. You must go. See Rymer: and make him understand—without telling him in so many words, you know—that there's nothing to fear from me, and he may call Ben back again. If the young man has begun to lead a new life, Heaven forbid that I, having sons myself, should be a stumbling-block in the way of it."

It was striking twelve when I reached Timberdale. Margaret said her father was poorly, having gone out in the storm of the previous day and caught a chill. He was in the parlour alone, cowering over the fire. In the last few hours he seemed to have aged years. I shut the door.

"What has happened?" I whispered. "I have come on purpose to ask you."

"That which I have been dreading all along," he said in a quiet, hopeless tone. "Benjamin has run away. He got some information, it seems, from the landlord of the Plough and Harrow, and was off the next hour."

"Well, now, the Squire sent me to you privately, Mr. Rymer, to say that Ben might come back again. He has nothing to fear."

"The Squire knows it, then?"

"Yes. Lee came up about it yesterday: Jelf had talked to him. Mr. Todhetley did not believe a word of it: he blew up Lee like anything for listening to such a tale; he means to blow up Jelf for repeating anything said by a vagabond like Cotton. Lee came round to his way of thinking. Indeed there's nothing to be afraid of. Jelf is eating his words. The Squire would not harm your son for the world."

Rymer shook his head. He did not doubt the Squire's friendly feeling, but thought it was out of his hands. He told me all he knew about it.

"Benjamin came to me yesterday morning in a great flurry, saying something was wrong, and he must absent himself. Was it about the bank-note, I asked—and it was the first time a syllable in regard to it had passed between us," broke off Rymer. "Jelf had given him a friendly hint of what had dropped from the man Cotton—you were in the shop that first day when he came in, Mr. Johnny—and Benjamin was alarmed. Before I had time to collect my thoughts, or say further, he was gone."

"Where is he?"

"I don't know. I went round at once to Jelf, and the man told me all. Jelf knows the truth; that is quite clear. He says he has spoken only to Lee; is sorry now for having done that, and he will hush it up as far as he can."

"Then it will be quite right, Mr. Rymer. Why should you be taking it in this way?"

"I am ill," was all he answered. "I caught a chill going round to the Plough and Harrow. So far as mental illness goes, we may battle with it to the end, strength from above being given to us; but when it takes bodily form—why, there's nothing for it but giving in."

Even while we spoke, he was seized with what seemed to be an ague. Mrs. Rymer appeared with some scalding broth, and I said I would run for Darbyshire.

A few days went on, and then news came up to Crabb Cot that Mr. Rymer lay dying. Robert Ashton, riding back from the hunt in his scarlet coat and white cords on his fine grey horse (the whole a mass of splashes with the thaw) pulled up at the door to say How d'ye do? and mentioned it amidst other items. It was just a shock to the Squire, and nothing less.

"Goodness preserve us!—and all through that miserable five-pound note, Johnny!" he cried in a wild flurry. "Where's my hat and top-coat?"

Away to Timberdale by the short cut through the Ravine, never heeding the ghost—although its traditional time of appearing, the dusk of evening, was drawing on—went the Squire. He thought Rymer must be ill through fear of him; and he accused me of having done my errand of peace badly.

It was quite true—Thomas Rymer lay dying. Darbyshire was coming out of the house as the Squire reached it, and said so. Instead of being sorry, he flew in a passion and attacked the doctor.

"Now look you here, Darbyshire—this won't do. We can't have people dying off like this for nothing. If you don't cure him, you had better give up doctoring."

"How d'you mean for nothing?" asked Darbyshire, who knew the Squire well.

"It can't be for much: don't be insolent. Because a man gets a bit of anxiety on his mind, is he to be let die?"

"I've heard nothing about anxiety," said Darbyshire. "He caught a chill through going out that day of the snow-storm, and it settled on a vital part. That's what ails him, Squire."

"And you can't cure the chill! Don't tell me."

"Before this time to-morrow, Thomas Rymer will be where there's neither killing nor curing," was the answer. "I told them yesterday to send for the son: but they don't know where he is."

The Squire made a rush through the shop and up to the bedroom, hardly saying, "With your leave," or, "By your leave." Thomas Rymer lay in bed at the far end; his white face whiter than the pillow; his eyes sunken; his hands plucking at the counterpane. Margaret left the room when the Squire went in. He gave one look; and knew that he saw death there.

"Rymer, I'd almost have given my own life to save you from this," cried he, in the shock. "Oh, my goodness! what's to be done?"

"I seem to have been waiting for it all along; to have seen the exposure coming," said Thomas Rymer, his faint fingers resting in the Squire's strong ones. "And now that it's here, I can't battle with it."

"Now, Rymer, my poor fellow, couldn't you—couldn't you make a bit of an effort to live? To please me: I knew your father, mind. It can't be right that you should die."

"It must be right; perhaps it is well. I can truly say with old Jacob that few and evil have the days of my life been. Nothing but disappointment has been my lot here; struggle upon struggle, pain upon pain, sorrow upon sorrow. I think my merciful Father will remember it in the last great account."

He died at five o'clock in the morning. Lee told us of it when he brought up the letters at breakfast-time. The Squire let fall his knife and fork.

"It's a shame and a sin, though, Johnny, that sons should inflict this cruel sorrow upon their parents," he said later. "Rymer has been brought down to the grave by his son before his hair was grey. I wonder how their accounts will stand at the great reckoning?"

CHAPTER III

HESTER REED'S PILLS

We were at our other and chief home, Dyke Manor: and Tod and I were there for the short Easter holidays, which were shorter in those days than they are in these.

It was Easter Tuesday. The Squire had gone riding over to old Jacobson's with Tod. I, having nothing else to do, got the mater to come with me for a practice on the church organ; and we were taking the round home again through the village, Church Dykely.

Easter was very late that year. It was getting towards the end of April: and to judge by the weather, it might have been the end of May, the days were so warm and glorious.

In passing the gate of George Reed's cottage, Mrs. Todhetley stopped.

"How are the babies, Hester?"

Hester Reed, sunning her white cap and clean cotton gown in the garden, the three elder children around, watering the beds with a doll's watering-pot, and a baby hiding its face on her shoulder, dropped a curtsy as she answered—

"They be but poorly, ma'am, thank you. Look up, Susy," turning the baby's face upwards to show it: and a pale mite of a face it was, with sleepy eyes. "For a day or two past they've not seemed the thing; and they be both cross."

"I should think their teeth are troubling them, Hester."

"Maybe, ma'am. I shouldn't wonder. Hetty, she seems worse than Susy. She's a-lying there in the basket indoors. Would you please spare a minute to step in and look at her, ma'am?"

Mrs. Todhetley opened the gate. "I may as well go in and see, Johnny," she said to me in an undertone: "I fear both the children are rather sickly."

The other baby, "Hetty," lay in the kitchen in a clothes-basket. It had just the same sort of puny white face as its sister. These two were twins, and about a year old. When they were born, Church Dykely went on finely at Hester Reed, asking her if she would not have had enough with one new child but she must go and set up two.

"It does seem very poorly," remarked Mrs. Todhetley, stooping over the young mortal (which was not cross just now, but very still and quiet), and letting it clasp its little fist round one of her fingers. "No doubt it is the teeth. If the children do not get better soon, I think, were I you, Hester, I should speak to Mr. Duffham."

The advice seemed to strike Hester Reed all of a heap. "Speak to Dr. Duffham!" she exclaimed. "Why, ma'am, they must both be a good deal worse than they be, afore we does that. I'll give 'em a dose o' mild physic apiece. I dare say that'll bring 'em round."

"I should think it would not hurt them," assented Mrs. Todhetley. "They both seem feverish; this one especially. I hear you have had Cathy over," she went on, passing to another subject.

"Sure enough us have," said Mrs. Reed. "She come over yesterday was a week and stayed till Friday night."

"And what is she doing now?"

"Well, ma'am, Cathy's keeping herself; and that's something. She has got a place at Tewkesbury to serve in some shop; is quite in clover there, by all accounts. Two good gownds she brought over to her back; and she's pretty nigh as lighthearted as she was afore she went off to enter on her first troubles."

"Hannah told me she was not looking well."

"She have had a nasty attack of—what was it?—neuralgy, I think she called it, and been obliged to go to a doctor," answered Hester Reed. "That's why they gave her the holiday. She was very well while she was here."

I had stood at the door, talking to the little ones with their watering-pot. As the mater was taking her final word with Mrs. Reed, I went on to open the gate for her, when some woman whisked round the corner from Piefinch Lane, and in at the gate.

"Thank ye, sir," said she to me: as if I had been holding it open for her especial benefit.

It was Ann Dovey, the blacksmith's wife down Piefinch Cut: a smart young woman, fond of fine gowns and caps. Mrs. Todhetley came away, and Ann Dovey went in. And this is what passed at Reed's—as it leaked out to the world afterwards.

The baby in the basket began to cry, and Ann Dovey lifted it out and took it on her lap. She understood all about children, having been the eldest of a numerous flock at home, and was no doubt all the fonder of them because she had none of her own. Mrs. Dovey was moreover a great gossip, liking to have as many fingers in her neighbours' pies as she could conveniently get in.

"And now what's amiss with these two twins?" asked she in confidential tones, bending her face forward till it nearly touched Mrs. Reed's, who had sat down opposite to her with the other baby. "Sarah Tanken, passing our shop just now, told me they warn't the thing at all, so I thought I'd run round."

"Sarah Tanken looked in while I was a-washing up after dinner, and saw 'em both," assented Mrs. Reed. "Hetty's the worst of the two; more peeky like."

"Which is Hetty?" demanded Ann Dovey; who, with all her neighbourly visits, had not learnt to distinguish the two apart.

"The one that you be a-nursing."

"Did the mistress of the Manor look at 'em?"

"Yes; and she thinks I'd better give 'em both some mild physic. Leastways, I said a dose might bring 'em round," added Hester Reed, correcting herself, "and she said it might."

"It's the very thing for 'em, Hester Reed," pronounced Mrs. Dovey, decisively. "There's nothing like a dose of physic for little ones; it often stops a bout of illness. You give it to the two; and don't lose no time. Grey powder's best."

"I've not got any grey powder by me," said Mrs. Reed. "It crossed my mind to try 'em with one o' them pills I had from Abel Crew."

"What pills be they?"

"I had 'em from him for myself the beginning o' the year, when I was getting the headache so much. They're as mild as mild can be; but they did me good. The box is upstairs."

"How do you know they'd be the right pills to give to babies?" sensibly questioned Mrs. Dovey.

"Oh, they be right enough for that! When little Georgy was poorly two or three weeks back, I ran out to Abel Crew, chancing to see him go by the gate, and asked whether one of his pills would do the child harm. He said no, it would do him good."

"And did it get him round?"

"I never gave it. Georgy seemed to be so much pearter afore night came, that I thought I'd wait till the morrow. He's a rare bad one to take physic, he is. You may cover a powder in treacle that thick, Ann Dovey, but the boy scents it out somehow, and can't be got to touch it. His father always has to make him; I can't. He got well that time without the pill."

"Well, I should try the pills on the little twins," advised Ann Dovey. "I'm sure they want something o' the sort. Look at this one! lying like a lamb in my arms, staring up at me with its poor eyes, and never moving. You may always know when a child's ill by its quietness. Nothing ailing 'em, they worry the life out of you."

"Both of them were cross enough this morning," remarked Hester Reed, "and for that reason I know they be worse now. I'll try the pill to-night."

Now, whether it was that Ann Dovey had any especial love for presiding at the ceremony of administering pills to children, or whether she only looked in again incidentally in passing, certain it was that in the evening she was for the second time at George Reed's cottage. Mrs. Reed had put the three elder ones to bed; or, as she expressed it, "got 'em out o' the way;" and was undressing the twins by firelight, when Ann Dovey tripped into the kitchen. George Reed was at work in the front garden, digging; though it was getting almost too dark to see where he inserted the spade.

"Have ye give 'em their physic yet?" was Mrs. Dovey's salutation.

"No; but I'm a-going to," answered Hester Reed. "You be just come in time to hold 'em for me, Ann Dovey, while I go upstairs for the box."

Ann Dovey received the pair of babies, and sat down in the low chair. Taking the candle, Mrs. Reed ran up to the room where the elder children slept. The house was better furnished than cottages generally are, and the rooms were of a fairly good size. Opposite the bed stood a high deal press with a flat top to it, which Mrs. Reed made a shelf of, for keeping things that must be out of the children's reach. Stepping on a chair, she put her hand out for the box of pills, which stood in its usual place near the corner, and went downstairs with it.

It was an ordinary pasteboard pill-box, containing a few pills—six or seven, perhaps. Mrs. Dovey, curious in all matters, lifted the lid and sniffed at the pills. Hester Reed was getting the moist sugar they were to be administered in.

"What did you have these here pills for?" questioned Ann Dovey, as Mrs. Reed came back with the sugar. "They bain't over big."

"For headache and pain in the side. I asked old Abel Crew if he could give me something for it, and he gave me these pills."

Mrs. Reed was moistening a teaspoonful of the sugar, as she spoke, with warm water. Taking out one of the pills she proceeded to crush it into small bits, and then mixed it with the sugar. It formed a sort of paste. Dose the first.

"That ain't moist enough, Hester Reed," pronounced Mrs. Dovey, critically.

"No? I'll put a drop more warm water."

The water was added, and one of the children was fed with the delectable compound—Hetty. Mrs. Dovey spoke again.

"Is it all for her? Won't a whole pill be too much for one, d'ye think?"

"Not a bit. When I asked old Abel whether one pill would be too much for Georgy, he said, No—two wouldn't hurt him. I tell ye, Ann Dovey, the pills be as mild as milk."

Hetty took in the whole dose by degrees. Susy had a similar one made ready, and swallowed it in her turn. Then the two babies were conveyed upstairs and put to bed side by side in their mother's room.

Mrs. Dovey, the ceremony being over, took her departure. George Reed came in to his early supper, and soon afterwards he and his wife went up to bed. Men who have to be up at five in the morning must go to rest betimes. The fire and candle were put out, the doors locked, and the cottage was steeped in quietness at a time when in larger houses the evening was not much more than beginning.

How long she slept, Mrs. Reed could not tell. Whether it might be the first part of the night, early or late, or whether morning might be close upon the dawn, she knew not; but she was startled out of her sleep by the cries of the babies. Awful cries, they seemed, coming from children so young; and there could be no mistaking that each was in terrible agony.

"Why, it's convulsions!" exclaimed George Reed, when he had lighted a candle. "Both of them, too!"

Going downstairs as he was, he hastily lighted the kitchen fire and put a kettle of water on. Then, dressing himself, he ran out for Mr. Duffham. The doctor came in soon after George Reed had got back again.

Duffham was accustomed to scenes, and he entered on one now. Mrs. Reed, in a state of distress, had put the babies in blankets and brought them down to the kitchen fire; the three elder children, aroused by the cries, had come down too, and were standing about in their night-clothes, crying with fright. One of the babies was dead—Hetty. She had just expired in her father's arms. The other was dying.

"What on earth have you been giving to these children?" exclaimed Duffham, after taking a good look at the two.

"Oh, sir, what is it, please?" sobbed Mrs. Reed, in her terror. "Convulsions?"

"Convulsions—no," said the doctor, in a fume. "It is something else, as I believe—poison."

At which she set up a shriek that might have been heard out of doors.

"Well, Hetty was dead, I say;" and Duffham could not do anything to save the other. It died whilst he stood there. Duffham repeated his conjecture as to poison; and Mrs. Reed, all topsy-turvy though she was, three-parts bereft of her senses, resented the implication almost angrily.

"Poison!" cried she. "How can you think of such a thing, sir!"

"I tell you that to the best of my belief these children have both died from some irritant poison," asserted Duffham, coolly imperative. "I ask what you have been giving them?"

"They have not been well this three or four days past," replied she, wandering from the point; not evasively, but in her mind's bewilderment. "It must have been their teeth, sir; I thought they were cutting 'em with fever."

"Did you give them any physic?"

"Yes, sir. A pill apiece when I put 'em to bed."

"Ah!" said Mr. Duffham. "What pill was it?"

"One of Abel Crew's."

This answer surprised him. Allowing that his suspicion of poison was correct, he assumed that these pills must have contained it; and he had never had cause to suppose that Abel Crew's pills were otherwise than innocent.

Mrs. Reed, her voice broken by sobs, explained further in answer to his questions, telling him how she had procured these pills from Abel Crew some time before, and had given one of the said pills to each of the babies. Duffham stood against the dresser, taking it all in with a solemn face, his cane held up to his chin.

"Let me see this box of pills, Mrs. Reed."

She went upstairs to get it. A tidy woman in her ways, she had put the box in its place again on the top of the press. Duffham took off the lid, and examined the pills.

"Do you happen to have a bit of sealing-wax in the house, Reed?" he asked presently.

George Reed, who had stood like a man bewildered, looking first on one, then on the other of his dead little ones, answered that he had not. But the eldest child, Annie, spoke up, saying that there was a piece in her little work-box; Cathy had given it her last week when she was at home.

It was produced—part of a small stick of fancy wax, green and gold. Duffham wrapped the pill-box up in the back of a letter that he took from his pocket, and sealed it with a seal that hung to his watch-chain. He put the parcel into the hand of George Reed.

"Take care of it," he said. "This will be wanted."

"There could not have been poison in them pills, sir," burst out Mrs. Reed, her distress increasing at the possibility that he might be right. "If there had been, they'd ha' poisoned me. One night I took three of 'em."

Duffham did not answer. He was nodding his head in answer to his own thoughts.

"And who ever heard of Abel Crew mixing up poison in his pills?" went on Mrs. Reed. "If you please, sir, I don't think he could do it."

"Well, that part of it puzzles me—how he came to do it," acknowledged Duffham. "I like old Abel, and shall be sorry if it is proved that his pills have done the mischief."

Mrs. Reed shook her head. She had more faith than that in Abel Crew.

Ever so many years before—for it was in the time of Sir Peter Chavasse—there appeared one day a wanderer at Church Dykely. It was hot weather, and he seemed to think nothing of camping out in the fields by night, under the summer stars. Who he was, or what he was, or why he had come, or why he stayed, nobody knew. He was evidently not a tramp, or a gipsy, or a travelling tinker—quite superior to it all; a slender, young, and silent man, with a pale and gentle face.

At one corner of the common, spreading itself between the village and Chavasse Grange, there stood a covered wooden shed, formerly used to impound stray cattle, but left to itself since the square space for the new pound had been railed round. By-and-by it was found that the wanderer had taken to this shed to sleep in. Next, his name leaked out—"Abel Crew."

He lived how he could, and as simply as a hermit. Buying a penny loaf at the baker's, and making his dinner of it with a handful of sorrel plucked from the fields, and a drink from the rivulet that ran through the wilderness outside the Chavasse grounds. His days were spent in examining roots and wild herbs, now and then in digging one up; and his nights chiefly in studying the stars. Sir Peter struck up a sort of speaking acquaintanceship with him, and, it was said, was surprised at his stock of knowledge and the extent of his travels; for he knew personally many foreign places where even Sir Peter himself had never been. That may have caused Sir Peter—who was lord of the manor and of the common included—to tolerate in him what it was supposed he would not in others. Anyway, when Abel Crew began to dig the ground about his shed, and plant roots and herbs in it, Sir Peter let him do it and never interfered. It was quite the opposite; for Sir Peter would sometimes stand to watch him at his work, talking the while.

In the course of time there was quite an extensive garden round the shed—comparatively speaking, you know, for we do not expect to see a shed garden as large as that of a mansion. It was fenced in with a hedge and wooden palings, all the work of Abel Crew's hands. Sir Peter was dead then; but Lady Chavasse, guardian to the young heir, Sir Geoffrey, extended to him the same favour that her husband had, and, if she did not absolutely sanction what he was doing, she at any rate did not oppose it. Abel Crew filled his garden with rare and choice and useful field herbs, the valuable properties of which he alone understood; and of ordinary sweet flowers, such as bees love to suck. He set up bee-hives and sold the honey; he distilled lavender and bergamot for perfumes; he converted his herbs and roots into medicines, which he supplied to the poor people around, charging so small a price for them that it could scarcely more than cover the cost of making, and not charging at all the very poor. At the end of about ten years from his first appearance, he took down the old shed, and built up a more convenient cottage in its place, doing it all with his own pair of hands. And the years went on and on, and Abel Crew and his cottage, and his herbs, and his flowers, and his bees, and his medicines, were just as much of an institution in the parish as was the Grange itself.

He and I became good friends. I liked him. You have heard how I take likes and dislikes to faces, and I rarely saw a face that I liked as I liked Abel Crew's. Not for its beauty, though it really was beautiful, with its perfect shape and delicately carved features; but for its unmistakable look of goodness and its innate refinement: perhaps also for the deep, far-seeing, and often sad expression that sat in the earnest eyes. He was old now—sixty, I dare say; tall, slender, and very upright still; his white hair brushed back from his forehead and worn rather long. What his original condition of life might have been did not transpire; he never talked of it. More than once I had seen him reading Latin books; and though he fell into the diction of the country people around when talking with them, he changed his tones and language when conversing with his betters. A character, no doubt, he was, but a man to be respected; a man of religion, too—attending church regularly twice on a Sunday, wet or dry, and carrying his religion into the little things of everyday life.

His style of dress was old-fashioned and peculiar. So far as I saw, it never varied. A stout coat, waistcoat, and breeches every day, all of one colour—drab; with leathern gaiters buttoned nearly to the knee. On Sundays he wore a suit of black silk velvet, and a frilled shirt of fine cambric. His breeches were tied at the knee with black ribbon, in which was a plain, glistening steel buckle; buckles to match shone in his shoes. His stockings were black, and in the winter he wore black-cloth gaiters. In short, on Sundays Abel Crew looked like a fine old-fashioned English gentleman, and would have been taken for one. The woman who got up his linen declared he was more particular over his shirt-frills than Sir Peter himself.

Strangers in the place would sometimes ask what he was. The answer was not easy to give. He was a botanist and herbalist, and made pills, and mixtures, and perfumes, and sold honey, and had built his cottage and planted out his garden, and lived alone, cooking his food and waiting on himself; doing all in fact with his own hands, and was very modest always. On the other side, he had travelled in his youth, he understood paintings, studied the stars, read his store of Latin and classical books, and now and then bought more, and was as good a doctor as Duffham himself. Some people said a better one. Certain it was, that more than once when legitimate medical nostrums had failed—calomel and blisters and bleeding—Abel Crew's simple decoctions and leaves had worked a cure. Look at young Mrs. Sterling at the Court. When that first baby of hers came to town—and a fine squalling young brat he was, with a mouth like a crocodile's!—gatherings arose in her chest or somewhere, one after another; it was said the agony was awful. Duffham's skill seemed to have gone a blackberrying, the other doctor's also, for neither of the two could do anything for her, and the Court thought she would have died of it. Upon that, some relation of old Sterling's was summoned from London—a great physician in great practice. He came in answer, and was liberal with his advice, telling them to try this and to try the other. But it did no good; and she only grew worse. When they were all in despair, seeing her increasing weakness and the prolonged pain, the woman who nursed her spoke of old Abel Crew; she had known him cure in these cases when the doctor could not; and the poor young lady, willing to catch at a straw, told them to send for Abel Crew. Abel Crew took a prepared plaster of herbs with him, green leaves of some sort, and applied it. That night the patient slept more easily than she had for weeks; and in a short time was well again.

But, skilful though he seemed to be in the science of herbs, as remedies for sickness and sores, Abel Crew never obtruded himself upon the ailing, or took money for his advice, or willingly interfered with the province of Duffham; he never would do it unless compelled in the interests of humanity. The patients he chiefly treated were the poor, those who could not have paid Duffham a coin worth thinking about. Duffham knew this. And, instead of being jealous of him, as some medical men might have been, or ridiculing him for a quack, Duffham liked and respected old Abel Crew. He was simple in his habits still: living chiefly upon bread and butter, with radishes or mustard and cress for a relish, cooking vegetables for his dinner, but rarely meat: and his drink was tea or spring water.

So that Abel Crew was rather a notable character amongst us; and when it was known abroad that two of his pills had caused the death of Mrs. Reed's twins, there arose no end of a commotion.

It chanced that the same night this occurred, just about the time in fact that the unfortunate infants were taking down the pills under the superintendence of their mother and the blacksmith's wife, Abel Crew met with an accident; though it was curious enough that it should be so. In taking a pan of boiling herbs off the fire, he let one of the handles slip out of his fingers; it sent the pan down on that side, spilled a lot of the stuff, and scalded his left foot on the instep. Therefore he was about the last person to hear of the calamity; for his door was not open as usual the following morning, and no one knocked to tell him of it.

Duffham was the first. Passing by on his morning rounds, the doctor heard the comments of the people, and it arrested him. It was so unusual a thing for Abel Crew not to be about, and for his door to be closed, that some of them had been arriving at a sensible conclusion—Abel Crew, knowing the mischief his pills had done, was shutting himself up within the house, unable to face his neighbours.

"Rubbish!" said Duffham. And he strode up the garden-path, knocked at the door with his cane, and entered. Abel had dressed, but was lying down on the bed again to rest his lame foot.

Duffham would have asked to look at it, but that he knew Abel Crew was as good at burns and scalds as he himself was. It had been doctored at once, and was now wrapped up in a handkerchief.

"The fire is nearly out of it," said Abel, "but it must have rest; by to-night I shall be able to dress it with my healing-salve. I am much obliged to you for coming in, sir: though in truth I don't know how you could have heard of the accident."

"Ah! news flies," said Duffham, evasively, knowing that he had not heard of the foot, or the neighbours either, and had come in for something altogether different. "What is this about the pills?"

"About the pills?" repeated Abel Crew, who had got up out of respect, and was putting on his coat. "What pills, sir?"

The doctor told him what had happened. Hester Reed had given one of his pills to each of her babies, and both had died of it. Abel Crew listened quietly; his face and his eyes fixed on Duffham.

"The children cannot have died of the pills," said he, speaking as gently as you please. "Something else must have killed them."

"According to Hester Reed's account, nothing can have done it but the pills," said Duffham. "The children had only taken their ordinary food throughout the day, and very little of that. George Reed came running to me in the night, but it was too late; one was dead before I got there. There could be no mistaking the children's symptoms—that both were poisoned."

"This is very strange," exclaimed Abel, looking troubled. "By what kind of poison?"

"Arsenic, I think. I—"

But here they were interrupted. Dovey, the blacksmith, hearing of the calamity, together with the fact that it was his wife who had assisted in administering the suspected doses, deemed it his duty to look into the affair a little, and to resent it. He had left his forge and a bar of iron red-hot in it, and come tearing along in his leather apron, his shirt-sleeves stripped up to the elbow, and his arms grimy. A dark-eyed, good-natured little man in general, was Dovey, but exploding with rage at the present moment.

"Now then, Abel Crew, what do you mean by selling pills to poison people?" demanded he, pushing back the door with a bang, and stepping in fiercely. Duffham, foreseeing there was going to be a contest, and having no time to waste, took his departure.

"I have not sold pills to poison people," replied Abel.

"Look here," said Dovey, folding his black arms. "Be you going to eat them pills, or be you not? Come!"

"What do you mean, Dovey?"

"What do I mean! Ain't my meaning plain? Do you own to having selled a box of pills to Hester Reed last winter?—be you thinking to eat that there fact, and deny of it? Come, Abel Crew!"

"I remember it well," readily spoke up Abel. "Mrs. Reed came here one day, complaining that her head ached continually, and her side often had a dull pain in it, and asked me to give her something. I did so; I gave her a box of pills. It was early in January, I think. I know there was ice on the ground."

"Then do you own to them pills," returned Dovey, more quietly, his fierceness subdued by Abel's civility. "It were you that furnished 'em?"

"I furnished the box of pills I speak of, that Hester Reed had from me in the winter. There's no mistake about that."

"And made 'em too?"

"Yes, and made them."

"Well, I'm glad to hear you say that; and now don't you go for to eat your words later, Abel Crew. Our Ann, my wife, helped to give them there two pills to the children; and I'm not a-going to let her get into trouble over it. You've confessed to the pills, and I'm a witness."

"My pills did not kill the children, Dovey," said Abel, in a pleasant tone, resting his lame foot upon an opposite chair.

"Not kill 'em?"

"No, that they did not. I've not made pills all these years to poison children at last."

"But what done it if the pills didn't?"

"How can I say? 'Twasn't my pills."

"Dr. Duffham says it was the pills. And he—"

"Dr. Duffham says it was?"

"Reed told me that the doctor asked outright, all in a flurry, what his wife had gave the babies, and she said she had gave 'em nothing but them there two pills of Abel Crew's. Duffham said the pills must have had poison in 'em, and he asked for the box; and Hester Reed, she give him the box, and he sealed it up afore their eyes with his own seal."

Abel nodded. He knew that any suspected medicine must in such a case be sealed up.

"And now that I've got that there word from ye, I'll say good-day to ye, neighbour, for I've left my forge to itself, and some red-hot iron in it. And I hope with all my heart and mind,"—the blacksmith turned round from the door to say more kindly, his good-nature cropping up again,—"that it'll turn out it warn't the pills, but some'at else: our Ann won't have no cause to be in a fright then." Which was as much as to say that Ann Dovey was frightened, you observe.

That same afternoon, going past the common, I saw Abel Crew in his garden, sitting against the cottage wall in the sun, his foot resting on a block of wood.

"How did it all happen, Abel?" I asked, turning in at the gate. "Did you give Mrs. Reed the wrong pills?"

"No, sir," he answered, "I gave her the right pills; the pills I make expressly for such complaints as hers. But if I had, in one sense, given her the wrong, they could not have brought about any ill effect such as this, for my pills are all innocent of poison."

"I should say it could not have been the pills that did the mischief, after all, then."

"You might swear it as well, Master Johnny, with perfect safety. What killed the poor children, I don't pretend to know, but my pills never did. I tried to get down as far as Reed's to inquire particulars, and found I could not walk. It was a bit of ill-luck, disabling myself just at this time."

"Shall you have to appear at the inquest to-morrow?"

He lifted his head quickly at the question—as though it surprised him. Perhaps not having cast his thoughts that way.

"Is there to be an inquest, Master Johnny?"

"I heard so from old Jones. He has gone over to see the coroner."

"Well, I wish the investigation was all over and done with," said he. "It makes me uneasy, though I know I am innocent."

Looking at him sitting there in the sun, at his beautiful face with its truthful eyes and its silver hair, it was next to impossible to believe he could be the author of the two children's death. Only—the best of us are liable to mistakes, and sometimes make them. I said as much.

"I made none, Master Johnny," was his answer. "When my pills come to be analyzed—as of course they must be—they will be found wholesome and innocent."

The inquest did not take place till the Friday. Old Jones had fixed it for the Thursday, but the coroner put it off to the next day. And by the time Friday morning dawned, opinion had veered round, and was strongly in favour of Abel Crew. All the parish had been to see him; and his protestations, that he had never in his life put any kind of poison into his medicines, made a great impression. The pills could not have been in fault, said everybody. Dr. Duffham might have sealed them up as a matter of precaution, but the mischief would not be found there.

In the middle of Church Dykely, next door to Perkins the butcher's, stood the Silver Bear Inn; a better sort of public-house, kept by Henry Rimmer. It was there that the inquest was held. Henry Rimmer himself and Perkins the butcher were two of the jurymen. Dobbs the blacksmith was another. They all dressed themselves in their Sunday-going clothes to attend it. It was called for two in the afternoon; and soon after that hour the county coroner (who had dashed up to the Silver Bear in a fast gig, his clerk driving) and the jury trooped down to George Reed's cottage and took a look at the two pale little faces lying there side by side. Then they went back again, and the proceedings began.

Of course as many spectators went crowding into the room as it would hold. Three or four chairs were there (besides those occupied by the jury at the table), and a bench stood against the wall. The bench was speedily fought for and filled; but Henry Rimmer's brother, constituting himself master of the ceremonies, reserved the chairs for what he called the "big people," meaning those of importance in the place. The Squire was bowed into one; and to my surprise I had another. Why, I could not imagine, unless it was that they remembered I was the owner of George Reed's cottage. But I did not like to sit down when so many older persons were standing, and I would not take the chair.

Some little time was occupied with preliminaries before what might be called the actual inquest set in. First of all, the coroner flew into a passion because Abel Crew had not put in an appearance, asking old Jones if he supposed that was the way justice must be administered in England, and that he ought to have had Crew present. Old Jones who was in a regular fluster with it all, and his legs more gouty than ever, told the coroner, calling him "his worship," that he had understood Crew meant to be present. Upon which the coroner sharply answered that "understanding" went for nothing, and Jones should know his business better.

However, in walked Abel Crew in the midst of the contest. His delayed arrival was caused by his difficulty in getting his damaged foot there; which had been accomplished by the help of a stick and somebody's arm. Abel had dressed himself in his black velvet suit; and as he took off his hat on entering and bowed respectfully to the coroner, I declare he could not be taken for anything but a courtly gentleman of the old school. Nobody offered him a chair. I wished I had not given up mine: he should have had it.

Evidence was first tendered of the death of the children, and of the terrible pain they had died in. Duffham and a medical man, who was a stranger and had helped at the post-mortem, testified to arsenic being the cause of death. The next question was, how had it been administered? A rumour arose in the room that the pills had been analyzed; but the result had not transpired. Every one could see a small paper parcel standing on the table before the coroner, and knew by its shape that it must contain the pill-box.

Hester Reed was called. She said (giving her evidence very quietly, just a sob and a sigh every now and then alone betraying what she felt) that she was the wife of George Reed. Her two little ones—twins, aged eleven months and a half—had been ailing for a day or two, seemed feverish, would not eat their food, were very cross at times and unnaturally still at others, and she came to the conclusion that their teeth must be plaguing them, and thought she would give them some mild physic. Mrs. Todhetley, the Squire's lady at Dyke Manor, had called in on the Tuesday afternoon, and agreed with her that some mild physic—

"Confine your statement to what is evidence," interrupted the coroner, sternly.

Hester Reed, looking scared at the check, and perhaps not knowing what was evidence and what not, went on the best way she could. She and Ann Dovey—who had been neighbourly enough to look in and help her—had given the children a pill apiece in the evening after they were undressed, mashing the pill up in a little sugar and warm water. She then put them to bed upstairs and went to bed herself not long after. In the night she and her husband were awoke by the babies' screams, and they thought it must be convulsions. Her husband lighted the fire and ran for Dr. Duffham; but one had died before the doctor could get there, and the other died close upon it.

"What food had you given them during the day?" asked the coroner.

"Very little indeed, sir. They wouldn't take it."

"What did the little that they did take consist of?"

"It were soaked bread, sir, with milk and some sprinkled sugar. I tried them with some potato mashed up in a spoonful o' broth at midday—we'd had a bit o' biled neck o' mutton for dinner—but they both turned from it."

"Then all they took that day was bread soaked in milk and sweetened with sugar?"

"Yes, it were, sir. But the bread was soaked in warm water and the milk and sugar was put in afterwards. 'Twas but the veriest morsel they'd take, poor little dears!"

"Was the bread—and the milk—and the sugar, the same that the rest of your household used?"

"In course it were, sir. My other children ate plenty of it. Their appetites didn't fail 'em."

"Where did you get the warm water from that you say you soaked the bread in?"

"Out o' the tea-kettle, sir. The water was the same that I biled for our tea morning and night."

"The deceased children, then, had absolutely no food given to them apart from what you had yourselves?"

"Not a scrap, sir. Not a drop."

"Except the pills."

"Excepting them, in course, sir. None o' the rest of us wanted physic."

"Where did you procure these pills?"

She went into the history of the pills. Giving the full account of them, as already related.

"By your own showing, witness, it must be three months, or thereabouts, since you had that box from Abel Crew," spoke the coroner. "How do you know that the two pills you administered to the deceased children came from the same box?"

Hester Reed's eyes opened wide. She looked as surprised as though she had been asked whether she had procured the two pills from the moon.

"Yes, yes," interposed one of the jury, "how do you know it was the same box?"

"Why, gentlemen, I had no other box of pills at all, save that," she said, when her speech came to her. "We've had no physic but that in the cottage since winter, nor for ever so long afore. I'll swear it was the same box, sirs; there can't be no mistake about it."

"Did you leave it about in the way of people?" resumed the coroner. "So that it might be handled by anybody who might come into your cottage?"

"No, sir," she answered, earnestly. "I never kept the pill-box but in one place, and that was on the top of the high press upstairs out of harm's way. I put it there the first night Abel Crew gave it me, and when I wanted to get a pill or two out for my own taking, I used to step on a chair—for it's too high for me to reach without—and help myself. The box have never been took from the place at all, sir, till Tuesday night, when I brought it downstairs with me. When I've wanted to dust the press-top, I've just lifted the pill-box with one hand and passed the duster along under it with the other, as I stood on the chair. It's the same box, sir; I'll swear to that much; and it's the same pills."

Strong testimony. The coroner paused a moment. "You swear that, you say? You are quite sure?"

"Sir, I am sure and positive. The box was never took from its place since Abel Crew gave it me, till I reached up for it on Tuesday evening and carried it downstairs."

"You had been in the habit of taking these pills yourself, you say?"

"I took two three or four times when I first had 'em, sir; once I took three; but since then I've felt better and not wanted any."

"Did you feel any inconvenience from them? Any pain?"

"Not a bit, sir. As I said to Ann Dovey that night, when she asked whether they was fit pills to give the children, they seemed as mild as milk."

"Should you know the box again, witness?"

"Law yes, sir, what should hinder me?" returned Hester Reed, inwardly marvelling at what seemed so superfluous a question.

The coroner undid the paper, and handed the box to her. She was standing close to him, on the other side his clerk—who sat writing down the evidence. "Is this the box?" he asked. "Look at it well."

Mrs. Reed did as she was bid: turned it about and looked "well." "Yes, sir, it is the same box," said she. "That is, I am nearly sure of it."

"What do you mean by nearly sure?" quickly asked the coroner, catching at the word. "Have you any doubt?"

"Not no moral doubt at all, sir. Only them pill-boxes is all so like one another. Yes, sir, I'm sure it is the same box."

"Open it, and look at the pills. Are they, in your judgment, the same?"

"Just the same, sir," she answered, after taking off the lid. "One might a'most know'em anywhere. Only—"

"Only what?" demanded the coroner, as she paused.

"Well, sir, I fancied I had rather more left—six or seven say. There's only five here."

The coroner made no answer to that. He took the box from her and put on the lid. We soon learnt that two had been taken out for the purpose of being analyzed.

For who should loom into the room at that juncture but Pettipher, the druggist from Piefinch Cut. He had been analyzing the pills in a hasty way in obedience to orders received half-an-hour ago, and came to give the result. The pills contained arsenic, he said; not enough to kill a grown person, he thought, but enough to kill a child. As Pettipher was only a small man (in a business point of view) and sold groceries as well as drugs, and spectacles and ear-trumpets, some of us did not think much of his opinion, and fancied the pills should have been analyzed by Duffham. That was just like old Jones: giving work to the wrong man.

George Reed was questioned, but could tell nothing, except that he had never touched either box or pills. While Ann Dovey was being called, and the coroner had his head bent over his clerk's notes, speaking to him in an undertone, Abel Crew suddenly asked to be allowed to look at the pills. The coroner, without lifting his head, just pushed the box down on the green cloth; and one of the jury handed it over his shoulder to Abel Crew.

"This is not the box I gave Mrs. Reed," said Abel, in a clear, firm tone, after diving into it with his eyes and nose. "Nor are these the pills."

Up went the coroner's head with a start. He had supposed the request to see the box came from a juryman. It might have been irregular for Abel Crew to be allowed so much; but as it arose partly through the coroner's own fault, he was too wise to make a commotion over it.

"What is that you say?" he asked, stretching out his hand for the box as eagerly as though it had contained gold.

"That this box and these pills are not the same that I furnished to Mrs. Reed, sir," replied Abel, advancing and placing the box in the coroner's hand. "They are not indeed."

"Not the same pills and box!" exclaimed the coroner. "Why, man, you have heard the evidence of the witness, Hester Reed; you may see for yourself that she spoke nothing but truth. Don't talk nonsense here."

"But they are not the same, sir," respectfully persisted Abel. "I know my own pills, and I know my own boxes: these are neither the one nor the other."

"Now that won't do; you must take us all for fools!" exploded the coroner, who was a man of quick temper. "Just you stand back and be quiet."

"Never a pill-box went out from my hands, sir, but it had my little private mark upon it," urged Abel. "That box does not bear the mark."

"What is the mark, pray?" asked the coroner.

"Four little dots of ink inside the rim of the lid, sir; and four similar dots inside the box near the edge. They are so faint that a casual observer might not notice them; but they are always there. Of all the pill-boxes now in my house, sir—and I suppose there may be two or three dozen of them—you will not find one but has the mark."

Some whispering had been going on in different parts of the room; but this silenced it. You might have heard a pin drop. The words seemed to make an impression on the coroner: they and Abel Crew were both so earnest.

"You assert also that the pills are not yours," spoke the coroner, who was known to be fond of desultory conversations while holding his inquests. "What proof have you of that?"

"No proof; that is, no proof that I can advance, that would satisfy the eye or ear. But I am certain, by the look of them, that those were never my pills."

All this took the jury aback; the coroner also. It had seemed to some of them an odd thing that Hester Reed should have swallowed two or three of the pills at once without their entailing an ache or a pain, and that one each had poisoned the babies. Perkins the butcher observed to the coroner that the box must have been changed since Mrs. Reed helped herself from it. Upon which the coroner, after pulling at his whiskers for a moment as if in thought, called out for Mrs. Reed to return.

But when she did so, and was further questioned, she only kept to what she had said before, strenuously denying that the box could have been changed. It had never been touched by any hands but her own while it stood in its place on the press, and had never been removed from it at all until she took it downstairs on the past Tuesday night.

"Is the room where this press stands your own sleeping-room?" asked the coroner.

"No, sir. It's the other room, where my three children sleep."

"Could these children get to the box?"

"Dear no, sir! 'Twould be quite impossible."

"Had any one an opportunity of handling the box when you took it down on Tuesday night?" went on the coroner after a pause.

"Only Mrs. Dovey, sir. Nobody else was there."

"Did she touch it?"

"She laid hold of it to look at the pills."

"Did you leave her alone with it?"

"No, sir. Leastways—yes, I did for a minute or so, while I went into the back'us to get the sugar and a saucer and spoon."

"Had she the box in her hands when you returned?"

"Yes, sir, I think she had. I think she was still smelling at the pills. I know the poor little innocents was lying one on one knee, and one on t'other, all flat, and her two hands was lifted with the box in 'em."

"It was after that that you took the pills out of it to give the children?"

"Yes, sir; directly after. But Ann Dovey wouldn't do nothing wrong to the pills, sir."

"That will do," said the coroner in his curt way. "Call Ann Dovey."

Ann Dovey walked forward with a face as red as her new bonnet-strings. She had heard the whole colloquy: something seemed, too, to have put her out. Possessing scant veneration for coroners at the best of times, and none for the jury at present assembled, she did not feel disposed to keep down her temper.

The few first questions asked her, however, afforded no opportunity for resentment, for they were put quietly, and tended only to extract confirmation of Mrs. Reed's evidence, as to fetching the pill-box from upstairs and administering the pills. Then the coroner cleared his throat.

"Did you see the last witness, Hester Reed, go into the back kitchen for a spoon and saucer?"

"I saw her go and fetch 'em from somewhere," replied Ann Dovey, who felt instinctively the ball was beginning, and gave the reins to her temper accordingly.

"Did you take charge of the pill-box while she was gone?"

"I had it in my hand, if you mean that."

"Did anybody come into the kitchen during that interval?"

"No they didn't," was the tart response.

"You were alone, except for the two infants?"

"I were. What of it?"

"Now, witness, did you do anything with that box? Did you, for instance, exchange it for another?"

"I think you ought to be ashamed o' yourselves, all on you, to sit and ask a body such a thing!" exploded Mrs. Dovey, growing every moment more resentful, at being questioned. "If I had knowed the bother that was to spring up, I'd have chucked the box, pills and all, into the fire first. I wish I had!"

"Was the box, that you handed to Hester Reed on her return, the same box she left with you? Were the pills the same pills?"

"Why, where d'ye think I could have got another box from?" shrieked Ann Dovey. "D'you suppose, sir, I carry boxes and pills about with me? I bain't so fond o' physic as all that comes to."

"Dovey takes pills on occasion for that giddiness of his; I've seen him take 'em; mayhap you'd picked up a box of his," spoke Dobbs the blacksmith, mildly.

That was adding fuel to fire. Two of a trade don't agree. Dovey and Dobbs were both blacksmiths: the one in Church Dykely; the other in Piefinch Cut, not much more, so to say, than a stone's-throw from each other. The men were good friends enough; but their respective ladies were apt to regard jealously all work taken to the rival establishment. Any other of the jurymen might have made the remark with comparative impunity; not so Dobbs. And, besides the turn the inquiry seemed to be taking, Mrs. Dovey had not been easy about it in her mind from the first; proof of which was furnished by the call, already mentioned, made by her husband on Abel Crew.

"Dovey takes pills on occasion, do he!" she shrilly retorted. "And what do you take, Bill Dobbs? Pints o' beer when you can get 'em. Who lamed Poole's white horse the t'other day a-shoeing him?"

"Silence!" sternly interrupted the coroner. While Dobbs, conscious of the self-importance imparted to him by the post he was now filling, and of the necessity of maintaining the dignity of demeanour which he was apt to put on with his best clothes, bore the aspersion with equanimity and a stolid face.

"Attend to me, witness, and confine yourself to replying to the questions I put to you," continued the coroner. "Did you take with you any pills or pill-box of your own when you went to Mrs. Reed's that evening?"

"No, I didn't," returned Ann Dovey, the emphasis culminating in a sob: and why she should have set on to shiver and shake was more than the jury could understand.

"Do you wear pockets?"

"What if I do?" she said, after a momentary pause. But her lips grew white, and I thought she was trying to brave it out.

"Had you a pocket on that evening?"

"Heaven be good to me!" I heard her mutter under her breath. And if ever I saw a woman look frightened nearly to death, Ann Dovey looked it then.

"Had you a pocket on that evening, witness?" repeated the coroner, sharply.

"Y—es."

"What articles were in it? Do you recollect?"

"It were a key or two," came the answer at length, her very teeth chattering and all the impudence suddenly gone out of her. "And my thimble, sir;—and some coppers; and a part of a nutmeg;—and—and I don't remember nothing else, sir."

"No box of pills? You are sure you had not that?"

"Haven't I said so, sir?" she rejoined, bursting into a flood of tears. For which, and for the sudden agitation, nobody could see any reason: and perhaps it was only that which made the coroner harp upon the same string. Her demeanour had become suspicious.

"You had no poison of any kind in your pocket, then?"

But he asked the question in jest more than earnest. For when she went into hysterics instead of replying, he let her go. He was used to seeing witnesses scared when brought before him.

The verdict was not arrived at that day. When other witnesses had been examined, the coroner addressed the jury. Ten of them listened deferentially, and were quite prepared to return a verdict of Manslaughter against Abel Crew; seemed red-hot to do it, in fact. But two of them dissented. They were not satisfied, they said; and they held out for adjourning the inquest to see if any more light could be thrown upon the affair. As they evidently had the room with them, the coroner yielded, and adjourned the inquest in a temper.

And then it was discovered that the name was not Crew but Carew. Abel himself corrected the coroner. Upon that, the coroner sharply demanded why he had lived under a false name.

"Nay, sir," replied Abel, as dignified as you please, "I have had no intention of doing so. When I first came to this neighbourhood I gave my name correctly—Carew: but the people at once converted it into Crew by their mode of pronunciation."

"At any rate, you must have sanctioned it."

"Tacitly I have done so. What did it signify? When I have had occasion to write my name—but that has been very rare—I have written it Carew. Old Sir Peter Chavasse knew it was Carew, and used to call me so; as did Sir Geoffry. Indeed, sir, I have had no reason to conceal my name."

"That's enough," said the coroner, cutting him short. "Stand back, Abel Carew. The proceedings are adjourned to this day week."

CHAPTER IV

ABEL CREW

Things are done in remote country places that would not be done in towns. Whether the law is understood by us, or whether it is not, it often happens that it is very much exceeded, or otherwise not acted upon. Those who have to exercise it sometimes show themselves as ignorant of it as if they had lived all their lives in the wilds of America.

Old Jones the constable was one of these. When not checked by his masters, the magistrates, he would do most outrageous things—speaking of the law and of common sense. And he did one in reference to Abel Crew. I still say Crew. Though it had come out that his name was Carew, we should be sure to call him Crew to the end.

The inquest might have been concluded at its first sitting, but for the two who stood out against the rest of the jury. Perkins the butcher and Dobbs the blacksmith. Truth to say, these two had plenty of intelligence; which could not be said of all the rest. Ten of the jury pronounced the case to be as clear as daylight: the infants had been poisoned by Abel Crew's pills: and the coroner seemed to agree with them—he hated trouble. But Dobbs and Perkins held out. They were not satisfied, they said; the pills furnished by Abel Crew might not have been the pills that were taken by the children; moreover, they considered that the pills should be "more officially" analyzed. Pettipher the druggist was all very well in his small way, but hardly up, in their opinion, to pronouncing upon pills when a man's life or liberty was at stake. They pressed for an adjournment, that the pills might be examined by some competent authority. The coroner, as good as telling them they were fools to their faces, had adjourned the inquest in suppressed passion to that day week.

"And I've got to take care of you, Abel Crew," said old Jones, floundering up on his gouty legs to Abel as the jury and crowd dispersed. "You've got to come along o' me."

"To come where?" asked Abel, who was hobbling towards home on his scalded foot, by the help of his stick and the arm of Gibbon the gamekeeper.

"To the lock-up," said old Jones.

"To the lock-up!" echoed Abel Crew.

"In course," returned old Jones. "Where else but the lock-up? Did you think it was to the pound?"

Abel Crew, lifting the hand that held his stick to brush a speck of dirt off his handsome velvet coat, turned to the constable; his refined face, a little paler than usual, gazing inquiringly at old Jones's, his silver hair glistening in the setting sun.

"I don't understand you, Mr. Jones," he said calmly. "You cannot mean to lock me up?"

"Well, I never!" cried old Jones, who had a knack of considering every suspected person guilty, and treating them accordingly. "You have a cheek, you have, Abel Crew! 'Not going to take me to the lock-up, Mr. Jones,' says you! Where would you be took to?"

"But there's no necessity for it," said Abel. "I shall not run away. I shall be in my house if I'm wanted again."

"I dare say you would!" said old Jones, ironically. "You might or you mightn't, you know. You be as good as committed for the killing and slaying o' them there two twins, and it's my business to see as you don't make your escape aforehand, Abel Crew."

Quite a company of us, sauntering out of the inquest-room, were listening by this time. I gave old Jones a bit of my mind.

"He is not yet committed, Jones, therefore you have no right to take him or to lock him up."

"You don't know nothing about it, Mr. Ludlow. I do. The crowner gave me a hint, and I'm acting on it. 'Don't you go and let that man escape,' says his worship to me: 'it'll be at your peril if you do.' 'I'll see to him, your worship,' says I. And I be a-doing of it."

But it was hardly likely that the coroner meant Abel Crew to be confined in that precious lock-up for a whole week. One night there was bad enough. At least, I did not think he meant it; but the crowd, to judge by their comments, seemed divided on the point.

"The shortest way to settle the question will be to ask the coroner, old Jones," said I, turning back to the Silver Bear. "Come along."

"You'd be clever to catch him, Master Johnny," roared out old Jones after me. "His worship jumped into his gig; it was a-waiting for him when he come out; and his clerk druv him off at a slapping pace."

It was true. The coroner was gone; and old Jones had it all his own way; for, you see, none of us liked to interfere with the edict of an official gentleman who held sway in the county and sat on dead people. Abel Crew accepted the alternative meekly.

"Any way, you must allow me to go home first to lock my house up, and to see to one or two other little matters," said he.

"Not unless you goes under my own eyes," retorted old Jones. "You might be for destroying your stock o' pills for fear they should bear evidence again' you, Abel Crew."

"My pills are, of all things, what I would not destroy," said Abel. "They would bear testimony for me, instead of against me, for they are harmless."

So Abel Crew hobbled to his cottage on the common, attended by old Jones and a tail of followers. Arrived there, he attended the first thing to his scalded foot, dressing it with some of his own ointment. Then he secured some bread and butter, not knowing what the accommodation at the lock-up might be in the shape of eatables, and changed his handsome quaint suit of clothes for those he wore every day. After that, he was escorted back to the lock-up.

Now, the lock-up was in Piefinch Cut, nearly opposite to Dovey the blacksmith's. The Squire remembered the time when the lock-up stood alone; when Piefinch Cut had no more houses in it than Piefinch Lane now has; but since then Piefinch Cut had been built upon and inhabited; houses touching even the sacred walls of the lock-up. A tape-and-cotton and sweetstuff shop supported it on one side, and a small pork-butcher's on the other. Pettipher's drug shop, should anybody be curious on the point, was next to the tape-and-cotton mart.

To see Abel Crew arriving in the custody of old Jones the constable, the excited stragglers after them, astonished Piefinch Cut not a little. Figg the pawnbroker—who was originally from Alcester—considered himself learned in the law. Anyway, he was a great talker, and liked to give his opinion upon every topic that might turn up. His shop joined Dovey's forge: and when we arrived there, Figg was outside, holding forth to Dovey, who had his shirt sleeves rolled up above his elbows as usual, his leather apron on. Mrs. Dovey stood listening behind, in the smart gown and red-ribboned bonnet she had worn at the inquest.

"Why—what on earth!—have they been and gone and took up Crew?" cried Figg in surprise.

"It is an awful shame of old Jones," I broke in; speaking more to Dovey than Figg, for Figg was no favourite of mine. "A whole week of the lock-up! Only think of it, Dovey!"

"But have they brought it in again' him, Master Johnny?" cried Dovey, unfolding his grimy arms to touch his paper cap to me as he spoke.

"No; that's what they have not done. The inquest is adjourned for a week; and I don't believe old Jones has a right to take him at all. Not legally, you know."

"That's just what her brought word," said Dovey, with a nod in the direction of his wife. "'Well, how be it turned, Ann?' says I to her when her come back—for I'd a sight o' work in to-day and couldn't go myself. 'Oh, it haven't turned no ways yet, Jack,' says her; 'it be put off to next week.' There he goes! right in."

This last remark applied to Abel Crew. After fumbling in his pocket for the two big keys, tied together with string, and then fumbling at the latch, old Jones succeeded in opening the door. Not being much used, the lock was apt to grow rusty. Then he stood back, and with a flourish of hands motioned Abel in. He made no resistance.

"They must know for certain as 'twere his pills what done it," struck in Mrs. Dovey.

"No, they don't," said I. "What's more, I do not think it was his pills. Abel Crew says he never put poison in his pills yet, and I believe him."

"Well, and no more it don't stand to reason as he would, Mr. Ludlow," said Figg, a man whose self-complaisance was not to be put down by any amount of discouragement. "I were just a-saying so to Dovey— Why have old Jones took him up?" went on Figg to Gibbon the gamekeeper, who came striding by.

"Jones says he has the coroner's orders for it," answered Gibbon.

"Look here, I know a bit about law, and I know a man oughtn't to be shut up till some charge is brought again' him," contended Figg. "Crew's pills is suspected, but he have not been charged yet."

"Anyway, it's what Jones has gone and done," said Gibbon. "Perhaps he is right. And a week's not much; it'll soon pass. But as to any pills of Abel Crew's having killed them children, it's just preposterous to think of it."

"What d'ye suppose did kill 'em, then, Richard Gibbon?" demanded Ann Dovey, a hot flush on her face, her tone full of resentment.

"That's just what has to be found out," returned Gibbon, passing on his way.

"If it hadn't been for Dobbs and Butcher Perkins holding out again' it, Crew 'ud ha' been brought in guilty safe enough," said Ann Dovey. And the tone was again so excited, so bitterly resentful against Dobbs and Perkins, that I could not help looking at her in wonder. It sounded just as though the non-committal of Abel were a wrong inflicted upon herself.

"No, he would not have been brought in guilty," I answered her; "he would have been committed for trial; but that's a different thing. If the matter could be sifted to the bottom, I know it would be found that the mischief did not lie with Abel Crew's pills. There, Mrs. Dovey!"

She was looking at me out of the corners of her eyes—for all the world as if she were afraid of me, or of what I said. I could not make her out.

"Why should you wish so particularly to bring it home to Crew?" I pointedly asked her; and Figg turned round to look at her, as if seconding the question.

"Me want particular to bring it home to Crew!" she retorted, her voice rising with temper; or perhaps with fear, for she trembled like an aspen leaf. "I don't want to bring it home particular to him, Mr. Ludlow. It were his pills, though, all the same, that did it."

And with that she whisked through the forge to her kitchen.

On the morning following I got old Jones to let me into the lock-up. The place consisted of two rooms opening into one another, and a small square space, no bigger than a closet, at the end of the passage, where they kept the pen and ink. For that small space had a window in it, looking on to the fields at the back; the two rooms had only skylights in the roof. In the inner room a narrow iron bedstead stood against the wall, a mattress and blanket on it. Abel was sitting on that when we went in.

"You must have been lively here last night, Abel!"

"Yes, very, sir," answered he, with a half-smile. "I did not really mind it; I am used to be alone. I could have done with fewer rats, though."

"Oh, are there rats here?"

"Lots of them, Master Johnny. I don't like rats. They came upon my face, and all about me."

"Why does old Jones not set traps for them? He considers this place to be under his special protection."

"There are too many for any trap to catch," answered Abel.

Old Jones had gone off to the desk in the closet, having placed some bread and butter and milk on the shelf for Abel. His errand there was to enter the cost of the bread in the account-book, to be settled for later. A prisoner in the lock-up was commonly treated to bread and water: old Jones had graciously allowed this one to pay for some butter and milk out of his own pocket.

"I don't want to treat 'em harsher nor I be obliged, Master Ludlow," he said to me, when coming in, in reference to the butter and the milk he was carrying. "Abel Crew have been known as a decent man ever since he come among us: and if he chooses to pay for the butter and the milk, there ain't no law against his having 'em. 'Tain't as if he was a burglar."

"No, he is not a burglar," I answered. "And you must mind that you do not get into the wrong box about him. There's neither law nor justice in locking him up, Jones, before he is charged."

"If I had never locked up nobody till they was charged, I should ha' been in the wrong box many a time afore now," said old Jones, doggedly. "Look at that there man last Christmas; what I caught prowling in the grounds at Parrifer Hall, with a whole set of house-breaking things concealed in his pockets! After I'd took him, and lodged him in here safe, it was found that he was one o' the worst characters in the county, only let out o' Worcester goal two days before. Suppose I'd not took him, Master Johnny? where 'ud the spoons at Parrifer Hall ha' been?"

"That was a different case altogether."

"I know what I'm about," returned Jones. "The coroner, he just give me a nod or two, looking at Crew as he give it. I knew what it meant, sir: a nod's as good as a wink to a blind horse."

Anyway, Jones had him, here in the lock-up: and had gone off to enter the loaf in the account-book; and I was sitting on the bench opposite Abel.

"It is a wicked shame of them to have put you here, Abel."

"It is not legal—as I believe," he answered. "And I am sure it is not just, sir. I swear those pills and that box produced at the inquest were none of mine. They never went out of my hands. Old Jones thinks he is doing right to secure me, I suppose, and he is civil over it; so I must not grumble. He brought me some water to wash in this morning, and a comb."

"But there's no sense in it. You would not attempt to escape; you would wait for the reassembling of the inquest."

"Escape!" he exclaimed. "I should be the first to remain for it. I am more anxious than any one to have the matter investigated. Truth to say, Master Johnny, my curiosity is excited. Hester Reed is so persistent in regard to their being the pills and box that I gave her; and as she is a truthful honest woman, one can't see where the mistake lies. There must be a mystery in it somewhere."

"Suppose you are committed to take your trial? And found guilty?"

"That I shall be committed, I look upon as certain," he answered. "As to being found guilty—if I am, I must bear it. God knows my innocence, and I shall hope that in time He will bring it to light."

"All the same, Abel, they ought not to put you in here."

"That's true, sir."

"And then there will be the lying in prison until the assizes—two or three good months to come! Don't go and die of it, Abel."

"No, I shall not do that," he answered, smiling a little. "The consciousness of innocence will keep me up."

I sat looking at him. What light could get in through the dusty skylight fell on his silver hair, which fell back from his pale face. He held his head down in thought, only raising it to answer me. Some movement in the closet betokened old Jones's speedy approach, and I hastened to assure Abel that all sensible people would not doubt his innocence.

"No one need doubt it, Master Johnny," he answered firmly, his eye kindling. "I never had a grain of arsenic in my house; I have never had any other poison. There are herbs from which poison may be distilled, but I have never gathered them. When it comes to people needing poison—and there are some diseases of the human frame that it may be good for—they should go to a qualified medical man, not to a herbalist. No. I have never, never had poison or poisonous herbs withing my dwelling; therefore (putting other reasons aside) it is impossible that those pills can have been my pills. God hears me say it, and knows that it is true."

Old Jones, balancing the keys in his hand, was standing within the room, listening. Abel Crew was so respectable and courteous a prisoner, compared with those he generally had in the lock-up, burglars, tipsy men, and the like, returning him a "thank you" instead of an oath, that he had already begun to regard him with some favour, and the assertion seemed to make an impression on him.

"Look here," said he. "Whose pills could they have been, if they warn't yours?"

"I cannot imagine," returned Abel Crew. "I am as curious about it as any one else—Master Ludlow here knows I am. I dare say it will come out sometime. They could not have been made up by me."

"What was that you told the coroner about your pill-boxes being marked?" asked old Jones.

"And so they are marked; all of them. The pill-box I saw there—"

"I mean the stock o' boxes you've got at home. Be they all marked?"

"Every one of them. When I have in a fresh lot of pill-boxes the first thing I do, on bringing them home, is to mark them."

"Then look here. You just trust me with the key of your place, and tell me where the boxes are to be found, and I'll go and secure 'em, and lay 'em afore the coroner. If they be all found marked, it'll tell in your favour."

The advice sounded good, and Abel Crew handed over his key. Jones looked solemn as he and I went away together.

"It's an odd thing, though, Master Johnny, ain't it, how the pison could ha' got into them there pills," said he slowly, as he put the big key into the lock of the outer door.

And we had an audience round us before the words were well spoken. To see the lock-up made fast when there was a prisoner within it, was always a coveted recreation in Piefinch Cut. Several individuals had come running up; not to speak of children from the gutters. Dovey stood gazing in front of his forge; Figg, who liked to be lounging about outside when he had no customers transacting delicate negotiations within, backed against his shop-window, and stared in concert with Dovey. Jones flourishing the formidable keys, crossed over to them.

"How do he feel to-day?" asked Figg, nodding towards the lock-up.

"He don't feel no worse appariently than he do other days," replied old Jones. "It be a regular odd thing, it be."

"What be odd?" asked Dovey.

"How the pison could ha' got into them there pills. Crew says he has never had no pison in his place o' no kind, herbs nor else."

"And I would pledge my word that it is the truth," I put in.

"Well, and so I think it is," said Dovey. "Last night George Reed was in here a-talking. He says he one day come across Abel Crew looking for herbs in the copse behind the Grange. Crew was picking and choosing: some herbs he'd leave alone, and some he dug up. Reed spied out a fine-looking plant, and called to him. Up comes Crew, trowel in hand, bends down to take a look, and then gives his head a shake. 'That won't do for me,' says he, 'that plant has poisonous properties,' says he; 'and I never meddles with them that has,' says he. George Reed told us that much in this here forge last night. Him and his wife have a'most had words about it."

"Had words about what?" asked old Jones.

"Why, about them pills. Reed tells her that if it is the pills what poisoned the young ones, she have made some mull o' the box Abel give her and got it changed. But he don't believe as 'twere the pills at all. And Hester Reed, she sticks to it that she never made no mull o' the box, and that the pills is the same."

At this juncture, happening to turn my head, I saw Mrs. Dovey at the door at the back of the forge, her face screwed round the doorpost, listening: and there was a great fear on it. Seeing me looking at her, she disappeared like a shot, and quietly closed the door. A thought flashed across me.

"That woman knows more about it than she will say! And it is frightening her. What can the mystery be?"

The children were buried on the Sunday afternoon, all the parish flocking to the funeral; and the next morning Abel Crew was released. Whether old Jones had become doubtful as to the legality of what he had done, or whether he received a mandate from the coroner by the early post, no one knew. Certain it was, that before nine o'clock old Jones held the lock-up doors open, and Abel Crew walked out. It was thought that some one must have written privately to the coroner—which was more than likely. Old Jones was down in the mouth all day, as if he had had an official blowing-up.

Abel and his stick went home. The rest and his own doctoring had very nearly cured the instep. On the Saturday old Jones had made a descent upon the cottage and cleared it of the pill-boxes. Jones found that every box had Abel's private mark upon it.

"Well, this is a curious start, Crew!" exclaimed Mr. Duffham, meeting him as he was turning in at his gate. "Now in the lock-up, and now out of it! It may be old Jones's notion of law, but it is not mine. How have you enjoyed it?"

"It would not have been so bad but for the rats, sir," replied Abel. "I could see a few stars shining through the skylight."

The days went on to the Thursday, and it was now the evening before the adjourned inquest. Tod and I, in consideration of the popular ferment, had taken the Squire at a favourable moment, and extracted from him another week's holiday. Opinions were divided: some believed in Crew, others in the poisoned pills. As to Crew himself, he was out in his garden as usual, attending to his bees, and his herbs and flowers, and quietly awaiting the good or the ill luck that Fate might have in store for him.

It was Thursday evening, I say; and I was taking tea with Duffham. Having looked in upon him, when rushing about the place, he asked me to stay. The conversation turned upon the all-engrossing topic; and I chanced to mention that the behaviour of Ann Dovey puzzled me. Upon that, Duffham said that it was puzzling him. He had been called in to her the previous day, and found her in a regular fever, eyes anxious, breath hysterical, face hectic. Since the day of the inquest she had been more or less in this state, and the blacksmith told Duffham he could not make out what had come to her. "Them pills have drove her mad, sir," were Dovey's words; "she can't get 'em off her mind."

The last cup of tea was poured out, and Duffham was shaking round the old black pot to see if he could squeeze out any more, when we received an interruption. Dovey came bursting in upon us straight from his forge; his black hair ruffled, his small dark face hot with flurry. It was a singular tale he had come to tell. His wife had been making a confession to him. Driven pretty nearly out of her mind by the weight of a secret, she could hold it no longer.

To begin at the beginning. Dovey's house swarmed with black-beetles. Dovey himself did not mind the animals, but Mrs. Dovey did; and no wonder, when she could not step out of bed in the night without putting her foot on one. But, if Dovey did not dislike black-beetles, there was another thing he did dislike—hated in fact; and that was the stuff called beetle-powder: which professed to kill them. Mrs. Dovey would have scattered some on the floor every night; but Dovey would not allow it. He forbid her to bring a grain of it into the house: it was nothing but poison, he said, and might chance to kill themselves as well as the beetles. Ann Dovey had her way in most matters, for Dovey was easy, as men and husbands go; but when once he put his veto on a thing, she knew she might as well try to turn the house round as turn him.

Now what did Ann Dovey do? On that very Easter Tuesday, as it chanced, as soon as dusk had set in, off she went to Dame Chad's general shop in Church Dykely, where the beetle-power was sold, and bought a packet of it. It seemed to her, that of the choice between two evils—to put up with the horrible black animals, or to disobey Dovey, the latter was the more agreeable. She could easily shake some of the powder down lightly of a night; the beetles would eat it up before morning, and Dovey would never know it. Accordingly, paying for the powder—a square packet, done up in blue paper, on which was labelled "Poison" in as large letters as the printer could get into the space—she thrust it into the depths of her gown-pocket—it was her holiday gown—and set off home again. Calling in at George Reed's cottage on her way, she there assisted, as it also chanced, in administering the pills to the unfortunate children. And perhaps her motive for calling in was not so much from a love of presiding at physic-giving, as that she might be able, when she got home, to say "At Reed's," if her husband asked her where she had been. It fell out as she thought. No sooner had she put foot inside the forge than Dovey began, "Where'st been, Ann?" and she told him at Reed's, helping with the sick little ones. Dovey's work was over for the night; he wanted his supper; and she had no opportunity of using the beetle-powder. It was left untouched in the pocket of her gown. The following morning came the astounding news of the children's death; and in the excitement caused by that, Mrs. Dovey lost sight of the powder. Perhaps she thought that the general stir might cause Dovey to be more wakeful than usual, and that she might as well let the powder be for a short time. It was safe where it was, in her hung-up gown. Dovey never meddled with her pockets: on or off, they were no concern of his.

But, on the Friday morning, when putting on this same holiday gown to attend the inquest, to which she had been summoned, what was her horror to find the packet burst, and her pocket filled with the loose powder. Mrs. Dovey had no greater love for beetle-powder in itself than she had for beetles, and visibly shuddered. She could not empty it out; there it had to remain; for Dovey, excited by his wife's having to give evidence, was in and out of her room like a dog in a fair; and she went off perforce with the stuff in her pocket. And when during her examination the questions took the turn they did take, and the coroner asked her whether she had had any poison in her pocket that night at George Reed's; this, with the consciousness of what had been that night in her pocket, of what was in her pocket at that very moment, then present, nearly frightened her into fits. From that hour, Ann Dovey had lived in a state of terror. It was not that she believed any of the beetle-powder could have got inside the ill-fated young ones (though she did not feel quite easy on the point), as that she feared the accusation might be shifted off Crew's shoulders and on to hers. On this Thursday evening she could hold out no longer; and disclosed all to Dovey.

Dovey burst upon us in a heat. He was as straightforward a man as ever lived, of an intensely honest nature, and could no more have kept it in, now that he knew it, than he could have given up all righteous dealing together. His chief concern was to tell the truth, and to restore peace to his wife. He went through the narrative to Duffham without stopping; and seemed not in the least to care for my being present.

"It ain't possible, sir, there ain't a moral possibility that any o' that there dratted powder could have come anigh the babies," wound up Dovey. "I should be thankful, sir, if you'd come down and quieten her a bit; her be in a fine way."

What with surprise, and what with the man's rapid speech, Duffham had not taken in one-half of the tale. He had simply sat behind the teapot and stared.

"My good fellow, I don't understand," he said. "A pocketful of poison! What on earth made her take poison to George Reed's?"

So Dovey went over the heads of the story again.

"'Twas in her pocket, sir, our Ann's, it's true; but the chances are that at that time the paper hadn't burst. None of it couldn't ha' got to them there two young ones."

To see the blacksmith's earnestness was good. His face was as eager, his tone as imploring, as though he were pleading for his life.

"And it 'ud be a work of charity, sir, if you'd just step down and see her. I'd pay handsome for the visit, sir; anything you please to charge. She's like one going right out of her mind."

"I'll come," said Duffham, who had his curiosity upon the point.

And the blacksmith set off on the run home again.

"Well, this is a curious thing!" exclaimed Duffham, when he had gone.

"Could the beetle-powder have poisoned the children?" I asked.

"I don't know, Johnny. It is an odd tale altogether. We will go down and inquire into it."

Which of course implied that he expected me to go with him. Nothing loath was I; more eager than he.

Finishing what was left of the tea and bread-and-butter, we went on to Piefinch Cut. Ann Dovey was alone, except for her husband and mother. She flung herself on the sofa when she saw us—the blacksmith's house was comfortably off for furniture—and began to scream.

"Now, just you stop that, Ann Dovey," said Duffham, who was always short with hysterics. "I want to come to the bottom of this business; you can't tell it me while you scream. What in the world possessed you to go about with your pocket full of poison?"

She had her share of sense, and knew Duffham was not one to be trifled with; so she told the tale as well as she could for sobbing.

"Have you mentioned this out of doors?" was the first question Duffham asked when it was over.

"No," interposed Dovey. "I told 'er afore I come to you not to be soft enough for that. Not a soul have heard it, sir, but me and her"—pointing to the old mother—"and you and Master Johnny. We don't want all the parish swarming about us like so many hornets."

"Good," said Duffham. "But it is rather a serious thing, I fear. Uncertain, at any rate."

"Be it, sir?" returned Ann, raising her heavy eyes questioningly. "Do you think so?"

"Why, you see, the mischief must have lain between that beetle-powder and Crew's pills. As Crew is so careful a man, I don't think it could have been the pills; and that's the truth."

"But how could the beetle-powder have got anigh the children out of my pocket, sir?" she asked, her eyes wild. "I never put my hand into my pocket while I sat there; I never did."

"You can't be sure of that," returned Duffham. "We may put our hands into our pockets fifty times a day without remembering it."

"D'you suppose, sir, I should take out some o' that there beetle-powder and cram it down the poor innocents' throats?" she demanded, on the verge of further screaming.

"Where is the powder?" questioned Duffham.

The powder was where it had been all along: in the gown-pocket. Want of opportunity, through fear of Dovey's eyes, or dread of touching the stuff, had kept her from meddling with it. When she took the gown off, the night of the inquest, she hung it up on the accustomed hook, and there it was still. The old mother went to the bedroom and brought it forward, handling it gingerly: a very smart print gown with bright flowers upon it.

Duffham looked round, saw a tin pie-dish, and turned the pocket inside out into it. A speckled sort of powder, brown and white. He plunged his fingers into it fearlessly, felt it, and smelt it. The blue paper it had been sold in lay amidst it, cracked all across. Duffham took it up.

"Poison!" read out he aloud, gazing at the large letters through his spectacles. "How came you to let it break open in your pocket, Ann Dovey?"

"I didn't let it; it braked of itself," she sobbed. "If you saw the black-beedles we gets here of a night, sir, you'd be fit to dance a hornpipe, you would. The floor be covered with 'em."

"If the ceiling was covered with 'em too, I wouldn't have that there dangerous stuff brought into the place—and so I've told ye often," roared Dovey.

"It's frightful uncomfortable, is black-beedles; mother knows it," said his wife, in a subdued voice—for Dovey in great things was master. "I thought if I just sprinkled a bit on't down, it 'ud take 'em away, and couldn't hurt nobody."

"And you went off on the sly that there Tuesday night and bought it," he retorted; "and come back and told me you had been to Reed's helping to physic the babies."

"And so I had been there, helping to physic 'em."

"Did you go straight to Reed's from the shop—with this powder?" asked Duffham.

"It was right at the bottom o' my pocket: I put it there as soon as Dame Chad had served me with it," sobbed Ann Dovey. "And I can be upon my Bible oath, Dr. Duffham, that I never touched it after; and I don't believe it had then burst. A-coming hasty out of Reed's back-gate, for I were in a hurry to get home, the pocket swung again' the post, and I think the blue paper must ha' burst then. I never knowed it had burst, for I'd thought no more about the beedles till I put on the gownd to go up to the inquest. Master Johnny, you be a-staring at me fearful, but I'm telling nothing but the naked truth."

She did seem to be telling the truth. And as to my "staring at her fearful," that was just her imagination. I was listening to the talk from the elbow of the wooden chair, on which I had perched myself. Duffham recommended Dovey to put the tin dish and its contents away safely, so that it did not get near any food, but not to destroy the stuff just yet. He talked a bit with Ann, left her a composing draught, and came away.

"I don't see that the powder could have had anything to do with the children's death," I said to him as we went along.

"Neither do I, Johnny!"

"Shall you have to declare this at the inquest to-morrow, Mr. Duffham?"

"I am sure I don't know," he answered, looking up at the sky through his spectacles, just as a perplexed owl might do. "It might only serve to complicate matters: and I don't think it's possible it could have been the powder. On the other hand, if it be proved not to have been the pills, we have only this poisonous powder to fall back upon. It is a strange affair altogether, take it in all its bearings."

I did not answer. The evening star was beginning to show itself in the sky.

"I must feel my way in this, Johnny: be guided by circumstances," he resumed, when we halted at the stile that led across the fields to the Manor. "We must watch the turn matters take to-morrow at the inquest. Of course if I find it necessary to declare it, I shall declare it. Meanwhile, lad, you had better not mention it to any one."

"All right, Mr. Duffham. Good-evening."

The jury went straggling into the Silver Bear by twos and threes. Up dashed the coroner's gig, as before, he and his clerk seated side by side. All the parish had collected about the doors, and were trying to push into the inquest-room.

Gliding quietly in, before the proceedings were opened, came Abel Crew in his quaint velvet suit, his silver hair gleaming in the sunlight, his pale face calm as marble. The coroner ordered him to sit on a certain chair, and whispered to old Jones. Upon which the constable turned his gouty legs round, marched up, and stood guard over Crew, just as though Abel were his prisoner.

"Do you see that, sir?" I whispered to Duffham.

"Yes, lad, and understand it. Crew's pills have been analyzed—officially this time, as the jury put it—and found to contain arsenic. Pettipher was right. The pills killed the children."

Well, you might have knocked me down with a feather. I had been fully trusting in Crew's innocence.

About the first witness called, and sworn, was the professional man from a distance who had analyzed the pills. He said that they contained arsenic. Not in sufficient quantity to hurt a grown-up person; more than sufficient to kill a little child. The coroner drew in his lips.

"I thought it must be so," he said, apparently for the benefit of the jury. "Am I to understand that these were improper pills to send out?—pills that no medical man would be likely to send?"

"Not improper at all, sir," replied the witness. "A medical man would prescribe them for certain cases. Not for children: to an infant one would be what it has been here—destruction."

I felt a nudge at my elbow, and turned to see the Squire's hot face close to mine.

"Johnny, don't you ever stand up for that Crew again. He ought to be hanged."

But the coroner, after a bit, seemed puzzled; or rather, doubtful. Led to be so, perhaps, by a question put by one of the jury. It was Perkins the butcher.

"If these pills were furnished by Abel Crew for Hester Reed, a growed woman, and she went and gave one of her own accord to the two babies, ought Crew to be held responsible for that?"

Upon which there ensued some cavilling. Some of the jury holding that he was not responsible; others that he was. The coroner reminded them of what Hester Reed had stated in her evidence—that she had asked Crew's opinion about the suitability of the pills for children, and he had told her they were suitable.

Hester Reed was called. As the throng parted to make way for her to advance, I saw Ann Dovey seated at the back of the room, looking more dead than alive. Dovey stood by her, having made himself spruce for the occasion. Ann would have gone off a mile in some opposite direction, but old Jones's orders to all the witnesses of the former day, to appear again, had been peremptory. They had been wanted before, he told them, and might be wanted again.

"You need not look such a scarecrow with fright," I whispered in Ann Dovey's ear, making my way to her side to reassure her, the woman was so evidently miserable. "It was the pills that did the mischief, after all—didn't you hear? Nothing need come out about your pocket and the powder."

"Master Johnny, I'm just about skeered out o' my life, I am. Fit to go and drown myself."

"Nonsense! It will be all right as far as you are concerned."

"I said it was Crew's pills, all along, I did; it couldn't have been anything else, sir. All the same, I wish I was dead."

As good try to console a post, seemingly, as Ann Dovey. I went back to my standing-place between the Squire and Duffham. Hester Reed was being questioned then.

"Yes, sir, it were some weeks ago. My little boy was ailing, and I ran out o' the house to Abel Crew, seeing the old gentleman go past the gate, and asked whether I might give him one of them there same pills, or whether it would hurt the child. Crew said I might give it freely; he said two even wouldn't hurt him."

"And did you give the pill?" asked the coroner.

"No, sir. He's a rare bad one to give physic to, Gregory is, and I let him get well without it."

"How old is he?"

"Turned of three, sir."

"You are absolutely certain, Mrs. Reed, that these pills, from which you took out two to give the deceased children, were the very self-same pills you had from Abel Crew?"

"I be sure and certain of it, sir. Nobody never put a finger upon the box but me. It stood all the while in the corner o' the press-shelf in the children's bedroom. Twice a week when I got upon a chair to dust the shelf, I see it there. There was nobody in the house but me, except the little ones. My husband don't concern himself with the places and things."

Circumstantial evidence could not well go farther. Mrs. Reed was dismissed, and the coroner told Abel Crew to come near the table. He did as he was bid, and stood there upright and manly, a gentle look on his face.

"You have heard the evidence, Abel Crew," said the coroner. "The pills have been analyzed and found to contain a certain portion of arsenic—a great deal more than enough to kill a child. What have you to say to it?"

"Only this, sir; only what I said before. That the pills analyzed were not my pills. The pills I gave to Mrs. Reed contained neither arsenic nor any other poison."

"It is showing great obstinacy on your part to repeat that," returned the coroner, impatiently. "Mrs. Reed swears that the pills were the same pills; and she evidently speaks the truth."

"I am sure she thinks she speaks it," replied Abel, gently. "Nevertheless, sir, I assure you she is mistaken. In some way the pills must have been changed whilst in her possession, box and all."

"Why, man, in what manner do you suppose they could have been changed?"

"I don't know, sir. All I do know is, that the pills and the box produced here last week were not, either of them, the pills and the box she had from me. Never a box went out from me, sir, but had my private mark on it—the mark I spoke of. Jones the constable searched my place whilst I was detained in the lock-up, and took away all the pill-boxes out of it. Let him testify whether he found one without the mark."

At this juncture a whole cargo of pill-boxes were shot out of a bag on the table by old Jones, some empty, some filled with pills. The coroner and jury began to examine them, and found the mark on all, lids and boxes.

"And if you'd be so good as to cause the pills to be analyzed, sir, they would be found perfectly free from poison," resumed Abel. "They are made from herbs that possess healing properties, not irritant; a poisonous herb, whether poisonous in itself, or one from which poison may be extracted, I never plucked. Believe me, sir, for I am telling the truth; the truth before Heaven."

The coroner said nothing for a minute or two: I think the words impressed him. He began lifting the lid again from one or two of the boxes.

"What are these pills for? All for the same disorder?"

"They were made up for different disorders, sir."

"And pray how do you distinguish them?"

"I cannot distinguish them now. They have been mixed. Even if returned to me I could not use them. I have a piece of furniture at home, sir, that I call my pill-case. It has various drawers in it, each drawer being labelled with the sort of pills kept in it: camomile, dandelion, and so on. Mr. Jones must be able to corroborate this."

Old Jones nodded. He had never seen nothing neater nor more exact in all his life, than the keeping o' them there pills. He, Mr. Jones, had tumbled the drawerfuls indiscriminately into his bag, and so mixed them.

"And they will be so much loss to me," quietly observed Abel. "It does not matter."

"Were you brought up to the medical profession?" cried the coroner—and some of us thought he put the question in irony.

"No, sir," replied Abel, taking it seriously. "I have learnt the healing art, as supplied by herbs and roots, and I know their value. Herbs will cure sometimes where the regular doctor fails. I have myself cured cases with them that the surgeons could not cure; cases that but for me, under God, might never have been cured in this world. I make no boast of it; any one else might do as much who had made herbs a study as I have."

"Are you making a fortune by it?" went on the coroner.

Abel shook his head.

"I have a small income of my own, sir, and it is enough for my simple wants. What little money I make by my medicines, and honey, and that—it is not much—I find uses for in other ways. I indulge in a new book now and then; and there are many poor people around who need a bit of help sometimes."

"You 'read' the stars, I am told, Abel Crew. What do you read in them?"

"The same that I read, sir, in all other of nature's works: God's wonderful hand. His wisdom, His power, His providence."

Perhaps the coroner thought to bring Abel to ridicule in his replies: if so, it was a mistake, for he seemed to be getting the worst of it himself. At any rate, he quitted the subject abruptly, brushed his energy up, and began talking to the jury.

The drift of the conversation was, so far as the room could hear it, that Crew's pills, and only Crew's, could have been the authors of the mischief to the two deceased children, whose bodies they were sitting upon, and that Crew must be committed to take his trial for manslaughter. "Hester Reed's evidence," he continued, "is so clear and positive, that it quite puts aside any suspicion of the box of pills having been changed—"

"The box had not my mark upon it, sir," respectfully spoke Abel Crew, his tone anxious.

"Don't interrupt me," rebuked the coroner, sharply. "As to the box not having what he calls his private mark upon it," he added to the jury, "that in my opinion tells little. Because a man has put a mark on fifty pill-boxes, he is not obliged to have put it on the fifty-first. An unintentional omission is readily made. It appears to me—"

"Am I in time? Is it all over? Is Abel Crew found guilty?"

This unceremonious interruption to the official speech came from a woman's voice. The door of the room was thrown open with a fling, considerably discomposing those who had their backs against it and were taken unawares, and they were pushed right and left by the struggles of some one to get to the front. The coroner looked daggers; old Jones lifted his staff; but the intruder forced her way forward with resolute equanimity. Cathy Reed: we never remembered to call her Parrifer. Cathy in her Sunday-going gown and a pink bonnet.

"How dare you?" cried the coroner. "What do you mean by this? Who are you?"

"I have come rushing over from Tewkesbury to clear Abel Crew," returned Cathy, recovering her breath after the fight. "The pills that killed the children were my pills."

The commotion this avowal caused in the room was beyond describing. The coroner stared, the jury all turned to look at the speaker, the crowd trod upon one another.

"And sorry to my heart I am that it should have been so," went on Cathy. "I loved those two dear little ones as if they were my own, and I'd rather my pills had killed myself. Just look at that, please, Mr. Coroner."

The ease with which Cathy spoke to the official gentleman, the coolness with which she put down a pill-box on the green cloth before him, took the room by surprise. As Ann Dovey remarked, later, "She must ha' learnt that there manner in her travels with young Parrifer."

"What is this?" questioned the coroner, curtly, picking up the box.

"Perhaps you'll ask Mr. Crew whether he knows it, sir, before I say what it is," returned Cathy.

The coroner had opened it. It contained seven pills; just the size of the other pills, and looking exactly like them. On the lid and on the box was the private mark spoken of by Abel Crew.

"That is my box, sir; and these—I am certain of it—are my pills," spoke Abel, earnestly, bending over the shoulder of the first juryman to look into the box. "The box and the pills that I gave to Mrs. Reed."

"And so they are, Abel Crew," rejoined Cathy, emphatically. "The week before last, which I was spending at home at father's, I changed the one pill-box for the other, inadvertent, you see"—with a nod to the coroner—"and took the wrong box away with me. And I wish both boxes had been in the sea before I'd done it."

Cathy was ordered to give her account more clearly, and did so. She had been suffering from illness, accompanied by neuralgia, and a doctor at Tewkesbury had prescribed some pills for it, one to be taken occasionally. The chemist who made them up told her they contained arsenic. He was about to write the directions on the box, when Cathy, who was in a hurry, snatched it from him, saying she could not wait for that bother, flung down the money, and departed. This box of pills she had brought with her on her visit to her father's, lest she should find occasion to take one; and she had put it on the shelf of the press, side by side with the other pill-box, to be out of the way of the children. Upon leaving, she took up the wrong box inadvertently: carrying away Abel Crew's pills, leaving her own. There lay the explanation of the mystery of the fatal mistake. Mrs. Reed had not known that Cathy had any pills with her; the girl, who was just as light-headed as ever, not having chanced to mention it; and Cathy had the grace to dust the room herself whilst she was there.

"When father and his wife sent me word about the death of the two little twins, and that it was some pills of Abel Crew's that had done it, I never once thought o' my pills," added Cathy. "They didn't as much as come into my head. But late last night I got lent to me last Saturday's Worcester Herald, and there I read the inquest, and what Crew had said about the marks he put on his pill-boxes, and mother's evidence about never having shifted the pill-box from its place on the press. 'Sure and I couldn't have changed the boxes,' thought I to myself; and upstairs I ran in a fright to look at the box I had brought away. Yes, there it was—Abel Crew's box with the marks on it; and I knew then that I had left my own pills at home here, and that they had killed the babies. As soon as I could get away this morning—which was not as soon as I wanted to—I started to come over. And that's the history—and the blessed truth."

Of course it was the truth. Abel's beautiful face had a glow upon it. "I knew I should be cleared in God's good time," he breathed. The Squire pounced upon him, and shook both his hands as if he would never let them go again. Duffham held out his.

So that was the end of the story. Cathy was reprimanded by the coroner for her carelessness, and burst into tears in his face.

"And thee come off home wi' thee, and see me chuck that there powder into the fire; and don't go making a spectacle o' th' self again," cried Dovey, sharply, in his wife's ear. "Thee just let me catch thee bringing in more o' the dratted stuff; that's all."

"I shall never look at a black-beedle again, Jack, without shivering," she answered; going in for a slight instalment of shivering there and then. "It might ha' come to hanging. Leastways, that's what I've been dreaming of."

CHAPTER V

ROBERT ASHTON'S WEDDING-DAY

The hall-clock was striking half-past five as we went out into the sharp night-air: Mr. and Mrs. Todhetley, I, and Tod. We were spending Christmas that year at Crabb Cot. Old Coney's dinner was fixed for six: but country people don't observe the fashion of dashing in at the last stroke of the hour. The weather was cold, and no mistake; the snow lay on the ground; the stars shone like silver. This was Tuesday, New Year's Day; and to-morrow, the second of January, Jane Coney would be married to Robert Ashton of Timberdale. The Ashtons were to dine to-night at the Farm, and we had been asked to meet them. If every one stood upon his own level, we should shoot up some degrees over the Coneys' heads in the scale of the world's ladder; for old Coney was only a plain farmer; and you've learnt by this time what the Squire was. But the Coneys were right-down good people, and made the best neighbours in the world.

We had only to cross the road slantwise, and old Coney had had it swept for us. It was an old-fashioned farm-house, full of nooks and angles, with one ugly, big room in it, oak-panelled. The cloth was laid there for to-night, the breakfast would be for the morrow. Old Coney and Mrs. Coney came out of the drawing-room to meet us: that was small and snug, with a running pattern of pale roses on its white-watered walls. He was jolly; she, plain, homely, and sensible.

Jane was quiet, like her mother; very well she looked, standing on the carpet in her pretty blue silk dress. Her brother Tom, a tall, strong young fellow with a red face, lifted her out of the way by the waist, that he might shake hands all round. The eldest daughter, Mary West, was staying there with her nurse and baby; she looked ill, and got up only for a minute from her chair by the fire. Her husband was a lawyer, in practice at Worcester. Another young lady was sitting near, with light frizzed hair: Mrs. James Ashton.

Before we had settled down, wheels were heard. It was Robert Ashton's dog-cart, bringing his two brothers, Charles and James; and Mary West's husband. Miss Jane's cheeks turned as red as a rose for nothing: Robert Ashton had not come with them.

I had better say who the Ashtons were. Old Ashton (the father) had lived at Timberdale Court always. It was one of the best farms in all Worcestershire. Old Ashton lived in good style, educated his children, and started them well in life. Lucy, the only girl, married a Captain Bird, who turned out to be a frightful scamp. Robert remained on the farm with his father; Charles was a clergyman; James a doctor in Worcester. Everybody respected Mr. Ashton. It was about three years now since he died, and he left a good pot of money behind him. Robert succeeded to the farm, and it was he who was to marry Jane Coney to-morrow.

They went upstairs with their carpet-bags, having come direct from Worcester by train; Robert Ashton's dog-cart had been waiting, as arranged, at Timberdale Station to bring them on. Mrs. James Ashton came over earlier in the day with Mrs. West. Robert and Charles Ashton were both fine young men, but the doctor was slight and short. Now I hope all that's clear; because it was necessary to say it.

What with talking and looking at the presents, the time passed. They were laid out on a table against the wall, on a snow-white damask cloth of rare beauty.

"Look here," whispered Mrs. Coney, taking up a scented blue-and-white case of satin ribbon and beads for holding pocket-handkerchiefs. "Poor Lucy Bird sent this. She must have made it herself, a thing like this, bought, would be as much as fifteen or sixteen shillings. It came almost anonymously: 'With best love and ever kind wishes for Robert and Jane,' written on it; but we knew Lucy's handwriting."

"Where are they now?" asked Mrs. Todhetley, in the same mysterious whisper.

"I fancy they are staying somewhere in Worcester. We should have liked to have Lucy over for the wedding; but—you know how it is: we could not ask him."

Mrs. Todhetley nodded. She wore her grey silk gown that night, which always seemed to make her look taller and thinner than ever, and a white lace cap with pink ribbons. A pink bow was in her light hair, and she had put on her beautiful earrings.

There is some thorn in most families, and Lucy was the one in that of Ashton. She was educated at the best school in Worcester, and came home at eighteen brimful of romance. It lay in her nature. You'd hardly have found so pretty and sentimental a girl in the county. Because her name was Lucy Ashton, she identified herself with Scott's Lucy Ashton, and looked out for a Master of Ravenswood. These sentimental girls sometimes come to grief, for they possess only three parts of their share of plain common-sense. The Master of Ravenswood came in the shape of Captain Bird, a tall, dark man, with a flaming coat and fierce moustache. He paid court to Lucy, and she fell in love with him before a week was over. The Ashtons turned their backs upon him: there was something in the man they did not like, in spite of the red coat and the black moustache. But he won Lucy over—he had heard of her fortune, you see—and she promised to marry him. She was a gentle, yielding, timid girl then; but her love was strong, and she ran away. She ran away and was married the same morning at St. Helen's church in Worcester, in which parish Bird had been staying. It was the talk of the county; but when the commotion had subsided, every one began to pity Lucy, saying she would have plenty of time and cause for repentance. After all, he was not a real captain now. He had sold out of the army; and there arose a rumour that he had done something wrong and was obliged to sell out.

Mr. Ashton had loved Lucy better than all his children. He forgave the marriage for Lucy's sake, and had them home on a visit, and presented her with a handsome sum. But he made a great mistake—I've heard the Squire say it often—in not settling it upon her. Bird spent it as soon as he well could; and he would have spent some more that came to Lucy when her father died, only that it was left in Robert Ashton's hands to be paid to her quarterly. People called Bird a blackleg: said he was about the worst man that ever stepped. Robert had offered Lucy a home at Timberdale Court, but she would not leave her husband: she had married him, she said, for better or worse. If he came to be transported—and he was going on for it—the chances were that Lucy would follow him to Van Diemen's Land.

"I say, there's six o'clock!" exclaimed Mr. Coney, as the hour struck. "Jane, what have you done with Robert?"

"Not anything, papa. He said he should be here half-an-hour before dinner."

"And it will soon be half-an-hour after it," returned old Coney. "If he does not make haste, we shall sit down without him."

The clock on the mantelpiece went ticking on, and struck half-past six. Dinner. The Squire led off the van with Mrs. Coney. Tod laid hold of Jane.

"I'll take Robert's place whilst I can, Jenny."

The oak-room was a surprise. It looked beautiful. The dark walls were quite covered with holly and ivy, mixed with the blossoms of laurustinus and some bright flowers. Old Thomas (borrowed from us) and the maids stood by the sideboard, which glittered with silver. The Coneys had their stores as well as other people, and did things well when they did them at all. On the table was a large codfish, garnished with horse-radish and lemon. Our names were before our places, and we took them without bustle, Robert Ashton's, next to Jane, being left vacant.

"For what—"

A faint shriek interrupted the Reverend Mr. Ashton, and the grace was interrupted. Lifting his head towards the quarter whence the shriek came, he saw his sister-in-law with a scared face.

"We are thirteen!" exclaimed Mrs. James Ashton. "I beg your pardon, Charles—I beg everybody's pardon; but indeed we must not sit down thirteen to dinner on New Year's Day. I would not for any money."

"What nonsense, my dear!" cried her husband, rather crossly. "Robert will be here directly."

It was of no use. The ladies took her part, saying they ought not to sit down. And there we all stood, uncertain what to do, the dinner hovering in mid-air like Mahomet's coffin, and not to be eaten.

"There are two days in the year when it is not well to sit down thirteen: New Year's Day and Christmas Day," said Mrs. Todhetley, and the rest held with her.

"Are we all to go back to the drawing-room, and leave our dinner?" demanded old Coney, in wrath. "Where the plague is Robert? Look here: those that won't sit down thirteen can go, and those that don't mind it can stop."

"Hear, hear!" cried the Squire.

But Jane Coney went gliding to her mother's side. "I will wait for Robert in the drawing-room, mamma, and you can sit down twelve. Yes, please; it is best so. Indeed I could not eat anything if I stayed."

"Shall we send you some dinner in, child?" asked Mr. Coney.

"No, thank you, papa. I should like best to take it with Robert when he comes."

"All right," said old Coney. "Johnny, you go over to that side, to make the table even. We'll have the grace now, parson."

And the parson said it.

It was a dinner that pleased the Squire's heart. He had a mortal objection to what he called kickshaws, meaning the superfluous dishes you find at a modern entertainment. The Coneys never had kickshaws, only a plain, substantial dinner, the best of its kind.

"Coney, I never taste such oyster-sauce as yours, go where I will," cried the Squire. "It can't be matched."

Old Coney winked, as much as to say he knew it. "The missis gives an eye to that, you see, Squire," he answered, in a side whisper. "She had been in the kitchen till you came."

The Squire took another ladleful. He went once or twice to every dish, and drank champagne with all of us. But still Robert Ashton did not come.

I slipped round to Mrs. Coney when the plum-pudding appeared, whispering that I would take a slice to Jane.

"So you shall, Johnny," she said, giving me some on a plate, and putting a mince-pie beside it. "She will have no luck unless she eats a little of both pudding and pie on the first day of the year."

Jane sat in a low elbow-chair before the fire, her head leaning on her hand, her hair a little tumbled. It was very pretty hair, dark chestnut, and her eyes were hazel. Robert Ashton was fair-haired and blue-eyed; Saxon all over, and very good-looking.

"I have brought you some pudding, Jane."

"Oh, Johnny! why did you leave the table? I can't eat it."

"But Mrs. Coney says you are to; and some mince-pie also, or you'll have no luck."

As if in obedience she ate a little of the pudding, cut a quarter of the mince-pie with her fork, and ate that.

"There, Johnny, that's quite enough for 'luck.' Go back now to your dinner; I dare say you've not had any pudding yourself."

"I'll stay with you, and finish this: as it is going begging."

She neither said yes nor no. She was looking frightfully uneasy.

"Are you vexed that Robert Ashton's not here, Jane?"

"I am not vexed, because I know he would have been here if he could. I think something has happened to him."

I stared at her. "What! because he is a little late in coming? Why, Jane, you must be nervous."

She kept looking into the fire, her eyes fixed. I sat on a stool on the other side of the hearth; the empty pudding-plate standing on the rug between us, where I had put it.

"Robert was sure to come for this dinner, Johnny, all being well, and to be in time."

"Tell me what you fear, Jane—and why?"

"I think I will tell you," she said, after a pause. "I should like to tell some one. I wish I had told Robert when he called this morning; but I was afraid he would laugh at me. You will laugh too."

And Jane Coney told it. In a low, dread voice, her eyes staring into the fire as before, just as though they could see through the blaze into the future.

Early that morning she had had a dream; a disagreeable, ugly dream about Robert Ashton. She thought he was in some frightful peril, that she cried to him to avoid it, or it would stop their marriage. He seemed not to take the least notice of her, but to go right on to it, and in the alarm this brought her, she awoke. I listened in silence, saying nothing to the end; no, nor then.

"The dream was so intensely real, Johnny. It seemed to be to-day; this very day then dawning; and we both of us knew that it was; the one before our marriage. I woke up in a fever; and but that it was night and not day, should have had difficulty in persuading myself at first that we were not really enacting the scene—it was, as I say, so vividly real. And Robert went out to the peril, never heeding me."

"What was the peril?"

"That's what I can't tell. A consciousness lay upon me that it was something very bad and frightful; but of its nature I saw nothing. I did not go to sleep again: it must have been about six o'clock, but the mornings are very dark, you know. I got up soon: what with this dinner-party and other things, there has been a great deal to do to-day, and I soon forgot my dream. Robert called after breakfast, and the sight of him put me in mind of it. I felt a great inclination to tell him to take especial care of himself; but he would only have laughed at me. He drove away direct to the Timberdale Station, to take the train for Worcester."

She did not say, though, what he had gone for to Worcester. To get the ring and licence.

"I have not felt the smallest fear of the dream all along, Johnny, since I awoke. Excepting for the few minutes Robert was here, I don't remember even to have thought of it. But when his brothers and Mr. West came in without him to-night, it flashed into my mind like a dart. I felt sure then that something had happened. I dare say we shall never be married now."

"Jane!"

"Well, Johnny Ludlow, I think it."

To me it seemed to be growing serious. There might be nothing at all in what she had said; most people would have said there was nothing; but, sitting there in the quiet room listening to her earnest voice, seeing her anxious face, a feeling came over me that there was. What had become of Robert Ashton? Where could he be?

"I wish you would give me that shawl of mamma's," she said, pointing to one on a chair. "I feel cold."

She was shivering when I put it over her pretty white shoulders and arms. And yet the fire was roaring to the very top of the grate.

"Alone here, while you were at dinner, I went over all sorts of probabilities," she resumed, drawing the shawl round her as if she were out in the snow. "Of course there are five hundred things that might happen to him, but I can only think of one."

"Well?" for she had stopped. She seemed to be speaking very unwillingly.

"If he walked he would be almost sure to take the near way, across the Ravine."

Was she ever coming to the point? I said nothing. It was better to let her go on in her own way.

"I dare say you will say the idea is far-fetched, Johnny. What I think is, that he may have fallen down the Ravine, in coming here."

Well, I did think it far-fetched. I'd as soon have expected her to say fallen down the chimney.

"Those zigzag paths are not very safe in good weather, especially the one on the Timberdale side," she went on. "With the snow on them, perhaps ice, they are positively dangerous. One false step at the top—and the fall might kill him."

Put in this way, it seemed feasible enough. But yet—somehow I did not take to it.

"Robert Ashton is strong and agile, Jane. He has come down the zigzag hundreds of times."

"I seem to see him lying there, at the bottom of the Ravine," she said, staring as before into the fire. "I—wish—some of you would go and look for him."

"Perhaps we had better. I'll make one. Who's this?"

It was Tom Coney. His mother had sent him to see after me. I thought I'd tell him—keeping counsel about the dream—that Robert Ashton might have come to grief in the Ravine.

"What kind of grief?" asked Tom.

"Turned a summersault down the zigzag, and be lying with a leg broken."

Tom's laugh displayed his small white teeth: the notion amused him excessively. "What else would you like to suppose, Johnny?"

"At any rate, Jane thinks so."

She turned round then, the tears in her eyes, and went up to Tom in an outburst of grief. It took him aback.

"Tom! Tom! if no one goes to see after him, I think I must go myself. I cannot bear the suspense much longer!"

"Why, Jenny girl, what has taken you?"

That had taken her. The fear that Robert Ashton might be lying disabled, or dead, in the Ravine. Tom Coney called Tod quietly out of the dining-room, and we started. Putting on our dark great-coats in silence, we went out at the back-door, which was nearest the Ravine. Jane came with us to the gate. I never saw eyes so eager as hers were, as she gazed across the snow in the moonlight.

"Look here," said Tom, "we had better turn our trousers up."

The expedition was not pleasant, I can assure you, especially the going down the zigzag. Jane was right about its being slippery: we had to hold on by the trees and bushes, and tread cautiously. When pretty near the bottom, Tod made a false step, and shot down into the snow.

"Murder!" he roared out.

"Any bones broken?" asked Tom Coney, who could hardly speak for laughing. Tod growled, and shied a handful of snow at him.

But the slip brought home to us the probability of the fear about Robert Ashton. To slip from where Tod did was fun; to slip from the top of the opposite zigzag, quite another thing. The snow here at the bottom was up to our calves, and our black evening trousers got rolled up higher. The moonlight lay cold and white on the Ravine: the clustering trees, thick in summer, were leafless now. Had any fellow been gazing down from the top, we must have looked, to him, like three black-coated undertakers, gliding along to a funeral.

"I'll tell you what," cried Tod: "if Ashton did lose his footing, he wouldn't come to such mortal grief. The depth of snow would save him."

"I don't believe he did fall," said Tom Coney, stoutly. "Bob Ashton's as sure-footed as a hare. But for Jane's being so miserable, I'd have said, flatly, I wouldn't come out on any such wild-goose errand."

On we went, wading through the snow. Some of us looked round for the ghost's light, and did not see it. But rumour said that it never came on a bright moonlit night. Here we were at last!—at the foot of the other zigzag. But Robert Ashton wasn't here. And, the best proof that he had not fallen, was the unbroken surface of the snow. Not so much as a rabbit had scudded across to disturb it.

"I knew it," said Tom Coney. "He has not come to grief at all. It stands to reason that a fellow must have heaps to do the day before his wedding, if it's only in burning his old letters from other sweethearts. Bob had a heap of them, no doubt; and couldn't get away in time for dinner."

"We had better go on to the Court, and see," I said.

"Oh, that be hanged!" cried the other two in a breath.

"Well, I shall. It's not much farther. You can go back, or not, as you like."

This zigzag, though steeper than the one on our side, was not so slippery. Perhaps the sun had shone on it in the day and melted the snow. I went up it nearly as easily as in good weather. Tod and Coney, thinking better of the turning back, came after me.

We should have been at Timberdale Court in five minutes, taking the short-cut over hedges and ditches, but for an adventure by the way, which I have not just here space to tell about. It had nothing to do with Robert Ashton. Getting to the Court, we hammered at it till the door was opened. The servant started back in surprise.

"Goodness me!" said she, "I thought it was master."

"Where is the master?" asked Tom.

"Not come home, sir. He has not been in since he left this morning."

It was all out. Instead of pitchpolling into Crabb Ravine and breaking his limbs, Bob Ashton had not got back from Worcester. It was very strange, though, what could be keeping him, and the Court was nearly in a commotion over it.

When we got back to the Farm, they were laying the table for the wedding-breakfast. Plenty of kickshaws now, and some lovely flowers. The ladies, helping, had their gowns turned up. This helping had not been in the evening's programme; but things seemed to have been turned upside down, and they were glad to seize upon it. Jane and her sister, Mrs. West, sat alone by the drawing-room fire, never saying a word to one another.

"Johnny, I don't half like this," whispered Mrs. Todhetley to me.

"Like what, good mother?"

"This absence of Robert Ashton."

I don't know that I liked it either.

Morning came. In an uncertainty such as this, people go to each other's houses indiscriminately. The first train came in from Worcester before it was well light; but it did not bring Robert Ashton. As to the snow on the ground, it was pretty well beaten now.

"He wouldn't travel by that slow parliamentary thing: he'll come by the express to South Crabb Junction," said Tom Coney, thinking he would cheer away the general disappointment. Jane we had not seen.

The express would be at the Junction between nine and ten. A whole lot of us went down there. It was not farther off than Timberdale Station, but the opposite way. I don't think one of us was more eager than another, unless it was the Squire. The thing was getting serious, he told us; and he went puffing about like a man looking for his head.

To witness the way he seized upon the doors when the express steamed in, and put his old red nose inside all the carriages, looking for Robert Ashton, was a rare sight. The guard laid hold of his arm, saying he'd come to damage. But Robert Ashton was not in the train.

"He may come yet," said old Coney, looking fit to cry. "There'll be a train in again at Timberdale. Or, he may drive over."

But every one felt that he would not come. Something told us so. It was only making believe to one another, saying he would.

"I shall go to Worcester by the next down train," said the Squire to old Coney.

"The next does not stop here."

"They'd better stop it for me," said the Squire, defiantly. "You can't come, Coney. You must remain to give Jane away."

"But if there's no bridegroom to give her to?" debated old Coney.

"There may be. You must remain on the strength of it."

The down train came up, and obeyed the signal to stop made by the station-master. The Squire, Tod, and Tom Coney got in, and it steamed on again.

"Now mind, I shall conduct this search," the Squire said to the others with a frown. "You young fellows don't know your right hand from your left in a business of this sort. We must go about it systematically, and find out the different places that Robert Ashton went to yesterday, and the people he saw." Tod and Tom Coney told us this later.

When they arrived at Worcester, the first man they saw at Shrubb Hill Station was Harry Coles, who had been seeing somebody off by the train, which was rather curious; for his brother, Fred Coles, was Robert Ashton's great chum, and was to be groom's-man at the wedding. Harry Coles said his brother had met Ashton by appointment the previous day, and went with him to the Registrar's office for the marriage licence—which was supplied to them by Mr. Clifton himself. After that, they went to the jeweller's, and chose the wedding-ring.

"Well, what after that?" cried the impatient Squire.

Harry Coles did not know what. His brother had come back to their office early in the afternoon—about one o'clock—saying Ashton was going, or had gone, home.

"Can't you tell which he said—going, or gone?" demanded the Squire, getting red.

"No, I can't," said Harry Coles. "I was busy with some estimates, and did not pay particular attention to him."

"Then you ought to have paid it, sir," retorted the Squire. "Your brother?—where is he?"

"Gone over to Timberdale ages ago. He started the first thing this morning, Squire; a big coat thrown over his wedding toggery."

The Squire growled, as a relief to his feelings, not knowing what in the world to do. He suddenly said he'd go to the Registrar's office, and started for Edgar Street.

Mr. Clifton was not there, but a clerk was. Yes, Mr. Ashton of Timberdale had been there the previous day, he said, in answer to the Squire, and had got his licence. The governor (meaning Mr. Clifton, who knew the Ashtons and the Coneys well) had joked a bit with young Ashton, when he gave it. As to telling where Ashton of Timberdale and Mr. Coles had gone to afterwards, the clerk did not know at all.

So there was nothing to be gathered at the Registrar's office, and the Squire turned his steps up the town again, Tod and Coney following him like two tame lambs; for he wouldn't let them make a suggestion or put in a word edgeways. He was on his way to the jeweller's now: but as he had omitted to ask Harry Coles which of the jewellers' shops the ring was bought at, he took them all in succession, and hit upon the right one after some difficulty.

He learnt nothing there, either. Mr. Ashton of Timberdale had bought the ring and keeper, and paid for them, the master said. Of course every one knew the young lady was Miss Jane Coney: he had brought one of her rings as a guide for size: a chased gold ring, with small garnet stones in it.

"I am not asking for rings and stones," interrupted the Squire, wrathfully. "I want to know if Mr. Ashton said where he was going to afterwards?"

"He said never a word about it," returned the master. "When they went out of here—young Fred Coles was with him—they took the way towards the Hop Market."

The Squire went to the Crown next—the inn used by the Ashtons of Timberdale. Robert Ashton had called in the previous day, about one o'clock, the waiter said, taking a little bread-and-cheese, observing that he had no time for anything else, and a glass of table-beer. Mr. Coles had come down Broad Street with him, as far as the inn door, when they shook hands and parted; Mr. Coles going back again. The waiter thought Mr. Ashton was not in the house above five minutes at the most.

"And don't you know where he went to next?" urged the Squire.

"No," the waiter replied. The impression on his mind was, that Mr. Ashton's business in Worcester was over, and that he was returning home again.

The Squire moved slowly up Broad Street, more gloomy than an owl, his hands in his pockets, his nose blue. He boasted of his systematic abilities, as applied to seekings and searchings, but he knew no more what to be at next than the man in the moon. Turning up the Cross, he came to an anchor outside the linen-draper's shop; propping his back against the window, as if the hanging silks had offended him. There he stood staring up at St. Nicholas's clock opposite.

"Tom," said he, virtually giving in, "I think we had better talk to the police. Here's one coming along now."

When the policeman was abreast, the Squire took his hands from his pockets, and pinned the man by his button-hole.

"Mr. Ashton of Timberdale?—oh, he has got into trouble, sir," was the man's ready answer. "He is before the magistrates now, on a charge of—"

The railway omnibus, coming along at the moment, partially drowned the word.

"Charge of what?" roared the Squire.

The policeman repeated it. The omnibus was making a frightful rattle, and the Squire only just caught it now. With a great cry he dashed over to the fly-stand, got into one, and ordered it to gallop away with him. Tom Coney and Tod barely escaped having to hang on behind.

"Drive like mad!" stamped the Squire.

"Yes, sir," said the man, obeying. "Where to?"

"Go on, will you, sir! To the deuce."

"To the police-court," corrected Tom Coney.

Arrived there, the Squire left them to pay the fare, and fought his way inside. The first thing his spectacles caught sight of distinctly was the fair Saxon face and fine form of Robert Ashton, standing, a prisoner, in the criminal dock.

At the Farm, things were in a state more easily imagined than described. The carriages came bowling up, bringing the guests. The four bridesmaids wore pale-blue silk, trimmed with white fur. Jane was dressed. In passing her door, I saw her. They had sent me up to fetch something from Tom's room.

"Is it not a mockery, Johnny?" she said, letting me enter. And her poor pale face looked more fit for a burying than a wedding, and her eyes had dark circles round them.

"If you mean your dress, Jane, I never saw anything less like a mockery, or more like a princess's in a fairy tale."

It was of rich white silk; a delicate wreath of myrtle and orange-blossoms on her chestnut hair. The veil lay upon the bed.

"You know what I mean, Johnny. There will be no wedding at North Crabb Church to-day—and nothing can have been more foolish than to prepare me for it. Oh, Johnny! if I could only go to sleep till ten years hence, and never wake up between!"

Before the gate waited the carriages, their postillions in scarlet jackets; the company, in their fine plumage, jostled each other in the nooks and corners of the house; the maids, wearing a bright uniform of purple gowns and white muslin aprons, ran about wildly. Every two minutes, old Coney went up to a staircase window that faced Timberdale, looking out to see whether Robert Ashton was coming—like Sister Anne, in "Bluebeard."

Twelve o'clock! It was like a knell booming out; and the carriages went away with the company. A fine ending to a wedding!

I was standing at the back-door, disconsolate as the moaning wind, when the Timberdale Station fly came rattling along. A gentleman put his head out of it, to tell the driver to stop. He got down, and came limping up to me. It was Mr. West's partner, old Lawyer Cockermuth, who had declined an invitation to the wedding, because of gout.

"Look here," said he, catching me by the shoulder, "I want to say half-a-dozen words to Mr. Coney. Can you manage to bring him out to me, or smuggle me into any little place where we can be alone? I suppose the house is chock-full of wedding-people."

"You have brought bad news of Robert Ashton!" I said, in sudden conviction. "What is it?"

"Well, so I have," he answered confidentially. "It will soon be known to every one, but I should like to break it to Coney first. I've come over to do it. Robert Ashton is in custody for murder!"

I felt my face turn as pale as a girl's. "For murder?"

Old Cockermuth's face grew long as he nodded. "He is in custody for nothing less than the murder of his brother-in-law, Bird. Yesterday—"

A smothered cry behind us, and I turned sharply. There stood Jane. She had seen Cockermuth's arrival, and came down, knowing he must have brought bad news. The white robe and wreath were gone, and she wore an everyday dress of violet merino.

"Now, my dear! my dear, be calm!" cried the old lawyer, in a fright. "For goodness' sake shut us in somewhere, Johnny Ludlow! We shall have the whole pack out upon us."

Some of the pack did come, before he could be shut up. And there we were—hearing that Robert Ashton had been taken up for murder.

It appeared that, after quitting the Crown on the previous day, he met his sister's husband, Captain Bird—from habit, people still accorded him his title. Captain Bird told him Lucy was dangerously ill, and asked him to go and see her. Robert went at once to their lodgings. What exactly happened there, no one as yet knew; but Robert and Bird got quarrelling. Robert did not come out again. In the morning (this morning) the neighbours heard a hue-and-cry; and on the door being opened by two policemen, Bird was found lying in the passage dead, as was supposed, and Robert Ashton was given into custody for his murder.

Jane touched me on the arm, and I followed her into the large, empty dining-room. That miserable breakfast! waiting for those who could not sit down to it. The evergreens on the walls seemed to look faded; the flowers on the table to have lost their first freshness.

"You see I was right, Johnny," she said. "That dream was a dream of warning. And sent as one."

It did look like it. But dreams are things you can't lay hold of; no, nor altogether believe in. Standing by the cold grate, she began to shiver. In the confusion, the servants had let the fire go out.

"I would forget the dream, if I were you, Jane. Where's the use of people having dreams—"

"Say warnings, Johnny."

"—if they cannot see how to make use of them? Call them warnings, an you like the word better. They are of no good at all."

"Oh, Johnny, if I could only die! It was hard enough to bear when he was only missing; but now—"

It was just as though she never meant to leave off shivering. I went to hunt for some sticks, and saw our cook, Molly, in the kitchen amongst the maids. Trust her for being in the thick of any gossip. Bringing the sticks back, I pushed them in, and they soon crackled up into a blaze. Jane sat down and watched them.

"I wouldn't be afraid, Jane, if I were you. There must be some mistake."

"I'm not afraid—in one sense. That Robert has done nothing wrong willingly, I know. But—he is rather passionate; and there's no telling how they might provoke him. If there is much prolonged suspense; a trial, or anything of that sort—well, I suppose I shall live through it."

How hopeless she looked! her head bent, her eyes cast down. Just then there was a cry outside for Jane. "Jane!"

"Go out, Johnny, and say I am all right. Pray to them to leave me alone. Tell mamma not to come in; I am easier by myself—and the fire's burning up. They have gone calling upstairs; they wouldn't think I am here."

Was there anything incoherent in her words? I looked at her narrowly. I suppose that they sounded something like it.

"One has been coming to soothe me, and another has been coming; I haven't known how to bear it. They mean it in kindness—great kindness; but I would so much rather be alone. You go now, Johnny."

So I shut her in. And whispered to Mrs. Coney that she was praying to be left.

I don't know how the day went on, except that it was miserably uncomfortable. We had some cold beef in the everyday dining-room, and old Coney, after saying he'd have given a thousand pounds out of his pocket for it not to have happened, went and smoked a pipe with Cockermuth in the best kitchen. Dusk began to come on.

Why! who was that—driving up in Robert Ashton's dog-cart? Robert! Robert himself? Yes, it was; and the Squire, and Tod, and Tom Coney with him. The dog-cart had gone to the station to wait for the Squire and the other two: they came, bringing Robert Ashton.

"Is it all right, Mr. Ashton?"

"Quite right, Johnny. You did not think it could be wrong, did you?"

"You are out on bail?"

"Out for good. There has been no real damage done. I wonder where Jane is?"

"I'll take you to her. She has been wishing she was dead."

No one in the house scented his presence. I opened the door of the large oak-room. Jane was kneeling on the hearthrug, her face buried in the cushion of the arm-chair. She started up at the noise, and stood like one turned to stone.

"Robert?"

I do believe she thought it was not real—his ghost, or something. He went up in silence, slightly smiling—he was always a quiet-mannered man—and holding out his hand.

"It is I, myself, Jane. You look as though you doubted it."

With a great cry she fell forward. Robert caught her to his breast. I was going away when he hastily called to me. For the first time in her life she had fainted away. The thing had been too much for her.

"Get some water, Johnny. Don't call any one. She'll soon come to."

There was water on the table; wine too. He gave Jane some of both. And then she listened to his story, leaning on his arm, and crying as softly and peacefully as a little child.

Those outside were listening to the wonderful tale. When I went out, they had gathered in the best kitchen, round the Squire, who had gone there in search of old Coney. The Squire's glowing face was a sight to be seen. Mrs. Coney had sat down on the mahogany bench; her hands lifted. Coney stood with his pipe held at arm's-length. As to Mrs. Todhetley, the tears were running down her cheeks in a stream.

It was quite true that Lucy Bird was very ill. Robert saw her in bed. As he was leaving, Bird began upon the old grievance—that he should have some of Lucy's money advanced in a lump. He wanted it for his cards and dice, you see. Robert told him, No: as he had told him all along. An associate of Bird's was there; a very bad man, named Dawler. They got Robert to take a friendly glass of wine—which purported to be sherry: and from that moment he lost all power, and partly consciousness. The wine was drugged. Their object, no doubt, had been to partly stupefy him, and so induce him to sign an undertaking to hand over the money to Bird. But they had made the potion a trifle too strong, not calculating the effect it would take on a young and habitually sober man. Robert fell into a deep sleep, from which it was impossible to arouse him all night: as to writing, his hands were as if dead. Late in the morning he awoke; and, bit by bit, realized where he was and what had passed. He was a little stupid even then, but sensible enough to remember that it was his wedding-day, and to foresee that he might have some trouble to get away from the house. On attempting to leave, Bird and Dawler placed themselves in the passage to prevent him. There was a hot contest. Robert Ashton, a stronger man than either of the others, but aware that all his strength was not then at his own command, seized a knotted stick, or club, that was lying in a corner, and lifted it to fight his way through. Dawler struck at it, to get it out of his hand, and struck it against Bird's head with frightful force. The fellow dropped as one dead, and the door was burst open by the neighbours and policemen. The excitement, perhaps the exertion, acting on Robert Ashton's only partly recovered state, turned him stupid again: the people took him to be drunk, and Dawler gave him in charge for murder.

That was the history. When the Squire had got into the police-court, Robert Ashton (who was nearly himself again through the remedies the doctor had given him in the police-station) was telling his tale. Dawler was contradicting him, and swearing hard and fast that it was a case of deliberate murder. The magistrates invited the Squire to a seat beside them: and the first thing he did was to break into a hot tantrum, vowing Robert Ashton couldn't be guilty. How it would have terminated no one knew, but Lucy saved him.

Lucy saved him. A wan, haggard young woman wrapped in an old shawl, staggered into the justice-room, to the front of the room. It was Lucy Bird. She had come crawling through the streets to tell the truth.

"My brother Robert did not attempt to strike any one," she said in low, weak, earnest tones. "He only held the club in his hand. I saw it all, for I stood by. It was Dawler who threw his weight upon the club, and struck down my husband. Robert fell too; pushed down by Dawler. This is the sole truth, before Heaven!"

They believed her. The best was, that Bird was not dead at all, only stunned; and the next to appear in court was himself, with a big white plaister on his forehead. Discovering his wife's flight to the magistrates, he thought it well to go after her: there was no knowing what plots might be in the wind. He had the grace to acknowledge that the blow was an accident. The whole bench shook hands with Robert Ashton, telling Bird and the other man significantly that they had better take care what they were about for the future: and the Squire brought him home in triumph.

"But where is Robert?" asked old Coney and the rest. Why, in there with Jane: where else should he be? They burst into the oak-room in a body, and found him trying on the ring.

"Why shouldn't we have a dinner to-night?" asked old Coney. "Last night's was only half a dinner, through one bother or another."

"Hear, hear!" cried the Squire. "Why not?"

The only thing against it was—as Mrs. Coney said—that no dinner was prepared. Unless they could put up with a cold one.

"And glad to do so," spoke up everybody. So the cold meats were brought from the larder, and the fowls from the breakfast-table, and laid in the everyday dining-parlour. The ladies were in their ordinary gowns, and there was no room for elbows, but we made up with laughter. Sixteen this evening; Fred Coles being there, and old Cockermuth, who sat down in spite of the gout. Afterwards we went off by the light of the stars to summon the company to the morrow's wedding; it was good to go knocking at the doors with the news. Whilst the servants at the Farm, with Molly to help them, began cooking fresh fowls for the breakfast-table.

And that's about all. There was never a better wedding seen, and the scarlet jackets of the post-boys dazzled one's eyes in the morning sun. Robert Ashton was calm and quiet in church; Jane too, and not a bit nervous. The chief speech at the breakfast was undertaken by the Squire, so you may give a guess what it was like; but it didn't spoil the wedding-cake.

Jane was shut up with her mother when the time came for starting, and came out in a flood of tears. She was leaving her childhood's home, you see. Robert would have hurried her straight to the carriage, but the company wouldn't be done out of their leave-taking. I was the last.

"Thank you for all, Johnny," she cried, wringing my hand as she went down the path. "They were all very kind to me yesterday, but it seemed that you were kindest."

In the next minute, both of them, with the door shut, and the carriage away towards South Crabb Junction. The people cheered, the cocks crew, and the old shoes flew after them in a shower.

CHAPTER VI

You remember what I, Johnny Ludlow, said in the last paper—that on our way to Timberdale Court we met with an adventure, which I had not then time to tell of. It was this.

After our race through Crabb Ravine by moonlight, looking for Robert Ashton, we went on to Timberdale Court as fast as the snowy ground would admit of, Joseph Todhetley and Tom Coney rushing on in front, I after them—they were older and stronger than I was. Not by the ordinary highway, but over fields and hedges and ditches, straight as the crow flies, wishing to save time. Instead of saving time, we lost it, for though the road, had we taken it, was longer, the snow was beaten there; whereas it was lying deep across the country and had to be waded through. But you can't always bring common-sense to bear at the moment it's wanted. And if we had looked like three undertakers at a funeral, stalking after one another in the Ravine, with our dark coats showing out against the white snow, I'm sure we must have looked still more like it in the open ground.

At the far corner of the square meadow was a cow-shed, unused since the autumn, when Ashton of Timberdale had caused the fields about here to be ploughed. Beyond the shed, touching its walls, ran a brook; and it brought us up. We had meant to take it at a flying leap; but the snow had melted there, and the brook was swollen. It was not agreeable to run the chance of pitching in, and it seemed that we should have to make for the gate, lower down. Standing for a moment to reconnoitre, there broke on our ears a low moan; and then another.

"I say," cried Tod, "is that the ghost?" I said in that last paper, as any one may see, that we had looked out for the ghost in the Ravine. The moaning came again.

"If I don't believe it is in the cow-shed!" exclaimed Tom Coney. And he went round to the door and shook it open.

Pitch dark inside and the same moaning, soft and low. Tom Coney had some lights in his pocket, and struck one. Well! we were astonished. On the ground lay a woman—or girl—and a very little child. She had a young face, with anxious eyes and feverish cheeks. She said she was dying, and so answered our questions; but we had to kneel down to hear her. She had walked across the country from somewhere in Gloucestershire, carrying her baby of a fortnight old, but the weakness and fever overtook her. Two nights ago she had crept into the shed, and lain there, unsuspected, ever since.

"But why did you leave your home?" inquired Tod.

"I couldn't stay for the shame," was the nearly inaudible answer: and but that our ears were good ones, we should not have caught it. If we would but fetch her a drop of water for the love of Christ, she said, as we got up.

It was impossible to help wondering whether God had not allowed Robert Ashton to be lost on purpose to bring us round there. But for our passing, both she and the baby must very soon have died, for the shed was quite out of the reach of any road likely to be traversed. We must have seemed to her like angels of mercy. Perhaps we were made use of as such that night.

"Have you lain here all that time—two nights and days—without food?" asked Tod, in his softest voice.

"Without food, sir, and without drink. Oh, for a drop of water! If you could only bring it me, I should die easier."

We got some clean snow and moistened her lips with it. She gave a sobbing cry as it trickled down her throat: Tom Coney said it was choking, but I thought it was joy. To a poor creature in a burning fever, lying without any sort of drink for days and nights, the fresh cold snow must have tasted like dew from heaven. She motioned that the baby should have some, but we were afraid: it looked to be dying.

What could be done with her? To carry her away was not practicable—and she seemed too ill besides. Tom Coney offered to cover up the baby under his coat and take it to the Court for food and shelter; but she clutched it closer to her side as it lay on her arm, and faintly said it couldn't do without her. Shutting the shed door again, we got quickly to Timberdale Court, found Robert Ashton was not at home, as you heard, and asked for the housekeeper, Mrs. Broom.

She was sitting in her little carpeted room, off the big kitchen, with one of the maids. They were sewing white bows on a lot of caps, and wondering what had become of the master. To be burst in upon by us, all three telling the story at once of the woman and child, pretty nearly scared good old Mother Broom's senses away.

"You are just playing a trick upon me, young gentlemen."

"It is as true as that we are here, Mrs. Broom; it is true as gospel. They'll both be dead if something's not done for them."

"Well, I never heard of such a thing," she exclaimed, beginning to stir about. "Lying in that cow-shed for two days without help! You ought to have brought the poor baby away with you, sirs."

"She wouldn't let it come."

"I wouldn't have minded her saying that. A fortnight-old baby lying in the shed in this cold!"

"I don't think it will make much difference in the long-run, whether the baby stays in the shed or comes out of it," said Tom Coney. "If it sees to-morrow's dawn, I shall wonder."

"Well, this is a fine start!" cried Mother Broom. "And the master never to have come home—that's another," she went on. For, what to do, she didn't know the least in the world, and was like a woman with a lost head.

We left the matter to her, carrying some things to the shed as we passed it on our way home—blankets and a pillow, fresh water, milk-and-water for the baby, and a candle and matches. One of the women-servants was to come after us, with hot broth and wine.

When we reached Crabb Cot, the dismay there at hearing Robert Ashton had not turned up, was diversified by this news, which we told of. Not that they thought very much of it: the woman was only a poor tramp, they said; and such things—fevers, and that—happen to poor tramps every day.

"Do you think the baby's dying?" asked Charles Ashton, the parson.

"I'm nearly sure it is," said Tom Coney.

"That's a kind of woman, you know, that ought to be committed for fourteen-days' hard labour," observed the Squire, fiercely, who was in a frightfully cross mood with the various mishaps and uncertainties of the evening. "Seems to be very sickly and humble, you say, Mr. Johnny! Hold your tongue, sir; what should you know about it? These women tramps bring death on their infants through exposure."

"And that's true," said old Coney. "I'd punish 'em, Squire, if I were a magistrate like you."

But what do you think Parson Ashton did? When the dog-cart had taken him and Mr. and Mrs. James Ashton to the Court—where they were to stay all night—he started off for the shed, and did not come away from it until he had baptized the baby.

We heard nothing more about it until the next day—and I don't suppose any one has forgotten what sort of a miserable day that was, at old Coney's Farm. How the wedding never took place, and Robert Ashton was still missing, and Jane Coney was dressed in her bridal robes for nothing, and the breakfast could not be eaten, and we guests staring in each other's faces like so many helpless dummies. What news we had of it then, came from Charles Ashton: he had been to the shed again that morning. Whilst the carriages stood waiting at the gate, the post-boys' scarlet jackets flaming in the sun, and the company indoors sat looking hopelessly for the bridegroom, Parson Ashton talked about it in a corner to Mrs. Coney and the Squire's wife: both of them in their grand silk plumage then, one plum-coloured, the other sea-green, with feathers for top-knots.

The little baby was dead, Charles Ashton said. The mother had been removed to a shelter in Timberdale village, and was being cared for. The doctor, called in to her, Darbyshire, thought she might get over it.

"You baptized the child, I hear, Charles?" said Mrs. Coney, to the parson.

"Oh yes."

"What did you name it?"

"Lucy. Something in the mother's face put me in mind of my sister, and it was the name I first thought of. I asked the mother what she would have it called. Anything, she answered; it did not matter. Neither did it, for the little thing was dying then. Hot-water bottles and other remedies were tried last night as soon as they could be had, to get warmth into the child—to renew its life, in fact; but nothing availed."

"Where was the woman taken to?"

"To Jael Batty's. Jael consented to take her in."

"I suppose it is but another case of the old, sad story?" groaned Mrs. Todhetley.

"Nothing else. And she, poor thing, is not much more than a girl."

"Now, Charles, I tell you what. It may be all very consistent for you clergymen—men of forgiveness, and that—to waste your compassion over these poor stray creatures, but I think it might do more good sometimes if you gave them blame," spoke Mrs. Coney, severely.

"There are times and seasons when you cannot express blame, however much it may be deserved," he answered. "The worst of it in these cases is, that we rarely know there exists cause for censure before it is too late for any censure to avail, or avert the evil."

What with the astounding events of the day, connected with the interrupted wedding, nothing more was said or thought of the affair. Except by Jane. When she and I were in the big dining-room together—I trying to blow up the fire, and she in full dread that Robert Ashton would have to be tried for his life at the Worcester Spring Assizes, and lie in prison until then—she suddenly spoke of it, interrupting the noise made by the crackling of the wood.

"So that poor baby's dead, Johnny! What a happy fate—not to grow up to trouble. Charles named it Lucy, I hear. I should like to see the poor mother."

"See her for what, Jane?"

"She is in distress, and so am I. I don't suppose she has a corner to turn to for comfort in the wide world. I have not."

It was not so very long after this that her distress was over. Robert Ashton arrived in triumph, and so put an end to it. One might suppose Jane would no longer have remembered that other one's distress; what with the impromptu dinner, where we had no room for our elbows, and the laughter, and the preparations for the next day's wedding.

But the matter had taken hold of Jane Coney's mind, and she reverted to it on the morrow before going away. When the wedding-breakfast was over, and she—nevermore Jane Coney, but Jane Ashton—had changed her dress and was saying good-bye to her mother upstairs, she suddenly spoke of it.

"Mamma, I want to ask you to do something for me."

"Well, my dear?"

"Will you see after that poor young woman who was found in the shed?"

Naturally Mrs. Coney was taken by surprise. She didn't much like it.

"After that young woman, Jane?"

"Yes; for me."

"Mrs. Broom has seen to her," returned Mrs. Coney, in a voice that sounded very frozen.

"Mother, dear," said Jane, "I was comparing myself with her yesterday; wondering which of us was the worst off, the more miserable. I thought I was. I almost felt that I could have changed places with her."

"Jane!" angrily interjected Mrs. Coney.

"I did. She knew the extent of her trouble, she could see all that it involved; I did not see the extent of mine. I suppose it is always thus—that other people's sorrows seem light when compared with our own. The reason must no doubt be that we cannot realize theirs, whilst we realize ours only too keenly."

"My dear, I don't care to talk of this."

"Nor I much—but hear me for a minute, mother. God has been so merciful to me, and she is still as she was, that I—I should like to do what I can for her when we come back again, and comfort and keep her."

"Keep her!"

"Keep her from want, I mean."

"But, child, she has been—you don't know what she has been," gravely rebuked Mrs. Coney.

"I think I do, mother."

"She is a poor outcast, Jane; with neither home to go to, nor friends to look upon her."

Jane burst into tears: they had been hardly kept down since she had begun to speak.

"Just so, mother. But what was I yesterday? If Robert had been tried for his life, and condemned, I should have felt like an outcast; perhaps been looked upon as no better than one by the world."

"Goodness, Jane, I wish you'd exercise your common sense," cried Mrs. Coney, losing patience. "I tell you she is an outcast, and has forfeited home and friends. She has been a great sinner."

"Mother, if she had a home and friends, there would be no need to succour her. As to sin—perhaps we can save her from that for the future. My gratitude for the mercy shown to me is such that I feel as if I could take her to my bosom; it seems to my mind that I ought to do something for her, that she has been thrown in my way that I should do it. Mother, it is my last petition to you: see after her a little for me until we come back again."

"Very well, dear; as you make this point of it," concluded Mrs. Coney, relenting just a little. And then Jane began to cry hysterically; and Tom Coney knocked at the door, saying time was up.

Mrs. Coney was not a hard-hearted woman, just the opposite: but only those who live in rural parts of the country can imagine the tricks and turns of regular tramps, and what a bad lot some of them are. They deceive you with no end of a plausible tale, and stare pitifully in your face whilst they tell it. Not long before this, a case had happened where both our house and the Coneys' had been taken in. A woman in jagged widows' garments presented herself at the door of Crabb Cot and asked to see the Squire. Her shoes wanted mending, and one side of her face was bandaged up. Mrs. Todhetley went to her. Of all pitiable tales that poor woman told the most: it would have melted a heart of stone. She came from near Droitwich, she said: her husband had worked under Sir John Pakington; that is, had been a labourer on part of his estate, Westwood Park. She lost her husband and grown-up son the past autumn with fever; she caught it herself, and was reduced to a skeleton, lost her cottage home through the things being seized for rent, and went to live with a married daughter in Oxfordshire. Cancer had appeared in her cheek, the daughter could not keep her, for she and all her children were down with sickness, and the husband had no work—and she, the widow, was making her way by easy walking-stages to Worcester, there to try and get into the infirmary. What she wanted at Crabb Cot was—not to beg, either money or food: money she could do without, food she could not eat—but to implore the gentleman (meaning the Squire) to give her a letter to the infirmary doctors, so that they might take her in.

I can tell you that she took us in—every one of us. The Squire, coming up during the conference, surrendered without fight. Questions were put to her about Droitwich and Ombersley, which she answered at once. There could be no mistaking that she knew all the neighbourhood about there well, and Sir John and Lady Pakington into the bargain. I think it was that that threw us off our guard. Mrs. Todhetley, brimming over with compassion, offered her some light refreshment, broth or milk. She said she could not swallow either, "it went against her," but she'd be thankful for a drink of water. Molly, the greatest termagant to tramps and beggars in general, brought out a half-pint bottle of store cordial, made by her own hands, of sweetened blackberry juice and spice, for the woman to put in her pocket and sip, on her journey to Worcester. Mrs. Todhetley gave her a pair of good shoes and some shillings, and two old linen handkerchiefs for the face; and the Squire, putting on his writing spectacles, wrote a letter to Mr. Carden, begging him to see if anything, in the shape of medical aid, could be done for the bearer. The woman burst into tears of thankfulness, and went away with her presents, including the letter, Molly the cross-grained actually going out to open the back-gate for her.

And now would anybody believe that this woman had only then come out of the Coneys' house—where she had been with the same tale and request, and had received nearly the same relief? We never saw or heard of her again. The note did not reach Mr. Carden; no such patient applied to the infirmary. She was a clever impostor; and we got to think that the cheek had only been rubbed up with a little blistering-salve. Many another similar thing I could tell of—and every one of them true. So you must not wonder at Mrs. Coney's unwillingness to interfere with this latest edition in the tramp line.

But she had given her promise: perhaps, as Jane put it, she could not do otherwise. And on the morning after the wedding she went over to Timberdale. I was sliding in the Ravine—for there was ice still in that covered spot, though the frost had nearly disappeared elsewhere—when I saw Mrs. Coney come down the zigzag by the help of her umbrella, and her everyday brown silk gown on.

"Are you here, Johnny! Shall I be able to get along?"

"If I help you, you will, Mrs. Coney."

"Take care. I had no idea it would be slippery here. But it is a long way round to walk by the road, and the master has taken out the pony-chaise."

"What wind is blowing you to Timberdale to-day?"

"An errand that I'm not at all pleased to go upon, Johnny; only Jane made a fuss about it before leaving yesterday. If I told the master he would be in a fine way. I am going to see the woman that you boys found in the shed."

"I fancied Jane seemed to think a good deal about her."

"Jane did think a good deal about her," returned Mrs. Coney. "She has not had the experience of this sort of people that I have, Johnny; and girls' sympathies are so easily aroused."

"There was a romance about it, you see."

"Romance, indeed!" wrathfully cried Mrs. Coney. "That's what leads girls' heads away: I wish they'd think of good plain sense instead. It was nothing but romance that led poor Lucy Ashton to marry that awful man, Bird."

"Why does Lucy not leave him?"

"Ah! it's easier to talk about leaving a man than to do it, once he's your husband. You don't understand it yet, Johnny."

"And shall not, I suppose, until I am married myself. But Lucy has never talked of leaving Bird."

"She won't leave him. Robert has offered her— Goodness me, Johnny, don't hurry along like that! It's nothing but ice here. If I were to get a tumble, I might be lamed for life."

"Nonsense, Mrs. Coney! It would be only a Christmas gambol."

"It's all very well to laugh, Johnny. Christmas gambols mean fun to you young fellows with your supple limbs; but to us fifty-year-old people they may be something else. I wish I had tied some list round my boots."

We left the ice in the Ravine, and she came up the zigzag path easily to the smooth road. I offered to take the umbrella.

"Thank you, Johnny; but I'd rather carry it myself. It's my best silk one, and you might break it. I never dare trust my umbrellas to Tom: he drives them straight out against trees and posts, and snaps the sticks."

She turned into Timberdale Court, and asked to see Mrs. Broom. Mrs. Broom appeared in the parlour with her sleeves turned up to the elbow, and her hands floury. She had been housekeeper during old Mr. Ashton's time.

"Look here," said Mrs. Coney, dropping her voice a little: "I've come to ask a word or two about that woman—from the shed, you know. Who is she?—and what is she?"

But the dropping of Mrs. Coney's voice was as nothing to the dropping of the housekeeper's face. The questions put her out uncommonly.

"I wish to my very heart, ma'am, that the woman—she's but a poor young thing at best!—had chosen any part to fall ill in but this! It's like a Fate."

"Like a what?" cried Mrs. Coney.

"And so it is. A Fate for this house. 'Tis nothing less."

"Why, what do you mean, Broom?"

Mother Broom bent her head forward, and said a word or two in Mrs. Coney's ear. Louder, I suppose, than she thought for, if she had intended me not to hear.

"Raves about Captain Bird!" repeated Mrs. Coney.

"He is all her talk, ma'am—George Bird. And considering that George Bird, blackleg though he has turned out to be, married the young lady of this house, Miss Lucy Ashton, why, it goes against the grain for me to hear it."

Mrs. Coney sat down in a sort of bewilderment, and gave me the silk umbrella. Folding her hands, she stared at Mother Broom.

"It seems as though we were always hearing fresh news about that man, Broom; each time it is something worse than the last. If he took all the young women within his reach, and—and—cut their heads off, it would be only like him."

"'George!' she moans out in her sleep. That is, in her dreaming, or her fever, or whatever it is. 'George, you ought not to have left me; you should have taken care of me.' And then, ma'am, she'll be quiet a bit, save for turning her head about; and begin again, 'Where's my baby? where's my baby?' Goodness knows 'twould be sad enough to hear her if it was anybody's name but Bird's."

"There might be worse names than his, in the matter of giving us pain," spoke Mrs. Coney. "As to poor Lucy—it is only another cross in her sad life."

"I've not told this to anybody," went on Mother Broom. "Jael Batty's three parts deaf, as the parish knows, and may not have caught Bird's name. It will vex my master frightfully for Miss Lucy's sake. The baby is to be buried to-day. Mr. Charles has stayed to do it."

"Oh, indeed!" snapped Mrs. Coney, and got up, for the baby appeared to be a sore subject with her. "I suppose the girl was coming across the country in search of Bird?"

Broom tossed her head. "Whether she was or not, it's an odd thing that this house should be the one to have to succour her."

"I am going," said Mrs. Coney, "and I half wish I had never come in. Broom, I am sorry to have hindered you. You are busy."

"I am making my raised pies," said Broom. "It's the second batch. What with master's coming marriage, and one thing and another, I did not get 'em done before the new year. Your Molly says hers beat mine, Master Ludlow; but I don't believe it."

"She does, does she! It's just like her boasting. Mrs. Todhetley often makes the pork-pies herself."

"Johnny," said Mrs. Coney, as we went along, she in deep thought: "that poor Lucy Bird might keep a stick for cutting notches—as it is said some prisoners used to do, to mark their days—and notch off her dreadful cares, that are ever recurring. Why, Johnny, what's that crowd for?"

The church stood on the right between Timberdale Court and the village. A regular mob of children seemed to be pressing round the gate of the churchyard. I went to look, leaving Mrs. Coney standing.

Charles Ashton was coming out of the church in his surplice, and the clerk, old Sam Mullet, behind him, carrying a little coffin. The grave was in the corner of the burial-ground, and Mr. Ashton went straight to it, and continued the service begun in the church. If it had been a lord's child, he could not have done it all in better order.

But there were no mourners, unless old Mullet could be called one. He put the coffin on the grass, and was in a frightful temper. I took off my hat and waited: it would have looked so to run away when there was no one else to stand there: and Mrs. Coney's face, as cross as old Mullet's, might be seen peering through the hedge.

"It's come to a pretty pass, when tramps' brats have to be put in the ground like honest folks's," grunted Sam, when Mr. Ashton had walked away, and he began to fling in the spadefuls of earth. "What must he needs go and baptize that there young atom for?—he ain't our parson; he don't belong to we in this parish. I dun-no what the world be a-coming to."

Mr. Ashton was talking to Mrs. Coney when I got up. I told him what a way Sam Mullet was in.

"Yes," said he. "I believe what I did has not given satisfaction in all quarters; so I waited to take the service myself, and save other people trouble."

"In what name is the dead child registered, Charles?" asked Mrs. Coney.

"Lucy Bird."

"Lucy Bird! Bird?"

"It was the name the mother gave me in one of her lucid intervals," answered the clergyman, shortly.

He hastened away, saying he must catch a train, for that his own parish was wanting him; but I fancied he did not care to be further questioned. Mrs. Coney stood still to stare after him, and would have liked to ask him how much and how little he knew.

Lucy Bird! It did sound strange to hear the name—as if it were the real Lucy Bird we knew so well. I said so to Mrs. Coney.

"The impudence of the woman must pass all belief," she muttered to herself. "Let us get on, Johnny? I would rather run a mile any other way than go to see her."

Leaving me on the wooden bench outside Jael Batty's door, she went in. It was remarkably lively: the farrier's shop opposite to look at, five hay-ricks, and a heap of children who strolled after us from the churchyard, and stayed to stare at me. Mrs. Coney came out again soon.

"It's of no use my remaining, Johnny. She can't understand a word said to her, only lies there rambling, and asking people to bring her baby. If she had any sense left in her, she might just go down on her knees in thankfulness that it's gone. Jael Batty says she has done nothing else but wail for it all the blessed morning."

"Well, it is only natural she should."

"Natural! Natural to mourn for that baby! Don't you say stupid things, Johnny. It's a great mercy that it has been taken; and you must know that as well as any one."

"I don't say it isn't; babies must make no end of noise and work; but you see mothers care for them."

"Don't be a simpleton, Johnny. If you take to upholding tramps and infants dying in sheds, goodness knows what you'll come to in time."

At the end of a fortnight, Ashton of Timberdale and his wife came home. It was a fine afternoon in the middle of January, but getting dusk, and a lot of us had gone over to the Court to see them arrive. Jane looked as happy as a queen.

"Johnny," she whispered, whilst we were standing to take some tea that Mother Broom (with a white cockade in her cap) brought in upon a silver tray, "how about that poor woman? She is not dead, I hope?"

I told Jane that she was better. The fever had gone down, but she was so weak and reduced that the doctor had not allowed her to be questioned. We knew no more of who she was than we had known before. Mrs. Coney overheard what I was saying, and took Jane aside.

There seemed to be a bit of a battle: Mrs. Coney remonstrating with a severe face, Jane holding out and flushing a little. She was telling Jane not to go to Jael Batty's, and representing why she ought not to go. Jane said she must go—her heart was set upon it: and began to re-tie her bonnet-strings.

"Mother dear, don't be angry with me in this the first hour of entering on my new home—it would seem like a bad omen for me. You don't know how strongly I have grown to think that my duty lies in seeing this poor woman, in comforting her if I can. It cannot hurt me."

"What do you suppose Robert would say? It is to him you owe obedience now, Jane, not to me."

"To him first, and to you next, my mother; and I trust I shall ever yield it to you both. But Robert is quite willing that I should go: he knows all I think about it."

"Jane, I wouldn't have said a word against it; indeed I had made up my mind that it was a good wish on your part; but now that we have discovered she is in some way connected with—with the Birds—why, I don't think Robert will like you to meddle with it. I'm sure I shrink from telling him."

Jane Coney—Ashton I mean: one can't get out of old names all at once—looked down in distress, thinking of the pain it would cause her husband for his sister's sake. Then she took her mother's hand.

"Tell Robert what you have told me, mamma. He will still let me go, I think; for he knows how much I wish it."

They had their conference away from us; Mrs. Coney, Robert Ashton, and Jane. Of course he was frightfully put out; but Jane was right—he said she should go all the same. Mrs. Coney shut her lips tight, and made no further comment.

"I promised her, you see, Mrs. Coney," he urged. "She has an idea in her head that—I'm sure I scarcely know what it is, except that her going is connected with Gratitude and Duty, and—and Heaven's blessing. Why, do you know we might have stayed away another week, but for this? I could have spared it; but she would come home."

"I never knew Jane take a thing up like this before," said Mrs. Coney.

"Any way, I suppose it is I who shall have to deal with it—for the sake of keeping it from Lucy," was Robert's answer. "I wish with all my heart Bird had been at the bottom of the sea before his ill-omened steps brought him to Timberdale! There's not, as I believe, another such scamp in the world."

Jane waited for nothing else. Shielded by the dusk of the evening, she went hastening to Jael Batty's and back again.

"I'll go down for her presently," said Robert. But she was back again before he started.

"I came back at once to set the misapprehension right," said Jane, her eyes bright with eagerness, her cheeks glowing. "Mother dear—Robert—Johnny—listen, all of you: that poor sick woman is George Bird's sister."

"Jane!"

"Indeed she is. Captain Bird used to talk to Lucy of his little sister Clara—I have heard you say so, Robert—in the old days when he first came here. It is she who is lying at Jael Batty's—Clara Bird."

The company sat down like so many lambs, Mrs. Coney's mouth and eyes alike opening. It sounded wonderful.

"But—Jane, child—there was still the baby!"

"Well—yes—I'm afraid so," replied Jane, in an uncomfortable hurry. "I did not like to ask her about that, she cries so. But she is Clara Bird; Captain Bird's sister, and Lucy's too."

"Well, I never!" cried Mrs. Coney, rubbing her face. "Poor misguided young thing—left to the guardianship of such a man as that, he let her go her own way, no doubt. This accounts for what Broom heard her say in the fever—'George, you should have taken care of me.'"

"Is she being taken care of now in her sickness, down at Jael Batty's?" spoke up Robert.

"Yes. For Jael, though three-parts deaf, is a kind and excellent nurse."

Robert Ashton wrote that night to Worcester; a sharp letter; bidding Captain Bird come over and see to his sister. The poor thing took to Jane wonderfully, and told her more than she'd have told any one else.

"I am twenty," she said, "and George is six-and-thirty; there is all that difference between us. Our father and mother were dead, and I lived with my aunt in Gloucestershire: where George lived, I did not know. He had been adopted by a wealthy relative in London, and went into the army. My mother had been a lady, but married beneath her, and it was her family who took to George and brought him up a gentleman. Mine was a hard, dull life. My aunt—she was my father's sister—counted ever-so-many children, and I had to nurse and see to them. Her husband was a master plumber and glazier. One day— it is fifteen months ago now—I shall never forget it—my brother George arrived. I did not know him: I had not seen him since I was thirteen, and then he was a fine handsome gentleman in an officer's regimentals. He was rather shabby now, and he had come to see if he could borrow money, but my aunt's husband would not lend him any; he told him he had much ado to keep his own family. I cried a good deal, and George said he would take me to London to his wife. I think he did it to spite them, because of their not lending the money, as much as to please me—he saw that I should be a loss there. We went up—and oh how nice I thought his wife! She was a kind, gentle lady, formerly Miss Lucy Ashton; but nearly always ailing, and afraid of George. George had gay acquaintances, men and women, and he let me go to theatres and balls with them. Lucy said it was wrong, that they were not nice friends for me; but I grew to like the gaiety, and she could do nothing. One night, upon going home from church, I found both George and Lucy gone from the lodgings. I had been spending the Sunday with some people they knew, the quietest of all their friends. There lay a note on the table from Lucy, saying they were obliged to leave London unexpectedly, and begging me to go at once—on the morrow—back to Gloucestershire, for which she enclosed a sovereign. I did not go: one invited me, and another invited me, and it was two months, good, before I went down. Ah me! I heard no more of George; he had got into some trouble in London, and was afraid to let it be known where he was. I have never heard of him or his wife to this hour. My aunt was glad to see me for the help I should be to her; but I felt ill always and could not do so much as I used. I didn't know what ailed me; I didn't indeed; I did not think it could be much; and then, when the time went on and it all happened, and they knew, and I knew, I came away with the baby because of the reproach and the shame. But George ought not to have left me to myself in London."

And when Jane Ashton repeated all this to Robert, he said Bird deserved to be hanged and quartered.

There came no answer from Captain Bird. Perhaps Ashton of Timberdale did not really expect any would come.

But on the Sunday afternoon, from the train that passed Timberdale from Worcester about the time folks came out of church, there descended a poor, weak woman (looking like a girl too) in a worn shawl that was too thin for the weather. She waited until the roads should be clear, as if not wanting to be seen, and then wrapped the shawl close around her arms and went out with her black veil down. It was Lucy Bird. And she was so pretty still, in spite of the wan thin cheeks and the faded clothes! There were two ways of getting to Jael Batty's from the station. She took the long and obscure one, and in turning the corner of the lane between the church and Timberdale Court, she met Robert Ashton.

But for her own movement, he might never have noticed her. It was growing dusk; and when she saw him coming, she turned sharp off to a stile and stood as if looking for something in the field. There's not much to stare at in a ploughed field at dusk, as Ashton of Timberdale knew, and he naturally looked at the person who had gone so fast to do it. Something in the cut of the shoulders struck him as being familiar, and he stopped.

"Lucy! Is it you?"

Of course it was no use her saying it was not. She burst into tears, trembling and shaking. Robert passed round her his good strong arm. He guessed what had brought her to Timberdale.

"Lucy, my dear, have you come over from Worcester?"

"Yes," she sobbed. "I shall be better in a minute, Robert. I am a little tired, and the train shook me."

"You should have sent me word, and I would have had a fly at the station."

Sent him word! It was good of Robert to pretend to say that; but he knew that she wouldn't have presumed to do it. It was that feeling on Lucy's part that vexed him so much. Since Bird had turned out the villain that he had, Lucy acted, even to her own family, as though she had lost caste, identifying herself with her husband, and humbling herself to them. What though she was part and parcel with the fellow, as Robert said, she was not responsible for his ill-doings.

"Lean on me, Lucy. You must have a good rest."

"Not that way," she said at the bottom of the lane, as he was turning to the Court. "I am going to Jael Batty's."

"When you have had some rest and refreshment at home."

"I cannot go to your home, Robert."

"Indeed but you can; and will," he answered, leading her on.

"I would rather not. Your wife may not care to receive me."

"Come and try her."

"Robert, I am not fit to see any one: I am not indeed. My spirits are low now, and I often burst into tears for nothing. I have been praying, all the way over, not to meet you. After what was done to you at our house but a week or two ago, I did not expect ever to have been noticed by you again. Jane must hate me."

"Does she! Jane and I have been concocting a charming little plot about you, Lucy. We are going to have your old room made ready, and the sweet-scented lavender sheets put on the bed, and get you over to us. For good, if you will stop; long enough to recruit your health if you will not. Don't you remember how you used to talk in the holidays about the home sheets; saying you only got them smelling of soap at school?"

A faint smile, like a shade, flitted over Lucy Bird's face at the reminiscence.

"I should not know the feel of fine white linen sheets now: coarse calico ones have had to content me this many a day. Let me turn, Robert! For my own sake, I would rather not meet your wife. You cannot know how I feel about seeing old friends; those who—who—"

Those who once knew me, she meant to say; but broke down with a sob. Robert kept walking on. Lucy was a great deal younger than he, and had been used to yield to him from the time she was a child. Well for her would it have been, that she had yielded to his opinion when Captain Bird came a-courting to Timberdale.

"You have company at your house, perhaps, Robert?"

"There's not a soul but Jane and me. The Coneys asked us to dine there to-day, but we thought we'd have the first Sunday to ourselves. We went to church this morning; and I came out after dinner to ask after old Arkwright: they fear he is dying."

She made no further opposition, and Robert took her into the Court, to the warm dining-room. Jane was not there. Robert put her into the arm-chair that used to be their father's, and brought her a glass of wine.

"No, thank you," she faintly said.

"You must take it, Lucy."

"I am afraid. My head is weak."

"A sign you want something good to strengthen it," he urged; and she drank the wine.

"And now take off your bonnet, Lucy, and make yourself at home, whilst I go to seek Jane," said he.

"Lucy is here," he whispered, when he had found his wife. "The merest shadow you ever saw. A wan, faded thing that one's heart bleeds to look upon. We must try and keep her for a bit, Jane."

"Oh, Robert, if we can! And nurse her into health."

"And deliver her from that brute she calls husband—as I should prefer to put it, Jane. Her life with him must be something woeful."

When they got in, she was leaning forward in the chair, crying silently. In the clear old room, with all its familiar features about her, memory could only have its most painful sway. Her grand old father with his grand old white hair used to sit where she was sitting; her brothers had each his appointed place; and she was a lovely bright child amongst them, petted by all; the sentimental girl with her head as brimful of romance as ever the other Lucy Ashton's had been, when she went out to her trysts with the Master of Ravenswood. Which had been the more bitter fate in after-life—that Lucy's or this one's?

Mrs. Ashton went quietly up, put her arms round Lucy, and kissed her many times. She untied the bonnet, which Lucy had not done, and gave it with the shawl to Robert, standing behind. The bright hair fell down in a shower—the bonnet had caught it—and she put her feeble hand up as if to feel the extent of the disaster. It made her look so like the sweet young sister they had all prized, that Robert turned to the window and gave a few stamps, as if his boots were cold.

How she cried!—tears that came from the very heart. Putting her face down on the arm of the chair, she let her grief have its way. Jane held her hand and stroked it lovingly. Robert felt inclined to dash his arms through the dark window-panes on which the fire-light played, in imaginary chastisement of the scamp, Bird.

"Could you lend me a shawl of your own, Jane?" she asked, by-and-by, when Robert said they would have tea in—and she glanced down at her shabby brown gown. "I don't wish the servants to see me like this."

Jane flew out and brought one. A handsome cashmere of scarlet and gold-colour, that her mother had given her before the wedding.

"Just for an hour or two, until I leave," said Lucy, as she covered herself up in it.

"You will not go out of this house to-night, Lucy."

"I must, Robert. You can guess who it was I came to Timberdale to see."

"Of course I can. She is going on all right and getting stronger; so there's no immediate haste about that. Mr. Bird would not—not come, I suppose."

Lucy did not answer. Robert was right—Bird would not come: his young sister might die where she was or be sheltered in the workhouse, for all the concern he gave himself. For one thing, the man was at his wits' end for money, and not too sure of his own liberty. But Lucy's conscience had not let her be still: as soon as she had scraped together the means for a third-class ticket, she came over.

"The poor girl has lain like a weight upon my mind, since the time when we abandoned her in London," confessed Lucy.

"Why did you abandon her?"

"It was not my fault," murmured Lucy; and Robert felt vexed to have asked the hasty question. "I hoped she went home, as I desired her; but I did not feel sure of it, for Clara was thoughtless. And those unsuspicious country girls cannot take care of themselves too well. Robert, whatever has happened I regard as our fault," she added, looking up at him with some fever in her eyes.

"As Mr. Bird's fault; not yours," corrected Robert—who, strange perhaps to say, observed courtesy of speech towards Bird when talking with Lucy: giving him in general a handle to his name. It might have sounded ironical, but that he couldn't help. "Did you never write to ascertain what had become of her, Lucy?"

"My husband would not let me. He is often in difficulties: and we never have a settled home, or address. What will be done with her, Robert?"

"She will stay where she is until she is strong; Jane wishes it; and then we shall see about the future. Something will turn up for her in some place or other, I've little doubt."

Jane glanced at her husband and smiled. Robert had given her a promise to help the girl to an honest living. But, as he frankly told his wife, had he known it was a sister of Bird's, he might never have done so.

"About yourself, Lucy; that may be the better theme to talk of just now," he resumed. "Will you remain here for good in your old home?"

The hot tears rushed to her eyes, the hot flush to her cheeks. She looked deprecatingly at both, as if craving pardon.

"I cannot. You know I cannot."

"Shall I tell you what Bird is, Lucy? And what he most likely will be?"

"To what end, Robert?" she faintly asked. "I know it without."

"Then you ought to leave him—for your own sake. Leave him before you are compelled to do so."

"Not before, Robert."

"But why?"

"Oh, Robert, don't you see?" she answered, breaking down. "He is my husband."

And nothing else could they get from her. Though she cried and sobbed, and did not deny that her life was a fear and a misery, yet she would go back to him; go back on the morrow; it was her duty. In the moment's anger Robert Ashton said he would wash his hands of her as well as of Bird. But Jane and Lucy knew better.

"What can have induced you and Robert to take up this poor Clara in the way you are doing—and mean to do?" she asked when she was alone with Jane at the close of the evening.

"I—owe a debt of gratitude; and I thought I could best pay it in this way," was Mrs. Ashton's timid and rather unwilling answer.

"A debt of gratitude! To Clara?"

"No. To Heaven."

CHAPTER VII

CHARLES VAN RHEYN

I shall always say it was a singular thing that I should chance to go back to school that time the day before the quarter opened. Singular, because I heard and saw more of the boy I am going to tell of than I otherwise might have heard and seen. I was present at his arrival; and I was present at his—well, let us say, at his departure.

The midsummer holidays were nearly up when Hugh was taken ill. Duffham was uncertain what the illness was going to be: so he pitched upon scarlatina. Upon that, the Squire and Mrs. Todhetley packed me back to school there and then. Not from any fear of my taking it; I had had it, and Tod too (and both of us were well again, I recollect, within a week or so); but if once the disease had really shown itself, Dr. Frost would not have liked us to return lest we might convey it to the school. Tod was in Gloucestershire. He was written to, and told not to return home, but to go straight to school.

Dr. Frost was surprised to see me. He said my coming back was quite right; and I am sure he tried to put me at ease and make me comfortable. Not a single boy had stayed the holidays that summer, and the doctor and I were alone. The school would open the following day, when masters and boys were alike expected to return. I had dinner with the doctor—he usually dined late during the holidays—and we played at chess afterwards.

Breakfast was just over the next morning when the letters came in. Amongst them was one from France, bearing the Rouen post-mark. Now the doctor, learned man though he was in classics and what not, could make nothing of French. Carrying the letter to the window, turning its pages over and back again, and staring at it through his spectacles, he at last brought it to me.

"You are a pretty good French scholar, Johnny; can you read this? I can't, I confess. But the paper's so thin, and the ink so pale, and the writing so small, I could scarcely see it if it were English."

And I had to go over it twice before I could make it out. As he said, the ink was pale, and it was a frightfully small and cramped handwriting. The letter was dated Rouen, and was signed curtly, "Van Rheyn," French fashion, without the writer's Christian name. Monsieur Van Rheyn wrote to say that he was about to consign his son, Charles Aberleigh Van Rheyn, to Dr. Frost's care, and that he would arrive quickly after the letter, having already departed on his journey under the charge of a "gentilhomme Anglais." It added that the son would bring credentials with him; that he spoke English, and was of partly English descent, through his mother, the late Madame Van Rheyn, née Aberleigh.

"Rather a summary way of consigning a pupil to my charge," remarked Dr. Frost. "Aberleigh?— Aberleigh?" he continued, as if trying to recollect something, and bending his spectacles over the letter. "She must have been one of the Aberleighs of Upton, I should think. Perhaps Hall knows? I have heard her mention the Aberleighs."

Ringing the bell, the housekeeper was sent for. Dr. Frost asked her what she knew of the Aberleighs of Upton.

"There's none of them left now to know, sir," answered Hall. "There never was but two—after the old mother died: Miss Aberleigh and Miss Emma Aberleigh. Good fortunes the young ladies had, sir, and both of them, I remember, married on the same day. Miss Aberleigh to Captain Scott, and Miss Emma to a French gentleman, Mosseer Van Rheyn."

"I should think, by the name, he was Dutch—or Flemish; not French," remarked the doctor.

"Anyway, sir, he was said to be French," returned Hall. "A dark sallow gentleman who wore a braided coat. The young ladies never came back to their home after the wedding-day, and the place was sold. Captain Scott sailed with his wife for Injee, and Mosseer Van Rheyn took Miss Emma off to his house in France."

"Do you recollect where his home was? In what part of France?"

"No, sir. And if I did, I should never be able to speak the name. Not long ago I heard it said that poor Miss Emma was dead—Mrs. Van Rheyn that is. A nice quiet girl, she was."

"Then I conclude the new pupil spoken of to me, must be the son of Monsieur Van Rheyn and Miss Emma Aberleigh," remarked the doctor, when Hall was dismissed. "You must help to make things pleasant for him, Johnny: it will be a change at first from his own home and country. Do you remember that other French boy we had here?"

I did. And the remembrance made me laugh. He used to lament every day that he had not a plate of soup for dinner, and to say the meat was tough.

Strolling out at the front iron gates in the course of the morning, wondering how long the boys were going to be before some of them put in an appearance, I caught sight of the first. He was walking up from the Plough and Harrow Inn, and must have come by the omnibus that plied backwards and forwards between the inn and the station. The Plough and Harrow man-of-all-work followed behind, carrying a large trunk.

Of all queer figures that boy looked the queerest. I wondered who he was, and whether he could really be coming as a pupil. His trousers and vest were nankeen, his coat was a sort of open blouse, and flew out behind him; the hat he wore was a tall chimney-pot with a wide brim. Off went the hat with a bow and a flourish of the arm, as he reached me and the gates.

"I ask your pardon, sir. This is, I believe, the pension of Dr. Frost?"

The French accent, though that was slight, the French manners, the French turn of the words, told me who it was. For a minute or two I really could not answer for staring at him. He seemed to have arrived with a shaved head, as if just out of gaol, or of brain-fever.

The hair was cut as closely as it could be cut, short of shaving: his face was red and round and covered with freckles: you could not have put a pin's point between them. Really and truly it was the most remarkable figure ever seen out of a picture. I could not guess his age exactly: something perhaps between twelve and fourteen. He was slender and upright, and to all appearance strong.

"I think you must be Charles Van Rheyn," I said then, holding out my hand to welcome him. "Dr. Frost is expecting you."

He put his hand into mine after a moment's hesitation, not seeming quite to understand that he might: but such a brightness came into his rather large and honest grey eyes, that I liked him from that hour, in spite of the clothes and the freckles and the shorn head. He had crossed to Folkestone by the night boat, he said, had come on to London, and the gentleman, who was his escort so far, had there put him into an early train to come on to his destination.

Dr. Frost was at the window, and came to the door. Van Rheyn stood still when within a yard of him, took his hat off with the most respectful air, and bowed his head half-way to the ground. He had evidently been brought up with a reverence for pastors and masters. The doctor shook hands. The first thing Van Rheyn did on entering the reception-parlour, was to produce from some inner pocket a large, square letter, sealed with two flaming red seals and a coat of arms; which he handed to the doctor. It contained a draft for a good sum of money in advance of the first three months' payment, and some pages of closely-written matter in the crabbed hand of Monsieur Van Rheyn. Dr. Frost put the pages aside to await the arrival of the French master.

"My father was unable to remit the exact amount of money for the trimestre, sir, not knowing what it would be," said young Van Rheyn. "And there will be the extra expenses besides. He will arrange that with you later."

"The end of the term would have been time enough to remit this," said the doctor, smiling. "It is not our custom to receive payment in advance."

"It is the custom in France, sir, I assure you. And, besides, I am to you a stranger."

"Not altogether a stranger; I believe I know something of your mother's family," said Dr. Frost. "How came your father to fix upon my school for you?"

"My mother knew of your school, sir: she and my father used to talk of placing me at it. And an English gentleman who came lately to Rouen spoke of it—he said he knew you very well. That again put into my father's head to send me."

It was the same Van Rheyn that they had thought—the son of Miss Emma Aberleigh. She had been dead two years.

"Are you a Protestant or a Roman Catholic?" questioned Dr. Frost.

"I am Protestant, sir: the same that my mother was. We attended the église of Monsieur le Pasteur Mons, of the Culte Evangélique."

The doctor asked him if he would take anything before dinner, and he chose a glass of eau sucrée. The mal-de-mer had been rather bad, he said, and he had not been able to eat since.

Evidently Hall did not approve of eau sucrée. She had never made eau sucary, she said, when sent to for it. Bringing in the water and sugar, she stood by to watch Van Rheyn mix it, her face sour, her lips drawn in. I am sure it gave her pleasure, when he asked for a few drops of orange-flower water, to be able to say there was not such a thing in the house.

"This young gentleman is the son of the Miss Emma Aberleigh you once knew, Hall," spoke the doctor, with a view no doubt to putting her on good terms with the new pupil.

"Yes, sir," she answered crustily. "He favours his mamma about the eyes."

"She must have had very nice eyes," I put in.

"And so she had," said Van Rheyn, looking at me gratefully. "Thank you for saying so. I wish you could have known her!"

"And might I ask, sir, what has become of the other Miss Aberleigh?" asked Hall of Van Rheyn. "The young lady who went off to Injee with her husband on the wedding-day."

"You would say my Aunt Margaret," he rejoined. "She is quite well. She and the major and the children will make the voyage to Europe next year."

After the eau sucrée came to an end, the doctor turned him over to me, telling me to take care of him till dinner-time, which that day would be early. Van Rheyn said he should like to unpack his box, and we went upstairs together. Growing confidential over the unpacking, he gave me scraps of information touching his home and family, the mention of one item leading to another.

His baptismal name in full, he said, was Charles Jean Aberleigh; his father's was Jean Marie. Their home was a très joli château close to Rouen: in five minutes you could walk there. It was all much changed since his mother died (he seemed to have loved her with a fervent love and to revere her memory); the last thing he did on coming away for England was to take some flowers to her grave. It was thought in Rouen that his father was going to make a second marriage with one of the Demoiselles de Tocqueville, whom his Aunt Claribelle did not like. His Aunt Claribelle, his father's sister, had come to live at the château when his mother died; but if that Thérèsine de Tocqueville came into the house she would quit it. The Demoiselles de Tocqueville had hardly any dot,—which would be much against the marriage, Aunt Claribelle thought, and bad for his father; because when he, Charles, should be the age of twenty-one, the money came to him; it had been his mother's, and was so settled: and his father's own property was but small. Of course he should wish his father to keep always as much as he pleased, but Aunt Claribelle thought the English trustees would not allow that. Aunt Claribelle's opinion was, that his father had at length decided to send him to a pension in England while he made the marriage; but he (Charles) knew that his mother had wished him to finish his education in England, and to go to one of the two colleges to which English gentlemen went.

"Here comes old Fontaine," I interrupted at this juncture, seeing his arrival from the window.

Van Rheyn looked up from his shirts, which he was counting. He seemed to have the tidiest ways in the world. "Who is it that you say? Fontaine?"

"Monsieur Fontaine, the French master. You can talk away with him in your native tongue as much as you like, Van Rheyn."

"But I have come here to speak the English tongue, not the French," debated he, looking at me seriously. "My father wishes me to speak and read it without any accent; and I wish it also."

"You speak it very well already."

"But you can hear that it is not my native tongue—that I am a foreigner."

"Yes."

"Well, I must learn to speak it without that—as the English do. It will be necessary."

I supposed he might allude to his future life. "What are you to be, Van Rheyn?" I inquired.

"What profession, do you ask? I need not be any: I have enough fortune to be a rentier—I don't know what you call that in English; it means a gentleman who lives on his money. But I wish, myself, to be an English priest."

"An English priest! Do you mean a parson?"

"Yes, I mean that. So you see I must learn the English tongue. My mother used to talk to me about the priests in her land—"

"Parsons, Van Rheyn."

"I beg your pardon: I forget. And I fear I have caught up the French names for things since my mother died. It was neither priest nor parson she used to call the English ministers."

"Clergymen, perhaps."

"That was it. She said the clergymen were good men, and she should like me to be one. In winter, when it was cold, and she had some fire in her chamber, I used to sit up there with her, after coming home from classe, and we talked together, our two selves. I should have much money, she said, when I grew to be a man, and could lead an idle life. But she would not like that: she wanted me to be a good man, and to go to heaven when I died, where she would be; and she thought if I were a clergyman I should have serious thoughts always. So I wish to be a clergyman."

He said all this with the utmost simplicity and composure, just as he might have spoken of going for a ride. There could be no mistaking that he was of a thoroughly straightforward and simple-minded nature.

"It might involve your living over here, Van Rheyn: once you were in Orders."

"Yes, I know. Papa would not mind. England was mamma's country, and she loved it. There was more peace in England than in France, she thought."

"I say, she must have been a good mother, Van Rheyn."

In a moment his grey eyes were shining at me through a mist of tears. "Oh, she was so good, so good! You can never know. If she had lived I should never have had sorrow."

"What did she die of?"

"Ah, I cannot tell. She was well in the morning, and she was dead at night. Not that she was strong ever. It was one Dimanche. We had been to the office, she and I—"

"What office?"

"Oh, pardon—I forget I am speaking English. I mean to church. Monsieur Mons had preached; and we were walking along the street towards home afterwards, mamma talking to me about the sermon, which had been a very holy one, when we met the Aunt Claribelle, who had come into the town for high mass at St. Ouen. Mamma asked her to come home and dine with us; and she said yes, but she must first go to say bon-jour to old Madame Soubitez. As she parted from us, there was suddenly a great outcry. It was fête at Rouen that Sunday. Some bands of music were to play on the estrade in the public garden, competing for a prize, consequently the streets were crowded. We looked back at the noise, and saw many horses, without riders, galloping along towards us; men were running after them, shouting and calling; and the people, mad with fright, tumbled over one another in the effort to get away. Later, we heard that these horses, frightened by something, had broken out of an hotel post-yard. Well, mamma gave just a cry of fear and held my hand tighter, as we set off to run with the rest, the horses stamping wildly after us. But the people pushed between us, and I lost her. She was at home before me, and was sitting at the side of the fountain, inside the château entrance-gate, when I got up, her face all white and blue, and her neck and throat beating, as she clung to the nearest lion with both hands. It alarmed me more than the horses had, for I had never seen her look so. 'Come in, mamma,' I said, 'and take a little glass of cordial;' but she could not answer me, she did not stir. I called one of the servants, and by-and-by she got a little breath again, and went into the house, leaning upon both of us, and so up to her chamber. Quite immediately papa came home: he always went into town to his club on the Sunday mornings, and he ran for Monsieur Petit, the médecin—the doctor. By seven o'clock in the evening, mamma was dead."

"Oh dear! What was the cause?"

"Papa did not tell me. He and Monsieur Petit talked about the heart: they said it was feeble. Oh, how we cried, papa and I! He cried for many days. I hope he will not bring home Thérèsine de Tocqueville!"

The dinner-bell rang out, and we went down. Dr. Frost was putting up the letter which old Fontaine had been translating to him. It was full of directions about Van Rheyn's health. What he was to do, and what not to do. Monsieur Van Rheyn said his son was not strong: he was not to be allowed to do gymnastics or "boxing," or to play at rough games, or take violent exercise of any kind; and a small glass of milk was to be given him at night when he went to bed. If the clothes sent over with him were not suitable to the school, or in accordance with the English mode, Dr. Frost was prayed to be at the trouble of procuring him new ones. He was to be brought well on in all the studies necessary to constitute the "gentilhomme," and especially in the speaking and reading of English.

Dr. Frost directed his spectacles to Charles Van Rheyn, examining him from top to toe. The round, red face, and the strongly-built frame appeared to give nothing but indications of robust health. The doctor questioned him in what way he was not strong—whether he was subject to a cough, or to want of appetite, and other such items. But Van Rheyn seemed to know nothing about it, and said he had always been quite well.

"The father fears we should make him into a muscular Englishman, hence these restrictions," thought Dr. Frost.

In the afternoon the fellows began to come in thick and threefold: Tod amongst them, who arrived about tea-time. To describe their amazement when they saw Van Rheyn is quite beyond me. It seemed that they never meant to leave off staring. Some of them gave him a little chaff, even that first night. Van Rheyn was very shy and silent. Entirely at his ease as he had been with me alone, the numbers seemed to daunt him; to strike him and his courage into himself.

On the whole, Van Rheyn was not liked. Once let a school set itself against a new fellow at first—and Van Rheyn's queer appearance had done that much for him—it takes a long time to bring matters round—if they ever are brought round at all. When his hair began to sprout, it looked exactly like pig's bristles. And that was the first nickname he got: Bristles. The doctor had soon changed his style of coat, and he wore jackets, as we did.

Charles Van Rheyn did not seem inclined to grow sociable. Shy and silent as he had shown himself to them that first evening, so he remained. True, he had no encouragement to be otherwise. The boys continually threw ridicule on him, making him into an almost perpetual butt. Any mistake in the pronunciation of an English word—Van Rheyn never made a mistake as to its meaning—they hissed and groaned at. I shall never forget one occasion. Being asked when that Indian lot intended to arrive (meaning the Scotts), and whether they would make the voyage in a palanquin (for the boys plied him with questions purposely) he answered, "Not in a palanquin, but in a sheep"—meaning ship. The uproar at that was so loud, that some of the masters looked in to know what was up.

Van Rheyn, too, was next door to helpless. He did not climb, or leap, or even run. Had not been used to it, he said. What had he been used to do, then, he was asked one day. Oh, he had sat out in the garden with his mother; and since her death, with Aunt Claribelle, and gone for an airing in the carriage three times a week. Was he a girl? roared the boys. Did he do patchwork? Not now; he had left off sewing when he was nine, answered Van Rheyn innocently, unconscious of the storm of mockery the avowal would invoke. "Pray, were you born a young lady?—or did they change you at nurse?" shouted Jessup, who would have kept the ball rolling till midnight. "I say, you fellows, he has come to the wrong school: we don't take in girls, do we? Let me introduce this one to you, boys—'Miss Charlotte.'" And, so poor Charley Van Rheyn got that nickname as well as the other. Miss Charlotte!

Latin was a stumbling-block. Van Rheyn had learnt it according to French rules and French pronunciation, and he could not readily get into our English mode. "It was bad enough to have to teach a stupid boy Latin," grumbled the under Latin master (under Dr. Frost), "but worse to have to un-teach him." Van Rheyn was not stupid, however; if he seemed so, it was because his new life was so strange to him.

One day the boys dared him to a game at leap-frog. Some of them were at it in the yard, and Van Rheyn stood by, looking on.

"Why don't you go in for it?" suddenly asked Parker, giving him a push. "There is to be a round or two at boxing this evening, why don't you go in for that?"

"They never would let me do these rough things," replied Van Rheyn, who invariably answered all the chaffing questions civilly and patiently.

"Who wouldn't? Who's 'they'?"

"My mother and my Aunt Claribelle. Also, when I was starting to come here, my father said I was not to exert myself."

"All right, Miss Charlotte; but why on earth didn't the respectable old gentleman send you over in petticoats? Never was such a thing heard of, you know, as for a girl to wear a coat and pantaloons. It's not decent, Miss Charlotte; it's not modest."

"Why do you say all this to me for ever? I am not a girl," said poor Van Rheyn.

"No? Don't tell fibs. If you were not a girl you'd go in for our games. Come! Try this. Leap-frog's especially edifying, I assure you: expands the mind. Won't you try it?"

Well, the upshot was, that they dared him to try it. A dozen, or so, set on at him like so many wolves. What with that, and what with their stinging ridicule, poor Van Rheyn was goaded out of his obedience to home orders, and did try it. After a few tumbles, he went over very tolerably, and did not dislike it at all.

"If I can only learn to do as the rest of you do, perhaps they will let me alone," he said to me that same night, a sort of eagerness in his bright grey eyes.

And gradually he did learn to go in for most of the games: running, leaping, and climbing. One thing he absolutely refused—wrestling.

"Why should gentlemen, who were to be gentlemen all their lives, fight each other?" he asked. "They would not have to fight as men; it was not kind; it was not pleasant; it was hard."

The boys were hard on him for saying it, mocking him fearfully; but they could not shake him there. He was of right blue blood; never caving-in before them, as Bill Whitney expressed it one day; he was only quiet and endured.

Whether the native Rouen air is favourable to freckles, I don't know; but those on Van Rheyn's face gradually disappeared over here. His complexion lost its redness also, becoming fresh and fair, with a brightish colour on the cheeks. The hair, growing longer, turned out to be of a smooth brown: altogether he was good-looking.

"I say, Johnny, do you know that Van Rheyn's ill?"

The words came from William Whitney. He whispered them in my ear as we stood up for prayers before breakfast. The school had opened about a month then.

"What's the matter with him?"

"Don't know," answered Bill. "He is staying in bed."

Cribbing some minutes from breakfast, I went up to his room. Van Rheyn looked pale as he lay, and said he had been sick. Hall declared it was nothing but a bilious attack, and Van Rheyn thought she might be right.

"Meaning that you have a sick headache, I suppose?" I said to him.

"Yes, the migraine. I have had it before."

"Well, look here, Charley," I went on, after thinking a minute; "if I were you, I wouldn't say as much to any of them. Let them suppose you are regularly ill. You'll never hear the last of it if they know you lie in bed for only a headache."

"But I cannot get up," he answered; "my head is in much pain. And I have fever. Feel my hand."

The hand he put out was burning hot. But that went with sick headaches sometimes.

It turned out to be nothing worse, for he was well on the morrow; and I need not have mentioned it at all, but for a little matter that arose out of the day's illness. Going up again to see him after school in the afternoon, I found Hall standing over the bed with a cup of tea, and a most severe, not to say horror-struck expression of countenance, as she gazed down on him, staring at something with all her eyes. Van Rheyn was asleep, and looked better; his face flushed and moist, his brown hair, still uncommonly short compared with ours, pushed back. He lay with his hands outside the bed, as if the clothes were heavy—the weather was fiery hot. One of the hands was clasping something that hung round his neck by a narrow blue ribbon; it seemed to have been pulled by him out of the opening in his night-shirt. Hall's quick eyes had detected what it was—a very small flat cross (hardly two inches long), on which was carved a figure of the Saviour, all in gold.

Now Hall had doubtless many virtues. One of them was docking us boys of our due allowance of sugar. But she had also many prejudices. And, of all her prejudices, none was stronger than her abhorrence of idols, as exemplified in carved images and Chinese gods.

"Do you see that, Master Ludlow?" she whispered to me, pointing her finger straight at the little cross of gold. "It's no better than a relict of paganism."

Stooping down, she gently drew the cross out of Van Rheyn's hot clasped hand, and let it lie on the sheet. A beautiful little cross; the face of our Saviour—an exquisite face in its expression of suffering and patient humility—one that you might have gazed upon and been the better for. How they could have so perfectly carved a thing so small I knew not.

"He must be one of them worshipping Romanics," said Hall, with horror, snatching her fingers from the cross as if she thought it would give her the ague. "Or else a pagan."

And the two were no doubt alike in Hall's mind.

"And he goes every week and says his commandments in class here, standing up before all the school! I wonder what the doctor—"

Hall cut short her complaints. Van Rheyn had suddenly opened his eyes, and was looking up at us.

"I find myself better," he said, with a smile. "The pain has nearly departed."

"We wasn't thinking of pains and headaches, Master Van Rheyn, but of this," said Hall, resentfully, taking the spoon out of the saucer, and holding it within an inch of the gold cross. Van Rheyn raised his head from the pillow to look.

"Oh, it is my little cross!" he said, holding it out to our view as far as the ribbon allowed, and speaking with perfect ease and unconcern. "Is it not beautiful?"

"Very," I said, stooping over it.

"Be you of the Romanic sex?" demanded Hall of Van Rheyn.

"Am I— What is it Mrs. Hall would ask?" he broke off to question me, in the midst of my burst of laughter.

"She asks if you are a Roman Catholic, Van Rheyn."

"But no. Why you think that?" he added to her. "My father is a Roman Catholic: I am a Protestant, like my mother."

"Then why on earth, sir, do you wear such a idol as that?" returned Hall.

"This? Oh, it is nothing! it is not an idol. It does me good."

"Good!" fiercely repeated Hall. "Does you good to wear a brazen image next the skin!—right under the flannel waistcoat. I wonder what the school will come to next?"

"Why should I not wear it?" said Van Rheyn. "What harm does it do me, this? It was my poor Aunt Annette's. The last time we went to the Aunt Claribelle's to see her, when the hope of her was gone, she put the cross into my hand, and bade me keep it for her sake."

"I tell you, Master Van Rheyn, it's just a brazen image," persisted Hall.

"It is a keepsake," dissented Van Rheyn. "I showed it to Monsieur Mons one day when he was calling on mamma, and told him it was a gift to me of the poor Tante Annette. Monsieur Mons thought it very pretty, and said it would remind me of the great Sacrifice."

"But to wear it next your skin," went on Hall, not giving in. Giving in on the matter of graven images was not in her nature. Or on any matter as far as that went, that concerned us boys. "I've heard of poor misdeluded people putting horse-hair next 'em. And fine torment it must be!"

"I have worn it since mamma died," quietly answered Van Rheyn, who did not seem to understand Hall's zeal. "She kept it for me always in her little shell-box that had the silver crest on it; but when she died, I said I would put the cross round my neck, for fear of losing it: and Aunt Claribelle, who took the shell-box then, bought me the blue ribbon."

"That blue ribbon's new—or almost new—if ever I saw new ribbon," cried Hall, who was in a mood to dispute every word.

"Oh yes. It was new when I left Rouen. I have another piece in my trunk to put on when this shall wear out."

"Well, it's a horrid heathenish thing to do, Master Van Rheyn; and, though it may be gold, I don't believe Miss Emma Aberleigh would ever have gave countenance to it. Leastways before she lived among them foreign French folks," added Hall, virtually dropping the contest, as Van Rheyn slipped the cross out of view within his night-shirt. "What she might have come to, after she went off there, Heaven alone knows. Be you going to drink this tea, sir, or be you not?"

Van Rheyn drank the tea and thanked her for bringing it, his gratitude shining also out of his nice grey eyes. Hall took back the cup and tucked him up again, telling him to get a bit more sleep and he would be all right in the morning. With all her prejudices and sourness, she was as good as gold when any of us were ill.

"Not bathe! Not bathe! I say, you fellows, here's a lark. Bristles thinks he'd better not try the water."

It was a terribly hot evening, close upon sunset. Finding ourselves, some half-dozen of us, near the river, Van Rheyn being one, the water looked too pleasant not to be plunged into. The rule at Dr. Frost's was, that no boy should be compelled to bathe against his inclination: Van Rheyn was the only one who had availed himself of it. It was Parker who spoke: we were all undressing quickly.

"What's your objection, Miss Charlotte? Girls bathe."

"They would never let me go into cold water at home," was the patient answer. "We take warm baths there."

"Afraid of cold water? well I never! What an everlasting pussy-cat you are, Miss Charlotte! We've heard that pussies don't like to wet their feet."

"Our doctor at Rouen used to say I must not plunge into cold water," said poor Van Rheyn, speaking patiently as usual, though he must have been nearly driven wild. "The shock would not be good for me."

"I say, who'll write off to Evesham for a pair of waterproofs to put over his shoes? Just give us the measure of your foot, Miss Charlotte?"

"Let's shut him up in a feather-bed!"

"Why, the water's not cold, you donkey!" cried Bill Whitney, who had just leaped in. "It's as warm as new milk. What on earth will you be fit for, Bristles? You'll never make a man."

"Make a man! What are you thinking of, Whitney? Miss Charlotte has no ambition that way. Girls prefer to grow up into young ladies, not into men."

"Is it truly warm?" asked Van Rheyn, gazing at the river irresolutely, and thinking that if he went in the mockery might cease.

I looked up at him from the water. "It is indeed, Van Rheyn. Quite warm."

He knew he might trust me, and began slowly to undress. We had continued to be the best of comrades, and I never went in for teasing him as the rest did; rather shielded him when I could, and took his part.

By the time he was ready to go in—for he did nothing nimbly, and undressing made no exception—some of us were ready to come out. One of Dr. Frost's rules in regard to bathing was stringent—that no boy should remain in the water more than three minutes at the very extent. He held that a great deal of harm was done by prolonged bathing. Van Rheyn plunged in—and liked it.

"It is warm and pleasant," he exclaimed. "This cannot hurt me."

"Hurt you, you great baby!" shouted Parker.

Van Rheyn had put his clothes in the tidiest manner upon the grass; not like ours, which were flung down any way. His things were laid smoothly one upon another, in the order he took them off, though I dare say I should not have noticed this but for a shout from Jessup.

"Halloa! What's that?"

Those of us who were out, and in the several stages of drying or dressing, turned round at the words. Jessup, buttoning his braces, was standing by Van Rheyn's heap, looking down at it. On the top of the flannel vest, exposed to full view, lay the gold cross with the blue ribbon.

"What on earth is it?" cried Jessup, picking it up; and at the moment Van Rheyn, finding all the rest out of the water, came out himself. "Is it a charm?"

"It is mine—it is my gold cross," spoke Van Rheyn, catching up one of the wet towels. The bath this evening had been impromptu, and we had only two towels between us, which Parker and Whitney had brought. In point of fact, it had been against rules also, for we were not expected to go into the river without the presence of a master. But just at this bend it was perfectly safe. Jessup passed the blue ribbon round his neck, letting the cross hang behind. This done, he turned himself about for general inspection, and the boys crowded round to look.

"What do you say it is, Bristles?"

"My gold cross."

"You don't mean to tell us to our faces that you wear it?"

"I wear it always," freely answered Van Rheyn.

Jessup took it off his neck, and the boys passed it about from one to another. They did not ridicule the cross—I think the emblem on it prevented that—but they ridiculed Van Rheyn.

"A friend of mine went over to the tar-and-feather islands," said Millichip, executing an aggravating war-dance round about Charley. "He found the natives sporting no end of charms and amulets—nearly all the attire they did sport—rings in the nose and chains in the ears. What relation are those natives to you, Miss Charlotte?"

"Don't injure it, please," pleaded Van Rheyn.

"We've an ancient nurse at home who carries the tip of a calf's tongue in her pocket for luck," shrieked Thorne. "And I've heard—I have heard, Bristles—that any fellow who arms himself with a pen'orth of blue-stone from the druggist's, couldn't have the yellow jaundice if he tried. What might you wear this for, pray?"

"My Aunt Annette gave it me as a present when she was dying," answered poor helpless Charley, who had never the smallest notion of taking chaff otherwise than seriously, or of giving chaff back again.

He had dressed himself to his trousers and shirt, and stood with his hand stretched out, waiting for his cross.

"In the Worcester Journal, one day last June, I read an advertisement as big as a house, offering a child's caul for sale," cried Snepp. "Any gentleman or lady buying that caul and taking it to sea, could never be drowned. Bristles thinks as long as he wears this, he won't come to be hanged."

"How's your grandmother, Miss Charlotte?"

"I wish you would please to let me alone," said he patiently. "My father would not have placed me here had he known."

"Why don't you write and tell him, Bristles?"

"I would not like to grieve him," simply answered Charley. "I can bear. And he does so much want me to learn good English."

"This cross is gold, I suppose?" said Bill Whitney, who now had it.

"Yes, it is gold," answered Van Rheyn.

"I wouldn't advise you to fall amongst thieves, then. They might ease you of it. The carving must be worth something."

"It cost a great deal to buy, I have heard my aunt say. Will you be so good as to give it me, that I may finish to dress myself?"

Whitney handed him the cross. Time was up, in fact; and we had to make a race for the house. Van Rheyn was catching it hot and sharp, all the way.

One might have thought that his very meekness, the unresisting spirit in which he took things, would have disarmed the mockery. But it did not. Once go in wholesale for putting upon some particular fellow in a school, and the tyranny gains with use. I don't think any of them meant to be really unkind to Van Rheyn; but the play had begun, and they enjoyed it.

I once saw him drowned in tears. It was at the dusk of evening. Charley had come in for it awfully at tea-time, I forget what about, and afterwards disappeared. An hour later, going into Whitney's room for something Bill asked me to fetch, I came upon Charles Van Rheyn—who also slept there. He was sitting at the foot of his low bed, his cheek leaning on one of his hands, and the tears running down swiftly. One might have thought his heart was broken.

"What is the grievance, Charley?"

"Do not say to them that you saw me," returned he, dashing away his tears. "I did not expect any of you would come up."

"Look here, old fellow: I know it's rather hard lines for you just now. But they don't mean anything: it is done in sport, not malice. They don't think, you see, Van Rheyn. You will be sure to live it down."

"Yes," he sighed, "I hope I shall. But it is so different here from what it used to be. I had such a happy home; I never had one sorrow when my mother was alive. Nobody cares for me now; nobody is kind to me: it is a great change."

"Take heart, Charley," I said, holding out my hand. "I know you will live it down in time."

Of all the fellows I ever met, I think he was the most grateful for a word of kindness. As he thanked me with a glad look of hope in his eyes, I saw that he had been holding the cross clasped in his palm; for it dropped as he put his hand into mine.

"It helps me to bear," he said, in a whisper. "My mother, who loved me so, is in heaven; my father has married Mademoiselle Thérèsine de Tocqueville. I have no one now."

"Your father has not married that Thérèsine de Tocqueville?"

"Why, yes. I had the letter close after dinner."

So perhaps he was crying for the home unhappiness as much as for his school grievances. It all reads strange, no doubt, and just the opposite of what might be expected of one of us English boys. The French bringing-tip is different from ours: perhaps it lay in that. On the other hand, a French boy, generally speaking, possesses a very shallow sense of religion. But Van Rheyn had been reared by his English mother; and his disposition seemed to be naturally serious and uncommonly pliable and gentle. At any rate, whether it reads improbable or probable, it is the truth.

I got what I wanted for Billy Whitney, and went down, thinking what a hard life it was for him—what a shame that we made it so. Indulged, as Van Rheyn must have always been, tenderly treated as a girl, sheltered from the world's roughness, all that coddling must have become to him as second nature; and the remembrance lay with him still. Over here he was suddenly cut off from it, thrown into another and a rougher atmosphere, isolated from country, home, home-ties and associations; and compelled to stand the daily brunt of this petty tyranny.

Getting Tod apart that night, I put the matter to him: what a shame it was, and how sorry I felt for Charley Van Rheyn; and I asked him whether he thought he could not (he having a great deal of weight in the school) make things pleasanter for him. Tod responded that I should never be anything but a muff, and that the roasting Van Rheyn got treated to was superlatively good for him, if ever he was to be made into a man.

However, before another week ran out, Dr. Frost interfered. How he obtained an inkling of the reigning politics we never knew. One Saturday afternoon, when old Fontaine had taken Van Rheyn out with him, the doctor walked into the midst of us, to the general consternation.

Standing in the centre of the schoolroom, with a solemn face, all of us backing as much as the wall allowed, and the masters who chanced to be present rising to their feet, the doctor spoke of Van Rheyn. He had reason to suspect, he said, that we were doing our best to worry Van Rheyn's life out of him: and he put the question deliberately to us (and made us answer it), how we, if consigned alone to a foreign home, all its inmates strangers, would liked to be served so. He did not wish, he went on, to think he had pitiful, ill-disposed boys, lacking hearts and common kindness, in his house: he felt sure that what had passed arose from a heedless love of mischief; and it would greatly oblige him to find from henceforth that our conduct towards Van Rheyn was changed: he thought, and hoped, that he had only to express a wish upon the point, to ensure obedience.

With that—and a hearty nod and smile around, as if he put it as a personal favour to himself, and wanted us to see that he did, and was not angry, he went out again. A counsel was held to determine whether we had a sneak amongst us—else how could Frost have known?—that Charley himself had not spoken, his worst enemy felt sure of. But not one could be pitched upon: every individual fellow, senior and junior, protested earnestly that he had not let out a syllable. And, to tell the truth, I don't think we had.

However, the doctor was obeyed. From that day all real annoyance to Charles Van Rheyn ceased. I don't say but what there would be a laugh at him now and then, and a word of raillery, or that he lost his names of Bristles and Miss Charlotte; but virtually the sting was gone. Charley was as grateful as could be, and seemed to become quite happy; and upon the arrival of a hamper by grande vitesse from Rouen, containing a huge rich wedding-cake and some packets of costly sweetmeats, he divided the whole amongst us, keeping the merest taste for himself. The school made its comments in return.

"He's not a bad lot after all, that Van Rheyn. He will make a man yet."

"It isn't a bit of use your going in for this, Van Rheyn, unless you can run like a lamplighter."

"But I can run, you know," responded Van Rheyn.

"Yes. But can you keep the pace up?"

"Why not?"

"We may be out for three or four hours, pelting like mad all the time."

"I feel no fear of keeping up," said Van Rheyn. "I will go."

"All right."

It was on a Saturday afternoon; and we were turning out for hare and hounds. The quarter was hard upon its close, for September was passing. Van Rheyn had never seen hare and hounds: it had been let alone during the hotter weather: and it was Tod who now warned him that he might not be able to keep up the running. It requires fleet legs and easy breath, as every one knows; and Van Rheyn had never much exercised either.

"What is just the game?" he asked in his quaintly-turned phrase. And I answered him—for Tod had gone away.

"You see those strips of paper that they have torn out of old copybooks, and are twisting? That is for the scent. The hare fills his pockets with it, and drops a piece of it every now and then as he runs. We, the hounds, follow his course by means of the scent, and catch him if we can."

"And then?" questioned Van Rheyn.

"Then the game is over."

"And what if you not catch him?"

"The hare wins; that's all. What he likes to do is to double upon us cunningly and lead us home again after him."

"But in all that there is only running."

"We vault over the obstructions—gates, and stiles, and hedges. Or, if the hedges are too high, scramble through them."

"But some hedges are very thick and close: nobody could get through them," debated Van Rheyn, taking the words, as usual, too literally.

"Then we are dished. And have to find some other way onwards, or turn back."

"I can do what you say quite easily."

"All right, Charley," I repeated: as Tod had done. And neither of us, nor any one else, had the smallest thought that it was not all right.

Millichip was chosen hare. Snepp turned cranky over something or other at the last moment, and backed out of it. He made the best hare in the school: but Millichip was nearly as fleet a runner.

What with making the scent, and having it out with Snepp, time was hindered; and it must have been getting on for four o'clock when we started. Which docked the run considerably, for we had to be in at six to tea. On that account, perhaps, Millichip thought he must get over the ground the quicker; for I don't think we had ever made so swift a course. Letting the hare get well on ahead, the signal was given, and we started after him in full cry, rending the air with shouts, and rushing along like the wind.

A right-down good hare Millichip turned out to be; doubling and twisting and finessing, and exasperating the hounds considerably. About five o'clock he had made tracks for home, as we found by the scent: but we could neither see him nor catch him. Later, I chanced to come to grief in a treacherous ditch, lost my straw hat, and tore the sleeve of my jacket. This threw me behind the rest; and when I pelted up to the next stile, there stood Van Rheyn. He had halted to rest his arms on it; his breath was coming in alarming gasps, his face whiter than a sheet.

"Halloa, Van Rheyn! What's up? The pace is too much for you."

"It was my breath," said he, when he could answer. "I go on now."

I put my hand on him. "Look here: the run's nearly over: we shall soon be at home. Don't go on so fast."

"But I want to be in at what they call the death."

"There'll be no death to-day: the hare's safe to win."

"I want to keep up," he answered, getting over the stile. "I said I could keep up, and do what the rest did." And off he was again, full rush.

Before us, on that side of the stile, was a tolerably wide field. The pack had wound half over it during this short halt, making straight for the entrance to the coppice at the other end. We were doing our best to catch them up, when I distinctly saw a heavy stone flung into their midst. Looking at the direction it came from, there crept a dirty ragamuffin over the ground on his hands and knees. He did not see us two behind; and he flung another heavy stone. Had it struck anyone's head it would have done serious damage.

Letting the chase go, I stole across and pounced upon him before he could get away. He twisted himself out of my hands like an eel, and stood grinning defiance and whistling to his dog. We knew the young scamp well: and could never decide whether he was a whole scamp, or half a natural. At any rate, he was vilely bad, was the pest of the neighbourhood, and had enjoyed some short sojourns in prison for trespass. Raddy was the name he went by; we knew him by no other; and how he got a living nobody could tell.

"What did you throw those stones for?"

"Shan't tell ye. Didn't throw 'em at you."

"You had better mind what you are about, Mr. Raddy, unless you want to get into trouble."

"Yah—you!" grinned Raddy.

There was nothing to be made of him; there never was anything. I should have been no match for Raddy in an encounter; and he would have killed me without the slightest compunction. Turning to go on my way, I was in time to see Van Rheyn tumble over the stile and disappear within the coppice. The rest must have nearly shot out of the other end by that time. It was a coppice that belonged to Sir John Whitney. Once through it, we were on our own grounds, and within a field of home.

I went on leisurely enough: no good to try to catch them up now. Van Rheyn would not do it, and he had more than half a field's start of me. It must have been close upon six, for the sun was setting in a ball of fire; the amber sky around it was nearly as dazzling as the sun, and lighted up the field.

So that, plunging into the coppice, it was like going into a dungeon. For a minute or two, with the reflection of that red light lingering in my eyes, I could hardly see the narrow path; the trees were dark, thick, and met overhead. I ran along whistling: wondering whether that young Raddy was after me with his ugly dog; wondering why Sir John did not—

The whistling and the thoughts came to a summary end together. At the other end of the coppice, but a yard or two on this side the stile that divided it from the open field, there was Charles Van Rheyn on the ground, his back against the trunk of a tree, his arms stretched up, clasping it. But for that clasp, and the laboured breathing, I might have thought he was dead. For his face was ghastly, blue round the mouth, and wore the strangest expression I ever saw.

"Charley, what's the matter?"

But he could not answer. He was panting frightfully, as though every gasp would be his last. What on earth was I to do? Down I knelt, saying never another word.

"It—gives—me—much—hurt," said he, at length, with a long pause between every word.

"What does?"

"Here"—pointing to his chest—towards the left side.

"Did you hurt yourself? Did you fall?"

"No, I not hurt myself. I fell because I not able to run more. It is the breath. I wish papa was near me!"

Instinct told me that he must have assistance, and yet I did not like to leave him. But what if delay in getting it should be dangerous? I rose up to go.

"You—you are not going to quit me!" he cried out, putting his feeble grasp on my arm.

"But, Charley, I want to get somebody to you," I said in an agony, "I can't do anything for you myself: anything in the world."

"No, you stay. I should not like to be alone if I die."

The shock the word gave me I can recall yet. Die! If there was any fear of that, it was all the more necessary I should make a rush for Dr. Frost and Featherston. Never had I been so near my wits' end before, in the uncertainty as to what course I ought to take.

All in a moment, there arose a shrill whistle on the other side the stile. It was like a godsend. I knew it quite well for that vicious young reptile's, but it was welcome to me as sunshine in harvest.

"There's Raddy, Van Rheyn. I will send him."

Vaulting over the stile, I saw the young man standing with his back to me near the hedge, his wretched outer garment—a sack without shape—hitched up, his hands in the pockets of his dilapidated trousers, that hung in fringes below the knee. He was whistling to his dog in the coppice. They must have struck through the tangles and briars higher up, which was a difficult feat, and strictly forbidden by law. It was well Sir John's agent did not see Mr. Raddy—whose eyes, scratched and bleeding, gave ample proof of the trespass.

"Yah!" he shrieked out, turning at the sound of me, and grinning fresh defiance.

"Raddy," I said, speaking in persuasive tones to propitiate him in my great need, "I want you to do something for me. Go to Dr. Frost as quickly as you are able, and say—"

Of all the derisive horrible laughs, his interruption was the worst and loudest. It drowned the words.

"One of the school has fallen and hurt himself," I said, putting it in that way. "He's lying here, and I cannot leave him. Hush, Raddy! I want to tell you,"—advancing a step or two nearer to him and lowering my voice to a whisper,—"I think he's dying."

"None o' yer gammon here; none o' yer lies"—and in proportion as I advanced, he retreated. "You've got a ambush in that there coppy—all the lot on you a-waiting to be down on me! Just you try it on!"

"I am telling you the truth, Raddy. There's not a soul in there but the one I speak of. I say I fear he is dying. He is lying helpless. I will pay you to go"—feeling in my pockets to see how much I had there.

Raddy displayed his teeth: it was a trick of his when feeling particularly defiant. "What'll yer pay me?"

"Sixpence"—showing it to him. "I will give it you when you have taken the message."

"Give it first."

Just for a moment I hesitated in my extremity, but I knew it would be only the sixpence thrown away. Paid beforehand, Raddy would no more do the errand than he'd fly. I told him as much.

"Then be dashed if I go!" And he passed off into a round of swearing.

Good Heavens! If I should not be able to persuade him! If Charles Van Rheyn should die for want of help!

"Did you ever have anybody to care for, Raddy? Did you ever have a mother?"

"Her's sent over the seas, her is; and I be glad on't. Her beated me, her did: I wasn't a-going to stand that."

"If you ever had anybody you cared for the least bit in the world, Raddy; if you ever did anybody a good turn in all your life, you will help this poor fellow now. Come and look at him. See whether I dare leave him."

"None o' yer swindles! Ye wants to get me in there, ye does. I warn't borned yesterday."

Well, it seemed hopeless. "Will you go for the sixpence, if I give it to you beforehand, Raddy?"

"Give it over, and see. Where the thunder have ye been?" dealing his dog a savage kick, as it came up barking. "Be I to whistle all day?" Another kick.

I had found two sixpences in my pocket; all its store. Bringing forth one, I held it out to him.

"Now listen, Raddy. I give you this sixpence now. You are to run with all your might to the house—and you can run, you know, like the wind. Say that I sent you—you know my name, Johnny Ludlow—sent you to tell them that the French boy is in the coppice dying;" for I thought it best to put it strong. "Dr. Frost, or some of them, must come to him at once, and they must send off for Mr. Featherston. You can remember that. The French boy, mind."

"I could remember it if I tried."

"Well, I'll give you the sixpence. And look here—here's another sixpence. It is all the money I have. That shall be yours also, when you have done the errand."

I slipped one of the sixpences back into my pocket, holding out the other. But I have often wondered since that he did not stun me with a blow, and take the two. Perhaps he could not entirely divest himself of that idea of the "ambush." I did not like the leering look on his false face as he sidled cautiously up towards the sixpence.

"Take a look at him; you can see him from the stile," I said, closing my hand over the sixpence while I spoke; "convince yourself that he is there, and that no trickery is meant. And, Raddy," I added, slowly opening the hand again, "perhaps you may want help one of these days yourself in some desperate need. Do this good turn for him, and the like will be done for you."

I tossed him the sixpence. He stole cautiously to the stile, making a wide circuit round me to do it, glanced at Van Rheyn, and then made straight off in the right direction as fast as his legs would carry him, the dog barking at his heels.

Van Rheyn was better when I got back to him; his breathing easier, the mouth less blue; and his arms were no longer clutching the tree-trunk. Nevertheless, there was that in his face that gave me an awful fear and made my breath for a moment nearly as short as his. I sat down beside him, letting him lean against me, as well as the tree, for better support.

"Are you afraid, Charley? I hope they'll not be long."

"I am not afraid with this," he answered with a happy smile—and, opening his hand, I saw the little cross clasped in it.

Well, that nearly did for me. It was as though he meant to imply he knew he was dying, and was not afraid to die. And he did mean it.

"You do not comprehend?" he added, mistaking the look of my face—which no doubt was desperate. "I have kept the Saviour with me here, and He will keep me with Him there."

"Oh—but, Charley! You can't think you are going to die."

"Yes, I feel so," he answered quite calmly. "My mother said, that last Sunday, might not be long after her. She drew me close to her, and held my hand, and her tears were falling with mine. It was then she said it."

"Oh, Charley! how can I help you?" I cried out in my pain and dread. "If I could only do something for you!"

"I would like to give you this," he said, half opening his hand again, as it rested on his breast, just to show me the cross. "My mother has seen how good you have always been for me: she said she should look down, if permitted, to watch for me till I came. Would you please keep it to my memory?"

The hardest task I'd ever had in my life was to sit there. To sit there quietly—helpless. Dying! And I could do nothing to stay him! Oh, why did they not come? If I could only have run somewhere, or done something!

In a case like this the minutes seem as long as hours. Dr. Frost was up sooner than could have been hoped for by the watch, and Featherston with him. Raddy did his errand well. Chancing to see the surgeon pass down the road as he was delivering the message at the house, he ran and arrested him. He put his ill-looking face over the stile, as they came up, and I flung him the other sixpence, and thanked him too. The French master came running; others came: I hardly saw who they were, for my eyes were troubled.

The first thing that Featherston did was to open Van Rheyn's things at the throat, spread a coat on the ground and put his head flat down upon it. But oh, there could be no mistake. He was dying: nearly gone. Dr. Frost knelt down, the better to get at him, and said something that we did not catch.

"Thank you, sir," answered Van Rheyn, panting again and speaking with pain, but smiling faintly his grateful smile. "Do not be sorrowful. I shall see my mother. Sir—if you please—I wish to give my cross to Johnny Ludlow."

Dr. Frost only nodded in answer. His heart must have been full.

"Johnny Ludlow has been always good for me," he went on. "He will guard it to my memory: a keepsake. My mother would give it to him—she has seen that Johnny has stood by me ever since that first day."

Monsieur Fontaine spoke to him in French, and Van Rheyn answered in the same language. While giving a fond message for his father, his voice grew feeble, his face more blue, and the lids slowly closed over his eyes. Dr. Frost said something about removing him to the house, but Featherston shook his head. "Presently, presently."

"Adieu, sir," said Van Rheyn faintly to Dr. Frost, and partly opening his eyes again, "Adieu, Monsieur Fontaine. Adieu, all. Johnny, say my very best adieux to the boys; tell them it has been very pleasant lately; say they have been very good comrades; and say that I shall see them all again when they come to heaven. Will you hold my hand?"

Taking his left hand in mine—the other had the gold cross in it—I sat on beside him. The dusk was increasing, so that we could no longer very well see his features in the dark coppice. My tears were dropping fast and thick, just as his tears had dropped that evening when I found him sitting at the foot of his bed.

Well, it was over directly. He gave one long deep sigh, and then another after an interval, and all was over. It seemed like a dream then in the acting; it seems, looking back, like a dream now.

He had died from the running at Hare and Hounds. The violent exercise had been too much for the heart. We heard later that the French family doctor had suspected the heart was not quite sound; and that was the reason of Monsieur Rheyn's written restrictions on the score of violent exercise. But, as Dr. Frost angrily observed, why did the father not distinctly warn him against that special danger: how was it to be suspected in a lad of hearty and healthy appearance? Monsieur Van Rheyn came over, and took what remained of Charles back to Rouen, to be laid beside his late wife. It was a great blow to him to lose his only son. And all the property went away from the Van Rheyn family to Mrs. Scott in India.

The school went into a state that night, when we got in from the coppice, and I gave them Van Rheyn's message. They knew something was up with him, but never suspected it could be death.

"I say, though," cried Harry Parker, in a great access of remorse, speaking up amidst the general consternation, "we would never have worried him had we foreseen this. Poor Van Rheyn!"

And I have his gold cross by me this day. Sometimes, when looking at it, a fancy comes over me that he, looking down from heaven, sees it too.

CHAPTER VIII

MRS TODHETLEY'S EARRINGS

Again we had been spending the Christmas at Crabb Cot. It was January weather, cold and bright, the sun above and the white snow on the ground. Mrs. Todhetley had been over to Timberdale Court, to the christening of Robert and Jane Ashton's baby: a year had gone by since their marriage. The mater went to represent Mrs. Coney, who was godmother. Jane was not strong enough to sit out a christening dinner, and that was to be given later. After some mid-day feasting, the party dispersed.

I went out to help Mrs. Todhetley from the carriage when she got back. The Squire was at Pershore for the day. It was only three o'clock, and the sun quite warm in spite of the snow.

"It is so fine, Johnny, that I think I'll walk to the school," she said, as she stepped down. "It may not be like this to-morrow, and I must see about those shirts."

The parish school was making Tod a set of new shirts; and some bother had arisen about them. Orders had been given for large plaits in front, when Tod suddenly announced that he would have the plaits small.

"Only— Can I go as I am?" cried Mrs. Todhetley, suddenly stopping in indecision, as she remembered her fine clothes: a silver-grey gown that shone like silver, white shawl of china crape, and be-feathered bonnet.

"Why, yes, of course you can go as you are, good mother. And look all the nicer for it."

"I fear the children will stare! But then—if the shirts get made wrong! Well, will you go with me, Johnny?"

We reached the school-house, I waiting outside while she went in. It was during that time of strike that I have told of before, when Eliza Hoar died of it. The strike was in full swing still; the men looked discontented, the women miserable, the children pinched.

"I don't know what in the world Joseph will say!" cried Mrs. Todhetley, as we were walking back. "Two of the shirts are finished with the large plaits. I ought to have seen about it earlier; but I did not think they would begin them quite so soon. We'll just step into Mrs. Coney's, Johnny, as we go home. I must tell her about the christening."

For Mrs. Coney was a prisoner from an attack of rheumatism. It had kept her from the festivity. She was asleep, however, when we got in: and Mr. Coney thought she had better not be disturbed, even for the news of the little grandson's christening, as she had lain awake all the past night in pain; so we left again.

"Why, Johnny! who's that?"

Leaning against the gate of our house, in the red light of the setting sun, was an elderly woman, dark as a gipsy.

"A tramp," I whispered, noticing her poor clothes.

"Do you want anything, my good woman?" asked Mrs. Todhetley.

She was half kneeling in the snow, and lifted her face at the words: a sickly face, that somehow I liked now I saw it closer. Her tale was this. She had set out from her home, three miles off, to walk to Worcester, word having been sent her that her daughter, who was in service there, had met with an accident. She had not been strong of late, and a faintness came over her as she was passing the gate. But for leaning on it she must have fallen.

"You should go by train: you should not walk," said Mrs. Todhetley.

"I had not the money just by me, ma'am," she answered. "It 'ud cost two shillings or half-a-crown. My daughter sent word I was to take the train and she'd pay for it: but she did not send the money, and I'd not got it just handy."

"You live at Islip, you say. What is your name?"

"Nutt'n, ma'am," said the woman, in the local dialect. Which name I interpreted into Nutten; but Mrs. Todhetley thought she said Nutt.

"I think you are telling me the truth," said the mater, some hesitation in her voice, though. "If I were assured of it I would advance you half-a-crown for the journey."

"The good Lord above us knows that I'm telling it," returned the woman earnestly, turning her face full to the glow of the sun. "It's more than I could expect you to do, ma'am, and me a stranger; but I'd repay it faithfully."

Well, the upshot was that she got the half-crown lent her; and I ran in for a drop of warm ale. Molly shrieked out at me for it, refusing to believe that the mistress gave any such order, and saying she was not going to warm ale for parish tramps. So I got the ale and the tin, and warmed it myself. The woman was very grateful, drank it, and disappeared.

"Joseph, I am so very sorry! They have made two of your shirts, and the plaits are the large ones you say you don't like."

"Then they'll just unmake them," retorted Tod, in a temper.

We were sitting round the table at tea, Mrs. Todhetley having ordered some tea to be made while she went upstairs. She came down without her bonnet, and had changed her best gown for the one she mostly wore at home: it had two shades in it, and shone like the copper tea-kettle. The Squire was not expected home yet, and we were to dine an hour later than usual.

"That Miss Timmens is not worth her salt," fired Tod, helping himself to some thin bread-and-butter. "What business has she to go and make my shirts wrong?"

"I fear the fault lies with me, Joseph, not with Miss Timmens. I had given her the pattern shirt, which has large plaits, you know, before you said you would prefer— Oh, we hardly want the lamp yet, Thomas!" broke off the mater, as old Thomas came in with the lighted lamp.

"I'm sure we do, then," cried Tod. "I can't see which side's butter and which bread."

"And I, not thinking Miss Timmens would put them in hand at once, did not send to her as soon as you spoke, Joseph," went on the mater, as Thomas settled the lamp on the table. "I am very sorry, my dear; but it is only two. The rest shall be done as you wish."

Something, apart from the shirts, had put Tod out. I had seen it as soon as we got in. For one thing, he had meant to go to Pershore: and the pater, not knowing it, started without him.

"Let them unmake the two," growled Tod.

"But it would be a great pity, Joseph. They are very nicely done; the stitching's beautiful. I really don't think it will signify."

"You don't, perhaps. You may like odd things. A pig with one ear, for example."

"A what, Joseph?" she asked, not catching the last simile.

"I said a pig with one ear. No doubt you do like it. You are looking like one now, ma'am."

The words made me gaze at Mrs. Todhetley, for the tone bore some personal meaning, and then I saw what Tod meant: an earring was absent. The lamp-light shone on the flashing diamonds, the bright pink topaz of the one earring; but the other ear was bare and empty.

"You have lost one of your earrings, mother!"

She put her hands to her ears, and started up in alarm. These earrings were very valuable: they had been left to her, when she was a child, in some old lady's will, and constituted her chief possession in jewellery worth boasting of. Not once in a twelvemonth did she venture to put them on; but she had got them out to-day for the christening.

Whether it was that I had gazed at the earrings when I was a little fellow and sat in her lap, I don't know; but I never saw any that I liked so well. The pink topaz was in a long drop, the slender rim of gold that encircled it being set with diamonds. Mrs. Todhetley said they were worth fifty guineas: and perhaps they were. The glittering white of the diamonds round the pink was beautiful to look upon.

The house went into a commotion. Mrs. Todhetley made for her bedroom, to see whether the earring had dropped on the floor or was lodging inside her bonnet. She shook out her grey dress, hoping it had fallen amidst the folds. Hannah searched the stairs, candle in hand; the two children were made to stand in corners for fear they should tread on it. But the search came to nothing. It seemed clear enough that the earring was not in the house.

"Did you notice, Johnny, whether I had them both in my ears when we went to the school?" the mater asked.

No, I did not. I had seen them sparkling when she got out of the carriage, but had not noticed them after.

I went out to search the garden-path that she had traversed, and the road over to the Coneys' farm. Tod helped me, forgetting his shirts and his temper. Old Coney said he remarked the earrings while Mrs. Todhetley was talking to him, and thought how beautiful they were. That is, he had remarked one of them; he was sure of that; and he thought if the other had been missing, its absence would have struck him. But that was just saying nothing; for he could not be certain that both were there.

"You may hunt till to-morrow morning, and get ten lanterns to it," cried Molly, in her tart way, meeting us by the bay-tree, as we went stooping up the path again: "but you'll be none the nearer finding it. That tramp got's the earring, Master Joe."

"What tramp?" demanded Tod, straightening himself.

"A tramp that Master Johnny there must needs give hot ale to," returned Molly. "I know what them tramps are worth. They'd pull rings out of ears with their own fingers, give 'em the chance: and perhaps this woman did, without the missis seeing her."

Tod turned to me for an explanation. I gave it, and he burst into a derisive laugh, meant for me and the mater. "To think we could be taken in by such a tale as that!" he cried: "we should never see tramp, or half-crown, or perhaps the earring again."

The Squire came home in the midst of the stir. He blustered a little, partly at the loss, chiefly at the encouragement of tramps, calling it astounding folly. Ordering Thomas to bring a lantern, he went stooping his old back down the path, and across to Coney's and back again; not believing any one had searched properly, and finally kicking the snow about.

"It's a pity this here snow's on the ground, sir," cried Thomas. "A little thing like an earring might easily slip into it in falling."

"Not a bit of it," growled the Squire. "That tramp has got the earring."

"I don't believe the tramp has," I stoutly said. "I don't think she was a tramp at all: and she seemed honest. I liked her face."

"There goes Johnny with his 'faces' again!" said the Squire, in laughing mockery: and Tod echoed it.

"It's a good thing you don't have to buy folks by their faces, Johnny: you'd get finely sold sometimes."

"And she had a true voice," I persisted, not choosing to be put down, also thinking it right to assert what was my conviction. "A voice you might trust without as much as looking at herself."

Well, the earring was not to be found; though the search continued more or less till bed-time, for every other minute somebody would be looking again on the carpets.

"It is not so much for the value I regret it," spoke Mrs. Todhetley, the tears rising in her meek eyes: "as for the old associations connected with it. I never had the earrings out but they brought back to me the remembrance of my girlhood's home."

Early in the morning I ran down to the school-house. More snow had fallen in the night. The children were flocking in. Miss Timmens had not noticed the earrings at all, but several of the girls said they had. Strange to say, though, most of them could not say for certain whether they saw both the earrings: they thought they did; but there it ended. Just like old Coney!

"I am sure both of them were there," spoke up a nice, clean little girl, from a back form.

"What's that, Fanny Fairfax?" cried Miss Timmens, in her quick way. "Stand up. How are you sure of it?"

"Please governess, I saw them both," was the answer; and the child blushed like a peony as she stood up above the others and said it.

"Are you sure you did?"

"Yes, I'm quite sure, please, governess. I was looking which o' the two shined the most. 'Twas when the lady was stooping over the shirt, and the sun came in at the window."

"What did they look like?" asked Miss Timmens.

"They looked—" and there the young speaker came to a standstill.

"Come, Fanny Fairfax!" cried Miss Timmens, sharply. "What d'you stop for? I ask you what the earrings looked like. You must be able to tell if you saw them."

"They were red, please, governess, and had shining things round them like the ice when it glitters."

"She's right, Master Johnny," nodded Miss Timmens to me: "and she's a very correct child in general. I think she must have seen both of them."

I ran home with the news. They were at breakfast still.

"What a set of muffs the children must be, not to have taken better notice!" cried Tod. "Why, when I saw only the one earring in, it struck my eye at once."

"And for that reason it is almost sure that both of them were in at the school-house," I rejoined. "The children did not particularly observe the two, but they would have remarked it directly had only one been in. Old Coney said the same."

"Ay: it's that tramp that has got it," said the Squire. "While your mother was talking to her, it must have slipped out of the ear, and she managed to secure it. Those tramps lay their hands on anything; nothing comes amiss to them; they are as bad as gipsies. I dare say this was a gipsy—dark as she was. I'll be off to Worcester and see the police: we'll soon have her found. You had better come with me, Johnny; you'll be able to describe her."

We went off without delay, caught a passing train, and were soon at Worcester and at the police-station. The Squire asked for Sergeant Cripp: who came to him, and prepared to listen to his tale.

He began it in his impulsive way; saying outright that the earring had been stolen by a gipsy-tramp. I tried to say that it might have been only lost, but the pater scoffed at that, and told me to hold my tongue.

"And now, Cripp, what's to be done?" he demanded, not having given the sergeant an opportunity to put in a word edgeways. "We must get the earring back; it is of value, and much prized, apart from that, by Mrs. Todhetley. The woman must be found, you know."

"Yes, she must be found," agreed the sergeant. "Can you give me a description of her?"

"Johnny—this young gentleman can," said the Squire, rubbing his brow with his yellow silk handkerchief, for he had put himself into a heat, in spite of the frosty atmosphere that surrounded us. "He was with Mrs. Todhetley when she talked to the woman."

"A thin woman of middle height, stooped a good deal, face pale and quiet, wrinkles on it, brown eyes," wrote the sergeant, taking down what I said. "Black poke bonnet, clean cap border, old red woollen shawl with the fringe torn off in places. Can't remember gown: except that it was dark and shabby."

"And, of course, sir, you've no clue to her name?" cried the sergeant, looking at me.

"Yes: she said it was Nutten—as I understood it; but Mrs. Todhetley thought she said Nutt." And I went on to relate the tale the woman told. Sergeant Cripp's lips extended themselves in a silent smile.

"It was well got up, that tale," said he, when I finished. "Just the thing to win over a warm-hearted lady."

"But she could not have halted at the gate, expecting to steal the earring?"

"Of course not. She was prowling about to see what she could steal, perhaps watching her opportunity to get into the house. The earring fell in her way, a more valuable prize than she expected, and she made off with it."

"You'll be able to hunt her up if she's in Worcester, Cripp," put in the pater. "Don't lose time."

"If she's in Worcester," returned Mr. Cripp, with emphasis. "She's about as likely to be in Worcester, Squire Todhetley, as I am to be at this present minute in Brummagem," he familiarly added. "After saying she was coming to Worcester, she'd strike off in the most opposite direction to it."

"Where on earth are we to look for her, then?" asked the pater, in commotion.

"Leave it to us, Squire. We'll try and track her. And—I hope—get back the earring."

"And about the advertisement for the newspapers, Cripp? We ought to put one in."

Sergeant Cripp twirled the pen in his fingers while he reflected. "I think, sir, we will let the advertisement alone for a day or two," he presently said. "Sometimes these advertisements do more harm than good: they put thieves on their guard."

"Do they? Well, I suppose they do."

"If the earring had been simply lost, then I should send an advertisement to the papers at once. But if it has been stolen by this tramp, and you appear to consider that point pretty conclusive—"

"Oh, quite conclusive," interrupted the pater. "She has that earring as sure as this is an umbrella in Johnny Ludlow's hand. Had it been dropped anywhere on the ground, we must have found it."

"Then we won't advertise it. At least not in to-morrow's papers," concluded Sergeant Cripp. And telling us to leave the matter entirely in his hands, he showed us out.

The Squire went up the street with his hands in his pockets, looking rather glum.

"I'm not sure that he's right about the advertisement, Johnny," he said at length. "I lay awake last night in bed, making up the wording of it in my own mind. Perhaps he knows best, though."

"I suppose he does, sir."

And he went on again, up one street, and down another, deep in thought.

"Let's see—we have nothing to do here to-day, have we, Johnny?"

"Except to get the pills made up. The mother said we were to be sure and not forget them."

"Oh, ay. And that's all the way down in Sidbury! Couldn't we as well get them made up by a druggist nearer?"

"But it is the Sidbury druggist who holds the prescription."

"What a bother! Well, lad, let us put our best leg foremost, for I want to catch the one-o'clock train, if I can."

Barely had we reached Sidbury, when who should come swinging along the pavement but old Coney, in a rough white great-coat and top-boots. Not being market-day, we were surprised to see him.

"I had to come in about some oats," he explained. And then the Squire told him of our visit to the place, and the sergeant's opinion about the advertisement.

"Cripp's wrong," said Coney, decisively. "Not advertise the earring!—why, it is the first step that ought to be taken."

"Well, so I thought," said the pater.

"The thing's not obliged to have been stolen, Squire; it may have been dropped out of the ear in the road, and picked up by some one. The offering of a reward might bring it back again."

"And I'll be shot if I don't do it," exclaimed the pater. "I can see as far through a millstone as Cripp can."

Turning into the Hare and Hounds, which was old Coney's inn, they sat down at a table, called for pen and ink, and began to draw out an advertisement between them. "Lost! An earring of great value, pink topaz and diamonds," wrote the Squire on a leaf of his pocket-book; and when he had got as far as that he looked up.

"Johnny, you go over to Eaton's for a sheet or two of writing-paper. We'll have it in all three of the newspapers. And look here, lad—you can run for the pills at the same time. Take care of the street slides. I nearly came down on one just now, you know."

When I got back with the paper and pills, the advertisement was finished. It concluded with an offer of £5 reward. Applications to be made to Mr. Sergeant Cripp, or to Squire Todhetley of Crabb Cot. And, leaving it at the offices of the Herald, Journal, and Chronicle, we returned home. It would appear on the next day, Saturday; to the edification, no doubt, of Sergeant Cripp.

"Any news of the earring?" was the Squire's first question when we got in.

No, there was no news of it, Mrs. Todhetley answered. And she had sent Luke Macintosh over to the little hamlet, Islip; who reported when he came back that there was no Mrs. Nutt, or Nutten, known there.

"Just what I expected," observed the pater. "That woman was a thieving tramp, and she has the earring."

Saturday passed over, and Sunday came. When the Worcester paper arrived on Saturday morning the advertisement was in it as large as life, and the pater read it out to us. Friday and Saturday had been very dull, with storms of snow; on Sunday the sun shone again, and the air was crisp.

It was about three o'clock, and we were sitting at the dessert-table cracking filberts, for on Sundays we always dined early, after morning service—when Thomas came in and said a stranger had called, and was asking if he could see Mrs. Todhetley. But the mater, putting a shawl over her head and cap, had just stepped over to sit a bit with sick Mrs. Coney.

"Who is it, Thomas?" asked the Squire. "A stranger! Tell him to send his name in."

"His name's Eccles, sir," said Thomas, coming back again. "He comes, he says, from Sergeant Cripp."

"My goodness!—it must be about the earring," cried the Squire.

"That it is, sir," said old Thomas. "The first word he put to me was an inquiry whether you had heard news of it."

I followed the pater into the study. Tod did not leave his filberts. Standing by the fire was a tall, well-dressed man, with a black moustache and blue silk necktie. I think the Squire was a little taken aback at the fashionable appearance of the visitor. He had expected to see an ordinary policeman.

"Have you brought tidings of Mrs. Todhetley's earring?" began the pater, all in a flutter of eagerness.

"I beg a thousand pardons for intruding upon you on a Sunday," returned the stranger, cool and calm as a cucumber, "but the loss of an hour is sometimes most critical in these cases. I have the honour, I believe, of speaking to Squire Todhetley?"

The Squire nodded. "Am I mistaken in supposing that you come about the earring?" he reiterated. "I understood my servant to mention Sergeant Cripp. But—you do not, I presume, belong to the police force?"

"Only as a detective officer," was the answer, given with a taking smile. "A private officer," he added, putting a stress upon the word. "My name is Eccles."

"Take a seat, Mr. Eccles," said the Squire, sitting down himself, while I stood back by the window. "I do hope you have brought tidings of the earring."

"Yes—and no," replied Mr. Eccles, with another fascinating smile, as he unbuttoned his top-coat. "We think we have traced it; but we cannot yet be sure."

"And where is it?—who has it?" cried the Squire, eagerly.

"It is a very delicate matter, and requires delicate handling," observed the detective, after a slight pause. "For that reason I have come over to-day myself. Cripp did not choose to entrust it to one of his men."

"I am sure I am much obliged to him, and to you too," said the Squire, his face beaming. "Where is the earring?"

"Before I answer that question, will you be so kind as to relate to me, in a few concise words, the precise circumstances under which the earring was lost?"

The pater entered on the story, and I helped him. Mr. Eccles listened attentively.

"Exactly so," said he, when it was over. "Those are the facts Cripp gave me; but it was only second-hand, you see, and I preferred to hear them direct from yourselves. They serve to confirm our suspicion."

"But where is the earring?" repeated the pater.

"If it is where we believe it to be, it is in a gentleman's house at Worcester. At least he may be called a gentleman. He is a professional man: a lawyer, in fact. But I may not give names in the present stage of the affair."

"And how did the earring get into his house?" pursued the Squire, all aglow with interest.

"News reached us last evening," began Mr. Eccles, after searching in his pockets for something that he apparently could not find: perhaps a note-case—"reached us in a very singular way, too—that this gentleman had been making a small purchase of jewellery in the course of yesterday; had been making it in private, and did not wish it talked of. A travelling pedlar—that was the description we received— had come in contact with him and offered him an article for sale, which he, after some haggling, purchased. By dint of questioning, we discovered this article to be an earring: one earring, not a pair. Naturally Mr. Cripp's suspicion was at once aroused: he thought it might be the very self-same earring that you have lost. We consulted together, and the result is, I decided to come over and see you."

"I'd lay all I've got it is the earring!" exclaimed the Squire, in excitement. "The travelling pedlar that sold it must have been that woman tramp."

"Well, no," returned the detective, quietly. "It was a man. Her husband, perhaps; or some confederate of hers."

"No doubt of that! And how can we get back the earring?"

"We shall get it, sir, never fear; if it be the earring you have lost. But, as I have just observed, it is a matter that will require extreme delicacy and caution in the handling. First of all, we must assure ourselves beyond doubt that the earring is the one in question. To take any steps upon an uncertainty would not do: this gentleman might turn round upon us unpleasantly."

"Well, let him," cried the Squire.

The visitor smiled his candid smile again, and shook his head. "For instance, if, after taking means to obtain possession of the earring, we found it to be coral set with pearls, or opal set with emeralds, instead of a pink topaz with diamonds, we should not only look foolish ourselves, but draw down upon us the wrath of the present possessor."

"Is he a respectable man?" asked the pater. "I know most of the lawyers—"

"He stands high enough in the estimation of the town, but I have known him do some very dirty actions in his profession," interrupted Mr. Eccles, speaking rapidly. "With a man like him to deal with, we must necessarily be wary."

"Then what are you going to do?"

"The first step, Squire Todhetley, is to make ourselves sure that the earring is the one we are in quest of. With this view, I am here to request Mrs. Todhetley to allow me to see the fellow-earring. Cripp has organized a plan by which he believes we can get to see the one I have been telling you of; but it will be of no use our seeing it unless we can identify it."

"Of course not. By all means. Johnny, go over and ask your mother to come in," added the Squire, eagerly. "I'm sure I don't know where she keeps her things, and might look in her places for ever without finding it. Meanwhile, Mr. Eccles, can I offer you some refreshment? We have just dined off a beautiful sirloin of beef: it's partly cold now, but perhaps you won't mind that."

Mr. Eccles said he would take a little, as the Squire was so good as to offer it, for he had come off by the first train after morning service, and so lost his dinner. Taking my hat, I dashed open the dining-room door in passing. Tod was at the nuts still, Hugh and Lena on either side of him.

"I say, Tod, do you want to see a real live detective? There's one in the study."

Who should be seated in the Coneys' drawing-room, her bonnet and shawl on, and her veil nearly hiding her sad face, but Lucy Bird—Lucy Ashton that used to be. It always gave me a turn when I saw her: bringing up all kinds of ugly sorrows and troubles. I shook hands, and asked after Captain Bird.

She believed he was very well, she said, but she had been spending the time since yesterday at Timberdale Court with Robert and Jane. To-day she had been dining with the Coneys—who were always kind to her, she added, with a sigh—and she was now about to go off to the station to take the train for Worcester.

The mater was in Mrs. Coney's bedroom with old Coney and Cole the doctor, who was paying his daily visit. One might have thought they were settling all the cases of rheumatism in the parish by the time they took over it. While I waited, I told Mrs. Bird about the earring and the present visit of Detective Eccles. Mrs. Todhetley came down in the midst of it; and lifted her hands at the prospect of facing a detective.

"Dear me! Is he anything dreadful to look at, Johnny? Very rough? Has he any handcuffs?"

It made me laugh. "He is a regular good-looking fellow—quite a gentleman. Tall and slender, and well-dressed: gold studs and a blue necktie. He has a ring on his finger and wears a black moustache."

Mrs. Bird suddenly lifted her head, and stared at me: perhaps the description surprised her. The mater seemed inclined to question my words; but she said nothing, and came away after bidding good-bye to Lucy.

"Keep up your heart, my dear," she whispered. "Things may grow brighter for you some time."

When I got back, Mr. Eccles had nearly finished the sirloin, some cheese, and a large tankard of ale. The Squire sat by, hospitably pressing him to take more, whenever his knife and fork gave signs of flagging. Tod stood looking on, his back against the mantelpiece. Mrs. Todhetley soon appeared with a little cardboard box, where the solitary earring was lying on a bed of wool.

Rising from the table, the detective carried the box to the window, and stood there examining the earring; first in the box, then out of it. He turned it about in his hand, and looked at it on all sides; it took him a good three minutes.

"Madam," said he, breaking the silence, "will you entrust this earring to us for a day or two? It will be under Sergeant Cripp's charge, and perfectly safe."

"Of course, of course," interposed the Squire, before any one could speak. "You are welcome to take it."

"You see, it is possible—indeed, most probable—that only one of us may be able to obtain sight of the other earring. Should it be Cripp, my having seen this one will be nearly useless to him. It is essential that he should see it also: and it will not do to waste time."

"Pray take charge of it, sir," said Mrs. Todhetley, mentally recalling what I had said of his errand to her and Lucy Bird. "I know it will be safe in your hands and Sergeant Cripp's. I am only too glad that there is a probability of the other one being found."

"And look here," added the Squire to Eccles, while the latter carefully wrapped the box in paper, and put it into his inner breast-pocket, "don't you and Cripp let that confounded gipsy escape. Have her up and punish her."

"Trust us for that," was the detective's answer, given with an emphatic nod. "She is already as good as taken, and her confederate also. There's not a doubt—I avow it to you—that the other earring is yours. We only wait to verify it."

And, with that, he buttoned his coat, and bowed himself out, the Squire himself attending him to the door.

"He is as much like a detective as I'm like a Dutchman," commented Tod. "At least, according to what have been all my previous notions of one. Live and learn."

"He seems quite a polished man, has quite the manners of society," added the mater. "I do hope he will get back my poor earring."

"Mother, is Lucy Bird in more trouble than usual?" I asked.

"She is no doubt in deep distress of some kind, Johnny. But she is never out of it. I wish Robert Ashton could induce her to leave that most worthless husband of hers!"

The Squire, after watching off the visitor, came in, rubbing his hands and looking as delighted as old Punch. He assumed that the earring was as good as restored, and was immensely taken with Mr. Eccles.

"A most intelligent, superior man," cried he. "I suppose he is what is called a gentleman-detective: he told me he had been to college. I'm sure it seems quite a condescension in him to work with Cripp and the rest."

And the whole of tea-time and all the way to church, the praises were being rung of Mr. Eccles. I'm not sure but that he was more to us that night than the sermon.

"I confess I feel mortified about that woman, though," confessed Mrs. Todhetley. "You heard him say that she was as good as taken: they must have traced the earring to her. I did think she was one to be trusted. How one may be deceived in people!"

"I'd have trusted her with a twenty-pound note, mother."

"Hark at Johnny!" cried Tod. "This will be a lesson for you, lad."

Monday morning. The Squire and Tod had gone over to South Crabb. Mrs. Todhetley sat at the window, adding up some bills, her nose red with the cold: and I was boxing Hugh's ears, for he was in one of his frightfully troublesome moods, when Molly came stealing in at the door, as covertly as if she had been committing murder.

"Ma'am! ma'am!—there's that tramp in the yard!"

"What?" cried the mater, turning round.

"I vow it's her; I know the old red shawl again," pursued Molly, with as much importance as though she had caught half the thieves in Christendom. "She turned into the yard as bold as brass; so I just slipped the bolt o' the door against her, and come away. You'll have her took up on the instant, ma'am, won't you?"

"But if she has come back, I don't think she can be guilty," cried Mrs. Todhetley, after a bewildered pause. "We had better see what she wants. What do you say, Johnny?"

"Why, of course we had. I'll go to her, as Molly's afraid."

Rushing out of hearing of Molly's vindictive answer, I went round through the snow to the yard, and found the woman meekly tapping at the kitchen-door—the old red shawl, and the black bonnet, and the white muslin cap border, all the same as before. Before I got quite up, the kitchen-door was cautiously drawn open, and Mrs. Todhetley looked out. The poor old woman dropped a curtsy and held out half-a-crown on the palm of her withered hand.

"I've made bold to call at the door to leave it, lady. And I can never thank you enough, ma'am," she added, the tears rising to her eyes; "my tongue would fail if I tried it. 'Tis not many as would have trusted a stranger; and, that, a poor body like me. I got over to Worcester quick and comfortable, ma'am, thanks to you, and found my daughter better nor I had hoped for."

The same feeling of reliance, of trust, arose within me as I saw her face and heard her voice and words. If this woman was what they had been fancying her, I'd never eat tarts again.

"Come in," said Mrs. Todhetley; and Molly, looking daggers as she heard it, approached her mistress with a whisper.

"Don't, ma'am. It's all a laid-out plan. She has heard that she's suspected, and brings back the half-crown, thinking to put us off the scent."

"Step this way," went on Mrs. Todhetley, giving no heed to Molly, except by a nod—and she took the woman into the little store-room where she kept her jam-pots and things, and bade her go to the fire.

"What did you tell me your name was," she asked, "when you were here on Friday?"

"Nutt'n, ma'am."

"Nutten," repeated the mater, glancing at me. "But I sent over to Islip, and no one there knew anything about you—they denied that any one of your name lived there."

"Why, how could they do that?" returned the woman, with every appearance of surprise. "They must have mistook somehow. I live in the little cottage, ma'am, by the dung-heap. I've lived there for five-and-twenty year, and brought up my children there, and never had parish pay."

"And gone always by the name of Nutten?"

"Not never by no other, ma'am. Why should I?"

Was she to be believed? There was the half-crown in Mrs. Todhetley's hand, and there was the honest wrinkled old face looking up at us openly. But, on the other side, there was the assertion of the Islip people; and there was the earring.

"What was the matter with your daughter, and in what part of Worcester does she live?" queried the mater.

"She's second servant to a family in Melcheapen Street, ma'am, minds the children and does the beds, and answers the door, and that. When I got there—and sick enough my heart felt all the way, thinking what the matter could be—I found that she had fell from the parlour window that she'd got outside to clean, and broke her arm and scarred her face, and frighted and shook herself finely. But thankful enough I was that 'twas no worse. Her father, ma'am, died of an accident, and I can never abear to hear tell of one."

"I—I lost an earring out of my ear that afternoon," said Mrs. Todhetley, plunging into the matter, but not without hesitation. "I think I must have lost it just about the time I was talking to you. Did you pick it up?"

"No, ma'am, I didn't. I should have gave it to you if I had."

"You did not carry it off with you, I suppose!" interrupted wrathful Molly; who had come in to get some eggs, under pretence that the batter-pudding was waiting for them.

And whether it was Molly's sharp and significant tone, or our silence and looks, I don't know; but the woman saw it all then, and what she was suspected of.

"Oh, ma'am, were you thinking that ill of me?"—and the hands shook as they were raised, and the white border seemed to lift itself from the horror-stricken face. "Did you think I could do so ill a turn, and after all the kindness showed me? The good Lord above knows I'm not a thief. Dear heart! I never set eyes, lady, on the thing you've lost."

"No, I am sure you didn't," I cried; "I said so all along. It might have dropped anywhere in the road."

"I never see it, nor touched it, sir," she reiterated, the tears raining down her cheeks. "Oh, ma'am, do believe me!"

Molly tossed her head as she went out with the eggs in her apron; but I would sooner have believed myself guilty than that poor woman. Mrs. Todhetley thought with me. She offered her some warm ale and a crust; but the old woman shook her head in refusal, and went off in a fit of crying.

"She knows no more of the earring than I know of it, mother."

"I feel sure she does not, Johnny."

"That Molly's getting unbearable. I wonder you don't send her away."

"She has her good points, dear," sighed Mrs. Todhetley. "Only think of her cooking! and of what a thrifty, careful manager she is!"

The Squire and Tod got home for lunch. Nothing could come up to their ridicule when they heard what had occurred, saying that the mother and I were two muffs, fit to go about the world in a caravan as specimens of credulity. Like Molly, they thought we ought to have secured the woman.

"But you see she was honest in the matter of the half-crown," debated Mrs. Todhetley, in her mild way. "She brought that back. It does not stand to reason that she would have dared to come within miles of the place, if she had taken the earring."

"Why, it's just the thing she would do," retorted the Squire, pacing about in a commotion. "Once she had got rid of the earring, she'd show up here to throw suspicion off herself. And she couldn't come without returning the half-crown: it must have gone nicely against the grain to return that."

And Mrs. Todhetley, the most easily swayed spirit in the world, began to veer round again like a weathercock, and fear we had been foolish.

"You should see her jagged-out old red shawl," cried Molly, triumphantly. "All the red a'most washed out of it, and the edges in tatters. I know a tramp when I sees one: and the worst of all tramps is them that do the tricks with clean hands and snow-white cap-borders."

The theme lasted us all the afternoon. I held my tongue, for it was of no use contending against the stream. It was getting dusk when Cole called in, on his way from the Coneys. The Squire laid the grievance before him, demanding whether he had ever heard of two people so simple as I and the mother.

"What did she say her name was?" asked Cole. "Nutten?—of Islip? Are you sure she did not say Norton?"

"She said Nutt'n. We interpreted it into Nutten."

"Yes, Johnny, that's how she would say it. I'll lay a guinea it's old Granny Norton."

"Granny Norton!" echoed the Squire. "She is respectable."

"Respectable, honest, upright as the day," replied Cole. "I have a great respect for old Mrs. Norton. She's very poor now; but she was not always so."

"She told us this morning that she lived in the cottage by the dung-heap," I put in.

"Exactly: she does so. And a nice dung-heap it is; the disgrace of Islip," added Cole.

"And you mean to say, Cole, that you know this woman—that she's not a tramp, but Mrs. Norton?" spoke the pater.

"I know Mrs. Norton of Islip," he answered. "I saw her pass my window this morning: she seemed to be coming from the railway-station. It was no tramp, Squire."

"How was she dressed?" asked Mrs. Todhetley.

"Dressed? Well, her shawl was red, and her bonnet black. I've never seen her dressed otherwise, when abroad, these ten years past."

"And—has she a daughter in service at Worcester?"

"Yes, I think so. Yes, I am sure so. It's Susan. Oh, it is the same person: you need not doubt it."

"Then what the deuce did Luke Macintosh mean by bringing word back from Islip that she was not known there?" fiercely demanded the Squire, turning to me.

"But Luke said he asked for her by the name of Nutt—Mrs. Nutt. I questioned him about it this afternoon, sir, and he said he understood Nutt to have been the name we gave him."

This was very unsatisfactory as far as the earring went. (And we ascertained later that poor Mrs. Norton was Mrs. Norton, and had been suspected wrongly.) For, failing the tramp view of the case, who could have sold the earring to the professional gentleman in Worcester?

"Cripp knows what he is about; never fear," observed the Squire. "Now that he has the case well in hand, he is sure to pull it successfully through."

"Yes, you may trust Cripp," said the doctor. "And I hope, Mrs. Todhetley, you will soon be gladdened by the sight of your earring again." And Cole went out, telling us we were going to have a thaw. Which we could have told him, for it had already set in, and the snow was melting rapidly.

"To think that I should have done so stupid a thing. But I have been so flustered this morning by that parson and his nonsense that I hardly know what I'm about."

The speaker was Miss Timmens. She had come up in a passion, after twelve o'clock school. Not with us, or with her errand—which was to bring one of the new shirts to show, made after Tod's fancy—but with the young parson. Upon arriving and unfolding the said shirt, Miss Timmens found that she had brought the wrong shirt—one of those previously finished. The thaw had gone on so briskly in the night that this morning the roads were all mud and slop, and Miss Timmens had walked up in her pattens.

"He is enough to make a saint swear, with his absurdities and his rubbish," went on Miss Timmens, turning from the table where lay the unfolded shirt, and speaking of the new parson; between whom and herself hot war waged. "You'd never believe, ma'am, what he did this morning"—facing Mrs. Todhetley. "I had got the spelling-class up, and the rest of the girls were at their slates and copies, and that, when in he walked amidst the roomful. 'Miss Timmens,' says he to me, in the hearing of them all, 'I think these children should learn a little music. And perhaps a little drawing might not come amiss to those who have talent for it.' 'Oh yes, of course,' says I, hardly able to keep my temper, 'and a little dancing as well, and let 'em go out on the green daily and step their figures to a fife and tambourine!' 'There's nothing like education,' he goes on, staring hard at me, as if he hardly knew whether to take my words for jest or earnest; 'and it is well to unite, as far as we can, the ornamental with the useful, it makes life pleasanter. It is quite right to teach girls to hem dusters and darn stockings, but I think some fancy-work should be added to it: embroidery and the like.' 'Oh, you great baby!' I thought to myself, and did but just stop my tongue from saying it. 'Will embroidery and music and drawing help these girls to scour floors, and cook dinners, and wash petticoats?' I asked him. 'If I had a set of young ladies here, it would be right for them to learn accomplishments; but these girls are to be servants. And all I can say, sir, is, that if ever those new-fangled notions are introduced, you'll have to find another mistress, for I'll not stop to help in it. It would just lead many a girl to her ruin, sir; that's what it would do, whoever lives to see it.' Well, he went away with that, ma'am, but he had put my temper up—talking such dangerous nonsense before the girls, their ears all agape to listen!—and when twelve o'clock struck, I was not half through the spelling-class! Altogether, it's no wonder I brought away the wrong shirt."

Miss Timmens, her errand a failure, began folding up the shirt in a bustle, her thin face quite fiery with anger. Mrs. Todhetley shook her head; she did not approve of nonsensical notions for these poor peasant girls any more than did the rest of us.

"I'll bring up the right shirt this evening when school's over; and if it suits we'll get on with the rest," concluded Miss Timmens, making her exit with the parcel.

"What the world will come to later, Mr. Johnny, if these wild ideas get much ground, puzzles me to think of," resumed Miss Timmens, as I went with her, talking, along the garden-path. "We shall have no servants, sir; none. It does not stand to reason that a girl will work for her bread at menial offices when she has had fine notions instilled into her. Grammar, and geography, and history, and botany, and music, and singing, and fancy-work!—what good will they be of to her in making beds and cleaning saucepans? The upshot will be that they won't make beds and they won't clean saucepans; they'll be above it. The Lord protect 'em!—for I don't see what else will; or what will become of them. Or of the world, either, when it can get no servants. My goodness, Master Johnny! what's that? Surely it's the lost earring?"

Close to the roots of a small fir-tree it lay: the earring that had caused so much vexation and hunting. I picked it up: its pink topaz and diamonds shone brightly as ever in the sun, and were quite uninjured. Mrs. Todhetley remembered then, though it had slipped her memory before, that in coming indoors after the interview with the woman at the gate, she had stopped to shake this fir-tree, bowed down almost to breaking with its weight of snow. The earring must have fallen from her ear then into the snow, and been hidden by it.

Without giving himself time for a mouthful of lunch, the Squire tore away to the station through the mud, as fast as his legs would carry him, and thence to Worcester by train. What an unfortunate mistake it would be should that professional gentleman have been accused, who had bought something from the travelling pedlar!

"Well, Cripp, here's a fine discovery!" panted the Squire, as he went bursting into the police-station and to the presence of Sergeant Cripp. "The lost earring has turned up."

"I'm sure I am very glad to hear it," said the sergeant, facing round from a letter he was writing. "How has it been found?"

And the Squire told him how.

"It was not stolen at all, then?"

"Not at all, Cripp. And the poor creature we suspected of taking it proves to be a very respectable old body indeed, nothing of the tramp about her. You—you have not gone any lengths yet with that professional gentleman, I hope!" added the Squire, dropping his voice to a confidential tone.

Cripp paused for a minute, as if not understanding.

"We have not employed any professional man at all in the matter," said he; "have not thought of doing so."

"I don't mean that, Cripp. You know. The gentleman you suspected of having bought the earring."

Cripp stared. "I have not suspected any one."

"Goodness me! you need not be so cautious, Cripp," returned the Squire, somewhat nettled. "Eccles made a confidant of me. He told me all about it—except the name."

"What Eccles?" asked Cripp. "I really do not know what you are talking of, sir."

"What Eccles—why, your Eccles. Him you sent over to me on Sunday afternoon: a well-dressed, gentlemanly man, with a black moustache. Detective Eccles."

"I do not know any Detective Eccles."

"Dear me, my good man, you must be losing your memory!" retorted the Squire, in wrath. "He came straight to me from you on Sunday; you sent him off in haste without his dinner."

"Quite a mistake, sir," said the sergeant. "It was not I who sent him."

"Why, bless my heart and mind, Cripp, you'll be for telling me next the sun never shone! Where's your recollection gone to?"

"I hope my recollection is where it always has been, Squire. We must be at cross-purposes. I do not know any one of the name of Eccles, and I have not sent any one to you. As a proof that I could not have done it, I may tell you, sir, that I was summoned to Gloucester on business last Friday directly after I saw you, and did not get back here until this morning."

The Squire rubbed his face, whilst he revolved probabilities, and thought Cripp must be dreaming.

"He came direct from you—from yourself, Cripp; and he disclosed to me your reasons for hoping you had found the earring, and your doubts of the honesty of the man who had bought it—the lawyer, you remember. And he brought back the other earring to you that you might compare them."

"Eh—what?" cried Cripp, briskly. "Brought away the other earring, do you say, sir?"

"To be sure he did. What else did you send him for?"

"And he has not returned it to you?"

"Returned it! of course not. You hold it, don't you?"

"Then, Squire Todhetley, you have been cleverly robbed of this second earring," cried Cripp, quietly. "Dodged out of it, sir. The man who went over to you must have been a member of the swell-mob. Well-dressed, and a black moustache!"

"He was a college man, had been at Oxford," debated the unfortunate pater, sitting on a chair in awful doubt. "He told me so."

"You did not see him there, sir," said the sergeant, with a suppressed laugh. "I might tell you I had a duke for a grandmother; but it would be none nearer the fact."

"Mercy upon us all!" groaned the Squire. "What a mortification it will be if that other earring's gone! Don't you think some one in your station here may have sent him, if you were out yourself?"

"I will inquire, for your satisfaction, Squire Todhetley," said the sergeant, opening the door; "but I can answer for it beforehand that it will be useless."

It was as Cripp thought. Eccles was not known at the station, and no one had been sent to us.

"It all comes of that advertisement you put in, Squire," finished up Cripp, by way of consolation. "The swell-mob would not have known there was a valuable jewel missing but for that, or the address of those who had missed it."

The pater came home more crestfallen than a whipped schoolboy, after leaving stringent orders with Cripp and his men to track out the swindler. It was a blow to all of us.

"I said he looked as much like a detective as I'm like a Dutchman," quoth Tod.

"Well, it's frightfully mortifying," said the Squire.

"And the way he polished off that beef, and drank down the ale! I wonder he did not contrive to walk off with the silver tankard!"

"Be quiet, Joe! You are laughing, sir! Do you think it is a laughing matter?"

"Well, I don't know," said bold Tod. "It was cleverly done."

Up rose the pater in a passion. Vowing vengeance against the swindlers who went about the world, got up in good clothes and a moustache; and heartily promising the absent and unconscious Cripp to be down upon him if he did not speedily run the man to earth.

And that's how Mrs. Todhetley lost the other earring.

CHAPTER IX

A TALE OF SIN

Part the First

If I don't relate this quite as usual, and it is found to be different from what I generally write, it is because I know less about it than others know. The history is Duffham's; not mine. And there are diaries in it, and all kinds of foreign things. That is, foreign to me. Duffham holds all the papers, and has lent them to me to use. It came about in this way.

"Whilst you are picking up the sea-breezes, Johnny," he said, when I called to tell him where I was going, "you can be getting on with another paper or two for us, I hope; for we like your stories."

"But I am going away for a rest, Mr. Duffham; not to work. I don't want to be ransacking memory for materials during any holiday, and then weaving them into what you call a story. Much rest that would be!"

"I'll give you the materials for one," he said; "plenty of them: it won't take much weaving; you'll have it all before your eyes. It will be nothing but play-work to you; just a bit of copying."

"But I don't care to put fiction on paper and send it forth as though it were true. What I tell of has mostly happened, you know."

Duffham laughed a little. "If everything told in print were as true as this, Johnny Ludlow, the world would have witnessed some strange events. Not that you'll find anything strange in this tale: it is quite matter-of-fact. There's no romance about it; nothing but stern reality."

"Well, let me see the papers."

Duffham went out of the surgery, and came back with his spectacles on, and carrying some papers tied up with pink tape.

"You'll find a sort of narrative begun, Johnny," he said, untying the tape, "for I tried my own hand at it. But I found I could not get on well. Writing manuscripts is not so much in my line as doctoring patients."

"Why, here's Lady Chavasse's name in it!" I exclaimed, glancing over the papers. "Is it about her?"

"You'll see who it's about and who it's not about, Johnny," he answered, rolling them up again. "I should like you to retain the title I have put to it."

"What is the title?"

Duffham undid the first sheet, and held it in silence for me to read. "A Tale of Sin." It took me aback. Sundry considerations naturally struck me.

"I say, Mr. Duffham, if it is about sin, and the people are still living, how will they like to see it talked about in print?"

"You leave the responsibility to me," he said; "I'll take it on my own shoulders. All you have to do is to put it into ship-shape, Johnny. That is a matter of course."

And so I took the papers. But the tale is Duffham's; not mine.

To begin with, and make it explainable, we have to go ever so many years back: but it won't be for long.

Duffham's predecessor as general practitioner at Church Dykely was a Mr. Layne. Some of the poor would spell it without the "y," "Lane," but the other was the proper way. This Mr. Layne was of rather good family, whilst his wife was only a small working farmer's daughter. Mr. Layne lived in a pretty red-brick house, opposite to Duffham's present residence. It stood a yard or two back from the path, and had woodbines and jessamine creeping up its walls; the door was in the middle, a window on each side; and there was a side-door round the little garden-path, that opened into the surgery. The house was his own.

Nearly a mile beyond the village, along the straight highway, stood the gates and lodge of a fine place called Chavasse Grange, belonging to Sir Peter Chavasse. He remained an old bachelor up to nearly the end of his life. And then, when it seemed to be getting time for him to prepare for the grave, he suddenly got married. The young lady was a Miss Gertrude Cust: as might have been read in the newspapers of the day, announcing the wedding.

But, when Sir Peter brought her home, the wonder to the neighbourhood was, what could have induced the young lady to have him; for she turned out to be a mere child in years, and very beautiful. It was whispered that her family, high, poor, and haughty, had wished her to make a different match; to a broken-down old nobleman, ten times richer than Sir Peter; but that she hated the man. Sir Peter had five thousand a-year, and his baronetcy was not of ancient creation. The new lady was found to be very pleasant: she went into the village often, and made acquaintance with everybody.

It was just about eight months after the marriage that Sir Peter died. The death was sudden. Mr. Layne was sent for in haste to the Grange, and found he was too late. Too late for Sir Peter: but Lady Chavasse, overcome with grief and terror, was in great need of his services.

There was a baby expected at the Grange. Not yet: in three or four months to come. And, until this child should be born, the baronetcy had to lie in abeyance. If it proved to be a boy, he would take his father's title and fortune; if a girl, both title and fortune would lapse to some distant cousin; a young man, compared with Sir Peter; who was in the navy, and was called Parker Chavasse.

And now we must give a line or two from one of the diaries I spoke of. It is Mr. Layne's: and it appears to have been partly kept as a professional note-book, partly as a private journal. At this time Mr. Layne was a middle-aged man, with three young children, girls; he had married later than some men do.

[From an Old Note-book of Mr. Layne's.]

May 18th.—Have had a fatiguing day. Upon getting home from my visit to Lady Chavasse, there were five different messages waiting for me. It never rains but it pours. Ten o'clock P.M., and I am dead tired; but I must write my notes before going to bed.

I wish I could get some strength and spirit into Lady Chavasse. This listlessness tells sadly against her. Over and over again it has been on the tip of my tongue to say it may go hard with her unless she uses more exertion; but I don't like to frighten her. Nearly four months now since Sir Peter died, and she has never been out but to church—and to that she goes in the pony-carriage. "My lady, you ought to walk; my lady, you must walk," say I. And it is just as though I spoke to the post at the lodge-gates.

I was much surprised by what she told me to-day—that there was no settlement made on her at her marriage. "Do you think my baby will be a boy, Mr. Layne?" she asked—as if it were possible for me to tell! "If it is not," she went on, "I shall have to turn out of my home here, and I have not another to go to in the wide world." And then it was, seeing my surprise, that she said there had been no settlement. "It was not my husband's intentional fault," she continued, "and I will never have him blamed, come what will. Things were unpleasant at my home, and we hurried on the marriage, he and I, so that he might take me out of it, and there was no time to get a settlement drawn up, even had we, either of us, thought of it, which we did not." Listening to this, the notion struck me that it must have been something like a runaway marriage; but I said nothing, only bade her take heart and hope for a boy. "I cannot imagine any lot in life now so delightful as this would be—that I and my baby-boy should live on in this charming place together—I training him always for good," she continued—and a faint pink came into her delicate cheek as she said it, a yearning look into her hazel eyes. "You would help me to keep him in health and make him strong, would you not, Mr. Layne?" I answered that I would do my best. Poor thing! she was only eighteen yesterday, she told me. I hope she'll be able to keep the place; I hope it won't go over her head to rough Parker Chavasse. And a rough-mannered man he is: I saw him once.

Coming home I met Thompson. The lawyer stopped, ever ready for a chat. I spoke about this expected child, and the changes its arrival might make. "It's quite true that Lady Chavasse would have to turn out," said he. "Every individual shilling is entailed. Books, plate, carriages—it all goes with the title. I'm not sure but Sir Peter's old clothes have to be thrown in too, so strict is the entail. No settlement on her, you say, Layne? My good fellow, old Peter had nothing to settle. He had spent his income regularly, and there lay nothing beyond it. I've heard that that was one of the reasons why the Custs objected to the match." Well, it seemed a curious position: I thought so as Thompson went off; but I don't understand law, and can take his word for it. And now to bed. If—

What's that? A carriage drawing up to the house, and the night-bell! I am wanted somewhere as sure as a gun, and my night's rest is stopped, I suppose. Who'd be a doctor? Listen! There's my wife opening the street-door. What does she call out to me? Lady Chavasse not well? A carriage waiting to take me to the Grange? Thank fortune at least that I have not to walk there.

May 22nd.—Four days, and nothing noted down. But I have been very busy, what with Lady Chavasse and other patients. The doubt is over, and over well. The little child is a boy, and a nice little fellow, too; healthy, and likely to live. He was born on the 20th. Lady Chavasse, in her gladness, says she shall get well all one way. I think she will: the mind strangely influences the body. But my lady is a little hard— what some might call unforgiving. Her mother came very many miles, posting across country, to see her and be reconciled, and Lady Chavasse refused to receive her. Mrs. Cust had to go back again as she came. I should not like to see my wife treat her mother so.

May 30th.—The child is to be named Geoffry Arthur. Sir Peter had a dislike to his own name, and had said he hoped never to call a boy of his by the same. Lady Chavasse, mindful of his every wish, has fixed on the other two. I asked her if they were the names of relatives: she laughed and said, No; she chose them because she thought them both nice-sounding and noble names.

The above is all that need be copied from Mr. Layne: one has to be chary of space. Little Sir Geoffry grew and thrived: and it was a pleasure, people say, to see how happy his mother and he were, and how she devoted herself to him. He had come to her in the midst of her desolation, when she had nothing else to care for in life. It was already seen that he would be much like his father, who had been a very good-looking man in his day. Little Geoffry had Sir Peter's fair complexion and his dark-blue eyes. He was a sweet, tractable child; and Lady Chavasse thought him just an angel come down from heaven.

Time went on. When Geoffry was about seven years old—and a very pretty boy, with fair curls—he went out surreptitiously on a fishing expedition, fell into the pond, and was nearly drowned. It left a severe cold upon him, which his nurse, Wilkins, said served him right. However, from that time he seemed to be less strong; and at length Lady Chavasse took him to London to show him to the doctors. The doctors told her he ought to be, for a time, in a warmer climate: and she went with him into Devonshire. But he still kept delicate. And the upshot was that Lady Chavasse let the Grange for a long term to the Goldingham family, and went away.

And so, many years passed. The Goldinghams lived on at the Grange: and Lady Chavasse nearly slipped out of remembrance. Mr. Layne fell into ill health as he grew older, and advertised for a partner. It was Duffham who answered it (a youngish man then) and they went into arrangements.

It is necessary to say something of Mr. Layne's children. There were four of them, girls. The eldest, Susan, married a Lieutenant Layne (some distant relative, who came from the West Indies), and went with him to India, where his regiment was serving, taking also her next sister, Eleanor. The third, Elizabeth, was at home; the young one, Mary, born several years after the others, was in a school as governess-pupil, or under-teacher. It is not often that village practitioners can save money, let alone make a fortune.

The next thing was, that Mr. Layne died. His death made all the difference to his family. Mr. Duffham succeeded to the practice; by arrangement he was to pay something yearly for five years to Mrs. Layne; and she had a small income of her own. She would not quit the house; it was hers now her husband was gone. Mr. Duffham took one opposite: a tall house, with a bow-window to the parlour: before that, he had been in apartments. Mary Layne came home about this time, and stayed there for some weeks. She had been much overworked in the school, and Mrs. Layne thought she required rest. She was a pleasing girl, with soft brown eyes and a nice face, and was very good and gentle; thinking always of others, never of self. Old Duffham may choose to deny it now he's grown older, but he thought her superior then to the whole world.

Matters were in this state when news spread that the Goldinghams had received notice to quit the Grange: Sir Geoffry, who would be of age the following year, was coming home to it with his mother. Accordingly the Goldinghams departed; and the place was re-embellished and put in order for the rightful owner. He arrived in April with Lady Chavasse: and I'll copy for you what Duffham says about it. Mr. Layne had then been dead about two years.

[From Mr. Duffham's Diary.]

April 29th.—The new people—or I suppose I ought to say the old people—reached the Grange yesterday, and I was called in to-day to the lady's-maid—Wilkins. My lady I don't like; Sir Geoffry I do. He is a good-looking, slight young man of middle height, with a fair refined face and honest eyes, blue as they tell me Sir Peter's used to be. An honourable, well-intentioned young fellow I am sure; affable and considerate as his mother is haughty. Poor Layne used to cry her up; he thought great things of her. I do not. It may be that power has made her selfish, and foreign travel imperious; but she's both selfish and imperious now. She is nice-looking still; and though she wants but a year of forty, and her son is only one-and-twenty, they are almost like brother and sister. Or would be, but for Sir Geoffry's exceeding consideration for his mother; his love and deference for her are a pattern to the young men of the present day. She has trained him to be obedient, that's certain, and to love her too: and so I suppose she has done her duty by him well. He came down the broad walk with me from the hall-door, talking of his mother: I had happened to say that the place must seem quite strange to Lady Chavasse. "Yes, it must," he answered. "She has exiled herself from it for my sake. Mr. Duffham," he continued warmly, "you cannot imagine what an admirable mother mine has been! She resigned ease, rest, society, to devote herself to me. She gave me a home-tutor, that she might herself watch over and train me; she went to and fro between England and foreign places with me everlastingly; even when I was at Oxford, she took a house a mile or two out, that we might not be quite separated. I pray Heaven constantly that I may never cross her in thought, word, or deed: but live only to repay her love." Rather Utopian this: but I honour the young fellow for it. I've only seen him for an hour at most, and am already wishing there were more like him in the world. If his mother has faults, he does not see them; he will never honour any other woman as he honours her. A contrast, this, to the contempt, ingratitude, and disrespect that some sons think it manly to show their best and truest earthly parent.

My lady is vexed, I can see, at this inopportune illness of her maid's; for the Grange is all upside down with the preparations for the grand fête to be held on the 20th of next month, when Sir Geoffry will come of age. Wilkins has been in the family for many years: she was originally the boy's nurse: and is quite the right hand of Lady Chavasse, so far as household management goes. Her illness just now is inopportune.

[End, for the present, of Mr. Duffham's Diary.]

Nothing was talked of, in the village or out of it, but the grand doings that were to usher in the majority of Sir Geoffry. As to Lady Chavasse, few people had seen her. Her maid's illness, as was supposed, kept her indoors; and some of the guests were already arriving at the Grange.

One morning, when it wanted about a week to the 20th, Mrs. Layne, making a pillow-case at her parlour window, in her widow's cap and spectacles, with the Venetian blind open to get all the light she could, was startled by seeing Lady Chavasse's barouche draw up to her door, and Lady Chavasse preparing to descend from it. Mrs. Layne instinctively rose, as to a superior, and took her glasses off: it has been said she was of a humble turn: and upon Lady Chavasse fixing her eyes upon her in what seemed some surprise, dropped a curtsy, and thought to herself how fortunate it was she happened to have put a clean new cap on. With that, Lady Chavasse said something to the footman, who banged the carriage-door to, and ordered the coachman across the road. Mrs. Layne understood it at once: she had come to the house in mistake for Duffham's. Of course, with that grand carriage to look at opposite, and the gorgeous servants, and my lady, in a violet velvet mantle trimmed with ermine, alighting and stepping in to Duffham's, Mrs. Layne let fall her pillow-case, and did no more of it. But she was not prepared, when Lady Chavasse came out again with Mr. Duffham, to see him escort her over the road to her gate. Mrs. Layne had just time to open her parlour-door, and say to the servant, "In the other room: show her ladyship into the other room," before she went off into complete bewilderment, and ran away with the pillow-case.

The other room was the best room. Mary Layne sat there at the old piano, practising. She had seen and heard nothing of all this; and rose in astonishment when the invasion took place. A beautiful lady, whom Mary did not know or recognize, was holding out a delicately-gloved hand to her, and saying that she resembled her father. It was Mary Layne's first meeting with Lady Chavasse: she had just come home again from some heavy place of teaching, finding her strength unequal to it.

"I should have known you, I think, for a daughter of Mr. Layne's had I met you in the street," said Lady Chavasse, graciously.

Mary was blushing like anything. Lady Chavasse thought her an elegant girl, in spite of the shabby black silk she was dressed in: very pretty too. At least, it was a nice countenance; and my lady quite took to it. Mrs. Layne, having collected her wits, and taken off her apron, came in then: and Mary, who was humble-minded also, though not exactly in the same way that her mother was, modestly retired.

My lady was all graciousness: just as much so that morning as she used to be. Perhaps the sight of Mrs. Layne put her in mind of the old days when she was herself suffering trouble in a widow's cap, and not knowing how matters would turn out for her, or how they would not. She told Mrs. Layne that she had, unthinkingly, bid her servants that morning drive to Mr. Layne's! and it was only when she saw Mrs. Layne at the window in her widow's cap, that she remembered the mistake. She talked of her son Geoffry, praising his worth and his goodness; she bade Mrs. Layne to the fête on the 20th, saying she must come and bring her two daughters, and she would take no denial. And Mrs. Layne, curtsying again—which did not become her, for she was short and stout—opened the front-door to her ladyship with her own hands, and stood there curtsying until the carriage had dashed away.

"We'll go on the 20th," she said to her daughters. "I didn't like to say nay to her ladyship; and I should be glad to see what the young heir's like. He was as pretty a boy as you'd wish to see. There'll no doubt be some people there of our own condition that we can mix with, and it will be in the open air: so we shan't feel strange."

But when the day arrived, and they had reached the Grange, it seemed that they felt very strange. Whether amidst the crowds they did not find any of their "own condition," or that none were there, Mrs. Layne did not know. Once, they came near Lady Chavasse. Lady Chavasse, surrounded by a bevy of people that Mrs. Layne took to be lords and ladies—and perhaps she was right—bowed distantly, and waved her hand, as much as to say, "Make yourselves at home, but don't trouble me:" and Mrs. Layne curtsyed herself to a respectful distance. It was a fine bright day, very warm; and she sat on a bench in the park with her daughters, listening to the band, looking at the company, and wondering which was the heir. Some hours seemed to pass in this way, and gradually the grounds grew deserted. People were eating and drinking in a distant tent—the lords and ladies Mrs. Layne supposed, and she did not presume to venture amongst them. Presently a young man approached, who had observed from a distance the solitary group. A fat old lady in widow's mourning; and the younger ones in pretty white bonnets and new black silks.

"Will you allow me to take you where you will find some refreshment?" he said, raising his hat, and addressing Mrs. Layne.

She paused before answering, taken aback by his looks, as she described it afterwards, for he put her in mind of Sir Peter. It was as nice a face as Sir Peter's used to be, clean-shaved, except for the light whiskers: and if those were not Sir Peter's kindly blue eyes, why, her memory failed her. But the dress puzzled Mrs. Layne: he wore a dark-blue frock-coat and grey trousers, a white waistcoat with a thin gold chain passed across it and a drooping seal: all very nice and gentlemanly certainly, but quite plain. What she had expected to see the heir attired in, Mrs. Layne never afterwards settled with herself: perhaps purple and miniver.

"I beg your pardon sir," she said, speaking at length, "but I think you must be Sir Geoffry?"

"Yes, I am Sir Geoffry."

"Lord bless me!" cried Mrs. Layne.

She told him who she was, adding, as an apology for being found there, that her ladyship had invited her and her girls, and wouldn't take a denial. Geoffry held out his arm cordially to lead her to the tent, and glanced behind at the "girls," remembering what his mother had said to him of one of them: "a sweet-looking young woman, Geoffry, poor Layne's daughter, quite an elegant girl." Yes, she was sweet-looking and elegant also, Geoffry decided. The elder one was like her mother, short, stout, and—Geoffry could not help seeing it—commonplace. He told Mrs. Layne that he could remember her husband still: he spoke of a ride the doctor had taken him, seated before him on his horse; and altogether in that short minute or two won, by his true affability, the heart of the doctor's widow.

The tent was crowded to confusion. Waiters were running about, and there was much rattle of knives and forks. Sir Geoffry could find only two places anywhere; at which he seated Mrs. Layne and her daughter Elizabeth, according to precedence.

"I will find you a place in the other tent, if you will come with me," he said to Mary.

She wished to refuse. She had a suspicion that the other tent was the one for the "lords and ladies," people who were altogether above her. But Sir Geoffry was holding up the canvas for her to pass out, and she was too timid to disobey. He walked by her side almost in silence, speaking a courteous word or two only, to put her at her ease. The band was playing "The Roast Beef of Old England."

But the other tent seemed in worse confusion as far as crowding went. Some one turned on her seat to accost Sir Geoffry: a slight, upright girl, with finely-carved features of that creamy white rarely seen, and a haughty expression in her very light eyes.

"You are being waited for, Geoffry. Don't you know that you preside?"

"No; nonsense!" he answered. "There's to be nothing of that sort, Rachel; no presiding. I am going to walk about and look out for stray people. Some of the strangers will get nothing, if they are not seen after. Could you make room for one by you?"

"Who is it?" she asked.

Sir Geoffry said a word in her ear, and she moved a few inches higher up. He stepped back to Mary Layne. She had been looking at the young lady, who was so richly dressed—in some thin material of shimmering blue and lace—and who was so utterly at her ease as to be sitting without her bonnet, which she had put at her feet.

"We have made a place for you," said Sir Geoffry. "I fear you will be a little crowded. Miss Layne, Rachel."

Mary waited to thank him before taking it. Her cheeks were full of blushes, her soft dark eyes went out to his. She felt ashamed that he should take so much trouble for her, and strove to say so. Sir Geoffry held her hand while he answered, his own eyes looking back again.

But Mary sat for some minutes before any one came to wait on her. The young lady whom Sir Geoffry had called Rachel was busy with her own plate, and did not observe. Presently, she looked round.

"Dear me! what are they about? Field!" she imperatively called to the butler, who was passing. He turned at once.

"My lady?"

"Have the goodness to attend here," said Lady Rachel, indicating the vacant space before Miss Layne. "This young lady has had nothing."

"So I really am amidst the lords and ladies," thought Mary, as the butler presented her with a card of the dishes, made out in French, and inquired what she would be pleased to take. She was inexperienced and shy; and did not know where to look or what to say. Lady Rachel spoke to her once or twice, and was civilly distant: and so the half-hour was got over. When Sir Geoffry's health was proposed by Lord L., the young baronet suddenly appeared in his rightful place at the head of the table. He thanked them all very heartily in a few words; and said he hoped he should live long, as they had all just been wishing him, live that he might repay his dear mother one tithe of the sacrifices she had made, and the love she had lavished on him.

The cheers broke forth as he finished, his eyes wet with the sincerity of his feeling, the music burst out with a crash, "See the conquering hero comes," and Mary Layne felt every nerve thrill within her; as if she would faint with the excess of unwonted emotion.

[Mr. Duffham's Diary.]

June 2nd.—The rejoicings are well over, and Sir Geoffry Chavasse is his own master. In law, at any rate; but it strikes me he will never know any will but his mother's. It's not that he possesses none of his own—rather the contrary, I fancy; but in his filial love and reverence he merges it in hers. It is, on the one hand, good to see; on the other, one can but fancy his ideal of the fifth commandment is somewhat exaggerated. Lady Chavasse on her part seems bound up in him. To him there is no sign of imperiousness, no assertion of self-will: and, so far as can be seen, she does not exact deference. "Geoffry, would you wish this?" she says. "Geoffry, would you like the other? My darling Geoffry, don't you think it might be well to do so-and-so?" No. It is a case of genuine filial respect and love; and one can but honour Lady Chavasse for have gained it.

My lady has condescended to be almost confidential with me. The illness of her maid has been a long and serious one, and I have had to be a good deal at the Grange. "Sir Geoffry is engaged to be married, Mr. Duffham," she said to me yesterday, when our conversation had turned—as it often does turn—on Sir Geoffry. I could not help showing some surprise: and, one word leading to another, I soon grasped the whole case. Not so much by what she directly said, as by the habit I have of putting two-and-two together.

Conspicuous amidst the guests at the fête on the 20th of May, was Lady Rachel Derreston: a cold, self-possessed girl, with strictly classical features, and the palest blue eyes I ever saw. It would be a very handsome face—and indeed is so—but for its cold, proud expression; she is the daughter of one of Lady Chavasse's sisters, who married the Earl of Derreston, and is now a very slenderly-portioned widow with some expensive daughters. It is to this Lady Rachel that Sir Geoffry is engaged. The engagement is not of his own seeking, or of hers; the two mothers settled it between them when the children were young; they have been brought up to look on each other as future husband and wife, and have done so as a matter-of-course. Neither of them, by what I can gather, has the slightest intention, or wish, to turn aside from fulfilling the contract: they will ratify it in just the same business manner and with the same calm feelings that they would take the lease of a house. It is not their fault: they should not have been led into it. Human nature is cross and contrary as a crab: had the two young people been thrown together now for the first time, and been warned not to fall in love with each other, the chances are they would have tumbled headlong into it before the week was out: as it is, they like each other as cousins, or brother and sister, but they'll never get beyond that. I can see. The two old sisters have a private understanding with each other—and my young Lady Rachel dutifully falls in with it—that after the marriage Lady Chavasse shall still live and rule at the Grange. Indeed she implied it when she let fall the words, perhaps unthinkingly—"Geoffry would never marry to put me out of my home here, Mr. Duffham." And I am sure that he never would.

Lady Rachel is here still. I often see her and Sir Geoffry together, indoors or out; but I have never yet seen a symptom of courtship on either side. They call each other "Geoffry" and "Rachel;" and are as indifferently familiar as brother and sister. That they will be sufficiently happy with a quiet, moonlight kind of happiness, is almost sure. I find that I am not at liberty to mention this engagement abroad: and that's why I say my lady has grown confidential with me.

June 29th.—Wilkins continues very ill; and it puts my lady about amazingly. The maid who has been taking Wilkins's duties, Hester Picker, is a country girl of the locality, Goody Picker's daughter; her services being as different from those of the easy, experienced Wilkins, as darkness is from light. "She manages my hair atrociously," cried my lady to me, one day, in her vexation; "she attempted to write a note for me in answer to inquiries for the character of my late page, and the spelling was so bad it could not be sent."

Lady Rachel has left. Sir Geoffry escorted her to her home (near Bath), stayed two days there, and came back again. And glad to be back, evidently: he does not care to be long separated from his mother. The more I see of this young fellow, the more I like him. He has no bad habits; does not smoke or swear: reads, rides, drives, loves flowers, and is ever ready to do a good turn for rich or poor. "You appear to have grown up quite strong, Sir Geoffry," I said to him to-day when we were in the greenhouse, and he leaped on a ledge to do something or other to the broken cord of the window. "Oh, quite," he answered. "I think I am stronger and heartier than most men: and I owe thanks for it to my mother. It was not only my health of body she cared for and watched over, but of mind. She taught me to love rational pursuits; she showed me how to choose the good, and reject the evil: it is she alone who has made me what I am."

July 5th.—Mary Layne is going to the Grange as companion to Lady Chavasse. "Humble companion," as my lady takes care to put it. It has been brought about in this way. Wilkins is slightly improving: but it will be months before she can resume her duties about Lady Chavasse: and my lady has at length got this opinion out of me. "Five or six months!" she exclaimed in dismay. "But it is only what I have lately suspected. Mr. Duffham, I have been thinking that I must take a companion; and now this has confirmed it. A humble companion, who will not object to do my hair on state occasions, and superintend Picker in trimming my dresses, especially the lace; and who will write notes for me when I desire it, and read to me when Sir Geoffry's not here; and sit with me if I wish it. She wouldn't dine with us, of course; but I might sometimes let her sit down to luncheon. In short, what I want is a well-educated, lady-like young woman, who will make herself useful. Do you happen to know of one?"

I mentioned Mary Layne. She has been wishing not to return to the heavy work and confinement of a school, where she had to sit up late, night after night, correcting exercises, and touching up drawings by gas-light. My lady caught at it at once. "Mary Layne! the very thing. I like the look of the girl much, Mr. Duffham; and of course she won't be above doing anything required of her: Layne, the apothecary's daughter, cannot be called a gentlewoman in position, you know."

She forgot I was an apothecary also; I'll give her that credit. But this is a specimen of the way my lady's exclusive spirit peeps out.

And so it is settled. And if Miss Mary had been suddenly offered a position in the Royal household, she could not have thought more of it. "Mr. Duffham, I will try my very best to satisfy Lady Chavasse," says she to me, in an ecstasy; "I will do anything and everything required of me: who am I, that I should be above it?" And by the glistening of her sweet brown eyes, and the rose-blush on her cheeks, it would seem that she fancies she is going into fairy-land. Well, the Grange is a nice place: and she is to have thirty guineas a-year. At the last school she had twenty pounds: at the first ten.

[End of the Diary for the present.]

Miss Layne entered the Grange with trepidation. She had never been inside the house, and at first thought it was fairy-land realized and that she was out of place in it. A broad flight of three or four steps led up to the wide entrance-door; the brilliant colours from the painted windows shone on the mosaic pavement of the hall; on the right were the grand drawing-rooms; on the left the dining-room and Sir Geoffry's library. Behind the library, going down a step or two was a low, shady apartment, its glass doors opening to a small grass plat, round which flowers were planted; and beyond it lay the fragrant herbary. This little room was called the garden-room; and on the morning of Miss Layne's arrival, after she had taken off her things, Hester Picker (who thought almost as much of the old surgeon's daughter as she did of my lady) curtsyed her into it, and said it was to be Miss Layne's sitting-room, when she was not with my lady.

Mary Layne looked around. She thought it charming. It had an old Turkey carpet, and faded red chairs, and a shabby checked cloth on the table, with other ancient furniture; but the subdued light was grateful after the garish July sun, and a sweetness came in from the herbs and flowers. Mary stood, wondering what she had to do first, and not quite daring to sit down even on one of the old red chairs. The Grange was the Grange, and my lady was my lady; and they were altogether above the sphere in which she had been brought up. She had a new lilac muslin dress on, fresh and simple; her smooth brown hair had a bit of lilac ribbon in it; and she looked as pretty and ladylike as a girl can look. Standing at the back, there beyond the able, was she, when Sir Geoffry walked in at the glass doors, his light summer coat thrown back, and a heap of small paper packets in his hands, containing seeds. At first he looked astonished: not remembering her.

"Oh, I beg your pardon!" he exclaimed, his face lighting up, as he took off his straw hat. "Miss Mary Layne, I think. I did not know you at the moment. My mother said she expected you to-day."

He came round to her with outstretched hand, and then put a chair for her, just as though she had been a duchess—or Lady Rachel Derreston. Mary did not take the chair: she felt strange in her new home, and as yet very timid.

"I am not sure what Lady Chavasse would wish me to do," she ventured to say, believing it might be looked upon as next door to a crime to be seen idle, in a place where she was to receive thirty guineas a-year. "There appears to be no work here."

"Get a book, and read!" cried Sir Geoffry. "I'll find you one as soon as I have put up these seeds. A box of new novels has just come from town. I hope you will make yourself at home with us, and be happy," he added, in his kindness.

"Thank you, sir; I am sure I shall."

He was putting up the seeds, when Lady Chavasse entered. She had a way of taking likes and dislikes, and she never scrupled to show either. On this first day, it seemed that she did not know how to make enough of Mary. She chose to forget that she was only to be the humble companion, and treated her as a guest. She carried her in to take luncheon with herself and Sir Geoffry; she made her play and sing; she showed her the drawing-rooms and the flower-gardens, and finally took her out in the barouche. She certainly did not ask her in to dinner, but said she should expect her to come to the drawing-room afterwards, and spend the evening. And Miss Layne, not ignorant of the customs obtaining in great houses, dressed herself for it in her one evening dress of white spotted muslin, and changed the lilac ribbon in her hair for blue.

So that, you perceive, the girl was inaugurated at the Grange as a young lady, almost as an equal, and not as a servant—as Lady Chavasse's true opinion would have classed her. That was mistake the first. For it led Sir Geoffry to make a companion of Miss Layne; that is, to treat her as though she belonged to their order; which otherwise he certainly would not have done. Had Miss Layne been assigned her true place at first—the place that Lady Chavasse meant her to fill, that of an inferior and humble dependent—Sir Geoffry, out of simple respect to the girl and to his mother, would have kept his distance.

As the time passed on they grew great friends. Lady Chavasse retained her liking for Mary, and saw no harm in the growing intimacy with Sir Geoffry. That was mistake the second. Both of them were drifting into love; but Lady Chavasse dreamt it not. The social gulf that spread itself between Sir Geoffry Chavasse, of Chavasse Grange, and Mary Layne, daughter of the late hard-worked village apothecary, was one that Lady Chavasse would have said (had she been asked to think about it) could never be bridged over: and for this very reason she saw no danger in the intercourse. She regarded Mary Layne as of a totally different caste from themselves, and never supposed but Sir Geoffry did so too.

And so time went on, on the wings of love. There were garden walks together and moonlight saunterings; meetings in my lady's presence, meetings without it. Sir Geoffry, going in and out of the garden-parlour at will, as he had been accustomed to do—for it was where all kinds of things belonging to him were kept: choice seeds, his fishing-rods, his collection of butterflies—would linger there by the hour together, talking to Mary at her work. And, before either of them was conscious of the danger, they had each passed into a dream that changed everything about them to Paradise.

Of course, Sir Geoffry, when he awoke to the truth—that it was love—ought to have gone away, or have contrived to get his mother to dismiss Miss Layne. He did nothing of the sort. And for this, some people—Duffham for one—held him even more to blame than for anything that happened afterwards. But how could he voluntarily blight his new happiness, and hers? It was so intense as to absorb every other feeling; it took his common sense away from him. And thus they went dreaming on together in that one spring-time (of the heart, not of the weather), and never thought about drifting into shoals and pitfalls.

In the autumn my lady went to the seaside in Cornwall, taking Mary as her maid, and escorted by her son. "Will you do for me what I want while I am away? I do not care to be troubled with Picker," she had said; and Mary replied, as in duty bound, that she would. It is inconvenient to treat a maid as a lady, especially in a strange place, and Mary found that during this sojourn Lady Chavasse did not attempt it. To all intents and purposes Mary was the maid now; she did not sit with her lady, she took her meals apart; she was, in fact, regarded as the lady's-maid by all, and nothing else. Lady Chavasse even took to calling her "Layne." This, the sudden dethroning of her social status, was the third mistake; and this one, as the first, was my lady's. Sir Geoffry had been led to regard her as a companion; now he saw her but as a servant. But, servant or no servant, you cannot put love out of the heart, once it has possession of it.

At the month's end they returned home: and there Mary found that she was to retain this lower station: never again would she be exalted as she had been. Lady Chavasse had tired of the new toy, and just carelessly allowed her to find her own level. Except that Miss Layne sat in the garden-parlour, and her meals were served there, she was not very much distinguished from Hester Picker and the other servants; indeed, Picker sometimes sat in the parlour too, when they had lace, or what not, to mend for my lady. Geoffry in his heart was grieved at the changed treatment of Miss Layne; he thought it wrong and unjust; and to make up for the mistake, was with her a great deal himself.

Things were in this position when Lady Chavasse was summoned to Bath: her sister, Lady Derreston, was taken ill. Sir Geoffry escorted her thither. Picker was taken, not Miss Layne. In the countess's small household, Mary, in her anomalous position—for she could not be altogether put with the servants—would have been an inconvenience; and my lady bade her make herself happy at the Grange, and left her a lot of fine needlework to get through.

Leaving his mother in Bath, Sir Geoffry went to London, stayed a week or so, and then came back to the Grange. Another week or two, and he returned to Bath to bring his mother home. And so the winter set in, and wore on. And now all that has to be told to the paper's end is taken from diaries, Duffham's and others. But for convenience' sake, I put it as though the words were my own, instead of copying them literally.

Spring came in early. February was not quite at an end, and the trees were beginning to show their green. All the month it had been warm weather; but people said it was too relaxing for the season, and they and the trees should suffer for it later. A good deal of sickness was going about; and, amongst others who had to give in for a time, was Duffham himself. He had inflammation of the lungs. His brother Luke, who was partner in a medical firm elsewhere, came to Church Dykely for a week or two, to take the patients. Luke was a plain-speaking man of forty, with rough hair and a good heart.

The afternoon after he arrived, an applicant came into the surgery with her daughter. It was Mrs. Layne, but the temporary doctor did not know her. Mrs. Layne never did look like a lady, and he did not mistake her for one: he thought it some respectable countrywoman: she had flung a very ancient cloak over her worn morning gown. She expressed herself disappointed at not seeing Mr. Duffham, but opened the consultation with the brother instead. Mrs. Layne took it for granted she was known, and talked accordingly.

Her daughter, whom she kept calling Mary, and nothing else, had been ailing lately; she, Mrs. Layne, could not think what was the matter with her, unless it was the unusually warm spring. She grew thinner and weaker daily; her cheeks were pale, her eyes seemed to have no life in them: she was very low in spirits; yet, in spite of all this, Mary had kept on saying it was "nothing." My Lady Chavasse—returning home from London yesterday, whither she had accompanied her son a week or two ago, and whom she had left there—was so much struck with the change she saw in Mary, who lived with her as humble companion, Mrs. Layne added, in a parenthesis, that she insisted on her seeing Dr. Duffham, that he might prescribe some tonics. And accordingly Mary had walked to her mother's this afternoon.

Mr. Luke Duffham listened to all this with one ear, as it were. He supposed it might be the warm spring, as suggested. However, he took Mary into the patients' room, and examined her; felt her pulse, looked at her tongue, sounded her chest, with all the rest of it that doctors treat their clients to; and asked her this, that, and the other—about five-and-twenty questions, when perhaps five might have done. The upshot of it all was that Mary Layne went off in a dead faint.

"What on earth can be the matter with her?" cried the alarmed mother, when they had brought her round.

Mr. Luke Duffham, going back to the surgery with Mrs. Layne, shut the doors, and told her what he thought it was. It so startled the old lady that she backed against the counter and upset the scales.

"How dare you say so, sir!"

"But I am sure of it," returned Mr. Luke.

"Lord be good to me!" gasped Mrs. Layne, looking like one terrified out of her seven senses. "The worst I feared was that it might be consumption. A sister of mine died of it."

"Where shall I send the medicine to?" inquired the doctor.

"Anywhere. Over the way, if you like," continued Mrs. Layne, in her perturbation.

"Certainly. Where to, over the way?"

"To my house. Don't you know me? I am the widow of your brother's late partner. This unhappy child is the one he was fondest of; she is only nineteen, much younger than the rest."

"Mrs. Layne!" thought Luke Duffham, in surprise, "I wish I had known; I might have hesitated before speaking plainly. But where would have been the good?"

The first thing Mrs. Layne did, was to shut her own door against Mary, and send her back to the Grange in a shower of anger. She was an honest old lady, of most irreproachable character; never needing, as she phrased it, to have had a blush on her cheek, for herself or any one belonging to her. In her indignation, she could have crushed Mary to the earth. Whatever it might be that the poor girl had done, robbed a church, or shot its parson, her mother deemed that she deserved hanging.

Mary Layne walked back to the Grange: where else had she to go? Broken-hearted, humiliated, weak almost unto death, she was as a reed in her mother's hands, yielding herself to any command given; and only wishing she might die. Lady Chavasse, compassionating her evident suffering, brought her a glass of wine with her own hand, and inquired what Mr. Duffham said, and whether he was going to give her tonics. Instead of answering, Mary went into another faint: and my lady thought she had overwalked herself. "I wish I had sent her in the carriage," said she kindly. And while the wish was yet upon her lips, Mrs. Layne arrived at the Grange, to request an audience of her ladyship.

Then was commotion. My lady talked and stormed, Mrs. Layne talked and cried. Both were united in one thing—heaping reproaches on Mary. They were in the grand drawing-room—where my lady had been sitting when Mrs. Layne was shown in. Lady Chavasse sat back, furious and scornful, in her pink velvet chair; Mrs. Layne stood; Mary had sunk on the carpet kneeling, her face bent, her clasped hands raised as if imploring mercy. This group was suddenly broken in upon by Sir Geoffry—who had but then reached the Grange from town. They were too noisy to notice him. Halting in dismay he had the pleasure of catching a sentence or two addressed to the unhappy Mary.

"The best thing you can do is to find refuge in the workhouse," stormed Lady Chavasse. "Out of my house you turn this hour."

"The best thing you can do is to go on the tramp, where you won't be known," amended Mrs. Layne, who was nearly beside herself with conflicting emotions. "Never again shall you enter the home that was your poor dead father's. You wicked girl!—and you hardly twenty years old yet! But, my lady, I can but think—though I know we are humble people, as compared with you, and perhaps I've no right to say it—that Sir Geoffry has not behaved like a gentleman."

"Hold your tongue, woman," said her ladyship. "Sir Geoffry—"

"Sir Geoffry is at least enough of a gentleman to take his evil deeds on himself, and not shift them on to others," spoke the baronet, stepping forward—and the unexpected interruption was startling to them all. My lady pointed imperatively to the door, but he stood his ground.

It was no doubt a bitter moment for him; bringing home to him an awful amount of self-humiliation: for throughout his life he had striven to do right instead of wrong. And when these better men yield to temptation instead of fleeing from it, the reacting sting is of the sharpest. The wisest and strongest sometimes fall: and find too late that, though the fall was so easy, the picking-up is of all things most difficult. Sir Geoffry's face was white as death.

"Get up, Mary," he said gently, taking her hand to help her in all respect. "Mrs. Layne," he added, turning to face the others; "my dear mother—if I may dare still to call you so—suffer me to say a word. For all that has taken place, I am alone to blame; on me only must it rest, The fault—"

"Sin, sir," interrupted Mrs. Layne.

"Yes. Thank you. Sin. The sin lies with me, not with Mary. In my presence reproach shall not be visited on her. She has enough trouble to bear without that. I wish to Heaven that I had never—Mrs. Layne, believe me," he resumed, after the pause, "no one can feel this more keenly than I. And, if circumstances permit me to make reparation, I will make it!"

Sir Geoffry wanted (circumstances permitting, as he shortly put it) to marry Mary Layne; he wished to do it. Taking his mother into another room he told her this. Lady Chavasse simply thought him mad. She grew a little afraid of him, lest he should set her and all high rules of propriety at nought, and do it.

But trouble like this cannot be settled in an hour. Lady Chavasse, in her great fear, conciliated just a little: she did not turn Miss Layne out at once, as threatened, but suffered her to remain at the Grange for the night.

"In any case, whatever may be the ending of this, it is not from my family that risk of exposure must come," spoke Sir Geoffry, in a tone of firmness. "It might leave me no alternative."

"No alternative?" repeated Lady Chavasse. "How?"

"Between my duty to you, and my duty to her," said Sir Geoffry. And my lady's heart fainted within her at the suggested fear.

They were together in the library at Chavasse Grange, Lady Chavasse and her only son Geoffry. It was early morning; they had sat in the breakfast-room making a show of partaking of the morning meal, each of them with that bitter trouble at the heart that had been known only—to my lady, at least—since the previous day. But the farce of speaking in monosyllables to one another could not be kept up—the trouble had to be dealt with, and without delay; and when the poor meal could not be prolonged by any artifice, Sir Geoffry held open the door for his mother to pass through, and crossed the hall with her to the library. Shut within its walls they could discuss the secret in safety; no eye to see them, no ear to hear.

Sir Geoffry mechanically stirred the fire, and placed a chair for his mother near it. The weather appeared to be changing. Instead of the unseasonable relaxing warmth that had been upon the earth up to the previous day, a cold north-east wind had set in, enough to freeze people's marrow. The skies were grey and lowering; the trees shook and moaned: winter was taking up his place again.

So much the better. Blue skies and brightness would hardly have accorded with Sir Geoffry's spirit. He might have to endure many cruel visitations ere he died, but never a one so cruel as this. No evil that Heaven can send upon us, or man inflict, is so hard to bear as self-reproach.

If ever a son had idolized a mother, it had surely been Geoffry Chavasse. They had been knit together in the strongest bonds of filial love. His whole thought from his boyhood had been her comfort: to have sacrificed himself for her, if needs must, would have been a cheerful task. When he came of age, not yet so very many months ago, he had resolved that his whole future life should be devoted to promote her happiness—as her life had been devoted to him in the days of his sickly boyhood. Her wishes were his; her word his law; he would have died rather than cause her a moment's pain.

And how had he, even thus early, fulfilled this? Look at him, as he leans against the heavy framework of the window, drawn back from it that the light may not fall on his subdued face. The brow is bent in grievous doubt; the dark-blue eyes, generally so honestly clear, are hot with trouble; the bright hair hangs limp. Yes; he would have died rather than bring his mother pain: that was his true creed and belief; but, like many another whose resolves are made in all good faith, he had signally failed, even while he was thinking it, and brought pain to her in a crushing heap. He hated himself as he looked at her pale countenance; at the traces of tears in her heavy eyes. Never a minute's sleep had she had the previous night, it was plainly to be seen; and, as for him, he had paced his chamber until morning, not attempting to go to rest. But there was a task close before him, heavier than any that had gone before; heavier even than this silent repentance—the deciding what was to be done in the calamity; and Sir Geoffry knew that his duty to his mother and his duty to another would clash with each other. All the past night he had been earnestly trying to decide which of the two might be evaded with the least sin— and he thought he saw which.

Lady Chavasse had taken the chair he placed for her; sitting upright in it, and waiting for him to speak. She knew, as well as he, that this next hour would decide their fate in life: whether they should still be together a loving mother and son; or whether they should become estranged and separate for ever. He crossed to the fireplace and put his elbow on the mantelpiece, shielding his eyes with his hand. Just a few words, he said, of his sense of shame and sorrow; of regret that he should have brought this dishonour on himself and his mother's home; of hope that he might be permitted, by Heaven and circumstances, to work out his repentance, in endeavouring daily, hourly constantly, to atone to her for it—to her, his greatly-loved mother. And then—lifting his face from the hand that had partially hidden it—he asked her to be patient, and to hear him without interruption a little further. And Lady Chavasse bowed her head in acquiescence.

"Nothing remains for me but to marry Miss Layne," he began: and my lady, as she heard the expected avowal, bit her compressed lips "It is the only course open to me; unless I would forfeit every claim to honour, and to the respect of upright men. If you will give your consent to this, the evil may be in a degree repaired; nothing need ever be known; Mary's good name may be saved—mine, too, if it comes to that—and eventually we may be all happy together—"

"Do not try me too much, Geoffry," came the low interruption.

"Mother, you signified that you would hear me to the end. I will not try you more than I can help; but it is necessary that I should speak fully. All last night I was walking about my room in self-commune; deliberating what way was open, if any, that it would be practicable to take—and I saw but this one. Let me marry her. It will be easy of accomplishment—speaking in reference to appearances and the world. She might go for a week or two to her mother's; for a month or two, if it were thought better and less suspicious; there is no pressing hurry. We could then be married quietly, and go abroad for a year or so, or for longer; and come back together to the Grange, and be your dutiful and loving children always, just as it was intended I and Rachel should be. But that you have liked Mary Layne very much, I might have felt more difficulty in proposing this."

"I have liked her as my servant," said Lady Chavasse, scornfully.

"Pardon me, you have liked her as a lady. Do you remember once saying—it was when she first came— that if you had had a daughter you could have wished her to be just like Mary Layne. Before I ever saw her, you told me she was a sweet, elegant young woman; and—mother—she is nothing less. Oh, mother, mother!" continued Sir Geoffry, with emotion, "if you will but forget your prejudices for my sake, and consent to what I ask, we would endeavour to be ever repaying you in love and services during our after-life. I know what a great sacrifice it will be; but for my sake I venture to crave it of you—for my sake."

A great fear lay upon Lady Chavasse: it had lain on her ever since the previous day—that he might carry this marriage out of his own will. So that she dared not answer too imperatively. She was bitterly hurt, and caught her breath with a sob.

"Do you want to kill me, Geoffry?"

"Heaven knows that I wish I had been killed, before I brought this distress upon you," was his rejoinder.

"I am distressed. I have never felt anything like it since your father died. No; not once when you, a child of seven, were given over in illness, and it was thought you would not live till morning."

Sir Geoffry passed his hand hastily across his eyes, in which stood the hot tears. His heart was sore, nearly unto breaking; his ingratitude to his mother seemed fearfully great. He longed to throw himself at her feet, and clasp her knees, and tell how deep for her was his love, how true and deep it always would be.

"Though the whole world had united to deceive me, Geoffry, I could never have believed that you would do so. Why did you pretend to be fond of Rachel?"

"I never pretended to be fonder of Rachel than I was. I liked her as a cousin, nothing more. I know it now. And—mother"—he added, with a flush upon his face, and a lowering of the voice, "it is better and safer that the knowledge should have come to me before our marriage than after it."

"Nonsense," said Lady Chavasse. "Once married, a man of right principles is always safe in them."

Sir Geoffry was silent. Not very long ago, he had thought himself safe in his. With every word, it seemed that his shame and his sin came more glaringly home to him.

"Then you mean to tell me that you do not like Rachel—"

"That I have no love for her. If—if there be any one plea that I can put forth as a faint shadow of excuse for what has happened, it lies in my love for another. Faint it is, Heaven knows: the excuse, not the love. That is deep enough: but I would rather not speak of it to you—my mother."

"And that you never will love Rachel?" continued Lady Chavasse, as though he had not interposed.

"Never. It is impossible that I can ever love any one but Mary Layne. I am grateful, as things have turned out, that I did not deceive Rachel by feigning what I could not feel. Neither does she love me. We were told to consider ourselves betrothed, and did so accordingly; but, so far as love goes, it has not been so much as mentioned between us."

"What else have you to say?" asked Lady Chavasse.

"I might say a great deal, but it would all come round to the same point: to the one petition that I am beseeching you to grant—that you will sanction the marriage."

Lady Chavasse's hands trembled visibly within their rich lace frills, as they lay passive on her soft dress of fine geranium cashmere. Her lips grew white with agitation.

"Geoffry!"

"My darling mother."

"I have heard you. Will you hear me?"

"You know I will."

"More than one-and-twenty years ago, my husband died within these walls; and I—I was not eighteen, Geoffry—felt utterly desolate. But, as the weeks went on, I said my child will be born, if God permit, and he will bring me comfort. You were born, Geoffry; you did bring me comfort: such comfort that I thought Heaven had come again. You best know, my son, what our life has been; how we have loved each other: how pleasantly time has flown in uninterrupted happiness. I have devoted myself, my time, my energies, everything I possessed, to you, my best treasure; I have given up the world for you, Geoffry; I had only you left in it. Is it fitting that you should fling me from you now; that you should blight my remaining days with misery; that you should ignore me just as though I were already dead—and all for the sake of a stranger?"

"But—"

"I have not finished, Geoffry. For the sake of a stranger, whom a few months ago neither you nor I had ever seen? If you think this—if you deem that you would be acting rightly, and can find in your heart to treat me so, why, you must do it."

"But what I wish and propose is quite different!" he exclaimed in agony. "Oh, mother, surely you can understand me—and the dilemma I am placed in?"

"I understand all perfectly."

"Ah yes!"

"Geoffry, there is no middle course. You must choose between me and—her. Once she and I separate—it will be to-day—we can never meet again. I will not tolerate her memory; I will never submit to the degradation of hearing her named in my presence. Our paths lie asunder, Geoffry, far as the poles: hers lies one way, mine another. You must decide for yourself which of them you will follow. If it be mine, you shall be, as ever, my dear and honoured son, and I will never, never reproach you with your folly: never revert to it; never think of it. If it be hers, why, then—I will go away somewhere and hide myself, and leave the Grange free for you. And I—I dare say—shall not live long to be a thorn in your remembrance."

She broke down with a flood of bitter sobs. Geoffry Chavasse had never seen his mother shed such. The hour was as trying to her as to him. She had loved him with a strangely selfish love, as it is in the nature of mothers to do; and that she should have to bid him choose between her and another—and one so entirely beneath her as Lady Chavasse considered Mary Layne to be—was gall and wormwood. Never would she have stooped to put the choice before him, even in words, but for her dread that he might be intending to take it.

"It is a fitting end, Geoffry—that this worthless girl should supplant me in your home and heart," she was resuming when her emotion allowed; but Geoffry stood forward to face her, his agitation great as her own.

"An instant, mother: that you may fully understand me. The duty I owe you, the allegiance and the love, are paramount to all else on earth. In communing with myself last night, as I tell you I was, my heart and my reason alike showed me this. If I must choose between you and Mary Layne, there cannot be a question in my mind on which side duty lies. In all honour I am bound to make her my wife, and I should do it in all affection: but not in defiance of you; not to thrust rudely aside the love and obligations of the past one-and-twenty years. You must choose for me. If you refuse your approval, I have no resource but to yield to your decision; if you consent, I shall thank you and bless you for ever."

A spasm of pain passed across the mouth of Lady Chavasse. She could not help saying something that arose prominently in her mind though it interrupted the question.

"And you can deem the apothecary Layne's daughter fit to mate with Sir Geoffry Chavasse?"

"No, I do not. Under ordinary circumstances, I should never have thought of such a thing. This unhappy business has a sting for me, mother, on many sides. Will you give me your decision?" he added, after a pause.

"I have already given it, Geoffry—so far as I am concerned. You must choose between your mother, between all the hopes and the home-interests of one-and-twenty years, and this alien."

"Then I have no alternative."

She turned her gaze steadily upon him. A sob rose in his throat as he took her hands, his voice was hoarse with emotion.

"To part from her will be like parting with life, mother. I can never know happiness again in this world."

But the decision was irrevocable. What further passed between Sir Geoffry and his mother in the remaining half-hour they spent together, how much of entreaty and anguish was spoken on his side, how much of passionate plaint and sorrow on hers, will never be known. But she was obdurate to the last letter: and Sir Geoffry's lot in life was fixed. Mary Layne was to be sacrificed: and, in one sense of the word, himself also: and there might be no appeal.

Lady Chavasse exacted from him that he should quit the Grange at once without seeing Miss Layne, and not return to it until Mary had left it for ever. Anything he wished to say to her, he was to write. On Lady Chavasse's part, she voluntarily undertook to explain to Miss Layne their conversation faithfully, and its result; and to shield the young lady's good name from the censure of the world. She would keep her for some time longer at the Grange, be tender with her, honour her, drive out with her in the carriage so that they might be seen together, subdue her mother's anger, strive to persuade Mr. Luke Duffham that his opinion had been mistaken, and, in any case, bind him down to secrecy: in short, she would make future matters as easy as might be for Mary, as tenaciously as though she were her own daughter. That she promised this at the sacrifice of pride and of much feeling, was indisputable; but she meant to keep her word.

However miserable a night the others had passed, it will readily be imagined that Mary Layne had spent a worse. She made no pretence of eating breakfast; and when it was taken away sat at her work in the garden-parlour, trying to do it; but her cold fingers dropped the needle every minute, her aching brow felt as though it were bursting. Good-hearted Hester Picker was sorry to see her looking so ill, and wished the nasty trying spring, hot one day, cold the next, would just settle itself down.

Mary rose from her chair, and went upstairs to her own bedroom for a brief respite: in her state of mind it seemed impossible to stay long quiescent anywhere. This little incidental occurrence frustrated one part of the understanding between Sir Geoffry and his mother—that he should quit the house without seeing Miss Layne. In descending, she chanced to cross the end of the corridor just as he came out of his mother's room after bidding her farewell. The carriage waited at the door, his coat was on his arm. Mary would have shrunk back again, but he bade her wait.

"You must allow me to shake her hand, and say just a word of adieu, mother; I am not quite a brute," he whispered. And Lady Chavasse came out of her room, and tacitly sanctioned it.

But there was literally nothing more than a hand-shake. Miss Layne, standing still in all humility, turned a little white, for she guessed that he was being sent from his home through her. Sir Geoffry held her hand for a moment.

"I am going away, Mary. My mother will explain to you. I have done my best, and failed. Before Heaven, I have striven to the uttermost, for your sake and for mine, to make reparation; but it is not to be. I leave you to my mother; she is your friend; and you shall hear from me in a day or two. I am now going to see Mrs. Layne. Good-bye: God bless you always!"

But, ere Sir Geoffry reached the hall, Lady Chavasse had run swiftly down, caught him, and was drawing him into a room. The fear had returned to her face.

"I heard you say you were going to call on Mrs. Layne. Geoffry, this must not be."

"Not be!" he repeated, in surprise. "Mother, I am obeying you in all essential things; but you cannot wish to reduce me to an utter craven. I owe an explanation to Mrs. Layne almost in the same degree that I owe it to you; and I shall certainly not quit Church Dykely until I have given it."

"Oh, well—if it must be," she conceded, afraid still. "You—you will not be drawn in to act against me, Geoffry?"

"No power on earth could draw me to that. You have my first and best allegiance; to which I bow before every other consideration, before every interest, whether of my own or of others. But for that, should I be acting as I am now? Fare you well, mother."

She heard the carriage-door closed; she heard Sir Geoffry's order to the footman. Even for that order, he was cautious to give a plausible excuse.

"Stop at Mrs. Layne's. I have to leave a message from her ladyship."

The wheels of the carriage crunched the gravel, bearing off Sir Geoffry in the storm of sleet—which had begun to fall—and Lady Chavasse passed up the stairs again. Taking the hand of Mary—who had stood above like a statue—never moving—she led her, gently enough, into her dressing-room, and put her in a comfortable chair by the fire; and prepared for this second interview.

Briefly, Lady Chavasse recounted what she had to say. Sir Geoffry had found himself obliged to choose between Miss Layne and her, his mother. Mary Layne sat with her hands before her face, and acknowledged that, if it came to such a choice, he had chosen rightly. And then, in forcible language, because it came from her heart, my lady drew a picture of the life-long happiness she and her son had enjoyed together, of her devotion and sacrifices for him, of his deep love and reverence for her: and she quietly asked Mary to put herself in imagination in her place, and say what her feelings would have been had a stranger come in to mar this. Had she any right to do this?—Lady Chavasse asked her—would she be justified in destroying the ties of a life, in thrusting herself between mother and son?—in invoking a curse, his mother's curse, on him? My lady did not spare her: but she spoke in no angry tone, rather in a piteous and imploring one: and Mary, feeling as if matters were being put to her own better feeling, sobbed, and shook, and shrunk within herself, and could have knelt at Lady Chavasse's feet for pardon in her distress and humiliation.

And that was the end of the wretched business—as Duffham phrases it in his diary—so far as the Grange and its people were concerned. Mary Layne stayed, perforce, two or three weeks longer at the house, and my lady made much of her: she took her out daily in her carriage; she said to her friends, in the hearing of her servants and the sympathizing Hester Picker, how vexatious it was that the relaxing, unseasonable weather had brought out the delicacy that was latent in Miss Layne's constitution, and that she feared she must let her go away somewhere for a change. Mary submitted to all. She was in such a self-abased frame of mind that had my lady desired her to immolate herself on a blazing pyre, she would have gone to it meekly. My lady had interviews with Mrs. Layne, and with Duffham (who had got well then), and with his brother Luke. At the two or three weeks' end, Miss Elizabeth Layne came by appointment to the Grange, and she and Mary were driven to the nearest station in my lady's own carriage on their way to the seaside: or to elsewhere, as it might be. And never an ill breath, in the Grange or out of it, transpired to tarnish the fair fame of Mary Layne.

But my lady was not honest in one respect. The letter that arrived for Mary from Sir Geoffry a day or two after his departure, was never given to her. My lady knew she might trust her son implicitly; he could only be straightforward and keep his word in all things; nevertheless, she deemed the fire the safest place for the weighty epistle of many sheets. On the other hand, Mary wrote to Sir Geoffry, saying that the alternative he had chosen was the only one possible to him. Nothing, no prayers of his, she said, would have induced her to put herself between him and his mother, even had he so far forgotten his duty as to urge it. It was a good and sensible letter, and none but a good and unselfish girl could have written it.

So that ended the dream and the romance. And I hope the reader does not forget that it is Duffham's diary that's telling all this, and not I. For though dreams and romance seem to be in Duffham's line, they are not in mine.

Part the Second

Not very long after the time that Mary Layne quitted Chavasse Grange—having closed all connection with it, never to be to it henceforth but as an utter stranger—her eldest sister, Susan, the wife of Captain Richard Layne, arrived in England from India with her children, four little ones; the eldest seven years old, the youngest eighteen months. The children had been ailing, and she brought them over for a twelvemonth's change. Mrs. Layne was a good deal worn herself, for the only nurse she had with her, a coloured woman, was sea-sick during the voyage. Her sister Eleanor, who originally went out with her to Calcutta, had made an excellent match; having married Allan McAlpin, the younger partner in the staid old firm of McAlpin Brothers, merchants of high standing, and wealthy men.

The first thing Mrs. Richard Layne did on arrival was to establish herself in lodgings in Liverpool, the port she landed at (in order to rest a week or two from the fatigues of the voyage) and send for her mother and sister Elizabeth. In answer came a letter from her mother, saying she was not equal to the journey and that Elizabeth was from home. It contained Elizabeth's present address, and also one or two items of news that startled young Mrs. Layne well-nigh out of her senses. Leaving her children to their nurse's care, she started for the address given, and found her two sisters, Elizabeth and Mary. The one living in a chronic state of outpouring sarcasm and reproach; the other meekly taking all as not a tithe of her just due.

After a day or two given to natural grief and lamentation, Mrs. Richard Layne took matters into her own capable hands. She considered that a more complete change would be good for Mary, and decided to convey her to the Continent. She wrote a long and confidential letter to her husband in India, of what she meant to do: and then she went back to Liverpool with Elizabeth, to leave the latter in charge of her own children and their coloured nurse, during her absence across the Channel. Mrs. Layne then returned to Mary, and they started together for France.

Shortly after this, old Mrs. Layne fell ill: and Elizabeth, when she found she must go home in consequence, left a responsible English nurse with the coloured woman and children. Not for several months afterwards did Mrs. Richard Layne and Mary return from abroad; and at the end of the twelvemonth they all went back to India—Mrs. Layne, her children, the native nurse, and Mary. Mary accompanied them in the capacity of governess.

After that a couple of years went on.

[From Miss Mary Layne's Journal, written in Calcutta, at the house of Captain Layne.]

June 10th.—Cool of the evening. Susan came to the schoolroom in the midst of the geography lesson this morning, and told me an old friend of mine at home had called, and I was to come into the verandah to see her. I never was more surprised. It was Jane Arkill; my chief friend in our old school-days. She has married a Mr. Cale, a doctor, who has just come out here to practise. Mrs. Cale says she shall never grow reconciled to the heat of India. While she sat telling us home news, she alternately wiped her pale face and stared at me, because I am so much altered. She thinks she should not have known me. It is not that my features have changed, she says, but that I have grown so much graver, and look so old. When people talk like this, I long to tell them that things have changed me; that I have passed through a fiery trial of sin and suffering; that my life is one long crucifixion of inward, silent repentance. When I first came out, two years ago, and people would say, "It must be the climate that is making Miss Layne look so ill," it seemed to me like the worst hypocrisy to let them think it was the climate, and not to tell the truth. This feeling came back again to-day, when Jane Arkill—I shall often forget to call her "Cale"—said my eyes had grown to have a sad look in them, and Susan answered that young ladies faded quickly in India; and that Mary would apply herself too closely to the children's studies in spite of remonstrance. Too closely? Why, if I devoted every hour of my life, night and day, to these dear children, I could never repay what their mother—or their father, either—has done for me.

My mother is very well, Jane says, but lame, and cannot get about much: she saw her only six weeks ago—for they came out by the overland route. Only six weeks ago!—to hear that one has seen my dear mother so recently as that, makes it seem almost as though I had seen her but yesterday. My darling mother!—whom my conduct so grieved and outraged at the time, and who was so quick to forgive me and to do so much for me. What a message she has sent me! "Give my love to dear Mary, and say I hope she is happy with her sisters." Elizabeth, too, sent me her love. "I saw your little Arthur, Mrs. Layne," Jane Cale then said to my sister: "he is a sweet little fellow; your mother and Elizabeth are so fond of him. They call him Baby Arthur." I felt my face growing whiter than death: but Susan, who was never I believe put out in her life, quietly sent me away with a message to the nurse—that she might bring the children. When I got back, Captain Layne had come in and had the baby on his shoulder: for nurse had made more haste than I. "None of your children here are so fair as the little one your wife left in England, Captain Layne," Jane Cale was saying, as she looked at them one by one. "You mean little Arthur," returned the Captain, in his ready kindness; "I hear he is fair." "Have you never seen him?" "No; how should I have seen him?" asked Captain Layne, laughing: "he was born over there, and my wife left him behind her as a legacy to her mother. It is rather a hazard, Mrs. Cale, as perhaps you know, to bring out very young infants to this country." Susan came to the rescue: she took the baby and put him on his feet, that Mrs. Cale should see how well he walked for his twelvemonth's age. But it did not answer. No doubt Jane thought that the more she told them about Baby Arthur in England, the better pleased they would be. How much difference was there, she asked, between this child and little Arthur—eighteen months?—and how much between Arthur and the one above him? "Oh," said the captain, "if it comes to months, you must ask my wife. Come here, sir," he called to Robert, who was tumbling over the little black bearer, "tell this lady how old you are, for I am sure I can't." "I'm over four," lisped Bobby. "Ah, I see," said Jane Cale, "Baby Arthur is just between them." "Exactly so," said Captain Layne: "Susan, I think these children may go to their own quarters now." They went at once, for I have trained them to be obedient, and I escaped with them. It is the first time any human tongue has spoken to me of Baby Arthur. I think if Captain Layne had looked at me I should have died: but he is ever kind. Never, by so much as a word, or look, or tone, since the hour when I first set foot on these shores, his wife's humbled sister, his children's meek governess—and it is more than good of him to entrust their training to me!—never has he betrayed that he as much as knew anything, still less thought of it.

Oh, how events have been smoothed for me!—how much more than I deserve have I to be thankful for!

[Letter from Captain Layne's Wife to her Mother at Church Dykely.]

Calcutta, September 2nd.

MY DARLING MOTHER,

I am sitting down to answer your letter, which arrived by last mail: for I am sure you must wonder at my long silence and think it an age since I wrote. But the truth is, I have had a touch of my old complaint—intermittent fever—and it left me very weak and languid. I know you have an untiring correspondent in Eleanor. Perhaps that makes me a little negligent in writing home, though I am aware it ought not to do so.

We were truly glad to welcome Mrs. Cale, because she had so recently come from you. I cannot say that I have seen much of her as yet, for it was just after she got out that my illness began; and when I grew better my husband sent me to the hills for a change. Mary went with me and the children. She is the greatest comfort. Mother dear, in spite of what we know of, I do not think Mary has her equal for true worth in this world. You say that Mrs. Cale, in writing home to you, described Mary as being so altered; so sad and subdued. Why, my dear mother, of course she is sad: how could it be otherwise? I do not suppose, in her more recent life, she has ever felt other than the most intense sadness of mind; no, not for one minute: and it is only to be expected that this must in time show itself in the countenance. I spoke to her about it one day; it is a long, long time ago now; saying I did not like to see her retain so much sadness. "It cannot be helped," she answered; "sadness must always follow sin."

And now I must tell you, even at the risk of being misunderstood—though I am sure you know me too well to fear I should seek to countenance or excuse wrong-doing—that I think Mary takes an exaggerated view of the past. She seems to think it can never be wiped out, never be palliated. Of course, in one sense, it never can: but I don't see why she need continue to feel this intense humiliation, as if she ought to have a cordon drawn round her gown to warn all good folks from its contact. Look again at that persistent fancy of hers, always to wear black; it is writing about her gown puts me in mind of it. Black, black, black: thin silk when the heat will allow, oftener a dreary, rusty-black-looking kind of soft muslin that is called here "black jaconite"—but I really don't know whether that's the way to spell the thing. During the late intense heat, we have talked her into a black-and-white muslin: that is, white, with huge black spots upon it in the form of a melon. Only once did I speak to her about wearing white as we do; I have never ventured since. She turned away with a shiver, and said white was no longer for her. Mother, dear, if any one ever lived to work out on earth their repentance for sin, surely it is Mary. The more I see of her innate goodness, the less can I understand the past. With her upright principles and strict sense of conscientiousness—and you know that Mary always had these, even as a child—I am unable to imagine how it could have been that— But I won't go into that. And it may be that the goodness, so remarkable, would not have come out conspicuously but for the trial.

Mrs. Cale gave us such a nice account of "Baby Arthur." She says he is very fair and pretty. She has talked to other people about him—and of course we cannot tell her not to talk. A brother-officer of my husband's said to me yesterday:

"I hear your little boy at home is charming, Mrs. Layne. When shall you have him out?"

"Not yet," I answered. "He was a very delicate baby, and I should not like to risk it."

"Ah," said Major Grant, "that is why you left him in England."

"My mother takes great care of him," I went on; "it would break her heart if I were to bring him away from her."

You will wonder at my writing all this: but it is so new a thing to hear "Baby Arthur" made a topic of discussion, and all through Mrs. Cale! Talking of children, Eleanor is, I think, getting somewhat over her long-continued disappointment. Four years she has been married, and has none. It is certainly a pity, when she and Allan McAlpin are so well off. Not a family in Calcutta lives in better style than they—people here talk of the house of McAlpin Brothers as we at home talk of Rothschild's and Baring's. I am sure they must be very rich, and poor Eleanor naturally thinks where is the use of the riches when there's no child to leave them to. Eleanor said to me the other day when she was here, "You might as well make over that child of yours to me, Susan,"—meaning Baby Arthur; "he does you no good, and must be a trouble to mamma and Elizabeth." Of course I laughed it off; saying that you and Elizabeth would not part with him for untold gold. And I believe it is so, is it not, dear mother? Do you remember when I first went to your house with the poor little infant, after his birth on the Continent, you took him out of my arms with an averted face, as if you would rather have thrown him on the floor, and Elizabeth turned away and groaned? "Mother," I said, "you may grow to love the child in time, and then you will be more ready to forgive and forget." And that has come to pass.

Mary has always been against our not telling the truth to Eleanor; she says, even yet, that she feels like a hypocrite before her; but I feel sure it was best and wisest. Eleanor is as sensitive in her way as Mary is; Eleanor holds a high position in the place; she and her husband are both courted, she for herself, he for his riches, for his high commercial name, for his integrity; and I know she would have felt the slur almost as keenly as Mary. It is true I do not like deliberate deceit; but there was really no need to tell her—it would not have answered any good end. Until Mrs. Cale talked, Eleanor scarcely remembered that there was a Baby Arthur; and now she seems quite jealous that he is mine and she cannot have him. I say to Eleanor that she must be contented with the good she has; her indulgent husband, her position. We poor officers' wives cannot compete with her in grandeur. By the way, talking of officers, you will be glad to hear that my husband expects his majority. It will be a welcome rise. For, with our little ones and our expenses, it is rather difficult at times to make both ends meet. We shall come into money some time from the West Indies; but until then every pound of additional pay is welcome.

Mrs. Cale told us another item of news; that is, she recounted it amidst the rest, little thinking what it was to us. That Sir G. C. is married, and living with his wife at the Grange with Lady C. You have been keeping the fact back, dear mother; either through not choosing to mention their names, or out of consideration to Mary. But I can assure you she was thankful to hear of it; it has removed a little of the abiding sting from her life. You cannot imagine how unselfish she is: she looks upon herself as the sole cause of all that occurred. I mean that she says it was through her going to the Grange. Had she not gone, the peace of mother and son would never have been disturbed. I think Lady C. was selfish and wrong; that she ought to have allowed Sir G. to do as he wished. Mary says no; that Lady C.'s comfort and her lifelong feelings were above every other consideration. She admires Lady C. more than I do. However, she is truly glad to hear that the marriage took place. Events have fallen now into their original course, and she trusts that the bitter episode in which she took part may be gradually forgotten at the Grange. The day we first heard of his marriage, I went hastily—and I fear you will say rudely—into Mary's room at night when she was preparing for rest, having omitted to tell her something I wished changed in Nelly's studies for the morning. She was on her knees, and rose up; the tears were literally streaming down her sweet face, "Oh, Mary, what is the matter?" I asked, in dismay. "I was only praying for God to bless them," she answered simply. Is she not a good, unselfish girl?

I could fill pages with her praises. What she has been to my children, during these two years she has had them in charge, I can never tell. She insisted upon being regarded and treated wholly as a governess; but, as my husband says, no real governess could be half so painstaking, untiring, and conscientious. She has earned the respect of all Calcutta, and she shrinks from it as if it were something to be shunned, saying, "If people did but know!" Nelly, from being the only girl, and perhaps also because she was the eldest and her papa loved her so, was the most tiresome, spoiled little animal in the world; and the boys were boisterous, and I am afraid frightfully impudent to the native servants: but since Mary took them in hand they are altogether different, fit to be loved. Richard often says he wishes he could recompense her.

And now I must bring my letter to a close, or you will be tired. The children all send love to grandmamma and Aunt Elizabeth: and (it is Miss Nelly calls out this) to little brother Arthur. Nelly is growing prettier every day: she is now going on for eleven. Young Richard promises to be as tall and fine a man as his father. I believe he is to be sent home next year to the school attached to King's College in London. Little Allan is more delicate than I like to see him; Bobby, a frightful Turk; baby, a dear little fellow. Master Allan's godfather, Eleanor's husband, gave him a handsome present on his last birthday— a railway train that would "go." He had sent for it from England: I am sure it never cost less than five pounds; and the naughty child broke it before the day was out. I felt so vexed; and downright ashamed to confess it to Eleanor. The Ayah said he broke it for the purpose, "to see what it was made of;" and, in spite of entreaties to the contrary, Richard was on the point of whipping him for the mischief, and Allan was roaring in anticipation, when Mary interposed, and begged to be let deal with him for it. What she said, or what she did, I don't know, I'm sure there was no whipping; but Master Allan was in a penitential and subdued mood for days after it, voluntarily renouncing some pudding that he is uncommonly fond of, because he had "not been good." Richard says that he would rather trust his children to Mary, to be made what they ought to be, than to any one under heaven. Oh, it is grievous— that her life should have been blighted!

My best love to you and Elizabeth, dearest mother, in which Richard begs to join; and believe me, your affectionate daughter,

SUSAN LAYNE.

P.S.—I have never before written openly on these private matters: we have been content tacitly to ignore them to each other, but somehow my pen has run on incautiously. Please, therefore, to burn this letter when you and Elizabeth shall have read it.[1]

[1] But old Mrs. Layne did not burn the letter: or else it would never have found its way into Duffham's collection. She was content to put it off from day to day just as people do put things off; and it was never done.—J.L.

[From Miss Mary Layne's Journal, about two years yet later.]

October 9th.—I quite tremble at the untoward turn things seem to be taking. To think that a noble gentleman should be casting his thoughts on me! And he is a gentleman, and a noble one also, in spite of that vain young adjutant, St. George's, slighting remark when Mr. McAlpin came in last night—"Here's that confounded old warehouseman!" It was well the major did not hear him. He has to take St. George to task on occasion, and he would have done it then with a will.

Andrew McAlpin is not an ordinary man. Head of a wealthy house, whose integrity has never been questioned; himself of unsullied honour, of handsome presence, of middle age, for surely, in his three-and-fortieth year, he may be called it—owner of all these solid advantages, he has actually turned his attentions upon me. Me! Oh, if he did but know!—if he could but see the humiliation it brings to this already too humiliated heart.

Has a glamour been cast over his sight—as they say in his own land? Can he not see how I shrink from people when they notice me by chance more than is usual? Does he not see how constantly I have tried to shrink from him? If I thought that this had been brought about by any want of precaution on my part, I should be doubly miserable. When I was assistant-teacher at school in England, the French governess, poor old Madame de Visme, confided to me something that she was in the habit of doing; it was nothing wrong in itself, but totally opposed to the arbitrary rules laid down, and, if discovered, might have caused her to be abruptly dismissed. "But suppose it were found out, madame?" I said. "Ah non, mon enfant," she answered; "je prends mes précautions." Since then I have often thought of the words: and I say to myself, now as I write, have I taken precautions—proper ones? I can hardly tell. For one thing, I was at first, and for some time, so totally unprepared; it would no more have entered my mind to suppose Mr. McAlpin would think of paying attention to me, than that the empty-headed Lieutenant St. George—who boasts that his family is better than anybody's in India, and intends to wed accordingly if he weds at all—would pay it.

When it first began—and that is so long ago that I can scarcely remember, nearly a year, though—Mr. McAlpin would talk to me about the children. I felt proud to answer him, dear little things; and I knew he liked them, and Allan is his brother's godchild, and Robert is Eleanor's. I am afraid that is where I was wrong: when he came talking, evening after evening, I should have been on my guard, and begged Susan to excuse me from appearing as often as she would. The great evil lies in my having consented to appear at all in company. For two years after I came out—oh, more than that; it must have been nearly three—I resolutely refused to join them when they were not alone. It was Major Layne's fault that the rule was broken through. One day, when invitations were out for an evening party, Susan came to me and said that the major particularly requested I would appear at it. "The fact is, Mary," she whispered, "there has been some talk at the mess: you are very much admired—your face, I mean—and some of them began wondering whether there was any reason for your never appearing in society; and whether you could really be my sister. Richard was not present—that goes without saying—the colonel repeated it to him afterwards in a joking way. But what the major says is this, Mary—that he knows India and gossiping tongues better than you do, and he desires for all our sakes, for yours of course especially, that you will now and then show yourself with us. You are to begin next Tuesday evening. Richard begs you will. And I have been getting you a black net dress, with a little white lace for the body—you cannot say that's too fine." The words "for all our sakes" decided it; and I said I would certainly obey Major Layne. What else could I do?

That was the beginning of it. Though I go out scarcely ever with the major and Susan, declining invitations on the plea of my duties as governess, it has certainly grown into a habit with me to spend my evenings with them when they are at home.

But I never supposed anything like this would come of it. It has always seemed to me as if the world could see me a little as I see myself, and not think of me as one eligible to be chosen. As soon as I suspected that Mr. McAlpin came here for me, I strove to show him as plainly as I might that he was making a mistake. And now this proves, as it seems to me, how wrong it was not to tell my sad story to Eleanor, but to let her think of me as one still worthy. Susan knows how averse I was to its suppression; but she overruled me, and said Richard thought with her. Eleanor would have whispered it to her husband, and he might have whispered to his brother Andrew, and this new perplexity have been spared. It is not for my own sake I am so sorry, but for his: crosses and vexations are only my due, and I try to take them patiently; but I grow hot with shame every time I think how he is deceived. Oh, if he would only speak out, and end it! that I might thank him and tell him it is impossible: I should like to say unfit. Susan might give him a hint; but when I urge her to do so, she laughs at me and asks, How can she, until he has spoken?

October 25th.—It has come at last. Mr. McAlpin, one of the best men amidst the honourable men of the world, has asked me to become his wife. Whilst I was trying to answer him, I burst into tears. We were quite alone. "Why do you weep?" he asked, and I answered that I thought it was because of my gratitude to him for his kindness, and because I was so unworthy of it. It was perhaps a hazardous thing to say—but I was altogether confused. I must have explained myself badly, for he could not or would not understand my refusal; he said he certainly should decline to take it: I must consider it well—for a week—or a month—as long as I liked, provided I said "Yes" at last. When the crying was over, I felt myself again; and I told him, just as quietly and calmly as I could speak, that I should never marry; never. He asked why, and as I was hesitating what reason to give, and praying to be helped to speak right in the emergency, we were interrupted.

Oh, if I could only tell him the naked truth, as I here write it! That the only one living man it would be possible for me to marry is separated from me wider than seas can part. The barrier was thrown up between us years ago, never to be overstepped by either of us: whilst at the same time it shut me out from my kind. For this reason I can never marry, and never shall marry, so long as the world, for me, endures.

November 19th.—This is becoming painful. Mr. McAlpin will not give me up. He is all consideration and respect, he is not obtrusive, but yet—he will not give me up. There can exist no good reason why I should not have him, he says; and he is willing to wait for months and years. Eleanor comes in with her remonstrances: "Whatever possesses you, Mary? You must be out of your mind, child, to refuse Andrew McAlpin. For goodness' sake, get a little common sense into your poor crotchety head." Allan McAlpin, in his half-earnest, half-joking way, says to me, "Miss Layne, I make a perfect husband; ask Eleanor if I don't; and I know Andrew will make a better." It is so difficult for me to parry these attacks. The children even have taken it up: and Richard to-day in the schoolroom called me Mrs. McAlpin. Susan has tried to shield me throughout. The major says not a word one way or the other.

A curious idea has come across me once or twice lately—that it might be almost better to give Mr. McAlpin a hint of the truth. Of course it is but an idea; one that can never be carried out; but I know that he would be true as steel. I cannot bear for him to think me ungrateful: and he must consider me both ungrateful and capricious. I respect him and like him very much, and he sees this: if I were at liberty as others are, I would gladly marry him: the great puzzle is, how to make him understand that it is not possible. I suppose the consciousness of my secret, which never leaves me, renders it more difficult for me to be decisive than it would be if I possessed none. Not the least painful part of it all is, that he brings me handsome presents, and will not take them back again. He is nearly old enough to be my father, he says, and so I must consider them as given to me in that light. How shall I stop it?—how convince him?

November 29th.—Well, I have done it. Last night there was a grand dinner at the mess; some strangers were to join it on invitation; Susan went to spend a quiet hour with the colonel's wife, and Mr. McAlpin came in, and found me alone. What possessed me I cannot tell: but I began to tremble all over. He asked what was the matter, and I took courage to say that I always now felt distressed to see him come in, knowing he came for my sake, and that I could not respond to him as he wished. We had never had so serious a conversation as the one that ensued. He begged me to at least tell him what the barrier was, and where it lay: I thought he almost hinted that it was due to him. "There is some particular barrier, I feel sure," he said, "although Eleanor tells me there is none." And then I took some more courage, inwardly hoping to be helped to speak for the best, and answered Yes, there was a barrier; one that could never be surmounted; and that I had tried to make him see this all along. I told him how truly I esteemed him; how little I felt in my own eyes at being so undeserving of the opinion of a good man; I said I should thank him for it in my heart for ever. Did the barrier lie in my loving another? he asked, and I hesitated there. I had loved another, I said: it was before I came out, and the circumstances attending it were very painful; indeed, it was a painful story altogether. It had blighted my life; it had isolated me from the world; it entirely prevented me from ever thinking of another. I do believe he gathered from my agitation something of the truth, for he was so kind and gentle. Eleanor knew nothing of it, I said; Major and Mrs. Layne had thought there was no need to tell her, and, of course, he would understand that I was speaking to him in confidence. Yes, he answered, in confidence that I should not find misplaced. I felt happier and more at ease with him than I had ever done, for now I knew that misapprehension was over; and we talked together on other matters peacefully, until Major Layne entered and brought a shock with him.

A shock for me. One of the guests at the mess came with him: a naval officer in his uniform: a big man of fifty or sixty years, with a stern countenance and a cloud of untidy white hair. "Where's Susan?" cried the major: "out? Come here, then, Mary: you must be hostess." And before I knew what or who it was, I had been introduced to Admiral Chavasse. My head was in a whirl, my eyes were swimming: I had not heard the name spoken openly for years. Major Layne little thought he was related to G. C.: Mr. McAlpin had no idea that this fine naval officer, Parker Chavasse, could be cousin to one of whom I had been speaking covertly, but had not named. The admiral is on cruise, has touched at Calcutta, and his vessel is lying in Diamond Harbour.

November 30th.—Oh dear! oh dear! That I should be the recipient of so much goodness, and not be able to appreciate it!

A message came to the schoolroom this morning; Miss Layne was wanted downstairs. It was Susan who sent, but I found Mr. McAlpin alone. He had been holding a confidential interview with Susan: and Susan, hearing how much I had said to him last night, confided to him all. Oh, and he was willing to take me still; to take me as I am! I fell down at his feet sobbing when I told him that it could not be.

[Private Note from Major Layne's Wife to her Mother at Church Dykely.]

Just half-a-dozen lines, my dear mother, for your eye alone: I enclose them in my ordinary letter, meant for the world in general as well as you. Mr. McAlpin knows all; but he was still anxious to make her his wife. He thinks her the best and truest girl, excellent among women. Praise from him is praise. It was, I am certain, a most affecting interview; but they were alone. Mary's refusal—an absolute one—was dictated by two motives. The one is that the old feelings hold still so much sway in her heart (and, she says, always will) as to render the idea of a union with any one else absolutely distasteful. The other motive was consideration for Andrew McAlpin. "I put it to you what it would be," she said to him, "if at any time after our marriage, whether following closely upon it, or in years to come, this story of mine should transpire? I should die with shame, with grief for your sake: and there could be no remedy. No, no; never will I subject you, or any one else, to that frightful chance."

And, mother, she is right. In spite of Mr. McAlpin's present disappointment, I know he thinks her so. It has but increased his admiration for her. He said to me, "Henceforth I shall look upon her as a dear younger sister, and give her still my heart's best love and reverence."

And this is the private history of the affair: I thought I ought to disclose it to you. Richard, while thinking she has done right, says it is altogether an awful pity (he means inclusive of the past), for she's a trump of a girl. And so she is.

Ever yours, dear mother,
SUSAN LAYNE.

Part the Third

It was a lovely place, that homestead of Chavasse Grange, as seen in the freshness of the summer's morning: and my Lady Chavasse, looking from her window as she dressed, might be thinking so. The green lawn, its dew-drops sparkling in the sun, was dotted with beds of many coloured flowers; the thrush and blackbird were singing in the surrounding trees; the far-off landscape, stretched around in the distance, was beautiful for the eye to rest upon.

Nearly hidden by great clusters of roses, some of which he was plucking, and talking at the same time to the head-gardener who stood by, was a good-looking gentleman of some five-and-twenty years. His light morning coat was flung back from the snowy white waistcoat, across which a gold chain passed, its seal drooping; a blue necktie, just as blue as his blue eyes, was carelessly tied round his neck. He might have been known for a Chavasse by those self-same eyes, for they had been his father's—Sir Peter's—before him.

"About those geraniums that you have put out, Markham," he was saying. "How came you to do it? Lady Chavasse is very angry; she wanted them kept in the pots."

"Well, Sir Geoffry, I only obeyed orders," replied the gardener—who was new to the place. "Lady Rachel told me to do it."

"Lady Rachel did? Oh, very well. Lady Chavasse did not understand that, I suppose."

Up went Lady Chavasse's window at this juncture. "Geoffry."

Sir Geoffry stepped out from the roses, and smiled as he answered her.

"Ask Markham about the geraniums, Geoffry—how he could dare to do such a thing without orders."

"Mother, Rachel bade him do it. Of course she did not know that you wished it not done."

"Oh," curtly replied Lady Chavasse. And she shut down the window again.

By this it will be seen that the wishes of the two ladies at Chavasse Grange sometimes clashed. Lady Rachel, though perhaps regarded as second in authority, was fond of having her own way, and took it when she could. Lady Chavasse made a show of deferring to her generally; but she had reigned queen so long that she found it irksome, not to say humiliating, to yield the smallest point to her son's wife.

They were sitting down to breakfast when Sir Geoffry went in, in the room that had once been the garden-parlour. It had been re-embellished since those days, and made the breakfast-room. Lady Chavasse was but in her forty-fourth year; a young woman, so to say, beautiful still, and excellently-well preserved. She wore a handsome dress of green muslin, with a dainty little cap of lace on her rich brown hair. Sir Geoffry's wife was in white; she looked just the same as when she was Rachel Derreston; her perfect features pale, and cold, and faultless.

Geoffry Chavasse laid a rose by the side of each as he sat down. He was the only one changed; changed since the light-hearted days before that episode of sin and care came to the Grange. It had soon passed away again; but somehow it had left its mark on him. His face seemed to have acquired a weary sort of look; and the fair bright hair was getting somewhat thin upon the temples. Sir Geoffry was in Parliament; but he had now paired off for the short remainder of the session. Sometimes they were all in London: sometimes Sir Geoffry would be there alone; or only with his wife: the Grange was their chief and usual home.

They began talking of their plans for the day. Sir Geoffry had to ride over some portion of the estate; Lady Rachel thought she must write some letters; Lady Chavasse, who said her head ached, intended to go out in her new carriage.

It was ordered to the door in the course of the morning: this pretty toy carriage, which had been a recent present from Geoffry to his mother. Low and lightly built, it was something like a basket-chaise, but much more elegant, and the boy-groom, in his natty postillion's dress, sat the horse. Lady Chavasse, a light shawl thrown over her green muslin, and a white bonnet on, stood admiring the turn-out, her maid, who had come out with the parasol, by her side.

"Wilkins," said her ladyship, suddenly, "run and ask Lady Rachel whether she is sure she would not like to go with me?"

The woman went and returned. "Lady Rachel's love and thanks, my lady, but she would prefer to get her letters done."

So Lady Chavasse went alone, taking the road to Church Dykely. The hedges were blooming with wild roses and woodbine, the sweet scent of the hay filled the air, the sky was blue and cloudless. But the headache was making itself sensibly felt; and my lady, remembering that she had often had these headaches lately, began wondering whether Duffham the surgeon could give her anything to cure them.

"Giles," she cried, leaning forward. And the groom turned and touched his cap.

"My lady?"

"To Mr. Duffham's."

So in the middle of the village, at Mr. Duffham's door, Giles pulled up. The surgeon, seeing who it was, came out, and handed his visitor indoors.

Lady Chavasse had not enjoyed a gossip with Mr. Duffham since before her last absence from home. She rather liked one in her coldly condescending way. And she stayed with him in the surgery while he made up some medicine for her, and told her all the village news. Then she began talking about her daughter-in-law.

"Lady Rachel seems well, but there is a little fractiousness perceptible now and then; and I fancy that, with some people, it denotes a state of not perfect health. There are no children, Mr. Duffham, you see. There have been no signs of any."

"Time enough for that, my lady."

"Well—they have been married for—let me recollect—nearly fourteen months. I do hope there will be children! I am anxious that there should be."

The surgeon happened to meet her eyes as she spoke, and read the anxiety seated in them.

"You see—if there were none, and anything happened to Sir Geoffry, it would be the case of the old days—my case over again. Had my child proved to be a girl, the Grange would have gone from us. You do not remember that; you were not here; but your predecessor, Mr. Layne, knew all about it."

Perhaps it was the first time for some three or more years past that Lady Chavasse had voluntarily mentioned the name of Layne to the surgeon. It might have been a slip of the tongue now.

"But nothing is likely to happen to Sir Geoffry, Lady Chavasse," observed Duffham, after an imperceptible pause. "He is young and healthy."

"I know all that. Only it would be pleasant to feel we were on the safe side—that there was a son to succeed. If anything did happen to him, and he left no son, the Grange would pass away from us. I cannot help looking to contingencies: it has been my way to do so all my life."

"Well, Lady Chavasse, I sincerely hope the son will come. Sir Geoffry is anxious on the point, I dare say."

"He makes no sign of being so. Sir Geoffry seems to me to have grown a little indifferent in manner of late, as to general interests. Yesterday afternoon we were talking about making some improvements at the Grange, he and I; Lady Rachel was indoors at the piano. I remarked that it would cost a good deal of money, and the question was, whether it would be worth while to do it. 'My successor would think it so, no doubt,' cried Sir Geoffry. 'I hope that will never be Parker Chavasse; I should not like him to reign here,' I said hastily. 'If it is, mother, I shall not be alive to witness it,' was his unemotional answer."

"Lady Chavasse, considering the difference between the admiral's age and Sir Geoffry's, I should say there are thirty chances against it," was Duffham's reply, as he began to roll up the bottle of mixture in white paper.

While he was doing this, a clapping of tiny hands attracted Lady Chavasse's attention to the window, which stood open. A little boy had run out of Mrs. Layne's door opposite, and stood on the pavement in admiration of the carriage, which the groom was driving slowly about. It was a pretty child of some three years old, or thereabouts, in a brown holland pinafore strapped round the waist, his little arms and legs and neck bare, and his light hair curling.

"Oh, g'andma, look! G'andma, come and look!" he cried—and the words were wafted distinctly to Lady Chavasse.

"Who is that child, Mr. Duffham? I have seen him sometimes before. Stay, though, I remember—I think I have heard. He belongs to that daughter of Mr. Layne's who married a soldier of the same name. A lieutenant, or some grade of that kind, was he not?"

"Lieutenant Layne then: Captain Layne now," carelessly replied Mr. Duffham. "Hopes to get his majority in time, no doubt."

"Oh, indeed. I sometimes wonder how people devoid of family connections manage to obtain rapid promotion. The grandmother takes care of the child, I suppose. Quite a charge for her."

Mr. Duffham, standing now by her side, glanced at Lady Chavasse. Her countenance was open, unembarrassed: there was no sign of ulterior thought upon it. Evidently a certain event of the past was not just then in her remembrance.

"How is the old lady?" she asked.

"Middling. She breaks fast. I doubt, though, if one of her daughters will not go before her."

Lady Chavasse turned quickly at the words.

"I speak of the one who is with her—Miss Elizabeth Layne," continued Mr. Duffham, busily rolling up the bottle. "Her health is failing: I think seriously; though she may linger for some time yet."

There was a pause. Lady Chavasse looked hard at the white knobs on the drug-drawers. But that she began to speak, old Duffham might have thought she was counting how many there were of them.

"The other one—Miss Mary Layne—is she still in that situation in India? A governess, or something of the kind, we heard she went out to be."

"Governess to Captain Layne's children. Oh yes, she's there. And likely to be, the people over the way seem to say. Captain and Mrs. Layne consider that they have a treasure in her."

"Oh, I make no doubt she would do her duty. Thank you; never mind sealing it. I will be sure to attend to your directions, Mr. Duffham."

She swept out to the carriage, which had now drawn up, and stepped over the low step into it. The surgeon put the bottle by her side, and saluted her as she drove away. Across the road trotted the little fellow in the pinafore.

"Did oo see dat booful tarriage, Mis'er Duffham? I'd like to 'ide in it."

"You would, would you, Master Arthur," returned the surgeon, hoisting the child for a moment on his shoulder, and then setting him on his feet again, as Miss Layne appeared at the door. "Be off back: there's Aunt Elizabeth looking angry. It's against the law, you know, sir, to run out beyond the house."

And the little lad ran over at once, obediently.

Nearly three years back—not quite so much by two or three months—Church Dykely was gratified by the intelligence that Captain Layne's wife—then sojourning in Europe—was coming on a short visit to her mother with her three or four weeks' old baby. Church Dykely welcomed the news, for it was a sort of break to the monotonous, jog-trot village life, and warmly received Mrs. Richard Layne and the child on their arrival. The infant was born in France, where Mrs. Richard Layne had been staying with one of her sisters—Mary—and whence she had now come direct to her mother's; Mary having gone on to Liverpool to join Mrs. Richard Layne's other children. The baby—made much of by the neighbours—was to remain with old Mrs. Layne: Mrs. Richard Layne did not deem it well to take so young a child to India, as he seemed rather delicate. Church Dykely said how generous it was of her to sacrifice her motherly feelings for the baby's good—but the Laynes had always been unselfish. She departed, leaving the child. And Baby Arthur, as all the place called him, lived and thrived, and was now grown as fine a little fellow for his age as might be, with a generous spirit and open heart. My Lady Chavasse (having temporarily forgotten it when speaking with Mr. Duffham) had heard all about the child's parentage just as the village had—that he was the son of Captain Richard Layne and his wife Susan. Chavasse Grange generally understood the same, including Sir Geoffry. There was no intercourse whatever between the Layne family and the Grange; there had not been any since Miss Mary Layne quitted it. My Lady Chavasse was in the habit of turning away her eyes when she passed Mrs. Layne's house: and in good truth, though perhaps her conscience reminded her of it at these moments, she had three-parts forgotten the unpleasant episode of the past.

And the little boy grew and thrived: and became as much a feature in Church Dykely as other features were—say the bridge over the mill-stream, or the butcher's wife—and was no more thought of, in the matter of speculation, than they were.

Miss Elizabeth Layne caught hold of the young truant's hand with a jerk and a reprimand, telling him he would be run over some day. She had occasion to tell it him rather often, for he was of a fearless nature. Mr. Duffham nodded across the road to Miss Elizabeth.

"Are you better to-day?" he called out. People don't stand on ceremony in these rural places.

"Not much, thank you," came the answer.

For Miss Elizabeth Layne had been anything but strong lately: her symptoms being very like those that herald consumption.

The time rolled on, bringing its changes. You have already seen it rolling on in Calcutta, for in this, the third part, we have had to go back a year or two.

Elizabeth Layne died. Mrs. Layne grew very feeble, and it was thought and said by every one that one of her daughters ought to be residing with her. There was only one left unmarried—Mary. Mary received news in India of this state of things at home, together with a summons from her mother. Not at all a peremptory summons. Mrs. Layne wrote a few shaky lines, praying her to come "if she would not mind returning to the place:" if she did mind it, why, she, the mother, must die alone as she best could. There was a short struggle in Mary Layne's heart; a quick, sharp battle, and she gave in. Her duty to her mother lay before aught else in God's sight; and she would yield to it. As soon as preparations for her voyage could be made, she embarked for England.

It was autumn when she got home, and Church Dykely received her gladly. Mary Layne had always been a favourite in the place, from the time her father, the good-hearted, hard-working surgeon, had fondly shown her, his youngest and fairest child, to the public, a baby of a few days old. But Church Dykely found her greatly changed. They remembered her as a blooming girl; she came back to them a grave woman, looking older than her years, and with a pale sweet countenance that seemed never to have a smile on it. She was only six-and-twenty yet.

Miss Layne took up her post at once by the side of her ailing mother. What with attending her and attending to Baby Arthur—whom she took into training at once, just as she had taken the children in India—she found her time fully occupied. The boy, when she returned, was turned five. She went out very rarely; never—except to church, or at dusk—when the family were at the Grange, for she seemed to have a dread of meeting them. Church Dykely wondered that Miss Layne did not call at the Grange, considering that she had been humble companion there before she went out, or that my lady did not come to see her; but supposed the lapse of time had caused the acquaintanceship to fall through.

Mary had brought good news from India. Her sister Eleanor, Mrs. Allan McAlpin, had a little girl, to the great delight of all concerned. Just when they had given it up as hopeless, the capricious infant arrived. Major Layne told his wife confidentially that Allan McAlpin was prouder of that baby than any dog with two tails.

And henceforth this was to be Mary Layne's home, and this her occupation—caring for her mother, so long as the old lady should be spared, and gently leading to good the child, Arthur. Mrs. Layne, lapsing into her dotage, would sit in her favourite place, the parlour window, open when the weather allowed it, watching people as they passed. Mary's smooth and bright brown hair might be seen in the background, her head drooping over the book she was reading to Mrs. Layne, or over her work when the old lady grew tired of listening, or over Master Arthur's lessons at the table. Not only lessons to fit him for this world did Mary teach him; but such as would stand him in good aid when striving onwards for the next. Twice a day, morning and evening, would she take the child alone, and talk to him of heaven, and things pertaining to it. Aunt Elizabeth's lessons had been chiefly on the score of behaviour: the other sort of instruction had been all routine, at the best. Mary remedied this, and she had an apt little scholar. Seated on her knee, his bright blue eyes turned up to her face, the child would listen and talk, and say he would be a good boy always, always. The tears wet his eyelashes at her Bible stories: he would put his little face down on her bosom, and whisper out a sobbing wish that Jesus would love him as He had loved the little children on earth. There is no safeguard like this seed sown in childhood: if withheld, nothing can replace it in after-life.

They grew the best and greatest friends, these two. Whether Mary loved him, or not, she did not say; she was ever patient and thoughtful with him, with a kind of grave tenderness. But the child grew to love her more than he had ever loved any one in his young life. One day, when he did something wrong and saw how it grieved her, his repentant sobs nearly choked him. It was very certain that Mary had found the way to his heart, and might mould him for good or for ill.

The child was a chatterbox. Aunt Elizabeth used to say he ought to have the tip of his tongue cut off. He seemed never tired of asking about papa and mamma in India, and Allan and Bobby and the rest, and the elephants and camels—and Dick the eldest, who was in London, at the school attached to King's College.

"When will they come over to see us, Aunt Mary?" he questioned one day, when he was on Mary's knee.

"If grandmamma's pretty well we, will have Dick down at Christmas."

"Is Dick to be a soldier like papa?"

"I think so."

"I shall be a soldier too."

There was an involuntary tightening of her hands round him—as if she would guard him from that.

"I hope not, Arthur. One soldier in a family's enough: and that is to be Richard."

"Is papa a very big, big brave man, with a flashing sword?"

"Major Layne is tall and very brave. He wears his sword sometimes."

"Oh, Aunt Mary, I should like to be a soldier and have a sword! When I can write well enough I'll write a letter to papa to ask him. I'd like to ride on the elephants."

"They are not as good to ride as horses."

"Is mamma as pretty as you?" demanded Master Arthur, after a pause.

"Prettier. I am pale and—" sad, she was going to say, but put another word—"quiet."

"When you go back to India, Aunt Mary, shall you take me? I should like to sail in the great ship."

"Arthur dear, I do not think I shall go back."

And so Miss Mary Layne—she was Miss Layne now—stayed on. Church Dykely would see a slender, grave young lady, dressed generally in black silk, whose sweet face seemed to have too careworn an expression for her years. But if her countenance was worn and weary, her heart was not. That seemed full of love and charity for all; of gentle compassion for any wrong-doer, of sympathy for the sick and suffering. She grew to be revered, and valued, and respected as few had ever been in Church Dykely: certainly as none had, so young as she was. Baby Arthur, clacking his whip as he went through the streets on his walks by the nurse Betsy's side, his chattering tongue never still; now running into the blacksmith's shed to watch the sparks; now perching himself on the top of the village stocks; and now frightening Betsy out of her senses by attempting to leap the brook—in spite of these outdoor attractions, Baby Arthur was ever ready to run home to Aunt Mary, as though she were his best treasure.

When Miss Layne had been about six months at her mother's, a piece of munificent good fortune befel her—as conveyed to her in official and unofficial communications from India. Andrew McAlpin—the head of the great McAlpin house in Calcutta, who had respected Mary Layne above all women, and had wished to marry her, as may be remembered—Andrew McAlpin was dead, and had left some of his accumulated wealth to Mary. It would amount to six hundred a-year, and was bequeathed to her absolutely: at her own disposal to will away when she in turn should die. In addition to this, he directed that the sum of one thousand pounds should be paid to her at once. He also left a thousand pounds to Mrs. Richard Layne—but that does not concern us. This good man's death brought great grief to Mary. It had been the result of an accident: he lay ill only a few weeks. As to the fortune—well, of course that was welcome, for Mary had been casting many an anxious thought to the future on sundry scores, and what little money she had been able to put by, out of the salary as governess at Major Layne's, was now nearly exhausted. She thought she knew why Mr. McAlpin had thus generously remembered her: and it was an additional proof of the thoughtful goodness which had ever characterized his life. Oh, if she could only have thanked him! if she had only known it before he died! He had been in the habit of corresponding with her since her return to Europe, for she and he had remained firm friends, but the thought of ever benefiting by him in this way had never entered her head. As how should it?—seeing that he was a strong man, and only in the prime of life. She mourned his loss: she thought she could best have spared any other friend; but all the regrets in the world would not bring him back to life. He was gone. And Allan McAlpin was now sole head of that wealthy house, besides inheriting a vast private fortune from his brother. Eleanor McAlpin, once Eleanor Layne, might well wish for more children amidst all her riches.

The first thing that Mary Layne did with some of this thousand pounds—which had been conveyed to her simultaneously with the tidings of the death—was to convey her mother to the seaside for a change, together with Baby Arthur and the nurse, Betsy. Before quitting home she held one or two interviews with James Spriggings, the house agent, builder, and decorator, and left certain orders with him. On their return, old Mrs. Layne did not know her house. It had been put into substantial repair inside and out, and was now one of the prettiest, not to say handsomest, in the village. All the old carpets were replaced by handsome new ones, and a great deal of the furniture was new. Pillars had been added to the rather small door, giving it an imposing appearance, iron outside railings had taken the place of the old ones. Mrs. Layne, I say, did not know her house again.

"My dear, why have you done it?" cried the old lady, looking about her in amazement. "Is it not a waste of money?"

"I think not, mother," was the answer. "Most likely this will be my home for life. Perhaps Arthur's home after me. At least it will be his until he shall be of an age to go out in the world."

Mrs. Layne said no more. She had grown of late very indifferent to outward things. Aged people do get so, and Mr. Duffham said her system was breaking up. The seaside air had done her good; they had gone to it in May, and came back in August. Mary added a third servant to the household, and things went on as before in their quiet routine.

One afternoon in September, when they had been at home about a month, Mary went out, and took Arthur. She was going to see a poor cottager who had nursed herself, Mary, when she was a child, and who had recently lost her husband. When they came to the gates of Chavasse Grange, past which their road lay, Master Arthur made a dead standstill, and wholly declined to proceed. The child was in a black velvet tunic, the tips of his white drawers just discernible beneath it, and his legs bare, down to the white socks: boys of his age were dressed so then. As bonny a lad for his six years as could be seen anywhere, with a noble, fearless bearing. Mary wore her usual black silk, a rich one too, with a little crape on it; the mourning for Mr. McAlpin. Arthur was staring over the way through the open gates of the Grange.

"I want to go in and see the peacock."

"Go in and see the peacock!" exclaimed Miss Layne, rather taken aback by the demand. "What can you mean, Arthur? The peacock is up by the house."

"I know it is. We can go up there and see it, Aunt Mary."

"Indeed we cannot, Arthur. I never heard of such a thing."

"Betsy lets me go."

The confession involved all sorts of thoughts, and a flush crossed Miss Layne's delicate face. The family were not at the Grange, as she knew: they had gone up to London in January, when Parliament met, and had never returned since: nevertheless she did not like to hear of this intrusion into the grounds of the nurse and child. The peacock had been a recent acquisition; or, as Arthur expressed it, had just "come to live there." When he had talked of it at home, Mary supposed he had seen it on the slopes in passing. These green slopes, dotted here and there with shrubs and flowers, came down to the boundary wall that skirted the highway. The avenue through the gates wound round abruptly, hiding itself beyond the lodge.

"Come, my dear. It is already late."

"But, Aunt Mary, you must see the peacock. He has got the most splendid tail. Sometimes he drags it behind him on the grass, and sometimes it's all spread out in a beautiful circle, like that fan you brought home from India. Do come."

Miss Layne did not reply for the moment. She was inwardly debating upon what plea she could forbid the child's ever going in again to see the peacock: the interdiction would sound most arbitrary if she gave none. All at once, as if by magic, the peacock appeared in view, strutting down the slopes, its proud tail, in all its glory, spread out in the rays of the declining sun.

It was too much for Arthur. With a shout of delight he leaped off the low foot-path, flew across the road, and in at the gates. In vain Mary called: in his glad excitement he did not so much as hear her.

There ensued a noise as of the fleet foot of a horse, and then a crash, a man's shout, and a child's cry. What harm had been done? In dire fear Mary Layne ran to see, her legs trembling beneath her.

Just at the sharp turn beyond the lodge, a group stood: Sir Geoffry Chavasse had Arthur in his arms; his horse, from which he had flung himself, being held and soothed by a mounted groom. The lodge children also had come running out to look. She understood it in a moment: Sir Geoffry must have been riding quickly down from the house, his groom behind him, when the unfortunate little intruder encountered him just at the turn, and there was no possibility of pulling up in time. In fact, the boy had run absolutely on to the horse's legs.

She stood, white, and faint, and sick against the wall of the lodge: not daring to look into the accident— for Mary Layne was but a true woman, timid and sensitive; as little daring to encounter Sir Geoffry Chavasse, whom she had not been close to but for a few months short of seven years. That it should have occurred!—that this untoward thing should have occurred!

"I wonder whose child it is?" she heard Sir Geoffry say—and the well-remembered tones came home to her with a heart-thrill. "Poor little fellow! could it have been my fault, or his? Dovey"—to the groom— "ride on at once and get Mr. Duffham here. Never mind my horse; he's all right now. You can lead him up to the house, Bill, my lad!"

The groom touched his hat, and rode past Mary on his errand. Sir Geoffry was already carrying the child to the Grange; Bill, the eldest of the lodge children, following with the horse. All in a minute, a wailing cry burst from Arthur.

"Aunt Mary! Aunt Mary! Oh, please let her come! I want Aunt Mary."

And then it struck Sir Geoffry Chavasse that a gentleman's child, such as this one by his appearance evidently was, would not have been out without an attendant. He turned round, and saw a lady in black standing by the lodge. The wailing cry began again.

"Aunt Mary! I want Aunt Mary."

There was no help for it. She came on with her agitated face, from which every drop of blood had faded. Sir Geoffry, occupied with the child, did not notice her much.

"I am so grieved," he began; "I trust the injury will be found not to be very serious. My horse—"

He had lifted his eyes then, and knew her instantly. His own face turned crimson; the words he had been about to say died unspoken on his lips. For a moment they looked in each other's faces, and might have seen, had the time been one of less agitation, how markedly sorrow had left its traces there. The next, they remembered the present time, and what was due from them.

"I beg your pardon: Miss Layne, I think?" said Sir Geoffry, contriving to release one hand and raise his hat.

"Yes, sir," she answered, and bowed in return.

He sat down on the bank for a moment to obtain a better hold of the child. Blood was dripping from one of the little velvet sleeves. Sir Geoffry, carrying him as gently as was possible, made all haste to the house. The window of what had been the garden-parlour stood open, and he took him into it at once. Ah, how they both remembered it. It had been refurnished and embellished now: but the room was the room still. Sir Geoffry had returned home that morning. His wife and Lady Chavasse were not expected for a day or two. Scarcely any servants were as yet in the house; but the woman who had been left in charge, Hester Picker, came in with warm water. She curtsied to Miss Layne.

"Dear little fellow!" she exclaimed, her tongue ready as of old. "How did it happen, sir?"

"My horse knocked him down," replied Sir Geoffry. "Get me some linen, Picker."

The boy lay on the sofa where he had been put, his hat off, and his pretty light brown hair falling from his face, pale now. Apparently there was no injury except to the arm. Sir Geoffry looked at Mary.

"I am a bit of a surgeon," he said. "Will you allow me to examine his hurt as a surgeon would? Duffham cannot be here just yet."

"Oh yes, certainly," she answered.

"I must cut his velvet sleeve up."

And she bowed in acquiescence to that.

Hester Picker came in with the linen. Before commencing to cut the sleeve, Sir Geoffry touched the arm here and there, as if testing where the damage might lie. Arthur cried out.

"That hurts you," said Sir Geoffry.

"Not much," answered the little fellow, trying to be brave. "Papa's a soldier, and I want to be a soldier, so I won't mind a little hurt."

"Your papa's a soldier? Ah, yes, I think I remember," said Sir Geoffry, turning to Mary. "It is the little son of Captain Layne."

"My papa is Major Layne now," spoke up Arthur, before she could make any answer. "He and mamma live in India."

"And so you want to be a soldier, the same as papa?" said Sir Geoffry, testing the basin of water with his finger, which Picker was holding, and which had been brought in very hot.

"Yes, I do. Aunt Mary there says No, and grandmamma says No; but—oh, what's that?"

He had caught sight of the blood for the first time, and broke off with a shuddering cry. Sir Geoffry was ready now, and had the scissors in his hand. But before using them he spoke to Miss Layne.

"Will you sit here whilst I look at it?" he asked, putting a chair with its face to the open window, and its back to the sofa. And she understood the motive and thanked him: and said she would walk about outside.

By-and-by, when she was tired of waiting, and all seemed very quiet, she looked in. Arthur had fainted. Sir Geoffry was bathing his forehead with eau-de-Cologne; Picker had run for something in a tumbler and wine stood on the table.

"Was it the pain?—did it hurt him very badly?" asked Mary, supposing that the arm had been bathed and perhaps dressed.

"I have not done anything to it; I preferred to leave it for Duffham," said Sir Geoffry—and at the same moment she caught sight of the velvet sleeve laid open, and something lying on it that looked like a mass of linen. Mary turned even whiter than the child.

"Do not be alarmed," said Sir Geoffry. "Your little nephew is only faint from the loss of blood. Drink this," he added, bringing her a glass of wine.

But she would not take it. As Sir Geoffry was putting it on the table, Arthur began to revive. Young children are elastic—ill one minute, well the next; and he began to talk again.

"Aunt Mary, are you there?"

She moved to the sofa, and took his uninjured hand.

"We must not tell grandmamma, Aunt Mary. It would frighten her."

"Bless his dear little thoughtful heart!" interjected Hester Picker. "Here comes something."

The something proved to be a fly, and it brought Mr. Duffham. Before the groom had reached the village, he overtook this said fly and the surgeon in it, who was then returning home from another accident. Turning round at the groom's news—"Some little child had run against Sir Geoffry's horse, and was hurt"—he came up to the Grange.

When Mr. Duffham saw that it was this child, he felt curiously taken aback. Up the room and down the room looked he; then at Sir Geoffry, then at Miss Layne, then at Hester Picker, saying nothing. Last of all he walked up to the sofa and gazed at the white face lying there.

"Well," said he, "and what's this? And how did it happen?"

"It was the peacock," Arthur answered. "I ran away from Aunt Mary to look at it, and the horse came."

"The dear innocent!" cried Hester Picker. "No wonder he ran. It's a love of a peacock."

"Don't you think it was very naughty, young sir, to run from your aunt?" returned Mr. Duffham.

"Yes, very; because she had told me not to. Aunt Mary, I'll never do it again."

The two gentlemen and Hester Picker remained in the room; Mary again left it. The arm was crushed rather badly; and Mr. Duffham knew it would require care and skill to cure it.

"You must send to Worcester for its best surgeon to help you," said the baronet, when the dressing was over. "I feel that I am responsible to Major Layne."

Old Duffham nearly closed his eyelids as he glanced at the speaker. "I don't think it necessary," he said; "no surgeon can do more than I can. However, it may be satisfactory to Major Layne that we should be on the safe side, so I'll send."

When the child was ready, Mary got into the fly, which had waited, and Mr. Duffham put him to lie on her lap.

"I hope, Miss Layne, I may be allowed to call to-morrow and see how he gets on," said Sir Geoffry, at the same time. And she did not feel that it was possible for her to say No. Mr. Duffham mounted beside the driver; to get a sniff, he said, of the evening air.

"How he is changed! He has suffered as I have," murmured Mary Layne to herself, as her tears fell on Baby Arthur, asleep now. "I am very thankful that he has no suspicion."

The child had said, "Don't tell grandmamma;" but to keep it from Mrs. Layne was simply impossible. With the first stopping of the fly at the door, out came the old lady; she had been marvelling what had become of them, and was wanting her tea. Mr. Duffham took her in again, and said a few words, making light of it, before he lifted out Baby Arthur.

A skilful surgeon was at the house the next day, in conjunction with Mr. Duffham. The arm and its full use would be saved, he said; its cure effected; but the child and those about him must have patience, for it might be rather a long job. Arthur said he should like to write to his papa in India, and tell him that it was his own fault for running away from Aunt Mary; he could write letters in big text hand. The surgeon smiled, and told him he must wait until he could use both arms again.

The doctors had not left the house many minutes when Sir Geoffry Chavasse called, having walked over from the Grange. Miss Layne sent her mother to receive him, and disappeared herself. The old lady, her perceptions a little dulled with time and age, and perhaps also her memory, felt somewhat impressed and flattered at the visit. To her it almost seemed the honour that it used to be: that one painful episode of the past seemed to be as much forgotten at the moment as though it had never had place. She took Sir Geoffry upstairs.

Arthur was lying close to the window, in the strong light of the fine morning. It was the first clear view Sir Geoffry had obtained of him. The garden-parlour at the Grange faced the east, so that the room on the previous evening, being turned from the setting sun, had been shady at the best, and the sofa was at the far end of it. As Sir Geoffry gazed at the child now, the face struck him as being like somebody's; he could not tell whose. The dark blue eyes especially, turned up in all their eager brightness to his, seemed quite familiar.

"He says I must not write to papa until I get well," said Arthur, who had begun to look on Sir Geoffry as an old acquaintance.

"Who does?" asked the baronet.

"The gentleman who came with Mr. Duffham."

"He means the doctor from Worcester, Sir Geoffry," put in old Mrs. Layne. She was sitting in her easy-chair near, as she had been previously; her spectacles keeping the place between the leaves of the closed Bible, which she had again taken on her lap; her withered hands, in their black lace mittens and frilled white ruffles, were crossed upon the Book. Every now and then she nodded with incipient sleep.

"I am so very sorry this should have happened," Sir Geoffry said, turning to Mrs. Layne. "The little fellow was running up to get a look at the peacock, it seems; and I was riding rather fast. I shall never ride fast round that corner again."

"But, Sir Geoffry, they tell me that the child ran right against you at the corner: that it was no fault of yours at all, sir."

"It was my fault, grandmamma," said Arthur. "And, Sir Geoffry, that's why I wanted to write to papa; I want to tell him so."

"I think I had better write for you," said Sir Geoffry, looking down at the boy with a smile.

"Will you? Shall you tell him it was my fault?"

"No. I shall tell him it was mine."

"But it was not yours. You must not write what is not true. If Aunt Mary thought I could tell a story, or write one, oh, I don't know what she'd do. God hears all we say, you know."

Sir Geoffry smiled—a sad smile—at the earnest words, at the eager look in the bright eyes. Involuntarily the wish came into his mind that he had a brave, fearless-hearted, right-principled son, such as this boy evidently was.

"Then I think I had better describe how it happened, and let Major Layne judge for himself whether it was my fast riding or your fast running that caused the mischief."

"You'll tell about the peacock? It had its tail out."

"Of course I'll tell about the peacock. I shall say to Major Layne that his little boy—I don't think I have heard your name," broke off Sir Geoffry. "What is it?"

"It's Arthur. Papa's is Richard. My big brother's is Richard too; he is at King's College. Which name do you like best?"

"I think I like Arthur best. It is my own name also."

"Yours is Sir Geoffry."

"And Arthur as well."

But at this juncture old Mrs. Layne, having started up from a nod, interposed to put a summary stop to the chatter, telling Arthur crossly that Mr. Duffham and the other doctor had forbid him to talk much. And then she begged pardon of Sir Geoffry for saying it, but thought the doctors wished the child to be kept quiet and cool. Sir Geoffry took the opportunity to say adieu to the little patient.

"May I come to see the peacock when I get well, Sir Geoffry?"

"Certainly. You shall come and look at him for a whole day if grandmamma will allow you to."

Grandmamma gave no motion or word of assent, but Arthur took it for granted. "Betsy can bring me if Aunt Mary won't; Betsy's my nurse. I wish I could have him before that window to look at while I lie here to get well. I like peacocks and musical boxes better than anything in the world."

"Musical boxes!" exclaimed Sir Geoffry. "Do you care for them?"

"Oh yes; they are beautiful. Do you know the little lame boy who can't walk, down Piefinch Cut? His father comes to do grandmamma's garden. Do you know him, Sir Geoffry? His name's Reuben."

"It's Noah, the gardener's son, sir," put in Mrs. Layne aside to Sir Geoffry. "He was thrown downstairs when a baby, and has been a cripple ever since."

But the eager, intelligent eyes were still cast up, waiting for the answer. "Where have I seen them?" mentally debated Sir Geoffry, alluding to the eyes.

"I know the name?" he answered.

"Well, Reuben has got a musical box, and it plays three tunes. He is older than I am: he's ten. One of them is 'The Blue Bells of Scotland.'"

Sir Geoffry nodded and went away. He crossed straight over to Mr. Duffham's, and found him writing a letter in his surgery.

"I hope the child will do well," said the baronet, when he had shaken hands. "I have just been to see him. What an intelligent, nice little fellow it is."

"Oh, he will be all right again in time, Sir Geoffry," was the doctor's reply, as he began to fold his letter.

"He is a pretty boy, too, very. His eyes are strangely like some one's I have seen, but for the life of me I cannot tell whose!"

"Really?—do you mean it?" cried Mr. Duffham, speaking, as it seemed, in some surprise.

"Mean what?"

"That you cannot tell."

"Indeed I can't. They puzzled me all the while I was there. Do you know? Say, if you do."

"They are like your own, Sir Geoffry."

"Like my own!"

"They are your own eyes over again. And yours—as poor Layne used to say, and as the picture in the Grange dining-room shows us also, for the matter of that—are Sir Peter's. Sir Peter's, yours, and the child's: they are all the same."

For a long space of time, as it seemed, the two gentlemen gazed at each other. Mr. Duffham with a questioning and still surprised look: Sir Geoffry in a kind of bewildered amazement.

"Duffham! you—you— Surely it is not that child!"

"Yes, it is."

He backed to a chair and stumbled into it, rather than sat down; somewhat in the same manner that Mrs. Layne had backed against the counter nearly seven years before and upset the scales. The old lady seemed to have aged since quicker than she ought to have done. but her face then had not been whiter than was Geoffry Chavasse's now.

"Good Heavens!"

The dead silence was only broken by these murmured words that fell from his lips. Mr. Duffham finished folding his note, and directed it.

"Sir Geoffry, I beg your pardon! I beg it a thousand times. If I had had the smallest notion that you were ignorant of this, I should never have spoken."

Sir Geoffry took out his handkerchief and wiped his brow. Some moisture had gathered there.

"How was I to suspect it?" he asked.

"I never supposed but that you must have known it all along."

"All along from when, Duffham?"

"From—from—well, from the time you first knew that a child was over there."

Sir Geoffry cast his thoughts back. He could not remember anything about the child's coming to Church Dykely. In point of fact, the Grange had been empty at the time.

"I understood that the child was one of Captain and Mrs. Layne's," he rejoined. "Every one said it; and I never had any other thought. Even yesterday at the Grange you spoke of him as such, Duffham."

"Of course. Miss Layne was present—and Hester Picker—and the child himself. I did not speak to deceive you, Sir Geoffry. When you said what you did to me in coming away, about calling in other advice for the satisfaction of Major Layne, I thought you were merely keeping up appearances."

"And it is so, then?"

"Oh dear, yes."

Another pause. Mr. Duffham affixed the stamp to his letter, and put the paper straight in his note-case. Sir Geoffry suddenly lifted his hand, as one whom some disagreeable reflection overwhelms.

"To think that I was about to write to Major Layne! To think that I should have stood there, in the old lady's presence, talking boldly with the child! She must assume that I have the impudence of Satan."

"Mrs. Layne is past that, Sir Geoffry. Her faculties are dulled: three-parts dead. That need not trouble you."

The baronet put aside his handkerchief and took up his hat to leave. He began stroking its nap with his coat-sleeve.

"Does my mother know of this, do you think?"

"I am sure she neither knows nor suspects it. No one does, Sir Geoffry: the secret has been entirely kept."

"The cost of this illness must be mine, you know, Duffham."

"I think not, Sir Geoffry," was the surgeon's answer. "It would not do, I fear. There's no need, besides: Miss Layne is rich now."

"Rich! How is she rich?"

And Mr. Duffham had to explain. A wealthy gentleman in India, some connection of the Laynes, had died and left money to Mary Layne. Six or seven hundred a year; and plenty of ready means. Sir Geoffry Chavasse went out, pondering upon the world's changes.

He did not call to see the invalid again; but he bought a beautiful musical box at Worcester, and sent it in to the child by Duffham. It played six tunes. The boy had never in his life been so delighted. He returned his love and thanks to Sir Geoffry; and appended several inquiries touching the welfare of the peacock.

The first news heard by Lady Chavasse and Lady Rachel on their coming home, was of the accident caused to Major Layne's little son by Sir Geoffry's horse. Hester Picker and the other servants were full of it. It happened to be the day that Sir Geoffry had gone to Worcester after the box, so he could not join in the narrative. A sweet, beautiful boy, said Hester to my ladies, and had told them he meant to be a soldier when he grew up, as brave as his papa. Lady Chavasse, having digested the news, and taken inward counsel with herself, decided to go and see him: it would be right and neighbourly, she thought. It might be that she was wishing to bestow some slight mark of her favour upon the old lady before death should claim her: and she deemed that the honour of a call would effect this. In her heart she acknowledged that the Laynes had behaved admirably in regard to the past; never to have troubled her or her son by word or deed or letter; and in her heart she felt grateful for it. Some people might have acted differently.

"I think I will go and see him too," said Lady Rachel.

"No, pray don't," dissented Lady Chavasse, hastily. "You already feel the fatigue of your journey, Rachel: do not attempt to increase it."

And as Lady Rachel really was fatigued and did not care much about it, one way or the other, she remained at home.

It was one of Mrs. Layne's worst days—one of those when she seemed three-parts childish—when Lady Chavasse was shown into the drawing-room. Mary was there. As she turned to receive her visitor, and heard the maid's announcement "Lady Chavasse," a great astonishment inwardly stirred her, but her manner remained quiet and self-possessed. Just a minute's gaze at each other. Lady Chavasse was the same good-looking woman as of yore; not changed, not aged by so much as a day. Mary was changed: the shy, inexperienced girl had grown into the calm, self-contained woman; the woman who had known sorrow, who had its marks impressed on her face. She had been pretty once, she was gravely beautiful now. Perhaps Lady Chavasse had not bargained for seeing her; Mary had certainly never thought thus to meet Lady Chavasse: but here they were, face to face, and each must make the best of it. As they did; and with easy courtesy, both being gentlewomen. Lady Chavasse held out her hand, and Mary put hers into it.

After shaking hands with Mrs. Layne—who was too drowsy properly to respond, and shut her eyes again—my lady spoke a few pleasant words of regret for the accident, of her wish to see the little patient, of her hope that Major and Mrs. Layne might not be allowed to think any care on Sir Geoffry's part could have averted it. Mary went upstairs with her. Lady Chavasse could only be struck with the improved appearance of the house, quite suited now to be the abode of gentle-people; and with its apparently well-appointed if small household.

The child lay asleep: his nurse, Betsy, sat sewing by his side. The girl confessed that she had allowed him sometimes to run in and take a look at the peacock. Lady Chavasse would not have him awakened: she bent and kissed his cheek lightly: and talked to Mary in a whisper. It was just as though there had been no break in their acquaintanceship, just as though no painful episode, in which they were antagonistic actors, had ever occurred between them.

"I hear you have come into a fortune, Miss Layne," she said, as she shook hands with Mary again in the little hall before departure. For Hester Picker had told of this.

"Into a great deal of money," replied Mary.

"I am glad to hear it: glad," came the parting response, whispered emphatically in Mary's ear, and it was accompanied by a pressure of the fingers.

Mr. Duffham was standing at his door, watching my lady's exit from Mrs. Layne's house, his eyes lost in wonder. Seeing him, she crossed over, and went in, Mr. Duffham throwing open the door of his sitting-room. She began speaking of the accident to Major Layne's little son—what a pity it was, but that she hoped he would do well. Old Duffham replied that he hoped so too, and thought he would.

"Mrs. Layne seems to be growing very old," went on Lady Chavasse. "She was as drowsy as she could be this afternoon, and seemed scarcely to know me."

"Old people are apt to be sleepy after dinner," returned the doctor.

And then there was a pause. Lady Chavasse (as Duffham's diary expresses it) seemed to be particularly absent in manner, as if she were thinking to herself, instead of talking to him. Because he had nothing else to say, he asked after the health of Lady Rachel. That aroused her at once.

"She is not strong. She is not strong. I am sure of it."

"She does not seem to ail much, that I can see," returned Duffham, who often had to hear this same thing said of Lady Rachel. "She never requires medical advice."

"I don't care: she is not strong. There are no children," continued Lady Chavasse, dropping her voice to a whisper; and a kind of piteous, imploring expression darkened her eyes.

"No."

"Four years married, going on for five, and no signs of any. No signs of children, Mr. Duffham."

"I can't help it, my lady," returned Duffham.

"Nobody can help it. But it is an awful misfortune. It is beginning to be a great trouble in my life. As the weeks and months and years pass on—the years, Mr. Duffham—and bring no hope, my very spirit seems to fail. 'Hope deferred maketh the heart sick.'"

"True."

"It has been the one great desire of my later years," continued Lady Chavasse, too much in earnest to be reticent, "and it does not come. I wonder which is the worst to be borne; some weighty misfortune that falls and crushes, or a longed-for boon that we watch and pray for in vain? The want of it, the eager daily strain of disappointment, has become to me worse than a nightmare."

Little Arthur Layne, attended by Betsy, spent a day at the Grange on his recovery, invited to meet the peacock. The ladies were very kind to him: they could but admire his gentle manners, his fearless bearing. Sir Geoffry played a game at ninepins with him on the lawn—which set of ninepins had been his own when a child, and had been lying by ever since. Betsy was told she might carry them home for Master Layne: Sir Geoffry gave them to him.

After that, the intercourse dropped again, and they became strangers as before. Except that Lady Chavasse would bow from her carriage if she saw Mrs. or Miss Layne, and Sir Geoffry raise his hat. The little boy had more notice: when they met him out, and were walking themselves, they would, one and all, stop and speak to him.

So this episode of the accident seemed to fade into the past, as other things had faded: and the time went on.

Part the Fourth

Autumn leaves were strewing the ground, autumn skies were overhead. A ray of the sun came slanting into the library, passing right across the face of Sir Geoffry Chavasse. The face had an older expression on it than his thirty years would justify. It looked worn and weary, and the bright hair, with its golden tinge, was less carefully arranged than it used to be, as if exertion were becoming a burden, or that vanity no longer troubled him; and his frame was almost painfully thin; and a low hacking cough took him at intervals. It might have been thought that Sir Geoffry was a little out of health, and wanted a change. Lady Chavasse, his mother, had begun to admit a long-repressed doubt whether any change would benefit him.

A common desk of stained walnut-wood was open on the table before him: he had been reading over and putting straight some papers it contained—notes and diaries, and so forth. Two or three of these he tore across and threw into the fire. Out of a bit of tissue paper, he took a curl of bright brown hair, recalling the day and hour when he had surreptitiously cut it off, and refused to give it up again to its blushing owner. Recalling also the happy feelings of that time—surreptitiously still, as might be said, for what business had he with them now? Holding the hair to his lips for a brief interval, he folded it up again, and took out another bit of paper. This contained a lady's ring of chased gold set with a beautiful and costly emerald. In those bygone years he had bought the ring, thinking to give it in payment of the stolen hair; but the young lady in her shyness had refused so valuable a present. Sir Geoffry held the ring so that its brightness glittered in the sun, and then wrapped it up again. Next he unfolded a diary, kept at that past period, and for a short time afterwards: then it was abruptly broken off, and had never since been written in. He smiled to himself as he read a page here and there—but the smile was full of sadness.

Lady Chavasse came into the room rather abruptly: Sir Geoffry shut up the diary, and prepared to close and lock the desk. There was a disturbed, restless, anxious look on my lady's face: there was a far more anxious and bitter pain ever making havoc with her heart.

"Why, Geoffry! have you got out that old desk?"

Sir Geoffry smiled as he carried it to its obscure place in a dark corner of the library. When he was about twelve years old, and they were passing through London, he went to the Lowther Arcade and bought this desk, for which he had been saving up his shillings.

"I don't believe any lad ever had so valuable a prize as I thought I had purchased in that desk, mother," was his laughing remark.

"I dare say it has a great deal of old rubbish in it," said Lady Chavasse, slightingly.

"Not much else—for all the good it can ever be. I was only glancing over the rubbish—foolish mementoes of foolish days. These days are weary; and I hardly know how to make their hours fly."

Lady Chavasse sighed at the words. He used to go shooting in the autumn—fishing—hunting once in a way, in the later season: he had not strength for these sports now.

Opening the desk he commonly used, a very handsome one that had been Lady Chavasse's present to him, he took a small book from it and put it into his breast-pocket. Lady Chavasse, watching all his movements, as she had grown accustomed to do, saw and knew what the book was—a Bible. Perhaps nothing had struck so much on my lady's fears as the habit he had fallen into of often reading the Bible. She had come upon him doing it in all kinds of odd places. Out amidst the rocks at the seaside where they had recently been staying—and should have stayed longer but that he grew tired and wanted to come home; out in the seats of this garden, amidst the roses, or where the roses had him with this small Bible. He always slipped it away when she or any one else approached: but the habit was casting on her spirit a very ominous shadow. It seemed to show her that he knew he must be drawing near to the world that the Bible tells of, and was making ready for his journey. How her heart ached, ached always, Lady Chavasse would not have liked to avow.

"Where's Rachel?" he asked.

"On her sofa, upstairs."

Sir Geoffry stirred the fire mechanically, his thoughts elsewhere—just as he had stirred it in a memorable interview of the days gone by. Unconsciously they had taken up the same position as on that unhappy morning: he with his elbow on the mantelpiece, and his face partly turned from his mother; she in the same chair, and on the same red square of the Turkey carpet. The future had been before them then: it lay in their own hands, so to say, to choose the path for good or for ill. Sir Geoffry had pointed out which was the right one to take, and said that it would bring them happiness. But my lady had negatived it, and he could only bow to her decree. And so, the turning tide was passed, not seized upon, and they had been sailing on a sea tolerably smooth, but without depth in it or sunshine on it. What had the voyage brought forth? Not much. And it seemed, so far as one was concerned, nearly at an end now.

"I fancy Rachel cannot be well, mother," observed Sir Geoffry, "She would not lie down so much if she were."

"A little inertness, Geoffry, nothing more. About Christmas?" continued Lady Chavasse. "Shall you be well enough to go to the Derrestons', do you think?"

"I think we had better let Christmas draw nearer before laying out any plans for it," he answered.

"Yes, that's all very well: but I am going to write to Lady Derreston to-day, and she will expect me to mention it. Shall you like to go?"

A moment's pause, and then he turned to her: his clear, dark-blue eyes, ever kind and gentle, looking straight Into hers; his voice low and tender.

"I do not suppose I shall ever go away from the Grange again."

She turned quite white. Was it coming so near as that? A kind of terror took possession of her.

"Geoffry! Geoffry!"

"My darling mother, I will stay with you if I can; you know that. But the fiat does not lie with you or with me."

Sir Geoffry went behind her chair, and put his arms round her playfully, kissing her with a strange tenderness of heart that he sought to hide.

"It may be all well yet, mother. Don't let it trouble you before the time."

She could not make any rejoinder, could not speak, and quitted the room to hide her emotion.

In the after-part of the day the surgeon, Duffham, bustled in. His visit was later than usual.

"And how are you, Sir Geoffry?" he asked, as they sat alone, facing each other between the table and the fire.

"Much the same, Duffham."

"Look here, Sir Geoffry—you should rally both yourself and your spirits. It's of no use giving way to illness. There's a certain listlessness upon you; I've seen it for some time. Shake it off."

"Willingly—if you will give me the power to do so," was Sir Geoffry's reply. "The listlessness you speak of proceeds from the fact that my health and energies fail me. As to my spirits, there's nothing the matter with them."

Mr. Duffham turned over with his fingers a glass paper-weight that happened to lie on the table, as if he wanted to see the fishing-boats on the sea that its landscape represented, and then he glanced at Sir Geoffry.

"Of course you wish to get well?"—with a slight emphasis on the "wish."

"Most certainly I wish to get well. For my mother's sake—and of course also for my wife's, as well as for my own. I don't expect to, though, Duffham."

"Well, that's saying a great deal," retorted Duffham, pretending to make a mockery of it.

"I've not been strong for some time—as you may have seen, perhaps: but since the beginning of May, when the intensely hot weather came in, I have felt as—as—"

"As what, Sir Geoffry?"

"As though I should never live to see another May, hot or cold."

"Unreasonable heat has that effect on some people, Sir Geoffry. Tries their nerves."

"I am not aware that it tries mine. My nerves are as sound as need be. The insurance offices won't take my life at any price, Duffham," he resumed.

"Have you tried them?"

"Two of the best in London. When I began to grow somewhat doubtful about myself in the spring, I thought of the future of those near and dear to me, and would have insured my life for their benefit. The doctors refused to certify. Since then I have felt nearly sure in my own mind that what must be will be. And, day by day, I have watched the shadow drawing nearer."

The doctor leaned forward and spoke a few earnest words of encouragement, before departing. Sir Geoffry was only too willing to receive them—in spite of the inward conviction that lay upon him, Lady Rachel Chavasse entered the library in the course of the afternoon. She wore a sweeping silk, the colour of lilac, and gold ornaments. Her face had not changed: with its classically-carved contour and its pale coldness.

"Does Duffham think you are better, Geoffry?"

"Not much, I fancy."

"Suppose we were to try another change—Germany, or somewhere?" she calmly suggested.

"I would rather be here than anywhere, Rachel."

"I should like you to get well, you know, Geoffry."

"I should like it too, my dear."

"Mamma has written to ask us to go into Somersetshire for Christmas," continued Lady Rachel, putting her foot, encased in its black satin shoe and white silk stocking, on the fender.

"Ay. My mother was talking about it just now. Well, we shall see between now and Christmas, Rachel. Perhaps they can come to us instead."

Lady Rachel turned her very light eyes upon her husband: eyes in which there often sat a peevish expression. It was not discernible at the present moment: they were coldly calm.

"Don't you think you shall be quite well by Christmas?"

"I cannot speak with any certainty, Rachel."

She stood a minute or two longer, and then walked round the room before the shelves, in search of some entertaining book. It was quite evident that the state of her husband did not bring real trouble to her heart. Was the heart too naturally cold?—or was it that as yet no suspicion of the seriousness of the case had penetrated to her? Something of both, perhaps.

Selecting a book, she was leaving the library with it when Sir Geoffry asked if she would not rather stay by the fire to read. But she said she preferred to go to her sofa.

"Are you well, Rachel?" he asked.

"My back feels tired, always. I suppose we are something alike, Geoffry—not over-strong," she concluded, with a smile.

That night Duffham made the annexed entry in his journal.

He does know the critical state he is in. Has known it, it seems, for some time. I suspected he did. Sir Geoffry's one that you may read as a book in his open candour. He would "get well if he could," he says, for his mother's sake. As of course he would, were the result under his own control: a fine young fellow of the upper ten, with every substantial good to make life pleasant, and no evil habits or thoughts to draw him backward, would not close his eyes on this world without a pang, and a struggle to remain a while longer in it.

I cannot do more for him than I am doing. All the faculty combined could not. Neither do I say, as he does, that he will not get better: on the contrary, I think there's just a chance that he will: and I honestly told him so. It's just a toss-up. He was always delicate until he grew to manhood: then he seemed to become thoroughly healthy and strong. Query: would this delicacy have come back again had his life been made as happy as it might have been? My lady can debate that point with herself in after-years: it may be that she'll have plenty of time to do it in. Sir Geoffry's is one of those sensitive natures where the mind seems almost wholly to influence the body; and that past trouble was a sharp blow to him. Upright and honourable, he could not well bear the remorse that fell upon him—it has been keenly felt, ay, I verily believe, until this hour: another's life was blighted that his might be aggrandized. My own opinion is, that had he been allowed to do as he wished, and make reparation, thereby securing his own happiness, he might have thrown off the tendency to delicacy still and always; and lived to be as old as his father, Sir Peter. Should my lady ever speak to me upon the subject, I shall tell her this. Geoffry Chavasse has lived with a weight upon him. It was not so much that his own hopes were gone and his love-dream wrecked, as that he had brought far worse than this upon another. Yes; my lady may thank herself that his life seems to have been wasted. Had there been children he might, in a degree, have forgotten what went before, and the mind would no longer have preyed upon the body. Has the finger of Heaven been in this? My pen ought to have written "specially in this:" for that Finger is in all things.

I hope he will get better. Yes, I do, in spite of a nasty doubt that crops up in my mind as I say it. I love him as I did in the old days, and respect him more. Qui vivra verra—to borrow a French phrase from young Master Arthur over the way. And now I put up my diary for the night.

Mrs. Layne was dead. Mary lived alone in her house now, with her servants and Arthur.

Never a woman so respected as she; never a lady, high or low, so revered and looked up to as Mary Layne. All the village would fly to her on an emergency; and she had both counsel and help to give. The poor idolized her. A noble, tender, good gentlewoman, with the characteristic humility in her bearing that had been observable of late years, and the gentle gravity on her thoughtful face. My lady, with all her rank and her show and her condescension, had never been half so much respected as this. The little boy—in knickerbockers now, and nine years old—was a great favourite; he also got some honour reflected on him through Colonel Layne. There had been a time of trouble in India, and Major Layne had grandly distinguished himself and gained honour and promotion. The public papers proclaimed his bravery and renown; and Arthur received his share of reflected glory. As the boy passed on his pony, the blacksmith, Dobbs, would shoot out from his forge to look after him, and say to the stranger whose horse had cast a shoe, "There goes the little son of the brave Colonel Layne: maybe you've heerd of his deeds over in Ingee." Perhaps the blacksmith considered he had acquired a sort of right in Arthur, since the pony—a sure-footed Welsh animal—was kept in the stable that belonged to his forge, and was groomed by himself or son. Miss Layne paid him for it; but, as the blacksmith said, it went again' the grain; he'd ha' been proud to do aught for her and the little gentleman without pay.

And somehow, what with one thing and another, my lady grew to think that if anything removed her from Chavasse Grange, Mary would take her place as best and chiefest in Church Dykely, and she herself would not be missed. But it was odd the thought should dawn upon her. Previsions of coming events steal into the minds of a great many of us; we know not whence they arise, and at first look on them only as idle thoughts, never recognizing them for what they are—advance shadows of the things to be.

One sunshiny afternoon, close upon winter, Arthur and Mr. Duffham went out riding. Mary watched them start; the doctor on his old grey horse (that had been her father's), and Arthur on his well-groomed pony. The lad sat well; as brave-looking a little gentleman, with his upright carriage, open face, and nice attire—for Mary was particular there—as had ever gratified a fond aunt's eye, or a blacksmith's heart.

Close by the gates of Chavasse Grange, they met Sir Geoffry and his mother strolling forth. Mr. Duffham's hopes had not been fulfilled. Outwardly there was not much change in the baronet, certainly none for the better; inwardly there was a great deal. He knew now how very certain his fate was, and that it might not be delayed for any great length of time; a few weeks, a few months: as God should will.

"Lady Rachel is not well," observed Sir Geoffry to the surgeon. "You must see her, Duffham. I suppose you can't come in now?"

"Yes, I can: I'm in no hurry," was the doctor's answer.

"May I come too, and see the peacock, Sir Geoffry? I'll wait here, though, if Mr. Duffham thinks I ought."

Of course the boy was told that the peacock would take it as a slight if he did not pay him a visit, and they all turned up the avenue. Arthur got off his pony and led it, and talked with Lady Chavasse.

"Why did you get off yet?" asked Sir Geoffry, turning to him.

"Lady Chavasse is walking," answered the boy, simply.

It spoke volumes for his innate sense of politeness. Sir Geoffry remembered that he had possessed the same when a child.

"Have you heard what papa has done?" asked Arthur, putting the question generally. "It has been in all the newspapers, and he is full colonel now. Did you read it, Sir Geoffry?"

"Yes, I read it, Arthur."

"And the Queen's going to thank papa when he comes to England, and to make him Sir Richard. Everybody says so. Dobbs thinks papa will be made general before he dies."

Dobbs was the blacksmith. They smiled at this. Not at the possibility for Colonel Layne, but at Dobbs.

"And, with it all, Aunt Mary does not want me to be a soldier!" went on the boy in rather an aggrieved tone. "Richard's enough, she says. Dick gets on well at King's College: he is to go to Woolwich next. I don't see the peacock!"

They had neared the house, but the gay plumaged bird, for which Arthur retained his full admiration, was nowhere in sight. Servants came forward and led the horses away. Mr. Duffham went on to see Lady Rachel: Arthur was taken into the garden-parlour by Sir Geoffry.

"And so you would like to be a soldier:" he said, holding the boy before him, and looking down at his bright, happy face.

"Oh, I should: very much. If papa says I'm not to be—or mamma—or Aunt Mary—if they should tell me 'No, no, you shall not,' why, it would be at an end, and I'd try and like something else."

"Listen, Arthur," said Sir Geoffry, in a low, earnest tone. "What you are to be, and what you are not to be, lie alike in the will of God. He will direct you aright, no doubt, when the time of choice shall come—"

"And that's what Aunt Mary says," interrupted the lad. "She says— There's the peacock!"

He had come round the corner, his tail trailing; the poor peahen following humbly behind him, as usual. Arthur went outside the window. The peacock had a most unsociable habit of stalking away with a harsh scream if approached; Arthur knew this, and stayed where he was, talking still with Sir Geoffry. When Lady Chavasse entered, he was deep in a story of the musical box.

"Yes, a wicked boy went into Reuben Noah's, and broke his box for the purpose. Aunt Mary is letting me get it mended for him with some sixpences I had saved up. Reuben is very ill just now—in great pain; and Aunt Mary has let me lend him mine—he says when he can hear the music, his hip does not hurt him so much. You are not angry with me for lending it, are you, Sir Geoffry?"

"My boy, I am pleased."

"Why should Sir Geoffry be angry—what is it to him?" cried Lady Chavasse, amused with the chatter.

"Sir Geoffry gave it to me," said Arthur, looking at her with wide-open eyes, in which the great wonder that any one should be ignorant of that fact was expressed. "Reuben wishes he could get here to see the peacock: but he can't walk, you know. I painted a beautiful one on paper and took it to him. Aunt Mary said it was not much like a real peacock; it was too yellow. Reuben liked it, and hung it up on his wall. Oh!"

For the stately peacock, stepping past the window as if the world belonged to him, suddenly threw wide his tail in an access of vanity. The tail had not long been renewed, and was in full feather. Arthur's face went into a radiant glow. Lady Chavasse, smiling at the childish delight, produced some biscuit that the peacock was inordinately fond of, and bade him go and feed it.

"Oh, Geoffry," she exclaimed in the impulse of the moment, as the boy vaulted away, "if you only had such a son and heir as that!"

"Ay. It might have been, mother. That child himself might have been Sir Arthur after me, had you so willed it."

"Been Sir Arthur after you!" she exclaimed. "Are you in a dream, Geoffry? That child!"

"I have thought you did not know him, but I never felt quite sure. He passes to the world for the son of Colonel Layne—as I trust he may so pass always. Don't you understand?"

It was so comical a thing, bringing up thoughts so astounding, and the more especially because she had never had the remotest suspicion of it, that Lady Chavasse simply stared at her son in silence. All in a moment a fiery resentment rose up in her heart: she could not have told at whom or what.

"I will never believe it, Geoffry. It cannot be."

"It is, mother."

He was leaning against the embrasure of the window as he stood, watching the boy in the distance throwing morsels of biscuit right into the peacock's mouth, condescendingly held wide to receive them. Lady Chavasse caught the strange sadness glistening in her son's eyes, and somehow a portion of her hot anger died away.

"Yes: there was nothing to prevent it," sighed Sir Geoffry. "Had you allowed it, mother, the boy might have been born my lawful son, my veritable heir. Other sons might have followed him: the probability is, there would have been half-a-dozen of them feeding the peacock now, instead of—of—I was going to say—of worse than none."

Lady Chavasse looked out at the boy with eager, devouring eyes: and whether there was more of longing in their depths, or of haughty anger, a spectator could not have told. In that same moment a vision, so vivid as to be almost like reality, stole before her mental sight—of the half-dozen brave boys crowding round the peacock, instead of only that one on whose birth so cruel a blight had been cast.

"A noble heir he would have made us, mother; one of whom our free land might have been proud," spoke Sir Geoffry, in a low tone of yearning that was mixed with hopeless despair. "He bears my name, Arthur. I would give my right hand—ay, and the left too—if he could be Sir Arthur after me!"

Arthur turned round. His cap was on the grass, his blue eyes were shining.

"He is frightfully greedy and selfish, Lady Chavasse. He will not let the peahen have a bit."

"A beautiful face," murmured Sir Geoffry. "And a little like what mine must have been at his age, I fancy. Sometimes I have thought that you would see the likeness, and that it might impart its clue."

"Since when have you known him?—known this?"

"Since the day after the accident, when my horse threw him down. Duffham dropped an unintentional word, and it enlightened me. Some nights ago I dreamt that the little lad was my true heir," added Sir Geoffry. "I saw you kiss him in the dream."

"You must have been letting your thoughts run on it very much," retorted Lady Chavasse, rather sharply.

"They are often running on it, mother: the regret for what might have been and for what is, never seems to leave me," was his reply. "For some moments after I awoke from that dream I thought it was reality: I believe I called out 'Arthur.' Rachel started, and inquired between sleeping and waking what the matter was. To find it was only a dream—to remember that what is can never be changed or redeemed in this world, was the worst pain of all."

"You may have children yet," said Lady Chavasse, after a pause. "It is not impossible."

"Well, I suppose not impossible," was the hesitating rejoinder. "But—"

"But you don't think it. Say it out, Geoffry."

"I do not think it. My darling mother, don't you see how it is with me?" he added, in an impulse of emotion—"that I am not to live. A very short time now, and I shall be lying with my father."

A piteous cry broke from her. It had to be suppressed. The ungrateful peacock, seeing no more dainty biscuit in store, had fluttered off with a scream, putting his tail down into the smallest possible compass; and Arthur came running back to the room. Mr. Duffham next appeared; his face grave, his account of Lady Rachel evasive. He suspected some latent disease of the spine, but did not wish to say so just yet.

The horse and pony were brought round. Arthur and the doctor mounted; Arthur turning round to lift his cap to Lady Chavasse and Sir Geoffry as he rode away. A noble boy in all his actions; sitting his pony like the young chieftain he ought to have been but for my lady's adverse will.

But Mr. Duffham was by no means prepared for an inroad on his privacy made that evening by my lady. She surprised him in his shabbiest parlour, when he was taking his tea: the old tin teapot on the Japan tray, and the bread-and-butter plate cracked across. Zuby Noah, Duffham's factotum, was of a saving turn, and never would bring in the best things except on Sundays. He had a battle with her over it sometimes, but it did no good. Duffham thought Lady Chavasse had come to hear about Lady Rachel, but he was mistaken.

She began with a despairing cry, by way of introduction to the interview; Zuby might have heard it as she went along the kitchen passage, but for her clanking pattens. The man-servant was out that evening, and Zuby was in waiting. Duffham, standing on the old hearthrug, found his arm seized by Lady Chavasse. He had never seen her in agitation like this.

"Is it to be so really? Mr. Duffham, can nothing be done? Is my son to die before my very eyes, and not be saved?"

"Sit down, pray, Lady Chavasse!" cried Duffham, trying to hand her into the chair that had the best-looking cushion on it, and wishing he had been in the other room and had not slipped on his worn, old pepper-and-salt coat.

"He ought not to die—to die and leave no children!" she went on, as if she were a lunatic. "If there were but one little son—but one—to be the heir! Can't you keep him in life? there may be children yet, if he only lives."

Her eyes were looking wildly into his; her fingers entwined themselves about the old grey cuffs as lovingly as though they were of silk velvet. No: neither Duffham nor any one else had ever seen her like this. It was as though she thought it lay with Duffham to keep Sir Geoffry in life and to endow Chavasse Grange with heirs.

"Lady Chavasse, I am not in the place of God."

"Don't you care for my trouble? Don't you care for it?"

"I do care. I wish I could cure Sir Geoffry."

Down sat my lady in front of the fire, in dire tribulation. By the way she stared at it, Duffham thought she must see in it a vision of the future.

"We shall have to quit the Grange, you know, if he should die: I and Lady Rachel. Better that I quitted it in my young life; that I had never had a male child to keep me in it. I thought that would have been a hardship: but oh, it would have been nothing to this."

"You shall take a cup of tea, Lady Chavasse—if you don't mind its being poured out of this homely tea-pot," said Duffham. "Confound that Zuby!" he cried, under his breath.

"Yes, I will take the tea—put nothing in it. My lips and throat are dry with fever and pain. I wish I could die instead of Geoffry! I wish he could have left a little child behind to bless me!"

Duffham, standing up whilst she took the tea, thought it was well that these trials of awful pain did not fall often in a lifetime, or they would wear out alike the frame and the spirit. She grew calm again. As if ashamed of the agitation betrayed, her manner gradually took a sort of hard composure, her face a defiant expression. She turned it on him.

"So, Mr. Duffham! It has been well done of you, to unite with Sir Geoffry in deceiving me! That child over the way has never been Colonel Layne's."

And then she went on in a style that put Duffham's back up. It was not his place to tell her, he answered. At the same time he had had no motive to keep it from her, and if she had ever put the question to him, he should readily have answered it. Unsolicited, unspoken to, of course he had held his peace. As to uniting with Sir Geoffry to deceive her, she deceived herself if she thought anything of the kind. Since the first moment they had spoken together, when the fact had become known to Sir Geoffry, never a syllable relating to it had been mentioned between them. And then, after digesting this for a few minutes in silence, she went back to Sir Geoffry's illness.

"It is just as though a blight had fallen on him," she piteously exclaimed, lifting her hand and letting it drop again. "A blight."

"Well, Lady Chavasse, I suppose something of the kind did fall upon him," was Duffham's answer.

And that displeased her. She turned her offended face to the doctor, and inquired what he meant by saying it.

So Duffham set himself to speak out. He had said he would, if ever the opportunity came. Reverting to what had happened some nine or more years ago, he told her that in his opinion Sir Geoffry had never recovered it: that the trouble had so fixed itself upon him as to have worked insensibly upon his bodily health.

"Self-reproach and disappointment were combined, Lady Chavasse; for there's no doubt that the young lady was very dear to him," concluded Duffham. "And there are some natures that cannot pick up again after such a blow."

She was staring at Duffham with open eyes, not understanding.

"You do not mean to say that—that the disappointment about her has killed Sir Geoffry?"

"My goodness, no!" cried Duffham, nearly laughing. "Men are made of tougher stuff than to die of the thing called love, Lady Chavasse. What is it Shakespeare says? 'Men have died, and worms have eaten them, but not for love.' There is no question but that Sir Geoffry has always had an inherent tendency to delicacy of constitution," he continued more seriously: "my partner Layne told me so. It was warded off for a time, and he grew into a strong, hearty man: it might perhaps have been warded off for good. But the blight—as you aptly express it, Lady Chavasse—came: and perhaps since then the spirit has not been able to maintain its own proper struggle for existence—in which lies a great deal, mind you; and now that the original weakness has shown itself again, he cannot shake it off."

"But—according to that—he is dying of the blight?"

"Well—in a sense, yes. If you like to put it so."

Her lips grew white. There rose before her mind that one hour of bitter agony in her lifetime and her son's, when he had clasped his pleading hands on hers, and told her in a voice hoarse with its bitter pain and emotion that if she decided against him he could never know happiness again in this world: that to part from one to whom he was bound by sweet endearment, by every tie that ought to bind man to woman, would be like parting with life. Entrenched in her pride, she had turned a deaf ear, and rejected his prayer: and now there had come of it what had come. Yes, as Lady Chavasse sat there, she had the satisfaction of knowing that the work was hers.

"A warmer climate?—would it restore him?" she exclaimed, turning her hot eyes on Mr. Duffham.

"Had it been likely to do so, Lady Chavasse, I should have sent him to one long ago."

She gathered her mantle of purple velvet about her as she rose up, and went out of the room in silence, giving Duffham her hand in token of friendship.

Duffham opened the front-door, and was confronted by a tall footman—with a gold-headed cane and big white silk calves—who had been waiting in the air for his lady. She took the way to the Grange; the man and his protecting cane stepping grandly after her.

"Sir Geoffry Chavasse."

Buried in her own reflections by the drawing-room fire, in the coming dusk of the winter's evening, Miss Layne thought her ears must have deceived her. But no. It was Sir Geoffry who advanced as the servant made the announcement; and she rose to meet him. Strangely her heart fluttered: but she had been learning a lesson in calmness for many years; he had too, perhaps; and they shook hands quietly as other people do. Sir Geoffry threw back his overcoat from his wasted form as he sat down.

Wasted more than ever now. Some weeks have gone on since my lady's impromptu visit to Mr. Duffham's tea-table; winter is merging into spring; and the most sanguine could no longer indulge hope for Sir Geoffry.

"You have heard how it is with me?" he began, looking at Mary, after recovering his short breath.

"Yes," she faintly answered.

"I could not die without seeing you, Mary, and speaking a word of farewell. It was in my mind to ask you to come to the Grange for half-an-hour's interview; but I scarcely saw how to accomplish it: it might have raised some speculation. So as the day has been fine and mild, I came to you."

"You should have come earlier," she murmured. "It is getting late and cold."

"I did come out earlier. But I have been with Duffham."

Moving his chair a little nearer to hers, he spoke to her long and earnestly. In all that was said there seemed to be a solemn meaning—as is often the case when the speaker is drawing to the confines of this world and about to enter on the next. He referred a little to the past, and there was some mutual explanation. But it seemed to be of the future that Sir Geoffry had come chiefly to speak—the future of Baby Arthur.

"You will take care of him, Mary?—of his best interests?" And the tears came into Mary Layne's eyes at the words. He could not really think it necessary to ask it.

"Yes. To the very utmost of my power."

"I am not able to leave him anything. You know how things are with us at the Grange. My wish would have been good—"

"It is not necessary," she interrupted. "All I have will be his, Sir Geoffry."

"Sir Geoffry! Need you keep up that farce, Mary, in this our last hour? He seems to wish to be a soldier: and I cannot think but that the profession will be as good for him as any other, provided you can like it for him. You will see when the time comes: all that lies in the future. Our lives have been blighted, Mary: and I pray God daily and hourly that, being so, it may have served to expiate the sin—my sin, my love, it was never yours—and that no shame may fall on him."

"I think it will not," she softly said, the painful tears dropping fast. "He will always be regarded as Colonel Layne's son: the very few who know otherwise—Mr. Duffham, Colonel and Mrs. Layne, and Lady Chavasse now—will all be true to the end."

"Ay. I believe it too. I think the boy may have a bright and honourable career before him: as much so perhaps as though he had been born my heir. I think the regret that he was not—when he so easily might have been—has latterly helped to wear me out, Mary."

"I wish you could have lived, Geoffry!" she cried from between her blinding tears.

"I have wished it also," he answered, his tone full of pain. "But it was not to be. When the days shall come that my mother is alone, except for Lady Rachel, and grieving for me, I want you to promise that you will sometimes see her and give her consolation. Something tells me that you can do this, Mary, that she will take it from you—and I know that she will need it sadly. Be kind to her when I am gone."

"Yes. I promise it."

"You are the bravest of us all, Mary. And yet upon you has lain the greatest suffering."

"It is the suffering that has made me brave," she answered. "Oh, Geoffry, I am getting to realize the truth that it is better to have too much of suffering in this world than too little. It is a truth hard to learn: but once learnt, it brings happiness in enduring."

Sir Geoffry nodded assent. He had learnt somewhat of it also—too late.

"I have begun a confidential letter to Colonel Layne, Mary, and shall post it before I die. To thank him for—"

The words were drowned in a gleeful commotion—caused by the entrance of Arthur. The boy came dashing in from his afternoon's study with the curate, some books under his arm.

"I have not been good, Aunt Mary. He said I gave him no end of trouble; and I'm afraid I did: but, you see, I bought the marbles going along, instead of in coming back, as you told me, and— Who's that!"

In letting his books fall on a side-table, he had caught sight of the stranger—then standing up. The fire had burnt low, and just for the moment even the young eyes did not recognize Sir Geoffry Chavasse. Mary stirred the fire into a blaze, and drew the crimson curtains before the window.

"What have you come for?" asked the little lad, as Sir Geoffry took his hand. "Are you any better, sir?"

"I shall never be better in this world, Arthur. And so you gave your tutor trouble this afternoon!"

"Yes; I am very sorry: I told him so. It was all through the marbles. I couldn't keep my hands out of my pockets. Just look what beauties they are!"

Out came a handful of "beauties" of many colours. But Mary, who was standing by the mantelpiece, her face turned away, bade him put them up again. Arthur began to feel that there was some kind of hush upon the room.

"I have been talking to Miss Layne about your future—for, do you know, Arthur, you are a favourite of mine," said Sir Geoffry. "Ever since the time when my horse knocked you down—and might have killed you—I have taken a very warm interest in your welfare. I have often wished that you—that you"—he seemed to hesitate in some emotion—"were my own little son and heir to succeed me; but of course that cannot be. I don't know what profession you will choose, or may be chosen for you—"

"I should like to be a soldier," interrupted Arthur, lifting his sparkling eyes to Sir Geoffry's.

"Your ideas may change before the time for choosing shall come. But a soldier may be as brave a servant of God as of his queen: should you ever become a soldier, will you remember this truth?"

"Yes," said Arthur, in a whisper, for the grave tones and manner impressed him with some awe.

Sir Geoffry was sitting down and holding Arthur before him. To the latter's intense surprise, he saw two tears standing on the wasted cheeks. It made him feel a sort of discomfort, and he began, as a relief, to play with the chain and seal that hung on the baronet's waistcoat. A transparent seal, with a plain device on it.

"Should you like to have them when I am gone, Arthur—and wear them in remembrance of me when you are old enough? I think it must be so: no one can have a better right to them than my little friend who once nearly lost his arm by my carelessness. I will see about it. But I have a better present than that—which I will give you now."

Taking from his pocket the small Bible that had been his companion for some months, he put it into Arthur's hands, telling him that he had written his name in it. And the child, turning hastily to the fly-leaf, saw it there: "Arthur Layne. From G. A. C." Lower down were the words: "Come unto Me all ye that labour and are heavy laden, and I will give you rest."

"Jesus said that!" cried the boy, simply.

"Jesus Christ. My Saviour and yours—for I am sure you will let Him be yours. Do not part with this Book, Arthur. Use it always: I have marked many passages in it. Should it be your fate ever to encamp on the battle-field, let the Book be with you: your guide and friend. In time you will get to love it better than any book that is to be had in the world."

The child had a tender heart, and began to cry a little. Sir Geoffry drew him nearer.

"I have prayed to God to bless you, Arthur. But you know, my child, He will only give His best blessing to those who seek it, who love and serve Him. Whatsoever may be your lot in life, strive to do your duty in it, as before God; loving Him, loving and serving your fellow-creatures; trusting ever to Christ's atonement. These are my last solemn words to you. Do you always remember them."

His voice faltered a little, and Arthur began to sob. "Oh, Sir Geoffry, must you die?"

Sir Geoffry seemed to be breathing fast, as though agitation were becoming too much for him. He bent his head and kissed the boy's face fervently: his brow, his cheeks, his lips, his eyelids—there was not a spot that Sir Geoffry did not leave a kiss upon. It quite seemed as though his heart had been yearning for those kisses, and as though he could not take enough of them.

"And now, Arthur, you must do a little errand for me. Go over to Mr. Duffham, and tell him I am coming. Leave the Bible on the table here."

Arthur went out of the house with less noise than he had entered it. Sir Geoffry rose.

"It is our turn to part now, Mary. I must be gone."

Her sweet face was almost distorted with the efforts she had been making to keep down emotion before the child. She burst into tears, as her hand met Sir Geoffry's.

"God bless you! God bless you always, my darling!" he murmured. "Take my thanks, once for all, for the manner in which you have met the past; there is not another woman living who would have done and borne as you have. This is no doubt our last meeting on earth, Mary; but in eternity we shall be together for ever. God bless you, and love you, and keep you always!"

A lingering hand-pressure, a steady look into each other's eyes, reading the present anguish there, reading also the future trust, and then their lips met—surely there was no wrong in it!—and a farewell kiss of pain was taken. Sir Geoffry went out, buttoning his overcoat across his chest.

A fly was waiting before Mr. Duffham's house; the surgeon and Arthur were standing by it on the pavement. Sir Geoffry got inside.

"Good-bye, Sir Geoffry!" cried the little lad, as Mr. Duffham, saying he should be at the Grange in the morning, was about to close the door. "I shall write and tell papa how good you've been, to give me your own Bible. I can write small-hand now."

"And fine small-hand it is!" put in old Duffham in disparagement.

Sir Geoffry laid his hand gently on Arthur's head, and kept it there for a minute. His lips were moving, but he said nothing aloud. Arthur thought he had not been heard.

"Good-bye, Sir Geoffry," he repeated.

"Good-bye, my child."

Sir Geoffry lay back in an easy-chair in front of the fire in his library. The end was near at hand now, but he was bearing up quite well to the last. Lady Chavasse, worn almost to a shadow with grief and uncertainty—for there were times yet when she actually entertained a sort of hope—sat away in the shade; her eyes watching every change in his countenance, her heart feeling ever its bitter repentance and despair.

Repentance? Yes, and plenty of it. For she saw too surely what might have been and what was—and knew that it was herself, herself only, who had worked out this state of things. Her self-reproach was terrible; her days and nights were one long dream of agony. Lady Rachel was not with them very much. She lay down more than ever in her own room; and Lady Chavasse had begun to learn that this almost continuous lying was not caused by inert idleness, but of necessity. The Grange was a sad homestead now.

The blaze from the fire flickered on Sir Geoffry's wasted face. Hers was kept in the shadow, or it might have betrayed the bitterness of her aching heart. He had been speaking of things that touched her conscience.

"Yes, it was a sin, mother. But it might have been repaired; and, if it had been, I believe God would have blessed us all. As it is—well, we did not repair it, you and I; and so—and so, as I take it, there has not been much of real blessing given to us here; certainly not of heartfelt comfort. I seem to see all things clearly now—if it be not wrong to say it."

Lady Chavasse saw them too—though perhaps not exactly in the way he meant. Never was the vision, of what might have been, more vividly before her than now as he spoke. She saw him, a hale happy man; his wife Mary, their children, a goodly flock, all at the Grange, and herself first amongst them, reigning paramount, rejoicing in her good and dutiful daughter-in-law. Oh, what a contrast between that vision and reality! A repressed groan escaped her lips; she coughed to smother it.

"Mother!"

"Well, Geoffry?"

"You need not have suppressed my last letter to Mary—the letter of explanation I wrote when I quitted her and the Grange. You might have been sure of me—that I would be true to my word to you."

No answer. There was a great deal that she would not suppress, besides the letter, if the time had to come over again. The log sparkled and crackled and threw its jets of flame upwards; but no other noise disturbed the room's stillness.

"Mother!"

"Well, Geoffry?"

"I should like the child, little Arthur, to have my watch and its appendages. Have you any objection?"

"None."

"It will be looked upon, you know, as a token of remembrance to the little fellow who had so sharp an illness through my horse."

"Yes."

"And—I have two desks, you know. The old one of common stained wood I wish sent to Miss Layne, locked as it is. The key I will enclose in a note. Let them be sent to her when I am dead."

"It shall be done, Geoffry."

"There's not much in the desk. Just a few odds and ends of papers; mementoes of the short period when I was happy—though I ought not to have been. Nothing of value; except a ring that I bought for her at Worcester at the time, and which she would not take."

"I promise it, Geoffry. I will do all you wish."

"Thank you. You have ever been my loving friend, mother."

"Ever, Geoffry?"

"Well—you did for the best there, mother; though it was a mistake. You acted for what you thought my welfare."

"Would you not like to see her, Geoffry?"

"I have seen her and bidden her farewell. It was the afternoon I went to Duffham's and you said that I stayed out too late. And now I think I'll lie down on the sofa, and get, if I can, a bit of sleep; I feel tired. To-morrow I will talk about you and Rachel—and what will be best for you both. I wish to my heart, for your sake and hers, that Rachel had borne a son; I am thinking of you both daily, and of what you will do when I am gone."

"I shall never know pleasure in life again, Geoffry," she cried, with a heartbroken sob. "Life for me will be, henceforth, one of mortification and misery."

"But it will not last for ever. Oh, mother! how merciful God is!—to give us the blessed hope of an eternal life of perfect happiness, after all the mistakes and tribulations and disappointments of this! My darling mother! we shall all be there in sweet companionship for ever."

They buried Sir Geoffry Chavasse by the side of his father—and any one who likes to go there may see his tomb against the graveyard wall of Church Dykely. My Lady Chavasse arranged the funeral. The Earl of Derreston and a Major Chavasse were chief mourners, with other grand people. Duffham's diary gives the particulars, but there is no space here to record them. Duffham was bidden to it; and brought Arthur Layne in his hand to the Grange, in obedience to a private word of my lady's—for she knew the dead, if he could look out of his coffin, would like to see Arthur following. So the procession started, a long line; the village gazing in admiration as it passed; and Dobbs the blacksmith felt as proud as ever was the

Grange peacock, when he saw Colonel Layne's little son in a coach, amidst the gentlefolks. 'Twere out of respect to the colonel's bravery, you might be sure, he told a select audience: and p'r'aps a bit because o' that back accident to the child hisself. And so, amidst pomps, and coaches, and comments, Geoffry Chavasse was left in his last home.

[Final matters extracted from Duffham's Diary.]

It is eighteen months now since Sir Geoffry died; and strange changes have taken place. The world is always witnessing such: you go up, and I go down.

Admiral Chavasse came home and took possession of the Grange. My lady had previously quitted it. She did not quit Church Dykely. It seemed indifferent to her where she settled down; and Lady Rachel Chavasse had become used to my attendance, and wished to stay. There was a small white villa to let on this side of the Grange, and they took it. Lady Rachel lies down more than ever; when she goes out it is in a Bath-chair. Old John Noah draws it. The spinal complaint is confirmed. I can do her no good; but I go in once or twice a week, and have a gossip. She is very fractious: and what with one thing and another, my Lady Chavasse has a trying life of it. They keep three servants only; no carriage—except the Bath-chair. What a change! what a change!

If ever there was a disappointed woman in this world, one who feels the humiliation of her changed position keenly, whose whole life is a long living repentance, it is Lady Chavasse. The picture of what might have been is ever in her mind; the reality of what is, lies around her. To judge by human fallibility, she has a long existence before her: not quite fifty yet, and her health rude: but in spirit she is a bowed, broken-down woman.

The Grange is let. Sir Parker Chavasse could not reconcile himself to living in a rural district, and went back to his ship. At first he shut the Grange up; now he has let it for a term to Mr. and Mrs. McAlpin, formerly of Calcutta. They live there with their children; in as good a style as ever the Chavasses did. Allan McAlpin has given up business, and spends his large fortune like the gentleman he is. She is Mary Layne's sister: a dainty and rather haughty woman. My lady looks out surreptitiously from the corner of her window as Mrs. McAlpin's carriage bowls along the road beyond the field. Colonel Layne's wife is also here just now, on a visit at the Grange; her husband, Sir Richard Layne, K.C.B., has returned to his duties in India. The whole county calls upon them and seems proud to do it, forgetting perhaps that they were only the daughters of my predecessor, Layne the apothecary. Yes! there are strange ups and downs in this world: and Mary Layne, so despised once, might not now be thought, even by my lady, so very unequal to Sir Geoffry Chavasse.

She does not go in for grandeur. But the village would like to lay its hands under her feet. Never was there so good, so unselfish, so sweet and humble-minded a woman as Mary. In a temporary indisposition that attacked her a few weeks ago, Mr. Dobbs, struck with consternation, gave, it as his opinion that Church Dykely "could afford to lose the whole biling of 'em, better than her." Lady Chavasse has seen her merit at last; and Mary's frequent presence in their house seems to bring light to the two lonely women. Arthur goes there too; my lady loves him, curious though the fact may sound. An incident occurred the other evening.

Miss Layne and Arthur were at tea there, when I happened to go in with some medicine. Mary had her work out, and sat talking in a low voice to Lady Rachel on her sofa; Lady Chavasse was watching Arthur, playing on the grass-plat. My lady rose up with a sudden cry:

"Take care of the wasp, Sir Arthur! Sir Arthur!"

I saw what painful reverie she had been lost in—the vision of that which might have been. It is apt to steal on her at sunset. Becoming conscious of the slip, she flushed slightly, and turned it off. Lady Rachel laughed; she thought it a good joke. Mary was more silent than usual that night, as I walked home by her and Arthur's side.

Here ends the history. Mary Layne lives on in her home, training Arthur, helping the sick and suffering, keeping her face steadily turned to another world. Never a one is there amidst us so respected as that good, grave lady, who blighted her life in early womanhood, and who carries its trace on her sad, sweet countenance, and its never-ceasing shame on her sorrowing heart.

That's all at last. You must be glad of it. Old Duffham shall not lead me blindfold into one of his spun-out histories again. The trouble I've had to cut it down! What with the diaries and letters, it was twice as long.

And he called it a tale of sin. I, Johnny Ludlow, think it is more like a tale of suffering.

CHAPTER X

A DAY OF PLEASURE

We all liked Captain Sanker; a post-captain in the navy, ages since on half-pay; who came into Worcestershire, and brought a letter of introduction to the Squire. He was about a seventeenth cousin of the Sankers of Wales, and a twenty-seventh of Mrs. Todhetley. The captain and his wife and family, six children, had lived in Ireland and the Channel Islands, and other cheap localities, making both ends of their income meet as well as they could—and nobody need be told how poor is the half-pay of naval officers, and what a fight and a struggle it is to rub along. At last, through the death of a relative of Mrs. Sanker, they dropped into quite a fortune, and came over to settle at Worcester.

A Dr. Teal, who had also recently come to Worcester, and was an old friend of Captain Sanker, proposed it to them. He wrote a flaming account of the pretty place that Worcester was, of the loveliness of the surrounding country; and of the great advantage the college school would be to the young Sankers, in giving them a free education if they could be got into it. The prospect of a free education for his boys took with the captain, and he lost no time in removing to Worcester, the Welsh Sankers giving him an introduction to us. We grew pretty intimate: calling on them when we went to Worcester for a day, and having them over to spend days with us.

All the young Sankers were got into the college school by degrees, and became four of the forty king's scholars. At that time—it is long past now—the school was not thought much of, for the boys were taught little but the classics, so entrance was easy: Latin, Greek, bad writing, and the first rule in arithmetic: there it ended. Captain Sanker thought the education first-rate, and had them all enrolled: Frederick, Daniel, King, and Toby. As to Toby, I fancy his real name was Alfred, but I never heard him called by it.

They had been in Worcester between one and two years, when Tod and I went over to them on a visit. The captain had come to spend a summer's day at Crabb Cot, and in his jolly, open-hearted fashion insisted on taking us two back with him. He was a short, stout man, with grey hair, and merry bright blue eyes all alight with smiles. The college school would be breaking up for its long holidays in a week or so, and it would have been better for us to have gone then; but the captain always did things on impulse, and had no more forethought than young Toby. The holidays were taken late that year, and would be very long, because the college hall, which was the schoolroom, would be wanted for the music-meeting in September.

The Sankers' was a funny household, and we pitched down amongst them without ceremony on either side. The house was at the corner of an open road, not very far from the cathedral. It was a commodious house as to size; but all the rooms were in an everlasting litter, so that you could never find a chair to sit down on. The captain was good-humoured always, going in and out a hundred times a day. There seemed to be no fixed hour for meals, and sometimes no meals to eat: Mrs. Sanker would forget to order them. She was a little lady, who went about as if she were dreaming, in a white petticoat and loose buff jacket; or else she'd be sitting aloft in the turret, darning stockings and saying poetry. She was the least excitable person I ever knew; all events, good and bad, she took as a matter of course: had the house caught fire she would have looked on quietly—as Nero did when Rome was burning. Why they called the room the turret did not appear. It had a great high beam running through it on the floor: and Mrs. Sanker would sit on that, reading poetry to us or telling her dreams, her light hair all down.

At seven o'clock the boys had to be in school. Being summer weather, that was no hardship. At nine they came in again with a rush, wild for breakfast. If Mrs. Sanker was not down to give it them, the four boys would begin and eat up the piles of bread-and-butter; upon which Hetta Sanker would call them tigers, and go to the kitchen to tell the maids to cut more. Which was the cook of the two servants and which the housemaid, they did not themselves seem to know: both did the work indiscriminately. Breakfast over, the boys went out again, Tod and I with them. At ten they must be in school. At one they came home to dinner; it might be ready, or it might not: if not, they'd go in and polish off anything cold that might be in the larder. It didn't seem to spoil their dinners. Afternoon school again until four o'clock; and then at liberty for good. Tea was at any time; a scrambling sort of meal that stayed on the table for hours, and was taken just as we chanced to go in for it. Jam and boiled eggs would be on the table, with the loaf and butter ad libitum. Sometimes toast and dripping, and there used to be a scuffle for that. As to dinner, when Mrs. Sanker forgot it, the servants would bring in a big dish of poached eggs, and we made it up with bread-and-cheese. Or Dan or Toby would be sent tearing off to High Street for a lot of penny pork-pies and apple-tarts. At night we had prayers, which the captain read.

Now I dare say that to people accustomed to a domestic life like clock-work, this would have been unbearable. I thought it delightful; as did Tod. It was like a perpetual picnic. But it was from one of these dinnerless episodes we found out that Captain Sanker had a temper. Generally speaking, he took disasters with equanimity.

It was on a Thursday. We were to have had four ducks for dinner, which the captain had bought at market the day before. Fine ducks that he was proud of: he carried them home himself, and brought them into the parlour to show us. On this day, Thursday, Tod and I had been into the Town Hall in the morning, listening to a trial before the magistrates—some fellow who had stolen his neighbour's clothes-props and cut them up for firewood. We reached home just as the boys and their books did, as hungry as they were. There was no cloth laid, and Fred shouted out for Biddy, asking whether we were to dine to-day or to-morrow. Biddy heard, and came rushing in with the cloth and knife-tray.

"What's for dinner besides the four ducks?" asked Dan. "Any pudding? Have you put plenty of stuffing?"

"Indeed then, and I don't think there's much for dinner," replied Biddy. "I've been in the turret with the missis all the morning, helping to stuff a pillow."

She laid the cloth, and Mrs. Sanker came mooning down in the short white petticoat and buff jacket, darning a sock of Dan's. The dreadful truth came out—busy over beds and pillows, nobody had thought of dinner, and the ducks were hanging in the larder, uncooked. Before speechless tongues could find words, Captain Sanker came in, bringing his friend Dr. Teal to taste the ducks. All the Teals were as intimate at the house as we were. Years before, when the captain was a middy, Dr. Teal had been assistant-surgeon on the same ship.

"They've a cold dinner at Teal's to-day," said the captain to his wife, as she was shaking hands with the doctor, "so he has come to share ours. Fine ducks they are, Teal!"

Then the news had to be told. The ducks were not cooked: dinner altogether had been forgotten.

I saw Captain Sanker's face turn white—quite white; but he did not say a word. Dr. Teal—a scientific Scotchman, who walked with his nose in the air and his spectacles turned to the skies, as if always looking for a lunar rainbow—made the best of it. Laughing, he said he would come in another day, and went out.

Then it began. Captain Sanker gave vent to passion in a way that startled me, and made Tod stare. I don't believe he knew for a few moments what he was doing or saying. Nora, the other servant—both girls had come with them from Ireland, and were as thoughtless as their mistress—came in with a dish of some hastily concocted pudding: a sort of batter. The captain, who still had his stick in his hand, lifted it and spattered the pudding all about the cloth. Then he stamped out of the house with a bang.

"Sit down, dears," said Mrs. Sanker, not at all moved, as she began to collect the pudding with a spoon. "Bring in the cheese, Nora, and do some eggs. Here's a corner seat for you, Johnny; can you squeeze in? The captain will have his dinner with the Teals, no doubt. He has been tasting the doctor's port wine, I think; or he wouldn't have been so put up."

And somehow we gathered, then or later, that the captain was easy as an old glove at all times and over all crosses, unless he was a little "put up" by artificial help. He told us himself one day (not, of course, alluding to anything of this sort) that he had had naturally an awful temper, would go into passions of absolute madness for a minute or two, when he was younger; but that he had by much self-restraint chiefly if not quite subdued it. It was true; and the temper never need be feared now unless he took anything to excite him. Dan had the same temper; but without the good-nature. And they said Hetta had; but we saw nothing of it in her. Hetta was eighteen, a nice-looking girl, who was governess to little Ruth, or pretended to be; but Ruth would manage to escape her lessons five days in the week. It was all the same to Mrs. Sanker whether she did them or whether she didn't.

At the time of this visit of ours to Worcester, the college school was in a ferment. Between the Cathedral and St. Peter's Church was situated a poor, back district called Frog Lane. It had been rechristened Diglis Street, but was chiefly called by the old name still. Crowded dwellings, narrow streets, noise and dirt— that's how the place struck me. The inhabitants were chiefly workmen belonging to the glove and china manufactories of the town. In this district was the parish school, always filled with boys, sons of the working-men, and under the superintendence of Mr. Jones, the portly parish clerk. Now there was wont to spring up from time to time a tide of animosity between these boys and the boys of the college school. Captain Sanker said it was the fault of the college boys: had they let the St. Peter's boys alone, St. Peter's boys would never have presumed to interfere with them: but the college boys could be downright contemptuous and overbearing when they pleased. They scornfully called the St. Peter's boys the Frogs, "charity boys;" and the Frogs retorted by calling them the College Caws—after the rooks that had their homes in the old trees of the college green and kept up a perpetual cawing. The animosity generally ended in a grand battle; and then hostilities would be dropped for months, perhaps years. One of these quarrels was going on while we were at Worcester; it had kept both schools in a ferment for some weeks, and there was every sign of a culminating fight. Of course we went in heart and soul with the king's scholars: but the boys on both sides held a code of honour—if you can call it so—that no stranger must take part in the engagements. The college boys were only forty, all told; the Frogs seemed to number four times as many.

Skirmishes took place daily—the scene being the top of Edgar Street. St. Peter's boys (let out of school at twelve, whereas the others did not get out till one) would collect in the narrow neck of their district opening on Edgar Street, and wait for the enemy. As soon as the college boys' steps were heard racing under the dark gateway of Edgar Tower, hisses and groans began. "Caw, caw, caw! Hiss, hiss, hiss! How's your Latin to-day?—what birchings has you had? Call yourselves gents, does you, you College Caws? You daren't come on fair, and fight it out with us, you Caws. Caw, caw, caw!" Sometimes the college boys would pass on, only calling back their contemptuous retorts; sometimes they'd halt, and a fierce storm of abuse would be interchanged, to the edification of Edgar Street in general and the clerks in Mr. Clifton's Registry Office. "You beggarly Frogs! We don't care to soil our hands with you! Had you been gentlemen, we'd have polished you off long ago, and sent you into next week. Croak, Frogs! Croak!" Not a third of the college boys need have taken Edgar Tower on their way home; through the cloisters and out by St. Michael's churchyard would have been their direct way; but they chose to meet the Frogs. Once in a way there'd be a single combat; but as a rule nothing came of it but abuse. When that was exhausted, each lot would rush home their separate ways: the Frogs back down Frog Lane; the others up the steps, or onwards down Edgar Street, as their road might lie, and remain apart till the same hour next day.

I have not said much yet about King Sanker. He was lame: something was wrong with his knee. Gatherings would come in it, and then he'd be in bed for weeks together. He was nearly thirteen then; next to Dan: and Dan was over fourteen. King was a nice little fellow, with mild eyes as blue as the captain's: Fred would order him to keep "out of the ruck" in the skirmishes with the Frogs, and he generally did. If it came to a fight, you see, King might have been hurt; he had no fighting in him, was frightened at it, and he could not run much. King was just like his mother in ideas: he would tell us his dreams as she did, and recite pieces of poetry a mile long. Dan and King slept together in the room next to ours; it was in the garret, close to the turret-room. King would keep us awake singing; sometimes chants, sometimes hymns, sometimes songs. They'd have let him try for the choir, but the head-master of the college school thought his knee would not do for it.

It was Saturday, and a pouring wet afternoon. Our visit was drawing to an end; on the following Wednesday we should bid the Sankers good-bye. Captain Sanker, always trying to find out ways of making folk happy, had devised a day of pleasure for the last day of our stay, Tuesday. We were to go to Malvern; a whole lot of us: ourselves, and the Teals, and the Squire, and Mrs. Todhetley, and take our dinner on the hill. It was so settled; and the arrangements were planned and made.

But this was yet only Saturday. We dined at twelve: whether for any one's convenience or that the servants made a mistake in an hour, I don't remember. It happened to be a saint's day, so the boys had no school; and, being wet, came home after morning service in the cathedral. After a jolly dinner of peas and bacon and pancakes, we looked at the skies for a bit, and then (all but Fred and Hetta) went up to the turret-room. Dan said the rain had come to spite us; for the whole school had meant to race to Berwick's Bridge after afternoon service and hold a mock review in the fields there. It was coming down in torrents, peppering the roof and the windows. Mrs. Sanker sat in the middle of the old beam, mending one of Toby's shirts, "Lalla Rookh" open on her knee, out of which she was singing softly; the floor was strewed with patches, and scissors, and tapes, and the combs were out of one side of her hair.

"Read it out loud to us, mamma," cried King.

"I can't spare time to read, King," she said. "Look here"—holding out the work, all rags and tatters. "If I don't mend this, Toby won't have a shirt to put on to-morrow."

"I shan't mind about that," said Toby.

"Oh, but, dear, I don't think you could go without a shirt. Has any one seen my cotton?"

"Then say something over to us that you know, mamma," returned King, as Toby found the cotton.

"Very well. I can do that and work too. Sit down, all of you."

We sat down, King and Toby on the floor before her, the rest of on the beam on either side her. Dan, who did not care for poetry, got some Brazil nuts out of his pocket and cracked them while he listened.

Mrs. Sanker might as well have read "Lalla Rookh." She began to recite "The Friar of Orders Grey." But what with gazing up at the sky through the rain to give it due emphasis, and shaking her head at pathetic parts, the sewing did not get on. She had finished the verse—

"Weep no more, lady, weep no more,
Thy sorrow is in vain;
For violets plucked, the sweetest showers
Will ne'er make grow again,"

—when King surprised us by bursting into tears. But as Mrs. Sanker took no notice, I supposed it was nothing unusual.

"You young donkey!" cried Dan, when the poem was finished. "You'll never be a man, King."

"It is such a nice verse, Dan," replied young King, meekly. "I whisper it over sometimes to myself in bed. Mamma, won't you say the 'Barber's Ghost'? Johnny Ludlow would like to hear that, I know."

We had the "Barber's Ghost," which was humorous, and we had other things. After that, Mrs. Sanker told a dreadful story about a real ghost, one that she said haunted her family, and another of a murder that was discovered by a dream. Some of the young Sankers were the oddest mixtures of timidity and bravery—personally brave in fighting; frightfully timid as to being alone in the dark—and I no longer wondered at it if she brought them up on these ghostly dishes.

"I should not like to have dreams that would tell me of murders," said King, thoughtfully. "But I do dream very strange dreams sometimes. When I awake, I lie and wonder what they mean. Once I dreamt I saw heaven—didn't I, mamma? It was so beautiful."

"Ay; my family have always been dreamers," replied Mrs. Sanker.

Thus, what with ghosts and poetry and talking, the afternoon wore on unconsciously. Dan suddenly started up with a shout—

"By Jove!"

The sun had come out. Come out, and we had never noticed it. It was shining as brightly as could be on the slates of all the houses. The rain had ceased.

"I say, we shall have the review yet!" cried Dan. "And, by Jupiter, that's the college bell! Make a rush, you fellows, or you'll be marked late. There's three o'clock striking."

The king's scholars thought it a great shame that they should have to attend prayers in the cathedral morning and afternoon on saints' days, instead of wholly benefiting by the holiday. They had to do it, however. The three went flying out towards the cathedral, and I gave King my arm to help him after them. Tod and I—intending to take part in the review at Berwick's Bridge—went to college also, and sat behind the surpliced king's scholars on the decani side, in the stalls next to the chanter.

But for a little mud, you'd hardly have thought there had been any rain when we got out again; and the sun was glowing in the blue sky. Not a single fellow was absent: even King limped along. We took the way by the Severn, past the boat-house at the end of the college boundaries, and went leisurely along the towing-path, intending to get into the fields beyond Diglis Wharf, and so onwards.

I don't believe there was a thought in any one's mind that afternoon of the enemy. The talk—and a good hubbub it was—turned wholly upon soldiers and reviews. A regular review of the Worcestershire militia took place once a year on Kempsey Ham, and some of the boys' heads got a trifle turned with it. They were envying Lord Ward, now, as they went along: saying they should like to be him, and look as well as he did, and sit his horse as proudly.

"Of course he's proud," squeaked out the biggest Teal, whose voice was uncertain. "Think of his money!—and his horses!—and see how good-looking he is! If Lord Ward hasn't a right to be proud, I should like to know who has. Why, he—oh, by George! I say, look here!"

Turning into the first field, we found we had turned into a company of Frogs. All the whole lot, it seemed. Caws and croaks and hoots and groans from either side rose at once on the air. Which army commenced hostilities, I couldn't tell; the one was as eager for it as the other; and in two minutes the battle had begun—begun in earnest. Up dashed the senior boy.

"Look here," said he to me and Tod; "you understand our rules. You must neither of you attempt to meddle in this. Stay and look on, if you please; but keep at a sufficient distance where it may be seen that you are simply spectators. These beggars shan't have it to say that we were helped."

He dashed back again. Tod ground his teeth with the effort it took to keep himself from going in to pummel some of the Frogs. Being upon honour, he had to refrain; and he did it somehow.

The Frogs had the blazing sun in their eyes; our side had it at their backs—which was against the Frogs. There were no weapons of any sort; only arms and hands. It looked like the scrimmage of an Irish row. Sometimes there was closing-in, and fighting hand to hand; sometimes the forces were drawn back again, each to its respective ground. During the first of these interludes, just as the sides were preparing to charge, a big Frog, with broad awkward shoulders, a red, rugged face, and a bleeding nose, came dashing forward alone into the ranks of the college boys, caught up poor lame helpless King Sanker, bore him bravely right through, and put him down in safety beyond, in spite of the blows freely showered upon him. Not a soul on our side had thought of King; and the college boys were too excited to see what the big Frog was about, or they'd perhaps have granted him grace to pass unmolested. King sat down on the wet grass for a bit, and gazed about him like a fellow bewildered. Seeing me and Tod he came limping round to us.

"It was good-natured of that big Frog, wasn't it, Johnny Ludlow?"

"Very. He'd make a brave soldier. I mean a real soldier."

"Perhaps I should have been killed, but for him. I was frightened, you see; and there was no way out. I couldn't have kept on my legs a minute longer."

The battle raged. The cawing and the croaking, that had been kept up like an array of trumpets, fell off as the fighting waxed hotter. The work grew too fierce and real for abuse of tongue. We could hear the blows dealt on the upturned faces. King, who had a natural horror of fighting, trembled inwardly from head to foot, and hid his face behind me. Tod was dancing with excitement, flinging his closed fists outward in imaginary battle, and roaring out like a dragon.

I can't say who would have won had they been left alone. Probably the Frogs, for there were a great many more of them. But on the other hand, none of them were so old as some of the college boys. When the fight was at the thickest, we heard a sudden shout from a bass, gruff, authoritative voice: "Now then, boys, how dare you!" and saw a big, portly gentleman in black clothes and a white necktie, appear behind the Frogs, with a stout stick in his hand.

It was Clerk Jones, their master. His presence and his voice acted like magic. Not a Frog of them all but dropped his blows and his rage. The college boys had to drop theirs, as the enemy receded. Clerk Jones put himself between the two sets of combatants.

The way he went on at both sides was something good to hear. Shaking his stick at his own boys, they turned tail softly, and then rushed away through the mud like wild horses, not waiting to hear the close: so the college boys had the pepper intended for the lot. He vowed and declared by the stick that was in his hand—and he had the greatest mind, he interrupted himself to say, to put it about their backs—that if ever they molested his boys again, or another quarrel was got up, he would appeal publicly to the dean and chapter. If one of the college boys made a move in future to so much as cast an insulting look towards a boy in St. Peter's School, that boy should go before the dean; and it would not be his fault (the clerk's) if he was not expelled the cathedral. He would take care, and precious good care, that his boys should preserve civility henceforth; and it was no great favour to expect that the college boys would do so. For his part he should feel ashamed in their places to oppress lads in an inferior class of life to themselves; and he should make it his business before he slept to see the head-master of the college school, and report this present disgraceful scene to him: the head-master could deal with it as he pleased.

Mr. Jones went off, flourishing his stick; and our side began to sum up its damages: closed eyes, scratched faces, swollen noses, and torn clothes. Dan Sanker's nose was as big as a beer barrel, and his shirt-front hung in ribbons. Fred's eyes were black. Toby's jacket had a sleeve slit up, and one of his boots had disappeared for good.

The spectacle we made, going home down the Gloucester Road, could not be easily forgotten. Folks collected on the pavement, and came to the windows and doors to see the sight. It was like an army of soldiers returning from battle. Bleeding faces, black eyes, clothes tattered and bespattered with mud. Farmers going back from market drew up their gigs to the roadside, to stare at us while we passed. One little girl, in a pony-chaise, wedged between a fat old lady in a red shawl and a gentleman in top-boots, was frightened nearly into fits. She shrieked and cried, till you might have heard her up at Mr. Allies's; and the old lady could not pacify her. The captain was out when we got in: and Mrs. Sanker took it all with her usual apathy, only saying we had better have come straight home from college to hear some more poetry.

An awful fuss was made by the head-master. Especially as the boys had to appear on Sunday at the cathedral services. Damages were visible on many of them; and their white surplices only helped to show the faces off the more. The chorister who took the solo in the afternoon anthem was decorated with cuttings of sticking-plaster; he looked like a tattooed young Indian.

The school broke up on the Monday: and on that day Mr. and Mrs. Todhetley drove into Worcester, and put up at the Star and Garter. They came to us in the afternoon, as had been agreed upon; dinner being ordered by Captain Sanker for five o'clock. It was rather a profuse dinner; fish and meat and pies and dessert, but quite a scramble of confusion: which none of the Sankers seemed to notice or to mind.

"Johnny dear, is it always like this?" Mrs. Todhetley could not help asking me, in a whisper. "I should be in a lunatic asylum in a week."

We started for Malvern on Tuesday at eleven o'clock. The Squire drove Bob and Blister in his high carriage: Dr. Teal, Captain Sanker, and Fred sitting with him. There was no railroad then. The ladies and the girls crammed themselves into a post-carriage from the Star, and a big waggonette was lent by some friend of Dr. Teal for the rest. The boys were losing the signs of their damages; nothing being very conspicuous now but Dan's nose. It refused to go down at all in size, and in colour was brighter than a rainbow. The Teals kept laughing at it, which made Dan savage; once he burst out in a passion, wishing all the Frogs were shot.

I remember that drive still. John Teal and I sat on the box of the post-carriage, the post-boy riding his horses. I remember the different features of the road as we passed them—not but that I knew them well before; I remember the laden orchards, and the sweet scent of the bean-fields, in flower then. Over the bridge from Worcester went we, up the New Road and through St. John's, and then into the open country; past Lower Wick, where Mrs. Sherwood lived, and on to Powick across its bridge. I remember that a hearse and three mourning-coaches stood before the Lion, the men refreshing themselves with drink; and we wondered who was being buried that day. Down that steep and awkward hill next, where so many accidents occurred before it was altered, and so on to the Link; the glorious hills always before us from the turning where they had first burst into view; their clumps of gorse and broom, their paths and their sheep-tracks growing gradually plainer to the sight the nearer we drew. The light and shade cast by the sun swept over them perpetually, a landscape ever changing; the white houses of the village, nestling amidst their dark foliage, looked fair for the eye to rest upon. Youth, as we all get to learn when it has gone by, lends a charm that later life cannot know: but never a scene that I have seen since, abroad or at home, lies on my memory with half the beauty as does that old approach to Malvern. Turning round to the left at the top of the Link, we drove into Great Malvern.

The carriages were left at the Crown. An old pony was chartered for some of the provisions, and we boys carried the rest. The people at St. Ann's Well had been written to, and the room behind the well was in readiness for us. Once the baskets were deposited there, we were at liberty till dinner-time, and went on up the hill. Turning a corner which had hidden the upper landscape from view, we came upon Dan Sanker, who had got on first. He was standing to confront us, his face big with excitement, his nose flaming.

"If you'll believe me, those cursed Frogs are here!"

In angry consternation—for the Frogs seemed to have no business to be at Malvern—we rushed on, turned another corner, and so brought ourselves into a wide expanse of upper prospect. Sure enough! About a hundred of the Frogs in their Sunday clothes were trooping down the hill. They had the start of us in arriving at Malvern, and had been to the top already.

"I'll—be—jiggered!" cried Dan, savagely. "What a horrid lot they are! Look at their sneaking tail-coats. Wouldn't I like to pitch into them!"

The college school wore the Eton jacket. Those preposterous coats, the tails docked to the size of the boys, did not improve the appearance of the Frogs. But as to pitching-in, Dan did not dare to do it after what had passed. It was his nose that made him so resentful.

"I desire that you will behave as gentlemen," said Captain Sanker, who was behind with the Squire, and bid us halt. "Those poor boys are here, I see; but they will not, I am sure, molest you, neither must you molest them. Civility costs nothing, remember. What are you looking so cross for, Dan?"

"Oh, well, papa, it's like their impudence, to come here to-day!" muttered Dan.

The captain laughed. "They may say it's like yours, to come, Dan: they were here first. Go on, lads, and don't forget yourselves."

Tod's whistle below was heard just then; and Dan, not caring to show his nose to the enemy, responded, and galloped back. We went on. The paths there are narrow, you know, and we expected to have all the string of Frogs sweeping past us, their coats brushing our jackets. But—perhaps not caring to meet us any more than we cared to meet them—most of them broke off on a detour down the steep of the hill, and so avoided us. About half-a-dozen came on. One of them was a big-shouldered, awkward, red-faced boy, taller than the rest of them and not unlike a real frog; he walked with his cap in his hand, and his brown hair stood on end like a porcupine's. Indisputably ugly was he, with a mouth as wide as a frying-pan; but it was a pleasant and honest face, for all that. King suddenly darted to him as he was passing, and pulled him towards Captain Sanker, in excitement.

"Papa, this is the one I told you of; the one who saved me and didn't mind the blows he got in doing it. I should have been knocked down, and my knee trampled on, but for him."

Out went Captain Sanker's hand to shake the boy's. He did it heartily. As to the Frog, he blushed redder than before with modesty.

"You are a brave lad, and I thank you heartily," said the captain, wringing his hand as though he'd wring it off. "You do honour to yourself, whoever you may be. There was not one of his own companions to think of him, and save him, and you did it in the midst of danger. Thank you, my lad."

The captain slid half-a-crown into his hand, telling him to get some Malvern cakes. The boy stood back for us to go by. I was the last, and he spoke as if he knew me.

"Good-day, Master Johnny."

Why, who was he? And, now I came to look at his freckled face, it seemed quite familiar. His great wide mouth brought me remembrance.

"Why, it's Mark Ferrar! I didn't know you at first, Mark."

"We've come over here for the day in two vans," said Mark, putting his grey cap on. "Eighty of the biggest of us; the rest are to come to-morrow. Some gent that's visiting at St. Peter's parsonage has given us the treat, sir."

"All right, Mark. I'm glad you thought of King Sanker on Saturday."

Ferrar touched his cap, and went vaulting down after his comrades. He was related to Daniel Ferrar, the Squire's bailiff, of whom you have heard before, poor fellow, and also to the Batleys of South Crabb. He used to come over to Crabb, that's where I had seen him.

Some donkeys came running down the hill, their white cloths flying. Captain Sanker stopped one and put King on him—for King was tired already. We soon got to the top then, and to Lady Harcourt's Tower. Oh, it was a glorious day! The great wide prospect around stood out in all its beauty. The vale of Herefordshire on the one side with its rural plains and woods basked in the sunshine, its crops of ruddy pears and apples giving token of the perry and cider to come; on the other side rose the more diversified landscape that has been so much told and talked of. Over the green meadows and the ripening corn-fields lay Worcester itself: the cathedral showing out well, and the summit of the high church-spire of St. Andrew's catching a glint of the sunlight. Hills caught the eye wherever it turned: Bredon Hill, Abberleigh Hills, the Old Hills; homesteads lay upon their lands, half hidden by their rick-yards and clustering trees; cattle and sheep browsed on the grass or lay in the shade to shelter themselves from the midday sun. To the right, on the verge of the horizon, far, far away, might be caught a glimpse of something that sparkled like a bed of stars—the Bristol Channel. It is not often you can discern that from Malvern, but this day that I am telling of was one of the clearest ever seen there; the atmosphere looking quite rarefied in spite of the sunlight.

King's donkey regaled himself with morsels of herbage, the donkey-boy lay stretched beside him, and we boys raced about. When an hour or two had passed, and we were as hot as fire and more hungry than hunters, we bethought ourselves of dinner. King got on his donkey again, and the rest of us whipped him up. When half-way down we saw Dr. Teal gesticulating and shouting, telling us to come on and not keep dinner waiting longer.

We had it in the room behind the well. It was a squeeze to sit round the table. Cold meats, and salad, and pastry, and all sorts of good things. Dan was next to me; he said he could hardly eat for thirst, and kept drinking away at the bottled ale.

"My dear," said Mrs. Todhetley to him by-and-by, "don't you think you had better drink some water instead—or lemonade? This bottled ale is very strong."

"I am afraid it is," said Dan. "I'll go in for the tarts now."

The room was stuffy; and after dinner a table was carried out to a sheltered place near the well: not much better than a little ledge of a path, but where we could not be overlooked, and should be quite out of the way of the hill-climbers. The bank rose perpendicularly above us, banks descended beneath to goodness knew where; there we sat at dessert, all sheltered. I think dark trees and shrubs overshaded us; but I am not altogether sure.

How it came about, I hardly know: but something was brought up about King's store of ballads, and he was asked to give us his favourite one, "Lord Bateman," for the benefit of the company. He turned very shy, but Captain Sanker told him not to be silly: and after going white and red for a bit, he began. Perhaps the reader would like to hear it. I never repeat it to myself, no, nor even a verse of it, but poor King Sanker comes before me just as I saw him that day, his back to the ravine below, his eyes looking at nothing, his thin hands nervously twisting some paper about that had covered the basket of raspberries.

Lord Bateman was a noble lord,
A noble lord of high degree:
He shipped himself on board a ship;
Some foreign country he would see.

He sailed east, he sailèd west,
Until he came unto Turkey,
Where he was taken, and put in prison
Until his life was quite weary.

In this prison there grew a tree:
It grew so very stout and strong:
And he was chained by the middle
Until his life was almost gone.

The Turk, he had one only daughter,
The fairest creature eye e'er did see:
She stole the keys of her father's prison,
And said she'd set Lord Bateman free.

"Have you got houses?—have you got lands
Or does Northumberland belong to thee?
And what would you give to the fair young I
Who out of prison would set you free?"

"Oh, I've got houses, and I've got lands,
And half Northumberland belongs to me;
And I'd give it all to the fair young lady
That out of prison would set me free."

Then she took him to her father's palace,
And gave to him the best of wine;
And every health that she drank to him
Was "I wish, Lord Bateman, you were mine.

"For seven long years I'll make a vow;
And seven long years I'll keep it strong:
If you will wed no other woman,
I will wed no other man."

Then she took him to her father's harbour,
And gave to him a ship of fame;
"Farewell, farewell to you, Lord Bateman;
I fear I never shall see you again."

When seven long years were gone and past,
And fourteen days, well known to me;
She packed up her gay gold and clothing,
And said Lord Bateman she would see.

When she came to Lord Bateman's castle,
So boldly there she rang the bell:
"Who's there, who's there?" cried the young proud porter:
"Who's there, who's there, unto me tell?"

"Oh, is this Lord's Bateman's castle?
And is his lordship here within?"
"Oh yes, oh yes," cried the young proud porter:
"He has just now taken his young bride in."

"Tell him to send me a slice of cake,
And a bottle of the best of wine;
And not to forget the fair young lady
That did release him when close confined."

Away, away went this young proud porter,
Away, away, away went he;

Until he came unto Lord Bateman,
When on his bended knees fell he.

"What news, what news, my young porter;
What news, what news have you brought unto me?"
"Oh, there is the fairest of all young ladies
That ever my two eyes did see.

"She has got rings on every finger,
And on one of them she has got three;
And she has as much gold round her middle
As would buy Northumberland of thee.

"She tells you to send her a slice of cake,
And a bottle of the best of wine;
And not to forget the fair young lady
That did release you when close confined."

Lord Bateman in a passion flew;
He broke his sword in splinters three;
"I'll give all my father's wealth and riches
Now, if Sophia has crossed the sea."

Then up spoke his young bride's mother—
Who never was heard to speak so free:
"Don't you forget my only daughter,
Although Sophia has crossed the sea."

"I own I've made a bride of your daughter
She's none the better nor worse for me;
She came to me on a horse and saddle,
And she may go back in a carriage and three."

Then another marriage was prepared,
With both their hearts so full of glee:
"I'll range no more to foreign countries,
Since my Sophia has crossed the sea."

King stopped, just as shyly as he had begun. Some laughed, others applauded him; and the Squire told us that the first time he had ever heard "Lord Bateman" was in Sconton's show, on Worcester racecourse, many a year ago.

After that, we broke up. I and some of the boys climbed up straight to Lady Harcourt's Tower again. A few Frogs were about the hills, but they did not come in contact with us. When we got back to St. Ann's the tea was ready in the room.

"And I wish to goodness they'd have it," cried Dan, "for I'm as thirsty as a fish. I've been asleep out there all the while on the bench in the sun. Can't we have tea, mother?"

"As soon as ever the gentlemen come back," spoke up Mrs. Teal, who seemed to like order. "They went down to look at the Abbey."

They were coming up then, puffing over the walk; Tod and Fred Sanker with them. We sat down to tea; and it was half over when the two young Sankers, King and Toby, were missed.

"Tiresome monkeys!" cried the captain. "I never came over here with a party yet, but we had to spend the last hour or two hunting some of them up. Well, I'll not bother myself over it: they shall find their way home as they can."

Toby ran in presently. He had only been about the hills, he said, and had not seen King.

"I dare say King's still in the place where we had dessert," said Hetta Sanker, just then thinking of it. "He stayed behind us all, saying he was tired. You boys can go and see."

I and Jim Teal ran off together. King was not there. One of the women at the well said that when she went out for the chairs and things, just before tea-time, nobody was there.

"Oh, he'll turn up presently," said the captain. And we went on with our tea, and forgot him.

It was twilight when we got down to the village to start for home. The Squire set off first: the same party with him as in the morning, except that Mrs. Teal took her husband's place. When they were bringing out the post-carriage, King was again thought of.

"He has stayed somewhere singing to himself," said Mrs. Sanker.

We went off in different directions, shouting our throats hoarse. Up as far as St. Ann's, and along the hill underneath, and in all the corners of the village: no King. It was getting strange.

"I should hope none of those impudent Frogs have made off with him!" cried Toby Sanker.

"They are capable of anything, mind you," added Dan.

One vanload of Frogs had started; the other was getting ready to start. The boys, gaping and listening about, saw and heard all our consternation at the dilemma we were in. Mrs. Todhetley, who did not understand the state of social politics, as between them and the college school, turned and inquired whether they had seen King.

"A delicate lad, who walks lame," she explained. "We think he must have fallen asleep somewhere on the hill: and we cannot start without him."

The Frogs showed themselves good-natured; and went tearing up towards the hill to look for King. In passing the Unicorn, a pleasure-party of young men and women, carrying their empty provision-baskets, came running downwards, saying that they had heard groaning under a part of the hill—and described where. I seemed to catch the right place, as if by instinct, and was up there first. King was lying there; not groaning then, but senseless or dead.

Looking upwards to note the position, we thought he must have fallen down from the place where we had sat at dessert. Hetta Sanker said she had left him there by himself, to rest.

"He must have dropped asleep, and fallen down," cried Dr. Teal.

King came to as they lifted him, and walked a few steps; but looked around and fell aside as though his head were dazed. Dr. Teal thought that there was not much the matter, and that he might be conveyed to Worcester. Ferrar helped to carry him down the hill, and the other Frogs followed. A fine fury their van-driver was in, at their having kept him waiting!

King was made comfortable along the floor of the waggonette, upon some rugs and blankets lent by the Crown; and so was taken home. When Captain Sanker found what had happened, he grew excited, and went knocking at half the doctors' doors in Worcester. Mr. Woodward was the first in, then Dr. Malden and Mr. Carden came running together. By what the captain had said, they expected to find all the house dead.

King seemed better in the morning. The injury lay chiefly in his head. We did not hear what the doctors made of it. He was sensible, and talked a little. When asked how he came to fall, all he said was that he "went over and could not save himself."

Coming in, from carrying the news of how he was to the Squire and Mrs. Todhetley at the Star, I found Mark Ferrar at the door.

"Mr. Johnny," said he, in a low voice, his plain face all concern, "how did it happen? Sure he was not pushed over?"

"Of course not. Why do you ask it?"

Ferrar paused. "Master Johnny, when boys are lame they are more cautious. He'd hardly be likely to slip."

"He might in walking. It's only a narrow ledge there. And his sister says she thinks he went to sleep when she left him. She was the last who saw him."

Mark's wide mouth went into all sorts of contortions, and the freckles shone in the sun in his effort to get the next words out.

"I fancy it was me that saw him last, Master Johnny. Leastways, later than his sister."

"Did you? How was that?"

"He must have seen me near the place, and he called to me. There was nobody there but him, and some chairs and a table and glasses and things. He asked me to sit down, and began telling me he had been saying 'Lord Bateman' to them all. I didn't know what 'Lord Bateman' meant, Master Johnny—and he said he would tell it me; he should not mind then, but he had minded saying it to the company. It was poetry, I found; but he stopped in the middle, and told me to go then, for he saw some of them coming—"

"Some of what?" I interrupted.

"Well, I took it to mean some of his grown-up party, or else the college boys. Anyway, he seemed to want me gone, sir, and I went off at once. I didn't see him after that."

"He must have fallen asleep, and somehow slipped over."

"Yes, sir. What a pity he was left in that shallow place!"

King seemed to have all his wits about him, but his face had a white, odd look in it. He lay in a room on the first floor, that belonged in general to the two girls. When I said Mark Ferrar was outside, King asked me to take him up. But I did not like taking him without speaking to Captain Sanker; and I went to him in the parlour.

"The idea of a Frog coming into our house!" cried resentful Dan, as he heard me. "It's like his impudence to stop outside it! What next? Let him wait till King's well."

"You hold your tongue, Dan," cried the captain. "The boy shall go up, whether he's a Frog, or whether he's one of you. Take him up, Johnny."

He did not look unlike a frog when he got into the room, with his wide, red, freckled face and his great wide mouth—but, as I have said, it was a face to be trusted. The first thing he did, looking at King, was to burst into a great blubber of tears.

"I hope you'll get well," said he.

"I might have been as bad as this in the fight, but for your pulling me out of it, Frog," said King, in his faint voice. And he did not call him Frog in any contempt, but as though it were his name: he knew him by no other. "Was that bump done in the battle?"

Mark had his cap off: on one side of his forehead, under the hair, we saw a big lump the size of an egg. "Yes," he answered, "it was got in the fight. Father thinks it never means to go down. It's pretty stiff and sore yet."

King sighed. He was gazing up at the lump with his nice blue eyes.

"I don't think there'll be any fighting in heaven," said King. "And I wrote out 'Lord Bateman' the other day, and they shall give it you to keep. I didn't finish telling it to you. He owned half Northumberland; and he married her after all. She had set him free from the prison, you know, Frog."

"Yes," replied Frog, quite bewildered, and looking as though he could not make top or tail of the story. "I hope you'll get well, sir. How came you to fall?"

"I don't think they expect me to get well: they wouldn't have so many doctors if they did. I shan't be lame, Frog, up there."

"Did you slip?—or did anybody push you?" went on Frog, lowering his voice.

"Hush!" said King, glancing at the door. "If papa heard you say that, he might go into a passion."

"But—was it a slip—or were you pushed over?" persisted Frog.

"My leg is always slipping: it has never been of much good to me," answered King. "When you come up there, and see me with a beautiful strong body and straight limbs, you won't know me again at first. Good-bye, till then, Frog; good-bye. It was very kind of you to carry me out of the fight, and God saw you."

"Good-bye, sir," said Frog, with another burst, as he put out his hand to meet poor King's white one. "Perhaps you'll get over it yet."

Tod and I took leave of them in the afternoon, and went up to the Star. The Squire wanted to be home early. The carriage was waiting before the gateway, the ostler holding the heads of Bob and Blister, when Captain Sanker came up in dreadful excitement.

"He's gone," he exclaimed. "My poor King's gone. He died as the clock was striking four."

And we had supposed King to be going on well! The Squire ordered the horses to be put up again, and we went down to the house. The boys and girls were all crying.

King lay stretched on the bed, his face very peaceful and looking less white than I had sometimes seen it look in life. On the cheeks there lingered a faint colour; his forehead felt warm; you could hardly believe he was dead.

"He has gone to the heaven he talked of," said Mrs. Sanker, through her tears. "He has been talking about it at intervals all day—and now he is there; and has his harp amongst the angels."

And that was the result of our Day of Pleasure! The force of those solemn words has rarely been brought home to hearts as it was to ours then: "In the midst of life we are in death."

CHAPTER XI

THE FINAL ENDING TO IT

Of all the gloomy houses any one ever stayed in, Captain Sanker's was the worst. Nothing but coffins coming into it, and all of us stealing about on tip-toe. King lay in the room where he died. There was to be an inquest: at which the captain was angry. But he was so excited and sorrowful just then as to have no head at all.

Which might well be excused in him. Picture what it was! Three carriages full of us had started on the Tuesday morning, expecting to have a day of charming pleasure on the Malvern Hills in the July sunshine; no more thinking of death or any other catastrophe, than if the world had never contained such! And poor King—poor lame King, whose weakness made him more helpless than were we strong ones, and who only on the previous Saturday had been plucked out of the fight in Diglis Meadow and been saved—King must fall asleep on a dangerous part of the hill and roll down it and come home to die! "Better King than any of the rest of you," cried Mrs. Sanker, more than once, in her dreamy way, and with her eyes dry, for she seemed tired of tears; "he could never have done battle with the world as you will have to do it; and he was quite ready for heaven."

Instead of going home with our people the day after the death, as Tod did, I had to wait at Worcester for the inquest. When the beadle (or whoever the officer might be; he had gold cord on his hat and white ribbed stockings below his breeches: which stockings might have been fellows to old Jones's of Church Dykely) came to Captain Sanker's to make inquiries the night of the death, and heard that I had been first up with King after his fall, he said I should have to give evidence. So I stayed on with them—much to my uneasiness.

If I had thought the Sankers queer people before, I thought them queerer now. Not one of the boys and girls, except Fred, cared to go alone by the door of the room where King lay. And, talking of King, it was not until I saw the name on the coffin-lid that I knew his name was not King, but Kingsley. He looked as nice and peaceful as any dead lad with a nice face could look; and yet they were afraid to pass by outside. Dan and Ruth were the worst. I did not wonder at her—she was a little girl; but I did at Dan. Fred told me that when they were children a servant used to tell them stories of ghosts and dreams and banshees; Hetta and he were too old to be frightened, but the rest had taken it all into their nature. I privately thought that Mrs. Sanker was no better than the fool of a servant, reciting to them her dreams and accounts of apparitions.

King died on the Wednesday afternoon. On Thursday afternoon the inquest took place. It was held at the Angel Inn, in Sidbury, and Mr. Robert Allies was the foreman. Boys don't give evidence on inquests every day: I felt shy and uncomfortable at having to do it; and perhaps that may be the reason why the particulars remain so strongly on my memory. The time fixed was three o'clock, but it was nearly four when they came down to look at King: the coroner explained to the jury that he had been detained. When they went back to the Angel Inn we followed them—Captain Sanker, Fred, and I.

All sorts of nonsense ran about the town. It was reported that there had been a fight with the Frogs on Malvern Hill, during which King had been pitched over. This was only laughed at by those who knew how foundationless it was. Not a shadow of cause existed for supposing it to have been anything but a pure accident.

The coroner and jury sat at a long table covered with green baize. The coroner had his clerk by him; and on one side Mr. Allies sat Captain Chamberlain, on the other side Mr. Allcroft. Dr. Teal and Mr. Woodward were present, and gave the medical evidence in a most learned manner. Reduced to plainness, it meant that King had died of an injury to the head.

When my turn came, what they chiefly asked me was, whether I had seen or heard any quarrelling with St. Peter's boys that day at Malvern. None whatever, I answered. Was I quite sure of that? pursued one—it was Mr. Allcroft. I did not think there had been, or could have been, I repeated: we and the charity boys had kept apart from each other all day. Then another of the jury, Mr. Stone, put some questions, and then Mr. Allen—I thought they were never going to believe me. So I said it was the opposite of quarrelling, and told of Captain Sanker's giving one of them half-a-crown because he had been kind to King on Saturday, and of some of the boys—all who had not gone home in the first van—having helped us to look for King at night. After they had turned me inside out, the coroner could say that these questions were merely put for form's sake and for the satisfaction of the public.

When the witnesses were done with, the coroner spoke to the jury. I suppose it was his charge. It seemed all as plain as a turnpike, he said: the poor little lame boy had slipped and fallen. The probability was that he had dropped asleep too near the edge of the perpendicular bank, and had either fallen over in his sleep, or in the act of awaking. He (the coroner) thought it must have been the former, as no cry appeared to have been made, or heard. Under these circumstances, he believed the jury could have no difficulty in arriving at their verdict.

The last word, "verdict," was still on his tongue, when some commotion took place at the end of the room. A working-man, in his shirt-sleeves and a leather apron on, was pushing in through the crowd at the door, making straight for the table and the coroner. Some of the jury knew him for John Dance, a glove-cutter at a Quaker gentleman's manufactory hard by. He begged pardon of the gentlefolk for coming amid 'em abrupt like that, he said, just as he was, but something had but now come to his hearing about the poor little boy who had died. It made him fear he had not fell of himself, but been flung over, and he had thought it his duty to come and tell it.

The consternation this suggestion created, delivered in its homely words, would not be easy to describe. Captain Sanker, who had been sitting against the wall, got up in agitation. John Dance was asked his grounds for what he said, and was entering into a long rigmarole of a tale when the coroner stopped him, and bade him simply say how it had come to his own knowledge. He answered that upon going home just now to tea, from his work, his son Harry, who was in St. Peter's School, told him of it, having been sent to do so by the master, Clerk Jones. His son was with him, waiting to be questioned.

The boy came forward, very red and sheepish, looking as though he thought he was going to be hung. He stammered and stuttered in giving his answers to the coroner.

The tale he told was this. His name was Henry Dance, aged thirteen. He was on the hill, not very far from St. Ann's Well, on the Tuesday afternoon, looking about for Mark Ferrar. All on a sudden he heard some quarrelling below him: somebody seemed to be in a foaming passion, and little King the lame boy called out in a fright, "Oh, don't! don't! you'll throw me over!" Heard then a sort of rustle of shrubs—as it sounded to him—and then heard the steps of some one running away along the path below the upright bank. Couldn't see anything of this; the bank prevented him; but did see the arm of the boy who was running as he turned round the corner. Didn't see the boy; only saw his left arm swaying; he had a green handkerchief in his hand. Could not tell whether it was one of their boys (St. Peter's) or one of the college boys; didn't see enough of him for that. Didn't know then that anything bad had happened, and thought no more about it at all; didn't hear of it till the next morning: he had been in the first van that left Malvern, and went to bed as soon as he got home.

The account was listened to breathlessly. The boy was in a regular fright while he told it, but his tones and looks seemed honest and true.

"How did you know it was King Sanker's voice you heard?" asked the coroner.

"Please, sir, I didn't know it," was the answer. "When I came to hear of his fall the next day, I supposed it must ha' been his. I didn't know anybody had fell down; I didn't hear any cry."

"What time in the afternoon was this?"

"Please, sir, I don't know exact. We had our tea at four: it wasn't over-long after that."

"Did you recognize the other voice?"

"No, sir. It was a boy's voice."

"Was it one you had ever heard before?"

"I couldn't tell, sir; I wasn't near enough to hear or to catch the words. King Sanker spoke last, just as I got over the spot."

"You heard of the accident the next morning, you say. Did you hear of it early?"

"It was afore breakfast, sir. Some of our boys that waited for the last van told me; and Ferrar, he told me. They said they had helped to look for him."

"And then it came into your mind, that it was King Sanker you had heard speak?"

"Yes, sir, it did. It come right into my mind, all sudden like, that he might have been throwed over."

"Well now, Mr. Harry Dance, how was it that you did not at once hasten to report this? How is it that you have kept it in till now?"

Harry Dance looked too confused and frightened to answer. He picked at the band of his grey cap and stood, first on one foot, then on the other. The coroner pressed the question sharply, and he replied in confusion.

Didn't like to tell it. Knew people were saying it might have been one of their boys that had pitched him over. Was afraid to tell. Did say a word to Mark Ferrar; not much: Ferrar wanted to know more, and what it was he meant, but didn't tell him. That was yesterday morning. Had felt uncomfortable ever since then, wanting to tell, but not liking to. This afternoon, in school, writing their copies at the desk, he had told Tom Wood'art, the carpenter's son, who sat next him; leastways, had said the college boy had not fell of himself, but been pitched over; and Tom Wood'art had made him tell it to another boy, Collins; and then the two had went up to the desk and told their master, Mr. Jones; and Mr. Jones, after calling him up to ask about it, had ordered him home to tell it all to his father; and his father said he must come and tell it here.

The father, John Dance, spoke up again to confirm this, so far as his part went. He was so anxious it should be told to the gentlemen at once, he repeated, that he had come out all untidy as he was, not stopping to put himself to rights in any way.

The next person to step forward was Mr. Jones, in his white cravat and black clothes. He stated that the two boys, Thomas Woodward and James Collins, had made this strange communication to him. Upon which he had questioned Dance, and at once despatched him home to acquaint his father.

"What sort of a boy is Harry Dance, Mr. Jones?" inquired the coroner. "A truthful boy?—one to be depended on? Some boys, as I dare say you know, are capable of romancing in the most unaccountable manner: inventing lies by the bushel."

"The boy is truthful, sir; a sufficiently good boy," was the reply. "Some of them are just what you describe; but Dance, so far as I believe, may be relied upon."

"Well, now, if this is to be credited, it must have been one of St. Peter's boys who threw the deceased over," observed a juryman at the other end. "Did you do it yourself, Harry Dance? Stand straight, and answer."

"No, sir; I shouldn't never like to do such a cowardly thing," was the answer, given with a rush of fear—if the look of his face might be trusted. "I was not anigh him."

"It must have been one of you. This is the result of that fight you two sets of boys held on Saturday. You have been harbouring malice."

"Please, sir, I wasn't in the fight on Saturday. I had went over to Clains on an errand for mother."

"That's true," said Clerk Jones. "Dance was not in the fight at all. As far as I can ascertain, there was no ill-feeling displayed on either side at Malvern; no quarrelling of any kind." And Captain Sanker, who was standing up to listen, confirmed this.

"The natural deduction to be drawn is, that if the deceased was flung over, it was by one of St. Peter's boys—though the probability is that he did not intend to inflict much injury," observed one of the jury to the rest. "Boys are so reprehensibly thoughtless. Come, Harry Dance! if you did not give him a push yourself, you can tell, I dare say, who did."

But Dance, with tears in his eyes, affirmed that he knew no more than he had told: he had not the least notion who the boy was that had been quarrelling with King. He saw none of the boys, St. Peter's boys or college boys, about the hill at that time; though he was looking out for them, because he wanted to find Ferrar: and he knew no more than the dead what boy it was who had run away, for he saw nothing but his arm and a green handkerchief.

"Did you find Ferrar after that?" resumed the coroner.

"Yes, sir; not long after. I found him looking for me round on t'other side of St. Ann's Well."

"By the way—on which side of St. Ann's Well is situated the spot where you heard the quarrel?"

"On the right-hand side, sir, looking down the hill," said the boy. And by the stress laid on the "down" I judged him to be given to exactness. "I know the place, sir. If you take a sideway path from the Well bearing down'ards, you come to it. It's shady and quiet there; a place that nobody hardly finds out."

"Did you say anything to Ferrar, when you found him, of what you had heard?"

"No, sir. I didn't think any more about it. I didn't think any harm had been done."

"But you did mention it to Ferrar the next morning?"

"Yes, sir, I had heard of it, then."

"What did you say?"

"I only said I was afeard he might have been throwed over. Ferrar asked me why, but I didn't like to say no more, for fear of doing mischief. It wasn't me," added Dance, appealing piteously to the jury. "I wouldn't have hurt a hair of his head: he was weak and lame."

"Is Ferrar here?" cried the coroner. "We must have him."

Ferrar was not there. And Mr. Jones, speaking up, said he had seen nothing of Ferrar since the previous day. He was informed that he had taken French leave to go off somewhere—which kind of leave, in point of fact, he added, Master Ferrar was much in the habit of taking.

"But where has he gone?" cried the coroner. "You don't mean he has decamped?"

"Decamped for the time being," said Mr. Jones. "He will no doubt put in an appearance in a day or two."

Not one of the jury but pricked up his ears; not one, I could see it in their faces, but was beginning to speculate on this absence of Ferrar's. The coroner was staring straight before him, speculating too: and just then Fred Sanker said something in a half-whisper.

"Ferrar was with my brother King at the spot where he fell from. As far as we know he was the last person who ever saw him alive."

"And not here!" cried the coroner. "Why is he not? Where does the neglect lie, I wonder? Gentlemen, I think we had better send round for his father, and ask an explanation."

In a small town like Worcester (small in comparison with great capitals) the inhabitants, rich and poor, mostly know one another, what they are, and where their dwelling is. Old Ferrar lived within a stone's-throw of the Angel; he was a china painter, employed by the Messrs. Chamberlain. Some one ran for him; and he came; a tidy-looking man in a good coat, with grey whiskers and grey hair. He bowed civilly to the room, and gave his name as Thomas Ferrar.

As far as anything connected with what took place at Malvern he was in total ignorance, he said. When his son Mark got home on the Tuesday night, he had told him that Captain Sanker's little boy had fallen down a part of the hill, and that he, Mark, had been one of those who helped to find him. In the afternoon of the same day they heard the little boy had died.

"Where is your son?" asked the coroner.

"I am not sure where he is," replied Thomas Ferrar. "When I and his brother got home from the factory on Wednesday evening, my daughter told me Mark had gone off again. Somebody had given him half-a-crown, I believe. With that in his pocket, he was pretty sure to go off on one of his rovings."

"He is in the habit of going off, then?"

"Yes, sir, he has done it on occasion almost ever since he could run alone. I used to leather him well for it, but it was of no use; it didn't stop it. It's his only fault. Barring that, he's as good and upright a lad as anybody need have. He does not go off for the purpose of doing harm: neither does he get into any."

"Where does he go to?"

"Always to one of two places; to South Crabb, or to his grandfather's at Pinvin. It's generally to South Crabb, to see the Batleys, who are cousins of my late wife's. They've boys and girls of Mark's own age, and he likes to be there."

"You conclude, then, that he is at one of these places now?"

"Sure to be, sir; and I think it's sure to be South Crabb. He was at Pinvin a fortnight ago; for I walked over on the Sunday morning and took him with me. Mark is of a roving turn; he is always talking of wanting to see the world. I don't believe he'll ever settle down to steady work at home."

"Well, we want him here, Mr. Ferrar; and must have him too. Could you send after him—and get him here by to-morrow?"

"I can send his brother after him, if you say it must be. The likelihood is that he will come home of himself to-morrow evening."

"Ay, but we must have him here in the afternoon, you see. We want to hear what he can tell us about the deceased. It is thought that he was the last person with him before the fall. And, gentlemen," added the coroner, turning to the jury, "I will adjourn proceedings to the same hour to-morrow—three o'clock."

So the inquest was adjourned accordingly, and the room slowly cleared itself. Very slowly. People stood in groups of threes and fours to talk to each other. This new evidence was startling: and the impression it made was, that one of the Frogs had certainly thrown King down.

The green handkerchief was mentioned. Coloured silk pocket-handkerchiefs were much patronized by gentlemen then, and the one used by Dr. Teal that day happened to be green. The doctor said he had missed his handkerchief when they were down at the Abbey before tea, but could not tell where he had left it. He found it in the room at St. Ann's when they got up again, and supposed it had been there all along. So that handkerchief was not much thought of: especially as several of the Frogs had green neckerchiefs on, and might have taken them off, as it was very hot. That a Frog had flung King over, appeared to be, to use the coroner's words on another part of the subject, as plain as a turnpike. The Sankers, one and all, adopted it as conclusive; Captain Sanker in particular was nearly wild, and said bitter things of the Frogs. Poor King still lay in the same room, and none of them, as before, cared to go by the door.

It must have been in the middle of the night. Anyway, it looked pitch-dark. I was asleep, and dreaming that we were sorting handkerchiefs: all colours seemed to be there but a green one, and that—the one being looked for—we could not find: when something suddenly woke me. A hand was grasping at my shoulder.

"Halloa! who's there?"

"I say, Johnny, I can't stop in my bed; I've come to yours. If you mind my getting in, I'll lie across the foot, and get to sleep that way."

The voice was Dan's, and it had no end of horror in it. He was standing by the bed in his night-shirt, shivering. And yet the summer's night was hot.

"Get in, if you like, Dan: there's plenty of room. What's the matter with your own bed?"

"King's there," he said, in a dreadful whisper, as he crept trembling in.

"King! Why, what do you mean?"

"He comes in and lies down in his place just as he used to lie," shivered Dan. "I asked Toby to sleep with me to-night, and Fred wouldn't let him. Fred ought to be ashamed; it's all his ill-nature. He's bigger than I am, one of the seniors, and he never cares whether he sleeps alone or not."

"But, Dan, you should not get these fancies into your head about King. You know it's not true."

"I tell you it is true. King's there. First of all, he stood at the foot of the bed and looked at me; and then, when I hid my face, I found he had got into it. He's lying there, just as he used to lie, his face turned to the wall."

"To begin with, you couldn't see him—him, or any one else. It's too dark."

"It's not dark. My room's lighter than this; it has a bigger window: and the sky was bright and the stars were out. Anyway, Johnny, it was light enough to see King—and there he was. Do you think I'd tell a lie over it?"

I can't say I felt very comfortable myself. It's not pleasant to be woke up with this kind of thing at the top of a house when somebody's lying dead underneath. Dan's voice was enough to give one the shivers, let alone his words. Some stars came out, and I could see the outline of the furniture: or perhaps the stars had been shining all along; only, on first awaking, the eye is not accustomed to the darkness.

"Try and go to sleep, Dan. You'll be all right in the morning."

To go to sleep seemed, however, to be far enough from Dan's thoughts. After a bit of uneasy turning and trembling—and I'm sure any one would have said his legs had caught St. Vitus's dance—he gave sleep up as a bad job, and broke out now and again with all sorts of detached comments. I could only lie and listen.

Wondered whether he should be seeing King always?—if so, would rather be dead. Wished he had not gone to sleep on that confounded bench outside St. Ann's Well—might have been at hand near King, and saved him, if he had not. It was that beastly bottled ale that made him. Wished bottled ale had not been invented. Wished he could wring Dance's neck—or Ferrar's—or that Wood'arts, whichever of the lot it was that had struck King. Knew it was one of the three. What on earth could have taken the Frogs to Malvern that day?—Wished every Frog ever born was hanged or drowned. Thought it must be Ferrar—else why had the fellow decamped? Thought the whole boiling of Frogs should be driven from the town—how dared they, the insolent charity beggars, have their school near the college school? Wondered what would be done to Ferrar if it was proved against him? Wished it had been Ferrar to fall down in place of King. Wished it had been himself (Dan) rather than King. Poor King!—who was always so gentle—and never gave offence to any of them—and was so happy with his hymns and his fancies, and his poetry!—and had said "Lord Bateman" for them that day when told to say it, and—and—

At this thought Dan broke fairly down and sobbed as though his heart were breaking. I felt uncommonly sorry for him; he had been very fond of King; and I was sorry for his superstition. What a mistake it seemed for Mrs. Sanker to have allowed them to grow up in it.

At three o'clock the next day the inquest met again. The coroner and jury, who seemed to have got thoroughly interested in the case now, kept their time to a minute. There was much stir in the neighbourhood, and the street was full before the Angel Inn. As to Frog Lane, it was said the excitement there had never been equalled. The report that it was one of St. Peter's boys who had done it, went echoing everywhere; no one thought of doubting it. I did not. Watching Harry Dance's face when he had given his evidence, I felt sure that every word he said was true. Some one had flung King over: and that some one, there could be no question of it, was one of those common adversaries, the Frogs. If King must have gone to sleep that afternoon, better that Dan, as he had said, or one of the rest of us, had stayed by to protect him!

Mark Ferrar had turned up. His brother found him at South Crabb. He came to the inquest in his best clothes, those he had worn at Malvern. I noticed then, but I had not remembered it, that he had a grass-green neckerchief on, tied with a large bow and ends. His good-natured, ugly, honest face was redder than ever as he stood to give his evidence. He did not show any of the stammering confusion that Dance had done, but spoke out with modest self-possession.

His name was Mark Ferrar, aged nearly fourteen (and looking ever so much older), second son of Thomas Ferrar, china painter. He had seen the deceased boy, King Sanker, at Malvern on Tuesday. When he and some more of St. Peter's boys were coming down the hill they had met King and his party. King spoke to him and told his father, Captain Sanker, that he was the Frog—the college boys called them Frogs—who had picked him up out of the fight on Saturday to save him from being crushed: and Captain Sanker thanked him and gave him half-a-crown to spend in Malvern cakes. Master Johnny Ludlow was with the Sankers, and saw and heard this. Did not buy the Malvern cakes: had meant to, and treat the rest of the boys; but dinner was ready near the foot of the hill when they got down, and forgot it afterwards. After dinner he and a lot more boys went up another of the beacons and down on the Herefordshire side. They got back about four o'clock, and had bread-and-butter and cider for tea. Then he and Harry Dance went up the hill again, taking two ways, to see which would be at St. Ann's Well first. Couldn't see Dance when he got up, thought he might be hiding, and went looking about for him. Went along a side-path leading off from St. Ann's; 'twas sheltered, and thought Dance might be there. Suddenly heard himself called to: looked onwards, and saw the lame boy, King Sanker, there, and some chairs and glasses on a table. Went on, and King asked him to sit down, and began talking to him, saying he had had to say "Lord Bateman" before them all. He, Ferrar, did not know what "Lord Bateman" was, and King said he would say it to him. Began to say it; found it was poetry verses: King had said a good many when he broke off in the middle of one, and told him to go then, for they were coming. Did not know who "they" meant, did not see or hear anybody himself; but went away accordingly. Went looking all about for Dance again; found him by-and-by on a kind of plateau on the other side of St. Ann's. They went up the hill together, and only got down again when it was time to start for Worcester. He did not go in the first van; there was no room; waited for the second. Saw the other party starting: heard that some one was missing: found it was King; offered to help to look for him. Was going up with the rest past the Unicorn, when some people met them, saying they'd heard groans. Ran on, and found it was

King Sanker. He seemed to have fallen right down from the place where he had been sitting in the afternoon, and where he, Ferrar, had left him.

Such in substance was the evidence he gave. Some of it I could corroborate, and did. I told of King's asking that Ferrar might go up to him the next day, and of his promising him "Lord Bateman," which he had got by him, written out.

But Ferrar was not done with. Important questions had to be asked him yet. Sometimes it was the coroner who put them, sometimes one or other of the jury.

"Did you see anything at all of the deceased after leaving him as you have described, Mark Ferrar?"

"No, sir. I never saw him again till night, when we found him lying under a part of the hill."

"When you quitted him at his bidding, did you see any boys about, either college boys or St. Peter's boys?"

"No, sir, I did not see any; not one. The hills about there seemed as lonely as could be."

"Which way did you take when you left him?"

"I ran straight past St. Ann's, and got on to the part that divides the Worcestershire beacon from the next. Waiting for Dance, I sat down on the slope, and looked at Worcester for a bit, trying how much of the town I could make out, and how many of the churches, and that. As I was going back toward St. Ann's I met Dance."

"What did Dance say to you?"

"He said he had been hunting for me, and wanted to know where I had hid myself, and I said I had been hunting for him. We went on up the hill then and met some more of our boys; and we stayed all together till it was time to go down."

"Did Dance say that he had heard sounds of quarrelling?"

"No, sir, never a word."

"What communication did Dance make to you on the subject the following morning?"

"Nothing certain, sir. Dance went home in the first van, and he didn't hear about King Sanker till the morning. I was saying then how we found him, and that he must have fell straight off from the place above. Dance stopped me, and said was it sure that he fell—was it sure he had not been pushed off? I asked why he said that, but he wouldn't answer."

"Did he refuse to answer?"

"I kept asking him to tell me, but he just said it was only a fancy that came to him. He had interrupted so eager like, that I thought he must have heard something. Later, I asked Master Johnny Ludlow whether the boy had been pushed off, but he said no. I couldn't get it out of my head, however."

"What clothes did you wear, witness, that day at Malvern?"

"These here that I've got on now, sir."

"Did you wear that same green neckerchief?"

"Yes, sir. My sister Sally bought it new for me to go in."

"Did you take it off at Malvern?"

"No, sir."

"Not at all?"

"No, sir. Some of them took their handkerchers off at dinner, because it was hot, but I didn't."

"Why did you not?"

For the first time Ferrar hesitated. His face turned scarlet.

"Come, speak up. The truth, mind."

"Sally had told me not to mess my new silk handkercher, for I wasn't likely to have another of one while; and I thought if I got untying and re-tying of it, I should mess it." It seemed quite a task to Ferrar to confess this. He feared the boys would laugh at him. But I think no one doubted that it was the true reason.

"You did not take it off while you were sitting with the deceased?"

"No, sir. I never took it off all day."

"Take it off now."

Mark Ferrar looked too surprised to understand the order, and did nothing. The coroner repeated it.

"Take off this here handkercher, sir? Now?"

"Yes. The jury wish to see it open."

Mark untied the bow and pulled it off, his very freckles showing out red. It was a three-cornered silk neckerchief, as green as grass.

"Was this like the kerchief you saw being swung about, Harry Dance?" asked the coroner, holding it up, and then letting it drop on the table.

Harry Dance gazed at it as it lay, and shook his head. "I don't think it were the one, sir," he said.

"Why don't you think it?"

"That there looks smaller and brighter, and t'other was bigger and darker. Leastways, I think it were."

"Was it more like this?" interrupted Dr. Teal, shaking out his handkerchief from his pocket.

"I don't know, sir. It seemed like a big handkerchief, and was about that there colour o' your'n."

Some inquiry was made at this point as to the neckerchiefs worn by the other boys. It turned out that two or three had worn very large ones, something the colour of Dr. Teal's. So that passed.

"One word, Harry Dance. Did you see Ferrar with his handkerchief off that day?"

"I didn't notice, sir: I don't remember. Some of us took 'em off on the hills—'twas very hot—and never put 'em on again all day."

The coroner and jury talked together, and then Harry Dance was told to repeat the evidence he had given the day before. He went over it again: the sounds of quarrelling, and the words in the voice he had supposed to be King's: "Oh, don't—don't! you'll throw me over."

"Had Ferrar his neckerchief on when you met him soon after this?" questioned Captain Chamberlain.

"I think he had, sir. I think if he had not I should ha' noticed it. I'm nearly as sure as I can be that it wasn't off."

When Dance was done with, Mark Ferrar was begun upon again.

"What induced you to go off from your home on Wednesday evening without notice?" asked the coroner.

"I went to South Crabb, sir."

"I don't ask you where you went, I ask why you went?"

"I go over there sometimes, sir. I told Sally I was going."

"Can't you understand my question? Why did you go?"

"Nothing particular made me go, sir. Only that I had got some money; and I was feeling so sorry that the little lame boy was dead, I couldn't bear to be still."

"You have been punished often, Mark Ferrar, for going off on these expeditions?" cried one of the jury.

"I used to be, sir. Father has leathered me for it at home, and Clerk Jones at school. I can't do without going out a bit. I wish I was a sailor."

"Oh, indeed! Well—is there one of your companions that you can suspect of having harmed this poor little boy—accidentally or otherwise?"

"No, sir. It is being said that he was pushed over in ill-feeling, or else by accident; but it don't seem likely."

"Did you push him over yourself?"

"Me!" returned Ferrar, in surprise. "Me push him over!"

"As far as we can learn yet, no one was with him there but you."

"I'd have saved him from it, sir, if I had been there, instead of harming him. When he sent me away he was all right, and not sitting anigh the edge. If it was me that had done it, sir, he'd not have asked for me to go up to him in his room—and shook hands—and said I should see him in heaven."

Mark Ferrar broke down at the remembrance, and sobbed like a child. I don't think one single person present thought it was he, especially the coroner and jury. But the question was—which of the other boys could it have been?

Several of them were called before the coroner. One and all declared they had done no harm to the deceased—had not been near him to do it—would not have done it if they had been—did not know he had been sitting in the place talked of—did not (most of them) know where the spot was now. In short, they denied it utterly.

Mr. Jones stepped forward then. He told the coroner and jury that he had done his best to come to the bottom of the affair, but could not find out anything. He did not believe one of his boys had been in it; they were mischievous enough, as he well knew, and sometimes deceitful enough; but they all seemed to be, and he honestly believed were, innocent of this.

The room was cleared while the jury deliberated. Their verdict was to the effect that Kingsley Sanker had died from falling over a portion of one of the Malvern hills; but whether the fall was caused by accident, or not, there was not sufficient evidence to show.

It was late when it was over. Growing dusk. In turning out of the inn passage to the street, I remember the great buzz around, and the people pushing one's elbows; and I can't remember much more. If one Frog was there, it seemed to me that there were hundreds.

I stayed at Captain Sanker's again that night. We all went up to bed after supper and prayers—which the captain read. He said he could not divest himself of the idea that it was a pure accident—for who would be likely to harm a helpless lad?—and that what Dance heard must have been some passing dispute connected with other people.

"Come along, Johnny: this one candle'll do for us both," cried Dan, taking up a bed candlestick and waiting for me to follow him.

I kept close to him as we went by the room—the room, you know—for Dan was worse than any of them for passing it. He and King had been much together. King followed him in age; they had always slept together and gone to school together; the rest were older or younger—and naturally Dan felt it most.

"I shan't be a minute, Johnny, and then you can take the candle," said he, when we got to the top. "Come in."

Before I had well turned round, after getting in, I declare Dan had rushed all his things off in a heap and leaped into bed. Poor King used not to be so quick, and Dan always made him put the light out.

"Good-night, Dan."

"Good-night, Johnny. I hope I shall get to sleep."

He put his head under the bedclothes as I went away with the candle. I was not long getting into bed either. The stars were bright in the sky.

Before there was time to get to sleep, Dan came bursting in, shivering as on the past night, and asking to be let get into the bed. I did not mind his being in the bed—liked it rather, for company—but I did think it a great stupid pity that he should be giving way to these superstitious fears as though he were a girl.

"Look here, Dan: I should be above it. One of the smallest of those Frogs couldn't show out more silly than this."

"He's in my bed again, Johnny. Lying down. I can't sleep there another night."

"You know that he is below in his coffin—with the room-door locked."

"I don't care—he's there in the bed. You had no sooner gone with the light than King crept in and lay down beside me. He used to have a way of putting his left arm over me outside the clothes, and he put it so to-night."

"Dan!"

"I tell you he did. Nobody would believe it, but he did. I felt it like a weight. It was heavy, just as dead arms are. Johnny, if this goes on, I shall die. Have you heard what mamma says?"

"No. What?"

"She says she saw King last night. She couldn't sleep; and by-and-by, happening to look out of bed, she saw him standing there. He was looking very solemn, and did not speak. She turned to awake papa, in spite of the way he goes on ridiculing such things, but when she looked next King had gone. I wish he was buried, Johnny; I shouldn't think he could come back into the house then. Should you?"

"He's not in it now—in that sense. It's all imagination."

"Is it! I should like you to have been in my bed, instead of me; you'd have seen whether it was imagination or not. Do you suppose his heavy arm across me was fancy?"

"Well, he does not come in here. Let us go to sleep. Good-night, Dan."

Dan lay still for a good bit, and I was nearly asleep when he awoke me sobbing. His face was turned the other way.

"I wish you'd kill me, Johnny."

"Kill you!"

"I don't care to live any longer without King. It is so lonely. There's nobody now. Fred's getting to be almost a man, and Toby's a little duffer. King was best. I've many a time snubbed him and boxed him, and I always put upon him; and—and now he's gone. I wish I had fallen down instead of him."

"You'll get over it, Dan."

"Perhaps. But it's such a thing to get over. And the time goes so slowly. I wish it was this time next year!"

"Do you know what some of the doctors say?"

"What do they say?" returned Dan, putting the tip of his nose out of bed.

"Dr. Teal told Captain Sanker of it; I was by and heard him. They think that poor King would not have lived above another year, or so: that there was no chance of his living to grow up. So you might have lost him soon in any case, Dan."

"But he'd have been here till then; he wouldn't have died through falling down Malvern Hill. Oh, and to think that I was rough with him often!—and didn't try to help him when he wanted it! and laughed at his poetry! Johnny, I wish you'd kill me! I wish it had been me to fall over instead of him!"

There was not one of them that felt it as keenly as Dan did: but the chances were that he would forget King the soonest. Dan was of that impetuous warm nature that's all fire at first; and all forgetfulness when the fire goes out.

I went home the next day to Crabb Cot. Mr. Coney came into Worcester to attend the corn-market, and offered to drive me back in his gig. So I took my leave of the Sankers, and my last look at poor King in his coffin. He was to be buried on Monday in St. Peter's churchyard.

The next news we had from Worcester was that Mark Ferrar had gone to sea. His people had wanted him to take up some trade at home; but Mark said he was not going to stay there to be told every day of his life that he killed King Sanker. For some of the Frogs had taken up the notion that it must have been he—why else, they asked, did the coroner and the rest of 'em want to see his green handkercher shook out? So his father, who was just as much hurt at the aspersions as Mark, allowed him to have his way and go to sea; in spite of Sally crying her eyes out, and foretelling that he would come home drowned. Mark was sent to London to some friend, who undertook to make the necessary arrangements; he was bound apprentice to the sea, and shipped off in a trading vessel sailing for Spain.

It was Michaelmas when we next went in to Worcester (save for a day at the festival), driving in from Dyke Manor: the Squire, Mrs. Todhetley, and I. You have heard the expedition mentioned before, for it was the one when we hired the dairymaid, Grizzel, at St. John's mop. That business over, we went down to Captain Sanker's and found them at home.

They were all getting pretty well over the death now, except Dan. Dan's grief and nervousness were as bad as ever. Worse, even. Captain and Mrs. Sanker enlarged upon it.

"Dan grieves after his brother dreadfully: they were always companions, you see," said the captain. "He has foolish fancies also: thinks he sees King continually. We have had to put him to sleep with Fred downstairs, for nothing would persuade him that King, poor fellow, did not come and get into his old place in bed. The night the poor lad was buried, Dan startled the whole house up; he flew down the stairs crying and shrieking, and saying that King was there. We don't know what to do: he seems to get worse, rather than better. Did you notice how thin he has become? You saw him as you came in."

"Like a bag of bones," said the Squire.

"Ay. Some days he is so nervous and ill he can't go to school. I never knew such a thing, for my part. I was for trying flogging, but his mother wouldn't have it."

"But—do you mean to tell us, Sanker, that he fancies he sees King's ghost?" cried the Squire, in great amazement.

"Well, I suppose so," answered the captain. "He fancies he sees him: and poor King, as far as this world's concerned, can be nothing but a ghost now. The other evening, when Dan had been commanded to the head-master's house for something connected with the studies and detained till after dark, he came rushing in with a white face and his hair all wet, saying he had met King under the elm-trees, as he was running back through the green towards Edgar Tower. How can you deal with such a case?"

"I should say flogging would be as good as anything," said the Squire, decidedly.

"So I thought at first. He's too ill for it now. There's nothing, hardly, left of him to flog."

"Captain Sanker, there is only one thing for you to do," put in Mrs. Todhetley. "And that is, consult a clever medical man."

"Why, my dear lady, we have taken him to pretty nearly all the medical men in Worcester," cried the captain. "He goes regularly to Dr. Hastings."

"And what do the doctors say?"

"They think that the catastrophe of King's unhappy death has seized upon the lad's mind, and brought on a sort of hypochondriacal affection. One of them said it was what the French would call a maladie des nerfs. Dan seems so full of self-reproach, too."

"What for?"

"Well, for not having made more of King when he was living. And also, I think, for having suffered himself to fall asleep that afternoon on the bench outside the Well: he says had he kept awake he might have been with King, and so saved him. But, as I tell Dan, there's nothing to reproach himself with in that: he could not foresee that King would meet with the accident. The doctors say now that he must have change of air, and be got away altogether. They recommend the sea."

"The sea! Do you mean sea-air?"

"No; the sea itself; a voyage: and Dan's wild to go. A less complete change than that, they think, will be of little avail, for his illness borders almost—almost upon lunacy. I'm sure, what with one thing and another, we seem to be in for a peck of misfortunes," added the captain, rumpling his hair helplessly.

"And shall you let him go to sea?"

"Well, I don't know. I stood out against it at first. Never meant to send a son of mine to sea; that has always been my resolution. Look at what I had to starve upon for ever so many years—a lieutenant's half-pay—and to keep my wife and bring up my children upon it! You can't imagine it, Squire; it's cruel. Dan's too old for the navy, however; and, if he does go, it must be into the merchant service. I don't like that, either; we regular sailors never do like it, we hold ourselves above it; but there's a better chance of getting on in it and of making money."

"I'm sure I am very sorry for it altogether," said Mrs. Todhetley. "A sailor cannot have any comfort."

"I expect he'll have to go," said the captain, ruefully: "he must get these ideas out of his head. It's such a thing, you see, for him to be always fancying he sees King."

"It is a dreadful thing."

"My wife had a brother once who was always seeing odd colours wherever he looked: colours and shadows and things. But that was not as bad as this. His doctor called it nerves: and I conclude Dan takes after him."

"My dear, I think Dan takes after your side, not mine," calmly put in Mrs Sanker, who had her light hair flowing and something black in it that looked like a feather. "He is so very passionate, you know: and I could not go into a passion if I tried."

"I suppose he takes after us both," returned Captain Sanker. "I know he never got his superstitious fancies from me, or from any one belonging to me. We may be of a passionate nature, we Sankers, but we don't see ghosts."

In a week or two's time after that, Dan was off to sea. A large shipping firm, trading from London to India, took him as midshipman. The ship was called the Bangalore; a fine vessel of about fourteen hundred tons, bound for some port out there. When Captain Sanker came back from shipping him off, he was full of spirits, and said Dan was cured already. No sooner was Dan amidst the bustle of London, than his fears and fancies left him.

It was some time in the course of the next spring—getting on for summer, I think—that Captain Sanker gave up his house in Worcester, and went abroad, somewhere into Germany. Partly from motives of economy, for they had no idea of saving, and somehow spent more than their income; partly to see if change would get up Mrs. Sanker's health, which was failing. After that, we heard nothing more of them: and a year or two went on.

"Please, sir, here's a young man asking to see you."

"A young man asking to see me," cried the Squire—we were just finishing dinner. "Who is it, Thomas?"

"I don't know, sir," replied old Thomas. "Some smart young fellow dressed as a sailor. I've showed him into your room, sir."

"Go and see who it is, Johnny."

It was summer-time, and we were at home at Dyke Manor. I went on to the little square room. You have been in it too. Opposite the Squire's old bureau and underneath the map of Warwickshire on the wall, sat the sailor. He had good blue clothes on and a turned-down white collar, and held a straw hat in his hand. Where had I seen the face? A very red-brown honest face, with a mouth as wide as Molly's rolling-pin. Wider, now that it was smiling.

He stood up, and turned his straw hat about a little nervously. "You've forgotten me, Master Johnny. Mark Ferrar, please, sir."

Mark Ferrar it was, looking shorter and broader; and I put out my hand to him. I take my likes and dislikes, as you have already heard, and can't help taking them; and Ferrar was one whom I had always liked.

"Please, sir, I've made bold to come over here," he went on. "Captain Sanker's left Worcester, they tell me, and I can't hear where he is to be found: and the Teals, they have left. I've brought news to him from his son, Mr. Dan: and father said I had better come over here and tell it, and maybe Squire Todhetley might get it sent to the captain."

"Have you seen anything of Mr. Dan, then?"

"I've been with him nearly all the time, Master Johnny. We served on the same ship: he as middy and I as working apprentice. Not but what the middies are apprenticed just as sure as we are. They don't do our rough work, the cleaning and that, and they mess apart; but that's pretty nigh all the difference."

"And how are you getting on, Mark?"

"First-rate, sir. The captain and officers are satisfied with me, and when I've served my four years I shall go up to pass for second mate. I try to improve myself a bit in general learning at odd moments too, sir, seeing I didn't have much. It may be of use to me if I ever get up a bit in life. Mr. Dan—"

"But look here, Ferrar," I interrupted, the recollection striking me. "How came you and Mr. Dan to sail together? You were on a small home-coasting barque: he went in an Indiaman."

"I was in the barque first of all, Master Johnny, and took a voyage to Spain and back. But our owners, hearing a good report of me, that I was likely to make a smart and steady sailor, put me on their big ship, the Bangalore. In a day or two Mr. Dan Sanker came on board."

"And how is he getting on? Does he—"

"If you please, Master Johnny, I'd like to tell what I've got to tell about him to the Squire," he interrupted. "It is for that, sir, I have come all the way over here."

So I called the Squire in. The following was the condensed substance of Ferrar's narrative. What with his way of telling it, and what with the Squire's interruptions, it was rather long.

"Mr. Dan joined the Bangalore the day we sailed, sir. When he saw me as one of the sailors he started back as if I shocked him. But in a week or two, when he had got round from his sea-sickness, he grew friendly, and sometimes talked a bit. I used to bring up Master King's death, and say how sorry I was for it—for you see, sir, I couldn't bear that he should think it true that I had had a hand in it. But he seemed to hate the subject; he'd walk away if I began it, and at last he said he couldn't stand the talking about King; so I let it be. Our voyage was a long one, for the ship went about from port to port. Mr. Dan—"

"What sort of a sailor did he make?" interrupted the Squire.

"Well, sir, he was a good smart sailor at his work, but he got to be looked upon as rather a queer kind of young man. He couldn't bear to keep his night watches—it was too lonely, he said; and several times he fell into trouble for calling up the hands when there was nothing to call them up for. At Hong Kong he had a fever, and they shaved his head; but he got well again. One evening, after we had left Hong Kong and were on our way to San Francisco, I was on deck—almost dark it was—when Mr. Dan comes down the rigging all in a heap, just as if a wild-cat was after him. 'There's King up there,' he says to me: and Mr. Conroy, do what he would, couldn't get him up again. After that he went about the ship peeping and peering, always fancying King was hiding somewhere and going to pounce out upon him. The captain said his fever was coming back: Mr. Dan said it was not fever, it was King. I told him one day what I thought—that Master King had been flung down; that it was not an accident—I felt as sure of it as though I had seen it done; and what I said seemed to put him up, sir. Who did I fancy had done it, or would do it? he asked me all in anger: and I said I did not know who, but if ever I got back to Worcester I'd leave not a stone unturned to find out. Well, sir, he got worse: worse in his fancies, and worse as to sickness. He was seeing King always at night, and he had dysentery and ague, and grew so weak that he could hardly stand. One of the cabin-boys took sick and died on board. The night he lay below, dead, Mr. Dan burst into the saloon saying it was King who was below, and that he'd never be got out of the ship again. Mr. Conroy—he was the chief mate, sir—humoured him, telling him not to fear, that if it was King he would be buried deep in the sea on the morrow: but Mr. Dan said he'd not stop in the sea, any more than he had stopped in his grave in St. Peter's churchyard at home; he'd be back in the ship again."

"Dan Sanker must have been mad," observed the Squire.

"Yes, sir, I think he was; leastways not right. In a day or two he had to be fastened down in his berth with brain-fever, and Mr. Conroy said that as he had known me in the past days I had better be the one to sit with him, for he couldn't be left. I was quite taken aback to hear what he said in his mutterings, and hoped it wasn't true."

"Did he get well again?"

"Just for a day or two, sir. The fever left him, but he was in the shockingest state of weakness you could imagine. The night before he died—"

The Squire started up. "Dan Sanker's not dead, Ferrar!"

"Yes he is, sir. It's what I have come to tell of."

"Goodness bless me! Poor Dan dead! Only think of it, Johnny!"

But I was not surprised. From the moment Ferrar first spoke, an instinct had been upon me that it was so. He resumed.

"Everything was done for him that could be, sir. We had a doctor on board—a passenger going to California—but he could not save him. He said when it came to such awful weakness as that, there could be no saving. Mr. Conroy and the other officers were very kind to him—the skipper too; but they could do nothing. All his fears seemed to be gone then; we could hardly hear his whispers, but he was sensible and calm. He said he knew God had forgave him for what he did, and would blot his sin out, and King had forgave him too, and had come to tell him so: he had been to him in the night and talked and smiled happily and said over to him a verse of 'Lord Bateman'—"

"And you say he was in his senses, Ferrar?"

"Yes, sir, that he was. That night he made a confession, Mr. Conroy and the doctor and me being by him. It was he that killed King."

"Bless my heart!" cried the Squire.

"He had seen me sitting with King that afternoon at Malvern, and heard him saying the verses to me. It put his temper up frightful, sir, I being one of their enemies the Frogs; but he says if he'd known it was me that snatched King out of the fight on Saturday, he'd not have minded so much. It must have been him that King saw coming, Master Johnny," added Ferrar, turning momentarily from the Squire to address me; "when he broke off in the midst of 'Lord Bateman,' and told me, all in a hurry, to go away. He waited till I was gone, and then rushed on to King and began abusing him and knocking him about. King was unsteady through his weak leg, and one of the knocks sent him over the bank. Dan says he was frightened almost to death; he caught up Dr. Teal's green handkercher from a chair and ran to the Well with it; he was too frightened to go and see after King, thinking he had killed him; and he sat down outside the Well and made as if he went to sleep. He never meant to hurt King, he said; it was only passion; but he had drunk a lot of strong ale and some wine upon it, and hardly knew what he was about. He said there was never a minute since but what he had been sorry for it, and he had been always seeing King. He asked me to show him the verses that had been given to me, that King wrote out, 'Lord Bateman'—for I had got them with me at sea, sir—and he kissed them and held them to him till he died."

"Dear, dear!" sighed the Squire.

"And that's all, sir," concluded Ferrar. "Mr. Conroy wrote out a copy of his confession, which I brought along with me to Worcester. Mr. Dan charged me to tell his father, and my own folks, and any other friends I liked that had thought me guilty, and I promised him. He was as placid as a child all the day after that, and died at sundown, so happy and peaceful that it was almost like heaven."

Ferrar broke off with a sob. Poor Dan!

And that was the final ending of the Day of Pleasure. He and King are together again.

CHAPTER XII

MARGARET RYMER

They had gone through the snow to evening service at North Crabb, the Squire, Mrs. Todhetley, and Tod, leaving me at home with one of my splitting headaches. Thomas had come in to ask if I would have the lamp, but I told him I would rather be without it. So there I sat on alone, beside the fire, listening to Hannah putting the children to bed upstairs, and looking sleepily out at the snowy landscape.

As the fire became dim, sending the room into gloom, the light outside grew stronger. The moon was high; clear and bright as crystal; what with that, and the perfectly white snow that lay on everything, the night seemed nearly as light as day. The grass plat outside was a smooth white plain, the clustering shrubs beyond it being also white.

I knew the fire wanted replenishing: I knew that if I sat on much longer, I should fall asleep; but sit on I did, letting the fire go, too listless to move. My eyes were fixed dreamily on the plain of snow, with the still moonlight lying across it. The room grew darker, the landscape lighter.

And asleep, in another minute, I should inevitably have been, but for a circumstance that suddenly arose. All in a moment—I saw not how or whence it came—a dark figure appeared on the grass plat, close before the bank of shrubs, right in front of me; the figure of a man, wrapped in a big great-coat. He was standing still and gazing fixedly at the house. Gazing, as it seemed (though that was impossible) at me. I was wide awake at once, and sitting bolt upright in the chair.

Yes, there could be no mistake; and it was no delusion. The man appeared to be a tall man, strong and muscular, with a mass of hair on his face. What could he want? Was it a robber reconnoitring the premises; peering and peeping to ascertain whether all the world was at church, before he broke in to rifle the house?

No one, void of such an experience, can imagine how dark he looked standing there, amidst the whiteness of all the scene around. In one sense, he stood out plainer than he could have done by daylight, because the contrast was greater. But this sort of light did not show his features, which were shrouded in obscurity.

Presently he moved. Looking to right and left, he took a step forward. Evidently he was trying to see whether the parlour where I sat was empty or occupied. Should I go out to him? Or should I fling up the window and ask what he wanted? I was not frightened: don't let any one think that: but watching him brought rather a creepy kind of sensation.

And, just then, as I left the chair quietly to open the window, I heard the catch of the garden-gate, and some one came whistling up the path. The man vanished as if by magic. Whilst I looked, he was gone. It seemed to me that I did not take my eyes off him; but where he went to, or what became of him, I knew not.

"Anybody at home?" called out Tom Coney, as he broke off his whistling and opened the hall-door.

"All right, Tom. Come along."

And, to tell the truth, I was not sorry to see Tom's hearty face. He had stayed away from evening service to sit with his mother.

"I say, Tom, did you see any fellow on the snow there, as you came in?"

"On the snow where?" asked Tom.

"There; just before the shrubs." And I pointed the spot out to him, and told him what had happened. Tom, one of the most practical fellows living, more so, I think, than even Tod, and with less imagination than an ostrich, received the account with incredulity.

"You dropped asleep, Johnny, and fancied it."

"I did not drop asleep, and I did not fancy it. When you came into the garden I was about to open the window and call to him."

"Those headaches are downright stupefying things, Johnny. Jane has them, you know. One day I remember she fell asleep with a bad one, and woke up and said the sofa was on fire."

"Tom, I tell you the man was there. A tall, strong-looking fellow, with a beard. He was staring at the house with all his might, at this room, as it seemed to me, wanting to come forward, I think, but afraid to. He kept close to the laurels, as if he did not wish to be seen, forgetting perhaps that they were white and betrayed him. When you opened the gate, he was there."

"It's odd, then, where he could have put himself," said Tom Coney, not giving in an inch. "I'll vow not a soul was there, man or woman, when I came up the path."

"That's true. He vanished in a moment. Whilst I was looking at him he disappeared."

"Vanished! Disappeared! You talk as though you thought it a ghost, Johnny."

"Ghost be hanged! It was some ill-doing tramp, I expect, trying to look if he might steal into the house."

"Much you know of the ways of tramps, Johnny Ludlow! Tramps don't come showing themselves on snow-lighted, open lawns, in the face and eyes of the front windows: they hide themselves in obscure hedges and byways. It's a case of headachy sleep, young man, and nothing else."

"Look here, Tom. If the man was there, his footprints will be there; if he was not, as you say, the snow will be smooth and level: come out and see."

We went out at once, Tom catching up a stick in the hall, and crossed the lawn. I was right, and Tom wrong. Sure enough, there were the footprints, plenty of them, indented in the deep snow. Tom gave in then.

"I wish to goodness I had seen him! The fellow should not have got off scot-free, I can tell him that. What tremendous feet he must have! Just look at the size, Johnny. Regular crushers."

"Don't you go and say again I was asleep! He must have stepped back and got away through these laurels; yes, here are the marks. I say, Tom"—dropping my voice to a whisper—"perhaps he's here now."

"We'll soon see that," said Tom Coney, plunging amidst the laurels with a crash, and beating about with the stick.

But there was no trace of him. Tom came out presently, covered with the beaten snow, and we went indoors; he veering round partly to his first opinion, and a little incredulous, in spite of the footprints.

"If any man was there, Johnny, how did he get away? I don't see, for my part, what he could possibly want. A thief would have gone to work in a different manner."

"Well, let it be so. I shall say nothing about it to them when they come home. Mrs. Todhetley's timid, you know, she would fancy the man was outside still, and be lying awake all night, listening for the smashing in of doors and windows."

Cracking the fire into a blaze; as much of a blaze, that is, as its dilapidated state allowed; I called Thomas to light the lamp and shut the shutters. When I told him of the affair, bidding him not mention it, he took a different view of it altogether, and put it down to the score of one of the younger maid-servants.

"They've got sweethearts, Master Johnny, the huzzies have; lots of sweethearts. One or the t'other of 'em is always a sidling sheepfaced up to the house, as though he didn't dare to say his soul was his own."

They came in from church before the fire had burnt up, and the Squire scolded me for letting it go so low. The coal we get in Worcestershire is the Staffordshire coal; it does not burn up in a minute as London coal does, but must have time.

Nothing of course was said about the man; I and Tom Coney—who stayed supper—held our tongues, as agreed upon. But I told Tod in going up to bed. He was sleepy, and did not think much of it. The fact was, as I could plainly perceive, that to any of them, when related, it did not seem to be much. They had not seen it as I had.

Timberdale Rectory, a cosy, old-fashioned house, its front walls covered with ivy, stood by itself amidst pasture-land, a field's length from the church. Mrs. Todhetley sent me there on the Monday morning, to invite the Rector, Herbert Tanerton, and his wife to dine with us the next evening, for we had a prime codfish sent as a present from London. The Squire and Tod had gone out shooting. It was January weather; cold and bright, with a frosty sky. Icicles drooped from the trees, and the snow in Crabb Ravine was above my ankles. The mater had said to me, "I should go the road way, Johnny;" but I did not mind the snow.

In Timberdale I met Margaret Rymer. She had her black cloak on, and her natty little black bonnet; and the gentle and refined face under it, with its mild brown eyes, put me more than ever in mind of her dead father.

Does any one remember her? I told something about her and her people early in this volume. When Thomas Rymer died, partly of a broken heart, Benjamin had again gone off, and Margaret continued to keep the business going. She understood the drugs thoroughly. During all the months that had elapsed since, the son had not made his appearance at home. Timberdale would say, "Why does not Benjamin come back to carry on affairs in his father's place?" but it had no satisfactory answer. Latterly, Timberdale had let Benjamin alone, and busied itself with Margaret.

Six months ago, the Reverend Isaac Sale had come to Timberdale as curate. He was a plain, dark little man of sterling worth, and some thirty years of age—older than the Rector. Margaret Rymer met him at the Sunday School, where she taught regularly, and he fell desperately in love with her—if it's not wrong to say that of a parson. As a rule, men and women like contrasts; and perhaps the somewhat abrupt-mannered man with the plain and rugged features had been irresistibly attracted by the delicate face of Margaret, and by her singularly gentle ways. In position she was not his equal; but Mr. Sale made no secret of his attachment, or that he wanted Margaret to be his wife. Mrs. Rymer entirely opposed it: how was the business to be kept going without Margaret, she demanded; or herself, either?

Mr. Sale had taken the curacy as a temporary thing. He was waiting for some expected appointment abroad. When it fell to him, Margaret Rymer would have to choose between sailing with him as his wife, or staying at home and giving him up for good. So said Timberdale.

After standing to talk a bit with Margaret, who had come out on an errand for her mother, I ran on to the Rectory. Mr. Tanerton and his wife were in the snug little bow-windowed front-room. He, spare and colourless, young yet, with cold grey eyes and thin light whiskers, sat by the blazing fire of wood and coal, that went roaring and sparkling up the chimney. Somehow Herbert Tanerton gave you the idea of being always in a chill. Well meaning, and kind in the main, he was yet severe, taking too much note of offences, and expecting all the world, and especially his own flock, to be better than gold.

His wife, kind, genial, and open-hearted, sat at the window, stitching a wristband for one of her husband's new shirts—he was as particular over them as he was over the parish sins—and glancing cheerfully out between whiles at the snowy landscape. When she was Grace Coney, and niece at the farm, we were very intimate; a nice, merry-hearted, capable girl, rather tall and slender, with bright dark hazel eyes, and a wide mouth that seemed always to be smiling to show its pretty white teeth. Seeing me coming, she ran to open the porch-door. As yet, she and Herbert had no children.

"Come in, Johnny! Is it not a lovely day? Herbert thinks it the coldest morning we have had; but I tell him that is because he does not feel very well. And he has been put out a little."

"What about?" I asked, as the Rector turned in his chair to shake hands with me. For she had said all that in his hearing.

"Oh, there are one or two things. Sam Mullett—"

"Where's the use of talking of the stupid old man, Grace?" cried the parson, crossly. "He is getting too old for his place."

"And Mr. Sale is going to leave," added Mrs. Tanerton, as I sat down by the table, after delivering the invitation. "The appointment he expected has been offered to him; it is a chaplaincy at the Bahama Islands. Mr. Sale has known of it for a week, and never told Herbert until yesterday."

"He spoke to me in the vestry after morning service," said the Rector, in an injured tone. "And he said at the same time that he was not sure he should accept it; it did not quite depend upon himself. I saw as clearly what he meant to imply as though he had avowed it; that it depended upon that girl, Margaret Rymer. It is a preposterous thing. The idea of a clergyman and a gentleman wanting to marry her! She keeps a chemist's shop!"

"It was her father who kept it," I said eagerly, for I liked Margaret Rymer, and did not care to hear her disparaged. "And he was a gentleman born."

"What has that to do with it?" retorted the parson, who was in one of his most touchy humours. "Had her grandfather been a duke, it would make no difference to what she is. Look at the mother!"

"Margaret is a lady in mind, in looks, and in manners," I persisted. "If I loved Margaret Rymer, I would marry her, though I were an archdeacon."

"That's just like you, Johnny Ludlow! you have no more sense than a child in some things," said the parson, crustily. Grace glanced up from her work and laughed; and looked as if she would like to take part with me.

"I never could have suspected Sale of such folly," went on the Rector, warming his hands over the blaze. "Grace, do you think that soup's ready?"

"I will see," answered Grace, putting the wristband on the little work-table; and she touched my shoulder playfully in passing.

Herbert Tanerton sat in silence; knitting his brow into lines. I took the chair on the other side the fireplace opposite to him, thinking of this and that, and fingering the tongs to help me: a habit I was often scolded for at home—that of fingering things.

"Look here, Mr. Tanerton. If they go all the way out to settle at the Bahamas, it will not signify there who Margaret has been here. Whether she may have helped in her father's business, or whether she may have been—as you said—a duke's granddaughter, and brought up accordingly, it will be all one to the Bahamas. Mr. Sale need not say to the Bahamas, 'My wife used to sell pennyworths of rhubarb and magnesia.'"

"It is not that," crossly responded the Rector—"what people will think or say; it is for Sale's own sake that I object. He cannot like the connection. A clergyman should marry in his own sphere."

"I suppose men are differently constituted, clergymen as well as others," said I, with deprecation, remembering that I was a plain, inexperienced lad, and he was the Rector of Timberdale. "Some persons don't care for social distinctions as others do, don't even see them: perhaps Mr. Sale is one."

"He cares for probity and honour—he would not choose to ally himself to crime, to disgrace," sternly spoke the Rector. "And he would do that in marrying Margaret Rymer. Remember what the son did, that ill-doing Benjamin," added he, dropping his voice. "You know all about it, Johnny. The affair of the bank-note, I mean."

And if Herbert Tanerton had said to me the affair of the moon and planets, I could not have been more surprised. "How did you get to know of it?" I asked, when speech came to me.

"Mr. Rymer told me on his death-bed. I was attending him spiritually. Of course, I have never spoken of it, even to my wife—I should not think of speaking of it; but I consider that it lies in my duty to disclose the facts to Mr. Sale."

"Oh no, don't—don't, please, Mr. Tanerton!" I cried out, starting up in a sort of distress, for the words seemed to take hold of me. "No one knows of it: no one but the Squire, and I, as you say, and Mrs. Rymer, and you, and Ben himself; Jelf's dead, you know. It need never be brought up again in this world; and I dare say it never will be. Pray don't tell Mr. Sale—for Margaret's sake."

"But I have said that I consider it my duty to tell him," replied the parson, steadily. "Here he comes!"

I turned to the window, and saw Sale trudging up to the parsonage through the snowy field pathway, his black hair and red rugged face presenting a sort of contrast to the white glare around. Ugly, he might be called; but it was a face to be liked, for all that. And the ring of his voice was true and earnest.

The affair of the bank-note had helped to kill Thomas Rymer, and sent Mr. Ben off on his wanderings again. It was a bit of ill-luck for Ben, for he had really pulled up, was reading hard at his medical books, and become as steady as could be. Never since then—some ten months ago now—had Ben been heard of; never had it been spoken of to man or woman. Need Herbert Tanerton disclose it to the curate? No: and I did not think he would do it.

"We were just talking of you," was the Rector's greeting to Mr. Sale, as the curate came into the room. "Bring a chair to the front of the fire: Johnny, keep your seat. I'm sure it's cold enough to make one wish to be in the fire to-day, instead of before it."

"What were you saying about me?" asked Mr. Sale, drawing forward the chair to sit down, as bidden, and giving me a nod in his short way.

"Have you come to tell me your decision—to go or stay?" asked the Rector, neglecting to answer the question.

"Not this morning. My decision is not yet made. I came to tell you how very ill Jael Batty is. I'm not at all sure that she will get over this bout."

"Oh," said the Rector, in a slighting tone, as if Jael Batty had no right to intrude herself into more momentous conversation. "Jael Batty is careless and indifferent in her duties, anything but what she ought to be, and makes her deafness an excuse for not coming to church. I'll try and get out to see her in the course of the day. She is always having these attacks. What we were speaking of was your friendship with Miss Rymer."

Herbert Tanerton, as I have said, meant to be kind, and I believe he had people's welfare at heart; but he had a severe way of saying things that seemed to take all the kindness out of his words. He was a great stickler for "duty," and if once he considered it was his duty to tell a fellow of his faults, tell he did, face to face, in the most uncompromising manner. He had decided that it was his duty to hold forth to

Mr. Sale, and he plunged into the discourse without ceremony. The curate did not seem in the least put out, but talked back again, quietly and freely. I sat balancing the tongs over the fender and listening.

"Miss Rymer is not my equal, you say," observed Sale. "I don't know that. Her father was a curate's son: I am a curate's son. Circumstances, it would seem, kept Mr. Rymer down in the world. Perhaps they will keep me down—I cannot tell."

"But you are a gentleman in position, a clergyman; Rymer served customers," retorted Mr. Tanerton, harping upon that bête noire of his, the chemist's shop. "Can't you perceive the difference? A gentleman ought to be a gentleman."

"Thomas Rymer was a gentleman, as I hear, in mind and manners and conduct; educated, and courteous, and—"

"He was one of the truest gentlemen I ever met," I could not help putting in, though it interrupted the curate. "For my part, when speaking with him I forgot the counter he served at."

"And a true Christian, I was about to say," added Mr. Sale.

There was a pause. Herbert Tanerton, who had been fidgeting in his chair, spoke:

"Am I mistaken in assuming that your acceptance of this chaplaincy depends upon Miss Rymer?"

"No, you are not mistaken," said Sale, readily. "It does depend upon her. If she will go with me—my wife—I shall accept it; if she will not, I remain at home."

"Margaret is as nice as her father was; she is exactly like him," I said. "Were I you, Mr. Sale, I should just take her out of the place and end it."

"But if she won't come with me?" returned he, with a half-smile.

"She is wanted at home," observed Herbert Tanerton, casting a severe look at me with his cold light eyes. "That shop could not get on without her." But Sale interrupted:

"I cannot imagine why the son is not at home to attend to things. It is his place to be there doing it, not his sister's. He is inclined to be wild, it is said, and given to roving."

"Wildness is not Benjamin Rymer's worst fault, or roving either," cried the Rector, in his hardest voice, though he dropped it to a low key. And forthwith he opened the ball, and told the unfortunate story in a very few words. I let the tongs fall with a rattle.

"I would not have mentioned this," pursued he, "but that I consider it lies in my duty to tell you of it. To any one else it would never be allowed to pass my lips; it never has passed them since Mr. Rymer disclosed it to me a day or two before he died. Margaret Rymer may be desirable in herself; but there's her position, and—there's this. It is for your own sake I have spoken, Mr. Sale."

Sale had sat still and quiet while he listened. There was nothing outward to show that the tale affected him, but instinct told me that it did. Just a question or two he put, as to the details, and then he rose to leave.

"Will you not let it sway you?" asked the Rector, perseveringly, as he held out his hand to his curate. And I was sure he thought he had been doing him the greatest good in the world.

"I cannot tell," replied Mr. Sale.

He went out, walked across the garden, and through the gate to the field, with his head down. A dreadful listlessness—as it seemed to me—had taken the place of his brisk bearing. Just for a minute I stood in the parlour where I was, feeling as though I had had a shower of ice thrown down upon me and might never be warm again. Saying a short good-morning, I rushed out after him, nearly upsetting Mrs. Tanerton in the hall, and a basin of soup she was carrying in on a plate. How cruel it seemed; how cruel! Why can't people let one another alone? He was half-way across the field when I overtook him.

"Mr. Sale, I want to tell you—I ought to tell you—that the story, as repeated to you by Mr. Tanerton, bears a worse aspect than the reality would warrant. It is true that Benjamin Rymer did change the note in the letter; but that was the best and the worst of it. He had become mixed up with some reckless men when at Tewkesbury, and they persuaded him to get the stolen note changed for a safe one. I am sure he repented of it truly. When he came home later to his father's, he had left all his random ways and bad companions behind him. Nobody could be steadier than he was; kind to Margaret, considerate to his father and mother, attentive to business, and reading hard all his spare time. It was only through an ill fellow coming here to hunt him up—one Cotton, who was the man that induced him to play the trick with the note—that he was disturbed again."

"How disturbed?"

"He grew frightened, I mean, and went away. That fellow Cotton deserved hanging. When he found that Ben Rymer would have nothing more to do with him, or with the rest of the bad lot, he, in revenge, told Jelf, the landlord of the Plough and Harrow (where Cotton ran up a score, and decamped without paying), saying that it was Ben Rymer who had changed the note—for, you see, it had always remained a mystery to Timberdale. Jelf—he is dead now—was foolish enough to let Ben Rymer know what Cotton had said, and Ben made off in alarm. In a week's time Mr. Rymer was dead. He had been ailing in mind and body for a long while, and the new fear finished him up."

A pause ensued. Sale broke it. "Did Miss Rymer know of this?"

"Of Ben and the bank-note? I don't believe she knows of it to this hour."

"No, I feel sure she does not," added Sale, speaking more to himself than to me. "She is truth and candour itself; and she has repeatedly said to me she cannot tell why her brother keeps away; cannot imagine why."

"You see," I went on, "no one knows of it, except myself, but Squire Todhetley and Mr. Tanerton. We should never, never think of bringing it up, any one of us; Mr. Tanerton only spoke of it, as he said, because he thought he ought to tell you; he will never speak of it again. Indeed, Mr. Sale, you need not fear it will be known. Benjamin Rymer is quite safe."

"What sort of a man is he, this Benjamin?" resumed Sale, halting at the outer gate of the field as we were going through it. "Like the father, or like the mother?"

"Like the mother. But not as vulgar as she is. Ben has been educated; she was not; and though he does take after her, there's a little bit of his father in him as well. Which makes a great difference."

Without another word, Mr. Sale turned abruptly off to the right, as though he were going for a country ramble. I shut the gate, and made the best of my way home, bearing back the message from the Rector and Grace—that they would come and help eat the codfish.

The Reverend Isaac Sale was that day sorely exercised in mind. The story he had heard shook his equanimity to the centre. To marry a young lady whose brother stood a chance of being prosecuted for felony looked like a very black prospect indeed; but, on the other hand, Margaret at least was innocent, and he loved and respected her with his whole heart and soul. Not until the evening was his mind made up; he had debated the question with himself in all its bearings (seated on the stump of a snowy tree); and the decision he arrived at, was—to take Margaret all the same. He could not leave her.

About nine o'clock he went to Mrs. Rymer's. The shop was closed, and Mr. Sale entered by the private door. Margaret sat in the parlour alone, reading; Mrs. Rymer was out. In her soft black dress, with its white frilling at the throat, Margaret did not look anything like her nearly twenty years. Her mild brown eyes and tale-telling cheeks lighted up at the entrance of the curate. Letting her nervous little hand meet his strong one, she would have drawn a chair forward for him, but he kept her standing by him on the hearthrug.

"I have come this evening to have some final conversation with you, Margaret, and I am glad your mother is out," he began. "Will you hear me, my dear?"

"You know I am always glad to hear you," she said in low, timid tones. And Mr. Sale made no more ado, but turned and kissed her. Then he released her hand, sat down opposite to her on the other side of the hearth, and entered on his argument.

It was no more, or other, than she had heard from him before—the whole sum and substance of it consisted of representations why he must accept this chaplaincy at the Bahamas, and why she must accompany him thither. In the midst of it Margaret burst into tears.

"Oh, Isaac, why prolong the pain?" she said. "You know I cannot go: to refuse is as painful to me as to you. Don't you see that I have no alternative but to remain here?"

"No, I do not see it," replied Mr. Sale, stoutly. "I think your mother could do without you. She is an active, bustling woman, hardly to be called middle-aged yet. It is not right that you should sacrifice yourself and your prospects in life. At least, it seems to me that it is not."

Margaret's hand was covering her face; the silent tears were dropping. To see him depart, leaving her behind, was a prospect intensely bitter. Her heart ached when she thought of it: but she saw no hope of its being otherwise.

"It is a week and a day since I told you that the promotion was at length offered me," resumed Mr. Sale, "and we do not seem to be any nearer a decision than we were then. I have kept it to myself and said nothing about it abroad, waiting for you to speak to me, Margaret; and the Rector—to whom I at length spoke yesterday—is angry with me, and says I ought to have told him at once. In three days from this— on Thursday next—I must give an answer: accept the post, or throw it up."

Margaret took her hand from her face. Mr. Sale could see how great was the conflict at work within her.

"There is nothing to wait for, Isaac. I wish there was. You must go by yourself, and leave me."

"I have told you that I will not. If you stay here, I stay."

"Oh, pray don't do that! It would be so intense a disappointment to you to give it up."

"The greatest disappointment I have ever had in life," he answered. "You must go with me."

"I wish I could! I wish I could! But it is impossible. My duty lies here, Isaac. I wish you could see that fact as strongly as I see it. My poor father always enjoined me to do my duty, no matter at what personal cost."

"It is your brother's duty to be here, Margaret; not yours. Where is he?"

"In London, I believe," she replied, and a faint colour flew into her pale face. She put up her handkerchief to hide it.

It had come to Margaret's knowledge that during the past few months her mother had occasionally written to Benjamin. But Mrs. Rymer would not allow Margaret to write or give her his address. It chanced, however, that about a fortnight ago Mrs. Rymer incautiously left a letter on the table addressed to him, and her daughter saw it. When, some days subsequently, Mr. Sale received the offer of the chaplaincy, and laid it and himself before Margaret, urging her to accompany him, saying that he could not go without her, she took courage to write to Benjamin. She did not ask him to return and release her; she only asked him whether he had any intention of returning, and if so, when; and she gave him in simple words the history of her acquaintanceship with Mr. Sale, and said that he wanted her to go out with him to the Bahamas. To this letter Margaret had not received any answer. She therefore concluded that it had either not reached her brother, or else that he did not mean to return at all to Timberdale; and so she gave up all hopes of it.

"Life is not very long, Margaret, and God has placed us in it to do the best we can in all ways; for Him first, for social obligations afterwards. But He has not meant it to be all trial, all self-denial. If you and I part now, the probability is that we part for ever. Amidst the world's chances and changes we may never meet again, howsoever our wills might prompt it."

"True," she faintly answered.

"And I say that you ought not to enforce this weighty penance upon me and yourself. It is for your brother's sake, as I look upon it, that you are making the sacrifice, and it is he, not you, who ought to be here. Why did he go away?"

"I never knew," said Margaret, lifting her eyes to her lover's, and speaking so confidingly and earnestly that, had he needed proof to convince him she was ignorant of the story he had that day been regaled with, it would have amply afforded it. "Benjamin was at home, and so steady and good as to be a comfort to papa; when quite suddenly he left without giving a reason. Papa seemed to be in trouble about it—it was only a few days before he died—and I have thought that perhaps poor Benjamin was unexpectedly called upon to pay some debt or other, and could not find the money to do it. He had not always been quite so steady."

"Well, Margaret, I think—"

A loud bang of the entrance-door, and a noisy burst into the room, proclaimed the return of Mrs. Rymer. Her mass of scarlet curls garnished her face on either side, and looked particularly incongruous with her widow's cap and bonnet. Mr. Sale, rising to hand her a chair, broke off what he had been about to say to Margaret, and addressed Mrs. Rymer instead; simply saying that the decision, as to her going out with him, or not going, could no longer be put off, but must be made.

"It has been made," returned Mrs. Rymer, disregarding the offered chair, and standing to hold her boots, one after the other, to the fire. "Margaret can't go, Mr. Sale; you know it."

"But I wish her to go, and she wishes it."

"It's a puzzle to me what on earth you can see in her," cried Mrs. Rymer, flinging her grey muff on the table, and untying her black bonnet-strings to tilt back the bonnet. "Margaret won't have any money. Not a penny piece."

"I am not thinking about money," replied the curate; who somehow could never keep his temper long in the presence of this strong-minded Amazon. "It is Margaret that I want; not money."

"And it's Margaret, then, that you can't have," she retorted. "Who is to keep the shop on if she leaves it?—it can't go to rack and ruin."

"I see you serving in it yourself sometimes."

"I can serve the stationery—and the pickles and fish sauce—and the pearl barley," contended she, "but not the drugs. I don't meddle with them. When a prescription comes in to be made up, if I attempted to do it I might put opium for senna, and poison people. I have not learnt Latin, as Margaret has."

"But, Mrs. Rymer—"

"Now we'll just drop the subject, sir, if it's all the same to you," loudly put in Mrs. Rymer. "I have told you before that Margaret must stay where she is, and keep the business together for me and her brother. No need to repeat it fifty times over."

She caught up her muff, and went out of the room and up the stairs as she delivered this final edict. Mr. Sale rose.

"You see how it is," said Margaret, in a low tone of emotion, and keeping her eyelids down to hide the tears. "You must go without me. I cannot leave. I can only say, God speed you."

"There are many wrongs enacted in this world, and this is one," he replied in a hard voice—not hard for her—as he took her hands in his, and stood before her. "I don't know that I altogether blame you, Margaret; but it is cruel upon you and upon me. Good-night."

He went out quite abruptly without kissing her, leaving her alone with her aching heart.

Tuesday afternoon, and the ice and the snow on the ground still. We were to dine at five o'clock—the London codfish and a prime turkey—and the Coneys were coming in as well as the Rector and his wife.

But Mrs. Coney did not come; old Coney and Tom brought in word that she was not feeling well enough; and the Tanertons only drove up on the stroke of five. As I helped Grace down from the pony-chaise, muffled up to the chin in furs, for the cold was enough to freeze an Icelander's nose off, I told her her aunt was not well enough to come.

"Aunt Coney not well enough to come!" returned Grace. "What a pity! Have I time to run in to see her before dinner, Johnny?"

"That you've not. You are late, as it is. The Squire has been telling us all that the fish must be in rags already."

Grace laughed as she ran in; her husband followed her unwinding the folds of his white woollen comforter. There was a general greeting and much laughter, especially when old Coney told Grace that her cheeks were as purple as his Sunday necktie. In the midst of it Thomas announced dinner.

The codfish came up all right, and the oyster sauce was in Molly's best style—made of cream, and plenty of oysters in it. The turkey was fine: the plum-pudding better than good. Hugh and Lena sat at the table; and altogether we had a downright merry dinner. Not a sober face amongst us, except Herbert Tanerton's: as to his face—well, you might have thought he was perpetually saying "For what we are going to receive—" It had struck eight ever so long when the last nut was eaten.

"Will you run over with me to my aunt's, Johnny?" whispered Grace as she passed my chair. "I should like to go at once, if you will."

So I followed her out of the room. She put her wraps on, and we went trudging across the road in the moonlight, over the crunching snow. Grace's foot went into a soft rut, and she gave a squeal.

"I shall have to borrow a shoe whilst this dries," said she. "Do you care to come in, Johnny?"

"No, I'll go back. I can run over for you presently."

"Don't do that. One of the servants will see me safe across."

"All right. Tell Mrs. Coney what a jolly dinner it was. We were all sorry she did not come."

Grace went in and shut the door. I was rushing back through our own gate, when some tall fellow glided out of the laurels, and put his hand on my arm. The moonlight fell upon his face and its reddish beard—

and, to my intense surprise, I recognized Benjamin Rymer. I knew him then for the man who had been dodging in and out of the shrubs the night but one before.

"I beg your pardon," he said. "It is, as I am well aware, a very unusual and unceremonious way of accosting you, or any one else, but I want particularly to speak with you, in private, Mr. Ludlow."

"You were here on Sunday night!"

"Yes. I saw the Squire and the rest of them go out to church, but I did not see you go, and I was trying to ascertain whether you were at home and alone. Tom Coney's coming in startled me and sent me away."

We had been speaking in a low key, but Ben Rymer dropped his to a lower, as he explained. When he went away ten months before, it was in fear and dread that the truth of the escapade he had been guilty of, in regard to the bank-note, was coming out to the world, and that he might be called upon to answer for it. His mother had since assured him he had nothing to fear; but Ben was evidently a cautious man, and preferred to ascertain that fact before showing himself openly at Timberdale. Knowing I was to be trusted not to injure a fellow (as he was pleased to say), he had come down here to ask me my opinion as to whether the Squire would harm him, or not. There was no one else to fear now Jelf was dead.

"Harm you!" I exclaimed in my enthusiasm, my head full of poor, patient Margaret; "why, the Squire would be the very one to hold you free of harm, Mr. Rymer. I remember his saying, at the time, Heaven forbid that he, having sons of his own, should put a stumbling-block in your path, when you were intending to turn over a new leaf. He will help you on, instead of harming you."

"It's very good of him," said Ben. "I was an awful fool, and nothing else. That was the only dangerous thing I ever did, and I have been punished severely for it. I believe it was nothing but the fear and remorse it brought that induced me to pull up, and throw ill ways behind me."

"I'm sure I am glad that you do," I answered, for something in Ben's tone seemed to imply that the bad ways were thrown behind him for good. "Are you thinking of coming back to Timberdale?"

"Not until I shall have passed for a surgeon—which will not be long now. I have been with a surgeon in London as assistant, since I left here. It was a letter from Margaret that induced me to come down. She—do you know anything about her, Mr. Johnny?"

"I know that a parson wants her to go out with him to the Bahamas; he is Tanerton's curate; and that the pills and powders stand in the way of it."

"Just so. Is he a good fellow, this parson?"

"Good in himself. Not much to look at."

"Maggie shall go with him, then. I should be the last to stand willingly in her way. You see, I have not known whether it was safe for me at Timberdale: or I should never have left Maggie to the shop alone. Does any one know of the past—my past—besides you and the Squire?"

"Yes; Herbert Tanerton knows of it; and—and the curate, Mr. Sale." And I told him what had passed only on the previous day, softening the Rector's speeches—and it seemed a curious coincidence, taken with this visit of Ben's, that it should have passed. His mouth fell as he listened.

"It is another mortification for me," he said. "I should like to have stood as well as might be with Margaret's husband. Perhaps, knowing this, he will not think more of her."

"I don't believe he will let it make any difference. I don't think he is the man to let it. Perhaps—if you were to go to him—and show him how straight things are with you now—and—"

I broke down in my hesitating suggestion. Ben was years older than I, miles taller and broader, and it sounded like the mouse attempting to help the lion.

"Yes, I will go to him," he said slowly. "It is the only plan. And—and you think there's no fear that Herbert Tanerton will get talking to others?"

"I'm sure there's none. He is indoors now, dining with us. I am sure you are quite safe in all respects. The thing is buried in the past, and even its remembrance will pass away. The old postman, Lee, thinks it was Cotton; the Squire persuaded him into the belief at the time. Where is Cotton?"

"Where all such rogues deserve to be—transported. But for him and his friends I should never have done much that's wrong. Thank you for the encouragement you give me."

He half put out his hand to endorse the thanks, and drew it back again; but I put mine freely into his. Ben Rymer was Ben Rymer, and no favourite of mine to boot; but when a man has been down and is trying to get up again, he deserves respect and sympathy.

"I was about here all last evening, hoping to get sight of you," he remarked, as he went out at the gate. "I never saw such light nights in all my life as these few last have been, what with the moon and the snow. Good-night, Mr. Johnny. By the way, though, where does the curate live?"

"At Mrs. Boughton's. Nearly the last house, you know, before you come to the churchyard."

Ben Rymer went striding towards Timberdale, putting his coat-collar well up, that he might not be recognized when going through the village, and arrived at the curate's lodgings. Mr. Sale was at home, sitting by the fire in a brown study, that seemed to have no light at all in it. Ben, as I knew later, sat down by him, and made a clean breast of everything: his temptation, his fall, and his later endeavours to do right.

"Please God, I shall get on in the world now," he said; "and I think make a name in my profession. I don't wish to boast—and time of course will alone prove it—but I believe I have a special aptitude for surgery. My mother will be my care now; and Margaret—as you are good enough to say you still wish for her— shall be your care in future. There are few girls so deserving as she is."

"I know that," said the curate. And he shook Ben's hand upon it as heartily as though it had been a duke royal's.

It was close upon ten when Ben left him. Mrs. Rymer about that same time was making her usual preparations before retiring—namely, putting her curls in paper by the parlour fire. Margaret sat at the table, reading the Bible in silence, and so trying to school her aching heart. Her mother had been cross and trying all the evening: which did not mend the inward pain.

"What are you crying for?" suddenly demanded Mrs. Rymer, her sharp eyes seeing a tear fall on the book.

"For nothing," faintly replied Margaret.

"Nothing! Don't tell me. You are frizzling your bones over that curate, Sale. I'm sure he is a beauty to look at."

Margaret made no rejoinder; and just then the young servant put in her head.

"Be there anything else wanted, missis?"

"No," snapped Mrs. Rymer. "You can be off to bed."

But, before the girl had shut the parlour-door, a loud ring came to the outer one. Such late summonses were not unusual; they generally meant a prescription to be made up. Whilst the girl went to the door, Margaret closed the Bible, dried her eyes, and rose up to be in readiness.

But instead of a prescription, there entered Mr. Benjamin Rymer. His mother stood up, staring, her hair a mass of white corkscrews. Ben clasped Margaret in his arms, and kissed her heartily.

"My goodness me!" cried Mrs. Rymer. "Is it you, Ben?"

"Yes, it is, mother," said Ben, turning to her. "Maggie, dear, you look as though you did not know me."

"Why, what on earth have you come for, in this startling way?" demanded Mrs. Rymer. "I don't believe your bed's aired."

"I'll sleep between the blankets—the best place to-night. What have I come for, you ask, mother? I have come home to stay."

Margaret was gazing at him, her mild eyes wide open, a spot of hectic on each cheek.

"For your sake, Maggie," he whispered, putting his arm round her waist, and bending his great red head (but not so red as his mother's) down on her. "I shall not much like to lose you, though, my little sister. The Bahamas are further off than I could have wished."

And, for answer, poor Margaret, what with one thing and another, sank quietly down in her chair, and fainted. Ben strode into the shop—as much at home amongst the bottles as though he had never quitted them—and came back with some sal volatile.

They were married in less than a month; for Mr. Sale's chaplaincy would not wait for him. The Rector was ailing as usual, or said he was, and Charles Ashton came over to perform the ceremony. Margaret was in a bright dark silk, a light shawl, and a plain bonnet; they were to go away from the church door, and the boxes were already at the station. Ben, dressed well, and looking not unlike a gentleman, gave her away; but there was no wedding-party. Mrs. Rymer stayed at home in a temper, which I dare say nobody regretted: she considered Margaret ought to have remained single. And after a day or two spent in the seaport town they were to sail from, regaling their eyes with the ships crowding the water, the Reverend Isaac Sale and his wife embarked for their future home in the Bahama Isles.

CHAPTER XIII

THE OTHER EARRING

"And if I could make sure that you two boys would behave yourselves and give me no trouble, possibly I might take you this year just for a treat."

"Behave ourselves!" exclaimed Tod, indignantly. "Do you think we are two children, sir?"

"We would be as good as gold, sir," I added, turning eagerly to the Squire.

"Well, Johnny, I'm not much afraid but that you would. Perhaps I'll trust you both, then, Joe."

"Thank you, father."

"I shall see," added the pater, thinking it well to put in a little qualification. "It's not quite a promise, mind. But it must be two or three years now, I think, since you went to them."

"It seems like six," said Tod. "I know it's four."

We were talking of Worcester Races. At that period they used to take place early in August. Dr. Frost had an unpleasant habit of reassembling his pupils either the race-week or the previous one; and to get over to the races was almost as difficult for Tod and for me as though they had been run in California. To hear the pater say he might perhaps take us this year, just as the Midsummer holidays were drawing to an end, and say it voluntarily, was as good as it was unexpected. He meant it, too; in spite of the reservation: and Dr. Frost was warned that he need not expect us until the race-week was at its close.

The Squire drove into Worcester on the Monday, to be ready for the races on Tuesday morning, with Tod, myself, and the groom—Giles; and put up, as usual, at the Star and Garter. Sometimes he only drove in and back on each of the three race-days; or perhaps on two of them: this he could do very well from Crabb Cot, but it was a good pull for the horses from Dyke Manor. This year, to our intense gratification, he meant to stay in the town.

The Faithful City was already in a bustle. It had put on its best appearance, and had its windows cleaned; some of the shop-fronts were being polished off as we drove slowly up the streets. Families were, like ourselves, coming in: more would come before night. The theatre was open, and we went to it after dinner; and saw, I remember, "Guy Mannering" (over which the pater went to sleep), and an after-piece with a ghost in it.

The next morning I took the nearest way from the hotel to Sansome Walk, and went up it to call on one of our fellows who lived near the top. His friends always let him stay at home for the race-week. A maid-servant came running to answer my knock at the door.

"Is Harry Parker at home?"

"No, sir," answered the girl, who seemed to be cleaning up for the races on her own account, for her face and arms were all "colly." "Master Harry have gone down to Pitchcroft, I think."

"I hope he has gone early enough!" said I, feeling disappointed. "Why, the races won't begin for hours yet."

"Well, sir," she said, "I suppose there's a deal more life to be seen there than here, though it is early in the day."

That might easily be. For of all solitary places Sansome Walk was, in those days, the dreariest, especially portions of it. What with the overhanging horse-chestnut trees, and the high dead wall behind those on the one hand, and the flat stretch of lonely fields on the other, Sansome Walk was what Harry Parker used to call a caution. You might pass through all its long length from end to end and never meet a soul.

Taking that narrow by-path on my way back that leads into the Tything by St. Oswald's Chapel, and whistling a bar of the sweet song I had heard at the theatre overnight, "There's nothing half so sweet in life as love's young dream," some one came swiftly advancing down the same narrow path, and I prepared to back sideways to give her room to pass—a young woman, with a large shabby shawl on, and the remains of faded gentility about her.

It was Lucy Bird! As she drew near, lifting her sad sweet eyes to mine with a mournful smile, my heart gave a great throb of pity. Faded, worn, anxious, reduced!—oh, how unlike she was, poor girl, to the once gay and charming Lucy Ashton!

"Why, Lucy! I did not expect to see you in Worcester! We heard you had left it months ago."

"Yes, we left last February for London," she answered. "Captain Bird has only come down for the races."

As she took her hand from under her shawl to respond to mine, I saw that she was carrying some cheese and a paper of cold cooked meat. She must have been buying the meat at the cook's shop, as the Worcester people called it, which was in the middle of High Street. Oh! what a change—what a change for the delicately-bred Lucy Ashton! Better that her Master of Ravenswood had buried his horse and himself in the flooded land, as the other one did, than have brought her to this.

"Where are you going to, down this dismal place, Lucy?"

"Home," she answered. "We have taken lodgings at the top of Sansome Walk."

"At one of the cottages a little beyond it?"

"Yes, at one of those. How are you all, Johnny? How is Mrs. Todhetley?"

"Oh, she's first-rate. Got no neuralgia just now."

"Is she at Worcester?"

"No; at Dyke Manor. She would not come. The Squire drove us in yesterday. We are at the Star."

"Ah! yes," she said, her eyes taking a dreamy, far-off look. "I remember staying at the Star myself one race-week. Papa brought me. It was the year I left school. Have you heard or seen anything of my brothers lately, Johnny Ludlow?"

"Not since we were last staying at Crabb Cot. We went to Timberdale Church one day and heard your brother Charles preach; and we dined once with Robert at the Court, and he and his wife came once to dine with us. But—have you not seen your brother James here?"

"No—and I would rather not see him. He would be sure to ask me painful questions."

"But he is always about the streets here, seeing after his patients, Lucy. I wonder you have not met him."

"We only came down last Saturday: and I go out as little as I can," she said; a hesitation in her tone and manner that struck me. "I did think I saw James's carriage before me just now as I came up the Tything. It turned into Britannia Square."

"I dare say. We met it yesterday in Sidbury as we drove in."

"His practice grows large, I suppose. You say Charles was preaching at Timberdale?" she added: "was Herbert Tanerton ill?"

"Yes. Ailing, that is. Your brother came over to take the duty for the day. Will you call at the Star to see the Squire, Lucy? You know how pleased he would be."

"N—o," she answered, her manner still more hesitating; and she seemed to be debating some matter mentally. "I—I would have come after dark, had Mrs. Todhetley been there. At least I think I would—I don't know."

"You can come all the same, Lucy."

"But no—that would not have done," she went on to herself, in a half-whisper. "I might have been seen. It would never have done to risk it. The truth is, Johnny, I ought to see Mrs. Todhetley on a matter of business. Though even if she were here, I do not know that I might dare to see her. It is—not exactly my own business—and—and mischief might come of it."

"Is it anything I can say to her for you?"

"I—think—you might," she returned slowly, pausing, as before, between her words. "I know you are to be trusted, Johnny."

"That I am. I wouldn't forget a single item of the message."

"I did not mean in that way. I shall have to entrust to you a private matter—a disagreeable secret. It is a long time that I have wanted to tell some of you; ever since last winter: and yet, now that the opportunity has come that I may do it, I scarcely dare. The Squire is hasty and impulsive, his son is proud; but I think I may confide in you, Johnny."

"Only try me, Lucy."

"Well, I will. I will. I know you are true as steel. Not this morning, for I cannot stop—and I am not prepared. Let me see: where shall we meet again? No, no, Johnny, I cannot venture to the hotel: it is of no use to suggest that."

"Shall I come to your lodgings?"

She just shook her head by way of dissent, and remained in silent thought. I could not imagine what it was she had to tell me that required all this preparation; but it came into my mind to be glad that I had chanced to go that morning to Harry Parker's.

"Suppose you meet me in Sansome Walk this afternoon, Johnny Ludlow? Say at"—considering—"yes, at four o'clock. That will be a safe hour, for they will be on the racecourse and out of the way. People will, I mean," she added hastily: but somehow I did not think she had meant people. "Can you come?"

"I will manage it."

"And, if you don't meet me at that time—it is just possible that I may be prevented coming out—I will be there at eight o'clock this evening instead," she continued. "That I know I can do."

"Very well. I'll be sure to be there."

Hardly waiting another minute to say good-morning, she went swiftly on. I began wondering what excuse I could make for leaving the Squire's carriage in the midst of the sport, and whether he would let me leave it.

But the way for that was paved without any effort of mine. At the early lunch, the Squire, in the openness of his heart, offered a seat in the phaeton to some old acquaintance from Martley. Which of course would involve Tod's sitting behind with me, and Giles's being left out altogether.

"Catch me at it," cried Tod. "You can do as you please, Johnny: I shall go to the course on foot."

"I will also," I said—though you, naturally, understand that I had never expected to sit elsewhere than behind. And I knew it would be easier for me to lose Tod in the crowd, and so get away to keep the appointment, than it would have been to elude the Squire's questioning as to why I could want to leave the carriage.

Lunch over, Tod said he would go to the Bell, to see whether the Letstoms had come in; and we started off. No; the waiter had seen nothing of them. Onwards, down Broad Street we went, took the Quay, and so got on that way to Pitchcroft—as the racecourse is called. The booths and shows were at this end, and the chief part of the crowd. Before us lay stretched the long expanse of the course, green and level as a bowling-green. The grand-stand (comparatively speaking a new erection there) lay on the left, higher up, the winning-chair and distance-post facing it. Behind the stand, flanking all that side of Pitchcroft, the beautiful river Severn flowed along between its green banks, the houses of Henwick, opposite, looking down upon it from their great height, over their sloping gardens. It was a hot day, the blue sky dark and cloudless.

"True and correct card of all the running horses, gentlemen: the names, weights, and colours o' the riders!" The words, echoing on all sides from the men who held these cards for sale, are repeated in my brain now; as are other sounds and sights. I was somewhat older then than I had been; but it was not very long since those shows, ranged round there side by side, a long line of them, held the greatest attraction for me in life. "Guy Mannering," the past night, had been very nice to see, very enjoyable; but it possessed not the nameless charm of that first "play" I went to in Scowton's Show on the racecourse. That charm could never come again. And I was but a lad yet.

The lightning with which the play opened had been real lightning to me; the thunder, real thunder. The gentleman who stood, when the curtain rose, gorgeously attired in a scarlet doublet slashed with gold (something between a king and a bandit), with uplifted face of terror and drawn sword, calling the war of the elements "tremendious," was to me a greater potentate than the world could almost contain! The young lady, his daughter, in ringlets and spangles, who came flying on in the midst of the storm, and fell at his feet, with upraised arms and a piteous appeal, "Alas! my father, and will you not consent to my marriage with Alphonso?" seemed more lovely to me than the Sultanas in the "Arabian Nights," or the Princesses in Fairyland. I sat there entranced and speechless. A new world had opened to me—a world of delight. For weeks and weeks afterwards, that play, with its wondrous beauties, its shifting scenes, was present to me sleeping and waking.

The ladies in spangles, the gentlemen in slashed doublets, were on the platforms of their respective shows to-day, dancing for the benefit of Pitchcroft. Now and again a set would leave off, the music ceasing also, to announce that the performance was about to commence. I am not sure but I should have gone up to see one, but for the presence of Tod and Harry Parker—whom we had met on the course. There were learned pigs, and spotted calves, and striped zebras; and gingerbread and cake stalls; and boat-swings and merry-go-rounds—which had made me frightfully sick once when Hannah let me go in one. And there was the ever-increasing throng, augmenting incessantly; carriages, horsemen, shoals of foot-passengers; conjurers and fortune-tellers; small tables for the game of "thimble-rig," their owners looking out very sharply for the constables who might chance to be looking for them; and the movable exhibitions of dancing dolls and Punch and Judy. Ay, the sounds and the sights are in my brain now. The bands of the different shows, mostly attired in scarlet and gold, all blowing and drumming as hard as they could blow and drum; the shouted invitations to the admiring spectators, "Walk up, ladies and gentlemen, the performance is just a-going to begin;" the scraping of the blind fiddlers; the screeching of the ballad-singers; the sudden uproar as a stray dog, attempting to cross the course, is hunted off it; the incessant jabber and the Babel of tongues; and the soft roll of wheels on the turf.

Hark! The bell rings for the clearing of the course. People know what it means, and those who are cautious hasten at once to escape under the cords on either side. The gallop of a horse is heard, its rider, in his red coat and white smalls, loudly smacking his whip to effect the clearance. The first race is about to begin. All the world presses towards the environs of the grand-stand to get a sight of the several horses entered for it. Here they come; the jockeys in their distinguishing colours, trying their horses in a brisk canter, after having been weighed in the paddock. A few minutes, and the start is effected; they are off!

It is only a two-mile heat. The carriages are all drawn up against the cords; the foot-passengers press it; horsemen get where they can. And now the excitement is at its height; the rush of the racers coming in to the winning-post breaks on the ear. They fly like the wind.

At that moment I caught sight of the sharply eager face of a good-looking, dashing man, got up to perfection—you might have taken him for a lord at least. Arm-in-arm with him stood another, well-got-up also, as a sporting country gentleman; he wore a green cut-away coat, top-boots, and a broad-brimmed hat which shaded his face. If I say "got-up," it is because I knew the one, and I fancied I knew the other. But the latter's face was partly turned from me, and hidden, as I have said, by the hat. Both watched the swiftly-coming racehorses with ill-concealed anxiety: and both, as well-got-up gentlemen at ease, strove to appear indifferent.

"Tod, there's Captain Bird."

"Captain Bird! Where? You are always fancying things, Johnny."

"A few yards lower down. Close to the cords."

"Oh, be shot to the scoundrel, and so it is! What a swell! Don't bother. Here they come."

"Blue cap wins!" "No! red sleeves gains on him!" "Yellow stripes is first!" "Pink jacket has it!" "By Jove! the bay colt is distanced!" "Purple wins by a neck!"

With a hubbub of these different versions from the bystanders echoing on our ears, the horses flew past in a rush and a whirl. Black cap and white jacket was the winner.

Amidst the crowding and the pushing and the excitement that ensued, I tried to get nearer to Captain Bird. Not to see him: it was impossible to look at him with any patience and contrast his dashing appearance with that of poor, faded Lucy's: but to see the other man. For he put me in mind of the gentleman-detective Eccles, who had loomed upon us at Crabb Cot that Sunday afternoon in the past winter, polished off the sirloin of beef, crammed the Squire with anecdotes of his college life, and finally made off with the other earring.

You can turn back to the paper called "Mrs. Todhetley's Earrings," and recall the circumstances. How she lost an earring out of her ear: a pink topaz encircled with diamonds. It was supposed a tramp had picked it up; and the Squire went about it to the police at Worcester. On the following Sunday a gentleman called introducing himself as Mr. Eccles, a private detective, and asking to look at the other earring. The Squire was marvellously taken with him, ordered in the beef, not long gone out from the dinner, and was as eager to entrust the earring to him as he was to take it. That Eccles had been a gentleman once—at least, that he had mixed with gentlemen, was easy to be seen: and perhaps had also been an Oxford man, as he asserted; but he was certainly a swindler now. He carried off the earring; and we had never seen him, or it, from that day to this. But I did think I saw him now on the racecourse. In the side face, and the tall, well-shaped figure of the top-booted country gentleman, with the heavy bunch of seals hanging from his watch-chain, who leaned on that man Captain Bird's arm, there was a great resemblance to him. The other earring, lost first, was found in the garden under a small fir-tree when the snow melted away, where it must have dropped unseen from Mrs. Todhetley's ear, as she stopped in the path to shake the snow from the tree.

But the rush of people sweeping by was too great. Captain Bird and he were nowhere to be seen. In the confusion also I lost Tod and Harry Parker. The country gentleman I meant to find if I could, and went looking about for him.

The carriages were coming away from their standing-places near the ropes to drive about the course, as was the custom in those days. Such a thing as taking the horses out of a carriage and letting it stay where it was until the end of the day was not known on Worcester racecourse. You might count the carriages-and-four there then, their inmates exchanging greetings with each other in passing, as they drove to and fro. It was a sight to see the noblemen's turn-outs; the glittering harness, the array of servants in their sumptuous liveries; for they came in style to the races. The meeting on the course was the chief local event of the year, when all the county assembled to see each other and look their best.

"Will you get up now, Johnny?"

The soft bowling of the Squire's carriage-wheels arrested itself, as he drew up to speak to me. The Martley old gentleman sat with him, and there was a vacant place by Giles behind.

"No, thank you, sir. I would rather be on foot."

"As you will, lad. Is your watch safe?"

"Oh yes."

"Where's Joe?"

"Somewhere about. He is with Harry Parker. I have only just missed them."

"Missed them! Oh, and I suppose you are looking for them. A capital race, that last."

"Yes, sir."

"Mind you take care of yourself, Johnny," he called back, as he touched up Bob and Blister, to drive on. I generally did take care of myself, but the Squire never forgot to remind me to do it.

The afternoon went on, and my search with it in the intervals of the racing. I could see nothing of those I wanted to see, or of Tod and Harry Parker. Our meeting, or not meeting, was just a chance, amidst those crowds and crowds of human beings, constantly moving. Three o'clock had struck, and as soon as the next race should be over—a four-mile heat—it would be nearly time to think about keeping my appointment with Lucy Bird.

And now once more set in all the excitement of the running. A good field started for the four-mile heat, more horses than had run yet.

I liked those four-mile heats on Worcester racecourse: when we watched the jockeys in their gay and varied colours twice round the course, describing the figure of eight, and coming in, hot and panting, at the end. The favourites this time were two horses named "Swallower" and "Master Ben." Each horse was well liked: and some betters backed one, some the other. Now they are off!

The running began slowly and steadily; the two favourites just ahead; a black horse (I forget his name, but his jockey wore crimson and purple) hanging on to them; most of the other horses lying outside. The two kept together all the way, and as they came in for the final run the excitement was intense.

"Swallower has it by a neck!" "No! Master Ben heads him!" "Ben wins! Swallower loses!" "Swallower has it! Ben's jockey is beat!" and so on, and so on. Amidst the shouts and the commotion the result was announced—a dead heat.

So the race must be run again. I looked at my watch (which you may be sure I had kept carefully buttoned up under my jacket), wondering whether I could stay for it. That was uncertain; there was no knowing how long an interval would be allowed for breathing-time.

Suddenly there arose a frightful commotion above all the natural commotion of the course. People rushed towards one point; horsemen galloped thither, carriages bowled cautiously in their wake. The centre of attraction appeared to be on the banks of the river, just beyond the grand-stand. What was it? What had occurred? The yells were deafening; the pushing fearful. At last the cause was known: King Mob was ducking some offender in the Severn.

To get near, so as to see anything of the fun, was impossible; it was equally impossible to gather what he had done; whether picked a pocket, or cheated at betting. Those are the two offences that on Pitchcroft were then deemed deserving of the water. This time, I think, it was connected with betting.

Soon the yells became louder and nearer. Execrations filled the air. The crowd opened, and a wretched-looking individual emerged out of it on the hard run, his clothes dripping, his hair hanging about his face like rat's tails.

On he came, the mob shouting and hallooing in his wake, and brushed close past me. Why! it was surely the country gentleman I had seen with Bird! I knew him again at once. But whether it was the man Eccles or not, I did not see; he tore by swiftly, his head kept down. A broad-brimmed hat came flying after him, propelled by the feet of the crowd. He stooped to catch it up, and then kept on his way right across the course, no doubt to make his escape from it. Yes, it was the same man in his top-boots. I was sure of that. Scampering close to his heels, fretting and yelling furiously, was a half-starved white dog with a tin kettle tied to its tail. I wondered which of the two was the more frightened—the dog or the man.

And standing very nearly close to me, as I saw then, was Captain Bird. Not running, not shouting; simply looking on with a countenance of supreme indifference, that seemed to express no end of languid contempt of the fun. Not a sign of recognition crossed his face as the half-drowned wight swept past him: no one could have supposed he ever set eyes on him before. And when the surging crowd had passed, he sauntered away in the direction of the saddling-place.

But I lost the race. Though I stayed a little late, hoping to at last see the horses come out for the second start, and to count how many of the former field would compete for it, the minutes flew all too swiftly by, and I had to go, and to put the steam on. Making a bolt across Pitchcroft and up Salt Lane, went I, full split, over the Tything, and so down to Sansome Walk. St. Oswald's clock was tinkling out four as I reached it.

Lucy did not come. She had indicated the spot where the meeting should be; and I waited there, making the best I could of it; cooling myself, and looking out for her. At half-past four I gave her up in my own mind; and when five o'clock struck, I knew it was useless to stay longer. So I began to take my way back slower than I had come; and on turning out by St. Oswald's, I saw the carriages and people flocking up on their way from Pitchcroft. The first day's racing was over.

There was a crowd at the top of Salt Lane, and I had to wait before I could get across. In the wake of a carriage-and-four that was turning out of it came Captain Bird, not a feather of his plumage ruffled, not a speck (except dust) on his superfine coat, not a wristband soiled. He had not been ducked, if his friend had.

"How d'ye do, Master Ludlow?" said he, with a grandly patronizing air, and a flourish of his cane, as if it were a condescension to notice me. And I answered him civilly; though he must have been aware I knew what a scamp he was.

"I wish he'd steal away to America some moonlight night," ran my thoughts, "and leave poor Lucy in peace."

The Squire's carriage dashed up to the hotel as I reached it, Tod sitting behind with Giles. I asked which of the two horses had won. Swallower: won by half-a-neck. The Squire was in a glow of satisfaction, boasting of the well-contested race.

And now, to make things intelligible, I must refer again for a minute or two to that past paper. It may be remembered that when "Detective Eccles" called on us that Sunday afternoon, asking to look at the fellow-earring to the one lost, Mrs. Todhetley had gone in to the Coneys', and the Squire sent me for her. When I arrived there, Lucy Bird was in the drawing-room alone, the mater being upstairs with Mrs. Coney. Poor Lucy told me she had been spending a day or two at Timberdale Court (her happy childhood's home), and had come over to dine with Mr. and Mrs. Coney, who were always kind to her, she added with a sigh; but she was going back to Worcester by the next train. I told her what I had come for—of the detective's visit and his request to see the other earring. Mrs. Todhetley felt nervous at meeting a real live detective, and asked me no end of questions as to what this particular one was like. I said he was no tiger to be afraid of, and described him as well as I could: a tall, slender, gentlemanly man, well-dressed; gold studs, a ring on his finger, a blue necktie, and a black moustache. Lucy (I had noticed at the time) seemed struck with the description; but she made no remark. Before we turned in at our gate we saw her leave the Coneys' house, and come stepping through the snow on her way to the station. Since then, until now, we had not seen anything of Lucy Bird.

The stars flickered through the trees in Sansome Walk as I turned into it. A fine trouble I had had to come! Some entertainment was in full swing that evening at the Saracen's Head—a sort of circus, combined with rope-dancing. Worcester would be filled with shows during the race-week (I don't mean those on Pitchcroft), and we went to as many as we could get money for. We had made the bargain with Harry Parker on the course to go to this one, and during the crowded dinner Tod asked the Squire's leave. He gave it with the usual injunctions to take care of ourselves, and on condition that we left our watches at home. So, there I was in a fix; neither daring to say at the dinner-table that I could not go, nor daring to say what prevented it, for Lucy had bound me to secrecy.

"What time is this thing going to be over to-night, Joe?" had questioned the Squire, who was drinking port wine with some more old gentlemen at one end of the table, as we rose to depart.

"Oh, I don't know," answered Tod. "About ten o'clock, I dare say."

"Well, mind you come straight home, you two. I won't have you getting into mischief. Do you hear, Johnny?"

"What mischief do you suppose, sir, we are likely to get into?" fired Tod.

"I don't know," answered the Squire. "When I was a young lad—younger than you—staying here for the races with my father—but we stayed at the Hop-pole, next door, which was the first inn then—I remember we were so wicked one night as to go about ringing and knocking at all the doors—"

"You and your father, sir?" asked Tod, innocently.

"My father! no!" roared the Squire. "What do you mean, Joe? How dare you! My father go about the town knocking at doors and ringing at bells! How dare you suggest such an idea! We left my father, sir, at the hotel with his friends at their wine, as you are leaving me with my friends here now. It was I and half-a-dozen other young rascals who did it—more shame for us. I can't be sure how many bell-wires we broke. The world has grown wiser since then, though I don't think it's better; and—and mind you walk quietly home. Don't get into a fight, or quarrel, or anything of that kind. The streets are sure to be full of rough people and pickpockets."

Harry Parker was waiting for us in the hotel gateway. He said he feared we should be late, and thought we must have been eating dinner for a week by the time we took over it.

"I'm not coming with you, Tod," I said; "I'll join you presently."

Tod turned round and faced me. "What on earth's that for, Johnny?"

"Oh, nothing. I'll come soon. You two go on."

"Suppose you don't get a place!" cried Parker to me.

"Oh, I shall get one fast enough: it won't be so crowded as all that."

"Now, look here, lad," said Tod, with his face of resolution; "you are up to some dodge. What is it?"

"My head aches badly," I said—and that was true. "I can't go into that hot place until I have had a spell of fresh air. But I shall be sure to join you later, if I can."

My headaches were always allowed. I had them rather often. Not the splitting, roaring pain that Tod would get in his head on rare occasions, once a twelvemonth, or so, when anything greatly worried him;

but bad enough in all conscience. He said no more; and set off with Harry Parker up the street towards the Saracen's Head.

The stars were flickering through the trees in Sansome Walk, looking as bright as though it were a frosty night in winter. It was cool and pleasant: the great heat of the day—which must have given me my headache—had passed. Mrs. Bird was already at the spot. She drew me underneath the trees on the side, looking up the walk as though she feared she had been followed. A burst of distant music crashed out and was borne towards us on the air: the circus band, at the Saracen's Head. Lucy still glanced back the way she had come.

"Are you afraid of anything, Lucy?"

"There is no danger, I believe," she answered; "but I cannot help being timid: for, if what I am doing were discovered, I—I—I don't know what they would do to me."

"You did not come this afternoon."

"No. I was very sorry, but I could not," she said, as we paced slowly about, side by side. "I had my shawl and bonnet on, when Edwards came in—a friend of my husband's, who is staying with him. He had somehow got into the Severn, and looked quite an object, his hair and clothes dripping wet, and his forehead bruised."

"Why, Lucy, he was ducked!" I cried excitedly. "I saw it all. That is, I saw the row; and I saw him when he made his escape across Pitchcroft. He had on a smart green cut-away coat, and top-boots."

"Yes, yes," she said; "I was sure it was something of that kind. When my husband came home later they were talking together in an undertone, Edwards cursing some betting-man, and Captain Bird telling Edwards that it was his own fault for not being more cautious. However, I could not come out, Johnny, though I knew you were waiting for me. Edwards asked, as impertinently as he dared, where I was off to. To buy some tea, I answered, but that it did not matter particularly, as I had enough for the evening. They think I have come out to buy it now."

"Do you mean to say, Lucy, that Captain Bird denies you free liberty?—watches you as a cat does a mouse?"

"No, no; you must not take up wrong notions of my husband, Johnny Ludlow. Bad though the estimation in which he is held by most people is, he has never been really unkind to me. Trouble, frightful trouble he does bring upon me, for I am his wife and have to share it, but personally unkind to me he has never yet been."

"Well, I should think it unkind in your place, if I could not go out when I pleased, without being questioned. What do they suspect you would be after?"

"It is not Captain Bird; it is Edwards. As to what he suspects, I am sure he does not know himself; but he seems to be generally suspicious of every one, and he sees I do not like him. I suppose he lives in general fear of being denounced to the police, for he is always doing what he calls 'shady' things; but he must know that he is safe with us. I heard him say to my husband the day before we left London, 'Why do you take your wife down?' Perhaps he thinks my brothers might be coming to call on me, and of course he does not want attention drawn to the place he may chance to be located in, whether here or elsewhere."

"What is his name, Lucy?"

"His name? Edwards."

"It's not Eccles, is it?"

She glanced quickly round as we walked, searching my face in the dusk.

"Why do you ask that?"

"Because, when I first saw him to-day on the racecourse with Captain Bird, he put me in mind of the fine gentleman who came to us that Sunday at Crabb Cot, calling himself Detective Eccles, and carried off Mrs. Todhetley's other earring."

Mrs. Bird looked straight before her, making no answer.

"You must remember that afternoon, Lucy. When I ran over to old Coney's for Mrs. Todhetley, you were there, you know; and I told you all about the earrings and the detective officer, then making his dinner of cold beef at our house while he waited for the mother to come home and produce the earring. Don't you remember? You were just going back to Worcester."

Still she said not a word.

"Lucy, I think it is the same man. Although his black moustache is gone, I feel sure it is he. The face and the tall slender figure are just like his."

"How singular!" she exclaimed, In a low tone to herself. "How strangely things come about!"

"But is it Eccles?"

"Johnny Ludlow," she said, catching my arm, and speaking in an excited, breathless whisper, "if you were to bring harm on me—that is, on him or on my husband through me, I should pray to die."

"But you need not be afraid. Goodness me, Lucy! don't you know that I wouldn't bring harm on any one in the world, least of all on you? Why, you said to me this morning that I was true as steel."

"Yes, yes," she said, bursting into tears. "We have always been good friends, have we not. Johnny, since you, a little mite of a child in a tunic and turned-down frill, came to see me one day at school, a nearly grown-up young lady, and wanted to leave me your bright sixpence to buy gingerbread? Oh, Johnny, if all people were only as loyal and true-hearted as you are!"

"Then, Lucy, why need you doubt me?"

"Do you not see the shadows of those leaves playing on the ground cast by the light of that gas-lamp?" she asked. "Just as many shadows, dark as those, lie in the path of my life. They have taught me to fear an enemy where I ought to look for a friend; they have taught me that life is so full of unexpected windings and turnings, that we know not one minute what new fear the next may bring forth."

"Well, Lucy, you need not fear me. I have promised you to say nothing of having met you here; and I will say nothing, or of what you tell me."

"Promise it me again, Johnny. Faithfully."

Just a shade of vexation crossed me that she should think it needful to reiterate this; but I would not let my face or voice betray it.

"I promise it again, Lucy. Faithfully and truly."

"Ever since last winter I have wanted to hold communication with one of you at your home, and to restore something that had been lost. But it had to be done very, very cautiously, without bringing trouble on me or on any one connected with me. Many a solitary hour, sitting by myself in our poor lodgings in London, have I deliberated whether I might venture to restore this, and how it was to be done: many a sleepless night have I passed, dwelling on it. Sometimes I thought I would send it anonymously by the post, but it might have been stolen by the way; sometimes it would occur to me to make a parcel of it and despatch it in that way. I never did either. I waited until some chance should bring me again near Mrs. Todhetley. But to-day I saw that it would be better to trust you. She is true also, and kind; but she might not be able to keep the secret from the Squire, and he—he would be sure to betray it, though perhaps not intentionally, to all Timberdale, and there's no knowing what mischief might come of it."

Light flashed upon me as she spoke. As surely as though it were already before me in black and white, I knew what she was about to disclose.

"Lucy, it is the lost earring! The man staying with you is Eccles."

"Hush!" she whispered in extreme terror, for a footstep suddenly sounded close to us. Lucy glided behind the tree we were passing, which in a degree served to hide her. How timid she was!—what induced it?

The intruder was a shop-boy with an apron on, carrying a basket of grocery parcels to one of the few houses higher up. He turned his head and gave us a good stare, probably taking us for a pair of lovers enjoying a stolen ramble by starlight. Setting up a shrill whistle, he passed on.

"I don't know what has come to me lately; my heart seems to beat at nothing," said poor Mrs. Bird, coming from behind the tree with her hand to her side. "And it was doubly foolish of me to go there; better that I had kept quietly walking on with you, Johnny."

"What is it that you are afraid of, Lucy?"

"Only of their seeing me; seeing me with you. Were they to do so, and it were to come out that the earring had been returned, they would know I had done it. They suspected me at the time—at least, Edwards did. For it is the earring I am about to restore to you, Johnny."

She put a little soft white paper packet in my hand, that felt as if it had wool inside it. I hardly knew whether I was awake or asleep. The beautiful earring that we had given up for good, come back again! And the sound of the drums and trumpets burst once more upon our ears.

"You will give it to Mrs. Todhetley when you go home, Johnny. And I must leave it to your discretion to tell her what you think proper of whence you obtained it. Somewhat of course you must tell her, but how much or how little I leave with you. Only take care you bring no harm upon me."

"I am sure, Lucy, that Mrs. Todhetley may be trusted."

"Very well. Both of you must be secret as the grave. It is for my sake, tell her, that I implore it. Perhaps she will keep the earring by her for a few months, saying nothing, so that this visit of ours into Worcestershire may be quite a thing of the past, and no suspicion, in consequence of it, as connected with the earring, may arise in my husband's mind. After that, when months have elapsed, she must contrive to let it appear that the earring is then, in some plausible way or other, returned to her."

"Rely upon it, we will take care. It will be managed very easily. But how did you get the earring, Lucy?"

"It has been in my possession ever since the night of the day you lost it; that Sunday afternoon, you know. I have carried it about with me everywhere."

"Do you mean carried it upon you?"

"Yes; upon me."

"I wonder you never lost it—a little thing like this!" I said, touching the soft packet that lay in my jacket pocket.

"I could not lose it," she whispered. "It was sewn into my clothes."

"But, Lucy, how did you manage to get it?"

She gave me the explanation in a few low, rapid words, glancing about her as she did it. Perhaps I had better repeat it in my own way; and to do that we must go back to the Sunday afternoon. At least, that will render it more intelligible and ship-shape. But I did not learn one-half of the details then; no, nor for a long time afterwards. And so, we go back again in imagination to the time of that January day, when we were honoured by the visit of "Detective Eccles," and the snow was lying on the ground, and Farmer Coney's fires were blazing hospitably.

Lucy Bird quitted the warm fires and her kind friends, the Coneys, and followed us out—me and Mrs. Todhetley—she saw us turn in at our own gate, and then she picked her way through the snow to the station at South Crabb. It was a long walk for her in that inclement weather; but she had been away from home (if the poor lodgings they then occupied in Worcester could be called home) two days, and was anxious to get back again. During her brief absences from it, she was always haunted by the fear of some ill falling on that precious husband of hers, Captain Bird; but he was nothing but an ex-captain, as you know. All the way to the station she was thinking about the earrings, and of my description of Detective Eccles. The description was exactly that of her husband's friend, Edwards, both as to person and dress; not that she supposed it could be he. When she left Worcester nearly two days before,

Edwards had just arrived. She knew him to be an educated man, of superior manners, and full of anecdote, when he chose, about college life. Like her husband, he had, by recklessness and ill-conduct, sunk lower and lower in the world, until he had to depend on "luck" or "chance" for a living.

Barely had Lucy reached the station, walking slowly, when the train shot in. She took her seat; and, after a short halt the train moved on again. At that moment there strode into the station that self-same man, Edwards, who began shouting furiously for the train to stop, putting up his hands, running and gesticulating. The train declined to stop; trains generally do decline to stop for late passengers, however frantically adjured; and Edwards was left behind. His appearance astonished Lucy considerably. Had he, in truth, been passing himself off as a detective officer to Squire Todhetley? If so, with what motive? Lucy could not see any motive, and still thought it could not be; that Edwards must be over here on some business of his own. The matter passed from her mind as she drew near Worcester, and reached their lodgings, which were down Lowesmoor way.

Experience had taught Lucy not to ask questions. She was either not answered at all, or the answer would be sure to give her trouble. Captain Bird had grown tolerably careless as to whether his hazardous doings reached, or did not reach, the ears of his wife, but he did not willingly tell her of them. She said not a word of having seen Edwards, or of what she had heard about the loss of Mrs. Todhetley's earring, or of the detective's visit to Crabb Cot. Lucy's whole life was one of dread and fear, and she never knew whether any remark of hers might not bear upon some dangerous subject. But while getting the tea, she did just inquire after Edwards.

"Has Edwards left?" she asked carelessly.

"No," replied Captain Bird, who was stretched out before the fire in his slippers, smoking a long pipe, and drinking spirits. "He is out on the loose, though, somewhere, to-day."

It was late at night when Edwards entered. He was in a rage. Trains did not run frequently on Sundays, and he had been kept all that time at South Crabb Junction, waiting for one. Lucy went upstairs to bed, leaving Edwards and her husband drinking brandy-and-water. Both of them had had quite enough already.

The matter of the earrings and the doubt whether Mr. Edwards had been playing at amateur detectiveship would have ended there, but for the accident of Lucy's having to come downstairs again for the small travelling-bag in which she had carried her combs and brushes. She had put it just inside the little back parlour, where a bed on chairs had been extemporized for Edwards, their lodgings not being very extensive. Lucy was picking up the bag in the dark, when some words in the sitting-room caught her ear; the door between the two rooms being partly open. Before a minute elapsed she had heard too much. Edwards, in a loud, gleeful, boasting tone, was telling how he had been acting the detective, and done the old Squire and his wife out of the other earring. Lucy, looking in through the opening, saw him holding it up; she saw the colours of the long pink topaz, and the diamonds flash in the candle-light.

"I thought I could relieve them of it," he said. "When I read that advertisement in the paper, it struck me there might be a field open to do a little stroke of business; and I've done it."

"You are a fool for your pains," growled Captain Bird. "There's sure to be a row."

"The row won't touch me. I'm off to London to-morrow morning, and the earring with me. I wonder what the thing will turn us in? Twenty pounds. There, put it in the box, Bird, and get out the dice."

The dice on a Sunday night!

Lucy felt quite sick as she went back upstairs. What would be the end of all this? Not of this one transaction in particular, but of all the other disgraceful transactions with which her husband was connected? It might come to some public exposure, some criminal trial at the Bar of Justice; and of that she had a horrible dread ever haunting her like a nightmare.

She undressed, and went to bed. One hour passed, two hours passed, three hours passed. Lucy turned and turned on her uneasy pillow, feeling ready to die. Besides her own anguish arising from their share in it, she was dwelling on the shameful wrong it did their kind friends at Crabb Cot.

The fourth hour was passing. Captain Bird had not come up, and Lucy grew uneasy on that score. Once, when he had taken too much (but as a general rule the ex-captain's delinquencies did not lie in that direction), he had set his shirt-sleeve on fire, and burnt his hands badly in putting it out. Slipping out of bed, Lucy put on her slippers and the large old shawl, and crept down to see after him.

Opening the sitting-room door very softly, she looked in. The candles were alight still, but had burnt nearly down to the socket; the dice and some cards were scattered on the table.

Edwards lay at full length on the old red stuff sofa; Captain Bird had thrown himself outside the bed in the other room, the door of which was now wide open, neither of them having undressed. That both were wholly or partially intoxicated, Lucy felt not a doubt of.

Well, she could only leave them as they were. They would come to no harm asleep. Neither would the candles: which must soon burn themselves out. Lucy was about to shut the door again, when her eye fell on the little pasteboard box that contained the earring.

Without a moment's reflection, acting on the spur of impulse, she softly stepped to the table, lifted the lid, and took the earring out.

"I will remedy the wrong they have done Mrs. Todhetley," she said to herself. "They will never suspect me."

Up in her room again, she lighted her candle and looked about for some place to conceal the earring; and, just as the idea to secure it had come unbidden to her, so did that of a safe place of concealment. With feverish hands she undid a bit of the quilting of her petticoat, one that she had but just made for herself out of an old merino gown, slipped the earring into the wadding, and sewed it up again. It could neither be seen nor suspected there; no, nor even felt, let the skirt be examined as it might. That done, poor Lucy went to bed again and at length fell asleep.

She was awakened by a commotion. It was broad daylight, and her husband (not yet as sober as he might be) was shaking her by the arm. Edwards was standing outside the door, calling out to know whether Mrs. Bird had "got it."

"What is the matter, George?" she cried, starting up in a fright, and for the moment completely forgetting where she was, for she had been aroused from a vivid dream of Timberdale.

"Have you been bringing anything up here from the sitting-room, Lucy?" asked Captain Bird.

"No, nothing," she replied promptly, and he saw that she spoke with truth. For Lucy's recollection had not come to her; she remembered nothing yet about the earring.

"There's something missing," said Captain Bird, speaking thickly.

"It has disappeared mysteriously off the sitting-room table. You are sure you have not been down and collared it, Lucy?"

The earring and the theft—her own theft—flashed into her memory together. Oh, if she could only avert suspicion from herself! And she strove to call up no end of surprise in her voice.

"Why, how could I have been down, George? Did you not see that I was fast asleep? What have you missed? Some money?"

"Money, no. It was—something of Edwards's. Had it close by him on the table when he went to sleep, he says—he lay on the sofa last night, and I had his bed—and this morning it was gone. I thought the house was on fire by the way he came and shook me."

"I'll look for it when I come down, if you tell me what it is," said poor Lucy. "How late I have slept! It must have been the cold journey."

"She has not got it," said Captain Bird, retreating to his friend outside, and closing the door on Lucy. "Knows nothing about it. Was asleep till I awoke her."

"Search the room, you fool," cried the excited Edwards. "I'd never trust the word of a woman. No offence to your wife, Bird, but it is not to be trusted."

"Rubbish!" said Captain Bird.

"Either she or you must have got it. It could not disappear without hands. The people down below have not been to our rooms, as you must know."

"She or I—what do you mean by that?" retorted Captain Bird; and a short sharp quarrel ensued. That the captain had not touched the earring, Edwards knew full well. It was Edwards who had helped him to reach the bed the previous night: and since then Bird had been in the deep sleep of stupor. But Edwards did think the captain's wife had. The result was that Captain Bird re-entered; and, ordering Lucy to lie still, he made as exact a search of the room as his semi-sobered faculties allowed. Lucy watched it from her bed. Amidst the general hunting and turning-over of drawers and places, she saw him pick up her gown and petticoats one by one and shake them thoroughly, but he found no signs of the earring.

From that time to this the affair had remained a mystery. There had been no one in the house that night, except the proprietor and his wife, two quiet old people who never concerned themselves with their lodgers. They protested that the street-door had been fast, and that no midnight marauder could have broken in and slipped upstairs to steal a pearl brooch (as Edwards put it) or any other article. So, failing other sources of suspicion, Edwards continued to suspect Lucy. There were moments when Bird did also: though he trusted her, in regard to it, on the whole. At any rate, Lucy was obliged to be most cautious. The quilted skirt had never been off her since, except at night: through the warm genial days of spring and the sultry heat of summer she had worn the clumsy wadded thing constantly: and the earring had never been disturbed until this afternoon.

"You see how it is, Johnny," she said to me, with one of her long-drawn sighs.

But at that moment the grocer's young man in the white apron came back down the walk, swinging his empty basket by the handle; and he took another good stare at us in passing.

"I mean as to the peril I should be in if you suffer the restoration of the earring to transpire," she continued in a whisper, when he was at a safe distance. "Oh, Johnny Ludlow! do you and Mrs. Todhetley take care, for my poor sake."

"Lucy, you need not doubt either of us," I said earnestly. "We will be, as you phrased it to-day, true as steel—and as cautious. Are you going back? Let me walk up to the top with you."

"No, no; we part here. Seeing us together might arouse some suspicion, and there is no absolute certainty that they may not come out, though I don't think they will. Edwards is for ever thinking of that earring: he does not feel safe about it, you perceive. Go you that way: I go this. Farewell, Johnny Ludlow; farewell."

"Good-night, Lucy. I am off to the circus now."

She went with a brisk step up the walk. I ran out by St. Oswald's, and so on to the Saracen's Head. The place was crammed. I could not get near Tod and Harry Parker; but they whistled at me across the sawdust and the fancy steeds performing on it.

We sat together in Mrs. Todhetley's bedroom at Dyke Manor, the door bolted against intruders: she, in her astonishment at the tale I told, hardly daring to touch the earring. It was Saturday morning; we had come home from Worcester the previous evening; and should now be off to school in an hour. Tod had gone strolling out with the Squire; which gave me my opportunity.

"You see, good mother, how it all is, and the risk we run. Do you know, I had half a mind to keep the earring myself for some months and say never a word to you; only I was not sure of pitching on a safe hiding-place. It would be so dreadful a thing for Lucy Bird if it were to get known."

"Poor Lucy, poor Lucy!" she said, the tears on her light eyelashes. "Oh, Johnny, if she could only be induced to leave that man!"

"But she can't, you know. Robert Ashton has tried over and over again to get her back to the Court—and tried in vain. See how it glitters!"

I was holding the earring so that the rays of the sun fell upon it, flashing and sparkling. It seemed more beautiful than it used to be.

"I am very, very glad to have it back, Johnny; the other was useless without it. You have not," with a tone of apprehension in her voice, "told Joseph?"

I shook my head. The truth was, I had never longed to tell anything so much in my life; for what did I ever conceal from him? It was hard work, I can assure you. The earring burning a hole in my pocket, and I not able to show Tod that it was there!

"And now, mother, where will you put it?"

She rose to unlock a drawer, took from it a small blue box in the shape of a trunk, and unlocked that.

"It is in this that I keep all my little valuables, Johnny. It will be quite safe here. By-and-by we must invent some mode of 'recovering the earring,' as poor Lucy said."

Lifting the lid of a little pasteboard box, she showed me the fellow-earring, lying in a nest of cotton. I took it out.

"Put them both into your ears for a minute, good mother! Do!"

She smiled, hesitated; then took out the plain rings that were in her ears, and put in those of the beautiful pink topaz and diamonds. Going to the glass to look at herself, she saw the Squire and Tod advancing in the distance. It sent us into a panic. Scuffling the earrings out of her ears, she laid them together on the wool in the cardboard box, put the lid on, and folded it round with white paper.

"Light one of the candles on my dressing-table, Johnny. We will seal it up for greater security: there's a bit of red sealing-wax in the tray." And I did so at her direction: stamping it with the seal that had been my father's, and which with his watch they had only recently allowed me to take into wearing.

"There," she said, "should any one by chance see that packet, though it is not likely, and be curious to know what it contains, I shall say that I cannot satisfy them, as it concerns Johnny Ludlow."

"Are you upstairs, Johnny? What in the world are you doing there?"

I went leaping down at Tod's call. All was safe now.

That's how the other earring came back. And "Eccles" had to be let off scot free. But I was glad he had the ducking.

CHAPTER XIV

ANNE [2]

[2] This paper, "Anne," ought to have been inserted before some of the papers which have preceded it, as the events it treats of took place at an earlier date.

"Why, what's the matter with you?" cried the Squire.

"Matter enough," responded old Coney, who had come hobbling into our house, and sat down with a groan. "If you had the gout in your great toe, Squire, as I have it in mine, you'd soon feel what the matter was."

"You have been grunting over that gout for days past, Coney!"

"So I have. It won't go in and it won't come out; it stops there on purpose to torment me with perpetual twinges. I have been over to Timberdale Parsonage this morning, and the walk has pretty nigh done for me."

The Squire laughed. We often did laugh at Coney's gout: which never seemed to be very bad, or to get beyond incipient "twinges."

"Better have stayed at home and nursed your gout than have pranced off to Timberdale."

"But I had to go," said the farmer. "Jacob Lewis sent for me."

Mr. Coney spoke of Parson Lewis, Rector of Timberdale. At this time the parson was on his last legs, going fast to his rest. His mother and old Coney's mother had been first cousins, which accounted for the intimacy between the parsonage and the farm. It was Eastertide, and we were spending it at Crabb Cot.

"Do you remember Thomas Lewis, the doctor?" asked old Coney.

"Remember him! ay, that I do," was the Squire's answer. "What of him?"

"He has been writing to the parson to take a house for him; he and his daughter are coming to live in old England again. Poor Lewis can't look out for one himself, so he has put it upon me. And much I can get about, with this lame foot!"

"A house at Timberdale?"

"Either in the neighbourhood of Timberdale or Crabb, Dr. Lewis writes: or he wouldn't mind Islip. I saw his letter. Jacob says there's nothing vacant at Timberdale at all likely to suit. We have been thinking of that little place over here, that the people have just gone out of."

"What little place?"

"Maythorn Bank. 'Twould be quite large enough."

"And it's very pretty," added the Squire. "Thomas Lewis coming back! Wonders will never cease. How he could reconcile himself to staying away all his life, I can't tell. Johnny lad, he will like to see you. He and your father were as thick as inkle weavers."

"Ay! Ludlow was a good friend to him while he was doing nothing," nodded old Coney. "As to his staying away, I expect he could not afford to live in England. He has had a legacy left him now, he tells the parson. What are you asking, Johnny?"

"Did I ever know Dr Lewis?"

"Not you, lad. Thomas Lewis went abroad ages before you were born, or thought of. Five-and-twenty years he must have been away."

"More than that," said the Squire.

This Thomas Lewis was half-brother to the Rector of Timberdale, but was not related to the Coneys. He served his time, when a boy, to a surgeon at Worcester. In those days young men were apprenticed to doctors just as they were to other trades. Young Lewis was steady and clever; but so weak in health that when he was qualified and ought to have set up on his own account, he could not. People were wondering what would become of him, for he had no money, when by one of those good chances that rarely fail in time of need, he obtained a post as travelling companion to a nobleman, rich and sickly, who was going to reside in the warmth of the south of France. They went. It brought up Thomas Lewis's health well; made quite another man of him; and when, a little later, his patron died, he found that he had taken care of his future. He had left the young surgeon a competency of two hundred a-year. Mr. Lewis stayed on where he was, married a lady who had some small means, took a foreign medical degree to become Dr. Lewis, and obtained a little practice amidst the English that went to the place in winter. They had been obliged to live frugally, though an income of from two to three hundred a-year goes a great deal farther over the water than it does in England: and perhaps the lack of means to travel had kept Dr. Lewis from visiting his native land. Very little had been known of him at home; the letters interchanged by him and the parson were few and far between. Now, it appeared, the doctor had again dropped into a legacy of a few hundred pounds, and was coming back with his daughter—an only child. The wife was dead.

Maythorn Bank, the pretty little place spoken of by Mr. Coney, was taken. It belonged to Sir Robert Tenby. A small, red-brick house, standing in a flower-garden, with a delightful view from its windows of the charming Worcestershire scenery and the Malvern Hills in the distance. Excepting old Coney's great rambling farm-homestead close by, it was the nearest house to our own. But the inside, when it came to be looked at, was found to be in a state of dilapidation, not at all fit for a gentleman's habitation. Sir Robert Tenby was applied to, and he gave directions that it should be put in order.

Before this was completed, the Rector of Timberdale died. He had been suffering from ailments and sorrow for a long while; and in the sweet spring season, the season that he had loved above all other seasons, when the May birds were singing and the May flowers were blooming, he crossed the river that divides us from the eternal shores.

Mr. Coney had to see to the new house then upon his own responsibility; and when it was finished and the workmen were gone out of it, he went over to Worcester, following Dr. Lewis's request, and ordered in a sufficiency of plain furniture. By the middle of June all was ready, a maid-servant engaged, and the doctor and his daughter were at liberty to come when they pleased.

We had just got home for the Midsummer holidays when they arrived. Old Coney took me to the station to meet them; he said there might be parcels to carry. Once, a French lady had come on a visit to the farm, and she brought with her fifteen small hand-packages and a bandbox.

"And these people are French, too, you see, Johnny," reasoned old Coney. "Lewis can't be called anything better, and the girl was born there. Can't even speak English, perhaps. I'm sure he has had time to forget his native tongue."

But they spoke English just as readily and fluently as we did; even the young lady, Anne, had not the slightest foreign accent. And there were no small packages; nothing but three huge trunks and a sort of large reticule, which she carried herself, and would not give up to me. I liked her looks the moment I saw her. You know I always take likes or dislikes. A rather tall girl, light and graceful, with a candid face, a true and sweet voice, and large, soft brown eyes that met mine frankly and fearlessly.

But the doctor! He was like a shadow. A tall man, with stooping shoulders, handsome, thin features, hollow cheeks, and scanty hair. But every look and movement bespoke the gentleman; every tone of his low voice was full of considerate courtesy.

"What a poor weak fellow!" lamented old Coney aside to me. "It's just the Thomas Lewis of the years gone by; no health, no stamina. I'm afraid he has only come home to die."

They liked the house, and liked everything in it; and he thanked old Coney very earnestly for the trouble he had taken. I never saw a man, as I learnt later, so considerate for the feelings of others, or so grateful for any little service rendered to himself.

"It is delightful," said Miss Lewis, smiling at me. "I shall call it our little château. And those hills in the distance are the beautiful Malvern Hills that my father has so often told me of!"

"How well you speak English!" I said. "Just as we do."

"Do you suppose I could do otherwise, when my father and my mother were English? It is in truth my native tongue. I think I know England better than France. I have always heard so much of it."

"But you speak French as a native?"

"Oh, of course. German also."

"Ah, I see you are an accomplished young lady, Miss Lewis."

"I am just the opposite," she said, with a laugh. "I never learnt accomplishments. I do not play; I do not sing; I do not draw; I do not—but yes, I do dance: every one dances in France. Ours was not a rich home, and my dear mother brought me up to be useful in it. I can make my own dresses; I can cook you an omelette, or—"

"Anne, this is Mr. Todhetley," interrupted her father.

The Squire had come in through the open glass doors, round which the jessamine was blooming. When they had talked a bit, he took me up to Dr. Lewis.

"Has Coney told you who he is? William Ludlow's son. You remember him?"

"Remember William Ludlow! I must forget myself before I could forget him," was the doctor's answer, as he took both my hands in his and held me before him to look into my eyes. The tears were rising in his own.

"A pleasant face to look at," he was pleased to say. "But they did not name him William?"

"No. We call him Johnny."

"One generation passes away and another rises up in its place. How few, how few of those I knew are now left to welcome me! Even poor Jacob has not stayed."

Tears seemed to be the fashion just then. I turned away, when released, and saw them in Miss Lewis's eyes as she stood against the window-sill, absently playing with the white jessamine.

"When they begin to speak of those who are gone, it always puts me in mind of mamma," she said in a whisper, as if she would apologize for the tears. "I can't help it."

"Is it long since you lost her?"

"Nearly two years; and home has not been the same to papa since. I do my best; but I am not my mother. I think it was that which made papa resolve to come to England when he found he could afford it. Home is but triste, you see, when the dearest one it contained has gone out of it."

It struck me that the house could not have had one dearer in it than Anne. She was years and years older than I, but I began to wish she was my sister.

And her manners to the servant were so nice—a homely country girl, named Sally, engaged by Mr. Coney. Miss Lewis told the girl that she hoped she would be happy in her new place, and that she would help her when there was much work to do. Altogether Anne Lewis was a perfect contrast to the fashionable damsels of that day, who could not make themselves appear too fine.

The next day was Sunday. We had just finished breakfast, and Mrs. Todhetley was nursing her toothache, when Dr. Lewis came in, looking more shadowy than ever in his black Sunday clothes, with the deep band on his hat. They were going to service at Timberdale, and he wanted me to go with them.

"Of course I have not forgotten the way to Timberdale," said he; "but there's an odd, shy feeling upon me of not liking to walk about the old place by myself. Anne is strange to it also. We shall soon get used to it, I dare say. Will you go, Johnny?"

"Yes, sir."

"Crabb Church is close by, Lewis," remarked the Squire, "and it's a steaming hot day."

"But I must go to Timberdale this morning. It was poor Jacob's church, you know for many years. And though he is no longer there, I should like to see the desk and pulpit which he filled."

"Ay, to be sure," readily acquiesced the Squire. "I'd go with you myself, Lewis, but for the heat."

Dr. Lewis said he should take the roadway, not the short cut through Crabb Ravine. It was a good round, and we had to start early. I liked Anne better than ever: no one could look nicer than she did in her trim black dress. As we walked along, Dr. Lewis frequently halted to recognize old scenes, and ask me was it this place, or that.

"That fine place out yonder?" he cried, stopping to point to a large stone house half-a-mile off the road, partly hidden amidst its beautiful grounds. "I ought to know whose it is. Let me see!"

"It is Sir Robert Tenby's seat—Bellwood. Your landlord, sir."

"Ay, to be sure—Bellwood. In my time it was Sir George's, though."

"Sir George died five or six years ago."

"Has Sir Robert any family? He must be middle-aged now."

"I think he is forty-five, or so. He is not married."

"Does he chiefly live here?"

"About half his time; the rest he spends at his house in London, He lives very quietly. We all like Sir Robert."

We sat in the Rector's pew, having it to ourselves. Herbert Tanerton did the duty, and gave a good sermon. Nobody was yet appointed to the vacant living, which was in Sir Hubert Tenby's gift. Herbert, meanwhile, took charge of the parish, and many people thought he would get it—as he did, later.

The Bellwood pew faced the Rector's, and Sir Robert sat in it alone. A fine-looking man, with greyish hair, and a homely face that you took to at once. He seemed to pay the greatest attention to Herbert Tanerton's sermon; possibly was deliberating whether he was worthy of the living, or not. In the pew behind him sat Mrs. Macbean, an old lady who had been housekeeper at Bellwood during two generations; and the Bellwood servants sat further down.

We were talking to Herbert Tanerton outside the church after service, when Sir Robert came up and spoke to the parson. He, Herbert, introduced Dr. Lewis to him as the late Rector's brother. Sir Robert shook hands with him at once, smiled pleasantly at Anne, and nodded to me as he continued his way.

"Do you like your house?" asked Herbert.

"I shall like it by-and-by, no doubt," was the doctor's answer. "I should like it now, but for the paint. The smell is dreadful."

"Oh, that will soon go off," cried Herbert.

"Yes, I hope so: or I fear it will make me ill."

In going back we took Crabb Ravine, and were at home in no time. They asked me to stay dinner, and I did so. We had a loin of lamb, and a raspberry tart, if any one is curious to know. Dr. Lewis had taken a fancy to me: I don't know why, unless it was that he had liked my father; and I'm sure I had taken one to them. But the paint did smell badly, and that's the truth.

In all my days I don't think I ever saw a man so incapable as Dr. Lewis; so helpless in the common affairs of life. What he would have done without Anne, I know not. He was just fit to sit down and be led like a child; to have said to him—Come here, go there; do this, do the other. Therefore, when he asked me to run in in the morning and see if he wanted anything, I was not surprised. Anne thought he might be glad of my shoulder to lean upon when he walked about the garden.

It was past eleven when I arrived there, for I had to do an errand first of all for the Squire. Anne was kneeling down in the parlour amidst a lot of small cuttings of plants, which she had brought from France. They lay on the carpet on pieces of paper. She wore a fresh white cotton gown, with black spots upon it, and a black bow at the throat; and she looked nicer than ever.

"Look here, Johnny; I don't know what to do. The labels have all come off, and I can't tell which is which. I suppose I did not fasten them on securely. Sit down—if you can find a chair."

The chairs and tables were strewed with books, most of them French, and other small articles, just unpacked. I did not want a chair, but knelt down beside her, asking if I could help. She said no, and that she hoped to be straight by the morrow. The doctor had stepped out, she did not know where, "to escape the smell of the paint."

I was deep in the pages of one of the books, "Les Contes de Ma Bonne," which Anne said was a great favourite of hers, though it was meant for children; and she had her head, as before, bent over the green sprigs and labels, when a shadow, passing the open glass doors, glanced in and halted. I supposed it must be the doctor; but it was Sir Robert Tenby. Up I started; Anne did the same quietly, and quietly invited him in.

"I walked over to see Dr. Lewis, and to ask whether the house requires anything else done to it," he explained. "And I had to come early, as I am leaving the neighbourhood this afternoon."

"Oh, thank you," said Anne, "it is very kind of you to come. Will you please to sit down, sir?" hastily taking the books off a chair. "Papa is out, but I think he will not be long."

"Are you satisfied with the house?" he asked.

"Quite so, sir; and I do not think it wants anything done to it at all. I hope you will not suppose we shall keep it in this state," she added rather anxiously. "When things are being unpacked, the rooms are sure to look untidy."

Sir Robert smiled. "You seem very notable, Miss Lewis."

"Oh, I do everything," she answered, smiling back. "There is no one else."

He had not taken the chair, but went out, saying he should probably meet Dr. Lewis—leaving a message for him, about the house, in case he did not.

"He is your great and grand man of the neighbourhood, is he not, Johnny?" said Anne, as she knelt down on the carpet again.

"Oh, he is grand enough."

"Then don't you think he is, considering that fact, very pleasant and affable? I'm sure he is as simple and free in manners and speech as we are."

"Most grand men—if they are truly great—are that. Your upstarts assume no end of airs."

"I know who will never assume airs, Johnny. He has none in him."

"Who's that?"

"Yourself."

It made me laugh. I had nothing to assume them for.

It was either that afternoon or the following one that Dr. Lewis came up to the Squire and old Coney as they were talking together in the road. He told them that he could not possibly stay in the house; he should be laid up if he did; he must go away until the smell of the paint was gone. That he was looking ill, both saw; and they believed he did not complain without cause.

The question was, where could he go? Mr. Coney hospitably offered him house-room; but the doctor, while thanking him, said the smell might last a long time, and he should prefer to be independent. He had been thinking of going with Anne to Worcester for a time. Did they know of lodgings there?

"Better go to an hotel," said the Squire. "No trouble at an hotel."

"But hotels are not always comfortable. I cannot feel at home in them," argued the poor doctor. "And they cost too much besides."

"You might chance to hit upon lodgings where you wouldn't be any more comfortable, Lewis. And they'd be very dull for you."

"There's Lake's boarding-house," put in old Coney, whilst the doctor was looking blank and helpless.

"A boarding-house? Ay, that might do, if it's not a noisy one."

"It's not noisy at all," cried the Squire. "It's uncommonly well conducted: sometimes there are not three visitors in the house. You and Miss Lewis would be comfortable there."

And for Lake's boarding-house Dr. Lewis and Anne took their departure on the very next day. If they had only foreseen the trouble their stay at it would lead to!

Lake's boarding-house stood near the cathedral. A roomy house, with rather shabby furniture in it: but in boarding-houses and lodgings people don't, as a rule, look for gilded chairs and tables. Some years before, Mrs. Lake, the wife of a professional man, and a gentlewoman, was suddenly left a widow with four infant children, boys, and nothing to keep them upon. What to do she did not know. And it often puzzles me to think what such poor ladies do do, left in similar straits.

She had her furniture; and that was about all. Friends suggested that she should take a house in a likely situation, and try for some lady boarders; or perhaps for some of the college boys, whose homes lay at a distance. Not to make too long a story of it, it was what she did do. And she had been in the house ever since, struggling on (for these houses mostly do entail a struggle), sometimes flourishing in numbers, sometimes down in the dumps with empty rooms. But she had managed to bring the children up: the two elder ones were out in the world, the two younger were still in the college school. Mrs. Lake was a meek little woman, ever distracted with practical cares, especially as to stews and gravies: Miss Dinah Lake (her late husband's sister, and a majestic lady of middle age), who lived with her, chiefly saw to the company.

But now, would any one believe that Dr. Lewis was "that shy," as their maid, Sally, expressed it—or perhaps you would rather call it helpless—that he begged the Squire to let me go with him to Lake's. Otherwise he should be lost, he said; and Anne, accustomed to French ways and habits, could not be of much use to him in a strange boarding-house: Johnny knew the house, and would feel at home there.

When Captain Sanker and his wife (if you have not forgotten them) first came to Worcester, they stayed at Lake's while fixing on a residence, and that's how we became tolerably well acquainted with the Lakes. This year that I am now writing about was the one that preceded the accident to King Sanker, told of earlier in the volume. And, in point of rotation, this paper ought to have appeared first.

So I went with Dr. Lewis and Anne. It was late in the afternoon when we reached Worcester, close upon the dinner-hour—which was five o'clock, and looked upon as quite a fashionable hour in those days. The dinner-bell had rung, and the company had filed in to dinner when we got downstairs.

But there was not much company staying in the house. Mrs. Lake did not appear at dinner, and Miss Dinah Lake took the head of the table. It happened more often than not that Mrs. Lake was in the kitchen, superintending the dinner and seeing to the ragouts and sauces; especially upon the advent of fresh inmates, when the fare would be unusually liberal. Mrs. Lake often said she was a "born cook;" which was lucky, as she could not afford to keep first-rate servants.

Miss Dinah sat at the head of the table, in a rustling green gown and primrose satin cap. Having an income of her own she could afford to dress. (Mrs. Lake's best gown was black silk, thin and scanty.) Next to Miss Dinah sat a fair, plump little woman, with round green eyes and a soft voice: at any rate, a soft way of speaking: who was introduced to us as Mrs. Captain Podd. She in turn introduced her daughters, Miss Podd and Miss Fanny Podd: both fair, like their mother, and with the same sort of round green eyes. A Mr. and Mrs. Mitchell completed the company; two silent people who seemed to do nothing but eat.

Dr. Lewis sat by Mrs. Captain Podd: and very pleasant and attentive the doctor found her. He was shy as well as helpless; but she talked to him freely in her low soft voice and put him altogether at his ease. My place chanced to be next to Miss Fanny Podd's: and she began at once to put me at my ease, as her mother was putting the doctor.

"You are a stranger here, at the dinner-table," observed Miss Fanny; "but we shall be good friends presently. People in this house soon become sociable."

"I am glad of that."

"I did not quite hear your name. Did you catch mine? Fanny Podd."

"Yes. Thank you. Mine is Ludlow."

"I suppose you never were at Worcester before?"

"Oh, I know Worcester very well indeed. I live in Worcestershire."

"Why!" cried the young lady, neglecting her soup to stare at me, "we heard you had just come over from living in France. Miss Dinah said so—that old guy at the head of the table."

"Dr. and Miss Lewis have just come from France. Not I. I know Miss Dinah Lake very well."

"Do you? Don't go and tell her I called her an old guy. Mamma wants to keep in with Miss Dinah, or she might be disagreeable. What a stupid town Worcester is!"

"Perhaps you do not know many people in it."

"We don't know any one. We had been staying last in a garrison town. That was pleasant: so many nice officers about. You could not go to the window but there'd be some in sight. Here nobody seems to pass but a crew of staid old parsons."

"We are near the cathedral; that's why you see so many parsons. Are you going to remain long in Worcester?"

"That's just as the fancy takes mamma. We have been here already six or seven weeks."

"Have you no settled home?"

Miss Fanny Podd pursed up her lips and shook her head. "We like change best. A settled home would be wretchedly dull. Ours was given up when papa died."

Thus she entertained me to the end of dinner. We all left the table together—wine was not in fashion at Lake's. Those who wanted any had to provide it for themselves: but the present company seemed to be satisfied with the home-brewed ale. Mrs. Captain Podd put her arm playfully into that of Dr. Lewis, and said she would show him the way to the drawing-room.

And so it went on all the evening: she making herself agreeable to the doctor: Miss Podd to Anne; Fanny to me. Of course it was highly good-natured of them. Mrs. Podd discovered that the doctor liked backgammon; and she looked for a moment as cross as a wasp on finding there was no board in the house.

"Quite an omission, my dear Miss Dinah," she said, smoothing away the frown with a sweet smile. "I thought a backgammon-board was as necessary to a house as chairs and tables."

"Mrs. Lake had a board once," said Miss Dinah; "but the boys got possession of it, and somehow it was broken. We have chess—and cribbage."

"Would you like a hand at cribbage, my dear sir?" asked Mrs. Podd of the doctor.

"Don't play it, ma'am," said he.

"Ah"—with a little sigh. "Julia, love, would you mind singing one of your quiet songs? Or a duet. Fanny, sweetest, try a quiet duet with your sister. Go to the piano."

If they called the duet quiet, I wondered what they called noisy. You might have heard it over at the cathedral. Their playing and singing was of the style known as "showy." Some people admire it: but it is a good thing ear-drums are not easily cracked.

The next day Mrs. Podd made the house a present of a backgammon-board: and in the evening she and Dr. Lewis sat down to play. Our number had decreased, for Mr. and Mrs. Mitchell had left; and Mrs. Lake dined with us, taking the foot of the table. Miss Dinah always, I found, kept the head.

"She is so much better calculated to preside than I am," whispered meek Mrs. Lake to me later in the evening; as, happening to pass the kitchen-door after dinner, I saw her in there, making the coffee. "What should I do without Dinah!"

"But need you come out to make the coffee, Mrs. Lake?"

"My dear, when I leave it to the servants, it is not drinkable. I am rather sorry Mrs. Podd makes a point of having coffee in an evening. Our general rule is to give only tea."

"I wouldn't give in to Mrs. Podd."

"Well, dear, we like to be accommodating when we can. Being my cousin, she orders things more freely than our ladies usually do. Dinah calls her exacting; but—"

"Is Mrs. Podd your cousin?" I interrupted, in surprise.

"My first cousin. Did you not know it? Her mother and my mother were sisters."

"The girls don't call you 'aunt.'"

"They do sometimes when we are alone. I suppose they think I am beneath them—keeping a boarding-house."

I had not much liked the Podds at first: as the days went on I liked them less. They were not sincere: I was quite sure of it; Mrs. Podd especially. But the manner in which she had taken Dr. Lewis under her wing was marvellous. He began to think he could not move without her: he was as one who has found a sheet-anchor. She took trouble of all kinds from him: her chief aim seemed to be to make his life pass pleasantly. She would order a carriage and take him for a drive in it; she'd parade the High Street on his arm; she sat with him in the Green within the enclosure, though Miss Dinah told her one day she had not the right of entrance to it; she walked him off to inspect the monuments in the cathedral, and talked with him in the cloisters of the old days when Cromwell stabled his horses there. After dinner they would play backgammon till bed-time. And with it all, she was so gay and sweet and gentle, that Dr. Lewis thought she must be a very angel come out of heaven.

"Johnny, I don't like her," said Anne to me one day. "She seems to take papa completely out of my hands. She makes him feel quite independent of me."

"You like her as well as I do, Anne."

"This morning I found him in the drawing-room; alone, for a wonder: he was gazing up in his abstracted way, as if wanting to discover what the pinnacles of the cathedral were made of, which appear to be so close, you know, from the windows of that room. 'Papa, you are lonely,' I said. 'Would you like to walk out?—or what would you like to do?' 'My dear, Mrs. Podd will see to it all,' he answered; 'don't trouble yourself; I am waiting for her.' It is just as though he had no more need of me."

Anne Lewis turned away to hide her wet eyelashes. For my part, I thought the sooner Mrs. Captain Podd betook herself from Lake's boarding-house, the better. It was too much of a good thing.

That same afternoon I heard some conversation not meant for me. Behind the house was a square patch of ground called a garden, containing a few trees and some sweet herbs. I was sitting on the bench there, underneath the high, old-fashioned dining-room windows, thinking how hot the sun was, wishing for something to do, and wondering when Dr. Lewis meant to send me home. He and Mrs. Podd were out together; Anne was in the kitchen, teaching Mrs. Lake some mysteries of French cookery. Miss Dinah sat in the dining-room, in her spectacles, darning table-cloths.

"Oh, have you come in!" I suddenly heard her say, as the door opened. And it was Mrs. Podd's voice that answered.

"The sun is so very hot: poor dear Dr. Lewis felt quite ill. He has gone up to his room for half-an-hour to sit quietly in the shade. Where are my girls?"

"I'm sure I don't know," replied Miss Dinah: and it struck me that her tone of voice was rather crusty. "Mrs. Podd, I must again ask you when you will let me have some money?"

"As soon as I can," said Mrs. Podd: who seemed by the sound, to have thrown herself upon a chair, and to be fanning her face with a rustling newspaper.

"But you have said that for some weeks. When is the 'soon' to be?"

"You know I have been disappointed in my remittances. It is really too hot for talking."

"I know that you say you have. But we cannot go on without some money. The expenses of this house are heavy: how are they to be kept up if our guests don't pay us? Indeed you must let me have part of your account, if not all."

"My dear sweet creature, the house is not yours," returned Mrs. Podd, in her most honeyed accents.

"I manage it," said Miss Dinah, "and am responsible for getting in the accounts. You know that our custom is to be paid weekly."

"Exactly, dear Miss Dinah. But I am sure that my cousin, Emma Lake, would not wish to inconvenience me. I am indebted to her; not to you; and I will pay her as soon as I can. My good creature, how can you sit stewing over that plain sewing this sultry afternoon?"

"I am obliged to," responded Miss Dinah. "We have not money to spend on new linen: trouble enough, it is, I can assure you, to keep the old decent."

"I should get somebody to help me. That young woman, Miss Lewis, might do it: she seems to have been used to all kinds of work."

"I wish you would shut that door: you have left it open," retorted Miss Dinah: "I don't like sitting in a draught, though it is hot. And I must beg of you to understand, Mrs. Podd, that we really cannot continue to keep you and your daughters here unless you can manage to give us a little money."

By the shutting of the door and the silence that ensued, it was apparent that Mrs. Podd had departed, leaving Miss Dinah to her table-cloths. But now, this had surprised me. For, to hear Mrs. Captain Podd and her daughters talk, and to see the way in which they dressed, one could not have supposed they were ever at a fault for ready-cash.

At the end of ten days I went home. Dr. Lewis no longer wanted me: he had Mrs. Podd. And I think it must have been about ten days after that, that we heard the doctor and Anne were returning. The paint smelt still, but not so badly as before.

They did not come alone. Mrs. Podd and her two daughters accompanied them to spend the day. Mrs. Podd was in a ravishing new toilette; and I hoped Lake's boarding-house had been paid.

Mrs. Podd went into raptures over Maythorn Bank, paint and all. It was the sweetest little place she had ever been in, she said, and some trifling, judicious care would convert it into a paradise.

I know who had the present care; and that was Anne. They got over about twelve o'clock; and as soon as she had seen the ladies' things off, and they were comfortably installed in the best parlour, its glass doors standing open to the fragrant flower-beds, she put on a big apron in the kitchen and helped Sally with the dinner.

"Need you do it, Anne?" I said, running in, having seen her crumbling bread as I passed the window.

"Yes, I must, Johnny. Papa bade me have a nice dinner served to-day: and Sally is inexperienced, you know: she knows nothing about the little dishes he likes. To tell you the truth," added Anne, glancing meaningly into my eyes for a moment, "I would rather be cooking here than talking with them there."

"Are you sorry to leave Worcester?"

"Yes, and no," she answered. "Sorry to leave Mrs. Lake and Miss Dinah, for I like them both: glad to be at home again and to have papa to myself. I shall not cry if we never see Mrs. Podd again. Perhaps I am mistaken: and I'm sure I did not think that the judging of others uncharitably was one of my faults; but I cannot help thinking that she has tried to estrange papa from me. I suppose it is her way: she cannot have any real wish to do it. However, she goes back to-night, and then it will be over."

"Who is at Lake's now?"

"No one—except the Podds. I am sorry, for I fear they have some difficulty to make both ends meet."

Was it over! Anne Lewis reckoned without her host.

I was running into Maythorn Bank the next morning, when I saw the shimmer of Anne's white garden-bonnet and her morning dress amidst the raspberry-bushes, and turned aside to greet her. She had a basin in her hand, picking the fruit, and the hot tears were running down her cheeks. Conceal her distress she could not; any attempt would have been worse than futile.

"Oh, Johnny, she is going to marry him!" cried she, with an outburst of sobs.

"Going to marry him!—who? what?" I asked, taking the basin from her hand: for I declare that the truth did not strike me.

"She is. Mrs. Podd. She is going to marry papa."

For a moment she held her face against the apple-tree. The words confounded me. More real grief I had never seen. My heart ached for her.

"Don't think me selfish," she said, turning presently, trying to subdue the sobs, and wiping the tears away. "I hope I am not that: or undutiful. It is not for myself that I grieve; indeed it is not; but for him."

I knew that.

"If I could only think it would be for his happiness! But oh, I fear it will not be. Something seems to tell me that it will not. And if—he should be—uncomfortable afterwards—miserable afterwards!—I think the distress would kill me."

"Is it true, Anne? How did you hear it?"

"True! Too true, Johnny. At breakfast this morning papa said, 'We shall be dull to-day without our friends, Anne.' I told him I hoped not, and that I would go out with him, or read to him, or do anything else he liked; and I reminded him of his small stock of choice books that he used to be so fond of. 'Yes, yes, we shall be very dull, you and I alone in this strange house,' he resumed. 'I have been thinking for some time we should be, Anne, and so I have asked that dear, kind, lively woman to come to us for good.' I did not understand him; I did not indeed, Johnny; and papa went on to explain. 'You must know that I allude to Mrs. Podd, Anne,' he said. 'When I saw her so charmed with this house yesterday, and we were talking about my future loneliness in it—and she lamented it, even with tears—one word led to another, and I felt encouraged to venture to ask her to share it and be my wife. And so, my dear, it is all settled; and I trust it will be for the happiness of us all. She is a most delightful woman, and will make the sunshine of any home.' I wish I could think it," concluded Anne.

"No; don't take the basin," I said, as she went to do so. "I'll finish picking the raspberries. What are they for?"

"A pudding. Papa said he should like one."

"Why could not Sally pick them? Country girls are used to the sun."

"Sally is busy. Papa bade her clear out that room where our boxes were put: we shall want all the rooms now. Oh, Johnny, I wish we had not left France! Those happy days will never come again."

Was the doctor falling into his dotage? The question crossed my mind. It might never have occurred to me; but one day at Worcester Miss Dinah had asked it in my hearing. I felt very uncomfortable, could not think of anything soothing to say to Anne, and went on picking the raspberries.

"How many do you want? Are these enough?"

"Yes," she answered, looking at them. "I must fill the basin up with currants."

We were bending over a currant-bush, Anne holding up a branch and I stripping it, when footsteps on the path close by made us both look up hastily. There stood Sir Robert Tenby. He stared at the distress on Anne's face, which was too palpable to be concealed, and asked without ceremony what was amiss.

It was the last feather that broke the camel's back. These words from a stranger, and his evident concern, put the finishing touch to Anne's state. She burst into more bitter tears than she had yet shed.

"Is it any trouble that I can help you out of?" asked Sir Robert, in the kindest tones, feeling, no doubt, as sorry as he looked. "Oh, my dear young lady, don't give way like this!"

Touched by his sympathy, her heart seemed to open to him: perhaps she had need of finding consolation somewhere. Drying her tears, Anne told her story simply: commenting on it as she had commented to me.

"It is for my father's sake that I grieve, sir; that I fear. I feel sure Mrs. Podd will not make him really happy."

"Well, well, we must hope for the best," spoke Sir Robert, who looked a little astonished at hearing the nature of the grievance, and perhaps thought Anne's distress more exaggerated than it need have been. "Dr. Lewis wrote to me last night about some alteration he wants to make in the garden; I have come to speak to him about it."

"Alteration in the garden!" mechanically repeated Anne. "I have heard nothing about it."

He passed into the house to the doctor. We picked on at the currants, and then took them into the kitchen. Anne sat down on a chair to strip them from their stalks. Presently we saw Sir Robert and the doctor at one end of the garden, the latter drawing boundaries round a corner with his walking-stick.

"Oh, I know," exclaimed Anne. "Yesterday Mrs. Podd suggested that a summer-house in that spot would be a delightful improvement. But I never, never could have supposed papa meant to act upon the suggestion."

Just so. Dr. Lewis wished to erect a summer-house of wood and trellis-work, but had not liked to do it without first speaking to his landlord.

As the days went on, Anne grew to feel somewhat reassured. She was very busy, for all kinds of preparations had to be made in the house, and the wedding was to take place at once.

"I think, perhaps, I took it up in a wrong light, Johnny," she said to me one day, when I went in and found her sewing at some new curtains. "I hope I did. It must have been the suddenness of the news, I suppose, and that I was so very unprepared for it."

"How do you mean? In what wrong light?"

"No one seems to think ill of it, or to foresee cause for apprehension. I am so glad. I don't think I can ever much like her: but if she makes papa happy, it is all I ask."

"Who has been talking about it?"

"Herbert Tanerton for one. He saw Mrs. Podd at Worcester last week, and thought her charming. The very woman, he said, to do papa good; lively and full of resource. So it may all be for the best."

I should as soon have expected an invitation to the moon as to the wedding. But I got it. Dr. Lewis, left to himself, was feeling helpless again, and took me with him to Worcester on the eve of the happy day. We put up at the Bell Hotel for the night; but Anne went direct to Lake's boarding-house. I ran down there in the evening.

Whether an inkling of the coming wedding had got abroad, I can't say; it was to be kept private, and had been, so far as any one knew; but Lake's house was full, not a room to be had in it for love or money. Anne was put in a sleeping-closet two yards square.

"It is not our fault," spoke Miss Dinah, openly. "We were keeping a room for Miss Lewis; but on Monday last when a stranger came, wanting to be taken in, Mrs. Podd told us Miss Lewis was going to the hotel with her father."

"My dear love, I thought you were," chimed in Mrs. Podd, as she patted Anne on the shoulder. "I must have mis-read a passage in your dear papa's letter, and so caught up the misapprehension. Never mind; you shall dress in my room if your own is not large enough. And I am sure all young ladies ought to be obliged to me, for the new inmate is a delightful man. My daughters find him charming."

"The room is quite large enough, thank you," replied Anne, meekly.

"Do you approve of the wedding, Miss Dinah?" I asked her later, when we were alone in the dining-room. "Do you like it?"

Miss Dinah, who was counting a lot of glasses on the sideboard that the maid had just washed and brought in, counted to the end, and then began upon the spoons.

"It is the only way we can keep our girls in check," observed she; "otherwise they'd break and lose all before them. I know how many glasses have been used at table, consequently how many go out to be washed, and the girl has to bring that same number in, or explain the reason why. As to the spoons, they get thrown away with the dishwater and sometimes into the fire. If they were silver it would be all the same."

"Do you like the match, Miss Dinah?"

"Johnny Ludlow," she said, turning to face me, "we make a point in this house of not expressing our likes and dislikes. Our position is peculiar, you know. When people have come to years of discretion, and are of the age that Mrs. Podd is, not to speak of Dr. Lewis's, we must suppose them to be capable of judging and acting for themselves. We have not helped on the match by so much as an approving word or look: on the other hand, it has not lain in our duty or in our power to retard it."

Which was, of course, good sense. But for all her caution, I fancied she could have spoken against it, had she chosen.

A trifling incident occurred to me in going back to the Bell. Rushing round the corner into Broad Street, a tall, well-dressed man, sauntering on before me, suddenly turned on his heel, and threw away his cigar. It caught the front of my shirt. I flung it off again; but not before it had burnt a small hole in the linen.

"I beg your pardon," said the smoker, in a courteous voice—and there was no mistaking him for anything but a gentleman. "I am very sorry. It was frightfully careless of me."

"Oh, it is nothing; don't think about it," I answered, making off at full speed.

St. Michael's Church stood in a nook under the cathedral walls: it is taken down now. It was there that the wedding took place. Dr. Lewis arrived at it more like a baby than a bridegroom, helpless and nervous to a painful degree. But Mrs. Podd made up for his deficiencies in her grand self-possession; her white bonnet and nodding feather seemed to fill the church. Anne wore grey silk; Julia and Fanny Podd some shining pink stuff that their petticoats could be seen through. Poor Anne's tears were dropping during the service; she kept her head bent down to hide them.

"Look up, Anne," I said from my place close to her. "Take courage."

"I can't help it, indeed, Johnny," she whispered. "I wish I could. I'm sure I wouldn't throw a damper on the general joy for the world."

The wedding-party was a very small one indeed; just ourselves and a stern-looking gentleman, who was said to be a lawyer-cousin of the Podds, and to come from Birmingham. All the people staying at Lake's had flocked into the church to look on.

"Pray take my arm. Allow me to lead you out. I see how deeply you are feeling this."

The ceremony seemed to be over almost as soon as it was begun—perhaps the parson, remembering the parties had both been married before, cut it short. And it was in the slight bustle consequent upon its termination that the above words, in a low, tender, and most considerate tone, broke upon my ear. Where had I heard the voice before?

Turning hastily round, I recognized the stranger of the night before. It was to Anne he had spoken, and he had already taken her upon his arm. Her head was bent still; the rebellious tears would hardly be kept back; and a sweet compassion sat on every line of his handsome features as he gazed down at her.

"Who is he?" I asked of Fanny Podd, as he walked forward with Anne.

"Mr. Angerstyne—the most fascinating man I ever saw in my life. The Lakes could not have taken him in, but for mamma's inventing that little fable of Anne's going with old Lewis to the Bell. Trust mamma for not letting us two girls lose a chance," added free-speaking Fanny. "I may take your arm, I suppose, Johnny Ludlow."

And after a plain breakfast in private, which included only the wedding-party, Dr. and Mrs. Lewis departed for Cheltenham.

Part the Second

"Johnny, what can I do? What do you think I can do?"

In the pretty grey silk that she had worn at her father's wedding, and with a whole world of perplexity in her soft brown eyes, Anne Lewis stood by me, and whispered the question. As soon as the bride and bridegroom had driven off, Anne was to depart for Maythorn Bank, with Julia and Fanny Podd; all three of them to remain there for the few days that Dr. and Mrs. Lewis purposed to be away. But now, no sooner had the sound of the bridal wheels died on our ears, and Anne had suggested that they should get ready for their journey home, than the two young ladies burst into a laugh, and said, Did she think they were going off to that dead-alive place! Not if they knew it. And, giving her an emphatic nod to prove they meant what they said, they waltzed to the other end of the room in their shining pink dresses to talk to Mr. Angerstyne.

Consternation sat in every line of Anne's face. "I cannot go there alone, or stay there alone," she said to me. "These things are not done in France."

No: though Maythorn Bank was her own home, and though she was as thoroughly English as a girl can be, it could not be done. French customs and ideas did not permit it, and she had been brought up in them. It was certainly not nice behaviour of the girls. They should have objected before their mother left.

"I don't know what you can do, Anne. Better ask Miss Dinah."

"Not go with you, after the arrangements are made—and your servant Sally is expecting you all!" cried Miss Dinah Lake. "Oh, you must be mistaken," she added; and went up to talk to them. Julia only laughed.

"Go to be buried alive at Maythorn Bank as long as mamma chooses to stay away!" she cried. "You won't get either of us to do anything of the kind, Miss Dinah."

"Mrs. Podd—I mean Mrs. Lewis—will be back to join you there in less than a week," said Miss Dinah.

"Oh, will she, though! You don't know mamma. She may be off to Paris and fifty other places before she turns her head homewards again. Anne Lewis can go home by herself, if she wants to go: I and Fanny mean to stay with you, Miss Dinah."

So Anne had to stay also. She sat down and wrote two letters: one to Sally, saying their coming home was delayed; the other to Dr. Lewis, asking what she was to do.

"And the gain is mine," observed Mr. Angerstyne. "What would the house have been without you?"

He appeared to speak to the girls generally. But his eyes and his smile evidently were directed to Anne. She saw it too, and blushed. Blushed! when she had not yet known him four-and-twenty hours. But he was just the fellow for a girl to fall in love with—and no disparagement to her to say so.

"Who is he?" I that evening asked Miss Dinah.

"A Mr. Angerstyne," she answered. "I don't know much of him, except that he is an independent gentleman with a beautiful estate in Essex, and a fashionable man. I see what you are thinking, Johnny: that it is curious a man of wealth and fashion should be staying at Lake's boarding-house. But Mr. Angerstyne came over from Malvern to see Captain Bristow, the old invalid, who keeps his room upstairs, and when here the captain persuaded him to stay for a day or two, if we could give him a room. That's how it was. Captain Bristow leaves us soon, and I suppose Mr. Angerstyne will be leaving too."

I had expected to go home the following day; but that night up came two of the young Sankers, Dan and King, and said I was to go and stay a bit with them. Leave to do so was easily had from home; for just as our school at old Frost's was reassembling, two boys who had stayed the holidays were taken with bad throats, and we were not to go back till goodness knew when. Tod, who was on a visit in Gloucestershire, thought it would be Michaelmas.

Back came letters from Cheltenham. Mrs. Lewis told her girls they might remain at Worcester if they liked. And Dr. Lewis wrote to Anne, saying she must not go home alone; and he enclosed a note to Mrs. Lake, asking her to be so kind as to take care of his daughter.

After that we had a jolly time. The Sankers and Lakes amalgamated well, and were always at one another's houses. This does not apply to Mrs. Lake and Miss Dinah: as Miss Dinah put it, they had no time for gadding down to Sanker's. But Mr. Angerstyne (who had not left) grew quite familiar there; the Sankers, who never stood on the slightest ceremony, making no stranger of him. Captain Sanker discovered that two or three former naval chums of his were known to Mr. Angerstyne; one dead old gentleman in particular, who had been his bosom friend. This was quite enough. Mr. Angerstyne had, so to say, the key of the house given him, and went in and out of it at will.

Every one liked Mr. Angerstyne. And for all the pleasurable excursions that now fell to our lot, we were indebted to him. Without being ostentatious, he opened his purse freely; and there was a delicacy in his manner of doing it that prevented its being felt. On the plea of wanting, himself, to see some noted spot or place in the neighbourhood, he would order a large post-carriage from the Star or the Crown, and invite as many as it would hold to accompany him, and bring baskets of choice fruit, or dainties from the pastry-cook's, to regale us on. Or he would tell the Sankers that King looked delicate: poor lame King, who was to die ere another year had flown. Down would come the carriage, ostensibly to take King for a drive; and a lot of us reaped the benefit. Mrs. Sanker was always of the party: without a chaperon, the young ladies could not have gone. Generally speaking the Miss Podds would come—they took care of that: and Anne Lewis always came—which I think Mr. Angerstyne took care of. The golden page of life was opening for Anne Lewis: she seemed to be entering on an Elysian pathway, every step of which was strewn with flowers.

One day we went to Holt Fleet. The carriage came down to the Sankers' in the morning, Mr. Angerstyne in it, and the captain stepped out of doors, his face beaming, to see the start. Once in a way he would be of the party himself, but not often. Mr. Angerstyne handed Mrs Sanker in, and then called out for me. I held back, feeling uncomfortable at being always taken, and knowing that Fred and Dan thought me selfish for it. But it was of no use: Mr. Angerstyne had a way of carrying out his own will.

"Get up on the box, Johnny," he said to me. And, close upon my heels, wanting to share the box with me, came Dan Sanker. Mr. Angerstyne pulled him back.

"Not you, Dan. I shall take King."

"King has been ever so many times—little wretch!" grumbled Dan. "It's my turn. It's not fair, Mr. Angerstyne."

"You, Dan, and Fred, and Toby, all the lot of you, shall have a carriage to yourselves for a whole day if you like, but King goes with me," said Mr. Angerstyne, helping the lad up.

He got in himself, took his seat by Mrs. Sanker, and the post-boy touched up his horses. Mrs. Sanker, mildly delighted, for she liked these drives, sat in her ordinary costume: a fancy shawl of some thick kind of silk crape, all the colours of the rainbow blended into its pattern, and a black velvet bonnet with a turned-up brim and a rose in it, beneath which her light hair hung down in loose curls.

We stopped at Lake's boarding-house to take up the three girls; who got in, and sat on the seat opposite Mrs. Sanker and Mr. Angerstyne: and then the post-boy started for Holt Fleet. "The place is nothing," observed Captain Sanker, who had suggested it as an easy, pleasant drive to Mr. Angerstyne; "but the inn is comfortable, and the garden's nice to sit or stroll in."

We reached Holt Fleet at one o'clock. The first thing Mr. Angerstyne did was to order luncheon, anything they could conveniently give us, and to serve it in the garden. It proved to be ham and eggs; first-rate; we were all hungry, and he bade them keep on frying till further orders. At which the girl who waited on us laughed, as she drew the corks of some bottled perry.

I saw a bit of by-play later on. Strolling about to digest the ham and eggs, some in one part of the grounds, which in places had a wild and picturesque aspect, some in another, Mr. Angerstyne suddenly seized Anne, as if to save her from falling. She was standing in that high narrow pathway that is perched up aloft and looks so dangerous, steadying herself by a tree, and bending cautiously forwards to look down. The path may be gone now. The features of the whole place may be altered; perhaps even done away with altogether; for I am writing of years and years ago. He stole up and caught her by the waist.

"Oh, Mr. Angerstyne!" she exclaimed, blushing and starting.

"Were you going to take a leap?"

"No, no," she smiled. "Would it kill me if I did?"

"Suppose I let you go—and send you over to try it?"

Ah, he would not do that. He was holding her all too safely. Anne made an effort to free herself; but her eyelids drooped over her tell-tale eyes, her conscious face betrayed what his presence was to her.

"How beautiful the river is from this, as we look up it!" she exclaimed.

"More than beautiful."

Julia Podd rushed up to mar the harmony. Never does a fleeting moment of this kind set in but somebody does mar it. Julia flirted desperately with Mr. Angerstyne.

"Mr. Angerstyne, I have been looking for you everywhere. Mrs. Sanker wants to know if you will take us for a row on the water. The inn has a nice boat."

"Mrs. Sanker does!" he exclaimed. "With pleasure. Are you fond of the water, Miss Lewis?"

Anne made no particular reply. She stood at a little distance now, apparently looking at the view; but I thought she wanted to hide her hot cheeks. Mr. Angerstyne caught her hand in his, playfully put his other hand within Miss Julia's arm, and so piloted them down. Ah, he might flirt back again with Julia Podd, and did; with Fanny also; but it was not to them his thoughts were given.

"Go on the water!" said Mrs. Sanker, who was sitting under the shade of the trees, repeating one of her favourite ballads to King in a see-saw tone. "I! Julia Podd must have misunderstood me. To go on the water might be nice for those who would like it, I said. I don't."

"Will you go?" asked Mr. Angerstyne, turning to Anne.

Anne shook her head, confessing herself too much of a coward. She had never been on any water in her life until when crossing over from France, and never wished to be. And Mr. Angerstyne ungallantly let the boat alone, though Julia and Fanny told him they adored the water.

We sat down in the shade by Mrs. Sanker; some on the bench by her side, some on the grass at her feet, and she recited for us the time-worn ballad she had begun for King: just as the following year she would recite things to us, as already told of, sitting on the floor beam of the turret-room. It was called "Lord Thomas." Should you like to hear it?

Lord Thomas he was a bold forester,
And a keeper of the king's deer;
Fair Ellenor, she was a fair young lady,
Lord Thomas he loved her dear.

"Come, read me a riddle, dear mother," said he,
"And riddle us both as one:
Whether fair Ellen shall be mine—
Or to bring the brown girl home?"

"The brown girl she hath both houses and lands;
Fair Ellenor, she has none:
Therefore I'd advise thee, on my blessing,
To bring the brown girl home."

Then he decked himself and he dressed himself,
And his merry men, all in green:
And as he rode through the town with them
Folks took him to be some king.

When he came to fair Ellenor's bower
So boldly he did ring;
There was none so ready as fair Ellen herself
To loose Lord Thomas in.

"What news, what news, Lord Thomas,
What news have you brought unto me?"
"I'm come to invite you to my wedding;
And that is bad news for thee."

"Oh, now forbid," fair Ellenor said,
"That any such thing should be done:
For I thought to have been the bride myself,
And that you would have been the bridegroom.

"Come, read me a riddle, dear mother," said she,
"And riddle us both as one:
Whether I shall go to Lord Thomas's wedding,
Or whether I shall tarry at home?"

"There's one may be thy friend, I know;
But twenty will be thy foe:
Therefore I charge thee, on my blessing,
To Lord Thomas's wedding don't go."

"There's one will be my friend, I know,
Though twenty should be my foe:
Betide me life, or betide me death,
To Lord Thomas's wedding I go."

Then she went up into her chamber
And dressed herself all in green:
And when she came downstairs again,
They thought it must be some queen.

When she came to Lord Thomas's castle
So nobly she did ring:
There was none so ready as Sir Thomas himself
To loose this lady in.

Then he took her by her lily-white hand
And led her across the hall;
And he placed her on the daïs,
Above the ladies all.

"Is this your bride, Lord Thomas?
I think she looks wondrous brown:
You might have had as fair a young maiden
As ever trod English ground."

"Despise her not," said Lord Thomas;
"Despise her not unto me;
I love thy little finger, Ellen,
Better than her whole body."

The brown girl, having a knife in her hand,
Which was both keen and sharp,
Between the long ribs and the short,
She pierced fair Ellenor's heart.

"Oh, what's the matter?" Lord Thomas said,
"I think you look pale and wan:
You used to have as fine a colour
As ever the sun shone on."

"What, are you blind, now, Thomas?
Or can't you very well see?
Oh, can't you see, and oh, can't you see my own heart's blood
Run trickling down to my knee?"

Then Lord Thomas, he took the brown girl by the hand,
And led her across the hall;
And he took his own bride's head off her shoulders,

And dashed it against the wall.

Then Lord Thomas, he put the sword to the ground,
The point against his heart:
So there was an end of those three lovers,
So sadly they did part!

Upon fair Ellenor's grave grew a rose,
And upon Lord Thomas's a briar:
And there they twixed and there they twined, till they came to the steeple-top;
That all the world might plainly see, true love is never forgot.

"Oh, how delightful these old ballads are!" cried Anne, as Mrs. Sanker finished.

"Delightful!" retorted Julia Podd. "Why, they are full of queer phrases and outrageous metre and grammar!"

"My dears, it is, I suppose, how people wrote and spoke in those old days," said Mrs. Sanker, who had given great force to every turn of the song, and seemed to feel its disasters as much as though she had been fair Ellen herself.

"Just so," put in Mr. Angerstyne. "The world was not full of learning then, as it is now, and we accept the language—ay and like it, too—as that of a past day. To me, these old ballads are wonderful: every one has a life's romance in it."

And that day at Holt Fleet, the only time I, Johnny Ludlow, ever saw the place, lives in my memory as a romance now.

As the days went on, there could be no mistake made by the one or two of us who kept our eyes open. I mean, as to Mr. Angerstyne's liking for Anne Lewis, and the reciprocal feelings he had awakened. With her, it had been a case of love at first sight; or nearly so. And that, if you may believe the learned in the matter, is the only love deserving the name. Perhaps it had been so with him: I don't know.

Three parts of their time they talked together in French, for Mr. Angerstyne spoke it well. And that vexed Julia and Fanny Podd; who called themselves good French scholars, but who somehow failed to understand. "They talk so fast; they do it on purpose," grumbled Fanny. At German Mr. Angerstyne was not apt. He spoke it a very little, and Anne would laughingly correct his mistakes, and repeat the German words slowly over, that he might catch the accent, causing us no end of fun. That was Anne's time of day, as Fanny Podd expressed it; but when it came to the musical evenings, Anne was nowhere. The other two shone like stars then, and did their best to monopolize Mr. Angerstyne.

That a fine gentleman, rich, and a man of the great world, should stay dawdling on at a boarding-house, puzzled Miss Dinah, who knew what was what. Of course it was no business of hers; she and Mrs. Lake were only too glad to have one who paid so liberally. He would run upstairs to sit with Captain Bristow; and twice a week he went to Malvern, sometimes not getting back in time for dinner.

The college school had begun again, and I was back at Lake's. For Tom and Alfred Lake, who had been away, were at home now: and nothing would do but I must come to their house before I went home—to which I was daily expecting a summons. As to the bride and bridegroom, we thought they meant to remain away for good; weeks had elapsed since their departure. No one regretted that: Julia and Fanny Podd considered Maythorn Bank the fag-end of the world, and hoped they might never be called to it. And Anne, living in the Elysian Fields, did not care to leave them for the dreary land outside their borders.

One evening we were invited to a tea-dinner at Captain Sanker's. The Miss Podds persisted in calling it a soirée. It turned out to be a scrambling sort of entertainment, and must have amused Mr. Angerstyne. Biddy had poured the bowl of sweet custard over the meat patties by mistake, and put salt on the open tartlets instead of sugar. It seemed nothing but fun to us all. The evening, with its mistakes, and its laughter, and its genuine hospitality, came to an end, and we started to go home under the convoy of Mr. Angerstyne, all the Sanker boys, except Toby, attending us. It was a lovely moonlight night; Mrs. Lake, who had come in at the tail of the soirée to escort the girls home, remarked that the moon was never brighter.

"Why, just look there!" she exclaimed, as we turned up Edgar Street, intending to take that and the steps homewards; "the Tower gates are open!" For it was the custom to close the great gates of Edgar Tower at dusk.

"Oh, I know," cried Fred Sanker. "The sub-dean gave a dinner to-night; and the porter has left the gates wide for the carriages. Who is good for a race round the green?"

It seemed that we all were, for the whole lot of us followed him in, leaving Mrs. Lake calling after us in consternation. The old Tower porter, thinking the Green was being charged by an army of ill-doers, rushed out of his den, shouting to us to come back.

Much we heeded him! Counting the carriages (three of them) waiting at the sub-dean's door, we raced onwards at will, some hither, some thither. King went back to Mrs. Lake. The evening coolness felt delicious after the hot and garish day; the moonlight brought out the lights and shades of the queer old houses and the older cathedral. Collecting ourselves together presently, at Fred Sanker's whoop, Mr. Angerstyne and Anne were missing.

"They've gone to look at the Severn, I think," said Dan Sanker. "I heard him tell her it was worth looking at in the moonlight."

Yes, they were there. He had Anne's arm tucked up under his, and his head bent over her that she might catch his whispers. They turned round at hearing our footsteps.

"Indeed we must go home, Mr. Angerstyne," said Julia Podd, who had run down after me, and spoke crossly. "The college clock is chiming a quarter to eleven. There's Mrs. Lake waiting for us under the Tower!"

"Is it so late?" he answered her, in a pleasant voice. "Time flies quickly in the moonlight: I've often remarked it."

Walking forward, he kept by the side of Julia; Anne and I followed together. Some of the boys were shouting themselves hoarse from the top of the ascent, wanting to know if we were lost.

"Is it all settled, Anne?" I asked her, jestingly, dropping my voice.

"Is what settled?" she returned. But she understood; for her face looked like a rose in the moonlight.

"You know. I can see, if the others can't. And if it makes you happy, Anne, I am very glad of it."

"Oh, Johnny, I hope—I hope no one else does see. But indeed you are making more of it than it deserves."

"What does he say to you?"

"He has not said anything. So you see, Johnny, you may be quite mistaken."

It was all the same: if he had not said anything yet, there could be no question that he meant soon to say it. We were passing the old elm-trees just then; the moonlight, flickering through them on Anne's face, lighted up the sweet hope that lay on it.

"Sometimes I think if—if papa should not approve of it!" she whispered.

"But he is sure to approve of it. One cannot help liking Mr. Angerstyne: and his position is undeniable."

The sub-dean's dinner guests were gone, the three carriages bowling them away; and the porter kept up a fire of abuse as he waited to watch us through the little postern-door. The boys, being college boys, returned his attack with interest. Wishing the Sankers good-night, who ran straight down Edgar Street on their way home, we turned off up the steps, and found Mrs. Lake standing patiently at her door. I saw Mr. Angerstyne catch Anne's hand for a moment in his, under cover of our entrance.

The morning brought news. Dr. and Mrs. Lewis were on their way to Maythorn Bank, expected to reach it that evening, and the young ladies were bidden to depart for it on the following day.

A wonderful change had taken place in Dr. Lewis. If they had doubted before whether the doctor was not falling into his dotage they could not doubt longer, for he was decidedly in it. A soft-speaking, mooning man, now; utterly lost in the shadow cast by his wife's importance. She appeared to be smiling in face and gentle in accent as ever, but she overruled every soul in the house: no one but herself had a will in it. What little strength of mind he might have had, his new bride had taken out of him.

Anne did not like it. Hitherto mistress of all things under her father, she found herself passed over as a nonentity. She might not express an opinion, or hazard a wish. "My dear, I am here now," Mrs. Lewis said to her once or twice emphatically. Anne was deposed; her reign was over.

One little thing, that happened, she certainly did not like. Though humble-minded, entirely without self-assertion, sweet-tempered and modest as a girl should be, she did not like this. Mrs. Lewis sent out invitations for dinner to some people in the neighbourhood, strangers to her until then; the table was too full by one, and she had told Anne that she could not sit down. It was too bad; especially as Julia and Fanny Podd filled two of the more important places, with bunches of fresh sweet-peas in their hair.

"Besides," Mrs. Lewis had said to Anne in the morning, "we must have a French side-dish or two, and there's no one but you understands the making of them."

Whether having to play the host was too much for him, or that he did not like the slight put upon his daughter, before the dinner was half over, the doctor fell asleep. He could not be roused from it. Herbert Tanerton, who had sat by Mrs. Lewis's side to say grace, thought it was not sleep but unconsciousness. Between them the company carried him into the other room; and Anne, hastening to send in her French dishes, ran there to attend upon him.

"I hope and trust there's nothing amiss with his heart," said old Coney doubtfully, in the bride's ear.

"My dear Mr. Coney, his heart is as strong as mine—believe me," affirmed Mrs. Lewis, flicking some crumbs off the front of her wedding-dress.

"I hope it is, I'm sure," repeated Coney. "I don't like that blue tinge round his lips."

They went back to the dinner-table when Dr. Lewis revived. Anne remained kneeling at his feet, gently chafing his hands.

"What's the matter?" he cried, staring at her like a man bewildered. "What are you doing?"

"Dear papa, you fell asleep over your dinner, and they could not wake you. Do you feel ill?"

"Where am I?" he asked, as if he were speaking out of a dream. And she told him what she could. But she had not heard those suspicious words of old Coney's.

It was some minutes yet before he got much sense into him, or seemed fully to understand. He fell back in the chair then, with a deep sigh, keeping Anne's hand in his.

"Shall I get you anything, papa?" she asked. "You had eaten scarcely any dinner, they say. Would you like a little drop of brandy-and-water?"

"Why was not your dress ready?"

"My dress!" exclaimed Anne.

"She said so to me, when I asked why you did not come to table. Not made, or washed, or ironed; or something."

Anne felt rather at sea. "There's nothing the matter with my dresses, papa," she said. "But never mind them—or me. Will you go back to dinner? Or shall I get you anything here?"

"I don't want to go back; I don't want anything," he answered. "Go and finish yours, my dear."

"I have had mine," she said, with a faint blush. For indeed her dinner had consisted of some bread-and-butter in the kitchen, eaten over the French stew-pans. Dr. Lewis was gazing out at the trees, and seemed to be in thought.

"Perhaps you stayed away from home rather too long, papa," she suggested. "You are not accustomed to travelling; and I think you are not strong enough for it. You looked very worn when you first came home; worn and ill."

"Ay," he answered. "I told her it did not do for me; but she laughed. It was nothing but a whirl, you know. And I only want to be quiet."

"It is very quiet here, dear papa, and you will soon feel stronger. You shall sit out of doors in the sun of a day, and I will read to you. I wish you would let me get you—"

"Hush, child. I'm thinking."

With his eyes still fixed on the outdoor landscape, he sat stroking Anne's hand abstractedly. Nothing broke the silence, except the faint rattle of knives and forks from the dining-room.

"Mind, Anne, she made me do it," he suddenly exclaimed.

"Made you do what, papa?"

"And so, my dear, if I am not allowed to remedy it, and you feel disappointed, you must think as lightly of it as you are able; and don't blame me more than you can help. I'll alter it again if I can, be sure of that; but I don't have a moment to myself, and at times it seems that she's just my keeper."

Anne answered soothingly that all he did must be right, but had no time to say more, for Mr. Coney, stealing in on tip-toe from the dining-room, came to see after the patient. Anne had not the remotest idea what it was that the doctor alluded to; but she had caught up one idea with dread of heart—that the marriage had not increased his happiness. Perhaps had marred it.

Maythorn Bank did not suit Mrs. Lewis. Ere she had been two weeks at it, she found it insufferably dull; not to be endured at any price. There was no fashion thereabout, and not much visiting; the neighbours were mostly simple, unpretending people, quite different from the style of company met with in garrison towns and pump-rooms. Moreover the few people who might have visited Mrs. Lewis, did not seem to take to her, or to remember that she was there. This did not imply discourtesy: Dr. Lewis and his daughter had just come into the place, strangers, so to say, and people could not practically recollect all at once that Maythorn Bank was inhabited. Where was the use of dressing up in peacock's plumes if nobody came to see her? The magnificent wardrobe, laid in during her recent honeymoon, seemed as good as wasted.

"I can't stand this!" emphatically cried Mrs. Lewis one day to her daughters. And Anne, chancing to enter the room unexpectedly at the moment, heard her say it, and wondered what it meant.

That same afternoon, Dr. Lewis had another attack. Anne found him sitting beside the pear-tree insensible, his head hanging over the arm of the bench. Travelling had not brought this second attack on, that was certain; for no man could be leading a more quiet, moping life than he was. Save that he listened now and then to some book, read by Anne, he had no amusement whatever, no excitement; he might have sat all day long with his mouth closed, for all there was to open it for. Mrs. Lewis's powers of fascination, that she had exercised so persistently upon him as Mrs. Podd, seemed to have deserted her for good. She passed her hours gaping, sleeping, complaining, hardly replying to a question of his, if he by chance asked her one. Even the soft sweet voice that had charmed the world mostly degenerated now into a croak or a scream. Those very mild, not-say-boo-to-a-goose voices are sometimes only kept for public life.

"I shall take you off to Worcester," cried Mrs. Lewis to him, when he came out of his insensibility. "We will start as soon as breakfast's over in the morning."

Dr. Lewis began to tremble. "I don't want to go to Worcester," said he. "I want to stay here."

"But staying here is not good for you, my dear. You'll be better at Mrs. Lake's. It is the remains of this paint that is making you ill. I can smell it still quite strongly, and I decidedly object to stay in it."

"My dear, you can go; I shall not wish to prevent you. But, as to the paint, I don't smell it at all now. You can all go. Anne will take care of me."

"My dear Dr. Lewis, do you think I would leave you behind me? It is the paint. And you shall see a doctor at Worcester."

He said he was a doctor himself, and did not need another; he once more begged to be left at home in peace. All in vain: Mrs. Lewis announced her decision to the household; and Sally, whose wits had been well-nigh scared away by the doings and the bustle of the new inmates, was gladdened by the news that they were about to take their departure.

"Pourtant si le ciel nous protège,
Peut-être encore le reverrai-je."

These words, the refrain of an old French song, were being sung by Anne Lewis softly in the gladness of her heart, as she bent over the trunk she was packing. To be going back to Worcester, where he was, seemed to her like going to paradise.

"What are you doing that for?"

The emphatic question, spoken in evident surprise, came from her stepmother. The chamber-door was open; Mrs. Lewis had chanced to look in as she passed.

"What are you doing that for?" she stopped to ask. Anne ceased her song at once and rose from her knees. She really did not know what it was that had elicited the sharp query—unless it was the singing.

"You need not pack your own things. You are not going to Worcester. It is intended that you shall remain here and take care of the house and of Sally."

"Oh, but, Mrs. Lewis, I could not stay here alone," cried Anne, a hundred thoughts rushing tumultuously into her mind. "It could not be."

"Not stay here alone! Why, what is to hinder it? Do you suppose you would get run away with? Now, my dear, we will have no trouble, if you please. You will stay at home like a good girl—therefore you may unpack your box."

Anne went straight to her father, and found him with Herbert Tanerton. He had walked over from Timberdale to inquire after the doctor's health.

"Could this be, papa?" she said. "That I am to be left alone here while you stay at Worcester?"

"Don't talk nonsense, child," was the peevish answer. "My belief is that you dream dreams, Anne, and then fancy them realities."

"But Mrs. Lewis tells me that I am not to go to Worcester—that I am to stay at home," persisted Anne. And she said it before Mrs. Lewis: who had come into the room then, and was shaking hands with the parson.

"I think, love, it will be so much better for dear Anne to remain here and see to things," she said, in that sweet company-voice of hers.

"No," dissented the doctor, plucking up the courage to be firm. "If Anne stays here, I shall stay. I'm sure I should be thankful if you'd let us stay: we should have a bit of peace and quiet."

She did not make a fuss before the parson. Perhaps she saw that to hold out might cause some unprofitable commotion. Treating Anne to a beaming smile, she remarked that her dear papa's wish was of course law, and bade her run and finish her packing.

And when they arrived the next day at Lake's, and Anne heard that Henry Angerstyne was in truth still there and knew that she should soon be in his presence, it did indeed seem to her that she had stepped into paradise. She was alone when he entered. The others had sought their respective chambers, leaving Anne to gather up their packages and follow, and she had her bonnet untied and her arms full of things when he came into the room. Paradise! she might have experienced some bliss in her life, but none like unto this. Her veins were tingling, her heart-blood leaping. How well he looked! how noble! how superior to other men! As he caught her hand in his, and bent to whisper his low words of greeting, she could scarcely contain within bounds the ecstasy of her emotion.

"I am so glad you are back again, Anne! I could not believe the good news when the letter came to Mrs. Lake this morning. You have been away two weeks, and they have seemed like months."

"You did not come over: you said you should," faltered Anne.

"Ay. And I sprained my foot the day you left, and have had to nurse it. It is not strong yet. Bad luck, was it not? Bristow has been worse, too. Where are you going?"

"I must take these things up to papa and Mrs. Lewis. Please let me go."

But, before he would release her hand, he suddenly bent his head and kissed her: once, twice.

"Pardon me, Anne, I could not help it; it is only a French greeting," he whispered, as she escaped with her face rosy-red, and her heart beating time to its own sweet music.

"What a stay Mr. Angerstyne is making!" exclaimed Fanny Podd, who had run about to seek Miss Dinah, and found her making a new surplice for Tom.

"Well, we are glad to have him," answered Miss Dinah, "and he has had a sprained ankle. We know now what is detaining him in Worcestershire. It seems that some old lady is lying ill at Malvern, and he can't get away."

"Some old lady lying ill at Malvern!" retorted Fanny, who liked to take Miss Dinah down when she could. "Why should that detain Mr. Angerstyne? Who is the old lady?"

"She is a relation of his: his great-aunt, I think. And I believe she is very fond of him, and won't let him go to any distance. All these visits he makes to Malvern are to see her. She is very rich, and he will come in for her money."

"I'm sure he's rich enough without it; he does not want more money," grumbled Fanny. "If the old lady would leave a little to those who need it, she might do some good."

"She would have to be made of gold and diamonds if she left some to all who need it," sighed Miss Dinah. "Mr. Angerstyne deserves to be rich, he is so liberal with his money. Many a costly dainty he causes us to send up to that poor sick Captain Bristow, letting him think it is all in the regular fare."

"But I think it was fearfully sly of him never to tell us why he went so much to Malvern—only you must always put in a good word for everybody, Miss Dinah. I asked him one day what his attraction was, that he should be perpetually running over there, and he gravely answered me that he liked the Malvern air."

Just for a few days, Dr. Lewis seemed to get a little better. Mrs. Lewis's fascinations had returned to her, and she in a degree kept him alive. It might have been from goodness of heart, or it might have been that she did not like to neglect him before people just yet, but she was ever devising plans for his amusement—which of course included that of herself and of her daughters. Mr. Angerstyne had not been more lavish of money in coach hire than was Mrs. Lewis now. Carriages for the country and flys for the town—that was the order of the day. Anne was rarely invited to make one of the party: for her there never seemed room. What of that?—when by staying at home she had the society of Mr. Angerstyne.

Whilst they were driving everywhere, or taking their pleasure in the town, shopping and exhibiting their finery, of which they seemed to display a new stock perpetually, Anne was left at liberty to enjoy her dangerous happiness. Dangerous, if it should not come to anything: and he had not spoken yet. They would sit together over their German, Anne trying to beat it into him, and laughing with him at his mistakes. If she went out to walk, she presently found herself overtaken by Mr. Angerstyne: and they would linger in the mellow light of the soft autumn days, or in the early twilight. Whatever might come of it, there could be no question that for the time being she was living in the most intense happiness. And about a fortnight of this went on without interruption.

Then Dr. Lewis began to droop. One day when he was out he had another of those attacks in the carriage. It was very slight, Mrs. Lewis said when they got back again; he did not lose consciousness for more than three or four minutes. But he continued to be so weak and ill afterwards that a physician was called in—Dr. Malden. What he said was known only to the patient and his wife, for nobody else was admitted to the conference.

"I want to go home," the doctor said to Anne the next morning, speaking in his usual querulous, faint tone, and as if his mind were half gone. "I'm sure I did not smell any paint the last time; it must have been her fancy. I want to go there to be quiet."

"Well, papa, why don't you say so?"

"But it's of no use saying so: she won't listen. I can't stand the racket here, child, and the perpetual driving out: the wheels of the carriages shake my head. And look at the expense! It frightens me."

Anne scarcely knew what to answer. She herself was powerless; and, so far as she believed, her father was; utterly so. Powerless in the hands of his new wife. Dr. Lewis glanced round the room as if to make sure there were no eavesdroppers, and went on in a whisper.

"I'm terrified, Anne. I am being ruined. All my ready-money's gone; she has had it all; she made me draw it out of the bank. And there, in that drawer, are two rolls of bills; she brought them to me yesterday, and there's nothing to pay them with."

Anne's heart fluttered. Was he only fancying these things in his decaying mind? Or, were they true?

"September has now come in, papa, and your quarter's dividends will soon be due, you know. Do not worry yourself."

"They have been forestalled," he whispered. "She owed a lot of things before her marriage, and the people would have sued me had I not paid them. I wish we were back in France, child! I wish we had never left it!" And, but for one thing, Anne would have wished it, too.

One afternoon, when it was getting late, Anne went into High Street to buy some ribbon for her hair. Mrs. Lewis and her party had gone over to Croome, some one having given her an order to see the gardens there. Lake's house was as busy as it could be, some fresh inmates of consequence being expected that evening; Anne had been helping Miss Dinah, and it was only at the last minute she could run out. In coming back, the ribbon bought, close to the college gates she heard steps behind her, and found her arm touched. It was by Mr. Angerstyne. For the past two days—nearly three—he had been absent at Malvern. The sight of him was as if the sun had shone.

"Oh!—is it you?—are you back again?" she cried, with as much quiet indifference as she could put on.

"I have just arrived. My aunt is better. And how are you, Anne?"

"Very well, thank you."

"Need you go in yet? Let us take a short stroll. The afternoon is delightful."

He called it afternoon, but it was getting on fast for evening: and he turned in at the college gates as he spoke. So they wound round St. Michael's Churchyard and passed on to the Dark Alley, and so down the long flight of steps that leads from it, and on to the banks of the Severn.

"How are you all going on at Lake's?" he asked presently, breaking the silence.

"Just as usual. To-day is a grand field-day," Anne added gaily: "at least, this evening is to be one, and we are not to dine until seven o'clock."

"Seven? So much the better. But why?"

"Some people of importance are coming—"

Mr. Angerstyne's laugh interrupted her. She laughed also.

"They are Miss Dinah's words: 'people of importance.' They will arrive late, so the dinner-hour is put off."

"Take care, Anne!"

A horse, towing a barge, was overtaking them. Mr. Angerstyne drew Anne out of the way, and the dinner and the new guests were forgotten.

It was almost dusk when they returned. The figures on the college tower were darkened, as they came through the large boat-house gateway: the old elm-trees, filled with their cawing rooks, looked weird in the dim twilight. Mr. Angerstyne did not turn to the Dark Alley again, but went straight up to the Green. He was talking of his estate in Essex. It was a topic often chosen by him; and Anne seemed to know the place quite well by this time.

"You would like the little stream that runs through the grounds," he was observing. "It is not, of course, like the grand river we have just left, but it is pleasant to wander by, for it winds in and out in the most picturesque manner possible, and the banks are overshadowed by trees. Yes, Anne, you would like that."

"Are you going through the cloisters?—is it not too late?" she interrupted, quite at a loss for something to say; not caring to answer that she should like to wander by the stream.

For he was crossing towards the little south cloister door: though onwards through the Green would have been their more direct road.

"Too late? No. Why should it be? You are not afraid of ghosts, are you?"

Anne laughed. But, lest she should be afraid of ghosts, he put her hand within his arm as they passed through the dark narrow passage beyond the postern; and so they marched arm-in-arm through the cloisters.

"To sit by that winding stream on a summer's day listening to its murmurs, to the singing of the birds, the sweet sighing of the trees; or holding low converse with a cherished companion—yes, Anne, you would like that. It would just suit you, for you are of a silent and dreamy nature."

There might not be much actual meaning in the words if you sat down to analyze them: but, to the inexperienced mind of Anne, they sounded very like plain speaking. At any rate, she took them to be an earnest that she should sometime sit by that stream with him—his wife. The dusky cloisters seemed to have suddenly filled themselves with refulgent light; the gravestones over which she was passing felt soft as the mossy glades of fairyland: ay, even that mysterious stone that bears on it the one terrible word "Miserrimus." Heaven was above her, and heaven beneath: there was no longer any prosaic earth for Anne Lewis.

"Good-night to you, gentlefolks."

The salutation was from the cloister porter; who, coming into close the gates, met them as they were nearing the west door. Not another word had passed until now: Mr. Angerstyne had fallen into silence. Anne could not have spoken to gain the world.

"Good-night to you, my man," he answered.

Lake's was in a bustle when they reached it. The luggage of the new people, who had just been shown to their chambers, was being taken in; the carriage containing Dr. and Mrs. Lewis was then just driving up. Anne felt alarmed as she caught sight of her father; he looked so very ill. Mr. Angerstyne, in his ready, kindly way, waited to help him down and give him his arm along the passage; he then ran up to his room, remarking that he had letters to write.

The people assembled for dinner in full fig, out of deference to the new-comers: who proved to be a Lady Knight, and a Mrs. and Miss Colter. Anne wore her pretty grey bridesmaid's dress, and the ribbon, just bought, in her hair. At the very last moment, Mr. Angerstyne came down, his hands full of the letters he had been writing.

"Why, are you here?" exclaimed Lady Knight: who seemed to be a chatty, voluble woman. "I am surprised."

Mr. Angerstyne, putting his letters on the side-table, until he could take them to the post, turned round at the address. A moment's stare, half doubt, half astonishment, and he went forward to shake Lady Knight's hand.

"What brings you here?" she asked.

"I have been here some little time. Old Miss Gibson is at Malvern, so I can't go far away."

There was no opportunity for more: dinner was waiting. Mr. Angerstyne and Anne sat side by side that evening; Lady Knight was opposite. Miss Dinah presided as usual, her best yellow cap perched on the top of her curls.

During an interval of silence between the general bustle and rattle of the dinner, for the two girls who waited (after their own fashion) had both run away with the fish to bring in the meat, Lady Knight looked across the table to put a question to Mr. Angerstyne.

"How is your wife?"

The silence dropped to a dead stillness. He appeared not to hear.

"How is your wife, Henry Angerstyne? Have you seen her lately?"

He could not pretend to be deaf any longer, and answered with angry curtness:

"No, I have not. She is all right, I suppose."

By the way the whole table stared, you might have thought a bombshell had fallen. Miss Dinah sat with her mouth open in sheer amazement, and then spoke involuntarily.

"Are you really married, Mr. Angerstyne?"

"Of course he is married," said Lady Knight, answering Miss Dinah. "All the world knows that. His wife is my cousin. I saw her at Lowestoft a few weeks ago, Henry. She was looking prettier than ever."

"Ah, Mr. Angerstyne, how sly you were, not to tell us!" cried Mrs. Lewis, playfully shaking her fan at him. "You— Oh, goodness me!"

A loud crash! Jenny the maid had dropped a hot vegetable dish on the floor, scattering the pieces and spilling the peas; and followed it up with a shriek and a scream. That took off the attention; and Mr. Angerstyne, coolly eating away at his bread, turned to make some passing remark to Anne.

But the words he would have said were left unspoken. No ghost ever seen, in cloisters or out of them, was whiter than she. Lips and fingers were alike trembling.

"You should be more careful!" he called to the maid in a tone of authority. "Ladies don't care to be startled in this way." Just as though Anne had turned white from the noise of the broken dish!

Well, it had been a dreadful revelation for her. All the sunshine of this world seemed to have gone out for ever; to have left nothing behind it but a misty darkness. Rallying her pride and her courage, she went on with her dinner, as the others did. Her head was throbbing, her brain on fire; her mind had turned to chaos. She heard them making arrangements for a picnic-party to the woods at Croome on the morrow; not in the least understanding what was said or planned.

"You did surprise us!" observed Mrs. Lewis to Lady Knight, when they were in the drawing-room after dinner, and Mr. Angerstyne had gone out to post his letters. "What could have been his motive for allowing us to think him a bachelor?"

"A dislike to mention her name," replied Lady Knight, candidly. "That was it, I expect. He married her for her pretty face, and then found out what a goose she was. So they did not get on together. She goes her way, and he goes his; now and then they meet for a week or two, but it is not often."

"What a very unsatisfactory state of things!" cried Miss Dinah, handing round the cups of coffee herself for fear of another upset. "Is it her fault or his?"

"Faults lie on both sides," said Lady Knight, who had an abrupt way of speaking, and was as poor as a church mouse. "She has a fearfully affronting temper of her own; those women with dolls' faces sometimes have; and he was not as forbearing as he might have been. Any way, that is the state of affairs between Mr. and Mrs. Angerstyne: and, apart from it, there's no scandal or reproach attaching to either of them."

Anne, sitting in a quiet corner, listened to all this mechanically. What mattered the details to her? the broad fact had been enough. The hum of conversation was going on all around; her father, looking somewhat the better for his dinner, was playing at backgammon with Tom Lake. She saw nothing, knew nothing, until Mr. Angerstyne dropped into the seat beside her.

"Shall you join this expedition to Croome to-morrow, Anne?"

Julia and Fanny were thumping over a duet, pedal down, and Anne barely caught the low-spoken words.

"I do not know," she answered, after a brief pause. "My head aches."

"I don't much care about it myself; rather the opposite. I shall certainly not go if you don't."

Why! he was speaking to her just as though nothing had occurred! If anything could have added to her sense of shame and misery it was this. It sounded like an insult, arousing all the spirit she possessed; her whole nature rose in rebellion against his line of conduct.

"Why have you been talking to me these many weeks as you have been talking, Mr. Angerstyne?" she asked in her straightforward simplicity, turning her face to his.

"There has been no harm in it," he answered.

"Harm!" she repeated, from her wrung heart. "Perhaps not to you. There has been at least no good in it."

"If you only knew what an interval of pleasantness it has been for me, Anne! Almost deluding me into forgetting my odious chains and fetters?"

"Would a gentleman have so amused himself, Mr. Angerstyne?"

But she gave him no opportunity of reply. Rising from her seat, and drawing her slight form to its full height, she looked into his face steadily, knowing not perhaps how much of scorn and reproach her gaze betrayed, then crossed the room and sat down by her father. Once after that she caught his eye: caught the expression of sorrow, of repentance, of deep commiseration that shone in every line of his face—for she could not altogether hide the pain seated in her own. And later, amidst the bustle of the general good-nights, she found her hand pressed within his, and heard his whispered, contrite prayer—

"Forgive me, Anne: forgive me!"

She lay awake all night, resolving to be brave, to make no sign; praying Heaven to help her to bear the anguish of her sorely-stricken heart, not to let the blow quite kill her. It seemed to her that she must feel it henceforth during all her life.

And before the house was well up in the morning, a messenger arrived post-haste from Malvern to summon Mr. Angerstyne to his aunt's dying bed. He told Miss Dinah, when he shook hands with her at parting, that she might as well send his traps after him, if she would be so kind, as he thought he might not be able to return to Worcester again.

And that was the ending of Anne Lewis's love. Not a very uncommon ending, people say. But she had been hardly dealt by.

Part the Third

The blinds of a house closely drawn, the snow drifting against the windows outside, and somebody lying dead upstairs, cannot be called a lively state of things. Mrs. Lewis and her daughters, Julia and Fanny Podd, sitting over the fire in the darkened dining-room at Maythorn Bank, were finding it just the contrary.

When Dr. Lewis, growing worse and worse during their sojourn at Lake's boarding-house at Worcester the previous autumn, had one day plucked up courage to open his mind to his physician, telling him that he was pining for the quiet of his own little cottage home, and that the stir and racket at Lake's was more than he could bear, Dr. Malden peremptorily told Mrs. Lewis that he must have his wish, and go. So she had to give in, and prepared to take him; though it went frightfully against the grain. That was in September, three months back; he had been getting weaker and more imbecile ever since, and now, just as Christmas was turned, he had sunk quietly away to his rest.

Anne, his loving, gentle daughter, had been his constant companion and attendant. He had not been so ill as to lie in bed, but a great deal had to be done for him, especially in the matter of amusing what poor remnant of mind was left. She read to him, she talked to him, she wrapped great-coats about him, and took him out to walk on sunshiny days in the open walk by the laurels. It was well for Anne that she was thus incessantly occupied, for it diverted her mind from the misery left there by the unwarrantable conduct of Mr. Angerstyne. When a girl's lover proves faithless, to dwell upon him and lament him brings to her a sort of painful pleasure: but that negative indulgence was denied to Anne Lewis: Henry Angerstyne was the husband of another, and she might not, willingly, keep him in her thoughts. To forget him, as she strove to do, was a hard and bitter task: but the indignation she felt at the man's deceit and cruel conduct was materially helping her. Once, since, she had seen his name in the Times: it was amongst the list of visitors staying at some nobleman's country-house. Henry Angerstyne. And the thrill that passed through her veins as the name caught her eye, the sudden stopping and then rushing violently onwards of her life's blood, convinced her how little she had forgotten him.

"But I shall forget him in time," she said to herself, pressing her hand upon her wildly-beating heart. "In time, God helping me."

And from that moment she redoubled her care and thought for her father; and he died blessing her and her love for him.

Anne felt the loss keenly; though perhaps not quite so much so as she would have felt it had her later life been less full of suffering. It seemed to be but the last drop added to her cup of bitterness. She knew that to himself death was a release: he had ceased to find pleasure in life. And now she was left amidst strangers, or worse than strangers; she seemed not to have a friend to turn to in the wide world.

Dr. Lewis had died on Monday morning. This was Tuesday. Mrs. Lewis had been seeing people to-day and yesterday, giving her orders; but never once consulting Anne, or paying her the compliment to say, Would you like it to be this way, or that?

"How on earth any human being could have pitched upon this wretched out-of-the-world place, Crabb, to settle down in, puzzles me completely," suddenly exclaimed Mrs. Lewis, bending forward to stir the fire.

"He must have been a lunatic," acquiesced Julia, irreverently alluding to the poor man who was lying in the room above.

"Not a decent shop in the place! Not a dressmaker who can cut out a properly-fitting skirt! Be quiet, Fanny: you need not dance."

"One does not know what to do," grumbled Fanny, ceasing to shuffle, and returning to her seat. "But I should like to know, mamma, about our mourning."

"I think I shall go to Worcester to-day and order it," spoke up Mrs. Lewis, briskly, after a pause. "Necessity has no law; and we cannot get proper things unless I do. Yes, we will go: I don't mind the weather. Julia, ring the bell."

Anne—poor Anne—came in to answer the bell. She had no choice: Sally was out on an errand.

"Just see that we have a tray in with the cold meat, Anne, at half-past twelve. We must go to Worcester about the mourning—"

"To Worcester!" involuntarily interrupted Anne, in her surprise.

"There's no help for it, though of course it's not the thing I would choose to do," said Mrs. Lewis, coldly. "One cannot provide proper things here: bonnets especially. I will get you a bonnet at the same time. And we must have a bit of something, hot and nice, for tea, when we come home."

"Very well," sighed Anne.

In the afternoon, Anne sat in the same room alone, busy over some black work, on which her tears dropped slowly. When it was growing dusk, Mr. Coney and the young Rector of Timberdale came in together. Herbert Tanerton did not forget that his late stepfather and Dr. Lewis were half-brothers. Anne brushed away the signs of her tears, laid down her work, and stirred the fire into a blaze.

"Now, my lass," said the farmer, in his plain, homely way, but he always meant kindly, "I've just heard that that stepmother of yours went off to Worcester to-day with those two dandified girls of hers, and so I thought I'd drop in while the coast was clear. I confess I don't like her: and I say that somebody ought to look a bit to you and your interests."

"And I, coming over upon much the same errand, met Mr. Coney at the gate," added Herbert Tanerton, with a smile as near geniality as he ever gave. "I wish to express my deep regret for your loss, Miss Lewis, and to assure you of my true sympathy. You will think my visit a late one, but I had a—a service this afternoon." He would not say a funeral.

"You are both very, very kind," said Anne, her eyes again filling, "and I thank you for thinking of me. I feel isolated from all: this place at best is strange to me after my life's home in France. It seems that I have not a friend in the world."

"Yes, you have," said the farmer; "and if my wife had not been staying with our sick daughter at Worcester, she'd have been in to tell you the same. My dear, you are just going, please, to make a friend of me. And you won't think two or three questions, that I should like to put, impertinent, will you?"

"That I certainly will not," said Anne.

"Well, now, to begin with: Did your father make a will?"

"Oh yes. I hold it."

"And do you chance to know how the property is left?"

"To me. No name but my own is mentioned in it."

"Then you'll be all right," said Mr. Coney. "I feared he might have been leaving somebody else some. You will have about two hundred and fifty pounds a-year; and that's enough for a young girl. When your father first came over, he spoke to me of his income and his means."

"I—I fear the income will be somewhat diminished from what it was," hesitated Anne, turning red at having to confess so much, because it would tell against her stepmother. "My father has had to sell out a good deal lately, to entrench upon his capital. I think the trouble it gave him hastened his end."

"Sell out for what?" asked old Coney.

"For bills, and—and debts, that came upon him."

"Her bills? Her debts?"

Anne did not expressly answer, but old Coney caught up the truth, and nodded his head in wrath. He as good as knew it before.

"Well, child, I suppose you may reckon, at the worst, on a clear two hundred a-year, and you can live on that. Not keep house, perhaps; and it would be very lonely for you also. You will have to take up your abode with some pleasant family: many a one would be glad to have you."

"I should like to go back to France," sighed Anne, recalling the misery that England had brought her: first in her new stepmother, then in Mr. Angerstyne, and now in her father's death. "I have many dear friends in France who will take every care of me."

"Well, I don't know," cried old Coney, with a blank look. "France may be very well for some people; but I'd almost as lieve go to the gallows as there. Don't you like England?"

"I should like it well, if I—if I could be happy in it," she answered, turning red again at the thought of him who had marred her happiness. "But, you see, I have no ties here."

"You must make ties, my lass."

"How much of the income ought I to pay over yearly to Mrs. Lewis, do you think?" she questioned. "Half of it?"

"Half! No!" burst forth old Coney, coughing down a strong word which had nearly slipped out. "You will give her none. None. A pretty idea of justice you must have, Anne Lewis."

"But it would be fair to give it her," argued Anne. "My father married her."

"Oh, did he, though! She married him. I know. Other folks know. You will give her none, my dear, and allow her none. She is a hard, scheming, deceitful brickbat of a woman. What made her lay hold of your poor weakened father, and play off upon him her wiles and her guiles, and marry him, right or wrong?" ran on old Coney, getting purple enough for apoplexy. "She did it for a home; she did it that she might get her back debts paid; that's what. She has had her swing as long as his poor life lasted, and put you down as if you were a changeling; we have all seen that. Now that her short day's over, she must go back again to her own ways and means. Ask the parson there what he thinks."

The parson, in his cold sententious way, that was so much more suited to an old bishop than a young rector, avowed that he thought with Mr. Coney. He could not see that Mrs. Lewis's few months of marriage entitled her (all attendant circumstances being taken into consideration) to deprive Miss Lewis of any portion of her patrimony.

"You are sure you have got the will all tight and safe?" resumed Mr. Coney. "I wouldn't answer for her not stealing it. Ah, you may laugh, young lassie, but I don't like that woman. Miss Dinah Lake was talking to me a bit the other day; she don't like her, either."

Anne was smiling at his vehement partisanship. She rose, unlocked a desk that stood on the side-table, and brought out a parchment, folded and sealed. It was subscribed, "Will of Thomas Lewis, M.D."

"Here it is," she said. "Papa had it drawn up by an English lawyer just before we left France. He gave it to me, as he was apt to mislay things himself, charging me to keep it safely."

"And mind you do keep it safely," enjoined old Coney. "It won't be opened, I suppose, till after the funeral's over."

"But wait a minute," interposed the clergyman. "Does not marriage—a subsequent marriage—render a will invalid?"

"Bless my heart, no: much justice there'd be in that!" retorted old Coney, who knew about as much of law as he did of the moon. And Mr. Tanerton said no more; he was not certain; and supposed the older and more experienced man might be right.

Anne sighed as she locked up the will again. She was both just and generous; and she knew she should be sure to hand over to Mrs. Lewis the half of whatever income it might give her.

"Well, my girl," said the farmer, as they prepared to leave, "if you want me, or anything I can do, you just send Sally over, and I'll be here in a jiffy."

"It is to be at Timberdale, I conclude?" whispered Herbert Tanerton, as he shook hands. Anne knew that he alluded to the funeral; and the colour came up in her face as she answered—

"I don't know. My father wished it; he said he wished to lie beside his brother. But Mrs. Lewis—here they come, I think."

They came in with snowy bonnets and red noses, stamping the slush off their shoes. It was a good walk from the station. Mrs. Lewis had expected to get a fly there; one was generally in waiting: but some one jumped out of the train before she did, and secured it. It made her feel cross and look cross.

"Such a wretched trapes!" she was beginning in a vinegar tone; but at sight of the gentlemen her face and voice smoothed down to oil. She begged them to resume their seats; but they said they were already going.

"We were just asking about the funeral," the farmer stayed to say. "It is to be at Timberdale?"

Up went Mrs. Lewis's handkerchief to her eyes. "Dear Mr. Coney, I think not. Crabb will be better."

"But he wished to lie at Timberdale."

"Crabb will be so much cheaper—and less trouble," returned the widow, with a sob. "It is as well to avoid useless expense."

"Cheaper!" cried old Coney, his face purple again with passion, so much did he dislike her and her ways. "Not cheaper at all. Dearer. Dearer, ma'am. Must have a hearse and coach any way: and Herbert Tanerton here won't charge fees if it's done at Timberdale."

"Oh, just as you please, my dear sir. And if he wished it, poor dear! Yes, yes; Timberdale of course. Anywhere."

They got out before she had dried her eyes—or pretended at it. Julia and Fanny then fetched in some bandboxes which had been waiting in the passage. Mrs. Lewis forgot her tears, and put back her cloak.

"Which is Anne's?" she asked. "Oh, this one"—beginning to undo one of the boxes. "My own will be sent to-morrow night. I bought yours quite plain, Anne."

Very plain indeed was the bonnet she handed out. Plain and common, and made of the cheapest materials; one that a lady would not like to put upon her head. Julia and Fanny were trying theirs on at the chimney-glass. Gay bonnets, theirs glistening with jet beads and black flowers. The bill lay open on the table, and Anne read the cost: her own, twelve shillings; the other two, thirty-three shillings each. Mrs. Lewis made a grab at the bill, and crushed it into her pocket.

"I knew you would prefer it plain," said she. "For real mourning it is always a mistake to have things too costly."

"True," acquiesced Anne; "but yet—I think they should be good."

It seemed to her that to wear this bonnet would be very like disrespect to the dead. She silently determined to buy a better as soon as she had the opportunity of doing so.

Of all days, for weather, the one of the funeral was about the worst. Sleet, snow, rain, and wind. The Squire had a touch of lumbago; he could not face it; and old Coney came bustling in to say that I was to attend in his place. Anne wanted Johnny Ludlow to go all along, he added; her father had liked him; only there was no room before in the coach.

"Yes, yes," cried the Squire, "Johnny, of course. He is not afraid of lumbago. Make haste and get into your black things, lad."

Well, it was shivery, as we rolled along in the creaky old mourning-coach, behind the hearse: Mr. Coney and the Podds' lawyer-cousin from Birmingham on one side; I and Cole, the doctor, opposite. The sleet pattered against the windows, the wind whistled in our ears. The lawyer kept saying "eugh," and shaking his shoulders, telling us he had a cold in his head; and looked just as stern as he had at the wedding.

All was soon over: Herbert Tanerton did not read slowly to-day: and we got back to Maythorn Bank. Cole had left us: he stopped the coach en route, and cut across a field to see a patient: but Mr. Coney drew me into the house with him after the lawyer.

"We will go in, Johnny," he whispered. "The poor girl has no relation or friend to back her up, and I shall stay with her while the will's read."

Mrs. Lewis, in a new widow's cap as big as a house, and the two girls in shining jet chains, were sitting in state. Anne came in the next minute, her face pale, her eyes red. We all sat down; and for a short time looked at one another in silence, like so many mutes.

"Any will to be read? I am told there is one," spoke the lawyer—who had, as Fanny Podd whispered to me, a wife at home as sour as himself. "If so, it had better be produced: I have to catch a train."

"Yes, there is a will," answered old Coney, glad to find that Anne, as he assumed, had mentioned the fact. "Miss Lewis holds the will. Will you get it, my dear?"

Anne unlocked the desk on the side-table, and put the will into Mr. Coney's hand. Without saying with your leave or by your leave, he broke the seals, and clapped on his spectacles.

"What's that?" Mrs. Lewis asked old Coney, from her seat on the sofa.

"Dr. Lewis's will, ma'am. Made in France, I believe: was it not, Miss Anne?"

"My dear, sweet creature, it is so much waste paper," spoke Mrs. Lewis, smiling sweetly upon Anne. "My deeply lamented husband's last will and testament was made long since he left France."

Pulling up the sofa-cushion at her elbow, she produced another will, and asked the lawyer if he would be good enough to unseal and read it. It had been made, as the date proved, at Cheltenham, the day after she and Dr. Lewis were married; and it left every earthly thing he possessed to "his dear wife, Louisa Jane Lewis."

Old Coney's face was a picture. He stared alternately at the will in his hands, at the one just read by the lawyer. Anne stood meekly by his side; looking as if she did not understand matters.

"That can't stand good!" spoke the farmer, in his honest indignation. "The money can't go to you, ma'am"—turning his burly form about to face Mrs. Lewis, and treading on my toes as he did it. "The money is this young lady's; part of it comes from her own mother: it can't be yours. Thomas Lewis must have signed the will in his sleep."

"Does a daughter inherit before a wife, dear sir?" cried Mrs. Lewis, in a voice soft as butter. "It is the most just will my revered husband could have made. I need the money: I cannot keep on the house without it. Anne does not need it: she has no house to keep."

"Look here," says old Coney, buttoning his coat and looking fiercely at the company. "It's not my wish to be rude to-day, remembering what place we came straight here from; but if you don't want to be put down as—as schemers, you will not lose an hour in making over the half of that income to Anne Lewis. It is what she proposed to do by you, madam, when she thought all was left to her," he added, brushing past Mrs. Lewis. "Come along, Johnny."

The time went on. Mrs. Lewis kept all the money. She gave notice to leave the house at Midsummer: but she had it on her hands until then, and told people she should die of its dulness. So far as could be known, she had little, if any, income, except that which she inherited from Dr. Lewis.

Anne's days did not pass in clover. Treated as of no moment, she was made fully to understand that she was only tolerated in what was once her own home; and she had to make herself useful in it from morning till night, just like a servant. Remembering what had been, and what was, Anne felt heart-broken, submitting patiently and unresistingly to every trial; but a reaction set in, and her spirit grew rebellious.

"Is there any remedy, I wonder?" she asked herself one night in her little chamber, when preparing for bed, and the day had been a particularly trying day. She had ventured to ask for a few shillings for some purpose or other, and was told she could not have them: being Easter-Monday, Sally had had a holiday, and she had been kept at work like a slave in the girl's place: Herbert Tanerton and his wife had come to invite her for a day or two to Timberdale, and a denial was returned to them without herself being consulted, or even allowed to see them. Yes, it had been a trying day. And in France Easter had always been kept as a fête.

"Is there not a remedy?" she debated, as she slowly undressed. "I have no home but this; but—could I not find one?"

She knew that she had no means of living, except by her own exertions; she had not even a rag to wear or a coin to spend, except what should come to her by Mrs. Lewis's bounty. And, whether that lady possessed bounty or not, she seemed never to possess ready-money. It appeared to Anne that she had been hardly dealt by in more ways than one; that the world was full of nothing but injustice and trouble.

"And I fancy," added Anne, thinking out her thoughts, "that they will be glad to get rid of me; that they want me gone. So I dare say there will be no objection made here."

With morning light, she was up and busy. It fell to her lot to prepare the breakfast: and she must not keep the ladies waiting for it one minute. This morning, however, she had to keep them waiting; but not through any fault of hers.

They grew impatient. Five minutes past nine: ten minutes past nine: what did Anne mean? Julia and Fanny were not much better dressed than when they got out of bed; old jackets on, rough and rumpled hair stuck up with hair-pins. In that respect they presented a marked contrast to Anne, who was ever trim and nice.

"I'm sure she must be growing the coffee-berries!" cried Fanny, as she flung the door open. "Is that breakfast coming to-day, or to-morrow?"

"In two minutes," called back Anne.

"Oh, what a dreary life it is out here!" groaned Mrs. Lewis. "Girls, I think we will go over to Worcester to-day, and arrange to stay a week at Lakes. And then you can go to the subscription ball at the Town Hall, that you are so wild over."

"Oh, do, do!" cried Julia, all animation now. "If I don't go to that ball, I shall die."

"I shall run away, if we don't; I have said all along I would not miss the Easter ball," spoke Fanny. "Mamma, I cannot think why you don't shut this miserable house up!"

"Will you find the rent for another?" coolly asked Mrs Lewis. "What can that girl be at with the coffee?"

It came in at last; and Anne was abused for her laziness. When she could get a word in, she explained that Sally had had an accident with the tea-kettle, and fresh water had to be boiled.

More indignation: Julia's egg turned out to be bad. What business had Anne to boil bad eggs? Anne, saying nothing, took it away, boiled another and brought it in. Then Mrs. Lewis fancied she could eat a thin bit of toasted bacon; and Anne must go and do it at the end of a fork. Altogether the breakfast was nearly at an end before she could sit down and eat her own bread-and-butter.

"I have been thinking," she began, in a hesitating tone, to Mrs. Lewis, "that I should like to go out. If you have no objection."

"Go out where?"

"Into some situation."

Mrs. Lewis, in the act of conveying a piece of bacon to her mouth, held it suspended in mid-air, and stared at Anne in amazement.

"Into what?"

"A situation in some gentleman's family. I have no prospect before me; no home; I must earn my own living."

"The girl's daft!" cried Mrs. Lewis, resuming her breakfast. "No home! Why, you have a home here; your proper home. Was it not your father's?"

"Yes. But it is not mine."

"It is yours; and your days in it are spent usefully. What more can you want? Now, Anne, hold your tongue, and don't talk nonsense. If you have finished your breakfast you can begin to take the things away."

"Mamma, why don't you let her go?" whispered Fanny, as Anne went out with some plates.

"Because she is useful to me," said Mrs. Lewis. "Who else is there to see to our comforts? We should be badly off with that incapable Sally. And who would do all the needlework? recollect how much she gets through. No, as long as we are here, Anne must stay with us. Besides, the neighbourhood would have its say finely if we let her turn out. People talk, as it is, about the will, and are not so friendly as they might be. As if they would like me to fly in the face of my dear departed husband's wishes, and tacitly reproach his judgment!"

But Anne did not give up. When she had taken all the things away and folded up the table-cloth, she came in again and spoke.

"I hope you will not oppose me in this, Mrs. Lewis. I should like to take a situation."

"And, pray, what situation do you suppose you could take?" ironically asked Mrs. Lewis. "You are not fitted to fill one in a gentleman's family."

"Unless it be as cook," put in Julia.

"Or seamstress," said Fanny. "By the way, I want some more cuffs made, Anne."

"I should like to try for a situation, notwithstanding my deficiencies. I could do something or other."

"There, that's enough: must I tell you again not to talk nonsense?" retorted Mrs. Lewis. "And now you must come upstairs and see to my things, and to Julia's and Fanny's. We are going to Worcester by the half-past eleven train—and you may expect us home to tea when you see us."

They went off. As soon as their backs were turned, Anne came running into our house, finding me and Mrs. Todhetley at the piano. It was pleasant Easter weather, though March was not out: the Squire and Tod had gone to Dyke Manor on some business, and would not be home till late. Anne told all her doubts and difficulties to the mater, and asked her advice, as to whether there would be anything wrong in her seeking for a situation.

"No, my dear," said the mother, "it would be right, instead of wrong. If—"

"If people treated me as they treat you, Anne, I wouldn't stay with them a day," said I, hotly. "I don't like toads."

"Oh, Johnny!" cried Mrs. Todhetley. "Never call names, dear. No obligation whatever, Anne, lies on you to remain in that home; and I think you would do well to leave it. You shall stay and dine with me and Johnny at one o'clock, Anne; and we will talk it over."

"I wish I could stay," said poor Anne; "I hardly knew how to spare these few minutes to run here. Mrs. Lewis has left me a gown to unpick and turn, and I must hasten to begin it."

"So would I begin it!" I cried, going out with her as far as the gate. "And I should like to know who is a toad, if she's not."

"Don't you think I might be a nursery governess, Johnny?" she asked me, turning round after going through the gate. "I might teach French, and English, and German: and I am very fond of little children. The difficulty will be to get an introduction. I have thought of one person who might give it me—if I could only dare to ask him."

"Who's that?"

"Sir Robert Tenby. He is of the great world, and must know every one in it. And he has always shown himself so very sociable and kind. Do you think I might venture to apply to him?"

"Why not? He could not eat you for it."

She ran on, and I ran back. But, all that day, sitting over her work, Anne was in a state of doubt, not able to make up her mind. It was impossible to know how Sir Robert Tenby might take it.

"I have made you a drop of coffee and a bit of hot toast and butter, Miss Anne," said Sally, coming in with a small tray. "Buttered it well. She's not here to see it."

Anne laughed, and thanked her; Mrs. Lewis had left them only cold bacon for dinner, and ordered them to wait tea until her return. But before the refreshment was well disposed of, she and the girls came in.

"How soon you are back!" involuntarily cried Anne, hoping Mrs. Lewis would not smell the coffee. "And how are they all at Lake's?"

Mrs. Lewis answered by giving a snappish word to Lake's, and ordered Anne to get tea ready. Fanny whispered the information that they were going to Worcester on the morrow to stay over the Easter ball; but not to Lake's. Anne wondered at that.

Upon arriving at Lake's that morning, Miss Dinah had received them very coolly; and was, as Mrs. Lewis remarked afterwards, barely civil. The fact was, Miss Dinah, being just-minded, took up Anne's cause rather warmly; and did not scruple to think that the beguiling poor weak-minded Dr. Lewis out of the will he made, was just a piece of iniquity, and nothing less. Perceiving Miss Dinah's crusty manner, Mrs. Lewis inquired after Mrs. Lake. "Where's Emma?" she asked.

"Very much occupied to-day. Can I do anything for you?"

"We are thinking of coming to you to-morrow for a week, Dinah; I and my two girls. They are wild to go to the Easter ball. Which rooms can you give us?"

"Not any rooms," spoke Miss Dinah, decisively. "We cannot take you in."

"Not take me in! When the servant opened the door to us she said the house was not full. I put the question to her."

"But we are expecting it to be full," said Miss Dinah, curtly. "The Beales generally come over to the ball; and we must keep rooms for them."

"You don't know that they are coming, I expect. And in a boarding-house the rule holds good, 'First come, first served.'"

"A boarding-house holds its own rules, and is not guided by other people's. Very sorry: but we cannot make room this time for you and your daughters."

"I'll soon see that," retorted Mrs. Lewis, getting hot. "Where's Emma Lake? I am her cousin, and shall insist on being taken in."

"She can't take you in without my consent. And she won't: that's more. Look here, Mrs. Podd—I beg your pardon—the new name does not always come pat to me. When you were staying here before, and kept us so long out of our money, it put us to more inconvenience than you had any idea of. We—"

"You were paid at last."

"Yes," said Miss Dinah; "with poor Dr. Lewis's money, I expect. We made our minds up then, Mrs. Lewis, not to take you again. At least, I did; and Mrs. Lake agreed with me."

"You will not have to wait again: I have money in my pocket now. And the girls must go to the ball on Thursday."

"If your pockets are all full of money, it can make no difference to me. I'm sorry to say I cannot take you in, Mrs. Lewis: and now I have said all I mean to say."

Mrs. Lewis went about the house, looking for Mrs. Lake, and did not find her. She, not as strong-minded as Miss Dinah, had bolted herself into the best bedroom, just then unoccupied. So Mrs. Lewis, not to be baffled as to the ball, went out to look for other lodgings, and found them in Foregate Street.

"But we shall be home on Saturday," she said to Anne, as they were starting this second time for Worcester, on the Wednesday morning, the finery for the ball behind them in two huge trunks. "I have to pay a great deal for the rooms, and can't afford to stay longer than that. And mind that you and Sally get the house in order whilst we are away; it's a beautiful opportunity to clean it thoroughly down: and get on as quickly as you can with the needlework."

"Why, my dear young lassie, I am not able to help you in such a thing as this. You had better see the master himself."

Anne had lost no time. Leaving Sally to the cleaning, she dressed and walked over on the Wednesday afternoon to Bellwood, Sir Robert Tenby's seat. She explained her business to Mrs. Macbean, the old family housekeeper, and asked whether she could help her into any good family.

"Nae, nae, child. I live down here all my days, and I know nothing of the gentlefolks in the great world. The master knows them all."

"I did think once of asking if I might see Sir Robert; but my courage fails me now," said Anne.

"And why should it?" returned the old lady. "If there's one man more ready than another to do a kindness, or more sociable to speak with, it's Sir Robert Tenby. He takes after his mother for that, my late dear lady; not after his father. Sir George was a bit proud. I'll go and tell Sir Robert what you want."

Sir Robert was in his favourite room; a small one, with a bright fire in it, its purple chairs and curtains bordered with gold. It was bright altogether, Anne thought as she entered: for he said he would see her. The windows looked out on a green velvet lawn, with beds of early flowers, and thence to the park; and, beyond all, to the chain of the Malvern Hills, rising against the blue sky. The baronet sat near one of the windows, some books on a small table at his elbow. He came forward to shake hands with Anne, and gave her a chair opposite his own. And, what with his good homely face and its smile of welcome, and his sociable, unpretending words, Anne felt at home at once.

In her own quiet way, so essentially that of a lady in its unaffected truth, she told him what she wanted: to find a home in some good family, who would be kind to her in return for her services, and pay her as much as would serve to buy her gowns and bonnets. Sir Robert Tenby, no stranger to the gossip rife in the neighbourhood, had heard of the unjust will, and of Anne's treatment by the new wife.

"It is, I imagine, impossible for a young lady to get into a good family without an introduction," said Anne. "And I thought—perhaps—you might speak for me, sir: you do know a little of me. I have no one else to recommend me."

He did not answer for the moment: he sat looking at her. Anne blushed, and went on, hoping she was not offending him.

"No one else, I mean, who possesses your influence, and mixes habitually with the great world. I should not care to take service in an inferior family: my poor father would not have liked it."

"Take service," said he, repeating the word. "It is as governess that you wish to go out?"

"As nursery governess, I thought. I may not aspire to any better position, for I know nothing of accomplishments. But little children need to be taught French and German; I could do that."

"You speak French well, of course?"

"As a native. German also. And I think I speak good English, and could teach it. And oh, sir, if you did chance to know of any family who would engage me, I should be so grateful to you."

"French, English, and German," said he, smiling. "Well, I can't tell what the great world, as you put it, may call accomplishments; but I think those three enough for anybody."

Anne smiled too. "They are only languages, Sir Robert. They are not music and drawing. Had my dear mamma suspected I should have to earn my own living, she would have had me educated for it."

"I think it is a very hard thing that you should have to earn it," spoke Sir Robert.

Anne glanced up through her wet eye-lashes: reminiscences of her mother always brought tears. "There's no help for it, sir; I have not a shilling in the world."

"And no home but one that you are ill-treated in—made to do the work of a servant? Is it not so?"

Anne coloured painfully. How did he know this? Generous to Mrs. Lewis in spite of all, she did not care to speak of it herself.

"And if people did not think me clever enough to teach, sir," she went on, passing over his question, "I might perhaps go out to be useful in other ways. I can make French cakes and show a cook how to make French dishes; and I can read aloud well, and do all kinds of needlework. Some old lady, who has no children of her own, might be glad to have me."

"I think many an old lady would," said he. The remark put her in spirits. She grew animated.

"Oh, do you! I am so glad. If you should know of one, sir, would you please to tell her of me?"

Sir Robert nodded, and Anne rose to leave. He rose also.

"If I could be so fortunate as to get into such a home as this, with some kind old lady for my friend and mistress, I should be quite happy," she said, in the simplicity of her heart. "How pleasant this room is! and how beautiful it is outside!"—pausing to look at the early flowers, as she passed the window.

"Do you know Bellwood? Were you ever here before?"

"No, sir, never."

Sir Robert put on his hat and went out with her, showing her some pretty spots about the grounds. Anne was enchanted, especially with the rocks and the cascades. Versailles, she thought, could not be better than Bellwood.

"And when you hear of anything, sir, you will please to let me know?" she said, in parting.

"Yes. You had better come again soon. This is Wednesday: suppose you call on Friday. Will you?"

"Oh, I shall be only too glad. I will be sure to come. Good-bye, Sir Robert: and thank you very, very much."

She went home with a light heart: she had not felt so happy since her father died.

"How good he is! how kind! a true gentleman," she thought. "And what a good thing he fixed Friday instead of Saturday, for on Saturday they will be at home. But it is hardly possible that he will have heard of any place by that time, unless he has one in his eye."

It was Friday afternoon before Anne could get to Bellwood, and rather late, also. She asked, as before, for Mrs. Macbean, not liking to ask direct for Sir Robert Tenby. Sir Robert was out, but was expected in every minute, and Anne waited in Mrs. Macbean's parlour.

"Do you think he has heard of anything for me?" was one of the first questions she put.

"Eh, my dear, and how should I know?" was the old lady's reply. "He does not tell me of his affairs. Not but what he talks to me a good deal, and always like a friend: he does not forget that my late leddy, his mother, made more of a friend of me than a servant. Many's the half-hour he keeps me talking in his parlour; and always bids me take the easiest seat there. I wish he would marry!"

"Do you?" replied Anne, mechanically: for she was thinking more of her own concerns than Sir Robert's.

"Why, yes, that I do. It's a lonely life for him at best, the one he leads. I've not scrupled to tell him, times and oft, that he ought to bring a mistress home— Eh, but there he is! That's his step."

As before, Anne went into the pretty room that Sir Robert, when alone, mostly sat in. Three or four opened letters lay upon the table, and she wondered whether they related to her.

"No, I have as yet no news for you," he said, smiling at her eager face, and keeping her hand in his while he spoke. "You will have to come again for it. Sit down."

"But if—if you have nothing to tell me to-day, I had better not take up your time," said Anne, not liking to appear intrusive.

"My time! If you knew how slowly time some days seems to pass for me, you would have no scruple about 'taking it up.' Sit here. This is a pleasant seat."

With her eyes fixed on the outer landscape, Anne sat on and listened to him. He talked of various things, and she felt as much at her ease (as she told me that same evening) as though she had been talking with me. Afterwards she felt half afraid she had been too open, for she told him all about her childhood's home in France and her dear mother. It was growing dusk when she got up to go.

"Will you come again on Monday afternoon?" he asked. "I shall be out in the morning."

"If I can, sir. Oh yes, if I can. But Mrs. Lewis, who will be at home then, does not want me to take a situation at all, and she may not let me come out."

"I should come without telling her," smiled Sir Robert. "Not want you to leave home, eh? Would you like to stay there to make the puddings? Ay, I understand. Well, I shall expect you on Monday. There may be some news, you know."

And, somehow, Anne took up the notion that there would be news, his tone sounded so hopeful. All the way home her feet seemed to tread on air.

On the Sunday evening, when they were all sitting together at Maythorn Bank, and Anne had no particular duty on hand, she took courage to tell of what she had done, and that Sir Robert Tenby was so good as to interest himself for her. Mrs. Lewis was indignant; the young ladies were pleasantly satirical.

"As nursery governess: you!" mocked Miss Julia. "What shall you teach your pupils? To play at cats' cradle?"

"Why, you know, Anne, you are not fit for a governess," said Fanny. "It would be quite—quite wicked of you to make believe to be one. You never learnt a note of music. You can't draw. You can't paint."

"You had better go to school yourself, first," snapped Mrs. Lewis. "I will not allow you to take such a step: so put all thought of it out of your head."

Anne leaned her aching brow upon her hand in perplexity. Was she so unfit? Would it be wicked? She determined to put the case fully before her kind friend, Sir Robert Tenby, and ask his opinion.

Providing that she could get to Sir Robert's. Ask leave to go, she dare not; for she knew the answer would be a point-blank refusal.

But fortune favoured her. Between three and four o'clock on Monday afternoon, Mrs. Lewis and her daughters dressed themselves and sailed away to call on some people at South Crabb; which lay in just the contrary direction to Bellwood. They left Anne a heap of sewing to do: but she left the sewing and went out on her own score. I met her near the Ravine. She told me what she had done, and looked bright and flushed over it.

"Mrs. Lewis is one cat, and they are two other cats, Anne. Tod says so. Good-bye. Good luck to you!"

"Eh, my dear, and I was beginning to think you didna mean to come," was Mrs. Macbean's salutation. "But Sir Robert is nae back yet, he has been out on horseback since the morning; and he said you were to wait for him. So just take your bonnet off, and you shall have a cup of tea with me!"

Nothing loth, Anne took off her outdoor things. "They will be home before I am, and find me gone out," she reflected; "but they can't quite kill me for it." The old lady rang her bell for tea, and thought what a nice and pretty young gentlewoman Anne looked in her plain black dress with its white frilling, and the handsome jet necklace that had been her mother's.

But before the tea could be made, Sir Robert Tenby's horse trotted up, and they heard him go to his sitting-room. Mrs. Macbean took Anne into his presence, saying at the same time that she had been about to give the young lady a cup of tea.

"I should like some tea, too," said Sir Robert; "Miss Lewis can take it with me. Send it in."

It came in upon a waiter, and was placed upon the table. Anne, at his request, put sugar and cream into his cup, handed it to him, and then took her own. He was looking very thoughtful; she seemed to fancy he had no good news for her, as he did not speak of it; and her heart went down, down. In a very timid tone, she told him of the depreciating opinion held of her talents at home, and begged him to say what he thought, for she should not like to be guilty of undertaking any duty she was not fully competent to fulfil.

"Will you take some more tea?" was all Sir Robert said in answer.

"No, thank you, sir."

"Another biscuit? No? We will send the tray away then."

Ringing the bell, a servant came in and removed the things. Sir Robert, standing at the window, and looking down at Anne as she sat, began to speak.

"I think there might be more difficulty in getting you a situation as governess than we thought for; one that would be quite suited to you, at least. Perhaps another kind of situation would do better for you."

Her whole face, turned up to him with its gaze of expectancy, changed to sadness; the light in her eyes died away. It seemed so like the knell of all her hopes. Sir Robert only smiled.

"If you could bring yourself to take it—and to like it," he continued.

"But what situation is it, sir?"

"That of my wife. That of Lady of Bellwood."

Just for a moment or two she simply stared at him. When his meaning reached her comprehension, her face turned red and white with emotion. Sir Robert took her hand and spoke more fully. He had learnt to like her very very much, to esteem her, and wished her to be his wife.

"I am aware that there is a good deal of difference in our ages, my dear; more than twenty years," he went on, while she sat in silence. "But I think you might find happiness with me; I will do my very best to insure it. Better be my wife than a nursery governess. What do you say?"

"Oh, sir, I do not know what to say," she answered, trembling a little. "It is so unexpected—and a great honour—and—and I am overwhelmed."

"Could you like me?" he gently asked.

"I do like you, sir; very much. But this—this would be different. Perhaps you would let me take until to-morrow to think about it?"

"Of course I will. Bring me your answer then. Bring it yourself, whatever it may be."

"I will, sir. And I thank you very greatly."

All night long Anne Lewis lay awake. Should she take this good man for her husband, or should she not? She did like him very much: and what a position it would be for her; and how sheltered she would be henceforth from the frowns of the world! Anne might never have hesitated, but for the remains of her love for Mr. Angerstyne. That was passing away from her heart day by day, as she knew; it would soon have passed entirely. She could never feel that same love again; it was over and done with for ever; but there was surely no reason why she should sacrifice all her future to its remembrance. Yes: she would accept Sir Robert Tenby: and would, by the help of Heaven, make him a true, faithful, good wife.

It was nearly dusk the next afternoon before she could leave the house. Mrs. Lewis had kept her in sight so long that she feared she might not find the opportunity that day. She ran all the way to Bellwood, anxious to keep her promise: she could not bear to seem to trifle, even for a moment, with this good and considerate man. Sir Robert was waiting for her in a glow of firelight. He came forward, took both her hands in his, and looked into her face inquiringly.

"Well?"

"Yes, sir, if you still wish to take me. I will try to be to you a loving wife; obedient and faithful."

With a sigh of relief, he sat down on a sofa that was drawn to the fire and placed her beside him, holding her hand still.

"My dear, I thank you: you have made me very happy. You shall never have cause to repent it."

"It is so strange," she whispered, "that you should wait all these years, with the world to choose from, and then think of me at last! I can scarcely believe it."

"Ay, I suppose it is strange. But I must tell you something, Anne. When quite a youth, only one-and-twenty, there was a young lady whom I dearly loved. She was poor, and not of much family, and my father forbade the union. She married some one else, and died. It is for the love of her I have kept single all these years. But I shall not make you the less good husband."

"And I—I wish to tell you that I once cared for some one," whispered Anne, in her straightforward honesty. "It is all over and done with; but I did like him very much."

"Then, my dear, we shall be even," he said, with a merry smile. "The one cannot reproach the other. And now—this is the beginning of April; before the month shall have closed you had better come to me. We have nothing to wait for; and I do not like, now that you belong to me, to leave you one moment longer than is needful with that lady whom you are forced to call stepmother."

How Anne reached home that late afternoon she hardly knew: she knew still less how to bring the news out. In the course of the following morning she tried to do so, and made a bungle of it.

"Sir Robert not going to get you a situation as governess!" interrupted Julia, before Anne had half finished. "Of course he is not. He knows you are not capable of taking one. I thought how much he was intending to help you. You must have had plenty of cheek, Anne, to trouble him."

"I am going to be his wife instead," said poor Anne, meekly. "He has asked me to be. And—and it is to be very soon; and he is coming to see Mrs. Lewis this morning."

Mrs. Lewis, sitting back in an easy-chair, her feet on the fender, dropped the book she was reading to stare at Anne. Julia burst into a laugh of incredulity. Her mother echoed it, and spoke—

"You poor infatuated girl! This comes of being brought up on French soup. But Sir Robert Tenby has no right to play jokes upon you. I shall write and tell him so."

"I—think—he is there," stammered Anne.

There he was. A handsome carriage was drawing up to the gate, the baronet's badge upon its panels. Sir Robert sat inside. A footman came up the path and thundered at the door.

Not very long afterwards—it was in the month of June—Anne and her husband were guests at a London crush in Berkeley Square. It was too crowded to be pleasant. Anne began to look tired, and Sir Robert whispered to her that if she had had enough of it, they would go home. "Very gladly," she answered, and turned to say good-night to her hostess.

"Anne! How are you?"

The unexpected interruption, in a voice she knew quite well, and which sent a thrill through her, even yet, arrested Anne in her course. There stood Henry Angerstyne, his hand held out in greeting, a confident smile, as if assuming she could only receive him joyfully, on his handsome face.

"I am so much surprised to see you here; so delighted to meet you once again, Miss Lewis."

"You mistake, sir," replied Anne, in a cold, proud tone, drawing her head a little up. "I am Lady Tenby."

Walking forward, she put her arm within her husband's, who waited for her. Mr. Angerstyne understood it at once; it needed not the almost bridal robes of white silk and lace to enlighten him. She was not altered. She looked just the same single-minded, honest-hearted girl as ever, with a pleasant word for all—except just in the moment when she had spoken to him.

"I am glad of it: she deserves her good fortune," he thought heartily. With all his faults, few men could be more generously just than Henry Angerstyne.

CHAPTER XV

THE KEY OF THE CHURCH

"Johnny, you will have to take the organ on Sunday."

The words gave me a surprise. I turned short round on the music-stool, wondering whether Mrs. Todhetley spoke in jest or earnest. But her face was quite serious, as she sat, her hands on her lap, and her lame finger—the fore-finger of the left hand—stretched out.

"I take the organ, good mother! What's that for?"

"Because I was to have taken it, Johnny, and this accident to my finger will prevent it."

We had just got home to Dyke Manor from school for the Michaelmas holidays. Not a week of them: for this was Wednesday afternoon, and we should go back the following Monday. Mrs. Todhetley had cut her finger very seriously in carving some cold beef on the previous day. Old Duffham had put it into splints.

"Where's Mr. Richards?" I asked, alluding to the church organist.

"Well, it is rather a long tale, Johnny. A good deal of dissatisfaction has existed, as you know, between him and the congregation."

"Through his loud playing."

"Just so. And now he has resigned in a huff. Mr. Holland called yesterday morning to ask if I would help them at the pinch by taking the organ for a Sunday or two, until matters were smoothed with Richards, or some fresh organist was found; and I promised him I would. In the evening, this accident happened to my finger. So you must take it in my place, Johnny."

"And if I break down?"

"Not you. Why should you?"

"I am out of practice."

"There's plenty of time to get up your practice between now and Sunday. Don't make objections, my dear. We should all do what little we can to help others in a time of need."

I said no more. As she observed, there was plenty of time between now and Sunday. And, not to lose time, I went off there and then.

The church stood in a lonely spot, as I think you know, and I took the way across the fields to it. Whistling softly, I went along, fixing in my mind upon the chants and hymns. Ours was rather a primitive service. The organ repertoire included only about a dozen chants and double that number of hymns. It had this advantage—that they were all familiar to the congregation, who could join in the singing at will, and the singers had no need to practise. Mr. Richards had lately introduced a different style of music, and it was not liked.

"Let me see: I'll make it just the opposite of Richards's. For the morning we will have the thirty-seventh psalm, 'Depend on God:' there's real music in that; and 'Jerusalem the Golden.' And for the afternoon, 'Abide with me,' and the Evening Hymn. Mornington's Chant; and the Grand Chant; and the— Halloa, Fred! Is it you?"

A lithe, straight-limbed young fellow was turning out of the little valley: on his way (as I guessed) from the Parsonage. It was Fred Westerbrook: old Westerbrook's nephew at the Narrow Dyke Farm—or, as we abbreviated it, the N. D. Farm.

"How are you, Johnny?"

His face and voice were alike subdued as he shook hands. I asked after Mr. and Mrs. Westerbrook.

"They are both well, for anything I know," he answered. "The N. D. Farm is no longer my home, Johnny."

Had he told me the Manor was no longer mine, I could not have been more surprised.

"Why, how is that, Fred?"

"They have turned me out of it."

"What—this morning?"

"This morning—no. Two months ago."

"And why? I never thought it would come to that."

"Because they wanted to get rid of me, that's why. Gisby has been the prime mover in it—the chief snake in the grass. He is worse than she is."

"And what are you doing?"

"Nothing: except knocking about. I'd be off to America to-morrow and try my luck there if I had a fifty-pound note in my pocket. I went up to the farm last week, and made an appeal to my uncle to help me to it, and be rid of me—"

"And would he?" I interrupted, too eager to let him finish.

"Would he!" repeated Fred, savagely. "He bade me go to a place unmentionable. He threatened to drive me off the premises if ever I put foot on them again."

"I am very sorry. What shall you do?" I asked.

"Heaven knows! Perhaps turn poacher."

"Nonsense, Fred!"

"Is it nonsense!" he retorted, taking off his low-crowned hat and passing his hand passionately over his wavy, auburn hair—about the nicest hair I ever saw. People said Fred was proud of it. He was a good-looking young fellow altogether; with a clear, fresh face, and steady grey eyes.

"You don't know what it is to be goaded, Johnny," he said. "I can tell you I am ripe for any mischief. And a man must live. But for one thing, I swear I wouldn't keep straight."

I knew what thing he meant quite well. "What does she say about it?" I asked.

"What can she say? My uncle has insulted her to her face, and made me out at the Parsonage to be a downright scamp. Oh, I go in for all that's bad, according to him, I assure you, Johnny Ludlow."

"Do you never see her?"

"It is chiefly by chance if I do. I have just been up there now, sitting for half-an-hour with her in the old study. There was no opportunity for a private word, though; the young ones were dodging around, playing at 'Salt Fish'—if you know the delectable game. Good-bye, Johnny lad."

He strode off with an angry fire in his eye. I felt very sorry for him. We all liked Fred Westerbrook. He had his faults, I suppose, but he was one of the most open-natured fellows in the world.

Dashing in at Clerk Bumford's for the key of the church, I sat down to the organ: an antiquated instrument, whose bellows were worked by the player's feet, as are some of the modern harmoniums; but, as far as tone went, it was not bad—rather rich and sweet. All through the practice my mind was running on Fred Westerbrook and his uncle. The parish had said long ago they would come to a blow-up some time.

The N. D. Farm stood about three-quarters of a mile on the other side the church, beyond Mr. Page's. It had a good house upon it, and consisted of two or three hundred acres of land. But its owner, Mr. Westerbrook, rented a great deal more land that lay contiguous to it, which rendered it altogether one of the most considerable farms round about. Up to fifty years of age, Mr. Westerbrook had not married. Fred, his dead brother's son, had been adopted by him, and was regarded as his heir. The farm had been owned by the Westerbrooks for untold-of years, and it was not likely a stranger in blood and name would be allowed to inherit it. So Fred had lived there as the son and heir, and been made much of.

But, to the surprise of every one, Mr. Westerbrook took it into his head to marry, although he was fifty years old. It was thought to be a foolish act, and the parish talked freely. She was a widow without children, of a grasping nature, and not at all nice in temper. A high-spirited boy of fourteen, as Fred was, would be hardly likely to get on with her. She interfered with him in the holidays, and thwarted him, and told sneaking tales of him to his uncle. It went on pretty smoothly enough, however, until Fred left school, which he did at eighteen, to take up his abode at home for good and busy himself about the farm. Upon the death of the bailiff some three years later, she sent for one Gisby, from a distance, and got Mr. Westerbrook to instal him in the bailiff's vacant place. This Gisby was a dark little man of middle age, and was said to be distantly related to her. He proved to be an excellent farmer and manager, and did his duty well; but from the first he and Fred were just at daggers-drawn. Presuming upon his relationship to the mistress, Gisby treated Fred in an off-hand manner, telling him sometimes to do this and not to do the other, as he did the men. Of course, Fred did not stand that, and offered to pitch him into next week unless he kept his place better.

But, as the years went on, the antagonism against Fred penetrated to Mr. Westerbrook. She was always at work with her covert whispers, as was Gisby with his outspoken accusations of him, and with all sorts of tales of his wrong-doing. They had the ear of the master, and Fred could not fight against it. Perhaps he did not try to do so. Whispering, and meanness, and underhand doing of any kind, were foreign to his nature; he was rather too outspoken, and he turned on his enemies freely and gave them plenty of abuse. It was Gisby who first told Mr. Westerbrook of the intimacy, or friendship, or whatever you may please to call it, though I suppose the right word would be love, between Fred and Edna Blake. Edna was one of a large family, and had come, a year or two ago, to live at the Parsonage, being niece to Mrs. Holland, the parson's wife. Mrs. Holland was generally ill (and frightfully incapable), and Edna had it all on her hands: the housekeeping, and the six unruly children, and the teaching and the mending, and often the cooking. They paid her twenty pounds a-year for it. But she was a charming girl, with one of the sweetest faces ever seen, and the gentlest spirit. Fred Westerbrook had found that out, and the two were deeply in love with one another. Old Mr. Westerbrook went into one of his passions when he heard of it, and swore at Fred. Edna was not his equal, he told him; Fred must look higher: she had no money, and her friends, as was reported, were only tradespeople. Fred retorted that Edna was a mine of wealth and goodness in herself, and he had never troubled himself to ask what her friends might be. However, to make short of the story, matters had grown more unpleasant for Fred day by day, and this appeared to be the end of it, turning him out of house and home. He was just twenty-four now. I don't wish to imply that Fred was without faults, or that he did nothing to provoke his uncle. He had been wild the last year or two, and tumbled into a few scrapes; but the probability is that he would have kept straight enough under more favourable circumstances. The discomfort at home drove him out, and he got associating with anything but choice company.

Making short work of my playing, I took the key back to Bumford's, and ran home. Tod was in the dining-room with the mother, and I told them of the meeting with Fred Westerbrook. Mrs. Todhetley seemed to know all about it, and said Fred had been living at the Silver Bear.

"What an awful shame of old Westerbrook!" broke out Tod. "To turn a fellow away from his home!"

"I am afraid there are faults on both sides," sighed Mrs. Todhetley, in her gentle way. "Fred has not borne a good character of late."

"And who could expect him to bear a good one?" fired Tod. "If I were turned out like a dog, should I care what I did? No! Old Westerbrook and that precious wife of his ought to be kicked. As to Gisby, the sneak, hanging would be too good for him."

"Don't, Joseph."

"Don't!" retorted Tod. "But I do. They deserve all the abuse that can be given them. I can see her game. She wants Westerbrook to leave the property to her: that's the beginning and the end of it; and to cut off poor Fred with a shilling."

"Of course we are all sorry for Fred, Joseph," resumed the mother. "Very sorry. I know I am. But he need not do reckless things, and lose his good name."

"Bother his good name!" cried Tod. "Look at their interference about Edna Blake. That news came out when we were at home at Midsummer. Edna is as good as they are."

"It is a hopeless case, I fear, Joseph. Discarded by his uncle, all his prospects are at an end. He has been all on the wrong track lately, and done many a sad thing."

"I don't care what he has done. He has been driven to it. And I'll stand up for him through thick and thin."

Tod flung out of the room with the last words. It was just like him, putting himself into a way for nothing. It was like somebody else too—his father. I began telling Mrs. Todhetley of the chants and hymns I had thought of, asking her if they would do.

"None could be better, Johnny. And I only wish you might play for us always."

A fine commotion arose next morning. We were at breakfast, when Thomas came in to say old Jones, the constable, wanted to see the Squire immediately. Old Jones was bade to enter; he appeared all on the shake, and his face as white as a sheet. There had been murder done in the night, he said. Master Fred Westerbrook had shot Gisby: and he had come to get a warrant signed for Fred's apprehension.

"Goodness bless me!" cried the Squire, dropping his knife and fork, and turning to face old Jones. "How on earth did it happen?"

"Well, your worship, 'twere a poaching affray," returned Jones. "Gisby the bailiff have had his suspicions o' the game, and he went out last night with a man or two, and met the fellows in the open field on this side the copse. There they was, in the bright moonlight, as bold as brass, with a bag o' game, Master Fred Westerbrook the foremost on 'em. A fight ensued—Gisby don't want for pluck, he don't, though he be undersized, and he attacked 'em. Master Fred up with his gun and shot him."

"Is Gisby dead?"

"No, sir; but he's a-dying."

"What a fool that Fred Westerbrook must be!" stormed the Squire. "And I declare I liked the young fellow amazingly! It was only last night, Jones, that we were talking of him here, taking his part against his uncle."

"He haven't been after much good, Squire, since he went to live at that there Silver Bear. Not but what the inn's as respectable—"

"Respectable!—I should like to know where you would find a more respectable inn, or one better conducted?" put in Tod, with scant ceremony. "What do you mean, old Jones? A gentleman can take up his abode at the Silver Bear, and not be ashamed of it."

"I have nothing to say again' it, sir; nor against Rimmer neither. It warn't the inn I was reflecting on, but on Master Fred himself."

"Anyway, I don't believe this tale, Jones."

"Not believe it!" returned Jones, aghast at the bold assertion. "Why, young Mr. Todhetley, the whole parish is a-ringing with it. There's Gisby a-dying at Shepherd's—which was the place he were carried to, being the nearest; and Shepherd himself saw young Mr. Fred fire off the gun."

"What became of the rascally poachers?" asked the Squire. "Who were they?"

"They got clean off, sir, every one on 'em. And they couldn't be recognized; they had blackened their faces. Master Fred was the only one who had not disguised hisself, which was just like his boldness. They left the game behind 'em, your worship: a nice lot o' pheasants and partridges. Pheasants too, the miscreants!—and October not in."

There was not much more breakfast for us. Tod rushed off, and I after him. As Jones had said, the whole parish was ringing with the news, and we found people standing about in groups to talk. The particulars appeared to be as old Jones had related. Gisby, taking Shepherd—who was herdsman on the N. D.

Farm—with him, and another man named Ford, had gone out to watch for poachers; had met half-a-dozen of them, including Fred Westerbrook, and Fred had shot Gisby.

The Silver Bear stood in the middle of Church Dykely, next door to Perkins the butcher's. It was kept by Henry Rimmer. We made for it, wondering whether Rimmer could tell us anything. He was in the tap-room, polishing the taps.

"Oh, it's true enough, young gentlemen!" he said, as we burst in upon him with questions. "And a dreadful thing it is. One can't help pitying young Mr. Westerbrook."

"Look here, Rimmer: do you believe he did it?"

"Why, in course he did, Master Johnny. There was no difficulty in knowing him: he was the only one of 'em not disguised. Shepherd says the night was as light as day. Gisby and him and Ford all saw young Mr. Westerbrook, and knew him as soon as the lot came in sight."

"Was he at home here last evening?" asked Tod.

"He was at home here, sir, till after supper. He had been out in the afternoon, and came in to his tea between five and six. Then he stayed in till supper-time, and went out afterwards."

"Did he come in later?"

"No, never," replied Rimmer, lowering his voice, as a man sometimes does when speaking very seriously. "He never came in again."

"They say Gisby can't recover. Is that true, or not?"

"It is thought he'll not live through the day, sir."

"And where can Westerbrook be hiding himself?"

"He's safe inside the hut of one or other of the poachers, I should say," nodded the landlord. "Not that that would be safe for him, or for them, if it could be found out who the villains were. I think I could give a guess at two or three of them."

"So could I," said Tod. "Dick Standish was one, I know. And Jelf another. Of course, their haunts will be searched. Don't you think, Rimmer, Mr. Fred Westerbrook would rather make off, than run the risk of concealing himself in any one of them?"

Rimmer shook his head. "I don't know about that, sir. He might not be able to make off. It's thought he was wounded."

"Wounded!"

"Gisby fired his own gun in the act of falling, and Shepherd thinks the charge hit young Mr. Westerbrook. The poachers were running off then, and Shepherd saw them halt in a kind of heap like, and he is positive that the one on the ground was Mr. Westerbrook. For that reason, sir, I should say the chances are he is somewhere in the neighbourhood."

Of course it looked like it. Strolling away to pick up anything else that people might be saying, we gave Fred our best wishes for his escape—in spite of the shot—and for effectually dodging old Jones and the rest of the Philistines. Tod made no secret of his sentiments.

"It's a thing that might have happened to you or to me, you see, Johnny, were we turned out of doors and driven to bay as Fred has been."

By the afternoon, great staring hand-bills were posted about, written in enormous text-hand, offering a reward of twenty pounds for the apprehension of Frederick Westerbrook. When old Westerbrook was incensed, he went in for the whole thing, and no mistake.

What with the bustle the place was in, and the excitement of the chase—for all the hedges and ditches, the barns and the suspected dwellings were being looked up by old Jones and a zealous crowd, anxious for the reward—it was not until after dinner in the evening that I got away to practice. Going along, I met Duffham, and asked after Gisby.

"I am on my way to Shepherd's now," he answered. "I suppose he is still alive, as they have not sent me word to the contrary."

"Is he sure to die, Mr. Duffham?"

"I fear so, Johnny. I don't see much chance of saving him."

"What a dreadful thing for Fred Westerbrook! They may bring it in wilful murder."

"That they will be sure to do. Good-evening, lad; I have no time to linger with you."

Bumford was probably looking out for the fugitive (and the reward) on his own score, as he was not to be seen; but I found the key inside the knife-box on the kitchen dresser, his store-place for it, opened the door, and went into the church.

On one side the church-door, as you entered, was an enclosed place underneath the belfry, that did for the vestry and for Clerk Bumford's den. He kept his store of candles in it, his grave-digging tools (for he was sexton as well as clerk), his Sunday black gown, and other choice articles. On the other side of the door, not enclosed, was the nook that contained the organ. I sat down at once. But I had come too late; for in half-an-hour's time the notes of the music and the keys were alike dim. Just then Bumford entered.

"Oh, you be here, be you!" said he, treating me, as he did the rest of the world, with slight ceremony. "I thought I heered the organ a-going, so I come on to see."

"You were not indoors, Bumford, when I called for the key."

"I were only in the field at the back, a-getting up some dandelion roots," returned old Bumford, in his usual resentful tone. "There ain't no obligation in me to be shut in at home everlasting."

"Who said there was?"

"Ain't it a'most too dark for you?"

"Yes, I shall have to borrow one of your candles."

Bumford grunted at this. The candles were not strictly his; they were paid for by the parish; but he set great store by them, and would have denied me one if he could. Not seeing his way clear to doing this, he turned away, muttering to himself. I took my fingers off the keys—for I had been playing while I talked to him—and followed. Bumford went out of the church, shutting the door with a bang, and I proceeded to search for the candlestick.

That was soon found: it always stood on the shelf; but it had no candle in it, and I opened the candle-box to take one out. All the light that came in was from the open slits in the belfry above. The next thing was to find the matches.

Groping about quietly with my hands on the shelf, for fear of knocking down some article or another, and wondering where on earth the match-box had gone to, I was interrupted by a groan. A dismal groan, coming from the middle of the church.

It nearly made me start out of my skin. My shirt-sleeves went damp. Down with us, the ghosts of the buried dead are popularly supposed to haunt the churches at night.

"It must have been the pulpit creaking," said I, gravely to myself. "Oh, here's the match—"

An awful groan! Another! Three groans altogether! I stood as still as death; calling up the recollection that God was with me inside the church as well as out of it. Frightened I was, and it is of no use to deny it.

"I wonder what the devil is to be the ending of this!"

The unorthodox words burst upon my ears, bringing a reassurance, for dead people don't talk, let alone their natural objection (as one must suppose) to mention the arch-enemy. The tones were free and distinct; and—I knew them for Fred Westerbrook's.

"Fred, is that you?" I asked in a half-whisper, as I went forward.

No sound; no answer.

"Fred! it's only I."

Not a word or a breath. I struck a match, and lighted a candle.

"You need not be afraid, Fred. Come along. I'll do anything I can for you. Don't you know me?—Johnny Ludlow."

"For the love of Heaven, put that light out, Johnny!" he said, feeling it perhaps useless to hold out, or else deciding to trust me, as he came down the aisle in a stooping position, so that the pews might screen him from the windows. And I put it out.

"I thought you had gone out of the church with old Bumford," said he. "I heard you both come away from the organ, and then the door was slammed, leaving the church to silence."

"I was searching after the candle and matches. When did you come here, Fred? How did you get in?"

"I got in last night. Is there much of a row, Johnny?"

"Pretty well. How came you to do it?"

"To do what?"

"Shoot Gisby."

"It was not I that shot him."

"Not you!"

"Certainly not."

"But—people are saying it was you. You were with the poachers."

"I was with the poachers; and one of them, like the confounded idiot that he was, pointed his gun and fired it. I recognized the cry for Gisby's, and knew that the charge must have struck him. I never had a gun in my hand at all, Johnny."

Well, I felt thankful for that. We sat down on the bench, and Fred told his tale.

After supper the previous night, he strolled out and met some fellow he knew, who lived two or three miles away. (A black sheep in public estimation, like himself.) It was a beautiful night. Fred chose to see him home, and stayed there, drinking a glass or two, till he knew not what hour. Coming back across the fields, he fell in with the poachers. Instead of denouncing them, he told them half in joke, half in earnest, that he might be joining their band himself before the winter was over. Close upon that, they fell in with the watchers, Gisby and the rest. Fred knew he was recognized, for Gisby called out his name; and that, Fred did not like: it made things look black against him. Gisby attacked them; a scuffle ensued, and one of the poachers used his gun. Then the poachers turned to run, Fred with them; a shot was fired after them and hit one of their body—but not Fred, as Rimmer had supposed. The man tripped as the shot struck him, and caused Fred to trip and fall; but both were up, and off, the next moment. Where the rest escaped to, Fred did not know; chance led him past the church: on the spur of the moment he entered it for refuge, and had been there ever since.

"And it is a great and good thing you did enter it, Fred," I said eagerly. "Gisby swears it was you who shot him, and he is dying; and Shepherd swears it too."

"Gisby dying?"

"He is. I met Duffham as I came here; he told me there was little, if any, chance of his life; he had been expecting news of his death all the afternoon. They have posted handbills up, offering a reward of twenty pounds for your apprehension, Fred; and—and I am afraid, and so is Duffham, that they will try you for wilful murder. The whole neighbourhood is being searched for you for miles round."

"Pleasant!" said Fred, after a brief silence. "I had meant to go out to-night and endeavour to ascertain how the land lay. Of course I knew that what could be put upon my back would be put; and there's no denying that I was with the poachers. But I did not think matters would be as bad as this. Hang it all!"

"But, Fred, how did you get in here?"

"Well," said he, "we hear talk of providential occurrences: there's nothing Mr. Holland is fonder of telling us about in his sermons than the guiding finger of God. If the means that enabled me to take refuge here were not providential, Johnny, I must say they looked like it. When I met you yesterday afternoon, you must remember my chancing to say that the little Hollands were playing at 'Salt Fish' in the study, while I sat there, talking to Edna?"

Of course I remembered it.

"Directly after I left you, Johnny," resumed Fred Westerbrook, "I put my hand in my coat-tail pocket for my handkerchief, and found a large key there. It was the key of the church, that the children had been hiding at their play; and I understood in a moment that Charley, whose turn it was to hide last, had made a hiding-place of my pocket. The parson keeps one key, you know, and Bumford the other—"

"But, Fred," I interrupted, the question striking me, "how came the young ones to let you come away with it?"

"Because, lad, their attention got diverted to something else. Ann brought in the tea-things, with a huge plate of bread-and-treacle: they screamed out in delight, and scuffled to get seats round the table. Well, I let the key lie in my pocket," went on Fred, "intending to take it back to-day. In the night, when flying from pursuit, not knowing who or how many might be after me, I felt this heavy key strike against me continually; and, in nearing the church, the thought flashed over me like an inspiration: What if I open it and hide there? Just as young Charley had hidden the key in my pocket, so I hid myself, by its means, in the church."

Taking a minute to think over what he said, it did seem strange. One of those curious things one can hardly account for; the means for his preservation were so simply natural and yet almost marvellous. Perhaps the church was the only building where he could have found secure refuge. Private dwellings would refuse to shelter him, and other places were sure to be searched.

"You are safe here, Fred. No one would ever think of seeking you here."

"Safe, yes; but for how long? I can't live without food for ever, Johnny. As it is, I have eaten none since last night."

My goodness! A shock of remorse came over me. When I was at old Bumford's knife-box, a loaf of bread stood on the dresser. If I had only secured it!

"We must manage to bring you something, Fred. You cannot stir from here."

Fred had taken the key out, having returned it to his pocket in the night when he locked himself in. He sat looking at it as he balanced it on his finger.

"Yes, you have served me in good need," he said to the key. "I shall turn out for a stroll during some quiet hour of the night, Johnny. To keep my restless legs curbed indoors for a whole day and night would be quite beyond their philosophy."

"Well, take care of yourself, if you do. There's not a soul in the place but is wild for the reward; and I dare say they will look for you by night more than by day. How about getting you in something to eat?"

"I don't know," he answered. "It would never do for you to be seen coming in here at night."

I knew that. Old Bumford would be down on me if no one else was. I sat turning over possibilities in my mind.

"I will come in betimes to-morrow morning under the plea of practising, Fred, and bring what I can. You must do battle with your hunger until then."

"I suppose I must, Johnny. Mind you lock the door when you come in, or old Bumford might pounce upon us. When I heard you unlock it on coming in this evening, I can tell you I shivered in my shoes. Fate is very hard," he added, after a pause.

"Fate is?"

"Why, yes. I have been a bit wild lately, perhaps, savage too, but I declare before Heaven that I have committed no crime, and did not mean to commit any. And now, to have this serious thing fastened upon my back! The world will say I have gone straight over to Satan."

I did not see how he would get it off his back either. Wishing him good-night and a good heart, I turned to go.

"Wait a moment, Johnny. Let me go back to my hiding-place first."

He went swiftly up the aisle, lighter now than it had been, for the moonlight was streaming in at the windows. Locking the church safely, I crossed the graveyard to old Bumford's. He was seated at his round table at supper: bread-and-cheese, and beer.

"Oh, Mr. Bumford, as I have to come into the church very early in the morning, or I shall never get my music up for Sunday, I will take the key home with me. Good-night."

He shouted out fifteen denials: How dared I think of taking the key out of his custody! But I was conveniently deaf, rushed off, and left him shouting.

"What a long practice you have been taking, Johnny!" cried Mrs. Todhetley. "And how hot you look. You must have run very fast."

The Squire turned round from his arm-chair. "You've been joining in the hunt after that scamp, Mr. Johnny;—you've not been in the church, sir, all this time. I hear there's a fine pack out, scouring the hedges and ditches."

"I got a candle from old Bumford's den," said I, evasively. And presently I contrived to whisper unseen to Tod—who sat reading—to come outside. Standing against the wall of the pigeon-house, I told him all. For once in his life Tod was astonished.

"What a stunning thing!" he exclaimed. "Good luck, Fred! we'll help you. I knew he was innocent, Johnny. Food? Yes, of course; we must get it for him. Molly, you say? Molly be shot!"

"Well, you know what Molly is, Tod. Let half a grain of suspicion arise, and it might betray him. If she saw us rifling her larder, she would go straight to the Squire; and what excuse should we have?"

"Look here, Johnny. I'll go out fishing to-morrow, you understand, and order her to make a lot of meat pasties."

"But he must have something to eat to-morrow morning, Tod: he might die of hunger, else, before night."

Tod nodded. He had little more diplomacy than the Squire, and would have liked to perch himself upon the highest pillar in the parish there and then, and proclaim Fred Westerbrook's innocence.

We stole round to the kitchen. Supper was over, but the servants were still at the table; no chance of getting to the larder then. Molly was in one of her tempers, apparently blowing up Thomas. There might be more chance in the morning.

Morning light. Tod went downstairs with the dawn, and I followed him. Not a servant was yet astir. He laid hold of a great tray, lodged it on the larder-floor, and began putting some things upon it—a cold leg of mutton and a big round loaf.

"I can't take in all that, Tod. It is daylight, you know, and eyes may be about: old Bumford's are sure to be. I can only take in what can be concealed in my pockets."

"Oh, bother, Johnny! You'd half famish him."

"Better half famish him than betray him. Some slices of bread and meat will be best—thick sandwiches, you know."

We soon cut into the mutton and the bread. Wrapping them in paper, I stowed the thick slices away in my pockets, leaving the rest of the loaf and meat on the shelves again.

"How I wish I could smuggle him in a bottle of beer!"

"And so you can, Johnny. Swear to old Bumford it is for your own drinking."

"He would know better."

"Wrap a sheet of music round the bottle, then. He could make nothing of that."

Hunting out a bottle, we went down to the cellar. Tod stooped to fill it from the tap. I stood watching the process.

"I've caught you, Master Johnny, have I! What be you about there, letting the ale run, I'd like to know?"

The words were Molly's. She had come down and found us out: suspecting something, I suppose, from seeing the cellar-door open. Tod rose up.

"I am drawing some beer to take out with me. Is it any business of yours? When it is, you may interfere."

I was nobody in the household—never turning upon them. She'd have gone on at me for an hour, and probably walked off with the beer. Tod was altogether different. He held his own authority, even with Molly. She went up the cellar-stairs, grumbling to herself.

"I want a cork for this bottle," said bold Tod, following her. And Molly, opening some receptacle of hers with a jerk, perforce found him one.

"Oh, and I shall want some meat pasties made to-day, for I think of going fishing," went on Tod. "Let them be ready by lunch-time. I have cut myself some slices of meat to go on with—if you chance to miss any mutton."

Molly, never answering, left her kitchen-grate, where she was beginning to crack up the huge flat piece of coal that the fire had been raked with the previous night, and stalked into the larder to see what depredations had been done. We tied up the bottle in paper on the parlour-table, and then wrapped it in a sheet of loose music. It looked a pretty thick roll; but nobody would be likely to remark that.

"I have a great mind to go with you and see him, Johnny," said Tod, as we went together down the garden-path.

"Oh, don't, Tod!" I cried. "For goodness' sake, don't. You know you never do go in with me, and it might cause old Bumford to wonder."

"Then, I'll leave it till after dark to-night, Johnny. Go in then, I shall."

Bumford was astir, but not down yet. I heard him coughing, through his open casement; for I went with a purpose round the path by his house, and called out to him. He looked out in his shirt-sleeves and a cotton night-cap.

"You see how early I am this morning. I'll bring you the key when I leave."

"Eugh!" growled Bumford. "No rights to ha' took it."

Locking the church-door securely after me, I went down the aisle, calling softly to Fred. He came forward from a dark, high-walled pew behind a pillar, where he had slept. You should have seen him devour the bread and meat, if you'd like to know what hunger means, and drink the bottle of beer. I sat down to practise. Had old Bumford not heard the sound of the organ, he might have come thundering at the door to know what I was about, and what the silence meant. Fred came with me, and we talked whilst I played. About the first question he asked was whether Gisby was dead; but I could not tell him. He said he had gone out cautiously in the night and walked about the churchyard for an hour, thinking over what he could do. "And I really had an unpleasant adventure, Johnny," he added.

"What was it?"

"I was pacing the path under the hedge towards Bumford's, when all at once there arose the sound of voices and steps on the other side of it—fellows on the look-out for me, I suppose."

I held my breath. "What did you do?"

"Crouched down as well as I could—fortunately the hedge is high—and came softly and swiftly over the grass and the graves to the porch. I only slipped inside just in time, Johnny: before I could close the door, the men were in the churchyard. The key has a trick of creaking harshly when turned in the lock, you know; and I declare I thought they must have heard it then, for it made a fearful noise, and the night was very still!"

"And they did not hear it?"

"I suppose not. But it was some minutes, I can tell you, before my pulses calmed down to their ordinary rate of beating."

He went on to say that the only plan he could think of was to endeavour to get away from the neighbourhood, and go out of the country. To stand his trial was not to be thought of. His word, that he had not been the guilty man, had never even had a gun in his hand that night, would go for nothing, against Gisby's word and Shepherd's. Whatever came of it, he would have to be out of the church before Sunday. The great question was: how could he get away unseen? I told him Tod was coming with me at night, and we would consult together. Locking up the church again, and the prisoner in it, I gladdened Bumford's heart by handing over the key, and ran home to breakfast.

Life yet lingered in Gisby; but the doctors thought he could not live through the day. The injury he had received was chiefly internal, somewhere in the region of the lungs. Fresh parties went out with fresh ardour to scour the country after Fred Westerbrook; and so the day passed. Chancing to meet Shepherd late in the afternoon, he told me Gisby still lived.

At sundown I went in to practise again, and took a big mould-candle with me, showing it to Bumford, that he might not be uneasy on the score of his stock in the vestry. As soon as dusk came on, and before the tell-tale moon was much up, I left the organ, opened the church-door, and stood at it, according to the plan concerted with Tod. He came swiftly up with his basket of provisions which he had got together by degrees during the day; and then we locked the door again. After Fred had regaled himself, we consulted together. Fred was to steal out of the church about one o'clock on Sunday morning, and make off across the country. But to do this with safety it was necessary he should be disguised. By that time the ardour of the night-searching might have somewhat passed; and the hour, one o'clock in the morning, was as silent and lonely a one as could be expected. It was most essential that he should not be recognized by any person who might chance to meet him.

"But you must manage one thing for me," said Fred, after this was settled. "I will not go away without seeing Edna. She can come in here with you to-morrow night."

We both objected. "It will be very hazardous, Fred. Old Bumford would be sure to see her: his eyes are everywhere."

"Tell him you want her to sing over the chants with you, Johnny. Tell him anything. But go away for an indefinite period, without first seeing her and convincing her that it is not guilt that sends me, I will not."

So there was no more to be said.

Getting provisions together seemed to have been easy compared with what we should have to get up now—a disguise. A smock-frock, say, and the other items of a day-labourer's apparel. But it was more easy to decide than to procure them.

"Mack leaves belongings of his in the barn occasionally," said Tod to me, as we walked home together. "We'll look to-morrow night."

It was our best hope. Failing that, there would be no possibility of getting a smock-frock anywhere; and Fred would have to escape in his coat turned inside out, or something of that sort. His own trousers, braced up high, and plastered with mud at the feet, would do very well, and his own wideawake hat, pulled low down on his face. There would be no more trouble about provisions, for what Tod had taken in would be enough.

Saturday. And Tod and I with our work before us. Gisby was sinking fast.

Late in the afternoon I went to the Parsonage, wondering how I should get to see Edna Blake alone. But Fortune favoured me—as it seemed to have favoured us throughout. The children were all at play in the nearest field. Edna was in what they called the schoolroom in her lilac-print dress, looking over socks and stockings, about a wheelbarrow-full. I saw her through the window, and went straight in. Her large dark eyes looked as sad and big as the hole she was darning; and her voice had a hopeless ring in it.

"Oh, Johnny, how you startled me! Nay, don't apologize. It is my fault for being so nervous and foolish. I can't think what has ailed me the last few days: I seem to start at shadows. Have—have you come to tell me anything?"

By the shrinking voice and manner, I knew what she feared—that Fred Westerbrook was taken. Looking round the room, I asked whether what we said could be heard.

"There's no one to hear," she answered. "Poor Mrs. Holland is in bed. Mr. Holland is out; and Anne is shut up, cleaning the kitchen."

"Well, then," I said, dropping my voice, "I have brought you a message from Fred Westerbrook."

Down went the socks in a heap. "Oh, Johnny!"

"Hush! No: he is not taken; he is in safe hiding. What's more, Edna, he is no more guilty than I am. He met the poachers accidentally that night just before the affray, and he never had a gun in his hands at all."

A prolonged, sobbing sigh, as if she were going to faint, and then a glad light in her eyes. She took up her work again. I went over to the seat next her, and told her all. She was darning all the while. With such a heap of mending the fingers must not be idle.

"To America!" she repeated, in answer to what I said. "What is he going to do for money to carry him there?"

"He talks of working his passage over. He has enough money about him, he says, to take him to the coast. Unfortunately, neither Tod nor I can help him in that respect. We have brought empty pockets from school, and shall have no money before the time of going back again. Will you go in and see him, Edna?"

"Yes," she said, after a minute's consideration. "And I will bring a roll of music in my hand, as you suggest, Johnny, for the satisfaction of Clerk Bumford's curiosity. I will be at the stile as near eight o'clock as I can, if you will come out there to meet me: but it is Saturday night, you know, when there's always a great deal to do."

Dinner was made later than usual that night at home: it had struck half-past seven before we got out, having secured another bottle of beer. The moon was rising behind the trees as we went into the barn.

Tod struck a match, and we looked about. Yes, Fortune was with us still. Hanging on the shaft of the cart, was Mack's smock-frock. It was anything but clean; but beggars can't be choosers. Next we descried a cotton neckerchief and a pair of boots; two clumsy, clod-hopping boots, with nails in the soles, and the outside leather not to be seen for patches.

"They must do," said Tod, with a rueful look. "But just look at the wretches, Johnny. I must smuggle these and the smock-frock into the church-porch, whilst you go round to old B.'s for the key."

"I have the key. I flung him a shilling this morning instead of the key, saying I might be wanting to practise at any hour to-day, and would give it him back to-night."

Going by the most solitary way, I let Tod into the church, and went to meet Edna Blake. She was already there, the roll of music in her hand. Bumford shot out of his house, and crossed our path.

"Good-evening, Mr. Bumford!" said she, cheerily. "I am come to try the hymns for to-morrow, with Johnny Ludlow."

"They'd need to be sum'at extra, they had, with all this here fuss of practising," returned Bumford, ungraciously. "Is the parson at home, Miss Blake?"

"Yes. He is in the little room, writing."

"'Cause I want to see him," said the clerk; and he stalked off.

"Do you know how Gisby is?" Edna asked me in a whisper.

"Dead by this time, I dare say. But I have not heard."

They were at the top of the church when we got in, laughing in covert tones; I guessed it was over those dreadful boots. Edna stood by me whilst I locked the door, and then we went at once to the organ and began the hymn. Old Bumford could not be too far off yet to catch the sounds. Presently Fred Westerbrook and Edna went into the aisle, and paced it arm-in-arm. I kept on playing; Tod, not knowing what to do with himself, whistled an accompaniment.

"How long shall I be away, Edna!" exclaimed Fred, in answer to her question. "Why, how can I tell? It may be for years; it may be for ever. I cannot come back, I suppose, whilst this thing is hanging over my head."

She was in very low spirits, and the tears began to drop from her eyes. Fred could see that much, as they paced through one of the patches of moonlight.

"You may not succeed in getting away."

"No, I may not. And do you know, Edna, there are moments when I feel half inclined not to attempt it, but to give myself up instead, and let the matter take its course. If I do get away, and get on in the States, so as to make myself a home, will you come out and share it with me?"

"Yes," she answered.

"I may do it. I think I shall. Few people know more about the cultivation of land than I do, and I will take care to put my shoulder to the wheel. Practical farmers get on well there if they choose, though they have to rough it at first. Be very sure of one thing, Edna: all my hopes and aims will be directed to one end—that of making a home for you."

She could not speak for crying.

"It may not be a luxurious home, neither may I make anything of a position. But if I make enough for comfort, you will come out to it?"

"I will," she said with a sob.

"My darling!"

Echo bore the words to us, softly though they were spoken. I played a crashing chord or two, after the manner of Richards.

"You may not hear from me," continued Fred. "I must not give any clue to where I am, and therefore cannot write—at least, not at present. Men accused of murder can be brought home from any part of the world. Only trust me, Edna. Trust me! though it be for years."

No fear but she would. She put a small packet in his hand.

"You must take it, Frederick. It is my last half-year's salary—ten pounds—and I chance to have it by me: a loan, if you will; but take it you shall. Knowing that you have a few pounds to help you away and to fall back upon, will make things a little less miserable for me."

"But, Edna—"

"I declare I will throw it away if you do not take it," she returned, warmly. "Do not be cruel to me, Frederick. If you knew how it will lighten my doubts and fears, you would not for a moment hesitate."

"Be it so, Edna. It will help me onwards. Truth to say, I did not see how I should have got along, even to the coast, unless I had begged on my way. It is a loan, Edna, and I will contrive to repay it as soon as may be."

So his boast of having money to take him to the coast had been all a sham. Poor Fred! They began to take leave of one another, Edna sobbing bitterly. I plunged into the "Hallelujah Chorus."

Tod let her out, and watched her safely across the churchyard. Then we locked the door again for the dressing-up, I playing a fugue between whiles. The first operation was that of cutting his hair short, for which we had brought the mater's big scissors. No labourer would be likely to possess Fred's beautiful hair, or wear it so long. Tod did it well; not counting a few notches, and leaving him as good as none on his head.

It was impossible to help laughing when we took a final look at him in the moonlight, Fred turning himself about to be inspected: his hair, clipped nearly to the roots, suggesting a suspicion that he had just come out of prison; his trousers, not reaching to the ankle, showing off the heavy, patched, disreputable boots; the smock-frock; and Mack's spotted cotton neckerchief muffled round his chin!

"Your own mother wouldn't know you, Fred."

"What a figure I shall cut if I am dropped upon and brought back!"

"Take heart, man!" cried Tod. "Resolve to get off, and you will get off."

"Yes, Fred, I think you will. You have been so helped hitherto, that I think you will be helped still."

"Thank you, Johnny. Thank you both. I will take heart. And if I live to return, I hope I shall thank you better."

Later we dared not stay; it was past nine now. I bade Fred good-bye, and God-speed.

"Between half-past twelve and one, mind, will be your time; you'll hear the clock strike," was Tod's parting injunction, given in a whisper. "Good luck to you, old fellow! I hope and trust you'll dodge the enemy. And as soon as you are clear of the churchyard, make off as if the dickens were behind you."

"Here's the key, Mr. Bumford," I said, while Tod stole off with his bundle the other way, Fred's boots, and hair, and all that. "You won't be bothered for it next week, for I shall be off to school again."

"Thought you'd took up your lodging inside for the night," grunted Bumford. "Strikes me, Master Ludlow, it's more play nor work with you."

"As it is with a good many of us, Bumford. Good-night!"

We walked home in the moonlight, silent enough, Tod handing me the bundles to carry. The Squire attacked us, demanding whether we had stayed out to look at the moon.

And I tossed and turned on my restless bed till the morning hours, thinking of poor Fred Westerbrook, and of whether he would get away. When sleep at last came, it brought me a very vivid dream of him. I thought he did not get away: he was unable to unlock the church-door. Whether Tod and I had double-locked it in leaving, I knew not; but Fred could not get it open. When Clerk Bumford entered the church in the morning, and the early comers of the congregation with him, there stood Fred, hopelessly waiting to be taken. I saw him as plainly in my dream as I had ever seen him in reality: with the dirty smock-frock, and the patched boots, and the clipped hair. Shepherd, who seemed to follow me in, darted forward and seized him; and in the confusion I awoke. Just for a minute I thought it was true—a scene actually enacted. Would it prove so?

CHAPTER XVI

THE SYLLABUB FEAST

"You have gone and done a fine thing, Master Johnny Ludlow!"

The salutation came from Clerk Bumford. He was standing at the church-door on Sunday morning, looking out as if he expected me, his face pale and stern. I had run on betimes: in fact, before the bell began.

"What have I done, Bumford?"

"Why, you just went and left this here church open last night! You never locked it up! When I come in but now, I found the door right on the latch; never as much as shut!"

Beginning to protest till all was blue that I had shut and locked the door—as I knew too well—caution pulled me up, and whispered me to take the blame.

"I'm sure I thought I locked it, Bumford. I never left it unlocked before, and I'll take care I never leave it so again."

"Such a thing as having the church open for a night was never heered of," he grumbled, turning away to ring out the first peal of the bell. "Why, I might have had all my store o' candles stole! there's nigh a pound on 'em, in here. And my black gownd—and the parson's gownd—and his surplice! Besides the grave-digging tools, and other odds and ends."

Shutting himself into his den underneath the belfry, and tugging away at the cords, the bell tinkled out, warning the parish that it was time to start for morning service. The bell-ringer was a poor old man named Japhet, who was apt to be a little late. Upon which Bumford would begin the ringing, and blow Japhet up when he came.

Not a soul was yet in church. I went down the middle aisle softly calling Fred Westerbrook's name. He did not answer; and I hoped to my heart he had got clear away. The open entrance-door seemed to indicate that he had; and I thought he might have left it undone in case he had to make a bolt back again. Nevertheless, I could not shake off the remembrance of my unpleasant dream.

Of all troublesome idiots, that Bumford was the worst. When I went back, after passing by all the remote nooks and corners, Japhet had taken his place at the bell, and he was telling the parson of my sins.

"Right on the latch all the blessed night, your reverence," protested Bumford. "We might have found the whole church ransacked this morning."

Mr. Holland, a mild man, with stout legs, and cares of his own, looked at me with a half-smile. "How was it, Johnny?"

"I have assured Bumford, sir, that it shall not happen again. I certainly thought I had locked it when I took him back the key. No harm has come of it."

"But harm might ha' come," persisted Bumford. "Look at all them candles in there! and the gownds and surplices! Pretty figures we should ha' cut, saving his reverence's presence, with nothing to put upon our backs this here blessed morning!"

"Talking of the key, I missed mine this morning," remarked Mr. Holland. "Have you taken it away for any purpose, Bumford?"

"What, the t'other church-key!" exclaimed Bumford. "Not I, sir. I'd not be likely to fetch that key when I've got my own—and without your reverence's knowledge either!"

"Well, I cannot find it anywhere," said Mr. Holland. "It generally lies on the mantelpiece at home, and it is not there this morning."

He went into the vestry with the last words. To hear that the church-key generally lay on the mantelpiece, was nothing; for the parson's house was not noticeable for order. There would have been none in it at all but for Edna.

Close upon that, arrived Shepherd, a folded paper in his hand. It contained a request that Gisby might be prayed for in the Litany.

"What, ain't he dead yet?" asked Bumford.

"No," returned Shepherd. "The doctors be afraid that internal inflammation's a-setting in now. Any way, he is rare and bad, poor man."

Next came in my set of singers, chiefly boys and girls from the parish school. But they sang better than such children generally sing; and would have sung very well indeed with an organist who had his head on his shoulders the proper way. Mrs. Todhetley had long taken pains with them, but latterly it had all been upset by Richards's crotchets.

"Now, look here," said I, gathering them before me. "We are not going to have any shrieking to-day. We sing to praise God, you know, and He is in the church with you and hears you; He is not a mile or two away, that you need shout out to be heard all that distance."

"Please, sir, Mr. Richards tells us to sing out loud: as loud as ever we can. Some on us a'most cracks our voices at it."

"Well, never mind Mr. Richards to-day. I am going to play, and I tell you to sing softly. If you don't, I shall stop the organ and let you shout by yourselves. You won't like that. To shout and shriek in church is more irreverent than I care to talk about."

"Please, sir, Mr. Richards plays the organ so loud that we can't help it."

"I wish you'd let Mr. Richards alone. You won't hear the organ loud to-day. Do you say your prayers when you go to bed at night?"

This question took them aback. But at last the whole lot answered that they did.

"And do you say your prayers softly, or do you shout them out at the top of your voices? To my mind, it is just as unseemly to shout when singing in church, as it would be when praying. This church has been like nothing lately but the ranter's chapel. There, take your seats, and look out the places in your Prayer-books."

I watched the different groups walk into church. Our people were pretty early. Tod slipped aside as they went up the aisle to whisper me a question—Had Fred got clear away? I told him I thought so, hearing and seeing nothing to the contrary. When the parson's children came in, Mrs. Holland was with them, so that Edna Blake was enabled to join the singers, as she did when she could. But it was not often Mrs. Holland came to church. Edna had dark circles round her eyes. They looked out at mine with a painful inquiry in their depths.

"Yes, I think it is all right," I nodded in answer.

"Mr. Holland has missed his church-key," she whispered. "Coming along to church, Charley suddenly called out that he remembered hiding it in Mr. Fred Westerbrook's coat-pocket. Mrs. Holland seemed quite put out about it, and asked me how I could possibly have allowed him to come into the study and sit there."

"There's old Westerbrook, Edna! Just look! His face is fiercer than usual."

Mrs. Westerbrook was with him, in a peach-coloured corded-silk gown. She made a point of dressing well. But she was just one of those women that no attire, good or bad, would set off: her face common, her figure stumpy. And so, one after another, the congregation all came in, and the service began. It caused quite a sensation when Mr. Holland made a pause, after turning to the Litany, and read out the announcement: "Your prayers are requested for Walter Gisby, who is dangerously ill." Men's heads moved, and bonnets fluttered.

"How I wish you played for us always, Johnny!" cried Miss Susan Page, looking in upon me to say it, as she passed out from her pew, when the service was over.

"Why, my playing is nothing, Miss Susan!"

"Perhaps not. I don't know. But it has this effect, Johnny—it sends us home with a feeling of peace in our hearts. What with Richards's crashing and the singers' shouting, we are generally turned out in a state of irritation."

After running through the voluntary, I found a large collection of people in the churchyard. Old Westerbrook was holding forth on the subject of Fred's iniquities to a numerous audience, the Squire making one of them. Mrs. Westerbrook looked simply malicious.

"No, I do not know where he is hiding," said the master of the N. D. Farm in answer to a question. "I wish I did know: I would hang him with all the pleasure in life. An ungrateful, reckless— What's that, Squire? You'd recommend me to increase the reward? Why, I have increased it. I have doubled it. Old Jones has my orders to post up fresh bills."

"If all's true that's reported, he can't escape very far; he had no money in his pocket," put in young Mr. Stirling, of the Court, who sometimes came over to our church. "By the way, who has been playing to-day?"

"Johnny Ludlow."

"Oh, have you, Johnny?" he said, turning to me. "It was very pleasant. And so was the singing."

"It would have been better had Mrs. Todhetley played—as she was to have done," I said, wishing they wouldn't bring me up before people, and knowing that my playing was just as simple as it could be, neither florid nor flowery.

"I have seen what Frederick Westerbrook was, this many a year past," broke in Mrs. Westerbrook in loud tones, as if resenting the drifting of the conversation from Fred's ill-doings. "Mr. Westerbrook knows that I have given him my opinion again and again. Only he would not listen."

"How could I believe that my own brother's son was the scamp you and Gisby made him out to be?" testily demanded old Westerbrook, who in his way was just as unsophisticated and straightforward as the Squire: and would have been as good-natured, let alone. "I'm sure till the last year or two Fred was as steady and dutiful as heart could wish."

"You had better say he is still," said she.

"But—hang it!—I don't say it, ma'am," fired old Westerbrook. "I should be a fool to say it. Unfortunately, I can't say it. I have lived to find he is everything that's bad—and I say that hanging's too good for him."

Mr. Holland came out of the church and passed us, halting a moment to speak. "I am on my way to pray by poor Gisby," he said. "They have sent for me."

"Gisby must need it," whispered Tod to me. "He has been a worse sinner than Fred Westerbrook: full of hatred, malice, and all uncharitableness."

And so he had been—in regard to Fred.

"Help! Thieves!—Robbers! Help!"

The shouts came from our yard, as we were sitting down to breakfast on Monday morning, and we rushed out. There stood Mack, in the greatest state of excitement possible; his eyes lifted, his arms at work, and his breath gone. The servants ran out before we did.

"Why! what on earth's the matter, Ben Mack?" demanded the Squire. "Have you gone mad?"

"We've had thieves in the barn, sir! Thieves! All my clothes is stole."

"What clothes?"

"Them what I left in't o' Saturday night, Squire. My smock-frock and my boots, and my spotted cotton neck-handkecher. They be gone, they be."

"Nonsense!" said the Squire, whilst I and Tod kept our faces. "We have not had thieves here, man."

"But, 'deed, and the things be gone, Squire. Clean gone! Not so much as a shred on 'em left! Please come and see for yourself, sir."

He turned, and went striding across the yard. The Squire followed, evidently at fault for comprehension; and the rest of us after him.

"It's a mercy as the horses and waggons bain't took!" cried Mack, plunging into the barn. "And the harness! look at it, a-hanging up; and that there wheelbarrer—"

"But what do you say is taken, Mack?" interrupted the Squire, cutting him short, and looking round the barn.

"All my traps, sir. My best smock-frock; and my boots, and my spotted cotton neck-handkecher. A beautiful pair o' boots, Squire, that I generally keeps here, in case I be sent off to Alcester, or Evesham, or where not, and have to tidy myself up a bit."

Tod backed out of the barn doubled up. Nearly choking at the "beautiful" boots.

"But why do you think they are stolen, Mack?" the Squire was asking.

"I left 'em safe here o' Saturday evening, sir, when I locked up the barn. The things be all gone now; you may see as they be, Squire. There bain't a vestige of 'em."

"Have any of the men moved them?"

"'Twas me as unlocked the barn myself but now, Squire. The key on't was on the nail where I put it Saturday night. If any of the men had unlocked it afore me this morning, they'd not ha' shut it up again. We've all been away at work too on t'other side o' the land since we come on at six o'clock. No, sir, it's thieves—and what will become of me? A'most a new smock-frock, and the beautifulest pair o' strong boots: they'd ha' lasted me for years."

Tod shrieked out at last, unable to help himself. Mack cast a reproachful glance at him, as if he thought the merriment too cruel.

"You must have been drinking on Saturday, Ben Mack, and fancied you left 'em here," put in Molly, tartly.

"Me been a-drinking!" retorted poor bereaved Mack, ready to cry at the aspersion. "Why, I'd never had a drop o' nothing inside my lips since dinner-time, save a draught of skim milk as the dairy-maid gave me. They was in that far corner, them boots; and the smock-frock was laid smooth across the shaft of this here cart, the handkecher folded a-top on't."

"Well, well, we must inquire after the things," remarked the Squire, turning to go back to breakfast. "I don't believe they are stolen, Mack: they'll be found somewhere. If you had lost yourself, you could not have made more noise over it. I'm sure I thought the ricks must be on fire."

Tod could hardly eat his breakfast for laughing. Every now and then he came out with the most unexpected burst. The pater demanded what there was to laugh at in Mack's having mislaid his clothes.

But, as the morning went on, the Squire changed his tone. When no trace could be discovered of the articles, high or low, he took up the opinion that we had been visited by tramps, and sent off for old Jones the constable. Jones sent back his duty, and he would come across as soon as he could, but he was busy organizing the search after Master Westerbrook, and posting up the fresh bills.

"Johnny, we must dispose of that hair of Fred's in some way," Tod whispered to me in the course of the morning. "To let any one come upon it would never do: they might fish and ferret out everything. Come along."

We went up, bolted ourselves in his room, and undid the hair. Fine, silky hair, not quite auburn, not quite like chestnut, something between the two, but as nice a colour as you would wish to see.

"Better burn it," suggested Tod.

"Won't it make an awful smell?"

"Who cares? You can go away if you don't like the smell."

"I shall save a piece for Edna Blake."

"Rubbish, Johnny! What good will it do her?"

"She may like to have it. Especially if she never sees him again."

"Make haste, then, and take a lock. It's quite romantic. I am going to put a match to it."

I chose the longest piece I could see, put it into an envelope, and fastened it up. Tod turned the hair into his wash-hand basin, and set it alight: the grate was filled up with the summer shavings. A frizzling and fizzing set in at once: and very soon a rare smell of singeing.

"Open the window, Johnny."

I had hardly opened it, when the handle of the door was turned and turned, and the panel thumped at. Hannah's voice came shrieking through the keyhole.

"Mr. Joseph!—Master Johnny! Are you both in there? What's the matter?"

"What should be the matter?" called back Tod, putting his hand over my mouth that I should not speak. "Go back to your nursery."

"There's something burning! My goodness! it's just as if all the blankets in the house were singeing! You've been setting your blankets on fire, Mr. Joseph!"

"And if I have!" cried Tod, blowing away at the hair to make it burn the quicker. "They are not yours."

"Good patience! you'll burn us all up, sir! Fire—fire!" shrieked out Hannah, frightened beyond her wits. "For goodness' sake, Miss Lena, keep away from the keyhole! Here, ma'am! Ma'am! Here's Mr. Joseph with all his blankets on fire!"

Mrs. Todhetley ran up the stairs, and her terrified appeal came to our ears through the door. Tod threw it open. The hair had burnt itself out.

"Why don't you go off for the parish engine?" demanded Tod of Hannah, as they came sniffing in. "Well, where's the fire?"

"But, my dears, something must be singeing," said Mrs. Todhetley. "Where is it?—what is it?"

"It can't be anything but the blankets," cried Hannah, choking and stifling. "Miss Lena, then, don't I tell you to keep outside, out of harm's way? Well, it is strong!"

Mrs. Todhetley put her hand on my arm. "Johnny, what is it? Where is the danger?"

"There's no danger at all," struck in Tod. "I suppose I can burn some old fishing-tackle rubbish in my basin if I please—horsehair, and that. You should not have the grates filled with paper, ma'am, if you don't like the smell."

She went to the basin, found the smell did come from it, and then looked at us both. I was smiling, and it reassured her.

"You might have taken it to the kitchen and burnt it there, Joseph," she said mildly. "Indeed, I was very much alarmed."

"Thanks to Hannah," said Tod. "You'd have known nothing about it but for her. I wish you'd just order her to mind her own business."

"It was my business, Mr. Joseph—smelling all that frightful smell of singeing! And if— Why, whose boots are these?" broke off Hannah.

Opening the closet to get out the hair, we had left Fred's boots exposed. Hannah's eyes, ranging themselves round in search of the singeing, had espied them. She answered her own question.

"You must have brought them from school in your box by mistake. Mr. Joseph. These are men's boots, these are!"

"I can take them back to school again," said Tod, carelessly.

So that passed off. "And it is the best thing we can do with the boots, Johnny, as I think," he said to me in a low tone when we were once more left to ourselves. "We can't burn them. They'd make a choicer scent than the hair made."

"I suppose they wouldn't fit Mack?"

Tod laughed.

"If he kept those other 'beautiful boots' for high days and holidays, what would he not keep these for? No, Johnny; they are too slender for Mack's foot."

"I wonder how poor Fred likes his clumsy ones?—how he contrives to tramp it in them?"

"I would give something to know that he was clear out of the country."

Dashing over to the Parsonage under pretence of saying good-bye to the children, I gave the envelope containing the lock of hair to Edna, telling her what it was. The colour rushed into her face, the tears to her eyes.

"Thank you, Johnny," she said softly. "Yes, I shall like to keep it—just a little memorial of him. Most likely we shall never meet again."

"I should just take up the other side of the question, Edna, and look forward to meeting him."

"Not here, at any rate," she answered. "How could he ever come back to England with this dreadful charge hanging over him? Good luck to you this term, Johnny Ludlow. Sometimes I think our school-days are our happiest."

We were to dine in the middle of the day, and start for school at half-past two. Tod boldly asked the Squire to give him a sovereign, apart from any replenishing of his pockets that might take place at starting. He wanted it for a particular purpose, he said.

And the pater, after holding forth a bit about thrift versus extravagance, handed out the sovereign. Tod betook himself to the barn. There sat Mack on the inverted wheelbarrow, at his dinner of cold bacon and bread, and looking most disconsolate.

"Found the things, Mack?"

"Me found 'em, Mr. Joseph! No, sir; and I bain't ever likely to find 'em, that's more. They are clean walked off, they are. When I thinks o' them there beautiful boots, and that there best smock-frock, I be fit to choke, I be!"

Tod was fit to choke, keeping his countenance. "What was their value, Mack?"

"They were of untold val'e, sir, to me. I'd not hardly ha' lost 'em for a one-pound note."

"Would a pound replace them?"

Mack, drawing his knife across the bread and bacon, looked up. Tod spoke more plainly.

"Could you buy new ones with a pound?"

"Bless your heart, sir, and where be I to get a pound from? I was just a-calkelating how long it 'ud take me to save enough money up—"

"I wish you'd answer my question, Mack. Would a pound replace the articles that have been stolen?"

"Why, in course it would, sir," returned Mack, staring. "But where be I—"

"Don't bother. Look here: there's a pound"—tossing the sovereign to him. "Buy yourself new ones, and think no more of the old ones."

Mack could not believe his eyes or ears. "Oh, Mr. Joseph! Well, I never! Sir, you be—"

"But now, understand this much, Mack. I only give you the money on one condition—that you say nothing about it. Tell nobody."

"Well, I never, Mr. Joseph! A whole golden pound! Why, sir, it'll set me up reg'lar in—"

"If you don't attend to what I am saying, Mack, I'll take it away again. You are not to tell any one that you have had it, do you hear?"

"Sir, I'll never tell a blessed soul."

"Very well. I shall expect you to keep your word. Once let it be known that your lost clothes have been replaced, and we should have the rest of the men losing theirs on speculation. So keep a silent tongue in your head; to the Squire as well as to others."

"Bless your heart, Mr. Joseph! I'll take care, sir. Nobody shan't know on't from me. When the wife wants to ferret out where I got 'em, I'll swear to her I've went in trust for 'em. And I'm sure I thank ye, sir, with all my—"

Tod walked away, cutting the thanks short.

As we were turning out at the gates on our way back to school, Tod driving Bob and Blister (which he much liked to do, though it was not always the Squire trusted him) and Giles sitting behind us, Duffham was coming along on his horse. Tod pulled up, and asked what was the latest news of Gisby.

"Well, strange to say, we are beginning to have some faint hopes of him," replied the doctor. "There's no doubt that at mid-day he was a trifle easier and better."

"That's good news," said Tod. "The man is a detestable sneak, but of course one does not want him to die. Save him if you can, Mr. Duffham—for Fred Westerbrook's sake. Good-bye."

"God-speed you both," returned Duffham. "Take care of those horses. They are fresh."

Tod gently touched the two with the whip, and called back a saucy word. He particularly resented any reflection on his driving.

A year went by. We were at home for the Michaelmas holidays again. And who should chance to call at the Manor the very day of our arrival but old Westerbrook.

Changes had taken place at the N. D. Farm. Have you ever observed that when our whole heart is set upon a thing, our entire aims and actions are directed to bringing it about, it is all quietly frustrated by that Finger of Fate that none of us, whether prince or peasant, can resist? Mrs. Westerbrook had been doing her best to move heaven and earth to encompass the deposition of Fred Westerbrook for her own succession, and behold she could not. Just as she had contrived that Fred should be crushed, and she herself put into old Westerbrook's will in his place, as the inheritor of the N. D. Farm and all its belongings, Heaven rendered her work nugatory by taking her to itself.

Yes, Mrs. Westerbrook was dead. She was carried off after a rather short illness: and Mr. Westerbrook was a widower, bereaved and solitary.

He was better off without her. The home was ten times more peaceful. He felt that: but he felt it to be very lonely; and he more than once caught himself wishing Fred was back again. Which of course meant wishing that he had never gone away, and never turned out to be a scamp.

Gisby did not die. Gisby had recovered in process of time, and was now more active on the farm than ever. Rather too active, its master was beginning dimly to suspect. Gisby seemed to haunt him. Gisby assumed more power than was at all necessary; and Gisby never ceased to pour into Mr. Westerbrook's ear reiterations of Fred's iniquity. Altogether, Mr. Westerbrook was growing a bit tired of Gisby. He had taken to put him down with curtness; and once when Gisby ventured to hint that it might be a convenient arrangement if he took up his abode in the house, Mr. Westerbrook swore at him. As to Fred, he was still popularly looked upon as cousin-german to the fiend incarnate.

Nothing had been heard of him. Nothing of any kind since that moonlight night when he had made his escape. Waiting for news from him so long, and waiting in vain, I, and Tod with me, had at last made up our minds that nothing more ever would be heard of him in this world. In short, that he had slipped out of it. Perhaps been starved out of it. Starved to death.

Well, Mr. Westerbrook called at the Manor within an hour of our getting home for Michaelmas, just twelve months after the uproar.

To me, he looked a good deal changed: his manner was quiet and subdued, almost as though he no longer took much interest in life; his hair had turned much greyer, and he complained of a continual pain in the left leg, which made him stiff, and sometimes prevented him from walking. Duffham called it a touch of rheumatism. Mr. Westerbrook fancied it might be an indication of something worse.

"But you have walked here, Westerbrook!" remarked the Squire.

"And shall walk back again—round by the village," he said. "It seems to me to be just this, Squire—that if I do not make an effort to walk while I can, I may be laid aside for good."

He gave a deep sigh as he spoke, as if he had the care of the whole parish upon him. The Squire began talking of the crop of oats on the N. D. Farm, saying what a famous crop it was.

"You'll net a good penny by them this year, Westerbrook."

"Passable," was the indifferent reply. "Good crops no longer bring me the satisfaction they did, Squire. I've nobody to save for now. Will you spend a day with me before you go back, young gentlemen?" he went on, turning to us. "Come on Friday. It is pretty lonely there. It wants company to enliven it."

And we promised we would go.

He said good-bye, and I went with him, to help him over the stile into the lane, on account of his stiffness—for that was the road he meant to take to Church Dykely. In passing the ricks he laid his hand on my shoulder.

"You won't mind a lonely day with a lonely old man?"

"We shall like it, sir. We will do our best to enliven you."

"It is not much that will do that now, Johnny Ludlow," said he. "When a man gets to my age, and feels his health and strength failing, it seems hard to be left all alone."

"No doubt it does, sir. I wish you had Fred back again!" I boldly added.

"Hush, Johnny! Fred is lost to me for good. He made his own bed, you know, and is lying on it. As I have to lie on mine—such as it is. Such as he left to me!"

"Do you know where Fred is, sir?"

"Do I know where Fred is?" he repeated in a tart tone. "How should I be likely to know? How could I know? I have never heard tidings of him, good or bad, since that wretched night."

We had reached the stile. Old Westerbrook rested his arms upon the top of it instead of getting over, tapping the step on the other side with his thick walking-stick.

"Gisby's opinion is that Fred threw himself into the first deep pond that lay in his way that night, and so put an end to his career for good," said he. "My late wife thought so too."

"Don't you believe anything of the kind, sir," said I, in hot impulse.

"It is what Gisby is always dinning into me, Johnny. I hate to hear him. With all Fred's faults, he was not one to fly to that extremity, under—"

"I am quite sure he was not, sir. And did not."

"Under ordinary circumstances, I was about to say," went on the old gentleman, with apathy, as he put one foot on the stile. "But when a man has the crime of murder upon his soul, there's no answering for what he may be tempted to do in his remorse and terror."

"It was not murder at all, sir. Gisby is well again."

"But it was thought to be murder at the time. Who would have given a brass button for Gisby's life that night? Don't quibble, Master Johnny."

"Gisby was shot, sir; there's no denying that, or that he might have died of it; but I am quite sure it was not Fred who shot him."

"Tush!" said he, testily. "Help me over."

I wished I dared tell him all. Jumping across myself, I assisted him down. Not that it would have answered any end if I did tell.

"Shall I walk with you as far as the houses, sir?"

"No, thank ye, lad. I want to be independent as long as I can. Come you both over in good time on Friday. Perhaps we can get an hour or two's shooting."

Friday came, and we had rather a jolly day than not, what with shooting and feasting. Gisby drew near to join us in the cover, but his master civilly told him that he was not wanted and need not hinder his time in looking after us. Never a word did old Westerbrook say that day of Fred, and he put on his best spirits to entertain us.

But in going away at night, when Tod had gone round to get the bag of partridges, which old Westerbrook insisted on our taking home, he suddenly spoke to me. We were standing at his front-door under the starlight.

"What made you say the other day that Fred was not guilty?"

"Because, sir, I feel sure he was not. I am as sure of it as though Heaven had shown it to me."

"He was with the gang of poachers: Gisby saw him shoot," said the old man, with emphasis.

"Gisby may have been mistaken. And Fred's having been with the poachers at the moment was, I think, accidental."

"Then why, if not guilty, did he go away?"

"Fear sent him. What would his word have been against Gisby's dying declaration? You remember what a hubbub there was, sir—enough to frighten any man away, however innocent he might be."

"Allow, for argument's sake, that your theory is correct, and that he was frightened into going into hiding, why does he not come out of it? Gisby is alive and well again."

Ah, I could not speak so confidently there. "I think he must be dead, sir," I said, "and that's the truth. If he were not, some of us would surely have heard of him."

"I see," said the old gentleman, looking straight up at the stars. "We are both of the same mind, Johnny—that he is dead. I say he might have died that night: you think he went away first and died afterwards. Not much difference between us, is there?"

I thought there was a great deal; but I could not tell him why. "I wish we could hear of him, sir—and be at some certainty."

"So do I, Johnny Ludlow. He was brought up at my knee; as my own child."

On our way home, Tod with the bag of game slung over his shoulder, we came upon Mr. Holland near the Parsonage, with Edna Blake and the children. They had been to Farmer Page's harvest-home. Whilst the parson talked to Tod, Edna snatched a moment with me.

"Have you heard any news, Johnny?"

"Of him? Never. We can't make it out."

"Perhaps we never shall hear," she sighed. "Even if he reached the coast in safety, he may not have got over to the other side. A great many wrecks took place about that time: our weekly paper was full of them. It was the time of the equinoctial gales, and—"

"Come along, Johnny!" called out Tod, at this juncture. "We must get on. Good-night, Edna: good-night, you youngsters."

The next day, Saturday, we went to Worcester, the Squire driving us, and there saw Gisby as large as life. The man had naturally great assumption of manner, and latterly he had taken to dress in the fashion. He was looming up High Street, booted and spurred, his silver-headed whip in his hand. Taking off his hat with an air, he wished the Squire a loud good-morning, as if the town belonged to him, and we were only subjects in it.

"I should think Westerbrook has never been fool enough to make his will in Gisby's favour!" remarked the Squire, staring after him. "Egad, though, it looks like it!"

"It is to be hoped, sir, that he would make it in Fred's," was Tod's rejoinder. And the suggestion put the pater out.

"Make it in Fred's," he retorted, going into one of his heats, and turning sharply round on the crowded pavement near the market-house, by which he came into contact with two women and their big butter-baskets. "What do you mean by that, sir? Fred Westerbrook is beyond the pale of wills, and all else. It's not respectable to mention his name. He—bless the women! What on earth are these baskets at?"

They seemed to be playing at bumps with the Squire; baskets thick and threefold. Tod went in to the rescue, and got him out.

It was a strange thing. It really was. Considering that for the past day or two something or other had arisen to bring up thoughts of Fred Westerbrook, it was strange that the strangest of all things in connection with him was yet to come.

Sitting round the fire after supper, upon getting home from Worcester—it is a long drive, you know—and Tod had gone up to bed, dead tired, who should walk in but Duffham. He would not sit down, had no time; but told his business hastily. Dick Standish was dying, and had something on his conscience.

"I would have heard his confession," said Duffham, "as I have heard that of many another dying man; but he seems to wish to make it to a magistrate. Either to a magistrate, or to old Mr. Westerbrook, he urged. But there's no time to go up to the N. D. Farm, so I came for you, Squire."

"Bless me!" cried the Squire, starting up in a commotion—for he thought a great deal of his magisterial duties, and this was a very unusual call. "Dick Standish dying! What can he have to say? He has been nothing but a poacher all his life, poor fellow! And what has Westerbrook to do with him?"

"Well," said Duffham, in his equable way, "it strikes me that what he wants to say may affect Fred. Perhaps Standish can clear him."

"Clear Fred Westerbrook!—clear an iniquitous young man who could turn poacher and murderer! What next will you say, Duffham? Here, Johnny, get my hat and coat. Dear me! Take down a confession! I wonder whether there'll be any ink there?"

"Let me go with you, sir!" I said eagerly. "I will take my little pocket-inkstand—and some paper—and—and—everything likely to be wanted. Please let me go!"

"Well, yes, you can, Johnny. Don't forget a Bible. Ten to one if he has one."

There were three brothers of these Standishes, Tom, Jim, and Dick, none of them particularly well-doing. Tom was no better than a sort of tramp, reappearing in the village only by fits and starts; Jim, who had married Mary Picker, was likewise given to roving abroad, until found and brought back by the parish; Dick, as the Squire phrased it, was nothing but a poacher, and made his home mostly with Jim and Mary.

The cottage—a tumble-down lodgment that they did not trouble themselves to keep in repair—was at our end of the parish half-a-mile away, and we put our best feet foremost.

Dick lay upon the low bed in the loft. His illness had been very short and sharp; it was scarcely a week yet since he was taken with it. Duffham had done his best; but the man was dying. Jim Standish was off on one of his roving expeditions, neither the parish nor the public knowing whither.

The Squire sat by the bed, taking down the man's confession at a small table, by the light of a small candle. I and Duffham stood to hear it; Mary Standish was sent down to the kitchen. What he said cleared Fred Westerbrook—Duffham had no doubt gathered so much before he came for the Squire.

Just what Fred had told us of the events of the night, Dick Standish confirmed now. He and other poachers were out, he said, his brother Tom for one. They had bagged some game, and were about to disperse when they encountered Mr. Fred Westerbrook. He stayed talking with them, walking the same way that they did, when lo! they all fell into the ambush planned by Gisby. A fight ensued; and he—he, Dick Standish, now speaking, conscious that he was dying—he fired his gun at them, and the shot entered Gisby. They ran away then and were not pursued; a gun was fired after them, and it struck his brother Tom, but not to hurt him very much: not enough to disable him. He and Tom made themselves scarce at once, before daylight; and they did not come back till danger was over, and Gisby about again. Old Jones and other folks had come turning the cottage inside out at the time in search of him (Dick), but his brother Jim swore through thick and thin that Dick had not been at home for ever so long. The Squire took all this down; and Dick signed it.

I was screwing the little inkstand up to return it to my pocket, when Mr. Holland entered, Mary Standish having sent for him. Leaving him with the sick man, we came away.

"Johnny, do you know, we might almost have made sure Fred Westerbrook was not guilty," said the Squire, quite humbly, as we were crossing the turnip-field. "But why on earth did he run away? Where is he?"

"I think he must be dead, sir. What news this will be for Mr. Westerbrook."

"Dear me yes! I shall go to him with it in the morning."

When the morning came—which was Sunday—the Squire was so impatient to be off that he could hardly finish his breakfast. The master of the N. D. Farm, who no longer had energy or health to keep the old early hours, was only sitting down to his breakfast when the Squire got there. In his well-meaning but hot way, he plunged into the narrative so cleverly that old Westerbrook nearly had a fit.

"Not guilty!" he stammered, when he came to himself. "Fred not guilty! Only met the poachers by accident!—was not the man that shot Gisby! Why, that's what Johnny Ludlow was trying to make me believe only a day or two ago!"

"Johnny was? Oh, he often sees through a stone wall. It's true, anyway, Westerbrook. Fred never had a gun in his hand that night."

"Then—knowing himself innocent, why on earth does he stay away?"

"Johnny thinks he must be dead," replied the Squire.

Old Westerbrook gave a groan of assent. His trembling hands upset a cupful of coffee on the table-cloth.

They came on to church together arm-in-arm. Mr. Holland joined them, and told the news—Dick Standish was dead: had died penitent. Penitent, so far as might be, in the very short time he had given to repentance, added the clergyman.

But knowing that Fred was innocent seemed to have renewed his uncle's lease of life. He was altogether a different man. The congregation felt quite electrified by some words read out by Mr. Holland before the General Thanksgiving: "Thomas Westerbrook desires to return thanks to Almighty God for a great mercy vouchsafed to him." Whispering to one another in their pews, under cover of the drooped heads, they asked what it meant, and whether Fred could have come home? The report of Dick Standish's confession had been heard before church: and Gisby and Shepherd received some hard words for having so positively laid the deed on Fred.

"I declare to goodness I thought it was Mr. Fred that fired!" said Shepherd, earnestly. "Moonlight's deceptive, in course: but I know he was close again' the gun."

Yes, he was close to the gun: Dick Standish had said that much. Mr. Fred was standing next him when he fired; Mr. Fred had tried to put out his arm to stop him, but wasn't quick enough, and called him a villain for doing it.

I was taking the organ again that day, if it concerns any one to know it, and gave them the brightest chants and hymns the books contained. The breach with Mr. Richards had never been healed, and the church had no settled organist. Sometimes Mrs. Holland took it; sometimes Mrs. Todhetley; once it was a stranger, who volunteered, and broke down over the blowing; and during the holidays, if we spent them at the Manor, it was chiefly turned over to me.

The Squire made old Westerbrook walk back to dine with us. Sitting over a plate of new walnuts afterwards—there was not much time for dessert on Sundays, before the afternoon service—Tod, calling upon me to confirm it, told all about Fred's hiding in the church, and how he had got away. But we did not say anything of the money given him by Edna Blake: she might not have liked it. The Squire stared with surprise, and seemed uncertain whether to praise us or to blow us up sharply.

"Shut up in the church for three days and nights! Nothing to eat, except what you could crib for him! Got away at last in Mack's smock-frock and boots! Well, you two are a pair of pretty conjurers, you are!"

"God bless 'em both for it!" cried old Westerbrook.

"But they ought to have told me, you know, Westerbrook. I could have managed much better—helped the poor fellow off more effectually."

Tod gave me a kick under the table. He was nearly splitting, at hearing the Squire say this.

The first thing Mr. Westerbrook did was to insert sundry advertisements in the Times and other newspapers, about a hundred of them, begging and imploring his dear nephew (sometimes he worded it his "dear boy") to return to him. Always underneath this advertisement wherever it appeared was inserted another: stating that all the particulars of the poaching affray which took place on a certain date (mentioning it) were known; that the poacher, Richard Standish, who shot Walter Gisby had confessed the crime, and that Gisby had not died of his wounds, but recovered from them. This was done with the view of letting Fred know that he might come back with safety. But he never came. The advertisements brought forth no answer of any kind.

The master of the N. D. Farm became very short with his bailiff as time went on. There was no reason to suppose that Gisby had intentionally accused Fred of the shot—he had really supposed it to come from Fred; nevertheless, Mr. Westerbrook took a great dislike to him, and was very short and crusty with him. Gisby did not like that, and they had perpetual rows. When we got home for the Christmas holidays, it was thought that Gisby would not be long on the N. D. Farm.

"Johnny, I want to tell you! I have had a letter. From him."

The whisper came from Edna Blake. It was Christmas Eve; and we were in the church, a lot of us, sticking the branches of holly in the pews. The leaves had never seemed so green or the berries so red.

"Not from Fred?"

"Yes, I have. It came addressed to me about a week ago, with a ten-pound Bank of England note enclosed. There was only a line or two, just saying he had not been able to return it before, but that he hoped he was at length getting on: and that if he did get on, he should be sure to write again later. It was signed F. W. That was all. Neither his name was mentioned, nor mine, nor any address."

"Where did it come from?"

"London, I think."

"From London! Nonsense, Edna!"

"The post-mark was London. You are welcome to see the letter. I have brought it with me."

Drawing the letter from her pocket under cover of her mantle, I took it to the porch. True enough; the letter had undoubtedly been posted in London. Calling Tod, we talked a little, and then told Edna that we both thought she ought to disclose this to Mr. Westerbrook.

"I think so too," she said, "but I should not like to tell him myself—though his manner to me lately has been very kind. Will you tell him, Johnny? I will lend you the letter to show him. He will be sure to want to see it."

"And he will have to know about the gold, Edna. The loan of that night."

"Yes; it cannot be helped. I have thought it all over, and I see that there's no help for its being known now. The letter alludes to it, you perceive."

After that the advertisements were resumed. Mr. Westerbrook put some solicitor in London to work, and they were inserted in every known paper. Also in some of the American and Australian papers.

Inquiries were made after Fred in London. But nothing came of it. As to old Westerbrook, he seemed to grow better, as if the suspense had stirred him up.

The months went on. Neither Fred nor news of him turned up. That he was vegetating somewhere beyond the pale of civilization, or else was at length really dead, appeared to be conclusive.

July. And we boys at home again for the holidays. The first news told us was, that Mr. Westerbrook and his bailiff had parted company. Gisby had said farewell to the N. D. Farm.

In the satisfaction of finding himself sole master, which he had not been for many a year, and to celebrate Gisby's departure, Mr. Westerbrook gave a syllabub feast, inviting to it old and young, grown people and children. Syllabub feasts were tolerably common with us.

It was an intensely hot day; the lawn was dotted with guests; most of them gathered in groups under the trees in the shade. Old Westerbrook, the Squire and Mrs. Todhetley, Parson and Mrs. Holland and Mr. Brandon were together under the great horse-chestnut tree. Edna Blake, of course, had the trouble of the parson's children, and I was talking to her. Little tables with bowls of syllabub on them and cakes and fruit stood about. By-and-by, at sunset or so, we were to go in to a high tea.

It was getting on for two years since the night of Fred Westerbrook's departure; and Edna was looking five times two years older. Worn and patient were the lines of her face. She was dressed rather poorly, as usual. She had never dressed much otherwise: but since that unlucky night her clothes had been made to last as I should think nobody else's clothes ever lasted. Whether that ten pounds had absorbed all her funds (as it most likely had), or whether Edna had been saving up for that visionary, possible voyage to America and the home with Fred that was to follow it, I knew not, but one never saw her in new things now. To-day she wore a muslin that once had had rose-red spots on it, but repeated washings had diluted them to a pale pink; and the pink ribbons on her hat had faded too. Not but that, in spite of all, she looked a lady.

"Have you a headache, Edna?"

"Just a little," she answered, putting her hand to her head. "Charley and Tom would race about as we came along, and I had to run after them. To be much under a blazing sun often gives me a headache now."

I wondered to myself why the parson and his wife could not have ordered Charley and Tom to be still. Fathers and mothers never think their children can tire people.

"I want some more syllabub, Edna," cried Charley, just then.

"And me too," put in little Miles Stirling.

She got up patiently; ladled some of the stuff into two of the custard-cups, and gave one to each of the children, folding her handkerchief under little Stirling's chin to guard his velvet dress. They stood at the table, two eager little cormorants, taking it in with their tea-spoons.

At that moment, the gate behind us opened, and a gentleman came in. We turned round to see who was arriving so late. A stranger. Some good-looking fellow, with auburn hair, a beard that shone like soft silk in the sun, and a bronzed face. To judge by his movements, he was struck with surprise at sight of the gay company, and stood in evident hesitation.

"Oh, Johnny!"

The low, half-terrified exclamation came from Edna. I turned to her. Her eyes were strained on the stranger; her face had turned white as death. He saw us then, and came towards us. We were the nearest to him.

"Do you know me, Edna?"

I knew him then: knew his voice. Ay, and himself also, now that I saw him distinctly. Edna did not faint; though she was white enough for it: she only put her hands together as one does in prayer, a joyous thankfulness dawning in her eyes.

"Frederick?"

"Yes, my darling. How strange that you should be the first to greet me! And you, Johnny, old fellow! You have grown!"

His two hands lay for a time in mine and Edna's. No one had observed him yet: we were at the end of the lawn, well under the trees.

"More syllabub, Edna!" shrieked out that greedy young Charley.

"And me want more, too," added little Miles; "me not had enough."

Edna drew her hand away to go to the table, a happy light shining through her tears. Fred put his arm within mine, and we went across the grass together.

The first to see him was Mr. Brandon. He took in the situation at once, and in a degree prepared Mr. Westerbrook. "Here's some bronzed young man coming up, Westerbrook," said he. "Looks like a traveller. I should not be surprised if it is your nephew; or perhaps one who brings news of him."

Old Westerbrook fell back in his chair, as Fred stood there with his two hands stretched out to him. Then he sprang up, burst into tears, and clasped Fred in his arms. Of all commotions! Mr. Brandon walked away out of it into the sun, putting his yellow silk handkerchief on his head. The Squire stared as if he had never seen a bronzed man before; Tod came leaping up, and the best part of the company after him.

"Edna, Edna!" called out Mr. Westerbrook, sitting back in his chair again, and holding Fred tightly. "Edna, I want you instantly."

She advanced modestly, blushing roses, her hat held in her hand by its faded strings. Mr. Westerbrook looked at her through his tears.

"Here he is, my dear—do you see?—come back to us at last. We must both welcome him. The homestead is yours from this day, Fred; I will have only just a corner in it. I am too old now for a busy life: you must be the acting master. And, Edna, my child, you will come here to be his helpmeet in it, and to take care of me in my declining years—my dear little daughter! Thank God for all things!"

Fred gave us just a brief summary of the past. Getting over to America without much difficulty, he had sought there for some remunerative work, and sought in vain. One of those panics that the Americans go in for had recently occurred in the States, and numbers of men were unable to get employment. After sundry adventures, and some semi-starvation, he at length made his way to the West Indies. A cousin of his late mother was, he knew, settled somewhere within the regions of British Guiana. He found him in Berbice, a small merchant of New Amsterdam. To him Fred told his whole story; and the old cousin gave him a berth in his counting-house. Office-work was new to Fred; but he did his best; and with the first proceeds of his pay he enclosed the ten pounds to Edna; the house forwarding the letter to their agents in London, to be posted there. Some months later, he chanced to see the advertisement for him in an English newspaper. As soon as he was able, he came off to answer it in person; and—here he was.

"All's well that ends well," remarked Mr. Brandon, in his dry way.

"And don't you go fraternizing with poachers again, Mr. Fred!" cried out the Squire. "See what it brought you to the last time."

"No, Squire; never again," answered Fred, pushing back his auburn hair (very long again), with a smile. "This one time has been quite enough."

"But you cannot have Edna, you know," said Mrs. Holland to him, with a disturbed face. "The Parsonage could not possibly get on without her."

"I am afraid the Parsonage will have to try, Mrs. Holland."

"I shall be obliged to keep my bed; that will be the end of it," said Mrs. Holland, gloomily. "Nobody can manage the children but Edna. When she is otherwise occupied, their noise is frightful: ten times more distracting than the worst toothache."

Fred said nothing further; she was looking so ruefully woebegone. Putting his arm into mine, he turned into a shady walk.

"Will you be my groomsman at the wedding, Johnny? But for you, my good friend, I don't know that I should have been saved to see this day."

"Nay, Fred, I think it was the key of the church that saved you. I will be your groomsman if you really and truly prefer to pitch upon me, rather than on some one older and better."

"Yes, you are right," he answered, lifting his hat, and glancing upwards. "It was the key of the church—under God."

CHAPTER XVII

"I tell you it is," repeated Tod. "One cannot mistake Temple, even at a distance."

"But this man looks so much older than he. And he has whiskers. Temple had none."

"And has not Temple grown older, do you suppose; and don't whiskers sprout and grow? You are always a muff, Johnny. That is Slingsby Temple."

We had gone by rail to Whitney Hall, and were walking up from the station. The Squire sent us to ask after Sir John's gout. It was a broiling hot day in the middle of summer. On the lawn before the house, with some of the Whitneys, stood a stranger; a little man, young, dark, and upright.

Tod was right, and I was wrong. It was Slingsby Temple. But I thought him much altered: older-looking than his years, which numbered close upon twenty-five, and more sedate and haughty than ever. We had neither seen nor heard of him since quitting Oxford.

"Oh, he's regularly in for it this time," said Bill Whitney, in answer to inquiries about his father, as they shook hands with us. "He has hardly ever had such a bout; can only lie in bed and groan. Temple, don't you remember Todhetley and Johnny Ludlow?"

"Yes, I do," answered Temple, holding out his hand to me first, and passing by Tod to do it. But that was Slingsby Temple's way. I was of no account, and therefore it did not touch his pride to notice me.

"I am glad to see you again," he said to Tod, cordially enough, as he turned to him; which was quite a gracious acknowledgment for Temple.

But it surprised us to see him there. The Whitneys had no acquaintance with the Temples; neither had he and Bill been special friends at college. Whitney explained it after luncheon, when we were sitting outside the windows in the shade, and Temple was pacing the shrubbery with Helen.

"I fancy it's a gone case," said Bill, nodding towards them.

"Oh, William, you should not say it," struck in Anna, in tones of remonstrance, and with her pretty blush. "It is not sure—and not right to Mr. Temple."

"Not say it to Tod and Johnny! Rubbish! Why, they are like ourselves, Anna. I say I think it is going to be a case."

"Helen with another beau!" cried free Tod. "How has it all come about?"

"The mother and Helen have been staying at Malvern, you know," said Whitney. "Temple turned up at the same hotel, the Foley Arms, and they struck up an intimacy. I went over for the last week, and was surprised to see how thick he was with them. The mother, who is more unsuspicious than a goose, told Temple, in her hospitable way, when they were saying good-bye, that she should be glad to see him if ever he found himself in these benighted parts: and I'll be shot if at the end of five days he was not here! If Helen's not the magnet, I don't know what else it can be."

"He appears to like her; but it may be only a temporary fancy that will pass away; it ought not to be talked about," reiterated Anna. "It may come to nothing."

"It may, or may not," persisted Bill.

"Will she consent to have him?" I asked.

"She'd be simple if she didn't," said Bill. "Temple would be a jolly fine match for any girl. Good in all ways. His property is large, and he himself is as sober and steady as any parson. Always has been."

I was not thinking of Temple's eligibility—that was undeniable; but of Helen's inclinations. Some time before she had gone in for a love affair, which would not do at any price, caused some stir at the Hall, and came to signal grief: though I have not time to tell of it here. Whitney caught the drift of my thoughts.

"That's over and done with, Johnny. She'd never let its recollection spoil other prospects. You may trust Helen Whitney for that. She is as shallow-hearted as—"

"For shame, William!" remonstrated Anna.

"It's true," said he. "I didn't say you were. Helen would have twenty sweethearts to your one, and think nothing of it."

Tod looked at Anna, and laughed gently. Her cheeks turned the colour of the rose she was holding.

"What's this about a boating tour?" he inquired of Whitney. It had been alluded to at lunch-time.

"Temple's going in for one with some more fellows," was the reply. "He has asked me to join them. We mean to do some of the larger rivers; take our tent, and encamp on the bank at night."

"What a jolly spree!" cried Tod, his face flushing with delight. "How I should like it!"

"I wish to goodness you were coming. But Temple has made up his party. It is his affair, you know. He talks of staying out a month."

"One get's no chance in this slow place," cried Tod, fiercely. "I'll emigrate, I think, and go tiger-hunting. Is it a secret, this boating affair?"

"A secret! No."

"What made you kick me under the table, then, when I would have asked particulars at luncheon?"

"Because the mother was present. She has taken all sorts of queer notions into her head—mothers always have them—that the boat will be found bottom upwards some day, and we under it. Failing that, we are to catch colds and fevers and agues from the night encampments. So we say as little about it as possible before her."

"I see," nodded Tod. "Look here, Bill, I should like to get up a boating party myself; it sounds glorious. How do you set about it?—and where can you get a boat?"

"Temple knows," said Bill, "I don't. Let us go and ask him."

They went across the grass, leaving me alone with Anna. She and I were the best of friends, as the reader may remember, and exchanged many a little confidence with one another that the world knew nothing of.

"Should you like it for Helen?" I asked, indicating her sister and Slingsby Temple.

"Yes, I think I should," she answered. "But William had no warrant for speaking as he did. Mr. Temple will only be here a few days longer: when he leaves, we may never see him again."

"But he is evidently taken with Helen. He shows that he is. And when a man of Slingsby Temple's disposition allows himself to betray anything of the kind, rely upon it he means something."

"Did you like him at Oxford, Johnny?"

"Well—I did and did not," was my hesitating answer. "He was reserved, close, proud, and unsociable; and no man displaying those qualities can be very much liked. On the other hand, he was exemplary in conduct, deserving respect from all, and receiving it."

"I think he is religious," said Anna, her voice taking a lower tone.

"Yes, I always thought him that. I fancy their mother brought them up to be so. But Temple is the last man in the world to display it."

"What with papa's taking up two rooms to himself now he has the gout, and all of us being at home, mamma was a little at fault what chamber to give Mr. Temple. There was no time for much arrangement, for he came without notice; so she just turned Harry out of his room, which used to be poor John's, you know, and put Mr. Temple there. That night Harry chanced to go up to bed later than the rest of us. He forgot his room had been changed, and went straight into his own. Mr. Temple was kneeling down in prayer, and a Bible lay open on the table. Mamma says it is not all young men who say their prayers and read their Bible nowadays."

"Not by a good many, Anna. Yes, Temple is good, and I hope Helen will get him. She will have position, too, as his wife, and a large income."

"He comes into his estate this year, he told us; in September. He will be five-and-twenty then. But, Johnny, I don't like one thing: William says there was a report at Oxford that the Temples never live to be even middle-aged men."

"Some of them have died young, I believe. But, Anna, that's no reason why they all should."

"And—there's a superstition attaching to the family, is there not?" continued Anna. "A ghost that appears; or something of that sort?"

I hardly knew what to answer. How vividly the words brought back poor Fred Temple's communication to me on the subject, and his subsequent death.

"You don't speak," said she. "Won't you tell me what it is?"

"It is this, Anna: but I dare say it's all nonsense—all fancy. When one of the Temples is going to die, the spirit of the head of the family who last died is said to appear and beckon to him; a warning that his own death is near. Down in their neighbourhood people call it the Temple superstition."

"I don't quite understand," cried Anna, looking earnestly at me. "Who is it that is said to appear?"

"I'll give you an instance. When the late Mr. Temple, Slingsby's father, was walking home from shooting with his gamekeeper one September day, he thought he saw his father in the wood at a little distance: that is, his father's spirit, for he had been dead some years. It scared him very much at the moment, as the keeper testified. Well, Anna, in a day or two he, Mr. Temple, was dead—killed by an accident."

"I am glad I am not a Temple; I should be always fearing I might see the sight," observed Anna, a sad, thoughtful look on her gentle face.

"Oh no, you wouldn't, Anna. The Temples themselves don't think of it, and don't believe in it. Slingsby does not, at any rate. His brother Fred told me at Oxford that no one must presume to allude to it in Slingsby's presence."

"Fred? He died at Oxford, did he not?"

"Yes, he died there, poor fellow. Thrown from his horse. I saw it happen, Anna."

But I said nothing to her of that curious scene to which I had been a witness a night or two before the accident—when poor Fred, to Slingsby's intense indignation, fancied he saw his father on the college staircase; fancied his father beckoned to him. It was not a thing to talk of. After that time Slingsby had seemed to regard me with rather a special favour; I wondered whether it was because I had not talked of it.

The afternoon passed. We went up to see Sir John in his gouty room, and then said good-bye to them all, including Temple, and started for home again. Tod was surly and cross. He had come out in a temper and he was going back in one.

Tod liked his own way. No one in the world resented interference more than he: and just now he and the Squire were at war. Some twelve months before, Tod had dropped into a five-hundred-pound legacy from a distant relative. It was now ready to be paid to him. The Squire wished it paid over to himself, that he might take care of it; Tod wanted to be grand, and open a banking account of his own. For the past two days the argument had held out on both sides, and this morning Tod had lost his temper. Lost it was again now, but on another score.

"Slingsby Temple might as well have invited me to join the boating lot!" he broke out to me, as we drew near home. "He knows I am an old hand at it."

"But if his party is made up, Tod? Whitney said it was."

"Rubbish, Johnny. Made up! They could as well make room for another. And much good some of them are, I dare say! I can't remember that Slingsby ever took an oar in his hand at Oxford. All he went in for was star-gazing—and chapels—and lectures. And look at Bill Whitney! He hates rowing."

"Did you tell Temple you would like to join them?"

"He could see it. I didn't say in so many words, Will you have me? Of all things, I should enjoy a boating tour! It would be the most jolly thing on earth."

That night, after we got in, the subject of the money grievance cropped up again. The Squire was smoking his long churchwarden pipe at the open window; Mrs. Todhetley sat by the centre table and the lamp, hemming a strip of muslin. Tod, open as the day on all subjects, abused Temple's "churlishness" for not inviting him to make one of the boating party, and declared he would organize one of his own, which he could readily do, now he was not tied for money. That remark set the Squire on.

"Ay, that's just where it would be, Joe," said he. "Let you keep the money in your own fingers, and we should soon see what it would end in."

"What would it end in?" demanded Tod.

"Ducks and drakes."

Tod tossed his head. "You think I am a child still, I believe, father."

"You are no better, where the spending of money's concerned," said the Squire, taking a long whiff. "Few young men are. Their fathers know that, and keep it from them as long as they can. And that's why so many are not let come into possession of their estates before they are five-and-twenty. This young Temple, it seems, does not come into his; Johnny, here, does not."

"I should like to know what more harm it would do for the money to lie in my name in the Old Bank than if it lay in yours?" argued Tod. "Should I be drawing cheques on purpose to get rid of it? That's what you seem to suppose, father."

"You'd be drawing them to spend," said the pater.

"No, I shouldn't. It's my own money, after all. Being my own, I should take good care of it."

Old Thomas came in with some glasses, and the argument dropped. Tod began again as we were going upstairs together.

"You see, Johnny," he said, stepping inside my room on his way, and shutting the door for fear of eavesdroppers, "there's that hundred pounds I owe Brandon. The old fellow has been very good, never so much as hinting that he remembers it, and I shall pay him back the first thing. To do this, I must have absolute possession of the money. A fine bobbery the pater would make if he got to know of it. Besides, a man come to my age likes to have a banking account—if he can. Good-night, lad."

Tod carried his point. He turned so restive and obstinate over it as to surprise and vex the Squire, who of course knew nothing about the long-standing debt to Mr. Brandon. The Squire had no legal power to keep the money, if Tod insisted upon having it. And he did insist. The Squire put it down to boyish folly, self-assumption; and groaned and grumbled all the way to Worcester, when Tod was taking the five-hundred-pound cheque, paid to him free of duty, to the Old Bank.

"We shall have youngsters in their teens wanting to open a banking account next!" said the pater to Mr. Isaac, as Tod was writing his signature in the book. "The world's coming to something."

"I dare say young Mr. Todhetley will be prudent, and not squander it," observed Mr. Isaac, with one of his pleasant smiles.

"Oh, will he, though! You'll see. Look here," went on the Squire, tapping the banker on the arm, "couldn't you, if he draws too large a cheque at any time, refuse to cash it?"

"I fear we could not do that," laughed Mr. Isaac. "So long as he does not overdraw his account, we are bound to honour his cheques."

"And if you do overdraw it, Joe, I hope the bank will prosecute you!—I would, I know," was the Squire's last threat, as we left the bank and turned towards the Cross, Tod with a cheque-book in his pocket.

But Mr. Brandon could not be paid then. On going over to his house a day or two afterwards, we found him from home. The housekeeper thought he was on his way to one of the "water-cure establishments" in Yorkshire, she said, but he had not yet written to give his address.

"So it must wait," remarked Tod to me, as we went home. "I'm not sorry. How the bank would have stared at having to pay a hundred pounds down on the nail! Conclude, no doubt, that I was going to the deuce headlong."

"By Jove!" cried Tod, taking a leap in the air.

About a week had elapsed since the journey to the Old Bank, and Tod was opening a letter that had come addressed to him by the morning post.

"Johnny! will you believe it, lad? Temple asks me to be of the boating lot, after all."

It was even so. The letter was from Slingsby Temple, written from Templemore. It stated that he had been disappointed by some of those who were to have made up the number, and if Todhetley and Ludlow would supply their places, he should be glad.

Tod turned wild. You might have thought, as Mrs. Todhetley remarked, that he had been invited to Eden.

"The idea of Temple's asking you, Johnny!" he said. "You are of no good in a boat."

"Perhaps I had better decline?"

"No, don't do that, Johnny. It might upset the party altogether, perhaps. You must do your best."

"I have no boating-suit."

"I will treat you to one," said Tod, munificently. "We'll get it at Evesham. Pity but my things would fit you."

So it was, for he had loads of them.

The Squire, for a wonder, did not oppose the scheme. Mrs. Todhetley (like Lady Whitney) did, in her mild way. As Bill said, all mothers were alike—always foreseeing danger. And though she was not Tod's true mother, or mine either, she was just as anxious for us; and she looked upon it as nearly certain that one of us would come home drowned and the other with the ague.

"They won't sleep on the bare ground, of course," said Duffham, who chanced to call that morning, while Tod was writing his letter of acceptance to Slingsby Temple.

"Of course we shall," fired Tod, resenting the remark. "What harm could it do us?"

"Give some of you rheumatic-fever," said Duffham.

"Then why doesn't it give it to the gipsies?" retorted Tod.

"The gipsies are used to it—born to it, as one may say. You young men must have a waterproof sheet to lie upon, or a tarpaulin, or something of the sort."

Tod tossed his head, disdaining an answer, and wrote on.

"You will have plenty of rugs and great-coats with you, of course," went on Duffham. "And I'll give you a packet of quinine powders. It is as well to be prepared for contingencies. If you find any symptoms of unusual cold, or shivering, just take one or two of them."

"Look here, Mr. Duffham," said Tod, dashing his pen down on the table. "Don't you think you had better attend us yourself with a medicine-chest? Put up a cargo of rhubarb—and magnesia—and castor oil—and family pills. A few quarts of senna-tea might not come in amiss. My patience! I believe you take us for delicate infants."

"And I should recommend you to carry a small keg of whisky amongst the boat stores," continued Duffham, not in the least put out. "You'll want it. Take a nip of it neat when you first get up from the ground in the morning. It is necessary you should, and it will ward off some evils that might otherwise arise. Johnny Ludlow, I'll put the quinine into your charge: mind you don't forget it."

"Of all the old women!" muttered Tod to me. "Had the pater been in the room, this might have set him against our going."

On the following day we went over to Whitney Hall, intending to take Evesham on our way back, and buy what was wanted. Surprise the first. Bill Whitney was not at home, and was not to be of the boating party.

"You never saw any one in such a way in your life," cried Helen, who could devote some time to us, now Temple was gone. "I must say it was too bad of papa. He never made any objection while Mr. Temple was here, but let poor William anticipate all the pleasure; and then he went and turned round afterwards."

"Did he get afraid for him?" cried Tod, in wonder. "I wouldn't have thought it of Sir John."

"Afraid! no," returned Helen, opening her eyes. "What he got was a fit of the gout. A relapse."

"What has the gout to do with Bill?"

"Why, old Featherston ordered papa to Buxton, and papa said he could not do without William to see to him there: mamma was laid up in bed with one of her bad colds—and she is not out of it yet. So papa went off, taking William—and you should just see how savage he was."

For William Whitney to be "savage" was something new. He had about the easiest temper in the world. I laughed, and said so.

"Savage for him, I mean," corrected Helen, who was given to talking at random. "Nothing puts him out. Some cross fellows would not have consented, and have told their fathers so to their faces. It is a shame."

"I don't suppose Bill cares much; he is no hand at rowing," remarked Tod. "Did he write to Temple and decline?"

"Of course he did," was Helen's resentfully spoken answer; and she seemed, to say the least, quite as much put out as Bill could have been. "What else could he do?"

"Well. I am sorry for this," said Tod. "Temple has asked me now. Johnny also."

"Has he!" exclaimed Helen, her eyes sparkling. "I hope you will go."

"Of course we shall go," said Tod. "Where's Anna?"

"Anna? Oh, sitting up with mamma. She likes a sick-room. I don't."

"You'd like a boat better—if Temple were in it," remarked Tod, with a saucy laugh.

"Just you be quiet," retorted Helen.

From Whitney Hall we went to Evesham, and hastily procured what we wanted. The next day but one was that fixed for our departure, and when it at last dawned, bright and hot, we started amidst the good wishes of all the house. Tod with a fishing-rod and line, in case the expedition should afford an opportunity for fishing, and I with Duffham's quinine powders in my pocket.

Templemore, the seat of the Temples, was on the Welsh borders. We were not going there, but to a place called Sanbury, which lay within a few miles of the mansion. Slingsby Temple and his brother Rupert were already there, with the boat and the tent and all the rest of the apparatus, making ready for our departure on the morrow. Our head-quarters, until the start, was at the Ship, a good, old-fashioned inn, and we found that we were expected to be Temple's guests there.

"I would have asked you to Templemore to dine and sleep," he observed, in cordial tones, "and my mother said she should have been pleased to see you; but to get down here in the morning would have been inconvenient. At least, it would take up the time that ought to be devoted to getting away. Will you come and see the boat?"

It was lying in a locked-up shed near the river. A tub-pair, large of its kind. Three of them were enough for it: and I saw that, in point of fact, I was not wanted for the working; but Temple either did not like to ask Tod without me, or else would not leave me out. The Temples might have more than their share of pride, but it was accompanied by an equal share of refined and considerate feeling.

"We shall make you useful, never fear," said he to me, with a smile. "And it will be capital boating experience for you."

"I am sure I shall like it," I answered. And I liked him better than I ever had in my life.

Numerous articles were lying ready with the boat. Temple seemed to have thought of every needful thing. A pot to boil water in, a pan for frying, a saucepan for potatoes, a mop and towing-rope, stone jugs for beer, milk, and fresh water, tins to hold our grog, and the like.

Amongst the stores were tea, sugar, candles, cheese, butter, a ham, some tinned provisions, a big jar of beer, and (Duffham should have seen it) a two-gallon keg of whisky.

"A doctor up with us said we ought to have whisky," remarked Tod. "He is nothing but an old woman. He put some quinine powders in Johnny's pocket, and talked of a waterproof sheet to sleep on."

"Quite right," said Temple. "There it lies."

And there it did lie, wrapped round the folded tent. A large waterproof tarpaulin to cover the ground, at night, and keep the damp from our limbs.

"Did you ever make a boating tour before, Temple?" asked Tod.

"Oh yes. I like it. I don't know any pleasure equal to that of camping out at night on a huge plain, where you may study all the stars in the heavens."

As Temple spoke, he glanced towards a small parcel in a corner. I guessed it was one of his night telescopes.

"Yes, it is," he assented; "but only a small one. The boat won't stretch, and we can only load it according to its limits."

Rupert Temple came up as we were leaving the shed. I had never seen him before. He was the only brother left, and Slingsby's heir presumptive. Why, I know not, but I had pictured Rupert as being like poor Fred—tall, fair, bright-looking as a man can be. But there existed not a grain of resemblance.

Rupert was just a second edition of Slingsby: little, dark, plain, and proud. It was not an offensive pride—quite the contrary: and with those they knew well they were cordial and free.

Those originally invited by Temple were his cousin Arthur Slingsby; Lord Cracroft's son; Whitney; and a young Welshman named Pryce-Hughes. All had accepted, and intended to keep the engagement, knowing then of nothing to prevent them. But, curious to say, each one in succession wrote to decline it later. Whitney had to go elsewhere with his father; Pryce-Hughes hurt his arm, which disabled him from rowing: and Arthur Slingsby went off without ceremony in somebody's yacht to Malta. As the last of the letters came, which was Whitney's, Mrs. Temple seemed struck with the coincidence of all refusing, or being compelled to refuse. "Slingsby, my dear," she said to her son, "it looks just as though you were not to go." "But I will go," answered Temple, who did not like to be baulked in a project more than anybody else likes it; "if these can't come, I'll get others who can." And he forthwith told his brother Rupert that there'd be room for him in the boat—he had refused him before; and wrote to Tod. After that, came another letter from Pryce-Hughes, saying his arm was better, and he could join the party at Bridgenorth or Bewdley. But it was too late: the boat was filled up. Temple meant to do the Severn, the Wye, and the Avon, with a forced interlude of canals, and to be out a month, taking it easily, and resting on Sundays.

"Catch Slingsby missing Sunday service if he can help it!" said Rupert aside to me.

We started in our flannel suits and red caps, and started well, but not until the afternoon, Temple steering, his brother and Tod taking the sculls. The water was very shallow: and by-and-by we ran aground. The stern of the boat swung round, and away went our tarpaulin; and it was carried off by the current before we could save it.

Well, that first afternoon there were difficulties to contend with, and one or other of the three was often in the water; but we made altogether some five or six miles. It was the hottest day I ever felt; and about seven o'clock, on coming to a convenient meadow, nearly level with the river, none of us were sorry to step ashore. Making fast the boat for the night, we landed the tent and other things, and looked about us. A coppice bounded the field on the left; right across, in a second field, stood a substantial farm-house, surrounded by its barns and ricks. Temple produced one of his cards, which was to be taken to the house, and the farmer's leave asked to encamp on the meadow. Rupert Temple and Tod made themselves decent to go on the errand.

"We shall want a bundle or two of straw," said Temple; "it won't do to lie on the bare ground. And some milk. You must ask if they will accommodate us, and pay what they charge."

They went off, carrying also the jar to beg for fresh water. Temple and I began to unfurl the tent, and to busy ourselves amongst the things generally.

"Halloa! what's to do here?"

We turned, and saw a stout, comely man, in white shirt-sleeves, an open waistcoat, knee-breeches and top-boots; no doubt the farmer himself. Temple explained. He and some friends were on a boating tour, and had landed there to encamp for the night.

"But who gave you leave to do it?" asked the farmer. "You are trespassing. This is my ground."

"I supposed it might be necessary to ask leave," said Temple, haughtily courteous; "and I have sent to yonder house—which I presume is yours—to solicit it. If you will kindly accord the permission, I shall feel obliged."

That Temple looked disreputable enough, there could be no denying. No shoes on, no stockings, trousers tucked up above the knee: for he had been several times in the water, and, as yet, had done nothing to himself. But two of our college-caps chanced to be lying exposed on the boat: and perhaps, Temple's tone and address had made their due impression. The farmer looked hard at him, as if trying to remember his face.

"It's not one of the young Mr. Temples, is it?" said he. "Of Templemore."

"I am Mr. Temple, of Templemore. I have sent my card to your house."

"Dash me!" cried the farmer, heartily. "Shake hands, sir. I fancied I knew the face. I've seen you out shooting, sir—and at Sanbury. I knew your father. I'm sure you are more than welcome to camp alongside here, and to any other accommodation I can give you. Will you shake hands, young gentleman?" giving his hand to me as he released Temple's.

"My brother and another of our party are gone to your house to beg some fresh water and buy some milk," said Temple, who did not seem at all to resent the farmer's familiarity, but rather to like it. "And we shall be glad of a truss or two of fresh straw, if you can either sell it to us or give it. We have had the misfortune to lose our waterproof sheet."

"Sell be hanged!" cried the farmer, with a jovial laugh. "Sell you a truss or two of straw! Sell you milk! Not if I know it, Mr. Temple. You're welcome, sir, to as much as ever you want of both. One of my men shall bring the straw down."

"You are very good."

"And anything else you please to think of. Don't scruple to ask, sir. Will you all come and take supper at my house? We've a rare round o' beef in cut, and I saw the missis making pigeon-pies this morning."

But Temple declined the invitation most decisively; and the farmer, perhaps noting that, did not press it. It was rare weather for the water, he observed.

"We could do with less heat," replied Temple.

"Ay," said the farmer, "I never felt it worse. But it's good for the corn."

And, with that, he left us. The other two came back with water and oceans of milk. Sticks were soon gathered from the coppice, and the fire made; the round pot, filled with water, was put on to boil for tea, and the tent was set up.

Often and often in my later life have I looked back to that evening. The meal over—and a jolly good one we made—we sat round the camp fire, then smouldering down to red embers, and watched the setting sun, Rupert Temple and Tod smoking. It was a glorious sunset, the west lighted up with gold and purple and crimson; the sky above us clear and dark-blue.

But oh, how hot it was! The moon came up as the sun went down, and the one, to our fancy, seemed to give out as much heat as the other. There we sat on, sipping our grog, and talking in the bright moonlight, Temple with his elbows on the grass, his face turned up towards the sky and the few stars that came out. The colours in the west gave place to a beautiful opal, stretching northwards.

It was singular—I shall always think so—that the conversation should turn on MacRae, the Scotchman who used to make our skin creep at Oxford with his tales of second-sight. We were not talking of Oxford, and I don't know how MacRae came up. Temple had been talking of astronomy; from that we got to astrology; so perhaps it was in that way. Up he came, however, he and his weird beliefs; and Rupert Temple, who had not enjoyed the honour of Mac's acquaintance, and had probably never heard his name before, got me to relate one or two of Mac's choice experiences.

"Was the man a fool?" asked Rupert.

"Not a bit of it."

"I'm sure I should say so. Making out that he could foresee people's funerals before they were dead, or likely to die."

"Poor Fred was three-parts of a believer in them," put in Temple, in a dreamy voice, as though his thoughts were buried in that past time.

"Fred was!" exclaimed Rupert, taking his brother up sharply. "Believer in what?"

"MacRae's superstitions."

"Nonsense, Slingsby!"

Temple made no rejoinder. In his eye, which chanced to catch mine at the moment, there sat a singular expression. I wondered whether he was recalling that other superstition of Fred's, that little episode a night or two before he died.

"We had better be turning in," said Temple, getting up. "It won't do to sit here too long; and we must be up betimes in the morning."

So we got to bed at last—if you can call it bed. The farmer's good straw was strewed thickly underneath us in the tent; we had our rugs; and the tent was fastened back at the entrance to admit air. But there was no air to admit, not a whiff of it; nothing came in but the moonlight. None of us remembered a lighter night, or a hotter one. I and Tod lay in the middle, the Temples on either side, Slingsby nearest the opening.

"I wonder who's got our sheet?" began Tod, breaking a silence that ensued when we had wished each other good-night.

No one answered.

"I say," struck in Rupert, by-and-by, "I've heard one ought not to go to sleep in the moonlight: it turns people luny. Do any of your faces catch it, outside there?"

"Go to sleep and don't talk," said Temple.

It might have been from the novelty of the situation, but the night was well on before any of us got to sleep. Tod and Rupert Temple went off first, and next (I thought) Temple did. I did not.

I dare say you've never slept four in a bed—and, that, one of littered straw. It's all very well to lie awake when you've a good wide mattress to yourself, and can toss and turn at will; but in the close quarters of a tent you can't do it for fear of disturbing the others. However, the longest watch has its ending; and I was just dropping off, when Temple, next to whom I lay, started hurriedly, and it aroused me.

"What's that?" he cried, in a half-whisper.

I lifted my head, startled. He was sitting up, his eyes fixed on the opening we had left in the tent.

"Who's there?—who is it?" he said again; and his low voice had a slow, queer sound, as though he spoke in fear.

"What is it, Temple?" I asked.

"There, standing just outside the tent, right in the moonlight," whispered he. "Don't you see?"

I could see nothing. The stir awoke Rupert. He called out to know what ailed us; and that aroused Tod.

"Some man looking in at us," explained Temple, in the same queer tone, half of abstraction, half of fear, his gaze still strained on the aperture. "He is gone now."

Up jumped Tod, and dashed outside the tent. Rupert struck a match and lighted the lantern. No one was to be seen but ourselves; and the only odd thing to be remarked was the white hue Temple's face had taken. Tod was marching round the tent, looking about him far and near, and calling out to all intruders to show themselves. But all that met his eye was the level plain we were encamped upon, lying pale and white under the moonlight, and all the sound he heard was the croaking of the frogs.

"What could have made you fancy it?" he asked of Temple.

"Don't think it was fancy," responded Temple. "Never saw any man plainer in my life."

"You were dreaming, Slingsby," said Rupert. "Let us get to sleep again."

Which we did. At least, I can answer for myself.

The first beams of the glorious sun awoke us, and we rose to the beginning of another day, and to the cold, shivery feeling that, in spite of the heat of the past night and of the coming day, attends the situation. I could understand now why the nip of whisky, as Duffham called it, was necessary. Tod served it out. Lighting the fire of sticks to boil our tea-kettle—or the round pot that served for a kettle—we began to get things in order to embark again, when breakfast should be over.

"I say, Slingsby," cried Rupert, to his brother, who seemed very sullen, "what on earth took you, that you should disturb us in the night for nothing?"

"It was not for nothing. Some one was there."

"It must have been a stray sheep."

"Nonsense, Rupert! Could one mistake a sheep for a man?"

"Some benighted ploughman then, 'plodding his weary way.'"

"If you could bring forward any ploughman to testify that it was he beyond possibility of doubt, I'd give him a ten-pound note."

"Look here," said Tod, after staring a minute at this odd remark of Temple's, "you may put all idea of ploughmen and every one else away. No one was there. If there had been, I must have seen him: it was not possible he could betake himself out of sight in a moment."

"Have it as you like," said Temple; "I am going to take a bath. My head aches."

Stripping, he plunged into the river, which was very wide just there, and swam towards the middle of it.

"It seems to have put Slingsby out," observed Rupert, alluding to the night alarm. "Do you notice how thoughtful he is? Just look at that fire!"

The sticks had turned black, and began to smoke and hiss, giving out never a bit of blaze. Down knelt Rupert on one side and I on the other.

"Damp old obstinate things!" he ejaculated. And we set on to blow at them with all our might.

"Where's Temple?" I exclaimed presently; looking off, and not seeing him. Rupert glanced over the river.

"He must be diving, Johnny. Slingsby's fond of diving. Keep on blowing, lad, or we shall get no tea to-day."

So we kept on. But, I don't know why, a sort of doubtful feeling came over me, and while I blew I watched the water for Temple to come up. All in a moment he rose to the surface, gave one low, painful cry of distress, and disappeared again.

"Good Heavens!" cried Rupert, leaping up and overturning the kettle.

But Tod was the quickest, and jumped in to the rescue. A first-rate swimmer and diver was he, almost as much at home in the water as out of it. In no time, as it seemed, he was striking back, bearing Temple. It was fortunate for such a crisis that Temple was so small and slight—of no weight to speak of.

By dint of gently rubbing and rolling, we got some life into him and some whisky down his throat. But he remained in the queerest, faintest state possible; no exertion in him, no movement hardly, no strength; alive, and that was about all; and just able to tell us that he had turned faint in the water.

"What is to be done?" cried Rupert. "We must get a doctor to him: and he ought not to lie on the grass here. I wonder if that farmer would let him be taken to the house for an hour or two?"

I got into my boots, and ran off to ask; and met the farmer in the second field. He was coming towards us, curious perhaps to see whether we had started. Telling him what had happened, he showed himself alive with sympathy, called some of his men to carry Temple to the farm, and sent back to prepare his wife. Their name we found was Best: and most hospitable, good-hearted people they turned out to be.

Well, Temple was taken there and a doctor was called in. The doctor shook his head, looked grave, and asked to have another doctor. Then, for the first time, doubts stole over us that it might be more serious than we had thought for. A dreadful feeling of fear took possession of me, and, in spite of all I could do, that scene at Oxford, when poor Fred Temple had been carried into old Mrs. Golding's to die, would not go out of my mind.

We got into our reserve clothes, as if conscious that the boating flannels were done with for the present, left one of the farmer's men to watch our boat and things, and stayed with Temple. He continued very faint, and lay almost motionless. The doctors tried some remedies, but they did no good. He did not revive. One of them called it "syncope of the heart;" but the other said hastily, "No, no, that was not the right name." It struck me that perhaps they did not know what the right name was. At last they said Mrs. Temple had better be sent for.

"I was just thinking so," cried Rupert. "My mother ought to be here. Who will go for her?"

"Johnny can," said Tod. "He is of no good here."

For that matter, none of us were any good, for we could do nothing for Temple.

I did not relish the task: I did not care to tell a mother that her son, whom she believes is well and hearty, is lying in danger. But I had to go: Rupert seemed to take it as a matter of course.

"Don't alarm her more than you can help, Ludlow," he said. "Say that Slingsby turned faint in the water this morning, and the medical men seem anxious. But ask her not to lose time."

Mr. Best started me on his own horse—a fine hunter, iron-grey. The weather was broiling. Templemore lay right across country, about six miles off by road. It was a beautiful place; I could see that much, though I had but little time to look at it; and it stood upon an eminence, the last mile of the road winding gradually up to its gates.

As ill-luck had it, or perhaps good-luck—I don't know which—Mrs. Temple was at one of the windows, and saw me ride hastily in. Having a good memory of faces, she recollected mine. Knowing that I had started with her sons in the boat, she was seized with a prevision that something was wrong, and came out before I was well off the horse.

"It is Mr. Ludlow, I think," she said, her plain dark face (so much like Slingsby's) very pale. "What ill news have you brought?"

I told her in the best manner I was able, just in the words Rupert had suggested, speaking quietly, and not showing any alarm in my own manner.

"Is there danger?" she at once asked.

"I am not sure that there is," I said, hardly knowing how to frame my answer. "The doctors thought you had better come, in case—in case of danger arising; and Rupert sent me to ask you to do so."

She rang the bell, and ordered her carriage to be round instantly. "The bay horses," she added: "they are the fleetest. What will you take, Mr. Ludlow?"

I would not take anything. But a venerable old gentleman in black, with a powdered bald head—the butler, I concluded—suggested some lemonade, after my hot ride: and that I was glad of.

I rode on first, piloting the way for the carriage, which contained Mrs. Temple. She came alone: her daughter was away on a visit—as I had learnt from Rupert.

Slingsby lay in the same state, neither better nor worse: perhaps the breathing was somewhat more difficult. He smiled when he saw his mother, and put out his hand.

The day dragged itself slowly on. We did not know what to do with ourselves; that was a fact. Temple was to be kept quiet, and we might not intrude into his room—one on the ground-floor that faced the east: not even Rupert. Mr. and Mrs. Best entertained us well as far as meals went, but one can't be eating for ever. Now down in the meadow by the boat—which seemed to have assumed a most forlorn aspect—and now hovering about the farm, waiting for the last report of Temple. In that way the day crept through.

"Is it here that Mr. Temple is lying?"

I was standing under the jessamine-covered porch, sheltering my head from the rays of the setting sun, when a stranger came up and put the question. An extraordinarily tall, thin man, with grey hair, clerical coat, and white neckcloth.

It was the Reverend Mr. Webster, perpetual curate of the parish around Templemore. And I seemed to know him before I heard his name, for he was the very image of his son, Long Webster, who used to be at Oxford.

"I am so grieved not to have been able to get here before," he said; "but I had just gone out for some hours when Mrs. Temple's message was brought to the Parsonage. Is he any better?"

"I am afraid not," I answered. "We don't know what to make of it; it all seems so sudden and strange."

"But what is it?" he asked in a whisper.

"I don't know, sir. The doctors have said something about the heart."

"I should like to see the doctors before I go in to Mrs. Temple. Are they here?"

"One of them is, I think. They have been going in and out all day."

I fetched the doctor out to him; and they talked together in low tones in the shaded and quiet porch. Not a ray of hope sat on the medical man's face: he as good as intimated that Temple was dying.

"Dear me!" cried the dismayed Mr. Webster.

"He seems to know it himself," continued the doctor. "At least, we fancy so, I and my brother-practitioner. Though we have been most cautious not to alarm him by any hint of the kind."

"I should like to see him," said the parson. "I suppose I can?"

He went in, and was shut up for some time alone with Temple. Yes, he said, when he came out again, Temple knew all about it, and was perfectly resigned and prepared.

You may be sure there was no bed for any of us that night. Temple's breathing grew worse; and at last we went in by turns, one of us at a time, to prop up the pillows behind, and keep them propped; it seemed to make it firmer and easier for him as he lay against them. Towards morning I was called in to replace Rupert. The shaded candle seemed to be burning dim.

"You can lie down, my dear," Mrs. Temple whispered to Rupert. "Should there be any change, I will call you."

He nodded, and left the room. Not to lie down. Only to sit over the kitchen fire with Tod, and so pass away the long hours of discomfort.

"Who is this now?" panted Slingsby, as I took my place.

"It is I. Johnny Ludlow. Do you feel any better?"

He made a little sound of dissent in answer.

"Nay, I think you look easier, my dear," said Mrs. Temple, gently.

"No, no," he said, just opening his eyes. "Do not grieve, mother. I shall be better off. I shall be with my father and Fred."

"Oh, my son, my son, don't lose heart!" she said, with a sob. "That will never do."

"I saw my father last night," said Temple.

The words seemed to strike her with a sort of shock. "No!" she exclaimed, perhaps thinking of the Temple superstition, and drawing back a step. "Pray, pray don't fancy that!"

"The tent was open to give us air," he said, speaking with difficulty. "I suddenly saw some one standing in the moonlight. I was next the opening; and I had not been able to get to sleep. For a moment I thought it was some man, some intruder passing by; but he took a strange likeness to my father, and I thought he beckoned—"

"We are not alone, Slingsby," interrupted Mrs. Temple, remembering me, her voice cold, not to say haughty.

"Ludlow knows. He knew the last time. Fred said he saw him, and I—I ridiculed it. Ludlow heard me. My father came for Fred, mother; he must have come for me."

"Oh, I can't—I can't believe this, Slingsby," she cried, in some excitement. "It was fancy—nervousness; nothing else. My darling, I cannot lose you! You have ever been dearer to me than my other children."

"Only for a little while, mother. It is God's will. That is our true home, you know; and then there will be no more parting. I am quite happy. I seem to be half there now. What is that light?"

Mrs. Temple looked round, and saw a faint streak coming in over the tops of the shutters. "It must be the glimmering of dawn in the east," she said. "The day is breaking."

"Ay," he answered: "my day. Where's Rupert? I should like to say good-bye to him. Yes, mother, that's the dawn of heaven."

And just as the sun rose, he went there.

That was the end of our boating tour. Ridicule has been cast on some of the facts, and will be again. It is a painful subject; and I don't know that I should have related it, but for its having led to another (and more lively) adventure, which I proceed to tell of.

CHAPTER XVIII

ROSE LODGE

It looked the prettiest place imaginable, lying under the sunlight, as we stood that first morning in front of the bay. The water was smooth and displayed lovely colours: now green, now blue, as the clouds passed over the face of the sky, now taking tinges of brown and amber; and towards evening it would be pink and purple. Further on, the waters were rippling and shining in the sun. Fishing-vessels stood out at sea, plying their craft; little cockle-shells, their white sails set, disported on it; rowing boats glided hither and thither. In the distance the grand waves of the sea were ebbing and flowing; a noble merchant-man, all her canvas filled, was passing proudly on her outward-bound course.

"I should like to live here," cried Tod, turning away at last.

And I'm sure I felt that I should. For I could watch the ever-changing sea from morning to night and not tire of it.

"Suppose we remain here, Johnny?"

"To live?"

"Nonsense, lad! For a month. I am going for a sail. Will you come?"

After the terrible break-up of our boating tour, poor Slingsby Temple was taken home to Templemore, ourselves going back to Sanbury to wait for the funeral, and for our black garments, for which we had sent. Rupert was fearfully cut up. Although he was the heir now, and would be chief of Templemore, I never saw any brother take a death more to heart. "Slingsby liked you much, Ludlow," said Rupert to me, when he came to us at the inn at Sanbury the day before the funeral, and the hot tears were in his eyes as he spoke. "He always liked you at Oxford: I have heard him say so. Like himself, you kept yourself free from the lawlessness of the place—"

"As if a young one like Johnny would go in for anything of the kind!" interrupted Tod.

"Young?" repeated Rupert Temple. "Well, I don't know. When I was there myself, some young ones—lads—went in for a pretty good deal. He liked you much, Ludlow."

And somehow I liked to hear Rupert say it.

Quitting Sanbury after the funeral, we came to this little place, Cray Bay, which was on the sea-coast, a few miles beyond Templemore. Our pleasure cut short at the beginning of the holiday, we hardly knew what to do with the rest of it, and felt like a couple of fish suddenly thrown out of water. Mrs. Temple, taking her son and daughter, went for change to her brother's, Lord Cracroft.

At Cray Bay we found one small inn, which bore the odd sign of the Whistling Wind, and was kept by Mrs. Jones, a stout Welshwoman. The bedroom she gave us enjoyed a look-out upon some stables, and would not hold much more than the two small beds in it. In answer to Tod's remonstrances, she said that she had a better room, but it was just now occupied.

The discomforts of the lodging were forgotten when we strolled out to look about us, and saw the beauties of the sea and bay. Cray Bay was a very primitive spot: little else than a decent fishing-place. It had not then been found out by the tour-taking world. Its houses were built anyhow and anywhere; its shops could be counted on your fingers: a butcher's, a baker's, a grocer's, and so on. Fishermen called at the doors with fish, and countrywomen with butter and fowls. There was no gas, and the place at night was lighted with oil-lamps. A trout-stream lay at the back of the village, half-a-mile away.

Stepping into a boat, on this first morning, for the sail proposed by Tod, we found its owner a talkative old fellow. His name was Druff, he said; he had lived at Cray Bay most of his life, and knew every inch of its land and every wave of its sea. There couldn't be a nicer spot to stop at for the summer, as he took it; no, not if you searched the island through: and he supposed it was first called Cray Bay after the cray-fish, they being caught in plenty there.

"More things than one are called oddly in this place," remarked Tod. "Look at that inn: the Whistling Wind; what's that called after?"

"And so the wind do hoostle on this here coast; 'deed an' it do," returned Druff. "You'd not forget it if you heered it in winter."

The more we saw of Cray Bay that day, the more we liked it. Its retirement just suited our mood, after the experience of only four or five days back: for I can tell you that such a shock is not to be forgotten all in a moment. And when we went up to bed that night, Tod had made up his mind to stay for a time if lodgings could be found.

"Not in this garret, that you can't swing a cat in," said he, stretching out his hands towards the four walls. "Madame Jones won't have me here another night if I can help it."

"No. Our tent in the meadow was ten times livelier."

"Are there any lodgings to be had in this place?" asked Tod of the slip-shod maid-servant, when we were at breakfast the next morning. But she professed not to know of any.

"But, Tod, what would they say at home to our staying here?" I asked after awhile, certain doubts making themselves heard in my conscience.

"What they chose," said Tod, cracking his fourth egg.

"I am afraid the pater—"

"Now, Johnny, you need not put in your word," he interrupted, in the off-hand tone that always silenced me. "It's not your affair. We came out for a month, and I am not going back home, like a bad sixpence returned, before the month has expired. Perhaps I shall tack a few weeks on to it. I am not dependent on the pater's purse."

No; for he had his five hundred pounds lying untouched at the Worcester Old Bank, and his cheque-book in his pocket.

Breakfast over, we went out to look for lodgings; but soon feared it might be a hopeless search. Two little cottages had a handboard stuck on a stick in the garden, with "Lodgings" on it. But the rooms in each proved to be a tiny sitting-room and a more tiny bedroom, smaller than the garret at the Whistling Wind.

"I never saw such a world as this," cried Tod, as we paced disconsolately before the straggling dwellings in front of the bay. "If you want a thing you can't get it."

"We might find rooms in those houses yonder," I said, nodding towards some scattered about in the distance. "They must be farms."

"Who wants to live a mile off?" he retorted. "It's the place itself I like, and the bay, and the— Oh, by George! Look there, Johnny!"

We had come to the last house in the place—a fresh-looking, charming cottage, with a low roof and a green verandah, that we had stopped to admire yesterday. It faced the bay, and stood by itself in a garden that was a perfect bower of roses. The green gate bore the name "Rose Lodge," and in the parlour window appeared a notice "To Let;" which notice, we both felt sure, had not been there the previous day.

"Fancy their having rooms to let here!" cried Tod. "The nicest little house in all the place. How lucky!"

In he went impulsively, striding up the short gravel-path, which was divided from the flower-beds by two rows of sea-shells, and knocked at the door. It was opened by a tall grenadier of a female, rising six feet, with a spare figure and sour face. She had a large cooking-apron on, dusted with flour.

"You have lodgings to let," said Tod; "can I see them?"

"Lodgings to let?" she repeated, scanning us up and down attentively; and her voice sounded harsh and rasping. "I don't know that we have. You had better see Captain Copperas."

She threw open the door of the parlour: a small, square, bright-looking room, rather full of furniture; a gay carpet, a cottage piano, and some green chairs being among the articles.

Captain Copperas came forward: a retired seaman, as we heard later; tall as the grenadier, and with a brown, weather-beaten face. But in voice and manners he, at any rate, did not resemble her, for they were just as pleasant as they could be.

"I have no lodgings," said he; "my servant was mistaken. My house is to let; and the furniture to be taken too."

Which announcement was of course a check to Tod. He sat looking very blank, and then explained that we only required lodgings. We had been quite charmed with Cray Bay, and would like to stay in it for a month or so: and that it was his misapprehension, not the servant's.

"It's a pity but you wanted a little house," said Captain Copperas. "This is the most compact, desirable, perfect little dwelling mortal man ever was in. Rent twenty-six pounds a-year only, furniture to be bought out-and-out for a hundred and twenty-five. It would be a little Eden—a paradise—to those who had the means to take it."

As he spoke, he regarded us individually and rather pointedly. It looked as much as to doubt whether we had the means. Tod (conscious of his five hundred pounds in the bank) threw his head up.

"Oh, I have the means," said he, as haughtily as poor Slingsby Temple had ever spoken. "Johnny, did you put any cards in your pocket? Give Captain Copperas one."

I laid one of Tod's cards on the table. The captain took it up.

"It's a great grief to me to leave the house," he remarked. "Especially after having been only a few months in it!—and laying in a stock of the best furniture in a plain way, purchased in the best market! Downright grief."

"Then why do you leave it?" naturally asked Tod.

"Because I have to go afloat again," said the sailor, his face taking a rueful expression. "I thought I had given up the sea for good; but my old employers won't let me give it up. They know my value as a master, and have offered me large terms for another year or two of service. A splendid new East Indiaman, two thousand tons register, and—and, in short, I don't like to be ungrateful, so I have said I'll go."

"Could you not keep on the house until you come back?"

"My sister won't let me keep it on. Truth to say, she never cared for the sea, and wants to get away from it. That exquisite scene"—extending his hand towards the bay, and to a steamer working her way onwards near the horizon—"has no charms for Miss Copperas; and she intends to betake herself off to our relatives in Leeds. No: I can only give the place up, and dispose of the furniture to whomsoever feels inclined to take it. It will be a fine sacrifice. I shall not get the one half of the money I gave for it: don't look to. And all of it as good as new!"

I could read Tod's face as a book, and the eager look in his eyes. He was thinking how much he should like to seize upon the tempting bargain; to make the pretty room we sat in, and the prettier prospect yonder, his own. Captain Copperas appeared to read him also.

"You are doubting whether to close with the offer or not," he said, with a frank smile. "You might make it yours for a hundred and twenty-five pounds. Perhaps—pardon me; you are both but young—you may not have the sum readily at command?"

"Oh yes, I have," said Tod, candidly. "I have it lying at my banker's, in Worcester. No, it's not for that reason I hesitate. It is—it is—fancy me with a house on my hands!" he broke off, turning to me with a laugh.

"It is an offer that you will never be likely to meet with again, sir."

"But what on earth could I do with the house and the things afterwards—allowing that we stayed here for a month or two?" urged Tod.

"Why, dispose of them again, of course," was the ready answer of Captain Copperas. "You'd find plenty of people willing to purchase, and to take the house off your hands. Such an opportunity as this need not go begging. I only wish I had not to be off all in a jiffy; I should make a very different bargain."

"I'll think of it," said Tod, as we got up to leave. "I must say it is a nice little nest."

In the doorway we encountered a tall lady with a brown face and a scarlet top-knot. She wore a thick gold chain, and bracelets to match.

"My sister, Miss Copperas," said the captain. And he explained to her in a few words our business, and the purport of what had passed.

"For goodness' sake, don't lose the opportunity!" cried she, impressively affectionate, as though she had known us all our lives. "So advantageous an offer was never made to any one before: and but for my brother's obstinately and wickedly deciding to go off to that wretched sea again, it would not be made now. Yes, Alexander," turning to him, "I do call it quite wicked. Only think, sir"—to Tod—"a house full of beautiful furniture, every individual thing that a family can want; a piano here, a table-cloth press in the kitchen; plate, linen, knives, forks; a garden full of roses and a roller for the paths; and all to go for the miserably inadequate sum of a hundred and twenty-five pounds! But that's my brother all over. He's a true sailor. Setting himself up in a home to-day, and selling it off for an old song to-morrow."

"Well, well, Fanny," he said, when he could get a word in edgeways to stem the torrent of eloquence, "I have agreed to go, and I must go."

"Have you been over the house?" she resumed, in the same voluble manner. "No? Then do pray come and see it. Oh, don't talk of trouble. This is the dining-room," throwing open a door behind her.

It was a little side-room, looking up the coast and over the fields; just enough chairs and tables in it for use. Upstairs we found three chambers, with their beds and other things. It all looked very comfortable, and I thought Captain Copperas was foolish to ask so small a sum.

"This is the linen closet," said Miss Copperas, opening a narrow door at the top of the stairs, and displaying some shelves that seemed to be well-filled. "Sheets, table-cloths, dinner-napkins, towels, pillow-cases; everything for use. Anybody, taking the house, has only to step in, hang up his hat, and find himself at home. Look at those plates and dishes!" she ran on, as we got down again and entered the kitchen. "They are very nice—and enough to dine ten people."

They were of light blue ware, and looked nice enough on the dresser shelves. The grenadier stood at the table, chopping parsley on a trencher, and did not condescend to take any notice of us.

Out in the garden next, amidst the roses—which grew all round the house, clustering everywhere. They were of that species called the cabbage-rose: large, and fragrant, and most beautiful. It made me think of the Roses by Bendemeer's stream.

"I should like the place of all things!" cried Tod, as we strolled towards the bay for a sail; and found Druff seated in his boat, smoking. "I say, Druff, do you know Captain Copperas? Get in, Johnny."

"Lives next door to me, at Rose Lodge," answered Druff.

"Next door! What, is that low whitewashed shanty your abode? How long has Copperas lived here?"

"A matter of some months," said Druff. "He came in the spring."

"Are they nice kind of people?"

"They be civil to me," answered Druff. "Sent my old missis a bottle o' wine in, and some hot broth t' other day, when she was ill. The captain—"

A sudden lurch put a stop to the discourse, and in a few minutes we glided out of the bay, Tod sitting in a brown reverie, his gaze fixed on the land and on Rose Lodge.

"My mind's made up, Johnny. I shall take the place."

I dropped my knife and fork in very astonishment. Our sail over, we were at dinner in the bar-parlour of the Whistling Wind.

"Surely you won't do it, Tod!"

"Surely I shall, lad. I never saw such a nice little nest in all my life. And there's no risk; you heard what Copperas said; I shall get my money back again when we want to leave it."

"Look here, Tod: I was thinking a bit whilst we sat in the boat. Does it not seem to you to be too good to be genuine?"

It was Tod's turn now to drop his knife and fork: and he did it angrily. "Just tell me what you mean, Johnny Ludlow."

"All that furniture, and the piano, and the carpets, and the plate and linen: it looks such a heap to be going for only a hundred and twenty-five pounds."

"Well?"

"I can't think that Copperas means it."

"Not mean it! Why, you young muff? There are the things, and he has offered them to me. If Copperas chooses to part with them for half their value, is it my place to tell him he's a fool? The poor man is driven into a corner through want of time. Sailors are uncommonly improvident."

"It is such an undertaking, Tod."

"It is not your undertaking."

"Of course it is a tremendous bargain; and it is a beautiful little place to have. But I can't think what the pater will say to it."

"I can," said Tod. "When he hears of it—but that will not be yet awhile—he will come off here post-haste to blow me up; and end by falling in love with the roses. He always says that there is no rose like a cabbage-rose."

"He will never forgive you, Tod; or me either. He will say the world's coming to an end."

"If you are afraid of him, Johnny, you can take yourself off. Hold up your plate for some more lamb, and hold your tongue."

There was no help for it; anything I could say would have no more weight with Tod than so much wasted water; so I did as he bade me, and held my tongue. Down he went to Captain Copperas ere his dinner was well swallowed, and told him he would take the house. The Captain said he would have a short agreement drawn up; and Tod took out his cheque-book, to give a cheque for the money there and then. But the Captain, like an honest man, refused to receive it until the agreement was executed; and, if all the same, he would prefer money down to a cheque. Cheques were all very good, no doubt, he said; but sailors did not much understand them. Oh, of course, Tod answered, shaking him by the hand; he would get the money.

Inquiring of our landlady for the nearest bank, Tod was directed to a town called St. Ann's, three miles off; and we started for it at once, pelting along the hot and dusty road. The bank found—a small one, with a glazed bow-window, Tod presented a cheque for a hundred and fifty pounds, twenty-five of it being for himself, and asked the clerk to cash it.

The clerk looked at the cheque then looked at Tod, and then at me. "This is not one of our cheques," he said. "We have no account in this name."

"Can't you read?" asked Tod. "The cheque is upon the Worcester Old Bank. You know it well by reputation, I presume?"

The clerk whisked into a small kind of box, divided from the office by glass, where sat a bald-headed gentleman writing at a desk full of pigeon-holes. A short conference, and then the latter came to us, holding the cheque in his hand.

"We will send and present this at Worcester," he said; "and shall get an answer the day after to-morrow. No doubt we shall then be able to give you the money."

"Why can't you give it me now?" asked Tod, in rather a fiery tone.

"Well, sir, we should be happy to do it; but it is not our custom to cash cheques for strangers."

"Do you fear the cheque will not be honoured?" flashed Tod. "Why, I have five hundred pounds lying there! Do you suppose I want to cheat you?"

"Oh, certainly not," said the banker, with suavity. "Only, you see, we cannot break through our standing rules. Call upon us the day after to-morrow, and doubtless the money will be ready."

Tod came away swearing. "The infamous upstarts!" cried he. "To refuse to cash my cheque! Johnny, it's my belief they take us for a couple of adventurers."

The money came in due course. After receiving it from the cautious banker, we went straight to Rose Lodge, pelting back from St. Ann's at a fine pace. Tod signed the agreement, and paid the cash in good Bank of England notes. Captain Copperas brought out a bottle of champagne, which tasted uncommonly good to our thirsty throats. He was to leave Cray Bay that night on his way to Liverpool to take possession of his ship; Miss Copperas would leave on the morrow, and then we should go in. And Elizabeth, the grenadier, was to remain with us as servant. Miss Copperas recommended her, hearing Tod say he did not know where to look for one. We bargained with her to keep up a good supply of pies, and to pay her twenty shillings a month.

"Will you allow me to leave one or two of my boxes for a few days?" asked Miss Copperas of Tod, when we went down on the following morning, and found her equipped for departure. "This has been so hurried a removal that I have not had time to pack all my things, and must leave it for Elizabeth to do."

"Leave anything you like, Miss Copperas," replied Tod, as he shook hands. "Do what you please. I'm sure the house seems more like yours than mine."

She thanked him, wished us both good-bye, and set off to walk to the coach-office, attended by the grenadier, and a boy wheeling her luggage. And we were in possession of our new home.

It was just delightful. The weather was charming, though precious hot, and the new feeling of being in a house of our own, with not as much as a mouse to control us and our movements, was satisfactory in the highest degree. We passed our days sailing about with old Druff, and came home to the feasts prepared by the grenadier, and to sit among the roses. Altogether we had never had a time like it. Tod took the best chamber, facing the sea; I had the smaller one over the dining-room, looking up coastwards.

"I shall go fishing to-morrow, Johnny," Tod said to me one evening. "We'll bring home some trout for supper."

He was stretched on three chairs before the open window; coat off, pipe in mouth. I turned round from the piano. It was not much of an instrument. Miss Copperas had said, when I hinted so to her on first trying it, that it wanted "age."

"Shall you? All right," I answered, sitting down by him. The stars were shining on the calm blue water; here and there lights, looking like stars also, twinkled from some vessels at anchor.

"If I thought they wouldn't quite die of the shock, Johnny, I'd send the pater and madam an invitation to come off here and pay us a visit. They would fall in love with the place at once."

"Oh, Tod, I wish you would!" I cried, eagerly seizing on the words. "They could have your room, and you have mine, and I would go into the little one at the back."

"I dare say! I was only joking, lad."

The last words and their tone destroyed my hopes. It is inconvenient to possess a conscience. Advantageous though the bargain was that Tod had made, and delightfully though our days were passing, I could not feel easy until they knew of it at home.

"I wish you would let me write and tell them, Tod."

"No," said he. "I don't want the pater to whirl himself off here and spoil our peace—for that's what would come of it."

"He thinks we are in some way with the Temples. His letter implied it."

"The best thing he can think."

"But I want to write to the mother, Tod. She must be wondering why we don't."

"Wondering won't give her the fever, lad. Understand me, Mr. Johnny: you are not to write."

Breakfast over in the morning, we crossed the meadows to the trout stream, with the fishing-tackle and a basket of frogs. Tod complained of the intense heat. The dark blue sky was cloudless; the sun beat down upon our heads.

"I'll tell you what, Johnny," he said, when we had borne the blaze for an hour on the banks, the fish refusing to bite: "we should be all the cooler for our umbrellas. You'll have a sunstroke, if you don't look out."

"It strikes me you won't catch any fish to-day."

"Does it? You be off and get the parapluies."

The low front window stood open when I reached home. It was the readiest way of entering; and I passed on to the passage to the umbrella-stand. The grenadier came dashing out of her kitchen, looking frightened.

"Oh!" said she, "it's you!"

"I have come back for the umbrellas, Elizabeth; the sun's like a furnace. Why! what have you got there?"

The kitchen was strewed with clothes from one end of it to the other. On the floor stood the two boxes left by Miss Copperas.

"I am only putting up Miss Copperas's things," returned Elizabeth, in her surly way. "It's time they were sent off."

"What a heap she must have left behind!" I remarked, and left the grenadier to her work.

We got home in the evening, tired out. The grenadier had a choice supper ready; and, in answer to me, said the trunks of Miss Copperas were packed and gone. When bed-time came, Tod was asleep at the window, and wouldn't awake. The grenadier had gone to her room ages ago; I wanted to go to mine.

"Tod, then! Do please wake up: it is past ten."

A low growl answered me. And in that same moment I became aware of some mysterious stir outside the front-gate. People seemed to be trying it. The grenadier always locked it at night.

"Tod! Tod! There are people at the gate—trying to get in."

The tone and the words aroused him. "Eh? What do you say, Johnny? People are trying the gate?"

"Listen! They are whispering to one another. They are trying the fastenings."

"What on earth does anybody want at this time of night?" growled Tod. "And why can't they ring like decent people? What's your business?" he roared out from the window. "Who the dickens are you?"

"Hush, Tod! It—it can't be the Squire, can it? Come down here to look after us."

The suggestion silenced him for a moment.

"I—I don't think so, Johnny," he slowly said. "No, it's not the Squire: he would be letting off at us already at the top of his voice; he wouldn't wait to come in to do it. Let's go and see. Come along."

Two young men stood at the gate. One of them turned the handle impatiently as we went down the path.

"What do you want?" demanded Tod.

"I wish to see Captain Copperas."

"Then you can't see him," answered Tod, woefully cross after being startled out of his sleep. "Captain Copperas does not live here."

"Not live here!" repeated the man. "That's gammon. I know he does live here."

"I tell you he does not," haughtily repeated Tod. "Do you doubt my word?"

"Who does live here, then?" asked the man, in a different tone, evidently impressed.

"Mr. Todhetley."

"I can take my oath that Captain Copperas lived here ten days ago."

"What of that? He is gone, and Mr. Todhetley's come."

"Can I see Mr. Todhetley?"

"You see him now. I am he. Will you tell me your business?"

"Captain Copperas owes me a small account, and I want it settled."

The avowal put Tod in a rage; and he showed it. "A small account! Is this a proper time to come bothering gentlemen for your small accounts—when folks are gone to bed, or going?"

"Last time I came in the afternoon. Perhaps that was the wrong time? Any way, Captain Copperas put me off, saying I was to call some evening, and he'd pay it."

"And I'll thank you to betake yourself off again now. How dare you disturb people at this unearthly hour! As to Captain Copperas, I tell you that he is no longer here."

"Then I should say that Captain Copperas was a swindler."

Tod turned on his heel at the last words, and the men went away, their retreating footsteps echoing on the road. I thought I heard the grenadier's window being shut, so the noise must have disturbed her.

"Swindlers themselves!" cried Tod, as he fastened the house-door. "I'll lay you a guinea, Johnny, they were two loose fellows trying to sneak inside and see what they could pick up."

Nevertheless, in the morning he asked the grenadier whether it was true that such men had come there after any small account. And the grenadier resented the supposition indignantly. Captain Copperas owed no "small accounts" that she knew of, she said; and she had lived with him and Miss C. ever since they came to Cray Bay. She only wished she had seen the men herself last night; she would have answered them. And when, upon this, I said I thought I had heard her shut her window down, and supposed she had been listening, she denied it, and accused me of being fanciful.

"Impudent wretches!" ejaculated Tod; "to come here and asperse a man of honour like Copperas."

That day passed off quietly, and to our thorough enjoyment; but the next one was fated to bring us some events. Some words of Tod's, as I was pouring out the breakfast coffee, startled me.

"Oh, by Jupiter! How have they found us out here?"

Looking up, I saw the postman entering the gate with a letter. The same thought struck us both—that it was some terrible mandate from the Squire. Tod went to the window and held out his hand.

"For Elizabeth, at Captain Copperas's," read out the man, as he handed it to Tod. It was a relief, and Tod sent me with it to the grenadier.

But in less than one minute afterwards she came into the room, bathed in tears. The letter was to tell her that her mother was lying ill at their home, some unpronounceable place in Wales, and begging earnestly to see her.

"I'm sorry to leave you at a pinch; but I must go," sobbed the grenadier. "I can't help myself; I shall start by the afternoon coach."

Well, of course there was nothing to be said against it. A mother was a mother. But Tod began to wonder what on earth we should do: as did I, for the matter of that. The grenadier offered to cook our luncheon before starting, which we looked upon as a concession.

"Let's go for a sail, Johnny, and leave perplexities to right themselves."

And a glorious sail we had! Upon getting back at one o'clock, we found a huge meat pie upon the luncheon-table, and the grenadier with her bonnet on. Tod handed her five shillings; the sum, as she computed, that was due to her.

We heard the bumping of her boxes on the stairs. At the gate stood the boy with the truck, ready to wheel them to the coach-office, as he had wheeled those of Miss Copperas. Tod was helping himself to some more pie, when the grenadier threw open the door.

"My boxes are here, gentlemen. Will you like to look at them?"

"Look at them for what?" asked Tod, after staring a minute.

"To see that I'm taking none of your property away inside them."

At last Tod understood what she meant, and felt inclined to throw the dish at her head. "Shut the door, and don't be a fool," said he. "And I hope you'll find your mother better," I called out after her.

"And now, Johnny, what are we to do?" cried he, when lunch was over and there was no one to take it away. "This is like a second edition of Robinson Crusoe."

We left it where it was, and went off to the shops and the Whistling Wind, asking if they could tell us of a servant. But servants seemed not to be forthcoming at a pinch; and we told our troubles to old Druff.

"My missis shall come in and see a bit to things for ye," said he. "She can light the fire in the morning, anyway, and boil the kettle."

And with the aid of Mother Druff—an ancient dame who went about in clogs—we got on till after breakfast in the morning, when a damsel came after the place. She wore a pink gauze bonnet, smart and tawdry, and had a pert manner.

"Can you cook?" asked Tod.

The substance of her answer was, that she could do everything under the sun, provided she were not "tanked" after. Her late missis was for ever a-tanking. Would there be any washing to do?—because washing didn't agree with her: and how often could she go out, and what was the wages?

Tod looked at me in doubt, and I slightly shook my head. It struck me that she would not do at any price. "I think you won't suit," said he to her.

"Oh," returned she, all impertinence. "I can go then where I shall suit: and so, good-morning, gentlemen. There's no call for you to be so uppish. I didn't come after your forks and spoons."

"The impudent young huzzy!" cried Tod, as she slammed the gate after her. "But she might do better than nobody, Johnny."

"I don't like her, Tod. If it rested with me, I'd rather live upon bread-and-cheese than take her."

"Bread-and-cheese!" he echoed. "It is not a question of only bread-and-cheese. We must get our beds made and the knives cleaned."

It seemed rather a blue look-out. Tod said he would go up again to the Whistling Wind, and tell Mother Jones she must find us some one. Picking a rose as he went down the path, he met a cleanly-looking elderly woman who was entering. She wore a dark apron, and old-fashioned white cap, and said she had come after the place.

"What can you do?" began Tod. "Cook?"

"Cook and clean too, sir," she answered. And I liked the woman the moment I saw her.

"Oh, I don't know that there's much cleaning to do, beyond the knives," remarked Tod. "We want our dinners cooked, you know, and the beds made. That's about all."

The woman smiled at that, as if she thought he knew little about it. "I have been living at the grocer's, up yonder, sir, and they can give me a good character, though I say it. I'm not afraid of doing all you can want done, and of giving satisfaction, if you'd please to try me."

"You'll do," said Tod, after glancing at me. "Can you come in at once?"

"As soon as you like, sir. When would you please to go for my character?"

"Oh, bother that!" said he. "I've no doubt you are all right. Can you make pigeon pies?"

"That I can, sir."

"You'll do then. What is your name?"

"Elizabeth Ho—"

"Elizabeth?" he interrupted, not giving her time to finish. "Why, the one just gone was Elizabeth. A grenadier, six feet high."

"I've been mostly called Betty, sir."

"Then we'll call you Betty too."

She went away, saying that she'd come back with her aprons. Tod looked after her.

"You like her, don't you, Johnny?"

"That I do. She's a good sort; honest as can be. You did not ask her about wages."

"Oh, time enough for that," said he.

And Betty turned out to be good as gold. Her history was a curious one; she told it to me one evening in the kitchen; in her small way she had been somewhat of a martyr. But God had been with her always, she said; through more trouble than the world knew of.

We had a letter from Mrs. Todhetley, redirected on from Sanbury. The chief piece of news it contained was, that the Squire and old Jacobson had gone off to Great Yarmouth for a fortnight.

"That's good," said Tod. "Johnny lad, you may write home now."

"And tell about Rose Lodge?"

"Tell all you like. I don't mind madam. She'll have leisure to digest it against the pater returns."

I wrote a long letter, and told everything, going into the minute details that she liked to hear, about the servants, and all else. Rose Lodge was the most wonderful bargain, I said, and we were both as happy as the days were long.

The church was a little primitive edifice near the sands. We went to service on Sunday morning; and upon getting home afterwards, found the cloth not laid. Tod had ordered dinner to be on the table. He sent me to the kitchen to blow up Betty.

"It is quite ready and waiting to be served; but I can't find a clean tablecloth," said Betty.

"Why, I told you where the tablecloths were," shouted Tod, who heard the answer. "In the cupboard at the top of the stairs."

"But there are no tablecloths there, sir," cried she. "Nor anything else either, except a towel or two."

Tod went upstairs in a passion, bidding her follow him, and flung the cupboard door open. He thought she had looked in the wrong place.

But Betty was right. With the exception of two or three old towels and some stacks of newspapers, the cupboard was empty.

"By Jove!" cried Tod. "Johnny, that grenadier must have walked off with all the linen!"

Whether she had, or had not, none to speak of could be found now. Tod talked of sending the police after her, and wrote an account of her delinquencies to Captain Copperas, addressing the letter to the captain's brokers in Liverpool.

"But," I debated, not quite making matters out to my own satisfaction, "the grenadier wanted us to examine her boxes, you know."

"All for a blind, Johnny."

It was the morning following this day, Monday, that, upon looking from my window, something struck me as being the matter with the garden. What was it? Why, all the roses were gone! Down I rushed, half dressed, burst out at the back-door, and gazed about me.

It was a scene of desolation. The rose-trees had been stripped; every individual rose was clipped neatly off from every tree. Two or three trees were left untouched before the front window; all the rest were rifled.

"What the mischief is the matter, Johnny?" called out Tod, as I was hastily questioning Betty. "You are making enough noise for ten, lad."

"We have had robbers here, Tod. Thieves. All the roses are stolen."

He made a worse noise than I did. Down he came, full rush, and stamped about the garden like any one wild. Old Druff and his wife heard him, and came up to the palings. Betty, busy in her kitchen, had not noticed the disaster.

"I see Tasker's people here betimes this morning," observed Druff. "A lot of 'em came. 'Twas a pity, I thought, to slice off all them nice big blows."

"Saw who?—saw what?" roared Tod, turning his anger upon Druff. "You mean to confess to me that you saw these rose-trees rifled, and did not stop it?"

"Nay, master," said Druff, "how could I interfere with Tasker's people? Their business ain't mine."

"Who are Tasker's people?" foamed Tod. "Who is Tasker?"

"Tasker? Oh, Tasker's that there man at the white cottage on t'other side the village. Got a big garden round it."

"Is he a poacher? Is he a robber?"

"Bless ye, master, Tasker's no robber."

"And yet you saw him take my roses?"

"I see him for certain. I see him busy with the baskets as the men filled 'em."

Dragging me after him, Tod went striding off to Tasker's. We knew the man by sight; had once spoken to him about his garden. He was a kind of nurseryman. Tasker was standing near his greenhouse.

"Why did I come and steal your roses?" he quietly repeated, when he could understand Tod's fierce demands. "I didn't steal 'em, sir; I picked 'em."

"And how dared you do it? Who gave you leave to do it?" foamed Tod, turning green and purple.

"I did it because they were mine."

"Yours! Are you mad?"

"Yes, sir, mine. I bought 'em and paid for 'em."

Tod did think him mad at the moment; I could see it in his face. "Of whom, pray, did you buy them?"

"Of Captain Copperas. I had 'em from the garden last year and the year afore: other folks lived in the place then. Three pounds I gave for 'em this time. The captain sold 'em to me a month ago, and I was to take my own time for gathering them."

I don't think Tod had ever felt so floored in all his life. He stood back against the pales and stared. A month ago we had not known Captain Copperas.

"I might have took all the lot: 'twas in the agreement; but I left you a few before the front winder," said Tasker, in an injured tone. "And you come and attack me like this!"

"But what do you want with them? What are they taken for?"

"To make otter of roses," answered Tasker. "I sell 'em to the distillers."

"At any rate, though it be as you say, I would have taken them openly," contended Tod. "Not come like a thief in the night."

"But then I had to get 'em afore the sun was powerful," calmly answered Tasker.

Tod was silent all the way home. I had not spoken a word, good or bad. Betty brought in the coffee.

"Pour it out," said he to me. "But, Johnny," he presently added, as he stirred his cup slowly round, "I can't think how it was that Copperas forget to tell me he had sold the roses."

"Do you suppose he did forget?"

"Why, of course he forgot. Would an honest man like Copperas conceal such a thing if he did not forget it? You will be insinuating next, Johnny Ludlow, that he is as bad as Tasker."

I must say we were rather in the dumps that day. Tod went off fishing; I carried the basket and things. I did wish I had not said so much about the roses to Mrs. Todhetley. What I wrote was, that they were brighter and sweeter and better than those other roses by Bendemeer's stream.

I thought of the affair all day long. I thought of it when I was going to bed at night. Putting out the candle, I leaned from my window and looked down on the desolate garden. The roses had made its beauty.

"Johnny! Johnny lad! Are you in bed?"

The cautious whisper came from Tod. Bringing my head inside the room, I saw him at the door in his slippers and braces.

"Come into my room," he whispered. "Those fellows who disturbed us the other night are at the gate again."

Tod's light was out and his window open. We could see a man bending down outside the gate, fumbling with the lock. Presently the bell was pulled very gently, as if the ringer thought the house might be asleep and he did not want to awaken it. There was something quite ghostly to the imagination in being disturbed at night like this.

"Who's there?" shouted Tod.

"I am," answered a cautious voice. "I want to see Captain Copperas."

"Come along, Johnny. This is getting complicated."

We went out to the gate, and saw a man: he was not either of the two who had come before. Tod answered him as he had answered them, but did not open the gate.

"Are you a friend of the captain's?" whispered the man.

"Yes, I am," said Tod. "What then?"

"Well, see here," resumed he, in a confidential tone. "If I don't get to see him it will be the worse for him. I come as a friend; come to warn him."

"But I tell you he is not in the house," argued Tod. "He has let it to me. He has left Cray Bay. His address? No, I cannot give it you."

"Very well," said the man, evidently not believing a word, "I am come out of friendliness. If you know where he is, you just tell him that Jobson has been here, and warns him to look out for squalls. That's all."

"I say, Johnny, I shall begin to fancy we are living in some mysterious castle, if this kind of thing is to go on," remarked Tod, when the man had gone. "It seems deuced queer, altogether."

It seemed queerer still the next morning. For a gentleman walked in and demanded payment for the furniture. Captain Copperas had forgotten to settle for it, he said—if he had gone away. Failing the payment, he should be obliged to take away the chairs and tables. Tod flew into a rage, and ordered him out of the place. Upon which their tongues went in for a pitched battle, and gave out some unorthodox words. Cooling down by-and-by, an explanation was come to.

He was a member of some general furnishing firm, ten miles off. Captain Copperas had done them the honour to furnish his house from their stores, including the piano, paying a small portion on account. Naturally they wanted the rest. In spite of certain strange doubts that were arising touching Captain Copperas, Tod resolutely refused to give any clue to his address. Finally the applicant agreed to leave matters as they were for three or four days, and wrote a letter to be forwarded to Copperas.

But the news that arrived from Liverpool staggered us more than all. The brokers sent back Tod's first letter to Copperas (telling him of the grenadier's having marched off with the linen), and wrote to say that they didn't know any Captain Copperas; that no gentleman of that name was in their employ, or in command of any of their ships.

As Tod remarked, it seemed deuced queer. People began to come in, too, for petty accounts that appeared to be owing—a tailor, a bootmaker, and others. Betty shed tears.

One evening, when we had come in from a long day's fishing, and were sitting at dinner in rather a gloomy mood, wondering what was to be the end of it, we caught sight of a man's coat-tails whisking up to the front-door.

"Sit still," cried Tod to me, as the bell rang. "It's another of those precious creditors. Betty! don't you open the door. Let the fellow cool his heels a bit."

But, instead of cooling his heels, the fellow stepped aside to our open window, and stood there, looking in at us. I leaped out of my chair, and nearly out of my skin. It was Mr. Brandon.

"And what do you two fine gentlemen think of yourselves?" began he, when we had let him in. "You don't starve, at any rate, it seems."

"You'll take some, won't you, Mr. Brandon?" said Tod politely, putting the breast of a duck upon a plate, while I drew a chair for him to the table.

Ignoring the offer, he sat down by the window, threw his yellow silk handkerchief across his head, as a shade against the sun and the air, and opened upon our delinquencies in his thinnest tones. In the Squire's absence, Mrs. Todhetley had given him my letter to read, and begged him to come and see after us, for she feared Tod might be getting himself into some inextricable mess. Old Brandon's sarcasms were keen. To make it worse, he had heard of the new complications, touching Copperas and the furniture, at the Whistling Wind.

"So!" said he, "you must take a house and its responsibilities upon your shoulders, and pay the money down, and make no inquiries!"

"We made lots of inquiries," struck in Tod, wincing.

"Oh, did you? Then I was misinformed. You took care to ascertain whether the landlord of the house would accept you as tenant; whether the furniture was the man's own to sell, and had no liabilities upon it; whether the rent and taxes had been paid up to that date?"

As Tod had done nothing of the kind, he could only slash away at the other duck, and bite his lips.

"You took to a closet of linen, and did not think it necessary to examine whether linen was there, or whether it was all dumb-show—"

"I'm sure the linen was there when we saw it," interrupted Tod.

"You can't be sure; you did not handle it, or count it. The Squire told you you would hasten to make ducks and drakes of your five hundred pounds. It must have been burning a hole in your pocket. As to you, Johnny Ludlow, I am utterly surprised: I did give you credit for possessing some sense."

"I could not help it, sir. I'm sure I should never have mistrusted Captain Copperas." But doubts had floated in my mind whether the linen had not gone away in those boxes of Miss Copperas, that I saw the grenadier packing.

Tod pulled a letter-case out of his breast-pocket, selected a paper, and handed it to Mr. Brandon. It was the cheque for one hundred pounds.

"I thought of you, sir, before I began upon the ducks and drakes. But you were not at home, and I could not give it you then. And I thank you very much indeed for what you did for me."

Mr. Brandon read the cheque and nodded his head sagaciously.

"I'll take it, Joseph Todhetley. If I don't, the money will only go in folly." By which I fancied he had not meant to have the money repaid to him.

"I think you are judging me rather hardly," said Tod. "How was I to imagine that the man was not on the square? When the roses were here, the place was the prettiest place I ever saw. And it was dirt-cheap."

"So was the furniture, to Copperas," cynically observed Mr. Brandon.

"What is done is done," growled Tod. "May I give you some raspberry pudding?"

"Some what? Raspberry pudding! Why, I should not digest it for a week. I want to know what you are going to do."

"I don't know, sir. Do you?"

"Yes. Get out of the place to-morrow. You can't remain in it with bare walls: and it's going to be stripped, I hear. Green simpletons, you must be! I dare say the landlord will let you off by paying him three months' rent. I'll see him myself. And you'll both come home with me, like two young dogs with their tails burnt."

"And lose all the money I've spent?" cried Tod.

"Ay, and think yourself well off that it is not more. You possess no redress; as to finding Copperas, you may as well set out to search for the philosopher's stone. It is nobody's fault but your own; and if it shall bring you caution, it may be an experience cheaply bought."

"I could never have believed it of a sailor," Tod remarked ruefully to old Druff, when we were preparing to leave.

"Ugh! fine sailor he was!" grunted Druff. "He warn't a sailor. Not a reg'lar one. Might ha' been about the coast a bit in a collier, perhaps—nothing more. As to that grenadier, I believe she was just another of 'em—a sister."

But we heard a whiff of news later that told us Captain Copperas was not so bad as he seemed. After he had taken Rose Lodge and furnished it, some friend, for whom in his good-nature he had stood surety to a large amount, let him in for the whole, and ruined him. Honest men are driven into by-paths sometimes.

And so that was the inglorious finale to our charming retreat by Bendemeer's stream.

CHAPTER XIX

LEE, THE LETTER-MAN

In a side lane of Timberdale, just off the churchyard, was the cottage of Jael Batty, whose name you have heard before. Side by side with it stood another cottage, inhabited by Lee, the assistant letter-carrier; or, as Timberdale generally called him, the letter-man. These cottages had a lively look-out, the farrier's shop and a few thatched hayricks opposite; sideways, the tombstones in the graveyard.

Some men are lucky in life, others are unlucky. Andrew Lee was in the latter category. He had begun life as a promising farmer, but came down in the world. First of all, he had to pay a heap of money for some man who had persuaded him to become his security, and that stripped him of his means. Afterwards a series of ill-fortunes set in on the farm: crops failed, cattle died, and Lee was sold up. Since then, he had tried at this and tried at that; been in turn a farmer's labourer, an agent for coal, and the proprietor of a shop devoted to the benefit of the younger members of the community, its speciality being bull's-eyes and besoms for birch-rods. For some few years now he had settled down in this cottage next door to Jael Batty's, and carried out the letters at fourteen shillings a-week.

There were two letter-men, Spicer and Lee. But there need not have been two, only that Timberdale was so straggling a parish, the houses in it lying far and wide. Like other things in this world, fortune, even in so trifling a matter as these two postmen, was not dealt out equally. Spicer had the least work, for he took the home delivery, and had the most pay; Lee did all the country tramping, and had only the fourteen shillings. But when the place was offered to Lee he was at a very low ebb indeed, and took it thankfully, and thought he was set up in riches for life; for, as you well know, we estimate things by comparison.

Andrew Lee was not unlucky in his fortunes only. Of his three children, not one had prospered. The son married all too young; within a year he and his wife were both dead, leaving a baby-boy to Lee as a legacy. The elder daughter had emigrated to the other end of the world with her husband; and the younger daughter had a history. She was pretty and good and gentle, but just a goose. Goose that she was, though, all the parish liked Mamie Lee.

About four years before the time I am telling of, there came a soldier to Timberdale, on a visit to Spicer the letter-carrier, one James West. He was related to Spicer's wife; her nephew, or cousin, or something of that sort; a tall, good-looking, merry-tempered dragoon, with a dashing carriage and a dashing tongue; and he ran away with the heart of Mamie Lee. That might not so much have mattered in the long-run, for such privilege is universally allowed to the sons of Mars; but he also ran away with her. One fine morning Mr. James West was missing from Timberdale, and Mamie Lee was missing also. The parish went into a rapture of indignation over it, not so much at him as at her; called her a "baggage," and hoping her folly would come home to her. Poor old Lee thought he had received his death-blow, and his hair turned grey swiftly.

Not more than twelve months had gone by when Mamie was back again. Jael Batty was running out one evening to get half-a-pound of sugar at Salmon's shop, when she met a young woman with a bundle staggering down the lane, and keeping under the side of the hedge as if she were afraid of falling, or else did not want to be seen. Too weak to carry the bundle, she seemed ready to sink at every step. Jael Batty, who had her curiosity like other people, though she was deaf, peered into the bent face, and brought herself up with a shriek.

"What, is it you, Mamie Lee! Well, the impedence of this! How on earth could you pick up the brass to come back here?"

"Are my poor father and mother alive? Do they still live here?" faltered Mamie, turning her piteous white face to Jael.

"They be both alive; but it's no thanks to you. If they—Oh, if I don't believe—What have you got in that ragged old shawl?"

"It's my baby," answered Mamie; and she passed on.

Andrew Lee took her in with sobs and tears, and thanked Heaven she had come back, and welcomed her unreasonably. The parish went on at him for it, showering down plenty of abuse, and asking whether he did not feel ashamed of himself. There was even a talk of his post as letter-carrier being taken from him; but it came to nothing. Rymer was postmaster then, though he was about giving it up; and he was a man of too much sorrow himself to inflict it needlessly upon another. On the contrary, he sent down cordials and tonics and things for Mamie, who had had a fever and come home dilapidated as to strength, and never charged for them. Thomas Rymer's own heart was slowly breaking, so he could feel for her.

The best or the worst of it was, that Mamie said she was married. Which assertion was of course not believed, and only added to her sin in the eyes of Timberdale. The tale she told was this. That James West had taken her straight to some town, where he had previously had the banns put up, and married her there. The day after the marriage they had sailed for Ireland, whither he had to hasten to join his regiment, his leave of absence having expired. At the end of some seven or eight months, the regiment was ordered to India, and he departed with it, leaving her in her obscure lodging at Cork. By-and-by her baby was born; she was very ill then; very; had fever and a cough, and sundry other complications; and what with lying ill eight weeks, and being obliged to pay a doctor and a nurse all that time, besides other expenses, she spent all the money Mr. James West left with her, and had no choice between starvation and coming back to Timberdale.

You should have heard how this account was scoffed at. The illness, and the baby, and the poverty nobody disputed—they were plain enough to be seen by all Timberdale; and what better could she expect, they would like to know? But when she came to talk about the church (or rather, old Lee for her, second-hand, for she was not at all a person now to be spoken to by Timberdale), then their tongues were let loose in all kinds of inconvenient questions. Which was the town?—and which was the church in it?—and where were her "marriage lines"? Mamie could give no answer at all. She did not know the name of the town, or where it was situated. James had taken her with him in the train to it, and that was all she knew; and she did not know the name of the church or the clergyman; and as to marriage lines, she had never heard of any. So, as Timberdale said, what could you make out of this, except one thing— that Mr. Jim West had been a deep rogue, and taken her in. At best, it could have been but a factitious ceremony; perhaps in some barn, got up like a church for the occasion, said the more tolerant, willing to give excuse for pretty Mamie if they could; but the chief portion of Timberdale looked upon the whole as an out-and-out invention of her own.

Poor Andrew Lee had never taken a hopeful view of the affair from the first; but he held to the more tolerant opinion that Mamie had been herself deceived, and he could not help being cool to Spicer in consequence. Spicer in retaliation threw all the blame upon Mamie, and held up Mr. James West as a paragon of virtue.

But, as the time went on, and no news, no letter or other token arrived from West, Mamie herself gave in. That he had deceived her she slowly became convinced of, and despair took hold of her heart. Timberdale might have the satisfaction of knowing that she judged herself just as humbly and bitterly as they judged her, and was grieving herself to a shadow. Three years had passed now since her return, and the affair was an event of the past; and Mamie wore, metaphorically, the white sheet of penitence, and hardly dared to show her face outside the cottage-door.

But you may easily see how all this, besides the sorrow, told upon Lee. Fourteen shillings a week for a man and his wife to exist upon cannot be called much, especially if they have seen better days and been used to better living. When the first grandchild, poor little orphan, arrived to be kept, Lee and his wife both thought it hard, though quite willing to take him; and now they had Mamie and another grandchild. This young one was named Jemima, for Mamie had called her after her faithless husband. Five people and fourteen shillings a-week, and provisions dear, and house-rent to pay, and Lee's shoes perpetually wanting to be mended! One or two generous individuals grew rather fond of telling Lee that he would be better off in the union.

It was November weather. A cold, dark, biting, sharp, drizzly morning. Andrew Lee got up betimes, as usual: he had to be out soon after seven to be ready for his letter delivery. In the kitchen when he entered it, he found his daughter there before him, coaxing the kettle to boil on the handful of fire, that she might make him his cup of tea and give him his breakfast. She was growing uncommonly weak and shadowy-looking now: a little woman, still not much more than a girl, with a shawl folded about her shivering shoulders, a hacking cough, and a mild, non-resisting face. Her father had lately told her that he would not have her get up in the morning; she was not fit for it: what he wanted done, he could do himself.

"Now, Mamie, why are you here? You should attend to what I say, child."

She got up from her knees and turned her sad brown eyes towards him: bright and sweet eyes once, but now dimmed with the tears and sorrow of the last three years.

"I am better up; I am indeed, father. Not sleeping much, I get tired of lying: and my cough is worse in bed."

He sat down to his cup of tea and to the bread she placed before him. Some mornings there was a little butter, or dripping, or mayhap bacon fat; but this morning he had to eat his bread dry. It was getting near the end of the week, and the purse ran low. Lee had a horror of debt, and would never let his people run into it for the smallest sum if he knew it.

"It's poor fare for you this morning, father; but I'll try and get a morsel of boiled pork for dinner, and we'll have it ready early. I expect to be paid to-day for the bit of work I have been doing for young Mrs. Ashton. Some of those greens down by the apple-trees want cutting: they'll be nice with a bit of pork."

Lee turned his eyes in the direction of the greens and the apple-trees; but the window was misty, and he could only see the drizzle of rain-drops on the diamond panes. As he sat there, a thought came into his head that he was beginning to feel old: old, and worn, and shaky. Trouble ages a man more than work, more than time; and Lee never looked at the wan face of his daughter, and at its marks of sad repentance, but he felt anew the sting which was always pricking him more or less. What with that, and his difficulty to keep the pot boiling, and his general state of shakiness, Lee was older than his years. Timberdale had fallen into the habit of calling him Old Lee, you see; but he was not sixty yet. He had a nice face; when it was a young face it must have been like Mamie's. It had furrows in it now, and his scanty grey locks hung down on each side of it.

Putting on his top-coat, which was about as thin as those remarkable sheets told of by Brian O'Linn, Lee went out buttoning it. The rain had ceased, but the cold wind took him as he went down the narrow garden-path, and he could not help shivering.

"It's a bitter wind to-day, father; in the north-east, I think," said Mamie, standing at the door to close it after him. "I hope there'll be no letters for Crabb."

Lee, as he pressed along in the teeth of the cruel east wind, was hoping the same. Salmon the grocer, who had taken the post-office, as may be remembered, when the late Thomas Rymer gave it up, was sorting the letters in the room behind the shop when Lee went in. Spicer, a lithe, active, dark-eyed man of forty-five, stood at the end of the table waiting for his bag. Lee went and stood beside him, giving him a brief good-morning: he had not taken kindly to the man since West ran away with Mamie.

"A light load this morning," remarked Mr. Salmon to Spicer, as he handed him his appropriate bag. "And here's yours, Lee," he added a minute after: "not heavy either. Too cold for people to write, I suppose."

"Anything for Crabb, sir?"

"For Crabb? Well, yes, I think there is. For the Rector."

Upon going out, Spicer turned one way, Lee the other. Spicer's district was easy as play; Lee's was a regular country tramp, the farm-houses lying in all the four points of the compass. The longest tramp was over to us at Crabb. And why the two houses, our own and Coney's farm, should continue to be comprised in the Timberdale delivery, instead of that of Crabb, people could never understand. It was so still, however, and nobody bestirred himself to alter it. For one thing, we were not often at Crabb Cot, and the Coneys did not have many letters, so it was not like an every-day delivery: we chanced to be there just now.

The letter spoken of by Salmon, which would bring Lee to Crabb this morning, was for the Reverend Herbert Tanerton, Rector of Timberdale. He and his wife, who was a niece of old Coney's, were now staying at the farm on a week's visit, and he had given orders to Salmon that his letters, during that week, were to be delivered at the farm instead of at the Rectory.

Lee finally got through his work, all but this one letter for the parson, and turned his steps our way. As ill-luck had it—the poor fellow thought it so afterwards—he could not take the short and sheltered way through Crabb Ravine, for he had letters that morning to Sir Robert Tenby, at Bellwood, and also for the Stone House on the way to it. By the time he turned on the solitary road that led to Crabb, Lee was nearly blown to smithereens by the fierce north-east wind, and chilled to the marrow. All his bones ached; he felt low, frozen, ill, and wondered whether he should get over the ground without breaking down.

"I wish I might have a whiff at my pipe!"

A pipe is to many people the panacea for all earthly discomfort; it was so to Lee. But only in the previous February had occurred that damage to Helen Whitney's letter, when she was staying with us, which the authorities had made much of; and Lee was afraid to risk a similar mishap again. He carried Salmon's general orders with him: not to smoke during his round. Once the letters were delivered, he might do so.

His weak grey hair blowing about, his thin and shrunken frame shivering and shaking as the blasts took him, his empty post-bag thrust into his pocket, and the Rector of Timberdale's letter in his hand, Lee toiled along on his weary way. To a strong man the walk would have been nothing, and not much to Lee in fairer weather. It was the cold and wind that tired him. And though, after giving vent to the above wish, he held out a little while, presently he could resist the comfort no longer, but drew forth his pipe and struck a match to light it.

How it occurred he never knew, never knew to his dying day, but the flame from the match caught the letter, and set it alight. It was that thin foreign paper that catches so quickly, and the match was obstinate, and the wind blew the flame about. He pressed the fire out with his hands, but a portion of the letter was burnt.

If Timbuctoo, or some other far-away place had been within the distance of a man's legs, Lee would have made straight off for it. His pipe on the ground, the burnt letter underneath his horrified gaze, and his hair raised on end, stood he. What on earth should he do? It had been only a pleasant young lady's letter last time, and only a little scorched; now it was the stern Rector's.

There was but one thing he could do—go on with the letter to its destination. It often happens in these distressing catastrophes that the one only course open is the least palatable. His pipe hidden away in his pocket—for Lee had had enough of it for that morning—and the damaged letter humbly held out in his hand, Lee made his approach to the farm.

I chanced to be standing at its door with Tom Coney and Tod. Those two were going out shooting, and the Squire had sent me running across the road with a message to them. Lee came up, and, with a face that seemed greyer than usual, and a voice from which most of its sound had departed, he told his tale.

Tom Coney gave a whistle. "Oh, by George, Lee, won't you catch it! The Rector—"

"The Rector's a regular martinet, you know," Tom Coney was about to add, but he was stopped by the appearance of the Rector himself.

Herbert Tanerton had chanced to be in the little oak-panelled hall, and caught the drift of the tale. A frown sat on his cold face as he came forward, a frown that would have befitted an old face better than a young one.

He was not loud. He did not fly into a passion as Helen Whitney did. He just took the unfortunate letter in his hand, and looked at it, and looked at Lee, and spoke quietly and coldly.

"This is, I believe, the second time you have burnt the letters?" and Lee dared not deny it.

"And in direct defiance of orders. You are not allowed to smoke when on your rounds."

"I'll never attempt to smoke again, when on my round, as long as I live, sir, if you'll only be pleased to look over it this time," gasped Lee, holding up his hands in a piteous way. But the Rector was one who went in for "duty," and the appeal found no favour with him.

"No," said he, "it would be to encourage wrong-doing, Lee. Meet me at eleven o'clock at Salmon's."

"Never again, sir, so long as I live!" pleaded Lee. "I'll give you my word of that, sir; and I never broke it yet. Oh, sir, if you will but have pity upon me and not report me!"

"At eleven o'clock," repeated Herbert Tanerton decisively, as he turned indoors again.

"What an old stupid you must be!" cried Tod to Lee. "He won't excuse you; he's the wrong sort of parson to do it."

"And a pretty kettle of fish you've made of it," added Tom Coney. "I wouldn't have minded much, had it been my letter; but he is different, you know."

Poor Lee turned his eyes on me: perhaps remembering that he had asked me, the other time, to stand his friend with Miss Whitney. No one could be his friend now: when the Rector took up a grievance he did not let it drop again; especially if it were his own. Good-hearted Jack, his sailor-brother, would have screened Lee, though all the letters in the parish had got burnt.

At eleven o'clock precisely the Reverend Herbert Tanerton entered Salmon's shop; and poor Lee, not daring to disobey his mandate, crept in after him. They had it out in the room behind. Salmon was properly severe; told Lee he was not sure but the offence involved penal servitude, and that he deserved hanging. A prosperous tradesman in his small orbit, the man was naturally inclined to be dictatorial, and was ambitious of standing well with his betters, especially the Rector. Lee was suspended there and then; and Spicer was informed that for a time, until other arrangements were made, he must do double duty. Spicer, vexed at this, for it would take him so much the more time from his legitimate business, that of horse doctor, told Lee he was a fool, and deserved not only hanging but drawing and quartering.

"What's up?" asked Ben Rymer, crossing the road from his own shop to accost Lee, as the latter came out of Salmon's. Ben was the chemist now—had been since Margaret's marriage—and was steady; and Ben, it was said, would soon pass his examination for surgeon. He had his hands in his pockets and his white apron on, for Mr. Ben Rymer had no false pride, and would as soon show himself to Timberdale in an apron as in a dress-coat.

Lee told his tale, confessing the sin of the morning. Mr. Rymer nodded his head significantly several times as he heard it, and pushed his red hair from his capacious forehead.

"They won't look over it this time, Lee."

"If I could but get some one to be my friend with the Rector, and ask him to forgive me," said Lee. "Had your father been alive, Mr. Rymer, I think he would have done it for me."

"Very likely. No good to ask me—if that's what you are hinting at. The Rector looks upon me as a black sheep, and turns on me the cold shoulder. But I don't think he is one to listen, Lee, though the king came to ask him."

"What I shall do I don't know," bewailed Lee. "If the place is stopped, the pay stops, and I've not another shilling in the world, or the means of earning one. My wife's ailing, and Mamie gets worse day by day; and there are the two little ones. They are all upon me."

"Some people here say, Lee, that you should have sent Mamie and her young one to the workhouse, and not have charged yourself with them."

"True, sir, several have told me that. But people don't know what a father's feelings are till they experience them. Mary was my own child that I had dandled on my knee, and watched grow up in her pretty ways, and I was fonder of her than of any earthly thing. The workhouse might not have taken her in."

"She has forfeited all claim on you. And come home only to break your heart."

"True," meekly assented Lee. "But the Lord has told us we are to forgive, not seven times, but seventy times seven. If I had turned her adrift from my door and heart, sir, who knows but I might have been turned adrift myself at the Last Day."

Evidently it was of no use talking to one so unreasonable as Lee. And Mr. Ben Rymer went back to his shop. A customer was entering it with a prescription and a medicine-bottle.

One morning close upon Christmas, Mrs. Todhetley despatched me to Timberdale through the snow for a box of those delectable "Household Pills," which have been mentioned before: an invention of the late Mr. Rymer's, and continued to be made up by Ben. Ben was behind the counter as usual when I entered, and shook the snow off my boots on the door-mat.

"Anything else?" he asked me presently, wrapping up the box.

"Not to-day. There goes old Lee! How thin he looks!"

"Starvation," said Ben, craning his long neck to look between the coloured globes at Lee on the other side the way. "Lee has nothing coming in now."

"What do they all live upon?"

"Goodness knows. Upon things that he pledges, and the vegetables in the garden. I was in there last night, and I can tell you it was a picture, Mr. Johnny Ludlow."

"A picture of what?"

"Misery: distress: hopelessness. It is several weeks now since Lee earned anything, and they have been all that time upon short commons. Some days on no commons at all, I expect."

"But what took you there?"

"I heard such an account of the girl—Mamie—yesterday afternoon, of her cough and her weakness, that I thought I'd see if any of my drugs would do her good. But it's food they all want."

"Is Mamie very ill?"

"Very ill indeed. I'm not sure but she's dying."

"It is a dreadful thing."

"One can't ask too many professional questions—people are down upon you for that before you have passed," resumed Ben, alluding to his not being qualified. "But I sent her in a cordial or two, and I spoke to Darbyshire; so perhaps he will look in upon her to-day."

Ben Rymer might have been a black sheep once upon a time, but he had not a bad heart. I began wondering whether Mrs. Todhetley could help them.

"Is Mamie Lee still able to do any sewing?"

"About as much as I could do it. Not she. I shall hear what Darbyshire's report is. They would certainly be better off in the workhouse."

"I wish they could be helped!"

"Not much chance of that," said Ben. "She is a sinner, and he is a sinner: that's what Timberdale says, you know. People in these enlightened days are so very self-righteous!"

"How is Lee a sinner?"

"How! Why, has he not burnt up the people's letters? Mr. Tanerton leads the van in banning him, and Timberdale follows."

I went home, questioning whether our folk would do anything to help the Lees. No one went on against ill-doings worse than the Squire; and no one was more ready than he to lend a helping hand when the ill-doers were fainting for want of it.

It chanced that just about the time I was talking to Ben Rymer, Mr. Darbyshire, the doctor at Timberdale, called at Lee's. He was a little, dark man, with an irritable temper and a turned-up nose, but good as gold at heart. Mamie Lee lay back in a chair, her head on a pillow, weak and wan and weary, the tears slowly rolling down her cheeks. Darbyshire was feeling her pulse, and old Mrs. Lee pottered about, bringing sticks from the garden to feed the handful of fire. The two children sat on the brick floor.

"If it were not for leaving my poor little one, I should be glad to die, sir," she was saying. "I shall be glad to go; hope it is not wrong to say it. She and I have been a dreadful charge upon them here."

Darbyshire looked round the kitchen. It was almost bare; the things had gone to the pawnbroker's. Then he looked at her.

"There's no need for you to die yet. Don't get that fallacy in your head. You'll come round fast enough with a little care."

"No, sir, I'm afraid not; I think I am past it. It has all come of the trouble, sir; and perhaps, when I'm gone, the neighbours will judge me more charitably. I believed with all my heart it was a true marriage— and I hope you'll believe me when I say it, sir; it never came into my mind to imagine otherwise. And I'd have thought the whole world would have deceived me sooner than James."

"Ah," says Darbyshire, "most girls think that. Well, I'll send you in some physic to soothe the pain in the chest. But what you most want, you see, is kitchen physic."

"Mr. Rymer has been very good in sending me cordials and cough-mixture, sir. Mother's cough is bad, and he sent some to her as well."

"Ah, yes. Mrs. Lee, I am telling your daughter that what she most wants is kitchen physic. Good kitchen physic, you understand. You'd be none the worse yourself for some of it."

Dame Lee, coming in just then in her pattens, tried to put her poor bent back as upright as she could, and shook her head before answering.

"Kitchen physic don't come in our way now, Dr. Darbyshire. We just manage not to starve quite, and that's all. Perhaps, sir, things may take a turn. The Lord is over all, and He sees our need."

"He dave me some pep'mint d'ops," said the little one, who had been waiting to put in a word. "Andy, too."

"Who did?" asked the doctor.

"Mr. 'Ymer."

Darbyshire patted the little straw-coloured head, and went out. An additional offence in the eyes of Timberdale was that the child's fair curls were just the pattern of those on the head of James the deceiver.

"Well, have you seen Mamie Lee?" asked Ben Rymer, who chanced to be standing at his shop-door after his dinner, when Darbyshire was passing by from paying his round of visits.

"Yes, I have seen her. There's no radical disease."

"Don't you think her uncommonly ill?"

Darbyshire nodded. "But she's not too far gone to be cured. She'd get well fast enough under favourable circumstances."

"Meaning good food?"

"Meaning food and other things. Peace of mind, for instance. She is just fretting herself to death. Shame, remorse, and all that, have taken hold of her; besides grieving her heart out after the fellow."

"Her voice is so hollow! Did you notice it?"

"Hollow from weakness only. As to her being too far gone, she is not so at present; at least, that's my opinion; but how soon she may become so I can't say. With good kitchen physic, as I've just told them, and ease of mind to help me, I'll answer for it that I'd have her well in a month; but the girl has neither the one nor the other. She seems to look upon coming death in the light of a relief, rather than otherwise; a relief to her own mental trouble, and a relief to the household, in the shape of saving it what she eats and drinks. In such a condition as this, you must be aware that the mind does not help the body by striving for existence; it makes no effort to struggle back to health; and there's where Mamie Lee will fail. Circumstances are killing her, not disease."

"Did you try her lungs?"

"Partially. I'm sure I am right. The girl will probably die, but she need not die of necessity; though I suppose there will be no help for it. Good-day."

Mr. Darbyshire walked away in the direction of his house, where his dinner was waiting: and Ben Rymer disappeared within doors, and began to pound some rhubarb (or what looked like it) in a mortar. He was pounding away like mad, with all the strength of his strong hands, when who should come in but Lee. Lee had never been much better than a shadow of late years, but you should have seen him now, with his grey hair straggling about his meek, wan face. You should have seen his clothes, too, and the old shoes, out at the toes and sides. Burning people's letters was of course an unpardonable offence, not to be condoned.

"Mamie said, sir, that you were good enough to tell her I was to call in for some of the cough lozenges that did her so much good. But—"

"Ay," interrupted Ben, getting down a box of the lozenges. "Don't let her spare them. They won't interfere with anything Mr. Darbyshire may send. I hear he has been."

But that those were not the days when beef-tea was sold in tins and gallipots, Ben Rymer might have added some to the lozenges. As he was handing the box to Lee, something in the man's wan and worn and gentle face put him in mind of his late father's, whose heart Mr. Ben had helped to break. A great pity took the chemist.

"You would like to be reinstated in your place, Lee?" he said suddenly.

Lee could not answer at once, for the pain at his throat and the moisture in his eyes that the notion called up. His voice, when he did speak, was as hollow and mild as Mamie's.

"There's no hope of that, sir. For a week after it was taken from me, I thought of nothing else, night or day, but that Mr. Tanerton might perhaps forgive me and get Salmon to put me on again. But the time for hoping that went by: as you know, Mr. Rymer, they put young Jelf in my place. I shall never forget the blow it was to me when I heard it. The other morning I saw Jelf crossing that bit of waste ground yonder with my old bag slung on his shoulder, and for a moment I thought the pain would have killed me."

"It is hard lines," confessed Ben.

"I have striven and struggled all my life long; only myself knows how sorely, save God; and only He can tell, for I am sure I can't, how I have contrived to keep my head any way above water. And now it's under it."

Taking the box, which Ben Rymer handed to him, Lee spoke a word of thanks, and went out. He could not say much; heart and spirit were alike broken. Ben called to his boy to mind the shop, and went over to Salmon's. That self-sufficient man and prosperous tradesman was sitting down at his desk in the shop-corner, complacently digesting his dinner—which had been a good one, to judge by his red face.

"Can't you manage to do something for Lee?" began Ben, after looking round to see that they were alone. "He is at a rare low ebb."

"Do something for Lee?" repeated Salmon. "What could I do for him?"

"Put him in his place again."

"I dare say!" Salmon laughed as he spoke, and then demanded whether Ben was a fool.

"You might do it if you would," said Ben. "As to Lee, he won't last long, if things continue as they are. Better give him a chance to live a little longer."

"Now what do you mean?" demanded Salmon. "Why don't you ask me to put a weathercock on yonder malthouse of Pashley's? Jelf has got Lee's place, and you know it."

"But Jelf does not intend to keep it."

"Who says he does not?"

"He says it. He told me yesterday that he was sick and tired of the tramping, and meant to resign. He only took it as a convenience, whilst he waited for a clerkship he was trying for at a brewery at Worcester. And he is to get that with the new year."

"Then what does Jelf mean by talking about it to others before he has spoken to me?" cried Salmon, going into a temper. "He thought to leave me and the letters at a pinch, I suppose! I'll teach him better."

"You may teach him anything you like, if you'll put Lee on again. I'll go bail that he won't get smoking again on his rounds. I think it is just a toss-up of life or death to him. Come! do a good turn for once, Salmon."

Salmon paused. He was not bad-hearted, only self-important.

"What would Mr. Tanerton say to it?"

Ben did not answer. He knew that there, after Salmon himself, was where the difficulty would lie.

"All that you have been urging goes for nonsense, Rymer. Unless the Rector came to me and said, 'You may put Lee on again,' I should not, and could not, attempt to stir in the matter; and you must know that as well as I do."

"Can't somebody see Tanerton, and talk to him? One would think that the sight of Lee's face would be enough to soften him, without anything else."

"I don't know who'd like to do it," returned Salmon. And there the conference ended, for the apprentice came in from his dinner.

Very much to our surprise, Mr. Ben Rymer walked in that same evening to Crabb Cot, and was admitted to the Squire. In spite of Mr. Ben's former ill-doings, which he had got to know of, the Squire treated Ben civilly, in remembrance of his father, and of his grandfather, the clergyman. Ben's errand was to ask the Squire to intercede for Lee with Herbert Tanerton. And the pater, after talking largely about the iniquity of Lee, as connected with burnt letters, came round to Ben's way of thinking, and agreed to go to the Rectory.

"Herbert Tanerton's harder than nails, and you'll do no good," remarked Tod, watching us away on the following morning; for the pater took me with him to break the loneliness of the walk. "He'll turn as cold to you as a stone the moment you bring up the subject, sir. Tell me I'm a story-teller when you come back if he does not, Johnny."

We took the way of the Ravine. It was a searching day; the wintry wind keen and "unkind as man's ingratitude." Before us, toiling up the descent to the Ravine at the other end, and coming to a halt at the stile to pant and cough, went a woebegone figure, thinly clad, which turned out to be Lee himself. He had a small bundle of loose sticks in his hand, which he had come to pick up. The Squire was preparing a sort of blowing-up greeting for him, touching lighted matches and carelessness, but the sight of the mild, starved grey face disarmed him; he thought, instead, of the days when Lee had been a prosperous farmer, and his tone changed to one of pity.

"Hard times, I'm afraid, Lee."

"Yes, sir, very hard. I've known hard times before, but I never thought to see any so cruel as these. There's one comfort, sir; when things come to this low ebb, life can't last long."

"Stuff," said the Squire. "For all you know, you may be back in your old place soon: and—and Mrs. Todhetley will find some sewing when Mamie's well enough to do it."

A faint light, the dawn of hope, shone in Lee's eyes. "Oh, sir, if it could be! and I heard a whisper to-day that young Jelf refuses to keep the post. If it had been anybody's letter but Mr. Tanerton's, perhaps— but he does not forgive."

"I'm on my way now to ask him," cried the pater, unable to keep in the news. "Cheer up, Lee—of course you'd pass your word not to go burning letters again."

"I'd not expose myself to the danger, sir. Once I got my old place back, I would never take out a pipe with me on my rounds; never, so long as I live."

Leaving him with his new hope and the bundle of firewood, we trudged on to the Rectory. Herbert and Grace were both at home, and glad to see us.

But the interview ended in smoke. Tod had foreseen the result exactly: the Rector was harder than nails. He talked of "example" and "Christian duty;" and refused point-blank to allow Lee to be reinstated. The Squire gave him a few sharp words, and flung out of the house in a passion.

"A pretty Christian he is, Johnny! He was cold and hard as a boy. I once told him so before his stepfather, poor Jacob Lewis; but he is colder and harder now."

At the turning of the road by Timberdale Court, we came upon Lee. After taking his faggots home, he waited about to see us and hear the news. The pater's face, red and angry, told him the truth.

"There's no hope for me, sir, I fear?"

"Not a bit of it," growled the Squire. "Mr. Tanerton won't listen to reason. Perhaps we can find some other light post for you, my poor fellow, when the winter shall have turned. You had better get indoors out of this biting cold; and here's a couple of shillings."

So hope went clean out of Andrew Lee.

Christmas Day and jolly weather. Snow on the ground to one's heart's content. Holly and ivy on the walls indoors, and great fires blazing on the hearths; turkeys, and plum-puddings, and oranges, and fun. That was our lucky state at Crabb Cot and at Timberdale generally, but not at Andrew Lee's.

The sweet bells were chiming people out of church, as was the custom at Timberdale on high festivals. Poor Lee sat listening to them, his hand held up to his aching head. There had been no church for him: he had neither clothes to go in nor face to sit through the service. Mamie, wrapped in an old bed-quilt, lay back on the pillow by the fire. The coal-merchant, opening his heart, had sent a sack each of best Staffordshire coal to ten poor families, and Lee's was one. Except the Squire's two shillings, he had had no money given to him. A loaf of bread was in the cupboard; and a saucepan of broth, made of carrots and turnips out of the garden, simmered on the trivet; and that would be their Christmas dinner.

Uncommonly low was Mamie to-day. The longer she endured this famished state of affairs the weaker she grew; it stands to reason. She felt that a few days, perhaps hours, would finish her up. The little ones were upstairs with their grandmother, so that she had an interval of rest; and she lay back, her breath short and her chest aching as she thought of the past. Of the time when James West, the handsome young man in his gay regimentals, came to woo her, as the soldier did the miller's daughter. In those happy days, when her heart was light and her song blithe as a bird's in May, that used to be one of her songs, "The Banks of Allan Water." Her dream had come to the same ending as the one told of In the ballad, and here she lay, deserted and dying. Timberdale was in the habit of prosaically telling her that she had "brought her pigs to a fine market." Of the market there could be no question; but when Mamie looked into the past she saw more of romance there than anything else. The breaking out of the church bells forced a rush of tears to her heart and eyes. She tried to battle with the feeling, then turned and put her cheek against her father's shoulder.

"Forgive me, father!" she besought him, in a sobbing whisper. "I don't think it will be long now; I want you to say you forgive me before I go. If—if you can."

And the words finished up for Lee what the bells had only partly done. He broke down, and sobbed with his daughter.

"I've never thought there was need of it, or to say it, child; and if there had been—Christ forgave all. 'Peace on earth and goodwill to men.' The bells are ringing it out now. He will soon take us to Him. Mamie, my forlorn one: forgiven; yes, forgiven; and in His beautiful world there is neither hunger, nor disgrace, nor pain. You are dying of that cold you caught in the autumn, and I shan't be long behind you. There's no longer any place for me here."

"Not of the cold, father; I am not dying of that, but of a broken heart."

Lee sobbed. He did not answer.

"And I should like to leave my forgiveness to James, should he ever come back here," she whispered: "and—and my love. Please tell him that I'd have got well if I could, if only for the chance of seeing him once again in this world; and tell him that I have thought all along there must be some mistake; that he did not mean deliberately to harm me. I think so still, father. And if he should notice little Mima, tell him—"

A paroxysm of coughing interrupted the rest. Mrs. Lee came downstairs with the children, asking if it was not time for dinner.

"The little ones are crying out for it, Mamie, and I'm sure the rest of us are hungry enough."

So they bestirred themselves to take up the broth, and take seats round the table. All but Mamie, who did not leave her pillow. Very watery broth, the carrots and turnips swimming in it.

"Say grace, Andy," cried his grandmother.

For they kept up proper manners at Lee's, in spite of the short commons.

"For what we are going to receive," began Andy: and then he pulled himself up, and looked round.

Bursting in at the door, a laugh upon his face and a white basin in his hands, came Mr. Ben Rymer. The basin was three parts filled with delicious slices of hot roast beef and gravy.

"I thought you might like to eat a bit, as it's Christmas Day," said Ben. "And here's an orange or two for you youngsters."

Pulling the oranges out of his pocket, and not waiting to be thanked, Ben went off again. But he did not tell them what he was laughing at, or the trick he had played his mother—in slicing away at the round of beef, and rifling the dish of oranges, while her back was turned, looking after the servant's doings in the kitchen, and the turning-out of the pudding. For Mrs. Rymer followed Timberdale in taking an exaggerated view of Lee's sins, and declined to help him.

Their faces had hardly done glowing with the unusual luxury of the beef, when I dropped in. We had gone that day to church at Timberdale; after the service, the Squire left the others to walk on, and, taking me with him, called at the Rectory to tackle Herbert Tanerton again. The parson did not hold out. How could he, with those bells, enjoining goodwill, ringing in his ears?—the bells of his own church. But he had meant to come round of his own accord.

"I'll see Salmon about it to-morrow," said he. "I did say just a word to him yesterday. As you go home, Johnny may look in at Lee's and tell him so."

"And Johnny, if you don't mind carrying it, I'll send a drop of beef-tea to Mamie," whispered Grace. "I've not dared to do it before."

So, when it was getting towards dusk, for the Squire stayed, talking of this and that, there I was, with the bottle of beef-tea, telling Lee the good news that his place would be restored to him with the new year, and hearing about Ben Rymer's basin of meat. The tears rolled down old Lee's haggard cheeks.

"And I had been fearing that God had abandoned me!" he cried, full of remorse for the doubt. "Mamie, perhaps you can struggle on a bit longer now."

But the greatest event of all was to come. Whilst I stood there, somebody opened the door, and looked in. A tall, fine, handsome soldier: and I did not at the moment notice that he had a wooden leg from the knee downwards. Ben's basin of beef had been a surprise, but it was nothing to this. Taking a glance round the room, it rested on Mamie, and he went up to her, the smile on his open face changing to concern.

"My dear lassie, what's amiss?"

"James!" she faintly screamed; "it's James!" and burst into a fit of sobs on his breast. And next the company was augmented by Salmon and Ben Rymer, who had seen James West go by, and came after him to know what it meant, and to blow him up for his delinquencies.

"Mamie not married!" laughed James. "Timberdale has been saying that? Why, what extraordinary people you must be! We were married at Bristol—and I've got the certificate in my knapsack at Spicer's: I've always kept it. You can paste it up on the church-door if you like. Not married! Would Mamie else have gone with me, do you suppose? Or should I have taken her?"

"But," said poor Lee, thinking that heaven must have opened right over his head that afternoon to shower down gifts, "why did you not marry her here openly?"

"Because I could not get leave to marry openly. We soldiers cannot marry at will, you know, Mr. Lee. I ought not to have done it, that's a fact; but I did not care to leave Mamie, I liked her too well; and I was punished afterwards by not being allowed to take her to India."

"You never wrote, James," whispered Mamie.

"Yes, I did, dear; I wrote twice to Ireland, not knowing you had left it. That was at first, just after we landed. Soon we had a skirmish with the natives out there, and I got shot in the leg and otherwise wounded; and for a long time I lay between life and death, only partly conscious; and now I am discharged with a pension and a wooden leg."

"Then you can't go for a soldier again!" cried Salmon.

"Not I. I shall settle at Timberdale, I think, if I can meet with a pretty little place to suit me. I found my poor mother dead when I came home, and what was hers is now mine. And it will be a comfortable living for us, Mamie, of itself: besides a few spare hundred pounds to the good, some of which you shall be heartily welcome to, Mr. Lee, for you look as if you wanted it. And the first thing I shall do, Mamie, my dear, will be to nurse you back to health. Bless my heart! Not married! I wish I had the handling of him that first set that idea afloat!"

"You'll get well now, Mamie," I whispered to her. For she was looking better already.

"Oh, Master Johnny, perhaps I shall! How good God is to us! And, James—James, this is the little one. I named her after you: Jemima."

"Peace on earth, and goodwill to men!" cried old Lee, in his thankfulness. "The bells said it to-day."

And as I made off at last to catch up the Squire, the little Mima was being smothered with kisses in her father's arms.

"Glory to God in the highest, and on earth peace, goodwill towards men!" To every one of us, my friends, do the Christmas bells say it, as Christmas Day comes round.

MRS HENRY WOOD (aka ELLEN WOOD) – A CONCISE BIBLIOGRAPHY

Danesbury House (1860)
East Lynne (1861)
The Elchester College Boys (1861)
A Life's Secret (1862)
Mrs. Halliburton's Troubles (1862)
The Channings (1862)
The Foggy Night at Offord: A Christmas Gift for the Lancashire Fund (1863)
The Shadow of Ashlydyat (1863)
Verner's Pride (1863)
Lord Oakburn's Daughters (1864)
Oswald Cray (1864)
Trevlyn Hold; or, Squire Trevlyn's Heir (1864)
William Allair; or, Running away to Sea (1864)
Mildred Arkell: A Novel (1865)
The Argosy (1865)
Elster's Folly: A Novel (1866)
St. Martin's Eve: A Novel (1866)
Lady Adelaide's Oath (1867)
Orville College: A Story (1867)
The Ghost of the Hollow Field (1867)
Anne Hereford: A Novel (1868)
Castle Wafer; or, The Plain Gold Ring (1868)
The Red Court Farm: A Novel (1868)
Roland Yorke: A Novel (1869)
Bessy Rane: A Novel (1870)
George Canterbury's Will (1870)
Dene Hollow (1871)
Within the Maze: A Novel (1872)
The Master of Greylands (1872)
Johnny Ludlow (1874)
Bessy Wells (1875)

Told in the Twilight: Containing 'Parkwater' and nine short stories (1875)
Adam Grainger: A Tale (1876)
Edina (1876)
Our Children (1876)
Parkwater: With four other tales (1876)
Pomeroy Abbey (1878)
Lady Adelaide (1879)
Johnny Ludlow, Second Series (1880)
A Tale of Sin and Other Tales (1881)
Court Netherleigh: A Novel (1881)
About Ourselves (1883)
Johnny Ludlow. Third Series (1885)
Lady Grace and Other Stories (1887)
The Story of Charles Strange (1888)
Featherston's Story. A Tale by Johnny Ludlow (1889)
The Unholy Wish and Other Stories (1890)
The House of Halliwell. A Novel (1890)
Ashley and Other Stories (1897)
Victor Serenus (1898)
Johnny Ludlow. Fifth series (1899)
Johnny Ludlow. Sixth series (1899)

Translations
Les Channing. Traduit de l'Anglais par Mme Abric-Encontre (1864)
Les Filles de Lord Oakburn: Roman traduit de l'anglais par L. Bochet (1876)
La Gloire des Verner: Roman traduit de l'anglais par L. de L'Estrive (1878)
Le Serment de Lady Adelaïde: Roman traduit de l'anglais par Léon Bochet (1878)